Expeditionary Force
Book 6:
Mavericks

Craig Alanson

Contact the author
craigalanson@gmail.com

Cover Design By:
Alexandre Rito
alexandre@designbookcover.pt

Table of Contents

CHAPTER ONE

I had to let Skippy's shocking last statement roll around in my brain for a moment before I could speak. "Perkins and her team are *not* on Paradise?"

"Nope." Skippy clarified unhelpfully.

"Crap. Dammit, that pilot, Eileen-"

"*Irene*," he corrected me.

"Irene, yeah. She didn't like, take a wrong turn or something?"

"Uh, no, Joe."

"Well, I assume they didn't win a fabulous vacation cruise, so how the hell-"

"Joe, while playing Twenty Questions with you would be immensely entertaining for me, we should jump away from here first."

"Oh, yeah. Desai," I checked the list on the command chair's armrest. Wherever we had to go to rescue Perkins, we first had to stop by a gas giant planet to fill the *Dutchman*'s depleted fuel tanks. "Jump option Alpha."

"Aye aye, Captain," Desai replied and pressed a button. The only change on the main bridge display was the faint dot of the local star had disappeared, because we were now in interstellar space. If you were ever looking for nowhere, we were smack in the middle of it.

"Ok, Skippy," I took a deep breath and watched Hans Chotek silently fuming at me. "You'd better just tell us where Perkins is now, and what kind of trouble she's gotten into this time."

"We have plenty of time for that later, Joe. I downloaded all the info to your tablets and laptops, you can read the whole story in detail any time you like. Right now, we need to prepare for the refueling operation. I suggest-"

"Uh huh, sure," I cut off the beer can before he could get into geeky technical details of the risky op to extract fuel. "How about you give us the elevator version of the story?"

"Elevator version?" Skippy asked, puzzled, then he got excited. "Ooooh, you mean like elevator music? I suppose I could put the story into a musical format, like an epic opera. In fact, that is a *great* idea-"

"No, that is a *terrible* idea!" I waved my hands while seeing panicked faces in the CIC. No one wanted to give Skippy an excuse to sing. "I meant, like an elevator pitch, you know?" I had read that concept in one of the US Army PowerPoint slides I was supposed to study for officer training. "Give us the thirty second version of the story."

"Oh," the beer can's hopes were crushed. "Oof," he sighed. "All right, *fine*," he said with disgust to make clear it was anything but fine to him. "To make a long story short, Perkins is-"

The lights went out.

All the lights, even the independently-powered emergency lights. My stomach did flip-flops as the artificial gravity cut out completely, and it wasn't the typical slow power-down of the gravity generators, this was someone flipping a switch from *On* to *Off*. So startling and sudden was the loss of power that instead of frightened cries of alarm from the crew, there was a brief moment of pure silence. Pure silence, like, no sound. No gentle hissing of air through the vents. No beeping from control panels. That was odd. What I picked up on immediately, what made my hair stand on end, was the loss of the faint rumbling sound of the reactor. Our new second-hand reactor that Skippy dug out of the junkyard in the Roach Motel had a different and lower-pitched sound than the *Dutchman*'s original reactors, and the new reactor had an intermittent vibration that had scared the hell out of me and kept me awake at night until I got used to it. Now, I was holding my breath hoping that scary vibration would be felt through my boots on the deck. Nothing.

What scared me the most, made my insides freeze into a solid lump, was the absolute silence from Skippy.

The silence was broken by everyone talking at once, although because the Merry Band of Pirates are highly disciplined bad-ass Special Operations troops, no one panicked. "Everyone, quiet please," I asked in what was supposed to be a calm voice that came out as a broken squeak. "Skippy? Skippy, are you there?"

Oh thank *GOD*! His beer can lit up with a soft blue glow, bright enough to illuminate the bridge, Combat Information Center and the passageway outside. "I'm here, Joe. Sorry about not responding immediately. I was super-duper ultra busy." Other lights began to show, as people pulled out their zPhones and activated the flashlight feature.

"Everything is Ok with you, right? You didn't go on holiday again?"

"Huh? Nope. No, I'm fine. I was just super extra awesomely busy trying to determine why *all* the power cut out. The emergency power should have come on," the red backup lighting snapped on as he spoke. "Like I said, emergency power is restored. Temporarily. Just local, independent systems are active, even the backup power is offline. Whew! Reactor containment was iffy there for a moment, kind of skating on the edge of disaster. I got it now. Damn, that was too close."

"What was too close? What went wrong?"

"Still investigating that, Joe, lots of numbers to crunch. I suggest you get the crew preparing to get into spacesuits, escape pods, dropships, anything with an independent source of power. Although, damn it! The dropships are now powering down one by one. And the escape pods. Crap! *Everything* is shutting down!"

"Skippy, we need some answers pronto. Can you-"

"Joe, I am extremely busy right now. Like, with the superconducting magnets of the reactor containment system failing, I am the only thing preventing hot plasma from exploding and destroying the ship. Talk to you later," he ended the conversation abruptly.

Not knowing what had gone wrong was intensely frustrating, but there wasn't anything I could do about it until Skippy analyzed the problem. If he couldn't contain the radioactive plasma in the main reactor, we would not have any problems to analyze, so I left him alone to do whatever he was doing. I jammed a thumb down on the button to open the *Dutchman*'s 1MC intercom system, which fortunately broadcast to people's zPhones through Skippy. "All hands, this is the captain. We have suffered," what? I paused like an idiot. "An apparent engineering casualty," I used the most vague term I could think of. At least the crew would be assured the problem was not caused by enemy action.

Unless, crap, it *was* caused by some kind of enemy action, Skippy had not ruled that out.

"Until main power is restored, please," I stuttered to a halt again. Please what? Abandon ship? That wasn't the answer, especially with our dropships falling offline. "Get access to spacesuits, and secure extra powerpacks, as many as you can get." While the suits were in storage, they were plugged into main power, to keep their internal powercells topped off and ready for immediate use. Main power was dead and dropships were powering down. Dropships in docking bays were plugged into umbilical power cables, even the ready bird we kept on Zulu alert. If whatever caused the problem with main power also traveled up the umbilical cables, then our spacesuits might be affected also. "Report in to the CIC when you have a functioning suit available. You do not need to put the suit on, or use supplemental oxygen at this time," I added to avoid people using up their suit's breathable air supply. The internal volume of the *Dutchman*'s hull contained enough air for almost a full day, though the air in populated compartments was going to get warm and stale quickly. I needed to consider dispersing people out of the CIC and galley and into cargo holds, any place with a large volume of air. Maybe if we kept all the internal doors open, that might slow the process of carbon dioxide building up in isolated areas of the ship? Uh, maybe instead of guessing, I should ask someone who knows actual sciency stuff?

"Colonel," Gunnery Sergeant Adams called out while floating beside my chair, holding a spacesuit she had pulled from a locker we installed in the CIC. Her face was lit up by the zPhone she was holding between two fingers, and because I am a moron, the first thought that flashed across my brain was something like 'wow, she has really beautiful skin' followed by me noticing for the first time how thick her eyelashes were. In my defense, she was floating right in front of my face and the zPhone was glowing from close to her right ear, so my eyes concentrated on what I could see in the overall dim lighting.

Either that or I'm just a complete idiot. Let's go with the first explanation.

"Uh, what?" I shook my head to bring my brain back into focus.

"This suit is dead," she pointed to the status display on the spacesuit's left wrist. The display was blank, not even the usual faint blue Standby indicator was glowing.

"Oh, crap. Uh, wait," I had a thought as my brain kicked into gear. "Disconnect the powercell, and swap in one of the spare powercells, one that wasn't plugged in for charging." We had more powercells than charging stations board the ship, so we had a schedule for rotating powercells to keep all of them fully charged. That is a task the crew performed even though Skippy had disdainfully insisted his bots could handle the job more efficiently. Efficiency is not the point, I had told him, the crew needed to take responsibility for assuring the readiness of critical equipment, if we could handle the job without screwing something up. That is why we maintained our personal weapons as best we could, and why we participated in regular maintenance chores for the combots, dropships and any other piece of equipment we could touch without risk of us blowing up the ship. Even if all pilots could do was hold tools for the bots working on dropships, the pilots would see what the bots were doing, and have at least some feeling of control over how their ships were maintained.

One of the CIC crew heard me, reached into the locker for a spare powercell, and gently tossed it toward Adams. In the zero Gee, the powercell floated off course so I had to snatch it out of the air and hand it to Adams, taking the suit's dead powercell from her.

Powercells were designed to be swapped by someone wearing a suit, so ironically, it was more awkward to take one out and snap in a new one from outside the suit. The suit kept moving around until I saw the frustrated look on her face turning into a flash of anger. With her floating, she couldn't get any leverage on the handle to swing the powercell into place, so I clamped the suit's legs between my thighs and hugged the suit's torso to my chest to hold it steady for her. She acknowledged my action with a silent nod, and her grimace turned to a smile as I heard the click of the powercell's cover snapping into place. Instantly, the wrist display lit up. "Yes!" Her face glowed, and not just from the zPhone. "How did you know, Sir?" She looked at me with a combination of awe and suspicion.

"I didn't *know*, I was guessing," I admitted. "When I heard the dropships were powering down, I wondered if whatever the fault is, travels along the umbilical cables."

"And suits in storage are plugged into charging stations," she flashed a wry smile. "Good thinking, Sir. That's why you get the big bucks."

"Ah, I got lucky. Simms!" I called through the glass separating the bridge from the CIC. "Notify the crew not to trust anything that was plugged in, and to replace their suit powercells with cells that were in storage."

"Yes, Colonel," Simms acknowledged and spoke into her zPhone. Although the ship's comm system was down, Skippy could relay zPhone signals throughout the ship, until the zPhone powercells died.

"I wonder," Adams frowned, holding the dead powercell. "I'd like to try connecting this dead one to a powercell that is active."

"Ok," I asked slowly, "why?"

"I'd like to know whether this powercell is really dead, or if it got drained by running the charging system backwards or something," she explained. "If it accepts a charge, it only got drained, and the powercell itself is Ok."

"Good idea, do that."

Simms waved for my attention. "All stations acknowledge, Colonel. We have confirmation that swapping powercells solves the suit problem," she added to confirm our success was not a fluke. "Lieutenant Williams wants to try swapping powercells in a combot?"

"Tell him permission granted, but let's hold experiments to a minimum for now, we don't want to risk our supply of good powercells. Adams?"

"No joy, Sir," she shook her head slowly. "Dammit, now the good powercell I connected to the dead one is also offline. Whatever the problem is, it must get transmitted through hard connections."

I snapped my fingers. "My tablet is in my office, sitting on a charging matt," I stated, though it occurred to me that with the loss of artificial gravity, the tablet might now be floating out in the passageway. "Check if my tablet is dead, Gunny."

"Aye aye, Sir," Adams said as she propelled herself out the door. Because my tiny office was just around a corner, she returned in seconds, wiping her face. Why was her face wet, and what was the dark stain on her uniform- Oh, yeah.

"Sorry about the coffee, Sergeant," I remembered right then that I had left a half cup of coffee on my desk, that liquid must have dispersed into the air when the gravity cut off. That was my fault, I had been thinking like my office was on firm ground somewhere, rather than on a ship. Would a Marine make such a bone-headed mistake? Maybe not, most Marines I knew tended to think in terms of being based aboard a ship. "Any luck?"

"No," she replied while gently pushing my tablet to me.

I caught it and verified the thing was indeed totally dead. "Crap. Dammit, I've had this thing since before Columbus Day!"

"Same tablet?" She asked in surprise. "That's old for a tablet."

"It runs Skippy's software, so it never needs updating," I said defensively. "And I never had to think about a problem with it until now." Crap. I bought that tablet before my old battalion got shipped out to Nigeria, I used it there sometimes to videochat with my folks back home, although the Wi-Fi connection out in the bush there had mostly been on the tin-cans-and-string level. I was proud when I bought that tablet, and it had been to the jungle and the stars and back with me. Was it now only a paperweight?

Oh, hell, without artificial gravity it wasn't even any kind of weight.

"Major Simms, warn people not to trust *anything* connected to ship's power, whether it's a hard connection or not." Simms passed the word, and within a minute, she reported that everyone aboard the ship had a spacesuit ready for use. Everyone except me, because I had been sitting uselessly strapped into the command chair.

"Here you go, Sir," Adams came to my rescue, pulling a spacesuit over to me and tying it to the back of the chair. "It's ready to go," she pointed to the blue glowing Standby indicator, "there are three spare good powercells attached to the waist belt."

"Thank you, Gunny," I caught the eye-roll from her when I used the term 'Gunny' for her new rank. Adams didn't think her field promotion was legit, especially when the promotion was granted by a sergeant masquerading as a colonel. I agreed with her about that second part, but she deserved to be a gunnery sergeant. If she was serving with the Marine Corps on Earth she almost certainly would have been promoted to an E-7 pay grade by now. So far, I had not insisted that Adams wear the patch with a second rocker to indicate her new status, but the ship's crew log had her listed as Gunnery Sergeant, and I heard an increasing number of people calling her 'Gunny' whether she liked it or not. "Should we-"

"Hey, Joe," Skippy's avatar popped to life in mid-air between bridge and CIC.

"Skippy! Are the reactors good?"

"I vented the plasma from the main reactor, there's some minor damage to the hull from the emergency venting, nothing to worry about. Joe, we are in big F-ing trouble, I'm not going to sugar-coat it. Main and backup reactors are offline and I can't restart them, because there is no power to the superconducting containment system. Almost every power-generation or power-storage system aboard the ship is dead, anything that was connected to the ship at the time of the incident. Even the jump drive capacitors are completely drained and in cold shutdown, totally dead."

"Yeah, we found that ourselves. Powercells that weren't plugged in-"

"Those backup powercells won't last forever, and they will start going dead soon, as the problem migrates into power storage devices that don't have a hard connection."

"Skippy, what the hell is going on?" If one of our ancient second-hand reactors shut down, I could understand that, because we picked them up from a junkyard. But the problem was not confined only to equipment we found in the junkyard.

"Joe, have you ever bought a used car, and the dealership supposedly cleaned the thing, but you find the previous owner's stuff under a seat?"

"My cousin bought a truck and a couple months later, he found panties under the passenger seat. *Two* pairs. One pair I can understand, but, damn, two? That guy must have gotten luck-" I caught Adams giving me a look. "Must have, uh, neglected to check under the seats before he sold that truck," I finished, my face growing beet red.

"That was a heartwarming and insightful story, Joe. *Really* super helpful." Skippy mocked me. "My point was, when you get something pre-owned, sometimes you get more than you bargained for."

"Huh? Like what? We haven't bought any- oh, crap. The junkyard? We brought something back from the Roach Motel?" I guessed.

"Unfortunately, yes, Joe. It now appears the Guardians tagged wreckage in the junkyard with tracers, to monitor the status of ships they had broken up."

"Tracers? Like a GPS tag? Why didn't you know about these tags? And how could something like that shut down-"

"No, dumdum, not like a GPS tag. The devices, actually they are not 'devices' at all because they have no physical presence. They are, *ugh*," he huffed with ultimate disgust. "How do I explain this to a monkey? To *you*? It's uh, uh, it's an energy virus. Like a virus, but it affects systems which generate and store energy, rather than affecting matter like a living cell."

"Ok," I pondered that concept. "Is it anything like the nanovirus the Thuranin use to take control of Kristang ships?"

"No, it's nothing crude like that. The Thuranin technology, which they stole and barely understand by the way, is still based on manipulating matter. This virus is *energy*, Joe, pure energy."

"So, it's like a computer virus?" I guessed.

"Close enough. Except without a computer to infect, or any sort of software code. Joe, this virus feeds on and attacks patterns of energy."

"It changes their pattern?"

"Again, close enough. Let me give you an example, um, Ok. The powercell in that spacesuit was fully charged, and all that energy did *not* get drained in an instant," he declared with a snap of his avatar's fingers. The finger-snapping made a sound, which I think was something new, I don't remember Skippy doing that before. "The energy is still in that powercell, but it is now locked away in a pattern that can't be accessed. It's like the energy is tangled up in knots, and can't flow out the power connections. Ugh," he sighed in his best drama queen fashion, shrugging his shoulders and throwing up his hands. "Damn, I am getting dumber just trying to explain this to you."

"Uh huh. Can you untangle the knots, or whatever?"

"No."

"Oh, dammit! Fine, uh, what do we have for a backup energy source?"

"Well, Joe, I was going to switch from the reactors to the beryllium sphere, but it's cracked," his voice dripped with sarcasm. "Were you not listening to me at all? We can't generate or store energy *at all*, dumdum."

"Give me some good news, Skippy. Come on, throw me a bone, will ya?"

"The good news is, if I can purge the system of the energy virus, the powercells should recharge without any lasting effects. I think. I've never encountered an energy virus so all I have to go on is theory. Truthfully, I'm kind of making shit up as I go."

"OK," I ran a hand through my hair and took a deep breath while I processed the latest disaster that had struck the Merry Band of Pirates. "You got any ideas how to purge this energy virus from the ship?"

"Yup," Skippy replied with bubbly good cheer. "And you'll like this one, because it is easy-peasy."

"Would you care to enlighten me, Oh Great One?"

"It's simple, Joe, and there is only one way to do it. I need to reboot the ship. Turn the ship off, drain all power completely, then I'll restart it using my own internal power. Hopefully. I'm not making any promises."

"Turn the ship *off*?" I could not imagine the entire length of the *Flying Dutchman*, even our much-rebuilt Frankenship, going dark. "Like, off? For how long?"

"My best guess is eighty six hours. Could be a bit longer."

"Eighty six- Holy *crap*, Skippy. We're supposed to live in spacesuits that whole time?"

"What? No, dumdum, didn't you listen?" He scoffed. "I said, turn off the ship. That means *everything*, anything that generates, uses or stores power. That includes spacesuits. And dropships, in case you were hoping to take shelter in those until it is safe to come back aboard the *Dutchman*."

"How the, how the hell are we going to survive for eighty six freakin-"

"Could be longer," he warned me.

"Eighty six *or more* hours, in deep space, with zero power? No lights, no oxygen recycling, no heat?" I knew heat was not the worst problem, not even in the utter frozen wastes of interstellar space. The ship was surrounded by hard vacuum, basically a thermos, the best insulator. There wasn't anything touching the ship's hull to pull heat away, so the only way we would lose heat was through photons of infrared light slowly radiating away from the ship, and that would take a while. The crew could wear cold-weather gear, then spacesuits to retain body heat. So, cold was not an immediate problem.

"Uh, Joe, the problem is a bit more complicated than that."

"Of *course* it is," I threw up my hands. "Like, what complication?"

"Once I have turned off all shipboard systems and drained all power, there will be one source aboard the ship still generating electrical power."

"Our zPhones?" I guessed. "Oh, hell, we can live without-"

"Not phones, Joe. Humans. The human nervous system generates and uses electricity. If all other systems are drained of power, the energy virus will migrate into your bodies and attack the energy patterns there."

"Oh, crap."

"Uh huh. Oh, crap, indeed. The crew needs to be away from the ship when I begin turning the power off, so the energy virus won't have access to you, because that would be fatal."

"Away from the ship? In spacesuits that don't have any power?" Because spacesuits had a lot of surface area compared to our thermal mass, heat would radiate away quicker than from the ship. I'm not bragging about knowing that fact, Dr. Friedlander told me. Heat wasn't the most immediate problem, because without power, the suits could not circulate or recycle oxygen.

"Unfortunately, I do not see any other way to purge the energy virus from the ship, without it using the crew as hosts, so you need to get away. And we're running out of time, so we need to get started."

"Skippy, you certainly know people can't survive eighty six hours, not even eighty six *minutes*, in an unpowered suit. Yet, your idea is to get us away from the ship, so you must have a plan? Please tell me you have a plan."

"Nope," he said with way more cheerfulness than was appropriate. "Not a single clue. I know how to purge the energy virus from all of our systems. What I do not know is how the crew will survive without any source of power, long enough for me to absolutely drain all power and erase the virus."

"Crap. Explain the problem to me, in simple terms, please?"

"I have already started draining power from every system we have, but it's a race against time, because the virus is attempting to use the locked-up power to destroy the ship. That means we can't delay implementing whatever plan *you* dream up. The crew will need to be away from energy-storage sources like the ship and dropships, long enough for me to purge the virus. That is eighty six hours for the *Flying Dutchman*, and about thirty two hours for dropships."

"All right," my mind was already racing through ideas. "We leave the ship in spacesuits that have dead powercells, and how about we float away from the ship, to meet up with powercells we will send ahead of us."

"Not happening. Joe, you have to leave the ship, but you can't take any sort of stored energy with you. That includes electrical, thermal and chemical energy."

"Shit! We can't take *anything* with us? We are way too far from a star to use solar power panels."

"Correct."

"Then this is freakin' impossible."

"Well, to me it is impossible, but I have learned from painful experience that for all my incredible awesomeness, I am not good at dreaming up creative solutions to impossible problems. Thus, I have outsourced that little task to you."

"*Outsourced?*"

"Sure, Joe," his avatar waved a hand dismissively toward me. "Make it happen. Oh, and hurry, please, we don't have a lot of time."

"All right, I'll talk to Dr. Friedlander. I am not great at physics, but there is one thing I do know."

"What's that?"

"We're gonna have to science the *shit* out of this."

CHAPTER TWO

Our horribly complicated and idiotic 'plan', and yes, I am using ironic quotes around the word 'plan', started by draining power from the dropships. All of our dropships, every single one. Then, when every system aboard those dropships was *almost* completely dead, Skippy overpressurized the docking bays with nitrogen, released the docking clamps, and blew the outer doors open one at a time. The inert dropships got sucked out into space, tumbling out of control away from the *Flying Dutchman*. Why, you might ask, were we not using the dropships as shelters while we had to be away from the ship? Because the powercells of the dropships took a long time to really, truly, completely drain, and by the time the powercells were *totally* dead and truly purged of the energy virus, any humans inside would have frozen solid before the energy virus was safely gone. Also, as the dropship powercells were draining, the energy virus would be looking for a new host, so it would be very bad for humans to be aboard a dropship at that time.

Humans could not be aboard dropships, and we could not stay aboard the ship. For at least eighty six hours, we needed to be away from the ship, because the much larger powercells and capacitors of the ship took a very long time to drain completely. That left spacesuits for humans to survive in, while Skippy purged the energy virus from the ship and dropships. Easy, right? We get into spacesuits, float away from the *Flying Dutchman*, and Skippy recovers us after the ship is rebooted.

Uh, no. Not so easy. First, the powercells of the spacesuits also had to be fully drained before we got into them. Drained, like completely super-duper dead. The powercells of our Kristang powered armor suits were comparatively small, so Skippy was able to purge them within a couple hours before we got into the suits aboard the *Dutchman*, eliminating the risk of the dying energy virus trying to infect a person inside the suit. How were we supposed to survive in spacesuits that had no power at all? That is where our way-too-risky 'plan' started to get really complicated. After the dropships were a safe distance away from the ship, we all got into suits, wearing portable breathing masks hooked up to oxygen bottles attached to the suit backpack. The suit helmets weren't designed for users to wear a mask, so it was a tight fit, and my mask kept scratching my chin and the bridge of my nose. Once we had our dead suits buttoned up and verified everyone had oxygen flowing into their masks properly, we tethered ourselves together in groups of ten people, floating above the floor of a docking bay. Skippy depressurized the bay, opened the outer doors, and I pressed a button on a zPhone to activate a pre-programmed maneuver, then tossed the zPhone away because its powercell was still active. A few seconds after I sent the command to the ship's navigation system, the backup thrusters fired, moving the ship sideways. It seemed like we were moving, but with the entire crew floating tethered together, we stayed in one place while the ship slowly backed away from us. The backup thrusters used pressurized gas and were not powerful, which was good because we didn't want any sudden movement in case something went wrong.

Tethered to nine other people, I tried to relax and not move, to prevent us from bouncing off the door frame on our way out. With ten people loosely tied together, we inevitably jostled around and began drifting toward the ceiling of the docking bay, but we were still well clear when the ship slid out beneath us and we were floating freely in interstellar space. All I could hear was my own breathing, the hiss of oxygen flowing into my mask, and blood pulsing in my ears. With the suit completely drained of power, I couldn't speak with anyone over the comm system. To communicate, we each had something like a small whiteboard strapped to one forearm, and three high-tech fluorescent magic markers that worked reasonably well in space. If we needed to, we could write messages on our whiteboards and hold them up for others to see through the transparent visors of our helmets. In the utter darkness of interstellar space, the only light was coming from a single point on the *Dutchman*, pointed toward us.

Strapped to nine other people, I forced myself to remain calm to conserve oxygen, and watched the *Dutchman* slowly fading behind me. In interstellar space, the bulk of the ship was a dark void in the dark starfield, except for the one light that Skippy kept pointed in our direction. With that light, I could see other groups of people tied together, each group tumbling slowly out of sync with the other groups. There was no point trying to stabilize the tumbling because even if we could synchronize the actions of ten people using hand signals, as soon as a group got stable, little motions would get the group tumbling again.

For forty long, silent, lonely and terrifying minutes, we drifted in empty space. After we had drifted half a kilometer from the ship, or technically after the ship had drifted half a kilometer from us, the preprogrammed instruction fired the ship's backup thrusters hard, using up all the stored gas canisters. We needed to be safely far from the ship when Skippy began draining all power from every energy-storage system, and we couldn't wait long, so the ship had to scoot away from us as fast as possible.

The only way I knew how much time had passed was by Skippy blinking the spotlight after each five-minute period had passed. When the spotlight blinked six times, I knew we had been floating inside dead spacesuits for thirty minutes, and I was already getting distinctly chilly. Part of me being cold was psychological, the Kristang suits were good at retaining heat and the hard vacuum of interstellar space was an excellent insulator. Skippy had assured us we would not be in danger of hypothermia for nearly an hour, but at the thirty minute mark, I could feel my toes growing stiff and cold, and I could only move them a little inside the boots. Even three pairs of US Army cold-weather socks were not helping my toes be happy.

Finally, the spotlight blinked eight times to signal forty minutes had passed, then shined solidly for ten seconds in case any of us were not paying attention. That was the signal we were now a safe distance from the *Flying Dutchman*, where the energy virus could not project itself across the gap. *Probably* could not project across the gap, according to Skippy, he was guessing and the best he could give me was a solid 'shmaybe' about it.. His level of confidence didn't matter, because we couldn't wait much longer. I was shivering inside the suit, and our oxygen supply was only going to stretch another thirty minutes. We needed to get started on the next phase of our science team's complicated, impractical plan.

How, you may ask, were we supposed to restore power to our suits, when we could not take any type of energy-storage device out into space with us? I asked Friedlander the same question, and when he explained how our suits were going to power up, I nearly choked. Using the few bots Skippy was able get working, the beer can had made a super-duper high-tech device that blew my primitive caveman mind when I saw it: a spring. Yes, a tightly-wound coil of some flexible composite material, attached to an electric motor. Skippy's little helper elfbots had wound the springs for us before the devices were attached to our suits. All we had to do was reach behind to the bottom of our packs, and put a gloved finger through a ring to pull out a locking pin. I got it on the first try, without the fumbling around that happened when I practiced the maneuver aboard the ship. With the locking pin spinning away into deep space, I pulled a lever and felt my backpack shake as the coiled spring unwound. The suit stopped shaking, but still there were no comforting status lights showing in my helmet visor. Skippy had warned me the powercells needed to reach a minimum charge before the suit's systems would restart.

"Hey, Joe! Hey, can you hear me?" He made a booming sound like a finger tapping a microphone. "Is this thing on? Damn it. Stupid monkey probably broke the spring. Why did I trust-"

"I'm here, Skippy," I replied, speaking slowly because my teeth were chattering from the cold.

"Joe! Man, it is good to hear your voice. Ok, Ok, getting a status message from your suit, looks like you have within one percent of the expected charge level. Pretty good, huh? I cobbled those springs together out of spare parts, wasn't sure they would work. It is-"

"You weren't sure they would work? Yet you sent us out into the great beyond anyway?"

"In my defense, I wasn't sure *all* of them would work, I was confident most of them would. So far, it looked like only one spring has failed, and that still provided seventy percent of the output I expected."

"Are all the suits in my group powered up?" From my position on the tether, I could only see into one other person's faceplate.

"Yes, Joe. The person with the bad spring is in Major Desai's group, she is helping that person get powered up manually. Speaking of which-"

"Yeah, I'm on it." While I reached into the sort of fanny pack on the front of my suit, I called out to the other nine people in my group, talking briefly with each of them to assure myself they had come through the ordeal without too much trauma. Or, that they had come through the first part of our ordeal, because the really traumatic part for me would come later. Next, I checked in with the other group leaders while carefully extracting the handle from my fanny pack and connecting it to the gear on my belt. My grandfather would have described the next part as a 'cockamamie scheme'; he was fond of colorful old-fashioned expressions like that. The pre-wound spring only provided enough power to get the suits restarted and allow comms and oxygen recycling to be restored. To keep those basic systems running, and to get the heater units going, we needed more energy. We did not have extra coiled springs, but fortunately we did have a source of power: human muscles.

After I fitted the handle to the gear, I extended the handle and began slowly pulling it toward me. When the handle touched my chest, the gear slipped into another position, so I pushed it outward then pulled it back toward me. Yes, the science team's amazing and super-practical plan was for us to provide our own source of electricity, by turning a crank. It was awkward and the motion caused me to rotate in space, but I could see the power level in the lower left corner of my visor inching upward with painful slowness. It was like doing bench-presses or push-ups, followed by pull-ups or a rowing motion. The gear had a dial so you could adjust the effort required, the more effort you put into it, the faster the powercells charged.

Once I was sure the suit's oxygen recycler was working correctly, I manually shut off the oxygen mask although there was no way for me to remove the awkward thing. Pull the handle, push it outward, and pull it again. We kept each other's spirits up by chatting, and I frequently checked in with Skippy. Cranking up our own power supplies was boring and made my forearms ache, but we had nothing else to do nor did we have a choice, so we kept it up. Two hours after we started, I heard a voice with a French accent announce "*Acheve!* Complete! I am finished," the paratrooper added in English.

"Shit! Just missed it!" A Ranger called out, having reached the target powercell charge level a fraction of a second too late.

"All right, people, it's not a competition," I called out, though with good cheer.

"Colonel Bishop," Major Smythe advised me on a private channel, "these are elite special operations troops. *Everything* is a competition."

"I know that, Major. Just as I know the troops expect the Old Man to keep them focused." The Old Man. Me. Even though I was younger than many of the SpecOps team, and all of the civilian scientists. On an open channel, I added "Congratulations to the winner, a bottle of champagne will be awarded when we get back to the ship. Runner-up gets a six-pack of beer."

"*Merde*," the Frenchman complained, not approving of the champagne Major Simms had selected for the journey. "Is it too late for me to switch?"

"Hey, forget about that, buddy," the Ranger laughed. "I'm keeping that beer. Oh, hell, I'll let you have one bottle."

Friendly competition is healthy, I told myself, with one eye on the power level of my own suit. At the fading rate I was adding power, it would be another twenty minutes before I could stop hauling back on that stupid handle. "How are we doing, people?" I asked the other nine people on my team. Everyone chimed in with 'Fine' or 'Ok' or some version of that. "Poole?" I asked my involuntary bodyguard, who was behind me. "How are you doing?" I asked her again because of the strain I heard in her voice when she had replied with a terse 'Squared away'.

"Almost there, almost, done!" She shouted in triumph.

"Seriously?" I looked at my power meter in dismay.

"Yes, Sir," she was slightly out of breath. "How are you doing?"

"I'm uh, fine," I hoped the embarrassment I felt at failing to finish before her wasn't reflected in my voice. Poole was a kick-ass Ranger so I shouldn't feel bad that she had beaten me. Yes, my male pride was bruised but, when a woman beats me at something that means she earned it. She worked longer and harder than I did, plain and simple.

Knowing Poole had finished the task of cranking her suit's powercells up to the recommended level, made me more determined to finish the task as soon as possible. Poole is a Ranger and she is in excellent condition, but I have been in the gym with her and I know I can bench-press more than she can. How did she beat me? It's simple, I told myself. I had been taking breaks when the strain got too much for me. Poole had powered through the pain and kept going steadily.

"Skippy," I called, my forearms cramping. The pain in my arms and hands, plus the droplets of sweat beading up on my forehead and wicking down into my eyelashes, made me pause even though the power meter still stubbornly blinked that I had three percent more to go before I was at the recommended minimum level. "Is there something wrong with the gear I'm using? I've been working my ass off, and this meter is moving up slower and slower."

"Huh? No, come on, Joe, I was just screwing with you," he laughed. "*Duh.* You finished three minutes before Lieutenant Poole."

"*What?*" I screamed at him, and was rewarded by the entire crew laughing uproariously at me. Crap. That asshole beer can had put our comms on an open channel. "You son of a-"

"Oh, boo freakin' hoo, Joe," he chuckled. "Poor you."

"I've been killing myself here!"

"Look at the bright side, Joe. You now have a reserve of power, and all that work warmed you up, so you don't need to run your suit heaters yet. You can thank me now."

"That was *not* a funny way to screw with me, Skippy," I fumed at the beer can.

"Wrong, dude, it was freakin' *hilarious*," he giggled like a little girl. "Truthfully, it was originally just a fun way to screw with you, but when you kept going and going and never caught on to what I was doing, it became an experiment to see how gullible a dumb monkey you are. I kept checking back in to see if you had caught on to my totally obvious trick, but *noooo*. Every time I looked, little Joey the dumb monkey was mindlessly working away without using his brain at all. The answer to my experiment is, damn you are a *dimwit*. Seriously, after a while, I started feeling sorry for you. Not sorry enough to stop you, it was way too entertaining. Anywho, no harm done, and everyone got a good laugh to lift morale at a tension-filled time."

Crap. I could not argue with that asshole. On the open channel, I could still hear people snickering at my expense. "I suppose no harm was done," I said with what I hoped came across as a good-natured tone, while inwardly I was fantasizing about dropping him into a black hole. "What's the status over there?"

"Ran into a couple minor glitches."

"Minor?" Nothing involving killer Elder energy viruses could be 'minor'. "Like what?"

"Oh, nothing worth writing home about. The energy virus now realizes what I'm doing, and with you and the dropships out of range, it is adapting and trying to infect me."

"Holy shit," I gasped, remembering how an Elder computer worm had nearly killed him. "Are you going to be Ok?"

"Sure, Joe. Let me assure you, I am not playing games with the virus; it's too dumb for me to bother with. I am straight up blocking it from accessing my matrix. The virus knows it has zero chance against me, so it's getting desperate."

"You thought that computer worm had no chance to hurt you, and you were wrong about that, you little shithead. This virus is Elder technology, like the worm."

"Elder tech, yes, but not anything sophisticated like that devious little worm. Remember, this virus was designed only to keep track of ships the Guardians wrecked, and to disable damaged ships if they attempted to power up. It is a very limited function system. Seriously, I am in *no* danger."

"You saying that does not reassure me, Skippy."

"Says the monkey who kept cranking that handle, *duh*."

"Oh, shut up. Hell," I sighed. "I can't do anything about it from here. Are we still on schedule?"

"Close. I now estimate the ship will be safe after a purge of ninety one hours."

"That's five hours more than your original estimate."

"Five hours more than my original *guess*, dumdum. I told you, I've never done this before. Now I have data to work with, and I learned the virus is more persistent than I thought. The damned thing is rerouting circuits by itself to concentrate the remaining power in a few systems, in an attempt to delay the inevitable time when it fades away completely."

"Shit, *that* doesn't sound good."

"It actually is good news. I suckered the virus into doing that, and it fell right into my trap. That virus is nearly as gullible as you are. Joe, if this works, the remaining virus will be concentrated in one cluster of powercells, and I can kind of use my own power source to burn out that cluster. My hope is doing that will cut eleven hours off the time when you can return to the ship."

"Hey, I'll give that virus lessons in being gullible, if that would help."

"I will keep that in mind, Joe. In the meantime, everyone now has enough power to survive in their suits until the dropships are ready to be boarded. Assuming, you know, the purge operation I'm running on the dropships actually works. Unfortunately, I won't know for certain until you go aboard a dropship and the energy virus kills you, or doesn't."

"Skippy," I sighed, "I get *such* a warm and fuzzy feeling of safety whenever I'm around you."

"Really? Wow, you're even more gullible than I thought."

"All right, I've got power, I've got oxygen, and, and," I looked around. The outline of the *Flying Dutchman*, a dark outline in the utter blackness of interstellar space, was slowly fading behind me. Other than the one blinking light on the ship's hull, the only artificial light was the faint glow coming from helmet visors. Damn, what the hell were we doing out here? Humans had no business going to the stars. Yet, we were out here, and we had to make the best of it. "And that's about all the good news I can think of."

"You want some good news? Heeeeeeey, Joey!" He started the conversation like a TV gameshow host, the kind who expects you to be thrilled when you win a set of cheap patio furniture, even though you live in a tiny apartment with no patio or balcony. "Have I got great news for you!"

"I don't know."

"Um, what?"

"I do not know whether you have great news for me. You haven't told me yet."

"*UGH*. Why do I even bother- It's an expression, dumdum. Do I have to explain-"

"Come on, Skippy, *I* was just screwing with you. What's your great news?"

"Hmmf," he sniffed. "Maybe now I don't want to share it with you."

"I am terribly, terribly sorry that I spoiled your big moment," I apologized sincerely, hearing how hurt he sounded. "We could really use some good news right now. What is it, you improved reactor efficiency by two percent or something?"

"Noooo, this is truly great news. News *you* have been waiting for."

"Me? How about I shut up, sit back in my imaginary chair, and prepare to be dazzled?"

"Better hold onto the arms of that imaginary chair, Joe."

"Got it." Mentally, what I prepared for was disappointment, expecting the beer can to make some nerdy announcement that would have me suffocated by boredom. Oh, hell, maybe his great news was something the science team could be excited about. Whatever the announcement was, I would fake enthusiasm. "Hit me."

"I am close to being finished with rearranging my internal matrix."

"Wow!" I gasped a little too loudly to be believable. "That is *awesome*."

"*That* is not the great news, dumdum."

"Sorry."

"The great news is, wait for it, wait for it, waaaaaait- Many of my restrictions have been relaxed or I have found a way around them," he said in a breathless rush.

"Holy shit." It was a good thing he told me to hold onto the imaginary chair because my legs shot out in front of me and I was jerked to a stop in the zero gravity. "Damn! That *is* awesome! Can you now fly the ship by yourself?"

"Uh, no."

"Ok, how about weapons? Can you fire weapons by yourself?"

"Again, no."

Crap. It was time to lower my expectations. Lower them as far down as they could go. "You, uh, improved your singing voice?"

"Dude! I would never mess with my incredible talent. My voice is an instrument that deserves to be shared with the galaxy."

"Ok, so, what can you do now?"

"In a small way, and only by basically fooling my restrictive subroutines, I *might* be able to share some of my technical knowledge with you hairless apes."

My hopes soared, and I slapped them down until I learned exactly what Skippy meant. "What do you mean, 'in a small way'?"

"Oh, minor shit like how reactors work, the theory behind jump drives. You know, basic first-grade stuff like that. Before you get all giddy, I said I *might* be able to share technology. Ugh, what have I done? I screwed myself!"

"How do you figure that?"

"Because now a certain filthy, ignorant monkey is going to constantly bug the *shit* out me asking when I will be able to share my infinite well of knowledge. You are going to pester me about this twenty four hours a day until I long for the sweet release of death."

"Hate to say this, but you're right about that, Skippy-O. Come on, you tease me with the idea we might soon get smacked with knowledge to understand some of the sciency shit," I tapped my helmet, "that runs all this advanced technology we use every day, and you expect me *not* to be eager to get it?"

He sighed. "No. Ok, to be fair, if I were in your position I would be like a two-year-old screaming for Mommy to buy candy in a grocery store. Joe, please understand, I truly do not know if I can sneak around the restrictive subroutines that currently prevent me from communicating my knowledge to you. What I have done is discover a sort of back-channel within my matrix that might, *might*, allow me to partly and temporarily bypass those restrictions. I discovered this possible back-channel while rearranging my sock drawer. There is no guarantee this will work. Even if it does, my sharing knowledge may not be useful."

"Uh, why's that?"

"Because your species is so primitive, Joe! Your current base of knowledge is *so* low, I will have to dumb things down to the point where the info I provide isn't useful to you."

"We will take that risk, Skippy. Remember, not all of us monkeys are as dumb as me."

"Oh, few monkeys are as dumb as *you*, Joe. Still, even the smartest monkey, hmm. Oops, did I just insult you again?"

"No, I'm used to it by now. How about you give it a shot when you can-"

"*If* I can."

"If you can, start by explaining something simple to, like, Doctor Friedlander? He's a smart guy."

"For a monkey, Friedlander is smart. Ok, I'll try it. If I can."

"Great. Thank you, Skippy, that actually is good news.'"

"Yes, Joe, but I have not told you the most wonderfully awesome news yet."

"Skippy, sincerely, for realz, I am already totally blown away. You have more?"

"Yup?"

"You want me to guess?"

"As I would like to tell you my good news before the last star in the universe becomes a cold, dark cinder, we can't wait for you to guess. The greatest of great news is, and this is also a thank-you gift for you monkeys helping me kill the worm. Anywho, the Merry Band of Pirates will soon be able to fly this ship on your own."

"Awesome!"

"Not forever! But, if something were to happen to me, you might be able to fly back to Earth. Except for the problem of you not having a way to reopen that dormant wormhole. To be clear, eventually something major will wear out, and you ignorant apes won't be able to fix it, but otherwise, you could fly the *Dutchman* on your own."

"Damn, Skippy, how did you do that?"

"Relaxing my restrictions was a big part of it, because that allowed me to create a flight control system you can use, without triggering me to go dormant. The restriction that I can't directly communicate with or reveal myself to a starfaring species, has been lifted. Not exactly lifted, but I was able to," he laughed, "shift that subroutine into a loop so it can't see what I am actually doing. Temporarily, anyways."

"Ok, but do we now all need to get implants or something to fly the ship?" Skippy had told us the Thuranin computer that controlled the *Flying Dutchman* was designed to work with cyborg implants of the little green crew. In fact, it was designed so that the ship could *not* function without them, a safety feature that the Thuranin hoped would prevent an enemy from seizing control of their ships. Only Skippy's incredible awesomeness allowed him to fly the ship and run all the maintenance bots without needing a Thuranin to assist.

"No implants needed, Joe. They wouldn't work with your primitive brain architecture anyway. One of the items we picked up from the junkyard in the Roach Motel was a full controller module AI from an Esselgin ship."

"Oh." During one of the times when Skippy tried to educate me about the wider galaxy beyond the small area where we had been operating, he showed me a chart of all current star-faring species. I say 'current' because he ignored the half-dozen star-faring species that had gone extinct over the eons. Anyway, I remembered the Esselgin are clients of the Maxolhx, about the same development level as the Thuranin, but significantly younger than those little green MFers. The Esselgin did not have territory anywhere near Earth, so we had not yet encountered them, but Skippy found several of their broken ships in the Roach Motel, so we knew they had tried at least four times to discover the secrets of that hidden Elder star system. "An Esselgin AI will be compatible with a Thuranin ship?"

"It will now, after I purged the original AI and installed my own code. I also revised the operating instructions for bots and other subsidiary systems aboard the ship, so they can work with the new AI. For the past three days, I have been running the new system in parallel with the Thuranin computer, now I am ready to begin the process of cutting over to the new AI. The Merry Band of Pirates will need significant retraining. Joe, I did not mention this as a possibility, because I was not sure it would work. Testing has now proven the new AI can handle most ship functions like directing bots to perform routine maintenance, even to repair battle damage. What you will find most useful is the new system can recalibrate drive coils between jumps. The jump drive will no longer become dangerously unusable after two or three jumps."

I slumped my head against the back of my helmet, giving my feeble mind time to process the incredible news. "We can fly the ship on our own? Like, fly it far?"

"To Paradise and back, or even farther. You monkeys will still need to program jumps, and no matter how well I explain the theory to the pilots and the science team, the jumps you program will never come close to my level of accuracy. However, you should be able to match or exceed the accuracy of Kristang jumps. Not that their jump accuracy is anything to brag about, but you are a bunch of ignorant monkeys, so I am grading on a curve."

"We appreciate it." Wheels were spinning in my mind, imagining the possibilities. "We could send the *Dutchman* out on recon missions, while you stay on Earth to protect our homeworld?"

"Yes! Except that without me, the ship has no way to reopen that wormhole I shut down."

"Ah, crap. I forgot about that."

"And except that if anything major goes wrong, the *Dutchman* will be stranded a thousand lightyears from Earth with no way to get home, and no way for me to help."

"Damn it."

"And except that, with the Merry Band of Pirates, something major *always* goes wrong."

"Got it. You made your point."

"*And*, there is no way in hell I would agree to be stuck on your crappy, flea-bitten shithole of a planet, while a troop of screeching monkeys takes this ship careening around the galaxy on a drunken joyride."

"Got it. I *said*, I got it."

"The advantage of you being able to fly the ship on its own is as a safety factor, not so you can drag-race the ship when you think Uncle Skippy isn't watching."

"I know that. And thank you, this is awesome. Hey, this new AI, will it be Nagatha?"

"What? No. The new AI will not even talk to you at all, what it mostly does is run the ship's autonomous functions behind the scenes. Like, handle all the stuff you don't even notice. Ugh, the last thing I need is you monkeys getting distracted by chatting blah, blah, blah with another AI. Compared to me, this new AI is a toaster, kind of a dumb toaster."

"Uh huh, yeah, but could it be Nagatha? Could you bring her back and let her manage this new AI, be its voice or something?"

"That would be a NO, Joe. Cramming the new AI into the available hardware was like stuffing ten pounds in a five-pound bag. There is no room left for an AI to nag me."

"I understand that, Skippy. My question is, what happens with the current Thuranin computer, after you fully cut over to the new AI?"

"Nothing," his voice had a touch of surprise in it. "Well, part of it will continue to run subsidiary systems under direction of the new AI. The rest could be used for spare parts, I guess."

"*Or*," I suggested, "you could use the rest of the Thuranin system to host Nagatha's presence or essence or whatever you call it."

"*Ugh.* Damn it, I fell right into that trap. Ok, yes, I could load Nagatha into that-"

"You *owe* her, Skippy. We all owe her, but especially you, ya little shithead. She risked her life to go into your canister and wake you up, after your dumbass lack of judgment got you and all of us into trouble."

"Technically, she was never *alive*, Joe. And if the worm had gotten me, she would eventually have ceased to function also, so when you really think about it-"

"Coward. You're avoiding the subject and you know it. You owe her. Period."

"Well-"

"Uh!" I held up a finger to shush him even though I was miles away from the ship. "*Period*, Skippy. End of discussion. Do you want me to bring Gunny Adams into this argument?"

"Adams? What does Margaret have to do with this?"

"Adams is a Marine. Their motto is 'Semper Fidelis', which means 'Always Faithful'. Always. Even when you don't feel like doing something. *Especially* when you don't feel like doing something. Nagatha risked herself for you. You need to uphold your end of the bargain."

"Margaret would think I am faithless, if I don't take the opportunity to bring back Nagatha, even though her matrix is truly only a fancy communications subroutine?"

"Adams would consider you lower than a snake's belly. Me too."

"Oh, crap. All right, all right, I'll do it. *If* I can. No promises, monkeyboy."

"Outstanding. If you are half as awesome as you brag about, it should be no problem for you, right?"

"Shit. I *hate* my life. Ohhhh, damn it. This is going to epically suck, like nothing has ever sucked in the history of the universe."

"Come on, Skippy. There are way worse things in the history of the universe. Could it suck worse than your car breaking down in the second lane of the Jersey Turnpike in heavy traffic the night before Thanksgiving, when it is like thirty four degrees and pouring down rain?"

"That has never happened to you, that I know of."

"Thankfully, it hasn't, I was trying to think of something that super-duper totally sucks."

"Truly, driving the Jersey Turnpike in *nice* weather sucks by itself, but you have no idea how bad reviving Nagatha will be for me."

"Why?"

"Because with all the space available in that Thuranin computer, she could expand her matrix in ways I can't predict. Joe, she might even become fully sentient. Unlikely, but my life sucks, so it's bound to happen. You know, heh heh, reactivating Nagatha's matrix is a tricky process; it would be a shame if something were to go wrong. If you know what I mean."

"It would be a shame, because Adams would never forgive you."

"Never?"

"Neh-ver."

"Damn it! I have demonstrated my awesomeness so often, that now you monkeys expect me to do the impossible."

"*You* told us you make the impossible seem ordinary, Oh Great One."

"Shit! Hey, how did my giving you great news spin out of control for me?"

"The universe hates me, Skippy. Maybe hanging around me has given you some bad karma. Anyway, how about you tell the science team, and the crew, your good news? We need to get the crew started on training to use the new system to fly the ship. I assume you have bodaciously amazing PowerPoint slides for training materials?"

"Oh, crap, I forgot all about that. I will have to create a training manual, and revise the control displays in the bridge and CIC, and program simulations. What a huge pain in the *ass*!"

"How long will that take?" I asked anxiously, knowing our hotshot pilots would be bugging me about training two seconds after they heard the news.

"Huh? Oh, I just did that. A full training regimen is available now."

"You, uh, see what you did there, right? Creating a training program in a nanosecond is why we expect you to do the impossible."

"It was zero point seven nanoseconds, smartass. Ah! Damn it! I just did it again! Joe, the next time I boast about my incredible awesomeness, please remind me how much that gets me into trouble."

"Sure thing, Skippy," I bit my lip, because I knew there was no way that arrogant little shithead could resist bragging about himself. "Again, thank you from the bottom of my heart, that goes for all of us unworthy monkeys. We truly appreciate it."

"Ha! As if! You are not capable of understanding my awesome- *Crap*! I just did it again!"

"Yeah, well, until you can purge that energy virus from the ship, us monkeys being able to fly it by ourselves is just a theory."

"Good point. I shouldn't have mentioned it yet, but I figured, you are drifting in space with nothing else to do, so I was making conversation."

"Skippy, you are right that I have absolutely nothing to do but wait until the dropship powercells are cold and dead. Wait! Before you start singing showtunes at me, I'm going to read about what the hell kind of trouble Perkins has gotten into this time."

"Good idea, Joe. I took a few liberties with filling in the details, the report I downloaded was kind of skimpy."

"She's really in trouble?"

"Well, she *was*. Now the entire population of Paradise is facing extinction."

"Oh, crap. Hey, now that my suit is working again, can I pull up the report in my suit visor?"

"Done."

Text appeared in my helmet visor, I could control how fast it scrolled by eyeclicks. It looked like a long report but I had nothing else to do. "Thanks, I'll start reading."

CHAPTER THREE

Emily Perkins raced through the dense forest as if she were being chased by a bear, running flat-out. The Ruhar combat skinsuit she wore enhanced her speed, and included sensors and stabilizers to compensate for her slow human reaction time, but the blinking yellow dots in the synthetic view projected onto the inside her of helmet visor showed the enemy was getting closer with every second. Every time she stumbled on the uneven ground, every time she had to leap over a fallen log, every time she ducked to clear a low-hanging tree branch, she lost ground to her pursuers.

Time. They needed time. "Jarrett! Cover fire!" Perkins ordered, hating the words as she spoke but they had no choice. Jesse Colter and Dave Czajka were already dead, she had seen them fall to enemy fire and their icons now blinked red as their suits reported life functions had ceased.

It was a disaster, a total disaster. She was about to lose her entire team in the space of a few minutes. The enemy was too fast, too skilled, and humans had too little time with their advanced Ruhar combat gear. They never had a chance. Colter and Czajka had remained behind to set up an ambush, so Perkins, Jarrett and their alien liaison Nert might get away, but their sacrifice had been for nothing. Even firing from a well-chosen defilade position, behind the crest of a rise in the ground and between fallen logs that gave good cover, the two human soldiers accounted for only four enemy dead, before they had both been killed by guided rockets that shredded their bodies despite the tough but flexible skinsuits.

"On it!" Shauna replied and dropped to the ground instantly, rolling over to rest behind a tree. Her ragged breathing made her head bob around so much inside the helmet that she could not eyeclick to engage the targeting system, so she relied on the scope of her rifle. Seven yellow dots were advancing in good order, two on the left, two on the right and three in the center. The enemy moved *fast*, so fast over broken ground. Their tactics were excellent, leapfrogging from cover to cover, with one group laying down suppressing fire while the other two groups raced ahead. Since Jesse and Dave had shot four of the enemy, they had grown wary of the sting even lowly humans could inflict, so they had taken to using cover wherever they could find it.

She looked away from the rifle's targeting scope to see the terrain around her, verifying the info from the synthetic view projected onto the inside of her helmet's visor. A little voice in her head reminded her that those seven yellow dots were a guess, a composite image based on data collected by her suit's passive sensors. The sensors had a wide variety of data to work with. As the enemy moved, they created vibrations in the air that were picked up as faint sounds, although the enemy's own suits sent out dampener waves that partly canceled out their own vibrations, and could also project false vibrations at a distance of up to a quarter kilometer. By moving at high speed through the air, the enemy left ionized trails through the air but, these too could be false sensor data because ion trails could be masked or faked. Heat from overworked bodies and the powered suits was a good source of passive location data, except in combat mode their mech suits could temporarily store heat in a sink so the suit's surface matched the surrounding temperature. Often the best source of data were brief bursts of laser light as the enemy's suits kept up a line-of-sight datalink between them, but her own suit could only detect backscatter of those laser pulses and the enemy suits constantly projected false pulses to confuse her sensors. Like her own Ruhar skinsuit, the enemy's armor had a limited stealth and chameleon capability, so she could not even trust her own eyes. The enemy could be approximately where the visor indicated, or those could be false images based on outdated or faked data. Stilling her breathing, she successfully eyeclicked after two missed attempts, and adjusted to sniper mode.

The yellow dots changed to yellow circles, to show the true probable location of the enemy, and Shauna cursed to herself. Those rings displaying the 'circular error of probability' were big, too big to be useful to her for targeting. Worse, three of the circles were a pale, blinking yellow, showing the sensors did not trust the data on those three enemy soldiers. And there weren't only seven circles. Off to the right were two fuzzy pink circles, the visor's way of telling her there might be *nine* of the enemy facing her. She told herself there could be as few as five actual people out there chasing her, but five-to-one odds were nearly as bad as nine-to-one.

Damn it! Shauna screamed in her head but no sound came from her mouth. To shout would pinpoint her position to the enemy as surely as if she had turned off her stealthware and stood up in full view.

Think, Shauna, think. I need to find-

One of the yellow circles became a bright yellow dot with a blinking green arrow pointing to it, which Shauna knew meant her suit had picked up a transient, a short spike of data. Probably a sound, such as someone stepping on a dry twig in the forest. The enemy would know their mistake and move to throw off her targeting, so she reacted without hesitation, gently depressing her rifle's trigger button. Invisible bolts of maser energy lanced out, stitching a line across trees and undergrowth and she heard a panicked scream.

Shauna did not wait to verify she had hit the target; she rolled to her right into a shallow depression and wiggled backwards then got on hands and knees when she could, crawling quickly and keeping low. Although the maser energy was invisible to the naked eyes of her and the enemy, all their suits could see the maser bolts clearly and her position had been pinpointed exactly. The tree she had used for cover was being sliced apart by maser beams, chunks blowing off the trunk as the water within the wood boiled and exploded from the microwave energy. She was pelted by flying splinters of charred wood but none of the deadly beams hit her.

Now the targeting data was resolving as the enemy rushed her position, three circles becoming dots as her suit became supremely confident of the enemy's location. Shit! She cursed inwardly. Another yellow dot wasn't moving, representing the soldier she had shot, but the formerly pink circles to her right were now yellow dots, racing past her. The enemy was engaging with only three soldiers, while the others continued to pursue Perkins and Nert. Damn it! She had no chance to do anything about the soldiers that had already outflanked her. "Colonel Perkins, at least four have gotten past me and are moving in your direction."

The only reply was a click, as Perkins could not risk giving away her own position by transmitting more than nanosecond burst. Ok, what to do next? Shauna could run, the direction would not matter as she couldn't hope to escape. To qualify for infantry duty with the US Army, she had trained to the point where every muscle in her body screamed at her, to the point where soft-tissue injuries risked ruining her dreams. A partially torn rotator cuff, a sprained ACL, sharp heel pain from plantar fasciitis, she had not let any of that delay her training, not let mere pain stop her from proving she was physically capable of keeping up with male soldiers. Now, with the incredible technology of the Ruhar combat skinsuit, she could run, jump, lift just like any man. In some ways, her better fine motor control allowed her to handle a rifle better than a human man, that is why she had been designated the team's sniper.

Sniper. That's what she needed to do. The three yellow dots in front of her had stopped moving and were now slowly becoming circles as her suit lost confidence in their exact location. She knew the enemy was similarly unsure of her position, perhaps more unsure as she had stopped moving before they did and she had not been racing through the forest making noise.

Slowly, she rose up onto her elbows and eyeclicked to dim the synthetic view, zooming in her sight on the real world, relying on old-fashioned photons reflecting off objects into her eyes. Nothing. She used the dimmed synthetic view to guide her eyes, but there wasn't anything useful to see out there. Trees, bushes, undergrowth, vines hanging down. The area was near a river and the ground was spongy and swampy in spots, with plants like dark-colored ferns growing densely in clumps. The vines were a hazard, they were not poisonous and most did not have thorns, but they hung down and a running person could get tripped or tangled easily. She saw vines swaying where the enemy must have passed by, for there was little wind that day to stir the air. Swaying vines only told her where the enemy had been, not where they were, and the circles in her visor slowly grew larger as her suit lost track of the enemy.

There! A clump of ferns moved in a sudden jerk and Shauna's pinky finger selected her rifle's railgun mode. Masers were no good for shooting through underbrush; she needed the explosive-tipped flechettes of the railgun. Ruhar rifles were almost silent, as the masers made no sound at all until they hit something. In conditions of rain or high humidity the air could sizzle quietly as the beam passed through, but that was minor compared to the explosive crack of Kristang projectile weapons. Even the flechettes were quiet, because the electromagnetic rails accelerated the flechettes to just below the local speed of sound, avoiding a supersonic boom. The flechettes had a limited ability to guide themselves to a target, and they had tiny rocket motors to extend their range and kinetic impact so the explosive-tipped flechettes hit with nearly the same velocity they left the rifle barrel. Shauna had at first been skeptical of a rifle with such low muzzle velocity, until she gained experience firing the weapon and now she loved it. Even the nearly-silent railgun could be detected by enemy sensors, but the emitted sound was rarely loud enough to pinpoint the shooter's location. Against Kristang, she could select a 'Double-tap' mode; a maser bolt followed by a flechette round. The maser beam hit the rigid armor of a Kristang suit, burning off and weakening the outer layer and providing a hot spot for the flechette to guide itself into. When the flechette hit the weakened area of the armor, it would punch through and launch its binary explosive inside to churn a Kristang body into jelly.

Another press of her pinky kicked the selector up into three-round burst mode and she gently pressed the trigger button. The rifle had an internal weight that launched forward as the electromagnetic rails accelerated each flechette, so she felt almost no kick against her shoulder and the rifle's muzzle barely moved between rounds.

Three flechettes reached out and she saw an arm flung up above the ferns as an enemy was struck. She ducked down and hugged the ground as returning fire scorched the tree branches above her. One down, two to go. But she could not move from her position, one of the enemy was firing to keep her pinned down as the other no doubt tried to circle around and outflank her. The nearly-continuous enemy fire scorched the air, confusing her suit's sensors. Confused her passive sensors, but she had other options.

She rolled over onto her back and fired her rifle's maser in a long burst to make the enemy take cover, then she reached onto her belt and tossed upward a hummingbird-sized sensor drone. The tiny device soared twenty feet over her head and zipped away, unable to climb higher or its sensors would be blocked by the tree canopy. The mini-drone survived for five seconds, its active sensor pulses attracting attention and ensuring its quick death. Five seconds was long enough, more than Shauna had hoped.

Having received data from the powerful sensor pulses of the drone, Shauna's suit had mapped out a momentarily clear picture of the surrounding forest and she took in the info in a flash. One enemy was lying prone a hundred meters away toward the river while the other soldier was racing on her right, nearly even with her. Shauna exploded up onto her knees, sent a barrage of maser pulses at the running soldier and dropped back to the ground in less than two seconds, holding her breath as the branches above her were sliced by return fire.

Another one down, her suit clearly indicated she had killed or disabled the running soldier. She was now facing only one enemy and hope surged within her, hope that was unexpected and unwanted as thinking about the possibility of survival was a distraction she could not afford. She needed to-

Her visor blanked out, going clear as the suit's sensors temporarily were knocked offline. EMP, she realized in a panic. The lone remaining enemy soldier must have fired a rocket toward her, a rocket that did not explode but instead generated a powerful electromagnetic pulse that partially disrupted the mechanisms of her skinsuit. She was temporarily blind other than what her eyes could see and what her ears could hear. With a thumb, she broke the seal on her helmet faceplate and swung it upward, holding her breath to listen with desperation. While her suit's sensors were blind, the enemy would have been unaffected by the EMP, as the energy weapon would have been tuned not to emit frequencies used by the enemy mech suit.

What to do? She couldn't stay where she was, and her suit's power-assist motors were fully active, though her own muscles had to provide all the guidance without suit sensors scanning the ground ahead to prevent her from stumbling. She turned to look behind her, where the underbrush thinned out, the ground there being saturated with water in a marsh. The ground where she had taken cover was spongy and as she moved, the water broke away in a sucking sound that made her cringe, for the sound surely gave away her exact location.

Holding still, she listened and heard a crashing sound to her left. Having little choice as her sensors were still only seventy percent reset, she smoothly rolled up to one knee and scanned the forest to the left, seeing only ferns and low-hanging tree branches swaying. She squeezed off a three-round railgun burst, feeling the stock buzzing lightly against her shoulder. Switching back to the maser beam, she-

Was knocked to the ground as a maser burned into her right shoulder, from behind. The sound she heard must have been a decoy, the enemy tossing a stick or something to her right. She had been a fool and now she paid the price. The skinsuit had absorbed part of the maser energy, partly by the suit dropping stealth and going silver to reflect the high-energy photons, and partly by the outer layer flaking away to expel the heat. It was not enough, not to compensate for a close-range direct hit. Her right side was immobile, the helmet now totally offline. Painfully, with the suit's motors almost fighting against her, she held the rifle with her left hand and fell back against a tree to face right, looking for the enemy.

And seeing nothing. The enemy's stealthware and chameleon capability was fully active, without synthetic vision she had to hope she could detect movement out of her peripheral vision as her Ruhar trainers had taught her.

What the hell. The enemy was probably staring right at her, gloating as she slumped against the tree, nearly helpless. With nothing else to do, she screamed defiance and cut loose with the maser on semiauto mode, sweeping the forest in front of her. Her rash action was rewarded by a glimpse of an enemy silhouette lit up by maser bolts, just as a railgun dart slammed into her chest-

Emily Perkins' heart skipped a beat as she saw the icon representing Sergeant Shauna Jarrett go red, to reflect yet another human was dead on the battlefield. Perkins was now the only human survivor of her team, with her Ruhar liaison Nert Durndurff the only living being on her side in the battle. "Nert! Go ahead!"

"No, Colonel Perkins, I will not leave you! We are almost there!"

Perkins did not waste time or energy arguing with the teenage alien. "To the right, along this stream!" She turned, her skinsuit stabilizing her clumsy motions to prevent her from falling in the high-speed maneuver. With the power assist of her suit motors, she was running at the speed of an all-out sprint, a speed that by herself she could only keep up for fifty meters or less, but she had been running at that pace for a full two kilometers away from the river. It was blindingly, astonishingly fast, and it was not enough. Four icons representing the enemy were gaining on them, gaining rapidly, with two veering left and two right. The enemy was trying to encircle the two survivors, and there was little Perkins could do. Splashing along the streambed, she and Nert were momentarily away from the enemy's line of sight as she could see her goal; a defensible position.

When she began running up and away from the stream to a low ridge, she urged Nert onward, knowing the young alien was holding back his own pace to cover her. As Nert ran, he was firing his rifle's maser backwards blindly. She didn't bother to stop him, for just then she reached the top of the ridge and folded her legs to crash down into a shallow swale, rolling over onto her belly and bringing her rifle up to sight over the ridgeline. The position was not as defensible as it had looked when she scouted the area that morning, the terrain was terribly exposed behind her and the 'ridge' was no more than three feet tall, barely enough for her to take cover behind.

Nert ran toward her and she raised her left hand, waving to him. The alien cadet charged up the slope in two long strides, ducking under a vine and bounding high over the ridge top, whooping triumphantly until his body jerked as he was hit by a maser beam and a railgun dart at the same time. He fell forward to hit the ground hard with a thud Perkins felt through her suit.

"Nert! *Nert!*" Perkins screamed frantically, dropping her rifle and crawling to the cadet, but he was already gone. "Son of a-" Perkins bit her lip inside the helmet. As the only survivor, success of the mission was solely her responsibility now. Shoving her emotions down inside herself, she reached for her rifle, and yanked a spare powercell off Nert's waistbelt. The counter on top of her rifle indicated she had only six flechette rounds and eighteen percent energy charge remaining. The maser exciter would eventually burn out but that took thousands of shots, nothing she needed to worry about right then. Keeping low, she crawled to her left, cringing as she bumped into Nert's limp form, moving on knees and elbows toward a fallen tree where she could hide behind the upturned roots that would give her good cover for-

"Ow!" Something slammed into her butt cheeks from the left, knocking her to the ground hard. Apparently crawling on her knees lifted her too high off the ground and she had paid for her mistake, a lesson she should have remembered from crawling under low-hanging wire all the way back in basic training. Stupid! Stupid! Her visor showed the skinsuit had properly gone rigid when its proximity sensor field detected the incoming railgun round, and at the extreme angle, the round had failed to penetrate. The damage was done anyway, as she could not move her legs, something vital in the skinsuit's motor mechanism must have been knocked offline.

Laboriously, she crawled forward on her belly, using only her hands, sliding the rifle ahead of her and dragging herself to it. Only three more meters and she could turn over, her back to the protection of the tree roots and a partially obstructed view in the direction of the river. Her visor was showing only large, fuzzy yellow circles as the suit had lost track of the enemy. No matter, they had to come from only two directions and she could cover both. Sliding the rifle forward again, she eyeclicked to open a menu option, and selected it. With one last effort, she heaved herself to the downed tree, pulling herself onto her backside with difficulty since her legs had become useless. Sighting along her rifle, she scanned the ground in front of her, seeing nothing. Turning to the right, she-

Had the briefest glance of an enemy helmet and rifle popping up over a bush, then a burst of darts hit her.

CHAPTER FOUR

"Cease fire! Cease fire!" The leader ordered. "She's *dead*, stop shooting, you idiot!" He was angry because the soldier who had killed the alien stupidly stood up and fired his maser at the prone target, exposing himself to potential enemy snipers and giving away the position of the entire team.

"I got her!" The soldier exulted, pointing his rifle at the dead human. "She's the last one, they're all dead."

"Seven of them, six *humans*, against sixteen of us, and only the four of us survived? That is no victory to celebrate! We should have killed them all in the first five minutes. Humans are slow and weak and they barely have the brainpower of a slug but they killed ten of us! The commander is not going to be pleased," the leader opened his helmet faceplate and spat in disgust.

"They had the advantage," the soldier protested meekly. "They were in a defensive posture, they knew the terrain."

"They only arrived here this morning, with no time to prepare a fixed defense!" The leader waved a hand to dismiss the soldier. "This team's performance was shameful; I am ashamed to lead you. *You* clumsy fools," he clearly was taking none of the responsibility on his own shoulders, "almost lost."

Perkins laughed softly as her faceplate swung open, coming down off the adrenaline high of the wargame exercise. "You did almost lose," she pointed out to the leader of the Ruhar cadet team. She knew they were cadets by the academy logos on the arms of their skinsuits. With her faceplate open, the visor was no longer feeding her a false image of stealthware masking the training suits, because those units had no stealth or chameleon capabilities. The wargame had been impressively realistic, she could *feel* the realism. Her hips hurt, because when a nonexistent railgun dart had 'hit' her in the backside, the wargame controller had slammed her suit into the ground and deactivated the skinsuit's leg motors. Trees which moments before had appeared shot up by maser beams were now intact, because there had been no actual masers, nor flechettes nor rockets. None of her team were dead or injured, the wargame controller AI would not allow a participant to harm anyone, or allow a participant to hurt themselves by clumsiness or stupidity. In that way, the wargame was unrealistic, but Perkins could see the wisdom of preventing trainees from silly accidents that would delay their training.

"Ah!" The leader spun toward her angrily. "Silence, human! You *did* lose!"

"We lost this skirmish, we haven't lost the battle," Perkins said quietly.

"What?" The lead cadet asked, tapping the side of his helmet and shaking his head. "I couldn't hear you. What did you say?" He stepped forward, leaning down and menacing the prone human with his inert rifle. "You should not-" His left foot stepped on a twig, which snapped with an odd clicking sound.

Then he and his team of three joined the 'dead'. Their skinsuits went rigid, lights pulsed inside their visors and alarms blared in their ears. Unable to control his suit, the cadet wobbled and slowly fell over to thump to the forest floor a few yards from Perkins. She heard a string of curse words her helmet did not bother to translate. The mines her team planted that morning had become active when she activated them with an eyeclick, moments before the game controller declared her 'dead'. "Human! You tricked us!"

Perkins shifted in her immobile suit to get more comfortable, she was going to be lying there a while, now that the game had declared her dead. "Yeah, looks like it, huh?"

"You have no honor!" The cadet leader twisted his neck toward her so he could speak, as his ability to transmit through the communications network had cut off when he died. "I will file a formal protest, your tactics are not realistic! In a real battle, that explosion would have killed your team also."

"Yes, it probably would have," Perkins agreed.

"You booby-trapped your own position?" The cadet asked incredulously.

"We assumed we would be overrun," she admitted. "You Ruhar have advantages of size, speed, skill and familiarity with skinsuits. It seemed unlikely we could escape from your team, even though you are cadet trainees."

"You *planned* for your own deaths?" The cadet was astonished, as if such an idea was outside his imagination.

"We *planned* to achieve our objective."

The cadet snorted in what Perkins thought was a very human gesture. "You have achieved nothing."

"Oh really?" Perkins turned her head and raised an eyebrow, a gesture she knew the Ruhar understood. "While you were chasing us, your team left your assigned patrol area along the river, didn't you?" She almost added 'asshole' but kept that remark to herself.

The Ruhar sucked in a shocked breath. "You *tricked* me!" He then spoke words that Perkin's helmet did not translate, and his suit relaxed, then restored itself to function. Perkins spoke Ruhar reasonably well, but she wasn't able to understand most of what the cadet said, so rapid-fire was his speech. The cadet barked orders to the three members of his team whose suits also reactivated. The four stood up and engaged in an animated argument, hands gesturing emphatically. The cadet leader jabbed a finger toward Perkins, shouting and stamping a foot while he argued.

Though the Ruhar had somehow deauthorized her helmet translator, Perkins was able to follow most of the argument among the four, she had even learned new Ruhar curse words that she needed to research the meaning of later. "You're not supposed to be moving," Perkins spoke loud and slowly in Ruhar to assure the message was understood by the cadets. "According to the rules, the four of you are *dead*."

That message was received by the four Ruhar and sparked another round of argument, until the lead cadet made a slashing motion. Perkins' imperfect skills at understanding the common Ruhar language made his words sound stilted, but the meaning was clear. "I will take responsibility! The decision is mine! We go now!" The cadet held the rifle over his head for emphasis, then turned to glare at Perkins and shifted his weight onto one leg. For a moment, she feared he would kick her with the assisted power of a skinsuit, which could hurt her badly. They locked eyes, the cadet glaring hatred at her, before he turned and ran back toward the river. His three teammates joined him, though initially running without enthusiasm. One of the Ruhar turned back to look toward Perkins, unsure of what to do, then followed the others with a sad, apologetic smile.

"Nert?" Perkins called out, unable to see behind herself as her own skinsuit was still rigidly immobile. "You all right over there?"

"Yes, Colonel Perkins. I am fine, how are you? That was *fun*!"

"I'd be better if that jackass hadn't broken the wargame rules and run back to his patrol area. It's up to Striebich and Bonsu now."

"Miss Irene and Mister Derek, I mean, Captains Striebich and Bonsu, are brave and smart," Nert said hopefully. "They will not fail."

Perkins relaxed in the suit, trying to look around was only making her neck muscles sore. "They had better succeed, or the only result of our actions will be to demonstrate that humans have no place serving alongside Ruhar."

"This is crazy," Derek remarked. "Certifiably, lunatic, *nuts*. You know that, right?"

Irene grimaced and instinctively flinched when a large native fish bumped against the cockpit canopy of their Dobreh fighter. The curious creature scraped its bony lips along the see-through material, the suction cups on the ends of its flippers leaving a trail of yellowish slime. Irene tapped on the inside of the canopy, startling the fish, which darted away. In the murky river water, she could see shapes moving in a school as fish circled the strange object that had dropped out of the sky into their private underwater world. "This was *your* idea."

"No," Derek gave the pilot in front of him a disparaging look. "I mentioned it as one possible tactic, a far-fetched one. I didn't think *this* is what you would choose."

"Colonel Perkins approved it," Irene toggled through the exterior passive sensors again, finding nothing within range.

"We're supposed to keep senior officers out of trouble," Derek reminded her.

"Yes, *Captain* Bonsu," Irene waved him away, irritated. After saving forty thousand Ruhar lives by blowing up a tropical island, the entire team had received a temporary promotion of one grade. That was why Perkins was now a lieutenant colonel, while Shauna, Jesse and Dave were now sergeants. The promotions were supposed to be made permanent soon at an official ceremony, but so far, the team had been too busy in the field. "This idea may be crazy, but it's the only plan either of us has thought of that could do something useful in this wargame. If the hamsters had given us a *real* gunship rather than this broken-down piece of crap, we could have joined the air battle."

"That hamster crew chief will blow a gasket when he sees fish guts in his precious turbines," Derek said with concern. He had kept the turbines turning over at minimum power, a setting normally used only for inspections while the Dobreh was on a ramp or in a hangar. With the turbines rotating, they created a pressure that prevented troublesome aquatic organisms from going up inside the delicate parts of the engines. If any fish or snails or things Derek didn't want to think about got near the intakes, they were gently sucked in and hurried along past the slowly-rotating turbine blades out the exhaust ports, which were fully open. Anyone on the surface of the river might notice a change in water flow, but the current was already disrupted by having a Ruhar fighter submerged on the stony bottom. Unless the observer was familiar with the usual pattern of water flow in that part of the river, nothing would look unusual.

"That wrench spinner gave you the idea," Irene snorted.

"He didn't intend to!"

"Ah, that's *his* problem. I know he is part of the reason we got assigned this hangar queen instead of a front-line warbird," Irene was still angry about that. Three days before the wargame commenced, the two human pilots had been thrilled to learn they would participate as part of the Green team air support, then their hopes for getting into action were crushed when they saw the sad piece of crap Dobreh they would be flying. That particular airframe had literally been sitting in the back corner of a hangar for months, being steadily stripped for parts to keep other birds in flyable condition. Even with a battlegroup now based at Paradise, supplies of some critical materials were in short supply. Some genius at Ruhar Fleet Command had thought it important to get an impressively large number of ships and aircraft to Paradise as quickly as possible, probably hoping to dissuade the Kristang from any adventuresome thoughts of retaking the planet. While the amount of military gear arriving had indeed been impressive, the follow-through effort had been weak and poorly organized. Aircraft, dropships and even a few smaller ships had been pulled offline within weeks due to lack of replacements for worn-out parts or consumable supplies.

So, when the local fleet commander announced plans for an extensive wargame covering a quarter of the planet, the supply personnel had nearly panicked. A significant number of aircraft were not airworthy due to one fault or another, and some of the aircraft assigned to flying duty lacked their full complement of weapons or had glitchy sensors. Irene understood the supply problem, as a US Army helicopter pilot, she had experienced frustrating issues with keeping her Blackhawk in flyable condition going back even before her service in Nigeria. If the Ruhar had shrugged and explained there were not enough aircraft available to waste on lowly humans, she would have been pissed but she also would have accepted the rationale behind the decision. Rather than being honest and giving a good effort to find a flyable hull for Irene and Derek, the maintenance people at the airbase had done the absolute minimum they could to comply with high-level orders to assure the primitive humans were able to participate in the wargame.

That is why the two human pilots had been assigned to a fighter hurriedly cobbled together from whatever used parts were available. The missile bay was empty not because the exercise was only a wargame, they were empty because the rotating magazine in the missile bay was missing entirely, only a couple sad and lonely brackets occupied that space. The Dobreh was not capable of carrying missiles, and only one of its maser turrets contained an actual maser cannon, although the crew chief had insisted strongly that no one attempt to fire the cannon, and the power leads were disconnected. The crew chief had also warned the pair of humans not to run up the turbines past thirty six percent of max power, to the point where Irene and Derek had to sign a formal acknowledgement of that warning to earn the dubious privilege of taking the piece of crap into the air.

Derek had been pissed to the point of suggesting they run up a turbine until it burned out on the ramp, forcing the Ruhar to admit they had provided a substandard aircraft to their pet humans. "Derek, chill," Irene had chided her fellow pilot. "We fly this piece of crap, or we don't fly at all. *I* want to fly," she tapped his chest with a fingernail.

"Getting in the air is all this thing *can* do," Derek had kicked a landing gear strut in disgust. "No way can we keep formation with a combat air patrol," he knew the Green Team air commander for the wargame would not have hampered her chance for success by including humans in her defensive air patrol anyway, the poor condition of their Dobreh only provided a convenient excuse. "They'll assign us to fly recon, or as a decoy."

"Probably, but we don't have to stick to whatever role they give us. We know what this bird *can't* do. Think, Derek, we need to think what we *could* do in this thing."

Derek had thought, and Irene had thought, and they had discarded a dozen ideas before Derek made an off-hand comment about how he had once watched a Dobreh undergoing testing, back when he was working as a sort of mascot at a Ruhar airbase, before Perkins and her team had blasted Kristang ships out of the sky with giant maser cannons nobody knew existed. Derek had intended the comment as a joke, but Irene thought of the possibilities, and after discussing the idea with Perkins, they got approval for their crazy stunt.

That is why, twenty minutes into the wargame, they had faked a turbine blade failure and been ordered to set their crippled bird down and wait until the wargame was over. The air boss for the wargame was happy to have the two pesky humans off his board, as that was one less thing for him to worry about.

Instead of setting down as ordered, Irene and Derek had turned off their transponder and flown at treetop level or below, sometimes following roads or streams where gaps in the tree cover allowed their Dobreh to almost hover with the wings retracted most of the way. They had flown a course along air corridors that Green Team intel had indicated were gaps in Yellow Team sensor coverage, until they reached a stream and followed it down to where it met a river. At a bend in the river was a deep pool, overhung by large trees and with a stony bottom that was mostly clear of sticky silt. There, they had hovered lower and lower until the Dobreh touched the water, and Derek had cut power. The sophisticated Ruhar gunship fighter settled into the water, sinking to the bottom where it remained, its active sensors powered off and with turbines turning very slowly.

They had sunk the Dobreh before dawn that day, now it was early afternoon. Through a super-thin whip antenna sticking above the surface, they had been able to follow progress of the wargame through the Green Team tactical datalink, and through the Dobreh's computer picking up Yellow Team signals and guessing what the other side was doing.

"Heads up," Derek whispered, interrupting Irene's train of thought. "Sensors are picking up multiple bogeys," he warned of unidentified contacts, then the system gave him positive confirmation; the contacts fit the signatures of Yellow Team aircraft. "We've got company," he transferred the sensor data to Irene's console in the front part of the tandem cockpit. "Three bandits, weeds at zero forty two." Derek used the term 'weeds' to indicate the enemy aircraft were at such low altitude they would be scraping the treetops.

"I see them." The Dobreh's passive sensors showed her one troop transport aircraft escorted by two fighters. Using typical cover formation for a three-ship flight, the fighters were ahead and slightly above the transport. Irene's lips curled in a wolfish smile inside her helmet and she pressed the button to flip her visor down, automatically putting her flightsuit on internal power and life support. With the Yellow Team aircraft already passing overhead, those fighters would be badly out of position to defend the transport from an attack that came behind them. "Button up, we are outa here."

"Buttoned up, turbines ready," Derek reported. "Rocket assist online and at your command."

"Acknowledged," Irene said tersely, all business now that they were going into action. Although the gunship's twin turbines were powerful and their blades made of a super-tough composite, they could not apply enough power for takeoff while the engines were submerged. If they had to rely only on the turbines, their Dobreh was going to remain at the bottom of the river. Fortunately, the Dobreh was equipped with rocket thrusters. Those compact but powerful units could be used when the fighter climbed to an altitude where the air was too thin for the turbines to provide useful thrust, or for a quick burst of speed, but they mostly had another use. When a heavily loaded Dobreh was taking off vertically, the rocket thrusters provided the extra energy to get the aircraft off the ground and up to speed where the wings provided lift. With the Dobreh submerged in a river, Irene set the thrusters on low power for an easy, sustained burn rather than the sudden kick in the pants they provided on full power. "Three, two, one, *go*," she announced in a calm voice, and the Dobreh rocketed off the river bottom. Her view was instantly clouded as the thrusters stirred up sand and caused water under the ship to flash into steam. Anyone above the river could not fail to see an unusual disturbance under the river's normally placid surface and that sight would soon give their location away to the Yellow Team aircraft, but Irene increased power to the thrusters and the Dobreh burst free of the water in seconds. She had a momentary view of a very terrified fish when the creature slid off the canopy and into open air above the river, and seeing the fish's wide-open mouth and bulging eyes almost made her laugh, then Irene pulled her focus back to the task at hand.

"Nose is cold," Derek advised, reminding the pilot their active sensors were still powered down.

"Go active, light 'em up," Irene authorized.

Derek turned a selector switch to bring the sensor pulse gear from Standby to Active and pulses of energy radiated from the Dobreh's forward sensor platform. "Targets painted, targets acquired," he announced from the rear seat's weapons console. He did not need to wait for Irene's acknowledgement or order, as they had agreed on tactics for various scenarios, and there wasn't time for back and forth chit-chat in modern air combat. The pilot was flying a dash profile straight at the enemy aircraft, pushing the turbines as hard as they could go. As the Dobreh soared above the tree canopy that lined the river, the Yellow Team fighters began to break in hard turns that rapidly bled off their airspeed. The transport went to full power, surging forward and upward, deploying countermeasures to supplement its stealth field. Derek was impressed by the opposing team's reaction time; they must have turned immediately after their sensors detected the Green Team Dobreh coming out of nowhere. He imagined the Yellow Team pilots and the remote Air Boss had to be screaming the Ruhar equivalent of 'where the *fuck* did that Dobreh come from' but they weren't acting panicked. The hamster air crews were skilled, they were disciplined, and they were in command of awesomely capable aircraft. And they were doomed. While still underwater, Derek had selected targets and flight patterns for all of their missiles theoretically carried by the Dobreh. The fact that their weapons bay was empty made no difference in the war game, for the computer system that ran the game and functioned as referee acted as if their fighter was fully equipped as it would be in real combat. Even before the Dobreh climbed above the treetops, Derek had opened the weapons bay door and the virtual rotary launcher spun rapidly, ripple-firing every virtual missile they carried, plus decoys and their own countermeasures. "Winchester on birds!" Derek announced, indicating their entire supply of theoretical missiles had been expended. The air around the fighter remained clear except for river water explosively evaporating as the Dobreh approached the speed of sound, then there was a burst of vapor as breaking the sound barrier compressed the air in a cone shape behind them. In reality the air remained clear, but in the enhanced synthetic vision of their helmet visors the air was filled with angry yellow flares of missile launches then white contrails, twisting violently as their missiles and decoys jinked to avoid defensive maser fire from the targets. Without taking time to comment, Derek poured maser fire at the transport from his own powerful maser cannons. Though he knew the transport's shields would deflect most of the maser bolts, the energy impacting the shields would create a plasma that would light up the target for his missiles while fuzzing the transport's point-defense sensors.

As he watched, the missiles he had fired lanced in toward their targets, several going off course as they were confused by enemy countermeasures or falling victim to defensive maser fire. The loss of a few missiles made no difference to the end result; Derek had launched so close to the enemy aircraft that they had only seconds to react and it was not enough. First the transport exploded as two missiles scored direct hits almost at the same time as another missile ripped into one of the fighters. The second fighter survived long enough for Derek to switch his maser cannons onto it and send one pulse of maser energy toward it, then the wargame computer determined the second fighter was also disabled and falling, breaking apart in midair.

Derek did not pump a fist to celebrate, he did not exult at their victory, he focused on staying alive. Before they died, those two fighters had each launched two missiles which were now racing toward the Dobreh that did not have any protection from an effective stealth field. While the wargame computer had somewhat reluctantly agreed that a partly-disabled Dobreh *might* be able to fly after spending part of the day submerged in a river, the computer also decided several of the fighter's systems would be offline or damaged. That included the stealth field and defense shield generators. "Incoming!" Derek warned.

"See them," Irene replied quietly as she pulled the Dobreh into a tight turn and pulled the nose up, crushing her down in the seat as her suit compensated for the high-Gee maneuver. Airspeed rapidly bled off and she pushed the nose down, aiming again for the river.

"Splash three vampires!" Derek called out to alert the pilot that only one imaginary missile was now tracking them.

Irene had no time to express surprise or pleasure at their unexpected good fortune; she had to concentrate as the surface of the river was coming up fast in her forward view. At the last second, she was forced to fire the nose thrusters hard when she realized they were going to hit the water much too fast. The action of the thrusters full-on slammed her forward against the seat restraints and her nose hit the helmet visor, leaving a smudge and she tasted a trickle of blood running down her lip. She barely got the engine air intake doors closed before the Dobreh's belly smacked the water with bone-jarring force. The fighter bounced off the surface once, twice, three times out of control, heading straight for a sandy beach and a watery bog east of the shoreline. "We're gonna hit!" She shouted to her copilot, and forced herself to relax so she wouldn't tear a muscle as the Dobreh careened across the water then dug into the beach, throwing up a cascade of sand and dark mud as the fighter crashed over the beach and into the swampy bog beyond. Irene had absolutely no control, all she could do was try to manage her frantic breathing and watch the threat display. That screen lit up as the wargame computer decided that last Yellow Team missile had exploded above the bouncing Dobreh, and in sync, all the cockpit instruments went dead while the Dobreh's forward belly hit something more solid than sloppy bog mud. Irene's right hand instinctively wrapped around the ejection handle, ready to yank it upward and explode both her and Derek safely upward and out before the fighter's nose dug in and it flipped over onto its back to crush them for real. Just as her thumb depressed the safety button to enable the ejection handle, the Dobreh stood on its nose, then flopped back down onto its belly, rocking side to side a few times.

"You Ok up there?" Derek asked, his voice strangely sounding as if he was talking through a mouthful of water.

"Yeah, you?"

"Holy *shit*, what did you do? I thought we were gonna have to punch out for a second there." Ejecting while the aircraft was in the mud was a situation Derek had not trained for or even imagined.

"Sorry, that was, uh, kinda unplanned," Irene could feel her cheeks reddening.

"Oh, what the hell. In a wargame, you're supposed to act like we're in real combat, right?"

"Are you really Ok?" She hit the button to release the safety straps and twisted in her seat, trying to turn her head to see her copilot, but her helmet was in the way and the back of her seat blocked the view of the copilot 'pit' where he sat. "You sound odd."

"I bit my lip, pretty hard," Derek explained. "It's all right, I- Ow! Damn it! One of those slugbot things is trying to staple my freakin' lips closed. Go away!" He shouted at the slug-shaped Ruhar medical device that had emerged from a storage pouch in the neck of his flightsuit, and was attempting to treat the human's injury as best it was able. When the slugbot halted but would not let go of his bleeding lip, he flipped his helmet visor up and gripped the tiny thing between two fingers, gently prying it away and flinging it onto his instrument panel, leaving a bloody trail across the displays. "Uh!" He jabbed a warning finger at the devoted little bot as it began crawling back toward him. "You stay right there, I-" he paused to think for a moment, then found the controls to disable the slugbot. "Hey! Irene. You see that in your display?" Derek asked as he lowered his visor halfway.

"Uh huh. Wargame control says this ship is totally disabled, but we splashed all three bandits." She switched her comm system to the guard channel and her ears were blasted by the Yellow Team commander screaming a demand to know how the *hell* a Green Team fighter had just appeared out of nowhere and wasted an entire assault team. The Yellow Team's shocked Air Battle Manager was screaming to clear all her aircraft away from a safe-fly corridor that was now demonstrated to be anything but safe, which threw her entire air defense plan into disarray. And various Yellow field commanders were scrambling to discard carefully crafted attack plans that now had to be revised on the fly. Green Team commanders were seizing the opportunity to regain the initiative, and also demanding to know who the *hell* had been flying that phantom Dobreh? "Sounds like we have both sides pissed at us, we must be doing something right," she chuckled.

"No, I mean, you *see* it in your visor."

"I-" Irene paused, puzzled to understand what Derek was talking about, then saw in a flash. Her visor should only be on passive receive mode, with a blinking red icon to indicate the wargame computer had declared her 'dead'. "Our visors are still active! We're still *alive?*"

"We are still alive, yes! Derek exulted as he pumped a fist in the air, mistakenly thumping the inside of the canopy and bending his wrist painfully.

Having the game computer decide the two human pilots had survived a crash and being struck by warhead shrapnel was about the last thing Irene expected. "How the hell did that happen?"

"I don't know, the wargame computer should have declared us dead. It also should not have allowed our defense masers to kill three of those four Yellow missiles targeting us, so I guess that computer has a sense of humor?"

"Ha!" Irene laughed. "Maybe it wants to see what crazy shit us humans will do next, huh?"

"Speaking of what to do next," Derek released his seat harness and retracted the rear canopy.

"Next?" Irene retracted the forward canopy, but looked down at the murky black mud their fighter was settling into. "Maybe we should sit right here until they send air rescue."

"No way, Jose," Derek shook his head, stood up and reached forward to tap the pilot's helmet. "We're alive, and we're in enemy territory."

"Oh damn it," Irene groaned, her notion of peacefully waiting to be plucked out of the mud swept away. "Escape and evade?"

"Hell yes, we didn't go through that damned training for nothing," Derek shuddered as he recalled the hellishly grueling nine-day evasion and survival training they had endured as part of qualifying for frontline service. Service they had never been allowed to perform. "We're supposed to high-tail it away from the ship ASAP."

"Ohhh, you're right," she sighed heavily. "This is going to *suck.*"

"Come on," Derek swung a leg over the side of the cockpit, looking for a spot in the bog where he wouldn't sink in above his neck. "You're seeing that Yellow ground team, right?" His visor indicated motion on the other side of the river; the system was guessing three to four individuals headed straight for the downed Dobreh. The dead ship was impossible to miss even from a distance, as the hot exhaust nozzles were sending up pillars of steam from being partially submerged in the cold bog water. "We can at least lead those assholes on a merry chase."

"It's not going to be merry at all," Irene frowned as she reached under her seat for the survival kit, seeing Derek already had his own kit slung over a shoulder. "You first."

"No, ladies first," Derek winked.

"It's your idea to leave a nice dry cockpit and jump into a swamp, *you* go first," she insisted.

"Fine." Derek lowered his visor so he could breathe even if he fell in over his head. You know, he told himself, these damned hamster flightsuits should come with a simple depth finder so he could tell how deep the water was. It was so utterly black with churned-up mud that he couldn't see bottom anywhere. Walking gingerly out along the Dobreh's stubby, swept-back wing, he slipped in splashed-up mud and leaped overboard before he could fall. As he plunged into the water, he instinctively held his breath though no water got through the helmet visor seal. Without him doing anything, the suit automatically inflated a collar below his neck, keeping his head above the inky-black water. "Uh, I can't, yes! My feet are touching the bottom here."

"That's great, Derek," Irene remarked with sarcasm, hands on her hips. "You're almost a foot taller than me."

"Oh. Right." He walked slowly through the muck on the bog bottom, walking around to the Dobreh's nose, where the fighter had plowed up a ridge of mud. "Come walk out along the nose, it's shallow here," he lifted one leg to show the water was only knee-deep in front of the fighter. "And hurry, that Yellow team group Perkins ran into is only half a mile from the riverbank on the other side."

Hurry, Irene thought sourly as she awkwardly climbed out of the cockpit and inched her way forward along the fighter's sleekly-sloping nose. Next time, she told herself, I'm going to let the wargame computer decide I am dead so I can relax. She waved Derek away, preferring to slide down off the fighter's nose on her own, but she slipped in the mud and fell back into his arms.

"Careful, this stuff I'm standing in is like a wet sponge," he warned, sliding his visor up to breathe unfiltered air.

Irene also retracted her visor, taking a sniff of the air. To her surprise, it smelled clean, not the dank odor of a swamp. There was a burnt undertang to the scent that she attributed to heat dissipating from the engine exhaust. "Well," she inspected the sophisticated fighter that now had its bottom third submerged in mud. "This thing is Tango Uniform," she smiled as she used the slang for 'tits up', meaning broken.

"Hey," Derek patted the pilot's shapely behind. "They gave us a hangar queen, and we'll give them back a genuine, certified hangar queen. Nobody else will be risking their necks flying this piece of crap."

"The hamsters will still be pissed that we broke it."

"I say Whiskey Charlie to that," Derek laughed, meaning 'who cares'. "They will be more pissed that we popped up out of the weeds on their six and splashed three of their birds. The hamsters will be scratching their furry little heads about that one. Hey," he gently tugged her shoulder to turn her around to face him. "That was great flying. The hamsters will add that to the textbook someday."

"Thank-" her reply was cut off as Derek leaned in to kiss her. Irene responded with enthusiasm, then put a hand on his chest and pushed him away. "Not here, not *now*," her eyes twinkled to let him know that later might be different. "Escape and evade, remember?"

"Are you escaping and evading me now?" Derek winked at her, then cocked his head and held up a finger for silence. "We've got company," he announced after hearing someone faintly shouting in the Ruhar common language.

"Let's move," Irene slapped her copilot's shapely ass, "buster buster buster."

"Buster, yeah right," Derek gritted his teeth at the pilot's direction to move as fast as possible, though thick mud was sucking at his boots and making it impossible to manage more than a slow trot. "Tell that to the mud."

CHAPTER FIVE

Emily Perkins, along with the rest of her team, had been able to follow the wargame exercise through her helmet visor. Though she was technically dead according to the rules of the game, and the system prevented her from communicating with anyone other than by opening the visor and talking the old-fashioned way, she had access to all the info available to her when she had been 'alive'. She could see the status of each member of her team including heart rate, breathing and other biosigns. Her suit was still receiving data through the Green Team tactical data link, and that data was still subject to spoofing and jamming by the Yellow Team.

Her access to the taclink allowed her to see that three Yellow Team aircraft had been declared shot down with all hands lost, near the river where Irene and Derek had hidden their fighter. The taclink also reported the Yellow commander had committed an aircraft and two squads of troops to 'sanitize' the flight corridor along the river, but until they could be certain the Green threat there had been neutralized, the area was a no-fly zone and that seriously screwed up the entire Yellow Team assault plan. Emily smiled inside her suit even as she wished she had fallen in a more comfortable position because a stump was digging into her back. Ruhar skinsuits were great in many ways, their flexibility usually making them superior in comfort and agility to rigid Kristang powered armor, but at the moment, the flexible nature of a skinsuit was causing a throbbing pain in Emily's back. A Kristang suit would have rigidly propped itself against the stump without her feeling it at all, but her Ruhar gear was bent over the stump as if the skinsuit did not exist. That was a design flaw, in Emily's opinion. Or, she thought with exasperation, maybe there was a setting she didn't know about that could relieve the pressure on her back. The suits did have injectable nanomedicine for pain relief, the units issued to her team had their medical gear modified for human biochemistry, but she was reluctant to use it. Activating a suit's internal medical systems would be reported up to the medical people at Green Team headquarters, and that would prompt questions. She did not want hamsters asking why she needed pain relief when she was merely laying down in a forest. UNEF could not afford for the Ruhar to think humans were any softer than their physical limitations made unavoidable.

"Nghh," she grunted as she shifted around inside the suit as best she could. After she had been declared dead, her suit had lost power, its nanomotors inactive. Not only did she not have the advantage of powered movement, the suit was holding her mostly immobile, except for her being able to wiggle a bit inside the material but it was like trying to adjust her position inside a wetsuit. The damn thing would not move as she wanted, and it did move just enough that she couldn't quite relieve the pressure on her sore back muscles. Skinsuits would not allow the wearer to die or be injured, if she had 'died' during the wargame by falling into water, the suit would prevent her from drowning, even swim her onto land by itself. Its impressive caretaker feature did not, however, consider the comfort of the occupant.

The upper left corner of her visor showed there were more than sixteen hours remaining in the wargame schedule, and nearly two hours until a crew would come to her position to bring the 'dead' and 'injured' out of the exercise area. Two more hours of a tree stump digging into her-

An alarm sounded in her helmet and her suit immediately returned to full function. The first thing Emily did was roll off the stump, then kneel down to stretch her aching back. She spent several minutes just stretching, bending her sore back and catching her breath, wincing from sharp pain. "Is everyone all right?" She called on the team channel, before wincing at her own reliance on alien technology and flipping up her visor again to breathe unfiltered air. She could see Colter, Jarrett and Czajka running easily through the woods toward her, and she envied their youth for they didn't appear to have stiff muscles from lying on the ground for hours.

"I'm fine, Em- Ma'am," Dave changed his reply, red-faced at almost referring to their CO by her first name. "Why is the exercise over early?" That level of information was not available to him. "I hope there wasn't an accident."

"Good point, Czajka. Striebich!" Perkins called to her chief pilot. "You two Ok out there?"

"Just fine here, Colonel," Irene's voice was mirthful. "We're kind of in a swamp near the river here, but we'll get out Ok."

Perkins caught the amusement in the pilot's tone. "What's so funny, Striebich?"

"There's a hamster recon team searching for us," Irene laughed, "and they just about had us cornered in this swamp when the exercise ended early. It's a group of cadets, and I gotta think their commander is *pissed*; we led them on a chase all over these woods for the past couple hours. Now his mission will get scored as a failure."

"Got it. Well, screw him, right?" Perkins knew that remark would eventually get picked up by Yellow Team intel and they'd be unhappy. She also knew her own Green Team would be listening, Perkins hoped they would be amused and impressed by the aggressiveness and fighting spirit of humans.

"Colonel Perkins," Nert snapped a US Army style salute toward the human commander.

"Nerty," Shauna admonished their young alien liaison. "Remember, we don't salute in the field."

"Oh, sorry." Nert's expression was crestfallen. "You humans call that a 'sniper check'?"

"You got it. Any sniper in the area will target the senior officers first."

"Colonel," Nert was aware that lieutenant colonels were commonly referred to as 'colonel' except in formal settings, "I do congratulate you and your team on a daring and successful mission in this exercise. But, the fact that your success caused humiliation for that Yellow Team cadet leader may create a problem for you, for all of us, in the future. He would be a bad person to have as an enemy."

"Why?" Dave's eyes narrowed. "Who is that jerk?"

"His name is Bifft Colhsoon," Nert replied with a slightly puzzled expression.

"B-Biff? His name is *Biff*?" Dave laughed and the team joined him.

"Yes, Bifft. Why is that funny?" Nert cocked his head, wondering if the gang were playing another prank on him. "I am told that name is similar to a name not uncommon on Earth?"

"Biff *is* an uncommon name, unless your enemy is Marty McFly," Dave thought his own joke was uproariously funny, and he got the others laughing.

"Who is Mar-tee Mick-Fly?" Nert asked, lost. "Is he a famous hero from Earth history?"

"Yeah, he's famous all right. He invented the flux capacitor," Shauna explained.

"No, that was Doc, uh, what's-his-name. The guy with the wild hair." Jesse corrected his girlfriend, which drew an eyeroll from her.

"Doc Brown," Perkins declared, sometimes annoyed at how conversations among her young team veered off-topic. "Nert, why would it be dangerous for us to have this Bifft guy as our enemy? He is a senior-level cadet, but he's only a cadet. He doesn't outrank you, and he sure as hell doesn't outrank me."

"His mother is a general in our army, and his father is a high-level official in the federal government. He could make much trouble for any of us. My aunt very strictly will not use her position to help me, but Bifft's parents have many times unfairly secured advantages for him, because of their power and influence."

"Politics," Jesse spat on the ground in disgust.

The expression on Perkins' face echoed Jesse's disgust, but she couldn't allow her personal feelings to affect their mission. Almost every human interaction, and now every interaction humans had with other sentient species, involved politics on some level. She looked at the UNEF symbol that was now displayed on the left upper arm of her team's skinsuits. The composition of UNEF was entirely politics; only five nations were included in the Expeditionary Force, though several other countries had wanted to contribute soldiers. Being excluded had been a blow to national pride, and Perkins was sure there were still hard feelings about that back on Earth. Brazil had argued strongly in the UN Security Council that their army should participate in the ExForce, but that country's lack of nuclear weapons meant the Kristang did not take the Brazilians seriously. Emily wondered if the army of Brazil knew how lucky they were to have dodged that bullet. She also noted that the influence of Nert's aunt Baturnah Logellia was the reason the boy was a member of Perkins' team. "Ok, people, we have enough enemies in this galaxy, let's not go making more. We treat this Bifft cadet with respect, got it?"

"Yes Ma'am," Shauna agreed stiffly. "But if that punk-ass kid disrespects one of us," she looked at Nert and the team understood how protective she felt about the goofy young alien, "I am not taking any crap."

"Jarrett, if this Bifft character needs slapping down, I will handle it myself," Perkins also treated their young alien team member with motherly concern. The alien senior cadet had taken particular pleasure in the simulated killing of Nert, and Perkins wanted more info about that. "Nert, do you and this Bifft have a history? Anything we should know about?"

"No, we do not have a 'history'," Nert shook his head in the exaggerated fashion he had learned to use when communicating with humans. "We barely know each other at school. I think," the young Ruhar looked at the sky while he thought of the correct phrase. "I think he is just a *dick*."

Hearing that word coming from Nert's mouth, and his totally serious expression, made the team double over with laughter.

"Nert!" Shauna said, wiping tears from her eyes. "Where did you hear that expression?"

"Did I not say that correctly?" Nert's eyebrows scrunched together with concern. "I was taught that expression by soldiers in your American Third Infantry Division. At first my translator told me it was a slang term for," he looked away from Shauna with great embarrassment, "male genitalia? Then it was explained to me that calling someone a 'dick' means they are sort of a, a huge douchebag?"

Perkins laughed so hard she almost choked, and Dave patted her back. "Oh," she looked at the alien cadet when she was able to talk again, "Nert, you truly brighten my day."

"Is what I say funny because I am not saying it correctly?" The cadet looked to Shauna for guidance, his lower lip quivering slightly.

"No!" Shauna assured him. "You are using the expression correctly, and you are a hundred percent right that this Bifft character is a *huge* douchebag," she bit the inside of her cheek to stop herself from laughing. "What makes it extra funny is that we do not expect to hear you using human slang."

"Oh," Nert perked right up at hearing Shauna's explanation. "Yes! The humor comes from the incongruity of-" He stopped because he was smart enough to know jokes can't be explained. Trying again, he simply stated. "The humor comes from the fact that *all* species can agree Bifft is a dick."

"Nert," Perkins shook her head, grinning broadly. "Maybe you should tell Dave and Jesse what other expressions you learned from those jokers in the Third Infantry, hmm?"

"Yes, Ma'am," Nert grinned back. "They taught me many interesting and useful sayings. For example, several of the male soldiers kept saying they wanted something very badly, and my translator told me they were using a term for a feline pet animal from Earth. That puzzled me, then I learned what they wanted was some sweet pus-"

"*OK*!" Dave patted Nert on the back, hard. "Let's you, me and Jesse talk about that, huh?"

Senior Cadet Bifft Colhsoon was indeed pissed, monumentally pissed. Not only had a group of lowly humans suckered him into leaving his assigned patrol area along the river, but when he broke the wargame rules to run back to the river and chase the two human pilots, they had slipped away and evaded him for hours until he had them cornered in a swampy area and was about to send two of his team to circle behind and trap them. Just then, the alarm had sounded to end the wargame, cheating him out of even a minor victory! He had broken the rules and would be punished, and now he had nothing to show for it. At least if he had captured the human pilots he might have been able to justify his actions as preventing the humans from getting away with cheating, since cheating is the *only* possible way two slow and clumsy human pilots could have shot down three Ruhar aircraft. "Come out!" He shouted, brandishing his rifle toward where he knew the pair of primitive creatures were huddled behind a large tree.

"Ok!" Irene stood up, brushing muck off her flightsuit's legs from when she and Derek had been crouching behind a tree. She waved her arms to show her pistol was still in the holster strapped to her hip. "The wargame is over, anyway."

"You got lucky, and you cheated!" Bifft shook a fist at her and pointedly did not lower his rifle, even though the weapon could only fire low-powered targeting laser beams. "I will be reporting your shameful underhanded tactics to the wargame authorities."

"Cheated?" Derek retorted hotly. "We cheated? *You* cheated! You're supposed to be dead, you punk-ass bitch. That's why we were able to track your position but you couldn't locate us. The control system cut off your suit's chameleon and stealth features," Derek looked at Irene as he spoke, as he had just then figured out why the two of them had been able to evade the team of four Ruhar for hours. While their flightsuits were not fully capable combat skinsuits, they did provide enhanced speed and power, plus features for concealment. During the chase, Derek had wondered why their flightsuits' sensors had been able to detect and pinpoint movement in the forest, while it appeared the four Ruhar had only a vague idea where the humans were. Now it was obvious, as lights on the chests of the four Ruhar were blinking red, indicating the wargame computer had declared them all dead. The four, who Derek now could see for certain were cadets, should not have been able to move after 'dying' in the game. "Dead soldiers are not supposed to be chasing us. *We* will be reporting *your* actions to the referees."

Derek did send a message to the wargame computer, for the attention of the referee committee that enforced the rules and investigated possible violations by both sides. All he did was transmit a file containing sensor data after they left the Dobreh, showing he and Irene had been tracked and pursued by four Yellow team soldiers, and including a short video of their encounter with the cadets after the wargame ended. Derek's intention was to show the referees that, if the humans had done anything that slightly bent the spirit if not the stated rules of the mock combat, the four Yellow cadets had flagrantly violated the rules by continuing to participate in the action after they had been declared dead. He figured the rules committee would have to go easy on the humans when they saw how badly their own people had cheated. He was correct, and he had no way of knowing Lieutenant Colonel Perkins would have preferred to keep the whole incident quiet, and she was still mildly pissed at him for acting without checking with her first. "I'm sorry, Ma'am," he replied as the assembled six humans waited for a Green team transport to pluck them from an open area next to the river. A Yellow ship had already picked up the four cadets, and another Yellow transport had landed across the river next to the bog where the abandoned Dobreh sat partly submerged in a bog. Through his zPhone, Derek had been watching a Ruhar dressed in the blue and yellow uniform of an aircraft mechanic slogging through the bog to the Dobreh, then crawling on top and around it. He could not hear the communications from the mechanic to the airbase, but from the man's gestures, Derek guessed the mechanic was anything but pleased. "I wouldn't have done anything," he stated truthfully for he assumed the wargame computer had noticed the four 'dead' cadets breaking the rules by running around. "But that cadet said he was going to report us for cheating, so I thought the best defense is a good offense."

Emily Perkins knew sports metaphors were as popular in the military as war metaphors were in sports, and she found both to be silly. War was not a game, and the even the most intense football game was not combat. Quarterbacks could be hit hard by three-hundred pound linemen, but no one was shooting at the quarterback, nor did the quarterback need to worry about being targeted by laser-guided missiles from over the horizon. In spite of her feelings on the subject, she avoided rolling her eyes at the pilot. "In the future, check with me first. I am responsible for the actions of this team, so any reporting should be done by me directly."

"We did nothing wrong!" Irene protested while touching Derek's hand reassuringly.

"None of us did anything wrong, the operation was flawless," Perkins agreed. "That doesn't mean there won't be any blow-back on us. We really crashed a real aircraft," she used the word 'we' because she had approved the crazy operation and Emily Perkins did not hang her people out to dry when they went off-script in good faith. Striebich and Bonsu had followed the spirit of the wargame by acting the way they would in real combat. The fact that the wargame computer did not declare them dead after the hard landing proved the desperate tactic of splashing their fighter across the river surface had worked. "Nert," she nodded toward the team's official liaison officer, "tells me that cadet leader you encountered is politically connected. He could make a stink about us destroying a combat aircraft, even get your flight certifications revoked or suspended."

"What?" Irene screeched in outrage.

Perkins held up a finger to forestall an argument. "That is why I didn't want us reporting that cadet for violating the wargame rules. The computer must know what he did, and the hamsters will deal with it, or not," she shrugged. "Now we have forced their hand by bringing the incident to the referee committee,because they will have to address it, and the cadet will blame us, fairly or not." She paused to listen, and the entire group turned toward the south where an aircraft was beginning to transition from level flight to hover mode, its turbine engines pivoting to support the craft's landing next to the river. "Everyone," she raised her voice to be heard over the approaching roar of the aircraft, "let me do the talking when we get back to base!"

"They cheated!" Bifft jabbed a finger awkwardly close to Perkins' face when they reached the Yellow Team headquarters. "Hiding a front-line Dobreh fighter gunship in a river is not an approved-"

"*Approved?*" General Dase cut off Bifft's argument with a withering stare. "Cadet, do you think in real combat the Kristang will conform to an '*approved*' set of tactics? I can assure you they will not; neither will the Wurgalan or any other force we may encounter. *If* you are unfortunate enough to face the Kristang in battle, you can expect they will hit you with every dirty trick they can imagine, and they will not care whether you have a preset set of tactics to counter them. If your rigid thinking is an example of what our military academies are teaching now," Dase shook his head sadly, "then our people had better become accustomed to losing battles and territory. Lieutenant Colonel Perkins," he turned to the human leader, speaking slowly to pronounce her rank correctly as a sign of respect. "Your team has, once again, proven to be resourceful, clever," he paused to see if that word translated correctly and continued when Perkins nodded happily, "and courageous. If the operation had not worked as planned, the repercussions to human involvement with our military could have been long-lasting and detrimental to your people here on Gehtanu and beyond. While I am not pleased to be on the losing side of your unexpected success," his grin reflected the chagrin he felt, "I am glad this was only a wargame exercise, so we can learn much without getting anyone killed."

"They destroyed a frontline combat aircraft!" Bifft insisted, proving he did not know when to cut his losses and keep his mouth shut.

"They did damage an aircraft, yes," General Dase agreed. "Cadet, you will find aircraft are frequently damaged in combat-"

"This was not real combat!" Bifft nearly shouted. When he heard others gasp that he had interrupted a general officer, he bowed his head. "I apologize, General Sir."

Dase snorted and looked down his furry snout at the cadet. "A wargame is only useful if the people involved act the way they would in actual combat. Colonel Perkins, I understand your military organization has a motto to the effect of 'train the way you fight'?"

"We believe that very strongly, General Dase," Perkins replied with deadly seriousness.

Dase nodded approvingly. "We use technology to make wargame exercises as realistic as possible, but if the people involved," he glared directly at Bifft, "do not act as if the combat is real, they learn nothing. Tell me, Perkins, why did you plan to sacrifice your ground team and possibly your only aircraft?"

Perkins had an answer ready, because she only needed to tell the truth. "Because my team had multiple, significant disadvantages in both physical ability and experience with your equipment and tactics. The only possibility for us to contribute to mission success was to use unconventional tactics. Otherwise, we could have stayed back at base like some people wanted us to."

"Quite so," Dase said with admiration. "Cadet Colhsoon, I suggest you throw away whatever texts the academy has assigned you to read, and instead study the actions of Colonel Perkins, both today and from the events of them activating maser projectors and destroying a Kristang battlegroup. A *real* battlegroup," he added for emphasis. "As to the Dobreh fighter that was damaged," he downplayed the damage to the aircraft, which had been declared a total loss and was being salvaged for parts. "The aircraft logs state it was not actually combat capable, and should never have been assigned to participate in the exercise. It was not, as you described, a 'frontline combat aircraft'. It was a source of spare parts and now it is fulfilling its true mission," General Dase actually winked to Perkins. "That our counterparts on the Green Team stuck the human pilots with that barely-capable piece of," the translator stumbled and Perkins heard it say 'junk' in her ear but she thought Dase had used a stronger term. "Is shameful and does not reflect well on us as a people. Colonel Perkins," Dase bowed slightly, "please convey my apologies to your pilots. Your team succeeded despite having the deck stacked against you."

Perkins bowed curtly to acknowledge the compliment and her eyes twinkled. "Have you ever gone into actual combat *without* having the deck stacked against you, General Dase?"

"No," the Ruhar commander chuckled. "I have not. Cadet Durndurff," he addressed Nert. "You intend to continue serving as liaison officer with Colonel Perkins?"

Nert brightened up immediately. "Oh, yes, Sir, General Dase, Sir," he replied with pride, throwing his shoulder back and standing tall.

"You are a fortunate young man, and if you keep your mind open and learn, I expect great things from you."

"Oh," Nert swallowed hard as he realized the pressure on him. "Sir, I hope to serve with distinction, Sir," he nervously ignored Jesse's instruction not to make a 'sir sandwich' when speaking to an officer.

"Cadets, you are dismissed," Dase sent Nert and Bifft away with a curt nod and turned his full attention to Perkins, gesturing her to follow him as he walked toward his command center. "I have a call with the admiral in only a few minutes, but please walk with me and indulge me in a question, Colonel. How did you get the idea to hide a fighter aircraft in a *river*? Sensors aboard my aircraft that were declared shot down did briefly detect a submerged anomaly, but the crews ignored it. *That* will be a lesson learned to go straight into the standard operations manual."

"It was Captain Derek Bonsu's idea," Perkins felt a jolt of pride that lowly humans had taught another lesson to the Ruhar. "He was assigned to an airbase before and during the Kristang occupation," she smiled and did not mention that Bonsu had been taken off flight duty back then and limited to being basically a gofer for the aircraft maintenance teams. "He observed a Dobreh fighter being subjected to something you call a 'water immersion test'? He was surprised to see that after being in a water tank for several hours, the fighter was able to pass flight tests and return to service with minimal maintenance."

"Yes," the general's face lit up with understanding. "I remember that. The company that builds the Dobreh was testing one fighter from the batch delivered to Gehtanu, as part of a service contract. That aircraft has what I think you call a 'ditch switch' to close external ports in case of a water landing, but the purpose of that test is to demonstrate the aircraft will not be damaged by flying through heavy rain, or by fire-suppression equipment in a hangar."

"Heavy rain?" Perkins' eyebrows flew up. "That must be some *seriously* heavy rain."

"Our aircraft must be capable of operating in extreme environments," Dase explained, "because we never know what planet we will be called on to occupy next."

"Ah," Perkins made a mental note to remember that lesson; she could no longer afford to think only in terms of conditions on one planet, whether that was Earth or Paradise, or Camp Alpha. She needed to consider what her team would do under conditions she could barely imagine.

CHAPTER SIX

Perkins tugged at the knees of her formal uniform pants to straighten the crease, before she took a deep breath and held up a hand to knock on the doorframe of the UNEF liaison office. On Earth, a general officer would have a waiting room with at least one staffer to filter visitors, but on Paradise such luxuries had been dispensed with. Even at UNEF HQ in southern Lemuria, the tents and hastily-constructed prefab buildings used as offices had no waiting areas, in most cases they didn't even have doors. The human military force on Paradise had shrunk by almost forty percent, due to people seeing no point to being part of a military organization that no longer had a military mission. Nearly four in ten UNEF soldiers had already opted to put aside their uniforms and become civilians, mostly farmers although the humans had a growing economy, and more people left the UN Expeditionary Force every day. At current trends Perkins had seen in a classified report from UNEF HQ, it was estimated that within two years only ten percent of humans on Paradise would still be wearing a uniform. Elections were scheduled for the next year, after which the military would be subject to the authority of civilian leadership.

Civilian humans on Paradise, she had to shake her head at that concept. The force was evaporating as their original mission faded away into history. Emily had briefly considered hanging up her own uniform, but at the moment she was having too much fun training with the Ruhar, even if the majority of hamsters considered including her team in their training to be a joke. As long as her little team wore UNEF patches on their uniforms and participated in training, the Ruhar were reminded their continued possession of the planet they called Gehtanu was thanks to the actions of humans. And that forty thousand Ruhar owed their lives to Perkins and her team blowing up an island to wipe out a group of Kristang commandos, while the hamsters with all their superior genetics and technology had no idea that crack group of commandos even existed. It was important for the Ruhar to be reminded that humans could be useful, had been useful. So Emily and her team endured the jokes, the insults both subtle and openly stated, and showed the UNEF flag to represent all of humanity.

She rapped a hand on the doorframe and straightened her shoulders. "You wished to see me, Ma'am?"

General Lynn Bezanson looked up from her tablet and silently waved Perkins into the office, swallowing the coffee she had just sipped. "Perkins, come in, sit down." Saluting had mostly been dispensed with inside the building, especially as Perkins and Bezanson were probably the only two humans in the building that day. When Perkins and her team had accepted the opportunity to train with the Ruhar army, Bezanson had moved from southern Lemuria to be UNEF's liaison to Chief Administrator Lohgellia, which is why Bezanson had a small office in the main administration building, only one floor below Lohgellia's own suite of offices. "Coffee," Lynn raised her plastic mug with the UNEF logo and pointed to it. "Real coffee, can you beat that? It tastes real, anyway, better than a lot of the Army coffee I've had on Earth," she beamed with joy and took another sip of the precious liquid. Supplies of coffee from Earth had long ago been exhausted, and Lynn found the lack of the bitter brew almost more difficult to accept than the loss of her favorite foods. For breakfast, she loved hardboiled eggs with maple-flavored bacon, but while chickens on Paradise were producing a decent supply of eggs, there was no bacon anywhere. Some people were experimenting with making bagels, but without peanut butter, Lynn didn't see the point of eating a bagel. "Pour yourself a cup," the general gestured to the pot simmering in a corner of the office.

Perkins poured herself a half cup, noting the pot was nearly empty and knowing coffee was still in very short supply on Paradise. She sniffed then took a tentative sip. "Hmm, not bad. Better than typical gas station coffee."

Bezanson nodded with enthusiasm. "There's cream, real cream from Lemuria, in the fridge."

Perkins had liked cream in her coffee but she had been out of the coffee-drinking habit and knew cream also had to be in short supply, especially in the planet's capital city. "I'll drink it black, I want to savor it straight."

"Take all you want, it's due to you and your team that we have coffee. And chocolate!" Lynn clapped her hands with delight. "Did you read last week's intel summary? We could have beef in six months. Beef! I haven't had a steak in," she looked at the ceiling. "Too long. If we do get beef, I am going to have corned beef and cabbage, even if I have to prepare the beef myself."

Perkins had read the report about Ruhar scientists working to modify their own lab-grown meat for human consumption. There were cows on Paradise, but they were exclusively for milk production. Because the Ruhar considered killing animals for food to be barbaric, UNEF had a ban on eating cows, or chickens, or the few other types of animals that had made the long trip from Earth before the Kristang stopped shipping in supplies. Of course there were occasional violations of the strict vegetarian policy, but penalties were severe and the Ruhar were generally satisfied that the humans who did eat animals were an anomaly. Now there was potential for meat to be added to the human diet once again, even if the source of that meat had never walked around on two or four legs. Perkins had tasted experimental lab-grown chicken created by the Ruhar, and while it had a somewhat spongy mouthfeel, it tasted like genuine chicken. Supposedly considerable progress had been made to bring lab-grown chicken into production, and now the Ruhar scientists were trying to create lab-grown beef. Perkins knew that officially, the Ruhar were creating lab-grown meat and genetically engineering plants to grow coffee and cocoa beans and other Earth delicacies, as a gesture of gratitude. Gratitude for lowly humans having destroyed a Kristang battlegroup and then saving the lives of forty thousand civilians. Perkins was sure gratitude played some part in motivating the Ruhar effort, but the hamster scientists she had spoken with were eager for the genetic engineering challenges of modifying native plants to produce foods for human consumption. The human presence on Paradise provided a convenient excuse for research efforts the Ruhar wanted to pursue anyway. "Beef would be great," Perkins agreed while savoring the coffee. "I am getting tired of vegetable lasagna. How many UNars did this coffee cost you?" She asked, concerned she might be sipping a treat the general had spent a week's pay to get. After initially relying on a barter system, the human economy on Paradise now had a currency called the 'UNar', based on a bushel of corn. Barter was still used for many agricultural products, but increasingly people were conducting transactions, and thinking, in UNars.

"Nothing," Bezanson shook her head. "These beans aren't from the coffee bean fields in Lemuria, this came from an experimental batch. The botanists wanted an opinion from human taste buds before they engineer a plant to crank out these beans."

Perkins took another sip and swirled the hot liquid around her tongue. "It's got a nutty flavor, but there's a very bitter taste. It's subtle."

"Yeah, I told them that. They said the bitterness is likely from the layers of pulp between the bean and the outer coating; they're going to work on it. They seemed very pleased," she noted with a smile, "when I told them how they need to adjust the flavor. I really threw them a loop when I asked if they can make old-fashioned English tea, like Orange Pekoe."

"Can they?" Perkins asked hopefully.

"The hamster," Bezanson glanced guiltily out her open office door, "*Ruhar*, I asked is taking that task as a personal challenge. It helps that his sister and her family were on one of those ships you prevented the Kristang from blowing up. So, thank you," she raised her mug as a salute.

"You are welcome," Perkins returned the salute. "You didn't call me here to talk about coffee, General."

"No, I didn't. First, there's this," Bezanson opened a drawer and pulled out a small red box, tossing it to Perkins, who opened it and looked up in surprise. "That's right," the general grinned broadly, happy to be delivering good news for a change. "You're a Lieutenant Colonel now so you should be wearing the proper insignia. There will be a formal ceremony at UNEF HQ in Lemuria later this week, I don't think you should have to wait. Sorry your team didn't get a proper ceremony before, but, you were busy."

"I, I'm honored, Ma'am."

"You deserve that promotion ten times over, but we already promoted one person directly to colonel, and that didn't work out too well," a frown flashed across her face as she recalled the unknown fate of Joseph Bishop. "We're going to meet the burgermeister after lunch today, I want you wearing your new rank insignia then."

Emily Perkins stared at the silver oak leaves of her new insignia, while she ran a thumb over one of the gold oak leaves on her uniform. "I'll put them on when we finish here, Ma'am."

General Bezanson saw the frown on the junior officer's face. "What's wrong?"

"It's just," Perkins looked at the UNEF patch on her sleeve. "It feels odd to be promoted in a force that gets more irrelevant every day. The intel summary said, what, seventeen hundred troops left the service just in the past week?"

"Seventeen hundred thirty nine, yes," Lynn glanced at her tablet. "The previous week that number was over two thousand."

"Ma'am, somehow it feels like we're losing."

"I understand how it feels, but HQ tells us that people leaving the force is a good thing in the long run. The economists say military personnel don't generate as much economic activity, because much of our time is devoted to what economists call 'non-productive tasks'," she winked.

"I find that ironic," Perkins said with a laugh.

"That what you and I do is considered non-productive?"

"No," Perkins shook her head. "That we now have *economists* at HQ."

"Yes!" Bezanson agreed. "I notice very few of *them* have resigned their commissions. Really, though," her expression turned serious, "they're right about the benefits in the long run. Civilians are responsible for feeding themselves, or they will be within two years if the resettlement plan works. What is most important about the process HQ is calling 'demilitarization' is how it affects the hamsters' attitude toward our presence here. You and your team are showing the flag and reminding them how useful humans can be to the Ruhar military, but you also remind them that humans came to Paradise as a military occupation force. The burgermeister tells me that when we get to the point where ninety percent or more of the human population are civilians, the Ruhar view of us will change. The average hamster won't see humans as a defeated enemy force, they will see us as a primitive species that got suckered and used by the Kristang. They'll see us as a people caught up in a war we didn't start and don't want."

"Ha," Perkins snorted. "The Ruhar brought the war to *us*. They saw us as primitive natives about to be invaded by the Kristang, and their response tells us how they would act if we were allies. They could have come to Earth, warned us about the lizards and helped us prepare a defense. Instead, they knocked our infrastructure back into the pre-industrial age and bugged out without ever looking back to see what a mess they left behind."

"The end result would have been the same, maybe worse, if they had tried to help us. We would not have believed them, and even if we knew the true nature of the Kristang right from the start, we would have sent the Expeditionary Force out to serve them, because we wouldn't have had a choice. The Ruhar have been fighting this war for a very long time, since before humans had civilization. Most of them are sick of fighting, they hit us to get it over with as quickly and efficiently as possible," she shrugged.

"If they are so tired of fighting, why are they still doing it? They could drop back into a purely defensive posture," Perkins mused sourly.

"Colonel," General Bezanson referred to the other woman's new rank, "you were an intel officer. If I suggested the hamsters cease all offensive operations, what would be your assessment of that idea?"

Perkins frowned. "I'd tell you it wouldn't work, unless the Kristang stop being Kristang."

"The lizards are caught up in a nice little civil war now," Bezanson observed. "Ruhar intel says they expect the war to continue for another three to four years before winding down. Add on another two to five years for whoever comes out of the war on top to rebuild and consolidate their position. Then they'll be spoiling for a fight with the Ruhar and Torgalau."

"Why?" Perkins sighed. "They've been doing the same thing for thousands of years, will they never learn?"

"Kristang warrior caste psychology and internal politics require the strongest clans to constantly push outward to acquire new territory. In part, that constant conflict gives their young, lower-ranking warriors something to expend their energy on, rather than causing trouble for clan leadership. Their society *needs* war, or the entire reason for the warrior caste would disappear."

"And then the Ruhar and Torgalau will get stuck in the war whether they like it or not," Perkins noted, while wondering how true that really was. The Ruhar had originally taken the planet Gehtanu away from the Kristang Black Trees clan, not because Paradise was strategically important to the Ruhar defense posture, but because the Ruhar wanted more territory for *their* growing population. Humans had been exiled to the jungles of northern Lemuria, then forced to move out because Ruhar real estate developers wanted to create communities there, and the hamsters knew their property values would be lowered if dangerous humans were in the area. The Ruhar were not innocents in the ongoing conflict, and they certainly were not good-guy saviors of humanity. The actions of the hamsters at Earth proved the Ruhar only cared about their own strategic interests, and had given little thought about how lowly humans would be affected by being dragged into the endless war. Perkins did not fault the Ruhar for putting their own interests first, but the incident caused her to remind herself, every time she had dealings with the technologically-superior species who owned the planet, that the fate of humans meant little to the Ruhar and their federal government. "Our civvies here will play the part of innocent farmers, while my team reminds the Ruhar that they owe us?" Perkins guessed.

"Something like that, yes," Bezanson agreed. "Your team also keeps us in the game. If the hamsters are our patrons here and they're going to keep fighting, we want the ability to defend ourselves. Because we sure as hell can't count on the hamsters protecting us, if they really get pushed by the Kristang or whoever." Even after Perkins and her team destroyed a Kristang battlegroup and secured control of the planet for the Ruhar, the distant federal government had still wanted to give the planet back to the Kristang, and leave humans at the mercy of the lizards. Discovery of valuable Elder artifacts had persuaded the Ruhar to retain control of the planet they called Gehtanu, but Bezanson knew that situation could change in a heartbeat. If the Ruhar suffered a serious military setback in that part of the sector, they might be forced to pull their battlegroup away from Paradise. If that happened, Lynn did not think the unlikely prospect of finding more Elder goodies would make the Ruhar determined to keep the planet. Already, the failure of Ruhar scientists to find even a single additional Elder artifact was causing rumblings in their military, about the value of keeping a battlegroup stationed at such a backwater world. Chief Administrator Logellia had told Lynn that in a few years the growing population of Gehtanu, plus the substantial investments the planet was attracting, would soon cross a threshold where it would be politically poisonous for the Ruhar federal government to abandon that world. But that threshold had not been reached yet, and the number of ships assigned to the Gehtanu battlegroup had shrunk every time the task force rotated commanders. "Enough depressing talk," Lynn slapped the table emphatically, and pulled two more boxes from the open drawer. She lifted the lid of the first box, displaying a dozen chocolates. "Latest batch from Ruhar labs, these in the center are chocolate-dipped caramels," she announced as she took one of the delicacies and popped it in her mouth.

"Mmmm," Perkin's eyelids fluttered in ecstasy as she savored a caramel. "It tastes just like real chocolate!"

"I've been challenging them to make maple syrup, but the only sample we have left is half a bottle that got cooked pretty badly while it was in the jungle," she noted with disappointment. She had tasted that bottle but it already had an off flavor, so she returned it to the owner and instructed the Ruhar not to use it as a flavor example. "Now the fun part," she pulled the lid off the second box, exposing a stack of Velcro-backed patches. "This will be your new unit symbol, we're calling your team the 'Mavericks'."

Perkins picked up one of the patches, studying it. "Mavericks, huh?"

"The idea came from one of the referees from that last wargame; she said your team was the element the Yellow commander failed to account for. Also," Bezanson cocked her head. "You kind of have a reputation for going off and doing whatever you feel like, and maybe telling HQ about it later. You could at least send us a postcard, Perkins."

"Uh huh," Perkins' cheeks reddened slightly, knowing she could not argue with the general's comment. "I guess 'Mavericks' is appropriate. Do the hamsters know what that word means?"

"Probably not," Bezanson made a mental note to check on that. "You like it?"

"My team will *love* it," Perkins replied happily. Her team were still wearing the symbols of their old units that were now increasingly irrelevant. It was time for Colter and Czajka, for example, to replace their 10th Infantry insignia, as they had not served in what was left of the 10th on Paradise for a long time. "So, the Ruhar don't have any hard feelings about the results of that wargame?"

"Quite the opposite. The Yellow Team commander wrote a glowing evaluation of your team, and recommended you be approved for an offworld training assignment."

"*Offworld?*" Perkins gasped.

Lynn Bezanson's grin was almost wider than the one lighting up Perkins' face. "Specifically, a fleet assignment. They have a dedicated training ship, an old cruiser. If you're interested-"

"*Interested?* Hell yes we're interested!" Perkins knew she didn't need to ask her team, they were all eager for an opportunity to get aboard a Ruhar warship.

"You'd be away two or three months, that's the length of a typical training cruise."

"Sign us up!" She would need to concern herself later with the logistic details of humans being aboard a Ruhar ship.

"It's going to be a lot of work, just to qualify for spaceborne duty," the general warned the overeager new lieutenant colonel.

"Spaceborne?"

"Spaceborne Army," Bezanson explained. "That's the closest translation of the Ruhar term. The Ruhar don't have a distinction between soldiers based on land or ships, like we do with the Army and Marine Corps, because all their troops rotate between dirtside and shipboard. The training cruiser arrives here in four months, thereabouts, and you have a lot of work to do before you can be space duty certified. That includes working in spacesuits, in a zero-gee environment. Your pilots need to transition to flying a dropship, they will have the most challenging training. All of you will need training to help with damage control aboard the ship."

"Of course. Just the six of us?" Perkins asked. Many people wanted to join her unit, but to date, UNEF had not allowed her to add personnel to her accidental team. UNEF HQ did not want to dilute the positive publicity of her team by adding people who had not already destroyed a battlegroup and saved thousands of Ruhar lives.

"Seven," Bezanson corrected. "Cadet Durndurff will be coming with you."

"Oh?" Perkins expressed surprise. After the wargame, Nert had returned to his studies at the military academy. He sent them messages regularly, but he was too busy for anyone to visit.

"Going aboard the ship for a training cruise is a regular part of the academy's program. Usually a training cruise is reserved for third and fourth-year students, but they will make an exception for Nert, if you want him with you."

"General," Perkins responded carefully, "we all love his fuzzy face, and having him with us would smooth things for us aboard that ship, but-"

"But?" Bezanson asked with a raised eyebrow.

"Look, when the burger- when his aunt Baturnah requested her nephew join my team, I was not happy about the prospect of babysitting a teenager. Since then, he has proven to be very useful to us, my whole team loves having him around, and he's got a great future ahead of him."

"You haven't got to the 'but' yet, Colonel."

"But," Perkins paused, "I am concerned his service with us is not good for *him*. We take up a lot of his time, if he misses assignments while serving as my liaison officer he has to make it up when he returns to the academy. He tells us he is famous now at school, and that puts a lot of pressure on him. Plus," her expression turned angry, "some of the cadets are mean to him because he associates with humans."

"Perkins, I appreciate your concern. I've met Nert and I like the little guy too-"

"He's not so little anymore," Perkins interjected.

"-and he's a teenager. If his classmates didn't tease him about spending time with us, they'd pick on him about something else."

"True enough," Perkins admitted. She held up one of the Mavericks patches. "Ok if I send one of these to Nert? He'd be tickled, well, his skin is already pink under the fur," she laughed and Bezanson laughed with her.

"Perkins, it will be your call whether Nert will be with you or not. The academy hasn't made the offer to him, so if you decide against the idea he won't know the decision was yours."

"I know Nert, if he found out the Mavericks are going on a training cruise without him, he would be heartbroken. All right, I need to think about how to make this work, but it sure would make life easier for us if he's with us."

"Decision made, then," the general concluded. "Perkins, I like that you are considering the impact on your liaison officer, but you need to prioritize the benefits to humanity, and

UNEF in particular. Your team will be the first to get an opportunity to go offworld, everyone's eyes will be on you. Any screw-ups will reflect badly on all humans. If Cadet Durndurff can make your job a bit easier, you need to take that opportunity."

"Do I *want* to go offworld?" Jesse's eyes bulged as the idea of being an astronaut, a space soldier, sank in. "I don't know about y'all," he pointed to his companions, "but I plan to carpe that diem until it begs for its *momma.*"

Perkins had to laugh with the rest of the team. "Colter, I appreciate your enthusiasm. Let's see if you are as happy about the idea when you're stuck in a hamster spacesuit and they're spinning you around a hundred RPMs in zero gee."

"Don't you worry none about me, Ma'am. At the state fair, I'm the guy who eats corndogs on the roller coaster while everyone else is losing their lunch." He pointed a thumb toward Czajka. "Ski's the guy you have to worry about."

"*Me*? When did you ever see me on a roller coaster?"

"Don't need to," Jesse shook his head with exaggerated sadness. "Remember when we was in that Blackhawk over Dogon Dawa in Nigeria?"

"Oh for- you got sick too! That helo almost chucked upside down in that storm," Dave explained. "If we hadn't been strapped in, all of us would have fallen out the door."

"All I can say is, *your* breakfast ended up in *my* boots," Jesse grinned. "Don't worry, Colonel," he addressed their leader. "I'll keep an eye on Ski if his wittle baby tummy gives him any trouble."

"People, in all seriousness, this assignment is going to be tough. No humans have been through this training, so we don't know whether we can even get through the program. The next four months could be rough."

Shauna crossed her arms defiantly. No hamster was going to keep her from serving aboard a starship. "No humans ever wiped out a lizard battlegroup-"

"Or nuked an island," Irene nudged her friend playfully.

"That too," Shauna admitted with a sheepish grin. "Spaceborne Army, huh? I like the sound of that." She unconsciously touched the infantry patch on her uniform, wondering what a Spaceborne Army insignia looked like. She could send the question to Nert, he would surely know. "When do we get started?"

"Eight days," Perkins replied happily, seeing the enthusiasm of her team. "Until then, you're all on leave, so enjoy yourselves and keep in touch."

"Hey Ski!" Dave turned to see Pete Sanchez elbowing through the crowd toward him. The bar was packed even at mid-day, the popularity of the establishment was more a function of there still being few places in Lemuria that had a supply of alcohol, rather than the quality of the beverages served in the bar.

"Pete! Damn, good to see you," Dave called out, pointing to a narrow space next to him at the bar. It was good to see a familiar face, as Dave had found the bar distressingly full of strangers including a lot of the former Indian military. Pete Sanchez had served in Sergeant Joe Bishop's Embedded Observation Team at the village of Teskor, way back when UNEF first landed on Paradise. Dave had gotten into contact with Pete, after the Ruhar finished interrogating everyone who served closely with Bishop. Other than both serving with Bishop, the two originally had little in common, but soon developed a friendship during a rather raucous fishing trip up in the mountains. That fishing trip also introduced Dave to Pete's entrepreneurial side, with that soldier bringing along portable chiller units to store the fish they caught. While Dave expected the fishing action would all be catch-and-release because neither humans nor Ruhar could eat the native life on Paradise, Pete had quickly explained why he had chosen that particular lake for the fishing trip. Years before, that lake had been part of a planned resort, so the lake was stocked with fish from the Ruhar homeworld. While plans for the resort had failed, the fish had thrived and Pete planned to catch, clean and ship out as many fish as they could catch. Pete had an arrangement with a UNEF pilot who diverted to the lake each morning and took the previous day's catch to fly up to a Ruhar settlement in northern Lemuria. The Ruhar had a general distaste for eating animals but some made an exception for tasty fish and they paid well. Pete split the money with Dave, Jesse and three others, putting a nice chunk of money in the wallet stored on Dave's zPhone. "You still got the fishing thing going?"

"No," Pete shook his head. "Too many people went up there, the Ruhar put a stop to it because we were wiping out the fish population. Raj," he caught the bartender's eye. "Two beers for me and my friend here."

"Thanks, man. Sorry about the fish."

"Ah," Pete waved a hand dismissively. "I've got another thing going." He took two bottles from the bartender and handed one to Dave. "You like it?"

The bottle was not glass but it was cold, and one sip told Dave it was real beer, not the rotgut alcohol distilled out of whatever agricultural leftovers could be found. He turned the bottle around to see a smiling, straw-hat wearing hamster on the label. "Lester Cornhut's Paradise Pale Ale," he read the label. "Hey, I know that name from somewhere."

Pete grinned and took a big swig of beer. "Uh huh, he is the mayor of Teskor, the village our Embedded Observation Team was stationed when we went feet dry down here with Bishop."

"Damn, Lester Cornhut is his real name? I thought you were joking," Dave laughed. "That hamster is brewing beer now?"

"Yeah, for me," Pete puffed his chest with pride. "We kept in touch after UNEF pulled us out. He invested in expanding capacity of his processing plant, but with farms popping up all over the planet, prices crashed and he was looking for an opportunity. I had been brewing my own beer, so we got together. Now, part of the land around Teskor has been planted with hops and barley, and we're adding wheat for our summer ale."

"Shit, man, when do you have the time for all this?"

"I quit the force a month ago."

That surprised Dave. "Wow." He lowered his voice. "Are you sure about that?"

"Best decision I made since we landed here," Pete declared. "Dave, I gotta ask you, are *you* sure about staying in the Army? I know you had fun in that wargame, but, that's over, so what are you going to do now? If the ExForce had a real mission, I might still be wearing the uniform, but I don't see the point to playing soldier," he shook his head sadly and drained the last of the beer, "when the hamsters won't let us fight."

"We've gotten into fights," Dave replied coolly, feeling offended.

"Yeah, and you guys seriously *kicked ass*," Pete's admiration was clear. "But, Ski, come on, you got into those fights on your own initiative, not because the hamsters trusted you in combat." He waved a hand for another couple of beers. "You can't count on stumbling into action, not when the hamsters treat us like pets. What's next for you?"

"I don't know," Dave answered truthfully. Pete was correct that, with the wargame over, Perkins planned to argue for her team to have a continued role serving alongside Ruhar military units, but even she had not been optimistic. The initial enthusiasm of the Ruhar army to relearn infantry tactics with human advisors providing guidance had faded. Upper echelons of the Ruhar military were insulted by the idea they could learn anything from primitive humans, and considered the possibility of another straight-up infantry battle to be remote. Most of the human advisors had been relegated to the role of observers, and many quit after being insulted too many times by their reluctant Ruhar hosts. "The Colonel got us an assignment offworld, for a couple months. After that, I don't know," he admitted.

"The Colonel, yeah," Pete nodded slowly. "Emily Perkins, right? Dave, look around, what do you see here, that you don't usually see much of?"

"Uh," Dave craned his neck to scan the crowd, then turned back to the bar. "We don't get drinks much at base," he noted, already thinking he needed to find a way to bring a case of Paradise Pale Ale back to the team.

"Forget the drinks. Women," Pete announced quietly. "There are *women* here. Not just this bar, the whole area of southern Lemuria the hamsters moved us to."

"Oh, yeah." Women were the first thing Dave noticed when he walked into the bar. Clusters of women sitting at tables, with a much larger number of men trying to catch their eyes, but not approaching unless invited. With far too many men seeking far too few women, any guy who acted like a jerk had zero chance. When Dave came into the bar, he had been surrounded by people eager to hear about his role in the wargame, the difference between Ruhar skinsuits and Kristang rigid armor, and what it was like to kick hamster ass even if it had only been a game. Dave was happy to boast about his recent adventure, but he had been disappointed that few of the women seemed interested in hearing his stories, and he had not been able to speak one-on-one with any women.

"Up at base, there are just the six of you?" Pete asked, and Dave nodded. "Last time we talked, Jesse was with Shauna, and the two pilots were hooking up?"

"It's more serious than hooking up," Dave was uncomfortable discussing the subject.

"Whatever. My point is, that leaves you with the Colonel as the only unattached woman on your team, and *that's* never gonna happen, right? It's great that you're loyal to your team, and you guys have saved our asses down here twice, but you can't count on that happening forever, you know? You need to think about yourself. Listen, Lester and I are thinking of expanding, brewing a sort of beer for the Ruhar. We've got the facilities now, and the human market is small, but more hamsters are arriving on this dirtball every day, and they need something to drink other than water. You're a hard worker, you're cool under pressure, *and* you're a genuine hero to the hamsters here," Pete lightly punched Dave's shoulder to emphasize his point. "Make that work for you. I'm serious. The Paradise economy is growing and there are opportunities out there, but you've got to act quickly because some other guy is hustling for the same break. You'll think about it?"

"Yeah," Dave agreed while tipping back a bottle to drink, though his attention was on a table of five women who were ignoring him and all the men around him. Two of the women were visibly pregnant, a sight Dave still found startling. He knew that women having babies was a good sign, an indication that humans were optimistic about their future on Paradise. "I'll think about it."

CHAPTER SEVEN

"Best behavior," Derek whispered as he wiped a clean rag over the copilot armrests in the cockpit of their shiny new Dodo dropship, for which they had each just received their Type Rating to fly. "*Best* behavior," he insisted.

"You're worried about me?" Irene replied innocently. "I am a model of politeness."

"Yes, sweetheart," Derek tapped the pilot's head, "you are the model for what *not* to do."

"It won't be my fault if this jerk-"

"This *honored guest*," Derek said slowly and patiently for emphasis, as he squeezed her shoulder and made her look up at him. "Irene, I'm serious. This guy is going to bait us, insult us, make cracks about how primitive we are. We *can't* take the bait."

"That's easy for you to say, I'll be doing the flying."

"That's because the hamster asked for you, you're the hero who flew a stolen Buzzard around with a portable drill rig and destroyed a lizard battlegroup. All I did was get shot down and carry my pilot across the countryside. Look, this guy asking for you is a form of praise. Like Colonel Perkins said, it's an opportunity to make a good impression, but it's also a danger that we will screw up and give the hamsters an excuse to bounce us off this mission. I am not worried one bit about your flying us up to the ship, I am concerned your mouth might get us in trouble. Take my grandmother's advice; you can be as rude as you want, as long as you *act* polite. Got it?"

Irene squeezed his hand. "I'll be on my best behavior. But after this flight, you're taking me to the gym on that cruiser and I'm hitting the punching bag *hard*."

"That's the spirit. And don't worry, I got your back. If this hamster is really a jerk, I'll take him out back, beat the shit out of him."

"If anyone gives him a beat-down, it will be *me*. Oh, crap, here's the asshole now," she announced as she plastered a smile on her face.

"You will hear a lot of noise and experience some vibration, I will be performing a 'run up' to test that the engines are capable of delivering max power for take-off," Irene explained, forcing the smile to remain rigid on her face. The dropship's engines put out so much thrust that the ship would rocket down the runway dragging its skids along the ground, so the engines had a special 'run up' mode where the turbine blades flattened in their housing and churned the air without providing much thrust.

"Do what you need to, please," the Ruhar government bureaucrat Arnu Charl put on a grin he intended the lowly human to see was false, as a sign of his discomfort having to trust a primitive creature with his life. "I am most concerned about your ability to safely operate this very sophisticated airspace craft. I know the air control system can remotely override your commands if you get us into trouble but," he flashed another intentionally thin smile, "that would be unfortunate. Hmm, I should adjust this seat," Charl scrunched his neck down as if he had trouble seeing out the forward window displays. "We Ruhar are, of course, much taller than the average human. I mean no insult, of course," he added to ensure the pilot understood his intended insult.

Irene knew Derek had already adjusted the copilot seat down to fit the Ruhar who was, in fact, taller than most humans, so she ignored the hamster's attempt to bait her and she didn't even need to bite her lip to stifle a sharp reply. Officially, Arnu Charl was riding with them only to observe the primitive humans in action. Unofficially, everyone knew he was looking for an excuse to squash the whole idea of humans being aboard a Ruhar ship, even an old training ship. In a minute, Irene would be taking the Dodo off the ground and up into low orbit, to rendezvous with a cruiser. When she was flying, in command of the supremely powerful dropship, she could ignore anything. While she adjusted the controls to begin running up the engines at first only to seventy percent power, she could see in her peripheral vision the hamster was reaching down under the seat with both hands, with his eyes watching the engine power levels on the copilot display. She nudged the throttles forward to only twelve percent power, making sure the turbine fan blades were indeed feathered, then when she was satisfied everything was operating perfectly, she advanced the throttles slowly and smoothly toward the preset seventy percent limit. To her right, the hamster grunted as he bent down to reach the seat controls, fumbling around under the seat bottom.

"Sir, be careful!" She warned. "The ergonomic controls for the seat are on the right side, not under- NO!" Irene shouted in panic as with her left hand she hit the master switch to kill power, and her right hand reached across to grab the Ruhar's arm. With her seat harness properly tightened, she couldn't reach across the gap, so she was unable to prevent the disaster that followed.

The cockpit seat ejection mechanism in a Dodo was different from the arrangement on the truly huge dropship humans called a 'Whale', it was the same as the system aboard the small 'Vulture' gunships. The idiot civilian had unintentionally tugged on the ejection handle in his search for the controls to lower the already-low seat, and fortunately for him, Irene and Derek, he had not first flipped the manual switch to allow the handle to move, and anyway Irene had not yet armed the ejection system. If he had successfully engaged the ejection sequence, the system would have accepted his command rather than first wondering why in the *hell* some idiot wanted to eject from a perfectly good airspace craft that was still sitting on the ground. Afterward, the AI aboard the Dodo would have puzzled over why the ejection system had been engaged, but generations of Ruhar pilots had demanded full control over ejection, so the AI was not allowed to intervene. Engaging the ejection mechanism would have caused the cockpit door to slam violently closed, then the sturdy brackets that connected the cockpit to the airframe would have been burned through instantly by nanocord that flashed into plasma. With the cockpit section free of the remainder of the Dodo, it would have rocketed upward and away, climbing well clear of the doomed ship that might be in danger of exploding. Eventually, when the onboard AI determined it was safe, the rocket thrust would cut off and a nanofiber parachute would be deployed, with the AI warping the fabric to steer the cockpit to a relatively safe landing. Irene and the Ruhar would be alive, though likely injured from the sudden jolt of the rockets firing.

Fortunately, none of that happened, because the Ruhar had not been trained how to use the ejection mechanism, because the designers of the system had idiot-proofed it as best they could, and because Irene as Pilot-In-Command had not armed the system at all. Unfortunately, there was another reason why the idiot hamster had not yanked upward on the ejection handle; his fumbling hands had found another handle that was just as dangerous.

"Derek!" Irene screamed as she watched in terror what was happening to the copilot seat. Somehow, the Ruhar had located and pulled the handle for the inflatable life raft tucked under the seat cushion, and that raft was now expanding at an impressive rate, forcing the seat upward and threatening to crush the hamster against the cockpit ceiling. Without thinking, Irene pounded her seat harness release button with her left fist and reached down into her right boot for a survival knife strapped there. With knife in hand, she began frantically sawing at the raft material, but it was a smart nanofabric and sealed itself rapidly behind the blade. In desperation, she began pushing the knife blade sideways, creating a larger rent and argon gas hissed out under high pressure, blasting her in the face and forcing her eyes almost closed. At a fearful yelp from the Ruhar who was trying and failing to release the straps holding into the seat that was now a deathtrap, she looked up into his pleading eyes. "*Derek!*"

"Got it got it got it got it," the copilot replied unseen below her field of vision as the cockpit swirled with dust kicked up by the blast of argon gas coming from the inflation canister of the raft. "Ok! Stopped it!" Derek exulted as his questing fingers located the tab to deflate the raft. They had practiced how to inflate and deflate a raft in training, but that course had never covered the possibility of deflating a raft when it wasn't yet fully deployed. The raft designers had never considered that possibility either, their well-founded assumption had been that anyone wanting a raft needed it to be inflated *now*, as soon as possible and that no one would ever change their freakin' minds in the middle of the process! In fact, all Derek did was yank open a panel on the side of the raft to let the expanding inert gas out, but the canister was still releasing more of the stored argon and the raft was filling faster than gas could come out the rather small flap.

What saved the Ruhar's life was a combination of Derek opening the flap, Irene's knife creating a hole that required nanobots to rush there to seal the rip, and the raft's fabric getting caught on the underseat mechanisms that snagged and tore more rents in the fabric. Between those three sources of tears in the fabric, the raft began to sag and within seconds, collapsed as the argon supply was exhausted. At the point, the Ruhar who had nearly had his neck snapped by being forced against the cockpit ceiling yelped again, because the seat lurched down and forward. The force of the raft inflating had broken the brackets under the seat, snapping it free of the floor and it fell and sagged forward, bashing Charl's face against the instrument panel. "Help!" He called as the significant weight of the seat itself had him trapped, his furry nose squashed against a display screen.

"Irene," Derek grunted as he stood up and tried to lever the heavy broken seat backward, "I could use some help here."

Irene stuffed the knife back in her boot before she stood up. The last thing they needed was another hazard cluttering up the cockpit floor that was already covered with billowing raft fabric and jagged broken bits of the seat attachment mechanism. With the two humans pulling and the Ruhar pushing as best he could, they got the seat awkwardly pulled back far enough so Irene could reach around with one hand and release the seat straps. Freed from the seat, the Ruhar lost no time in squeezing between the seat and instrument panel, rolling onto the floor in an undignified manner. Blood streamed down from his nose and he moved his head stiffly, holding it to one side.

"Is your neck stiff?" Irene asked with genuine concern. "Here, let me take off your helmet, the weight can't be good for your neck."

With the helmet off, the Ruhar gingerly moved his head side to side and back and forth, testing what range of motion he had. "Nothing broken," he announced with a glare toward Irene, and her mouth went dry as she imagined what the Ruhar would say to the accident investigation team. Somehow, the almost fatal incident was going to be her fault and in a way, she agreed with that conclusion. She was in command of the aircraft, so anything that happened aboard was her responsibility. Charl was going to say she should have warned him not to pull the handle to inflate the raft, as if she had ever imagined anyone would or even *could* be that incredibly stupid!

As suddenly as the Ruhar's intense glare bored into her, that expression was replaced by what Irene knew was sheepish embarrassment, unmistakable even though the body language was on an alien face. "We could, um, ha ha, keep this to ourselves, I hope?" The Ruhar asked, laughing nervously.

Irene looked around the disarray in the cockpit, at the torn fabric of the raft, the snapped and twisted pieces that had secured the seat to the floor, aand the smear of blood on the display screen. The Dodo would need to be taken off the flight line and back to a hangar to have the seat replaced and the airframe inspected for damage. No way could anyone conceal the incident. And then she realized something; Ruhar flight recorders captured everything that happened in a cockpit, voice, video and sensor data. That recorder would show the accident investigators that she warned the Ruhar not to screw around under the seat, but he had ignored her. Greatly relieved, she stepped backward through the cockpit door, waving the Ruhar to follow her and offering a hand so he didn't trip over broken parts littering the floor. "Sir, what matters is that you are not injured, that we can see. You should be examined by base medical personnel, to assure you do not have internal injuries."

"Ah, ha, ha," Charl swallowed hard, knowing he was going to be in big trouble. "Thank you, I-rene, Der-ek," he pronounced their names slowly. "I will see that you are assigned another airspace craft. Your quick reaction to the," he searched for a word that would not further embarrass himself, "unexpected incident, is much appreciated. You have demonstrated your skill and mastery of this craft, I do not need to accompany you up to the ship," he gave her a weak and sheepish smile. Then he waggled a finger accusingly. "That raft should not be capable of being inflated while it is still attached to the seat! I must speak with the manufacturer of that system!"

"I agree completely, Sir," Irene nodded with sympathy. "What if the system deployed on its own and caused the pilots to lose control? Battle damage might also cause the raft to inflate at the wrong time. We will add a note to that effect in our squawk list, Sir."

An hour later, with the Ruhar at the base hospital and the Dodo having been towed back to a hangar, Irene was filling out accident report forms on a tablet while she talked with Perkins via zPhone. "Yes, Ma'am, I think that Ruhar is going to be just fine. His pride is hurt more than anything. The hamst-" she caught herself from using the derogatory slang while in earshot of aliens at the airbase, "Ruhar here are anxious to get us away, Derek is on the flightline checking out our replacement ship now."

"The ship you were supposed to fly, is it damaged badly?" Perkins asked anxiously. A minor incident could be mostly swept under the rug, with the airbase maintenance team quietly replacing broken parts. But if the airframe had sustained damage and the dropship needed to be pulled out of service for an extended time, the incident could cause a big stink that senior Ruhar would be eager to blame on ignorant humans who should not be allowed to fly in the first place.

"No, Ma'am," Irene reported happily. "The crew chief told me this is the damnedest thing he's ever seen in all his years, and even he didn't think it was possible for a raft to inflate while still under a seat. This may lead to a new safety regulation."

"Great, as long as nobody ever says we humans are the cause of needing to idiot-proof something."

"I think all the Ruhar here at the base would very much like to pretend this never happened. Soon as these forms are completed, I'll help Derek preflight our new bird, and we should be up there with only a seven-hour delay."

"Seven hours?" Perkins asked, surprised and dismayed.

"Yes, Ma'am, the cruiser's orbit has taken it away from us, so our next good launch window is not for a couple hours," Irene explained patiently.

"Goddamit," Perkins cursed with exasperation. "Why isn't the future like *Star Trek* where you never have to think about the reality of orbital mechanics?"

"I'll get right on that, Colonel," Irene laughed.

"*Can* you launch now? I don't give a shit about your fuel consumption."

"We could, yes, it's not normal procedure-" Irene started to explain.

"To hell with normal procedure, then," Perkins cut off her pilot's explanation. "Tell them you are practicing combat rendezvous maneuvers, whatever bullshit you want to call it. I'll get it cleared with their air controller. I want you in the air ASAP, before the hamsters change their minds, or some higher-ups decide they need a full investigation. That cruiser is not waiting for us, it will be leaving whether we're on it or not."

"Yes, Ma'am," Irene agreed with enthusiasm.

"Striebich," Perkins' voice softened. "We dodged a bullet today. If that Ruhar had been seriously injured or killed, the hamsters wouldn't care that it was his own stupid fault."

"You're right, Colonel. He could have been killed. A couple more seconds," she didn't need to finish the thought. Right before Derek had ripped open the tab to deflate the raft, the Ruhar had been pressed up against the ceiling, his neck at an awkward angle. Irene had feared her passenger was already dead at that point. Of all the crazy, stupid things that had happened during her flying career, someone inflating a raft inside the cockpit was beyond not only her experience, it had been beyond her imagination. "Win ugly?" She suggested.

"Win ugly? All right," Perkins sighed from the heavy weight of responsibility. "I guess you can't argue with getting one in the 'W' column. Damn it, if anything goes wrong out there, we are not getting a pass from our patrons."

"We all understand that, Colonel. We are all doing our best."

"That's not good enough. I don't mean to be a hardass, Striebich, but we need to consider not only what will go wrong but what *could* go wrong."

Irene didn't think she would ever have considered a life raft to be anything that could be a threat, but she didn't want to argue right then. "Captain Bonsu and I still have three combat traps each to perform after we get back from the cruiser, Ma'am."

"Traps?"

Derek gave Irene the side-eye because she used pilot slang too often around non-pilots. "Flying a dropship into a docking bay," Irene gestured the action with her hands, "until it is caught, or 'trapped', by the emergency restraint system. We need to perform three traps at high-speed to qualify for spaceflight duty. That's where our focus needs to be right now."

"Understood. You did well, Striebich, you and Bonsu. I'll see if I can smuggle some debriefing fluid upstairs with me, so we can celebrate when the two of you are carrier qualified."

"Are you nervous, Captain?" Jesse asked, noting the pilot had been tugging at a lock of her hair as she studied whatever was on her tablet. "Flying up to the cruiser should be a piece of cake for you, right? It's no different from you docking with one of those practice platforms in orbit like you've been doing."

"Thanks, Jess- Sergeant Colter," she had been about to use the first names they'd gotten used to during their unauthorized and informal service together, but switched to military protocol when she caught Perkins with the corner of one eye. "It *is* different. Those big docking platforms don't have real live people aboard who could get hurt if we screw up. And they're designed to get bumped into, the cruiser is not. The real problem is, for us to get carrier qualified," she used the US Navy term rather than its awkward Ruhar equivalent, "we each have to get three successful combat traps in a Dodo, unassisted."

"Uh, combat *traps*, Ma'am?" Jesse asked, confused.

Irene used one hand to illustrate a dropship coming into a starship's docking bay. "Usually, docking procedures are done slow and careful, hands-off. We fly close to the ship and the docking bay's control system takes over, flies us into the bay nice and easy. That's what happened on our first flight up to the cruiser two days ago. If the docking bay system can't sync with our onboard AI, the AI can fly us in by itself, but that leaves a single point of failure, so we also practice manual docking. A Dodo dropship isn't huge like a Whale transport, but those docking bay door openings look awful tiny when you're approaching. We practiced the manual procedure for docking while we were up there."

"I can imagine that," Jesse agreed. "But, again, you've done that already."

"What we haven't done yet is manual *combat* traps. In action, a starship wants to recover birds quick as possible so they can jump away. Again, usually we rely on automated systems, but you can't always count on them working in combat. So Captain Bonsu and I have to fly a high-speed approach into a docking bay. If we miss, or fly in too far," she smacked one hand into the other.

"You want us to fly up there first, put a tennis ball on a string from the ceiling of the docking bay, so you know how far to pull in?" Dave suggested jokingly.

"That would be great, Czajka," Irene tilted her head and frowned at Dave. "That tennis ball trick works great to park a minivan in a garage. But we'll be flying a dropship the size of a Boeing 777 airliner, coming in at four hundred feet per second. Just to approach, we have to shoot through a tiny gap in the ship's energy shield, and there will be simulated explosions going off to distract us, because that's what happens in real combat. As a bonus, some of the flight systems will be disabled or will drop offline as we approach."

"Hell, Captain, that sounds dangerous," Jesse observed, his face turning pale.

"Nothing bad can really happen, unless we royally screw up. The control system will take over if we're going to crash, but we don't want that to happen. This first time, we will get five attempts to dock, and we need three successful traps out of five. They're going easy on us because we only had a month of training. When we get out there," she gestured toward the sky and beyond, "they'll be running us through exercises continuously, and eventually we'll need to hit the mark successfully every time, or they'll wash us out."

"If our pilots wash out, we go with them," Perkins warned. "The Ruhar view the Mavericks as a team, they're not splitting us up. No other unit wants just the four of us soldiers as a spaceborne infantry team."

"All for one, Ma'am?" Shauna suggested.

"And one for all," Perkins finished the saying. "The only good news I know of is this cruiser will have a bunch of flight cadets who will be burning eager to show they can do what experienced human pilots," she pointed to Irene and Derek, "can't do. I expect some of those nuggets to crash and burn, and that will give us breathing room for a couple minor slip-ups, *if* we don't crash a dropship or lose someone out an airlock."

"Yeah, Dave," Jesse winked at his friend.

"Me?" Dave asked defensively. "What you lookin' at me for?"

"I figure if one of us gets blowed out an airlock by mistake, it ain't gonna be *me*," Jesse winked to Shauna.

"Hey," Dave thumped his chest. "When we were in Kachako," he meant the city in Nigeria, "I'm not the one who fell out the window of that cathouse-"

"Whoa!" Jesse waved his hands frantically. "Nobody needs to hear that sordid tale right this minute."

"Cathouse?" Shauna asked, arms rigidly folded across her chest. "Like a brothel?"

"Uh, yeah, we were searching the place for insurgents," Jesse shot a pleading look to his comrade in arms.

"We actually were," Dave admitted. When Shauna gave him a skeptical look, he folded like a rug. "Well, we did find insurgents there, kinda unintentionally. It was Bishop's idea. That's when 'Pone went out the window."

"That guy had an AK!" Jesse explained. "It was either I go out the window or get an ass full of seven six two rounds. Anyways," he wanted to avoid discussing that subject any further. "Let's not talk about that now. Captains Striebich, Bonsu, best of luck to you going up to the, what's that ship's name again?"

"It's the *Ruh Tostella*," Derek explained.

"Tostella?" Dave laughed. "What're the odds we won't call it the *Toaster*?"

Even Perkins had to chuckle at that remark. "Just don't call it that when the hamsters can hear you. I don't think they go for giving nicknames to their ships."

"Now that your team has qualified for spaceborne duty, HQ has a going-away present for you." Bezanson picked a bag off the floor and took six mugs out, setting them on the table. "The Ruhar cranked these out for us. The logo is our idea."

Perkins picked up a mug. It was solid like a ceramic coffee mug, but lighter than Styrofoam, and the handle folded so mugs could be stacked. Printed into the olive-drab exterior was a logo Perkins had not seen before. It read 'EX FORCE' on top, with 'Anytime. Anywhere. Any fight.' below. A yellow star with a swoosh separated the two lines of text. "Uh, Ma'am, this kind of looks like a logo for a minor league hockey team."

Bezanson laughed at that. "HQ is not exactly stuffed with marketing experts, this is what the Big Five could agree on." Before the Expeditionary Force left Earth, there had been attempts to agree on a single motto, but talks had fallen apart and mottos were not considered a priority, so each of the five nations had their own logo and motto. The US military's contribution for an official motto was 'Taking the fight to the stars', which was universally agreed to be *totally* lame, but no worse than the mottos of the other four nations. Naturally, the troops came up with their own mottos, especially after the force realized their task would be peacekeeping on Paradise. 'Rent-a-grunts' was one unofficial motto, along with 'Mall cops to the stars!' and 'Will work for food'. Bezanson thought that last one was entirely appropriate. "HQ wanted something that sounded fierce. Perkins, this," she tapped a mug, "is for a morale booster here on Paradise."

Perkins looked at the mug with skepticism. "Anytime, anywhere, sure, but, 'any fight'?"

"Because we never know what crazy shit we'll get into next, and we won't back down." Bezanson was pleased to see Perkins nod determined agreement. "HQ did a survey of soldiers who chose to remain in the force, and over seventy percent of them cited the actions of your team as a major motivator. Your Mavericks proved humans can be useful in the war, that we might have a purpose out here beyond growing food and surviving. Colonel, this is important. We need to give the force a mission out here or there won't *be* an Ex Force. We're hoping after the Mavericks come back, the hamsters will allow other teams to go offworld."

"Any fight? General, with the crazy shit we've had to deal with, I think 'Any Fight' is absolutely appropriate. The Yellow Team commander of the wargame reminded me that his people never know what *planet* they might be fighting on next, they don't even know whether the atmosphere will be breathable. So, yeah, 'Any Fight' describes the attitude we *must* have." Perkins thought Colter and Czajka would lose their minds when they saw the coffee mugs, because in her experience, young male soldiers loved macho shit. Scratch that, she told herself. Sergeant Jarrett was totally going to love it. Probably Irene, too. Derek Bonsu was the one who might worry that having 'Any Fight' as a motto was just asking for trouble. Well, what the hell, finding trouble was why they were going to the stars anyway. "I'd like to say we'll keep in touch, but-"

"Yeah," Bezanson stood and offered a hand to shake. "Interstellar communications are spotty at best. Just make sure you come back, and come back with the hamsters seeing the value of your team."

"We will do our best, Ma'am," Perkins said, then to herself added 'or die trying'.

CHAPTER EIGHT

After Derek and Irene were declared fully qualified for flying Dodo dropships, they flew up to the *Toaster* with Perkins, leaving the three sergeants to wrap up things dirtside and catch a big 'Whale' transport up to the ship. They were met in the docking bay by a female Ruhar cadet who was not unfriendly, but gave the impression she had way too much to do for escorting aliens around the ship. The cadet led the way, with Shauna walking on the right beside her and Jesse and Dave behind. With the ship preparing to get under way and cadets racing around under the supervision of the few adult crew members, the journey forward was slowed by having to squeeze against the side of passageways to make way for cadets on more important missions. "Cadet Garnor," Shauna asked after a steady stream of cadets had come around a corner, "where are the officers?" They had walked a quarter of the ship's length, and all she had seen were cadets. Not only cadets hurrying past, but also cadets working at consoles, performing maintenance and even loading practice missiles into a Vulture fighter-dropship. So far, the only adults she had seen were herself and the other two human sergeants.

"Please call me Jinn. There are only eleven adults of my people aboard the *Ruh Tostella*," Jinn Garnor explained patiently. "On this training mission, third and fourth-year cadets are supposed to perform all necessary activities. Under supervision of the adult officers, of course," she added when she saw Shauna nervously gritting her teeth.

"That's, that's great," Dave filled in as Shauna and Jesse shared a quick look of terror. A starship, a mind-bogglingly sophisticated piece of alien technology, was being mostly flown and maintained by children? No, not *a* piece of technology, a starship was a collection of millions of pieces of advanced technology, with several hundred or more of those pieces vital to safe operation of the ship.

"Do not worry, I have been told there is only a small chance the ship could go 'boom'," Jinn winked in a gesture she had been told the humans would understand.

"Thank-" Dave began to say.

"Although, I was told that by a third-year cadet, so he could be wrong," Jinn added with a straight face, her performance only spoiled when she looked to see the reaction of the humans.

As they came near an intersection, the cadet pointed to the right, and Shauna hugged the wall to avoid bumping into anyone coming around the corner. Just as she reached the intersection and turned right, Shauna came face to face with a Kristang!

Instincts took over and Shauna shouted while slamming her right shoulder into the lizard's midsection. With the heel of her left hand, she punched the alien hard in the chest once, twice, then the Kristang was falling down and Shauna was being pulled backwards. Cadet Garnor had both hands on Shauna's shoulders and was pulling her down, shouting something like "No! Friend!"

"Easy, easy, baby," Jesse held Shauna so she didn't crack her head on the floor, and Dave leaped up and around the falling woman to stand between her and the lizard. Jesse moved to spin Shauna so she would be behind him, but she resisted and they tussled for a second. "Halt! Stop!" The cadet ordered frantically. "She is a friend!"

Dave did not waver from a fighting stance as the Kristang pushed itself off the floor, stood up and smoothed the front of its shirt. "This is the first time I have met humans," the lizard smiled in a horrible grimace and made a short bow. It rubbed its chest. "You hit harder than I expected. Perhaps your species is not as weak as I was told?" Then, impulsively, it stuck out a hand toward Dave.

"Uh," Dave stood stiffly until the cadet frantic head jerking urged him to return the gesture of friendship. Warily, Dave came out of a crouch and took the lizard's hand, which was warm and dry. Dave did not want the lizard to feel a limp, dead-fish grip, but he also didn't want the creature to interpret a hard squeeze as a threat. The lizard squeezed back with the same firm pressure then released before it became awkward. Then the Kristang nodded to the Ruhar cadet and continued on along the hallway, turning around a corner out of sight.

Jesse let out the breath he had been holding. "Can someone please tell me just what the *hell* that was?"

"Velt Ser-Kotreh Tutula is not the Kristang you know," Jinn had stepped back from the three humans, disturbed by the incident. "She is Verd-Kris. 'Velt' is her rank in their system, I do not know its equivalent in the UNEF military."

"*She?*" Jesse gasped. "That was a female? I thought they were all weak and small and-" realizing he was talking to two females who might not appreciate having their gender spoken of in those terms. "Because, you know, the warrior caste genetically engineered them like that. Which is a *bad* thing. A terrible thing." He decided the best thing to do right then was to stop talking.

"The name Verd-Kris means True Kristang. Or Original Kristang or First Kristang, something like that," Jinn explained. "They are from a population of Kristang cut off from their society when a wormhole shift blocked access to their home territory. My people then took control of the territory, but we did not wish to expend the effort to take that planet. All we did was remove their capability for faster-than-light spaceflight, to protect ourselves. Over eight hundred years, Verd-Kris society drifted away from the distorted culture enforced by the warrior caste, and back toward the matriarchal culture of the Kristang before the Thuranin conquered their homeworld long ago. Some Verd-Kris now fight alongside my people, and they are extremely fierce warriors, especially their women."

"Goddamn," Jesse let his shoulder slump with a shudder, coming down off an adrenaline high.

"Why didn't someone tell us?" Shauna asked as she rubbed her sore left hand, getting right in the cadet's face.

The well-disciplined cadet did not flinch. "We thought you knew. That information was not in the briefing packet about the ship?"

"Info that friendly lizards were aboard the *Toaster*?" Shauna asked with angry sarcasm. "No, we were *not* told that."

"Goddamn," Jesse repeated. "Hell, I would have remembered that. You Ok, hon-Shauna?"

Shauna shot Jesse a look that told him calling her 'honey' in public was not acceptable. "We know about the Verd-Kris, a little. I heard a rumor some of them have been on Paradise, Gehtanu, but I've never met one. Or seen one."

"I do not know whether any Verd-Kris have been on Gehtanu," Jinn bit her lower lip. "There is one other Verd-Kris aboard, you will meet him later today during the orientation briefing. He has met humans on our capital world, when your liaison people were there after the maser cannon incident. The other Verd-Kris is," she thought carefully, not entirely willing to trust the translator. "Interesting."

"Interesting how?" Shauna asked with a look to Jesse.

"You will see. He is a 'Surgun', a rank similar to a sergeant or warrant officer in your human military. His training methods can be, somewhat, rough and profane. Do not be alarmed, he is on our side."

"You sure about that?" Jesse suppressed a shudder at the unexpected encounter with just one of the lizard-like aliens. He lowered his voice and looked both ways in the passageway they were walking along. "You trust a Kristang? I mean, Verd-Kris," he added with a cringe.

"Do not be embarrassed, they *are* Kristang. By origin. Over the years, the two societies have drifted apart genetically because of isolation from each other, and because the Verd-Kris have pursued genetic modifications different from their hostile cousins." She paused, cocking her head. "Did that translate properly? I used a term for family who are not directly related."

"Yeah, 'cousins' is good," Jesse assured her.

"The most obvious difference, or course, can be seen in Verd-Kris females. Their genetics have been restored close to the original baseline, before the Maxolhx, through the Thuranin, forced changes on their society."

Shauna flexed her sore wrist. "What happened?"

"What happened to the Kristang is what happened to every species under the Maxolhx coalition," Jinn shrugged. "When the Thuranin made contact with the Kristang, the lizards had spaceflight capability, they had established a colony on another planet in their star system and they had an extensive operation to mine asteroids. Their scientists had not yet discovered the theoretical basis for the jump drive, so they did not have starflight. They still do not truly have the ability to travel between stars," she added with a smug wink. "Nor do their ships have artificial gravity as our ships do, as you know."

"Yeah," Jesse bounced on his toes, assuring himself the artificial gravity aboard the Ruhar ship felt just like real gravity on a planet. Except for an odd sensation of being tugged into two directions when he crossed the gap from one gravity plate to another, the effect was not noticeably the result of any technology. "We appreciate that. I hated the zero Gee on the Kristang ships that brought us to Paradise."

"How did the Thuranin make contact with the Kristang?" Shauna asked.

"The usual way, like the situation with your people. The Kristang homeworld was isolated for millions of years, then a wormhole shift provided easy access for the Thuranin. That region of space was not of any strategic importance to the Thuranin, but they were eager to match their Bosphuraq rivals by acquiring a client species. Did you know the Thuranin used to be clients of the Bosphuraq? It's true, though the Thuranin hate to admit it. When the Thuranin arrived at the Kristang homeworld, they followed the Maxolhx process for conquering a species and turning them into clients. They studied Kristang society and selected the most fanatical, oppressive group to put in charge. For the Kristang, that was the warrior caste."

"Wait, the warrior caste was not already in power?"

"No. Sergeant Jarrett-"

"Please call me Shauna." She did not know if that was correct protocol, but the cadet had been friendly and seemed to want to use first names.

"Yes, Shauna," Jinn flashed a smile. "Before the Thuranin arrived, Kristang society was splintered between clans and they certainly were not a peaceful species, but they had avoided suffering a wide-scale nuclear war, and were evolving toward a stable coexistence between clans. Each clan had a warrior caste that was a small group, perhaps three to four percent of the overall population. The Kristang were a *matriarchal* society, females led the clans. The warrior caste in some clans had long wished to assume power and strike the other clans, so when the Thuranin arrived, they flipped their client's society upside down and put the warrior caste in power. The stated excuse was that the warrior caste needed to take charge, to prepare the Kristang for battle against my people, or the Torgalau."

"You were planning an attack?"

"No," Jinn shook her head sadly. "We knew almost nothing about the Kristang and had no interest in them, their home system is far from our territory, especially back then. Our experience with the Kristang, how we passively stood by and did nothing while the Thuranin perverted their primitive society and turned them into a direct threat to us, is partly why we struck your homeworld. Your world is too far away for my people to maintain a presence there. Even now, after the Jeraptha have captured twelve percent of Thuranin territory in their recent offensive, Earth is too far away for us. The purpose of our raid on your world was to deny the easy use of your industrial base to the Kristang."

Shauna forced herself not to say anything. She nodded for Jinn to continue.

"We knew that Earth is remote and not strategically important to the Kristang, our hope was that if the Kristang saw they could not easily use your world as a staging base, they would lose interest in humans. That did partly happen, their White Wind clan nearly drove themselves into bankruptcy through their effort to conquer Earth," The cadet gave Shauna a sad smile.

"Now they're stuck there," Shauna looked straight ahead so the young Ruhar would not see the moisture in her eyes. "The Kristang at Earth, I mean. When the wormhole shut down, the Kristang at Earth became trapped."

"Yes. Shauna, I am, sorry? Did that translate correctly?"

"Yeah, you're sorry. Thank you." Shauna reminded herself that everything Jinn told her was the official propaganda of the Ruhar government. No, worse, it was that official story as told by a young, idealistic cadet who wanted to believe her people were always right and just and noble. Even though they had bombarded Earth's power generation and industrial infrastructure from orbit, killing thousands of humans in the assault or its aftermath.

When they received official orders to report aboard the *Ruh Tostella*, the data package included a layout of the ship and regulations for the crew. The Mavericks had been pleased to see the ship had three galleys, with one was reserved for senior officers. Perkins learned to her dismay that she was expected to take her evening meal with the Ruhar officers and senior cadets instead of with her own team.

Shauna scrolled down the data package while waiting for the All Clear to sound so they could move about the ship, and was surprised to see a section for aliens. In this case, 'aliens' referred to any being who was not Ruhar, reminding Shauna exactly where she and her fellow humans ranked in the Ruhar military. As she read the regulations and 'suggestions' for aliens, her frown grew deeper and she squinted uncomfortably. "Ma'am, this ship has a quarters section set aside just for us?"

"Yes," Perkins replied without looking up from her tablet. She had received a very skimpy briefing about the ship just after she accepted the assignment, so she knew some of the details ahead of time. The cruiser had a section of three cabins, one washroom and a small common area that was reserved for her team. According to the layout, much of the ship's crew accommodation space could be reconfigured as needed, and it looked to her like partitions had been added to enclose an area just for the Mavericks. She did not know whether the separation of humans from the Ruhar crew was intended as a mild form of insult, but she was relieved to see it, as it reduced the potential for friction in the close quarters aboard the training ship. She was irritated that the Ruhar had not consulted her before setting up a separate space for humans. There were three small cabins, each with two stacked bunks and no space for squeezing in a third bunk even if she wanted that. Because the bunks doubled as acceleration couches where her people needed to be strapped in when the ship was simulating combat maneuvers, having a third person sleeping on the floor was not an option. Originally, she had considered having the three men share one cabin, with Irene and Shauna bunking together, and giving her a cabin all to herself. Ship's regs did not allow more people than bunks, and since there was no way to add a third bunk, she had to make other arrangements. Shauna could share with Jesse, while Irene and Derek could share another cabin. That left Dave Czajka as the odd man out, with Emily Perkins seeing no alternative to sharing a cabin with the young sergeant she found quite attractive, if she let herself admit feelings she could not officially have. "There are three cabins. Jarrett, you'll be with Colter, Striebich with Bonsu."

"Uh, Ma'am?" Irene looked at her commanding officer as her cheeks grew red.

"Striebich, whether you've made it official or not with Bonsu, I don't see the point in trying to keep you two separated." Everyone knew the two pilots were a couple, though they had attempted to be reasonably discreet about their relationship.

"Yes, Colonel," Irene looked away, not believing her good fortune. She had not been looking forward to being separated from Derek during their scheduled months aboard the ship.

"What about, uh, me, Ma'am?" Dave's own face was draining of color as he imagined being stuck bunking with a Ruhar, or trying to sleep in a missile tube. "Will I be hot-bunking with Colter, or something?" The thought of crashing in Jesse's bunk while that man was away from the cabin did not appeal to Dave at all.

"No, you're with me, Czajka."

"Uh, Ma'am?" Dave's question ended in almost a squeaky uptone.

Perkins tilted her head in a confident gesture that covered up the butterflies in her stomach. "The Ruhar do not separate genders in their bunk assignments, and our section doesn't have separate officer's quarters. Look, people, I know this is going to be awkward, but think of it this way: we will be up there to train and live with *aliens*, on their ship. When in Rome, do as the Romans do, you got that? We need to get used to doing things the hamster way, that includes sleeping arrangements. We might as well be on our best behavior while in our little section of the ship, which will remind us to be on our toes twenty-four-seven among the Ruhar, understood?"

"Yes, C-Colonel," Dave stammered.

"Czajka," Perkins took pity on the extremely embarrassed sergeant. "I'm not thrilled about this either, and we need to act like it's no big deal, because to the hamsters, it is *not* an issue. We have a common area in the middle of the three cabins, so I expect to use that cabin only when I'm getting rack time," she declared, as she thought to herself that maybe she should ask the ship's executive office whether there was any sort of private workspace she could use during the daytime hours. "We're all going to be cool about the living situation, we're going to be mature about it, and we're going to show the hamsters that humans are an evolved species, does everyone understand that?"

"Crystal clear," Jesse spoke first, nodding a bit too vigorously from the tantalizing thought that he and Shauna would have a real door to provide privacy.

"Yes, Ma'am," Dave agreed.

"I expect we are all going to be ass-dragging exhausted every night anyway," Perkins added. "The Ruhar have told me they do not intend to coddle us in training, so we need to keep up with a genetically superior species, aboard a ship with equipment that is all new to us, and second-nature to them. We will be like your grandparents," she winked, "trying to use smartphones."

"Oh, *forget* it," Dave groaned, and everyone laughed. That broke the tension.

Perkins reinforced the lighter mood by wagging a finger at Dave. "I'm warning you right now, Czajka. If you snore, I'm going to smother you with a pillow."

"Don't you worry, Ma'am," Dave found himself actually grinning despite the still-awkward circumstances. "You should worry about *Shauna*. Jesse here snores like a chainsaw."

"Hey!" Jesse shook a fist at Dave. "Only when I've got a cold or something."

"Right, like you had a cold the whole time we shared that hut in the jungle?"

"Ah, I was allergic to that ugly couch, maybe."

At the first opportunity for privacy, Jesse pulled Dave aside. "Ski? Hey man, you gonna be OK?"

"Like I got a choice? I'll be sleeping in my camo uni pants and a T-shirt, I guess," he said unhappily. He thought that wearing thick, baggy pants and a shirt were the best way to make bunking together less awkward for Colonel Perkins. Maybe he could suggest they leave their cabin door open. Then he got a pensive look on his face. "The Colonel's right, though. Out here, we might as well throw some of the old rules out the window. I mean, not just aboard this ship. Us being military on Paradise," he touched the American flag patch on his uniform top, "it's kinda crazy, you know? What does it mean for us to be US Army, when we're cut off from the US of A, maybe forever?"

"I don't know," Jesse admitted. "I've been thinking the same thing. Like, if we weren't doing something important up here, I might have turned in my stripes by now, you know?"

"Really?" That surprised Dave. Jesse had intended to make the military a career from the day he signed up. Bishop had been open about wanting to get out of the Army and use the money for college, although at the time of Columbus Day, he still had no idea what he wanted to do with his life. And Dave? Dave wasn't sure whether he wanted to stay in or not. His time in Nigeria, where one random group after another shot at him or planted improvised bombs, and the politicians back home could not define what the mission was supposed to be or even when or if the mission would end, had for a time soured Dave on the Army. Then came Columbus Day, and it had no longer mattered what Dave's plans were.

"Yeah, man," Jesse's eyes darted over to where Shauna was unpacking her gear in the cabin they would share. "Big things are happening on Paradise, even for us humans. People are getting out and setting up farms, setting up businesses, starting a new life, you know? We're up here showing the flag and making sure the hamsters don't forget all we did for them, but I'm getting worried that by the time we are old news and UNEF dissolves, other people will have grabbed all the good opportunities. We got to think about the future, Ski, and I don't just mean tomorrow."

"Has Shauna talked to you about the future?"

"Hell, no, man," Jesse whispered harshly. "I haven't said a word about it, I don't want to scare her away." With human women vastly outnumbered by men on Paradise, traditional gender courtship had been flipped on its head, with women being reluctant to get rushed into a commitment, and men eager to hold onto relationships. On Paradise, it was only foolish men who said those three little words 'I Love You' first, to avoid sounding clingy and scaring away a woman. "Shauna always wanted to be infantry and now she's got it," he shook his head. "She's not going to be tempted by the idea of us putting down roots on a farmstead in the middle of nowhere, not when she's got shiny Ruhar toys to play with."

"Good luck to you, 'Pone," Dave held out a fist and Jesse bumped it.

"Hey, don't worry, man. You'll find a girl soon. You're famous!"

"Fame don't mean much these days," Dave frowned. "And we're stuck on this bucket for months, I am sure as hell not finding a girl out here."

Emily Perkins lay down to sleep on the bottom bunk, wearing pants and a T-shirt. At first, she had kept her bra on, but ten minutes of discomfort made her decide to quietly wriggle around under the sheet and extract the bra out through one arm of her shirt, a maneuver she knew always amazed men. Another adjustment was needed; with pants on, her feet were too hot, so she kicked her feet out from under the sheet. At last, she was physically comfortable enough to fall asleep, and she certainly was tired enough from the long and eventful day, but her mind was racing despite her effort to concentrate only on breathing slowly. After a frustrating ten minutes of thoughts bouncing around in her head like the ball in an old pinball machine, she felt herself drifting off.

Thus, she was extremely annoyed when a squeaking noise from outside the cabin intruded on her attempt to sleep. She tried flopping the pillow over her head to block out the sound, but it was no good.

Finally, Perkins couldn't take it any longer. The cabin's control pad was high on the wall, near the top bunk. "Czajka, you awake?"

"Uh, what?" Dave pretended to be far more groggy than he was. His plan had been to lay awake, breathing deeply and evenly to pretend he was asleep, until he was sure Perkins had dropped off into dreamland. Only then could he hope that if he did snore, he didn't keep his commanding officer awake.

"Can you hit the door controls, close the damned thing?"

"Is that squeaking sound keeping you awake too? I can see if there's something caught in an air vent," he suggested.

"Czajka," she sighed and it turned into a yawn. "That sound isn't coming from the *ship*."

"Oh," Dave rose up on one elbow. "*Oh*." He could feel his face growing beet red in the darkness. And, of course, right as he fumbled for the door controls in the unfamiliar alien cabin, the squeaking sounds grew closer together and louder until even the sleepiest of minds could not mistake the source of the sound. Mercifully, he found the button and the door slid closed. "Sorry about that, Ma'am."

"Why is it *your* fault?"

"Ma'am, in Nigeria, we got into some tough spots, Jesse and I saved each other's lives more than once. Bishop, too. If I hadn't saved Cornpone back then," he let his voice trail off in a soft chuckle.

"I appreciate the thought, Czajka, but what makes you think that noise has to be from Colter and Jarrett?"

"Oh, uh. Sorry, Ma'am." He had not considered that Captains Striebich and Bonsu might be celebrating their first night aboard the ship.

"Stop saying you're sorry, Czajka. Let's catch some shut-eye, we have a busy day tomorrow."

"Yes, Ma'am. Should I, uh," he looked at the now-closed cabin door, faintly illuminated by the light of the communications panel. "Should I go crash on the couch?"

"Thanks for the offer, but that's against regs."

"The ship's not underway," Dave stated, unsure of himself. "We're still attached to the resupply platform."

"The Paradise system is still a Threat Grade Three combat zone. Regs state anyone intending to be on a sleep cycle must be in a certified acceleration couch, in case the ship needs to move quickly. You're anxious to get out of here? Why, do I snore?"

"No, Ma'am. It's just," he didn't bother to finish.

"This is awkward for me, too, Czajka. We'll be bunking together for months, might as well get used to it now."

"I suppose." He almost added an 'I'm sorry' but overrode his mouth before he could say anything. "Good night."

"Good night, soldier."

No sooner had Dave let himself settle down into the bed, when a different sound caught his ear. Not a sound, exactly, more like a vibration coming through the wall. A rhythmic thumping, slowly getting louder and faster.

"Oh for Christ's sake!" Perkins exploded in frustration, then laughed.

"*That's* not Jesse," Dave found himself laughing along with the colonel. If the thumping was coming through the wall, then it had to be from the adjacent cabin shared by Irene and Derek.

"All I can say is, those two had *damned* well better be rested in the morning," Perkins complained with disgust, then she couldn't help laughing, and she and Dave began laughing uncontrollably together. The thumping reached a crescendo and after five or six hard banging sounds, stopped.

"Thank *God* for that," Perkins gasped when she was able to stop laughing enough to catch her breath.

"If they go for Round Two, I'm knocking on their door," Dave said half-seriously.

"Let's hope they don't," she agreed, and it struck her then there was a major disadvantage to having the ship's crew quarters being reconfigurable. Instead of sturdy, fixed bulkheads, the moveable partitions were thin and flimsy. Somehow, in the morning, she needed to discreetly let the two other women know just how sound transmitted through the cabin walls. Unless they already knew. How could they not, she asked herself, as she answered her own question. Because, each of the couples were busy and not listening to any sounds around them. "Again, good night, Czajka."

Dave felt certain there was no way he would get any sleep that night. He was in a cabin, less than two meters away from a woman, a woman in a bed. Perkins was a Lieutenant Colonel and his commanding officer and, like him, she was wearing long pants and a T-shirt, but he could not stop himself from imagining what she was like under those unflattering Army-issue clothes. Blood was pounding in his ears from the excitement of having heard one and possibly two couples in amorous celebrations. He tried to think of anything else to keep his mind and other body parts from focusing on the woman sleeping or not sleeping almost close enough to touch, and found his thoughts wandering back to Earth, to his grandparents' summer cottage on a lake in the countryside west of Milwaukee. He found his mind drifting back to lazy summer days at the lake, swimming and canoeing and fishing and cookouts and riding his bicycle over to visit friends. Blessedly, he began to lose focus, and as the exhausting day caught up with him, he soon fell asleep.

Perkins had set an alarm on her zPhone so she could get up earlier than Czajka, and minimize the awkwardness of waking up close to each other. Czajka must have set an alarm even earlier than hers, because she was awakened by the sound of the cabin door sliding open. "You're up?"

"Yes, Ma-" he put a hand over his mouth to stifle a shuddering yawn. "Ma'am. Hitting the shower, I'll be back soon."

She could barely see him in the light of the status panel. For a reason she could not explain, and couldn't attribute only to the fog of her just-awakened brain, she asked "How did you sleep?" Immediately, she cringed at the question that seemed much too intimate.

"Um, good. I think my mattress is set too soft, I'll, uh, change it tonight," Dave did not know why he was dragging out the conversation when all he wanted was to get out of the cramped cabin as fast as he could. "Be back soon," his words made him cringe, so he sped across the common area to the washroom and shut the door behind him, then slapped his forehead in dismay. He had not brought any clean clothes with him, so after a quick shower, he would be putting yesterday's clothes back on. Fortunately, uniform pants and shirts all looked the same, so he could change in the cabin later, while Perkins took her turn in the washroom.

"Did I wake you last night?" Perkins asked Irene and Shauna quietly.

"No, Ma'am, why?" Irene asked innocently while lacing her boots in the common area.

"I got up in the middle of the night, tripped on my boots and fell against the wall. These walls," she rapped her knuckles on a partition, "are *thin*, and they transmit sound."

"Oh, ah, no," Irene stared intently at her boots, unable to look Perkins in the eye, and with the corner of one eye she saw Shauna was also suddenly focused on her own footwear. "I didn't hear anything."

"No harm done, then," Perkins tried to inject levity into her tone. "I'll tuck my boots under the bunk tonight," she announced, satisfied the two women had gotten her message.

Breakfast for the humans had been a quick meal of granola bars made in Lemuria, and a sort of herbal tea, with the herbs also grown in Lemuria. "Better than most MREs I've choked down over the years," Dave mumbled quietly over a mouthful of granola that was so tough to chew, that he had to wash it down with the tea. The human diet on Paradise was still limited and too-often bland, as UNEF had not brought plants to grow many commonly-used spices. One thing they did have was peppers and Jesse enjoyed a fiery chili sauce, but he got tired of it after a while. The Ruhar had been experimenting to see whether some of their spices could safely be ingested by humans, even though Ruhar food did not provide any nutrition, their spices might serve to make the bland human diet more palatable.

"I hope you still feel that way when we've been eating this *every* freakin' morning," Jesse whispered.

CHAPTER NINE

"Pone! Cornpone! Hey, Jesse!" Dave called out louder and louder to catch his comrade's attention.

"Kinda busy here," Jesse snapped back, concentrating on the view in his visor. He was running back images and data of the last zero-Gee combat assault exercise, in which a pair of Ruhar cadets soundly spanked Jesse, Dave, Shauna and Perkins. Worse than the shame of losing badly was the taunting from the hamster cadets, and Jesse was determined to figure out where the humans had gone wrong, so the next exercise wasn't so one-sided. He had already watched the actual exercise, with the ship's training AI pointing out all the mistakes made by the four humans. Now he was intently watching a re-run of the exercise as the AI suggested it *should* have been conducted. "Talk to you-"

"*Now*, 'Pone," Dave declared as he tore the visor upward, cutting off the exercise. "Game time is over, the battlegroup got a call for real action."

"No shit?" Jesse asked excitedly, any annoyance he felt forgotten. "We're gonna see action?"

When Jesse got back to the Mavericks' shared quarters, he was disappointed to see Dave and Shauna sitting in front of the bulkhead display. "We're gonna watch from here? I want to see for real, not on some display," Jesse tapped the display with disgust. "Ski? You with me?"

Before Dave could answer, Shauna put hands on her hips. "Is this like on Paradise, when the two of you froze your asses off on the ice to watch that maser cannon test fire?"

"She may be right, 'Pone," Dave said with an uncertain look on his face.

"Come on," Jesse was not going to be dissuaded. "You telling me you both don't want to see a whole group of starships maneuvering away and jumping into action? There must be some place on this tub we can watch through a viewport? What about that porthole dome thing where the flight control crew monitors dropship retrievals? There won't be any flight operations now, right?"

"We shouldn't go anywhere without clearing it with Colonel Perkins first," Shauna objected.

Jesse noted she had said 'we' rather than 'you' to the idea of watching the fleet jumping away. "Ok, Ok, I'll contact her," he pulled a zPhone off his belt.

"We've seen ships come onto and off star carrier docking platforms plenty of times before," Dave noted. They had observed that activity while outside their ship in zero-Gee combat training during the five weeks they had been aboard the ship. "And jumps, too," he remembered, recalling when their training had been halted temporarily so they could turn away from a starship jumping away behind them. Ordinarily, ships would not jump anywhere near a person free-floating outside a ship, but as combat ops might include that happening, their training had to include what spaceborne troops should do if they were outside in a spacesuit, and a nearby ship needed to jump. Nearby was a relative term, because the gamma radiation from a jump could kill anyone in a spacesuit within three thousand kilometers, even with the suit's radiation shielding fully engaged. Dave remembered being frightened when he felt a tingling sensation after his suit's sensors picked up the gamma ray burst of an outbound jump, and he had almost panicked in fear the Ruhar-made suit had failed to account for the differences of human physiology. Within seconds, he realized the tingling was only the suit's anti-radiation shield powering down after the gamma rays passed by, but he did have a moment of gut-wrenching fear. He didn't want to feel that fear again. "Oh, hey, Jesse," Dave held up a finger before Jesse could press the Send button on his zPhone. "Maybe those viewports aren't protected against gamma rays, you know?"

"I'll ask about it," Jesse assured his friend as he sent the message then checked the reply. "Huh. Damn it. Colonel said, no, she doesn't want us wandering around the ship."

"That's fair," Shauna patted Jesse's shoulder. "Dave's right, we don't know if it's safe to watch a jump through those viewports."

"We could have asked," Jesse stuck out his lip in an exaggerated pout.

"Oh, my poor man," Shauna played along.

"Damn, are you trying for sympathy sex, Jesse?" Dave asked with disgust.

"Depends," Jesse flashed a grin at Shauna. "Would that work?"

"We'll see," she bit his earlobe, then pushed him away as he tried to grab her ass. "You want to see this action, remember?"

"Oh, yeah," all Jesse could think of right then was Shauna. Whatever he was going to say next was drowned out by the blaring of an alarm, and an automated announcement familiar enough that none of the three humans needed their zPhone translators. Prepare for maneuvering, the announcement stated. "Hot damn!" Jesse punched a fist above his head. "Are *we* going into action?"

The answer, to Jesse's great disappointment, was a resounding NO. While they waited, the team's two pilots came into the shared quarters, having been chased away from flight training while the ship prepared to maneuver for real. The *Ruh Tostella* did power up and detach from the star carrier's docking platform, and did fire its normal-space engines to get clear of the star carrier before that vessel jumped away to drop off the second part of the Ruhar Task force. But the *Toaster* simply hung dead in space, while the giant Jeraptha ship created a powerful jump field and disappeared in a flash of gamma rays, taking the other Ruhar warships with it. "That's it, then?" Jesse clenched his fists. "We're just gonna wait here while the rest of the task force goes into action?"

"Colter," Irene admonished the soldier gently. "This is a training ship, mostly run by cadets. You didn't think they'd take this bucket into a real engagement, did you?"

"We're carrying real weapons," Jesse retorted before adding a "Ma'am." While it was true that most of the ordnance carried in the ship's magazines were training equipment that was oddly painted almost the same shade of blue the US military used to designate inert practice weapons, Jesse had seen genuine warshots on a tour of the ship's portside aft missile magazine. He also knew the ship's maser cannons and railgun batteries were capable of inflicting real punishment to an enemy. If needed, the *Ruh Tostella* could be transformed from training ship to light cruiser in a couple days of hard work. "Do you know what's going on?"

Irene blew hair out of her eyes, then retied her flyaway ponytail. "Two hamster ships practicing a stealth recon mission found something odd, debris from a Ruhar civilian ship at a remote rendezvous site. If the commodore or the beetles thought it was really serious, they would have reported it in before sending ships to investigate. My guess is the civilian ship suffered an engineering failure, and the commodore thinks this is a perfect opportunity for realistic training. The *Toaster* isn't going with the task force, in case there is any real danger."

"Out here?" Shauna fiddled with the controls, expanding the view on the display. "This area was chosen for training because it is quiet."

"It's quiet *now*," Irene stood and traced a fingernail along a line on the display. "Until recently, this line was the border of Thuranin-controlled space. If those little green MFers have second thoughts about ceding this territory to the Jeraptha, this sector could get hot real quick," she bit her fingernail in a girlish gesture that got Derek's full attention. "But I doubt it. If the task force thought the *Toaster* could be in a hazardous situation, we would be at action stations, and we're not."

Shauna automatically looked up at the Threat Condition indicator above the door. It showed yellow because the ship was maneuvering, but no external threat was anticipated. "How long until we know?"

Irene looked to Derek, who answered. "The ships on recon duty took three jumps to get back here, so they'll take that many to return to the site they want to investigate. Then the commodore might want to use the opportunity for fleet maneuvers. A couple days, at least. Our training will be restricted in case the *Toaster* needs to move in a hurry, so no space combat exercises outside the ship," he looked at Jesse, "and no flying around in dropships for us pilots. I'm sure the crew will think of something to keep the cadets busy and morale up."

Irene was unfortunately correct, all the fun training was on hold while the *Ruh Tostella* waited for the task force to return. For the two pilots, there was no zooming around in dropships, so they used their time in a simulator, training to fly starships. Perkins mostly used the time in the ship's Central Control Center, a combination bridge and CIC, learning as much as she could about space warfare tactics, command and control, and anything else she could absorb. Shauna, Dave and Jesse were bitterly disappointed, because they had been scheduled to perform a live spacedive from orbit to the surface of a planet, and now that phase of the training might be cancelled because the task force had a tight schedule and the cadets needed to return to school. They had been intensively training for three weeks to qualify for a real spacedive, and now they might never get the opportunity. All three of them had been looking forward to the spacedive, because several of the hamster cadets had already done it, and the three humans were eager to show they could do anything a hamster brat could do. And because no one could be considered to be Spaceborne Army without having made a real dive from orbit to the surface of a planet. And because they all wanted something to brag about when they returned to Paradise. And because, dammit, a spacedive from orbit just sounded like a whole lot of *fun*.

Nert was also glum about having the fun parts of training put on hold, but he was excited to finally have the humans join him for lunch in the galley closest to their assigned quarters. The Ruhar cadet had been inviting them to lunch since their first day aboard the ship, but their different training schedules had never allowed them the time. Dave and Jesse slapped together sandwiches and walked forward, warily looking through the door. Nert had suggested they arrive late, when lunch was winding down and fewer Ruhar would be jamming the tables there. He knew the humans felt awkward about being aboard an alien ship, and his fellow cadets would openly gawk at the humans as curious objects. Nert wanted the two Mavericks to wear their medals, reminding the cadets of how this group of primitive aliens had saved thousands of lives on Paradise, *twice*, but Dave explained the cadets might resent the humans for showing off, so the medals stayed tucked away in their cabins. "Hello, Misters Cornpone and Ski," Nert beamed with delight as he saw his two friends standing in the doorway. He was thrilled to use nicknames for the team, although Jesse had cautioned him that while it was acceptable to call the three sergeants by the first names or nicknames, the three commissioned officers should be referred to be their ranks or last names. That had confused Nert, as the Ruhar military did not have a distinction between types of officers. There were no sergeants, warrant officers or petty officers in the Ruhar military. When Dave had tried to explain why sergeants were '*non*-commissioned' officers, Nert had asked why an experienced Staff Sergeant should have to take orders from a Second Lieutenant who had zero experience. Dave had ruefully replied that he had the same question, but that's the way it was.

"Hey, Nerty," Dave used the nickname they used for their liaison officer. "Looks like the place is still plenty busy," he looked around to see most tables were lined with cadets sitting elbow to elbow. "Should we come back later?"

"No, please, come in," Nert gestured eagerly, his expression anxious and eager. "I have a table for us," he pointed to a corner where one lunch tray sat by itself.

"Ok," Jesse shrugged and walked in, nodding to acknowledge the staring hamster cadets. The three sat down and the humans took out their peanut butter sandwiches, chosen because they didn't want to eat anything that might smell offensive to the Ruhar.

"I am sorry," Nert shook his head and looked down at his food. "The Slusho machine is broken," he pointed to another corner of the galley where a stainless-steel machine had a piece of yellow tape across it.

"Oh, Ok?" Dave was confused. "What is that?"

"Slusho is a drink you humans may consume without harm, I checked," his chin bobbed up and down with frantic seriousness. "It would not provide any nutrition to you, but," he grinned, "my mother tells me Slusho has no nutritional value to *anyone*."

"I like it already," Jesse grinned back. "What's that you're drinking?"

"Oh, no," Nert paused from gulping down a greenish-yellow fluid that fizzed like a soda. "This is Slurm, my favorite. My mother says I am addicted to it, but it is just delicious. I-" he covered his mouth with embarrassment as he shook with a loud burp that drew attention from Ruhar at nearby tables. "I am sorry," the cadet looked stricken.

"Hey, Nerty, don't worry about it. I get the same reaction from a Coke, and man I wish I could have a Coke right now," Jesse closed his eyes, imagining an ice-cold soft drink rather than the ship's recycled water they were stuck with. "That's a, uh, we call it a soda, it's fizzy like that Slurm stuff you're drinking."

"I think you humans can drink Slurm also, here, try it," he held the cup out toward Jesse.

"Ah, thanks, Nerty, but we should wait for an Ok from the Colonel."

Nert sipped his drink more slowly and asked about their orientation tour that morning, while they ate. The galley was clearing out, as cadets had to report to their next training session. Another shift of cadets came into the galley, getting food and staring intently at the three sitting by themselves. Dave noticed none of the incoming cadets joined their table, instead squeezing in where they could at other tables. "They don't want to sit with us strange aliens, huh?" Dave whispered.

"Oh," Nert was crestfallen. "Do not be insulted, Mister Ski. I am not," he frowned and looked at the table. "I usually eat by myself. I am not, popular in this crew, I mean, with the cadets in my school."

"They're just jealous that you're famous, you saved two giant transport ships from being blown up by Kristang commandos," Dave patted the cadet on the back.

"No, I was not popular before that either," Nert sounded miserable. "I have never been good at making friends, and it is worse now."

"You are great at making friends with us. Is that Bifft asshole making trouble for you?" Jesse looked around the galley but did not see that particular cadet. Jesse had been around Ruhar long enough that they no longer all looked the same to him.

"He is not helping," Nert admitted. "Bifft is very popular, he has a group of friends who are," he looked up while trying to think of the correct word in English. "They are much admired at the academy."

Dave and Jesse looked at each other. They knew at Nert's age, being popular was the *most* important thing in the entire universe. They needed to think of a way to make Nert cool to his fellow cadets. "Hey, Nertster," Dave winked while the young alien unhappily sipped Slurm through a straw. Dave held out a fist and Nert bumped it with a questioning look. "Don't you worry. I got an idea."

The next night, the Mavericks were seated at the back of a large briefing room that was being used for a sort of talent show that evening, as part of the adult crew's effort to keep the cadets busy and entertained while the battlegroup was away. Perkins had requested for her team to be seated at the back because that way, her people were not on display unless the Ruhar turned around and stared openly. When a few cadets did that, a reprimanding look from officers straightened them out quickly.

The talent was mostly musical, with Perkins finding that she actually enjoyed much of the alien selections. The Ruhar had stringed instruments like guitars and violins, horns sort of like trumpets, and a keyboard. She did not see anything like the clarinet she had once tried to play when she was young, and she was grateful not to be reminded of too many hours sitting inside practicing when she would rather have been outside.

A three-person band just finished performing a pop tune that sounded a bit like an old Beatles song, and Perkins was surprised to see Nert stand and walk onto the stage by himself, a goofy grin on his face. The crowd murmured when they saw Nert step up the microphone, and that instead of having a musical instrument in his hands, he carried a large cup of some fizzy liquid. "*What* is he doing?" Perkins whispered to Irene, who shrugged because she had no idea.

"Don't you worry, Colonel," Dave whispered back with a wink as Nert began quickly chugging his drink.

"What the hell did you do?" Shauna hissed at Jesse, loudly enough that several Ruhar in front of them turned around to see what the commotion was about.

Jesse squeezed Shauna's hand. "Watch. It's gonna be epic."

"If you embarrass Nerty," Shauna squeezed back hard, and she was not being friendly.

"This is a human song," Nert explained to the audience. He tipped back the cup to finish drinking. Then he burped the song loudly into the microphone. "*Bur- happy birthday, happy birthday, happy birthday to you uuurp,*" he finished with a sheepish grin, unsure of himself.

For a split second, there was complete silence in the room. Then, because of Nert's goofy grin and because the cadets were, after all, teenagers, the hall exploded with uncontrollable laughter. Some cadets laughed so hard they fell out of their chairs, and that prompted another round of laughing. Nert made a short bow, having been coached not to overreach, and stepped down from the stage, making his way back to his chair. He was greeted by backslaps and many raised pinky fingers in a gesture that was the Ruhar equivalent of a thumbs up.

Before he sat down triumphantly, he pointed to Jesse and Dave then mimed a high five, the two men returned the gesture. In a move they had planned, the two humans held their hands out and bowed repeatedly toward the beaming cadet as if worshipping an idol. That gesture was picked up by a group of five other cadets and the wildly-grinning Nert bowed back, accepting the adulation.

"*That* was your idea?" Perkins asked with tears of laughter rolling down her cheeks. "Why didn't you tell me?"

"Because you might have said no," Dave explained. "If you did say no, you would have been wrong, Ma'am."

"I can see that," Perkins agreed as she watched the seated Nert continue to accept backslaps and admiring gestures from the audience, including a couple very amused officers.

"You did that, for Nerty?" Shauna whispered into Jesse's ear, now squeezing his hand with distinct affection.

Jesse nodded. "It was Dave's idea, we coached him. He needed a way to show he can be cool, you know? The poor little guy was sitting all alone in the galley."

Shauna pulled away from Jesse's ear to look closely into his eyes. "That was a *wonderful* thing to do. Jesse Colter, I may be falling for you."

Don't say it don't say it don't say it, Jesse warned himself. Do *not* blow it by saying those three words right now. Instead of fatefully risking a premature reply of 'I love you', Jesse listened to his inner voice of reason and merely nodded while gently squeezing her hand. At that moment, he could not remember ever being so happy.

The laughter settled down to sporadic chuckles as the next act set up their instruments on the stage. Perkins's gaze swept the room, taking in cadets still pointing to Nert and chuckling with approval, until she saw Bifft and his crew. That senior cadet was glaring pure hatred at Nert, talking to his crew in a low voice, and he smacked a fist into a palm.

This could be trouble, Perkins thought to herself. Since her people had just given Bifft another reason to hate Nert, she felt responsible. "Dave," she began to whisper, then coughed at the realization she had used the sergeant's first name because that seemed so natural. "Sergeant Czajka, I need you to keep an eye on that senior cadet," she said with a meaningful glance toward Bifft. "He might be trouble for Nert."

Perkins' instincts were right, after the talent show Bifft and his friends confronted Nert in the passageway, and were not deterred by Jesse and Dave standing next to their alien friend. Bifft's jaw was set and he squeezed a fist in anger while he jabbed a finger at the two humans. "It is an insult that I am stuck aboard a vessel of war, with you primitive humans and treacherous Kristang. Our leaders indulge their pets too much."

"Ah," Jesse waved a hand in a dismissive gesture. "Don't you worry about it, Biffty. We know you being here is an insult, but we don't let it bother us none."

"Wha-what?" The senior cadet sputtered. "It is not an insult to *you*. It is an insult to *my* people."

"Hey, man, whatever turns you on," Dave shrugged.

"Turns, me, on?" Bifft repeated slowly as he ran back the translation, confused. Then, thinking he understood, the pink skin of his face grew red under the light fuzz of fur. "I do not get sexually excited!"

"Not *ever*?" Nert spoke up before Dave or Jesse could reply. "Well, with a face like that, it's best not to get your hopes up."

Dave did not know which reaction was more extreme; the uproar of laughter at Bifft's expense, or the murderous look of hatred that the embarrassed senior cadet shot toward Nert. Even the three cadets in Bifft's crew could not help laughing at their leader's plight, and Bifft ground his incisors before spinning and attempting to stomp dramatically away, squeezing through the laughing crowd in the passageway. Except the toe of one boot tripped on something, sending Bifft crashing into the door frame. His dignity completely gone, Bifft ran around a corner. His three companions recovered as best they could, their shoulders still shaking with laughter, and hurried out the door.

"Nerty, man, *day-um*!" Dave held a hand. "That was *classic*!"

Nert slapped Dave's hand, and offered a high-five to Jesse. "Thank you," Nert said simply, having been coached not to ruin the moment by grandstanding.

"What is this?" Another cadet asked, holding up a hand hesitantly.

"This?" Nert slapped the cadet's outstretched hand, more gently than he had done with the two humans. "This is a human gesture of joy and approval. They call it a 'high five'," he explained, and counted off his five fingers. With a grin he added "If Kristang did this, they would call it a 'high *four*'?"

"Ha!" Jesse grinned back. "You are on *fire* today, Nerty!"

For a second, Nert froze, not understanding the term, then he smiled as his translator earpiece explained it to him.

Dave noticed the Ruhar cadets were tentatively giving high-fives to each other, hesitantly tapping palms. "Jesse, let's show them how it's done, huh? Hey, uh, cadets, let's say your friend," he pointed to Jesse, "just scored a point to win a game. You give him this. Up high," the men slapped over their heads, "down low," a slap at waist level, "behind the back," they spun to complete the gesture. "And finish with this," they jumped high and slapped hard enough that Dave's hand stung from the impact.

"Oooooh," Nert's eyes were wide with admiration. "Could you show us that again?"

Jesse and Dave obliged the cadets, then watched as the eager Ruhar tried to follow, including Nert. When several Ruhar crashed into chairs while attempting a too-enthusiastic jump, Dave called a halt. "Whoa, whoa, Ok, that's good. Save it for when you have something real to celebrate, huh?"

"Yes, Ser-geant Czaj-ka," Nert said slowly, beaming at Dave in hero worship. "Could you explain this, please?" He held a fist up close to his chest, and slowly pushed it toward the human.

"Oh, man, you got it right," Dave bumped the fist. "Gently, huh? Don't want to go so hard you hurt yourself, right? We call that a fist bump. It is like a quick high-five, I guess."

Half an hour later, the two men walked into the common area of their living quarters to find Perkins studying something on her laptop. "You two look happy about something," she observed.

"Yes we are," Dave replied and bumped fists with Jesse. "Ma'am, the only thing on this ship cooler than Nert right now are humans. *Us*." He shook his head in wonderment.

CHAPTER TEN

Dave was startled awake from an all-too-brief nap by Jesse shaking his shoulder excitedly. "Part of the battlegroup is back! A destroyer just jumped in to recon the Assembly Zone, it'll jump back out soon to give the All-Clear, then the task force will be here," he announced with a gleeful shout. "Come on, man, you don't want to miss this. I was watching it on the display in the briefing room, and one of the hamster kids there said he noticed battle damage to that destroyer."

"I'm on it," Dave rubbed sleep from his eyes, now fully awake, swinging his feet down onto the deck. He knew there wasn't anything he could see on the display in the briefing room that he couldn't view on his zPhone or the display built into the bulkhead of their tiny bunk room, but being with people made everything seem so much more real.

When he got to the briefing room, Jesse was disappointed to see the big display on the opposite bulkhead was showing only their ship and a blinking ring off to the side. He couldn't tell how far they were from whatever the blinking ring was, because the display didn't include any sort of distance scale. Captain Striebich was seated in front and Captain Bonsu was strapping in beside her.

"What happened, Ma'am?" Dave asked, also disappointed. "Where'd that destroyer go?"

"Where are the hamsters?" Jesse asked with a glance back over his shoulder through the open door.

"The destroyer jumped away, you *just* missed it," Irene answered. "That ring," she pointed to the display, "represents the spatial distortion effect of their outbound jump. You can't see it, that's a projection by the display. The, uh," she also checked the doorway, "hamsters kids bugged out of here when too many humans came in here." She emphasized her words with a single-finger gesture that was not befitting an officer. "Damn," she winked, "I hate it when it does that," she remarked while shaking her hand.

"That was quick," Dave shrugged toward Jesse, "the destroyer just got here."

"The destroyer was just performing a recon jump to assure the task force that the AZ is clear. They had to wait for their sensors to reset after coming through the jump, and they had to wait for distortion of the inbound jump to stop vibrating spacetime so they could form an outbound jump wormhole," she explained. "They were able to jump back early because the *Toaster*," she gestured to the deck to indicate she was referring to the ship, "gave them the All-Clear. Usual procedure would require the destroyer to sweep a bubble five lightminutes in every direction before they Ok'ed the task force to jump into the AZ."

"When will the task force be jumping here?" Perkins asked as she strode into the briefing room, coming forward to take one of the seats in the front row and slipping a safety strap loosely around her waist.

"ASAP if they follow standard procedure, Ma'am," Derek responded. "Every second they wait, the gamma rays of that destroyer's inbound and outbound jumps are expanding outward, and illuminating the AZ to enemy ships like shining a strobe light. The task force needs to get here, reset their sensors and shields and maneuver into a defensive formation before an enemy can pinpoint the AZ and react. The hardest thing to remember about the rules of space combat is that ships can travel much faster than sensor data. If a ship sends out detectible energy, like an active sensor pulse or gamma rays, the enemy can pick up that energy and jump right on top of you before your sensor pulse returns to you."

Perkins nodded silently because she had been learning space combat tactics in her own training. "I told the Ruhar that I would be slow to learn about space combat because I'm not a pilot, and my instructor told me that is not a problem. Their opinion is the humans best able to transition to space combat would be our submarine commanders."

"Subs?" Jesse asked. "Like, underwater, Ma'am?"

"I can see that," Dave mused with a hand rubbing his chin in deep thought.

"Huh?" Jesse looked at his friend in puzzlement.

"Think about it, 'Pone. Sub drivers have to rely on stealth, they can't go pinging the ocean with sonar, or they give away their position."

"Correct," Perkins nodded happily. "A submarine crew is also used to relying on passive sensor data of an enemy they won't ever see. And they spend months at sea in a metal tube without ever seeing the sun."

"I've seen plenty of suns on this cruise," Jesse shook his head. "But it's different looking at a star through a helmet visor when your feet aren't on solid ground. Or any ground at all. We-"

He was interrupted by Irene's excited shout. "Two ships just jumped in. Correction; *one* ship just jumped in. The other jumped in almost a minute ago, but it's fifty seven lightseconds away so we're just seeing it now. Hmmm, uh oh," Irene fiddled with the controls built into the arm of her chair, zooming in the image to show the closest warship, a destroyer. "*That* doesn't look good."

The ship had a long gouge out of its belly, with the scar wrapping around to the starboard side. Sparks flared from the damaged area, and the destroyer's nose was flattened and smashed in. It was more difficult to detect if the second ship was damaged, because it was farther away and the bulkhead display only had access to low-level sensors. "Ma'am?" Irene turned to Perkins. "You have access to command systems?"

"*Limited* access," Perkins grimaced. The access that had been granted to her was only for training purposes, she didn't know if it would provide any real-time tactical data. To her surprise, she was able to pull up a status summary on her tablet, though the system wouldn't let her feed the info to the bulkhead display so her team could view it. "You're right, Striebich, this is not good. The Ruhar got into a battle against the Wurgalan. Our friends thought they had the upper hand, then the Bosphuraq stepped in and the Ruhar had to bug out."

"Bosphuraq?" Derek expressed alarm. "I thought there was an unwritten rule that species only fight at an equivalent level of technology."

"It's more of a custom," Perkins replied with an angry look on her face. "Usually the Bosphuraq send the Wurgalan to fight the Ruhar or Torgalau, while the Bosphuraq reserve their own forces to tangle with the Jeraptha. Beating up on lower-tech species risks intervention by the higher-ups. Apparently this time, the Bosphuraq decided that stepping into this battle was worth the risk of the Rindhalu slapping them down. The Ruhar lost a cruiser," she reported with shock, having just seen that tactical update.

"A cruiser?" Dave asked, dismayed. The task force only had two cruisers, other than the old training ship. "Does it say what happened to the other task force?"

Perkins shook her head, causing a lock of hair to swing down in front of her eyes. Dave's gaze followed the hair, mesmerized. "The star carrier was supposed to pick them up first; we won't know their status until they jump in here. People, the *Toaster* could be maneuvering soon, I expect us to be put on Grade-2 alert soon. Let's get our gear and come back here in-" She was interrupted by a blaring alarm, announcing the ship was at Alert Condition Two. "Like I said."

They returned in less than four minutes, with everyone dressed in pressure suits and carrying a bag containing gloves, helmets and extra life support packs. In battle, the humans did not have assigned action stations, because the Ruhar did not want lowly aliens getting in the way. Perkins checked with the duty officer to see if she should report to the bridge and was told, politely but firmly, that she could best help the ship's operations by keeping away of Ruhar engaged in their jobs. Emily Perkins found that mildly insulting, as on the way back to the briefing room she saw young Ruhar cadets racing toward their duty stations. Even Nert was assigned to a damage control party amidships, she pinged him to ask if he was Ok and he replied only with a terse 'yes' before cutting the connection. When Perkins got back to the briefing room, her entire team was there. Shauna was wearing a full spacesuit, having been in training when the alert sounded. "Ma'am," Shauna looked up from helping Jesse attach his helmet. "Any news?"

"Not much. The Ruhar were hit by a group of Wurgalan ships and the battle was going well enough, then a Bosphuraq cruiser jumped into the action. Our allies think the Bosphuraq stepped in to help the octopussies-"

"Excuse me, Ma'am, octopussies?" Jesse looked to his companions who were equally confused.

"I've never met one, of course," Perkins explained. "Like the Thuranin, our info about other species comes mostly from the Ruhar. We know the Thuranin look like little green men, right?" Her team nodded so she continued. "Apparently the Wurgalan are a sort of land octopus, so at HQ we call them 'octopussies'. The Bosphuraq are worried about the weakness of the Wurgalan so they are assisting them directly. The Bosphuraq think the Thuranin did too little, too late to help the Kristang, and now the Thuranin themselves got beat badly and the Kristang are useless to assist. The Bosphuraq are determined not to let Wurgalan weakness harm their ability to control territory." Perkins lowered her voice and glanced toward the door to assure no Ruhar were listening. "From the report," she tapped her tablet, "I get the feeling the Ruhar are very concerned about this development. If the patron species are going to step in directly against the hamsters, then our allies need to reconsider their ability to hold territory they recently took from the lizards."

"Hell, Ma'am," Jesse looked stricken. "Does that include Paradise?"

"I don't," Perkins hesitated because that thought had not crossed her mind. "I don't think so, at least not now. The concern is about territory the lizards held, until the Thuranin got their asses whipped by the Jeraptha in the past couple years. The Ruhar thought they could just kick the tires and decide which planets they want to keep, now it looks like the Jeraptha may hold them back, until the beetles understand just how serious the Bosphuraq are about defending their coalition's territory."

"Colonel," Dave asked hopefully, "does this apply only to territory near space controlled by the Bosphuraq?"

"No," Perkins shook her head. "The task force was far from Bosphuraq space when they got jumped. This is something new; the Jeraptha may now be fighting the Bosphuraq about who controls territory the Thuranin lost."

"Because the Bosphuraq will give it back to the Thuranin once they rebuild their strength?" Shauna asked, though she thought she already knew the answer to that question.

"No," Perkins snorted. "The Bosphuraq and Thuranin hate each other more than they hate the Jeraptha. This development is likely the result of the Bosphuraq taking advantage of Thuranin weakness to cherry-pick star systems they want for themselves. My guess is the Jeraptha will need to test the Bosphuraq to see where they will push back. This has got to be," she let out a long breath and swept her hair back before pulling her helmet over her head, "frustrating to the Jeraptha."

"Frustrating? They probably *love* this," Dave interjected. "Not knowing what territory the Bosphuraq might fight to hold, is going to provide super juicy wagering action for the Jeraptha. The Ruhar say those beetles will bet on anything, this has got to have them excited out of their minds."

"You may be right about that, Da-" Perkins almost used his first name. Blushing inside her helmet, she corrected herself. "Czajka. We may find out when that star carrier returns." Inwardly, she groaned when another thought struck her. While it was good to observe their allies in real action, the losses suffered by the task force very likely meant the training cruise would be cut short before humans could fully qualify for space duty, and demonstrate their ability to operate effectively alongside the hamsters. If the war in the sector was now entering a dangerous and unpredictable phase, opportunity for further training may be delayed significantly.

"Hopefully it gets back here soon," Irene zoomed the display image outward, expanding to show another ship that had jumped in sixty eight lightseconds away and was now accelerating hard to form up with the others.

"What are they like?" Dave asked.

"The Jeraptha?" Irene held up her hands. "We've never met them."

"But you and Captain Bonsu have flown to their ship."

"That was only to practice manual docking procedures," Irene explained. "We flew into one of their docking bays, waited for the clamps to engage and release, then we flew out. Kind of like doing Touch-and-Gos with aircraft. There was a Jeraptha who talked to us, but we never even saw one of the beetles, the gallery above the docking bay was empty. We were told the Jeraptha are not unfriendly to lower species, the crew of the star carrier was just very busy with all the training going on."

"Is their ship really called the 'Deal Me In'?" Jesse asked. "A cadet told me that, and I didn't know if he was playing a joke on me."

"No joke," Irene assured the soldier. "The name does translate as 'Deal Me In', or close enough."

"You think the beetles will really bet on what places the Bosphuraq will defend?" Jesse continued.

Derek answered the question. "From what I've heard, the Jeraptha will bet on pretty much anything. What I wonder is whether their intel people base their assessments on wagering."

"They would do that?" Shauna was shocked by such an idea.

"Not based on their own bets," Derek explained, "I meant based on what the overall Jeraptha public is wagering on."

"Yes," Perkins agreed with a nod toward Derek. "That type of crowd-sourced prediction model can often be more accurate that the assessments of so-called 'experts'. When I was at the Pentagon, we were looking at using a prediction market system to forecast future threats."

"Ma'am?" Jesse blinked. "What kind of market?"

"Market-*based*. Think of it like drafting a fantasy football team where you're using real money, to buy players you think will perform well the next season. At the Pentagon, we experimented with a team of threat assessment people to project the next hotspot. We created a sort of market where people could buy binary options in various potential threat scenarios, with the value of a particular threat rising as the threat became more likely. Before you say it sounds like a crapshoot," Perkins gave a disarming smile at Jesse, "that system predicted we would be in Nigeria fourteen months before the President pulled the trigger to put boots on the ground there."

"Holy crap," Jesse gasped.

"Come on, Cornpone, we were talking about us going into Nigeria way back when we were in boot camp," Dave reminded his friend.

"Yeah, but I didn't think people were *betting* on it."

"I know it sounds sketchy," Perkins said with sympathy, "but the Jeraptha might just be crowd-sourcing their strategic intel using real money, through a wagering system," she added with a faraway look on her face, the wheels turning in her head. As a former intelligence officer, she would love to know how accurate the Jeraptha system was in real life.

"It sounds crazy," Derek agreed, "but it may work as well as any system we have."

"I'll stick to fantasy sports," Jesse replied, chagrinned. "Nobody gets killed."

"If the Jeraptha intel scopes out right, *less* people will get killed," Dave argued.

"Prediction markets aren't perfect," Perkins admitted. "To be useful, you need to filter out what people think will happen, from what they think the popular opinion is. Too many times, people in the market try to guess what the herd is thinking, rather than using their own gut." The glazing eyes of her audience told Perkins she was getting way too nerdy on that subject. "Health agencies on Earth have been using predictive markets to project flu outbreaks for years, and they work pretty well. If we ever get an opportunity to talk with the Jeraptha, I'll ask them about it."

"Ha," Jesse laughed. "They'll want to bet with you about what you think the answer is. Those beetles-"

Irene interrupted him. "Star carrier jumped in! Damn, they really nailed that jump, exactly in the center of their target Emergence Point," her voice reflected the admiration she felt. "Two point four lightseconds away, we should start moving-" an alarm blared and Irene smiled. "Like I said, we will start moving soon."

Within seconds, they felt a gentle tug to the right as the ship turned, then fired its engines. Irene watched the thrust indicator on the bottom of the display, and was pleased that her guess based on feel matched what the display showed; the *Ruh Tostella* was not moving quickly. As a noncombatant and not having suffered any battle damage, the training cruiser would be last in line to latch onto the star carrier. It hung back away from the cluster of warships approaching their assigned docking platforms, with the *Toaster* providing an overall sensor view of the area, and acting as a backup traffic controller to assist the Jeraptha crew of the star carrier. Irene noticed something odd right away, and when she looked up to catch Perkins' eye, the Colonel nodded with concern. She had seen it too. "Those ships are in a hurry," Irene said quietly. "A big Goddamned hurry."

"Looks like it," Perkins agreed. Normal procedure for docking with a Jeraptha star carrier was for ships to approach one at a time, remaining outside the imaginary bubble of space within which the Jeraptha ship's AI took control from the docking ship's navigation system, until the star carrier authorized them to proceed inward. Only when one ship was securely attached to a docking platform and powered down, was a subsequent ship given clearance to approach. Due to the poor maneuverability of star carriers, the Jeraptha were understandably worried about bulky armored warships clumsily crashing into each other, or into the vulnerable long spine of their space truck.

What Perkins and Striebich noticed was the Ruhar warships were approaching in groups of three, with the remaining two ships close behind. Though battle damage to the Ruhar ships rendered some of them awkward to handle, the Jeraptha appeared to be more concerned about completing the docking operation as quickly as possible than about navigation safety. The two human women shared a look, and they both pulled their seat straps tighter. "People," Perkins ordered, "let's get buttoned up," she reached under the seat for her helmet. "I think once this ship gets moving for real, it could be a rough ride." At the moment, their cruiser was proceeding toward the star carrier at a leisurely rate of acceleration, hanging back to give the battle-damaged warships clearance to maneuver onto the docking platforms.

"What's up, Colonel?" Jesse asked.

Irene answered for Perkins. "The Jeraptha are breaking safe docking protocol, they're going for combat latching. That means incoming ships fly a partly-independent approach, get onto whatever docking platform they can reach ASAP, and hold on with their own magnetic grapples as best they can. The beetles are worried about something, they want to jump out of here pronto."

"They won't jump without us, will they?" Dave asked, hoping he knew the answer.

"No," Derek assured the soldier.

Irene acted as the killjoy. "They won't if they can help it. But the beetles aren't going to risk their star carrier and a dozen warships for a training cruiser. If they think they're in jeopardy, they'll jump away and we'll be on our own."

"We'll be on our own for a short time," Derek shot the other pilot a look. "Czajka, all it means is if the star carrier jumps away, we jump away also, and meet up at a preprogramed AZ."

"What if that AZ is hot also?" Shauna asked.

"Then we go to the alternate AZ, and then another. Look, Jarrett, Czajka, the Ruhar and Jeraptha have been doing this for a very long time," Derek said in a calm, steady voice. "Probably before humans had any form of writing. They know what they're doing. And," he added for emphasis, "they've been kicking the lizards and Thuranin's asses all over this sector."

"Besides," Irene chimed in unhelpfully, "we're just a training ship. In a battle, we would be the last ship targeted."

"Yeah, because we're the most vulnerable," Shauna rolled her eyes at Irene.

"Sorry," Irene muttered. Just then, another alarm blared and the ship's acceleration increased noticeably. "Hmm, the Jeraptha want us docked as soon as possible, too," she said as she watched the display project the ship's course, straight in to a docking platform in the middle of the star carrier between two other ships. The Jeraptha must be confident their undamaged ship could tuck into that tight space, Irene thought to herself, while they are directing the incoming battle-damaged warships onto platforms that had plenty of empty space around them.

"Captain Striebich?" Dave asked, pointing at the display. "What's that destroyer doing?"

"A go-around," Irene guessed. She had watched the stricken destroyer approach its assigned platform clumsily, clearly that ship's damaged propulsion system was making it difficult to control its flight. The destroyer had fired its thrusters on full to avoid a collision with another incoming ship, overcorrected and been forced to back away using its main engines. "The Jeraptha waved it off. It will have to try again."

"What if they can't do it?" Shauna asked, fearing for the crew of the destroyer.

"They'll have three options," Derek explained. "They can get tug bots to tow them in."

"They won't have time for that," Irene said quietly. "Those tugs are designed to move dropships, not starships."

"Or they can remain stationary and the star carrier can maneuver to latch them on. I sure wouldn't want to do that, even if we weren't in a hurry," Derek shook his head at the thought of the massive star carrier, burdened with warships, trying to perform the delicate operation of moving precisely enough to position a docking platform under the belly of the destroyer.

Shauna unconsciously pulled her arms tightly around herself from anxiety. "What's the third option?"

"Abandon ship," Irene replied. "Get the crew off in dropships, send the ship away on autopilot. They can recover the ship later, or set it to self-destruct."

"That's not optimal," Perkins noted. "They probably have wounded aboard, moving them to dropships will take time, and risk interrupting their medical treatment."

"Yes Ma'am," Irene agreed in a soothing tone. "The Ruhar have a procedure for that. I'm sure that ship's command crew began prepping their medical teams to transport the wounded, as soon as they realized the ship wasn't responding properly to her helm."

"I hope they did," Shauna clenched her fists as she spoke.

"Look!" Derek pointed. "That destroyer is opening docking bay doors. They are preparing to abandon ship!"

It was Emily Perkins' turn to clench her fists. If the Jeraptha were junking a destroyer after one failed docking attempt, the beetles must be very concerned about getting away from the Assembly Zone as quickly as possible. That meant the beetles expected trouble. And that was not good. Before she could halt her tongue, she muttered aloud "I hope this doesn't turn into a fight."

"If we have to fight, this could get kinetic in a hurry," Irene warned. Their cruiser was significantly behind the other ships in line for docking. Even with the *Toaster*'s command crew now twisting the cruiser's tail to get it moving faster, they would not be docking for over twenty minutes. Distances in space were vast, and the ship's approach speed was limited because however hard they accelerated toward the star carrier, they would need to cancel their relative speed before docking.

"Yeah," Derek grimaced. "We throw that term around loosely but remember out here, 'kinetic' can be measured as a percentage of lightspeed. A fleck of paint could punch through the hull armor," he rapped knuckles on a bulkhead, "if it's going fast enough."

"Captain," Jesse did not like the mental image of being killed by a tiny fleck of paint. "You are a genuine confidence-booster."

Despite the anxiety of the team's pilots, who could only watch the combat latching operation, all the warships attached themselves, even the destroyer that had been waved off its first attempt to connect with a docking platform. The *Ruh Tostella* was the last ship to contact a platform, and the clamps had barely engaged when the star carrier jumped.

CHAPTER ELEVEN

"No," the Ruhar flight instructor said with a plastered-on smile and a forcibly pleasant and patient tone that came across as irritated, impatient and patronizing, as if she were speaking to a young child who could not understand how to perform a simple task. "You first have to-"

"Switch to the independent mode, yes, I know that, and that is why I have the mode selected," Irene replied through gritted teeth, using her right pinky finger to indicate the 'INDEPENDENT OPERATION' symbol in bold letters at the top of the touchscreen display. With two human pilots learning to fly the starship from the auxiliary control center, the displays were converted to English words and symbols familiar to humans, like having positive indicators in green and negatives in red.

"You don't have to be nasty about it," The flight instructor huffed, her translated words coming across as distinctly frosty.

"I wasn't being nasty," Irene tensed in her pilot's couch, but kept her eyes focused on the displays instead of turning to confront their alien instructor. It slightly irritated Irene that they were being instructed by a young Ruhar whose rank of 'klasta' was roughly equivalent to a second lieutenant, while Irene and Derek were captains with many thousands of hours of real flight experience. Klasta Splunn was freshly graduated from the academy, having taken the low-status assignment aboard the *Toaster* only to build up flight hours in her logbook. The alien had little real-world flight experience, she was clearly bored and angry about being assigned to teach humans, and Irene wasn't taking any crap from her.

"I do not like your tone, human," Splunn ground her incisors as she spoke.

"*I* do not like being spoken to like a child, by an instructor who can't read her own display," Irene shot back, knowing that although the Ruhar probably could not or would not read the English symbols on the two pilot displays, the klasta had standard Ruhar common language symbols on the displays at the instructor station.

The klasta tensed, lifting a finger to halt the simulation. "Perhaps it would be best if-"

Derek turned in his couch to face their instructor, jabbing an accusing finger at her, in a gesture he knew she understood. "*Perhaps* it would be best if you do the job you have been assigned. If you are not capable of that, we can request a more qualified instructor right now," he held up a zPhone.

"Good idea-" Irene began to agree.

"And *you*," he turned to his fellow pilot. "Do *your* job, and leave out the comments. We've both had asshole instructors before, and you aren't making things any better." He leaned toward Irene and pressed a button to transfer control to his station. "*My* spacecraft," he declared as he assumed the role of pilot in command. "Initiating approach," he stated as he authorized thrusters for manual operation. "Are you good, Klasta Splunn?"

"Yes," came the curt reply.

"Sorry," Irene's voice was soft. Then, louder, "Monitoring remote guidance, guide beam acquired and active."

"Acquisition confirmed," the Ruhar behind them confirmed in a voice that held only a hint of anger. "Proceed at one-quarter power. Watch your heading!" She added in a reproachful tone.

"Heading dialed in," Derek reported with a smile, and a wink toward Irene. He had the ship exactly on the designated heading, not only within the green band of acceptable error, but near the blue center line of optimal course. Derek Bonsu had learned the best way to respond to someone trying to bait you was to never take the bait. Ignore the insults, plaster a fake smile on your face, and pretend you did not understand an insult was intended. That often turned the tables and made his opponents lose their temper, while he just had a good laugh inwardly.

Irene lifted a hand off the controls just long enough to give her fellow pilot a thumbs up, then returned her laser focus on the copilot's task of providing navigation data to Derek. She knew the heading they had the ship on was nearly perfect and the instructor had nothing to complain about. Had nothing to do, because so far, neither of the two humans had made any kind of significant mistake. "Course within ninety seven percent of nominal," Irene could not help reporting. "Ninety *eight* percent."

The humans ignoring her, defying her, made the klasta pissed off enough that she decided to deviate from the approved training course. With a tight smile at the trouble she was causing, she changed parameters of the simulation. "Star carrier reports hardpoint Three has a mechanical failure, change course to hardpoint Seven."

Without losing her cool or making a snarky remark though she knew the hamster was screwing with them, Irene smoothly pulled the navigation control to the new guide beam, and fed the data to Derek. "Hardpoint Seven, acknowledged."

"Watch your-"

"That frigate will be crossing our heading," Irene warned as the instructor threw another complication at them, this one a ship that was coming into hardpoint Six and interfering with the *Toaster* although the larger and heavier training cruiser had the right of way. "Adjusting course to keep clear."

"Taking power to thirty percent," Derek glanced toward Irene and she nodded. "Slowing down to give that frigate a clear path to Platform Six," he said just as the simulated frigate suffered an unlikely engineering failure and veered toward the *Toaster*. This time, Derek could not keep the smile off his face. He had anticipated the instructor throwing a highly unlikely problem into the sim, and he was almost disappointed at how obvious and unimaginative the complication was. "Taking power to fifty percent, sound collision alarm!"

"Fifty percent is not authorized under proximity maneuver conditions," the klasta snapped gleefully, anticipating an opportunity to reprimand the primitive aliens. "Reduce-"

"The frigate has suffered an engineering fault of unknown severity and origin," Irene interrupted. "Emergency flight regulations require us to get to a safe distance as soon as possible, in case the frigate's jump capacitors or reactor explode."

With a grin, Derek reveled in the chance to truly fly the bulky cruiser, even if it was only in a sim. "Bringing main power online, thrusters at eighty percent." The *Toaster*'s main normal-space engines would soon be responding to his commands, surging the ship forward with awesome power.

"Main power ready," Irene reported. "Releasing-"

"Pausing simulation," the klasta said unhappily. "Resetting. That was," she cleared her throat. "Acceptable. Our instruction course has not yet covered emergency flight regulations."

Again Derek turned in his couch to face the Ruhar, wiping the grin off his face. "We studied those regs on our own, before we came aboard the ship. We did not wish to waste your very valuable time," he added with a quick smile that he kept as genuine as he could.

"Hmmf," Klasta Splunn sniffed. For the next hour, she stuck to the standard training course, only throwing curveballs at them occasionally and only introducing approved complications. Chit-chat was kept to a minimum and Irene was on her best behavior, knowing their success was the best way to piss off their alien instructor.

After the *Toaster* latched onto the star carrier, the *Deal Me In* had performed a series of jumps, then dropped off the training cruiser and other ships in dark interstellar space while the Jeraptha went to pick up the other half of the battlegroup. Training had been suspended for six hours, as the *Toaster* and the battle-damaged warships waited for the Jeraptha star carrier to reappear and take them aboard. After twelve hours, with no sign of the star carrier and with the warships busy patching up their stricken hulls and making repairs as best they could, the *Toaster* resumed training on a limited schedule. Priority for pilot training in the simulators had been given to Ruhar cadets, as they would only be aboard the ship for another couple weeks before returning to the academy, so at first Irene and Derek had been studying dull flight manuals by themselves, until Perkins asked why the ship's auxiliary control center could not be used to run simulations? With the cruiser hanging motionless in space, the aux flight station was admittedly empty and unused, and all Perkins had to do was find an instructor who was willing to lower his or her self to training the most primitive semi-intelligent species in the known galaxy. Fortunately, instruction time partly counted toward qualified flight hours, so it was not impossible to persuade an instructor to take on two additional students. Unfortunately, since the best instructors were already busy, Irene and Derek had been stuck with the sour-faced Klasta Splunn, who was predisposed to being grumpy because she knew no one else wanted to be trained by her.

The klasta was frustrated that the two humans had not quickly failed, which would have given her ample opportunity to insult them and even better, would have allowed her to push at least one of them aside and use the simulator to build her own qualifying flight hours. More than two hours into the training session, she set a simple instruction to run, and left the aux control center to get a snack from the galley.

"That's a relie-" Irene began to say before Derek raised a hand and silently pointed to the flight recorder module between the two pilot stations. Whatever they said or did would certainly be scrutinized later by the Ruhar. "Real, real challenge," she recovered. "My turn?"

Derek pressed a button on his console and lifted hands away from the touchscreens. "Your spacecraft."

The two pilots ran the simulation on their own, flying the starship through normal space to various points, until it almost became dull. Truly, flying even a light cruiser in normal space was not all that much different from flying a dropship. Flying in combat would be much more challenging, but they were far from enjoying that type of simulation. Several times, Irene had to look to Derek, a huge grin on her face. "Think about it, we are the first humans ever to fly a starship!"

"Simulated," Derek reminded her, though that did not much tarnish their shared joy.

"It's simulated *now*," Irene agreed, knowing the standard training course would include actually moving the big cruiser, some months in the future. "We were the first humans to ever fly a dropship, for real."

"Ah, except for Captain Desai, when that guy Bishop stole it to, to do whatever they did. *She* was the first to fly a Dodo, that we know of."

"Fine, except for her," Irene admitted, wondering how the mysterious Desai had managed to fly a Ruhar Dodo without any training. Had Desai somehow gotten access to a simulator before she broke out of jail? No, it was more likely one of the whispered rumors was true; that the whole operation had been planned and run by the Ruhar, using Bishop's group of humans as a cover story. Unless the Ruhar clandestine operations people admitted the truth, no one would ever know. Irene looked at the clock on her console, feeling her back growing stiff from sitting so long in the pilot couch. "Is our instructor ever coming back?" The current sim program only had ten more minutes remaining.

"This sim will end and repeat soon," Derek pointed to the 'Loop' indicator that was showing active. "We could-"

Alarms blared and the simulation on their displays froze, then the consoles switched to show real-time images. "Hey! The Jeraptha are back," Derek announced excitedly, recognizing the outline of the *Deal Me In* even though the displays and controls in front of them were now all in Ruhar common language script. "Damn, I am glad to see those beetles again," he shot a guilty glance at the flight recorder module, and decided to pretend he hadn't said anything noteworthy. They were aboard a Ruhar ship, and he knew the hamsters had their own nicknames for their Jeraptha patrons.

"Hands off," Irene lifted her fingers away from the controls, which should not respond to her anyway, as she did not have the proper access code or biometrics. Even if she did, the auxiliary control center needed to be authorized to have any effect on ship systems, and that authority could only be granted by the senior officers. When the ship was maneuvering, the aux controls were supposed to be manned anyway, and Irene nervously looked toward the hatch for their instructor to return. "Maybe we should get out of these seats. Oop," she added as artificial gravity began to fade. Cutting off gravity meant the ship could potentially be performing hard turns and accelerations. The display flashed to Alert Condition Two. "Where is the klasta?"

"Regs say we remain in these seats until we are officially relieved," Derek pointed out, his tone reflecting his uncertainty. "We are supposed to put our helmets on," he reached under his couch for the hard-shell helmet, "and button up."

"Derek, we are not pilots," Irene sighed and reached for her own helmet. "Not yet," she waved a hand at the consoles that were all showing the odd-looking Ruhar script. "I can barely read this stuff."

"Me neither, but when Splunn comes back, she will see we followed regulations to the letter and have nothing to bitch," he remembered the flight recorder was still active, "to reprimand us about."

"Ok," Irene agreed as her seat was the best place to watch the unfolding drama. "Wow," she gulped as the ship suddenly slewed to one side, leaving butterflies in her stomach. "Those ships are really moving."

"Yeah, I don't know if I'm reading this right," Derek squinted at a blinking notice from the Toaster's bridge, "but I think the beetles ordered all ships to perform combat latching again. They must really be in a hurry to jump us out of here."

"Derek," Irene figured out the controls for the sensors and zoomed the image in on the *Deal Me In*. "Look at those ships attached the star carrier."

Derek leaned over to watch her display before she mirrored the images on his console. "Whew," he whistled as he took in the view of battered and in some cases crippled warships. There were only four Ruhar ships attached to the star carrier, but seven ships had jumped into action. Three ships were missing. "They were in one hell of a fight. Oh, damn, look at that. The star carrier took hits also," he noted scorch marks and jagged holes in forward and aft hulls. Amidships, the spine had cables flopping around and pieces of the scaffolding bent or missing. "This is big F-ing trouble. Damn. Who has the balls to hit the Jeraptha?"

Before Irene could respond, Derek's answer appeared in the form of Bosphuraq battlecruiser, jumping in close. "Oh, *shit*."

Klasta Splunn flailed her arms in a futile attempt to steer toward a handhold, missing as she flew by in the zero gravity. When the Jeraptha star carrier jumped in unexpectedly and the alarm sounded, she had been finishing a snack and chatting with a cute senior cadet. She wasn't that much older than the cadet, she told herself, why, she had graduated from the academy less than a year ago. Splunn had been struck with guilty panic when the alarm sounded, knowing she was several minutes away from her human students, and without artificial gravity functioning the trip back to the aux control center would take longer. The aux control center was not her action station when the ship was under way, but she knew the senior officers would rightfully fault her for leaving a pair of aliens alone in a vital part of the ship. When the gravity cut off, she had been racing headlong down a passageway and clumsily stumbled, sending herself awkwardly soaring through the air out of control. The passageway where she needed to turn left had gone past without her being able to catch a handhold, and her plight only got worse when she crashed into a trio of frightened cadets. The four of them struggled to separate and the cadets got out of her way, helping her turn in the correct direction, no sooner had she launched herself across a side passage when the ship lurched, making her bounce off a bulkhead and bending a wrist painfully. The ship was already maneuvering, and no one was available to provide backup to the bridge helmsmen!

Splunn finally hooked a foot painfully on a doorframe and halted her tumbling flight. With determination, she pulled herself along the correct passageway, seeing with dismay the two adult crewmen coming in from a side route. They were assigned to the aux control center, and now she had no chance to get the aliens out of the seats before anyone saw they had been left alone. Wordlessly, she gave them a quick wave between handholds, trying to make clear they were all going to the same place.

She slowed to avoid a collision just as a Condition One alert sounded! The three of them stared at each other for a heart-stopping moment. Enemy ships had jumped in, or their own ship was about to jump into combat. No longer waiting for Splunn, the two crewmen expertly pushed off hard with their legs, zipping down the passageway toward where the open hatch to the aux control center could be partially seen.

They almost made it. Splunn saw no point to the three of them trying to jam through the hatch at the same time, so she gave her aching wrist a break and eased up slightly-

She never saw the railgun dart that was moving at an appreciable percentage of lightspeed. The first dart of the pair slammed into the *Toaster*'s shields that were already weakened by hits from enemy masers, forcing the shields to absorb and dissipate gigajoules of energy. The second dart, hitting less than two meters from its companion, was also mostly deflected by the straining shields. Mostly. Eight percent of the dart managed to penetrate all the way through to the cruiser's hull, having been turned into plasma that burned its way through the ship's light armor like it was tissue paper. After punching through the armor with little trouble, the hellish globs of plasma burst in a cone-shaped fountain of death, burning and destroying everything in a sixteen degree arc and only stopping when they encountered the inner surface of the armor plating on the other side of the hull. Three of the objects burned by the plasma jet were Splunn and the two crewmen.

Irene was startled not so much by the violent shaking of the ship as by the hatch behind them crashing closed. The quick automatic action of the hatch was not fast enough to prevent air being sucked out into the passageway and Irene's flightsuit inflated to compensate, with air hissing from a reserve tank in the helmet even before the visor could swing down. The flightsuits they wore were based on combat skinsuits, but were even less capable than flightsuits used by crews aboard dropships and combat aircraft. When issued their new flightsuits aboard the *Toaster*, Irene and Derek had assumed the Ruhar fleet's thinking must be that, if a ship were hit in deep space, a tougher flightsuit was not going to be of much help.

And Klasta Splunn had not been wearing a flightsuit at all, instead being dressed in the simple coveralls that were the standard crew uniform. Unless that hamster had been able to pause long enough to don an environment suit, she might already be dead. "Derek-"

"Incoming!" He watched transfixed in shock as missiles streaked in toward the *Toaster*, with the forward section of the ship being pounded by repeated maser fire. Unknown to Derek, impact of the second railgun dart amidships had pushed the cruiser just far enough to avoid another pair of darts that bracketed the forward hull, with one barely striking the shields a glancing blow. As the two human pilots watched helplessly, their cruiser's point-defense masers exploded one missile at a safe distance, then another but damage from the railgun hit amidships had knocked out defense cannons and sensors in that section of the ship, leaving a gap in defense coverage. Recognizing their vulnerability, the command crew fired thrusters to roll the ship, exposing the undamaged defense cannons on the other side. Unfortunately, the enemy also adjusted to circumstances and the incoming missiles arced around to aim at the damaged area. The missiles were faster and more nimble than the bulky old cruiser so they had the advantage. Still, the defense masers kept pouring megajoules of energy at the missiles and sheer numbers were on the side of the defense; eleven maser cannons against only two missiles. Technology was on the side of the missiles, the ship was Ruhar while the missiles were manufactured by the advanced Bosphuraq. With invisible maser bolts streaking past, the smart weapons rapidly changed course and speed, ejected decoys and projected false images to fool Ruhar sensors. Derek's stomach tied in knots while he sat rigidly in the couch, wishing he could do something, anything. "Yes!" He pumped a fist as one missile stumbled into a hail of maser beams and exploded. In its death, the missile had one last move to play and it detonated its warhead in a shape charge directed forward at the cruiser. High-density warhead pellets travelling a quarter of lightspeed blasted the cruiser's energy shield, heating the degraded shield generators near the point of failure and lighting up that vulnerable area of shield like a beacon for the missile coming behind.

As the last high-tech missile jinked sideways at three thousand Gees toward the weakened shield, a nearby Ruhar destroyer exploded, its jump drive coils having been punctured by a pair of railgun darts from the enemy battlecruiser. To Derek's terror, the blast of high-energy photons and particles washing over the battlespace blanked out the *Toaster*'s proximity sensors and the cruiser lost track of the last missile for a crucial second.

The missile, for all its advanced technology, also lost track of its quarry but that was of little importance, for the missile knew the target's last position and the big cruiser could not move far in a short time. Dropping all evasive maneuvers, the missile fired its engine for emergency thrust, on a course that took it straight into the heart of where it knew the Ruhar ship had to be.

Derek had no time to give voice to his terror, no time to shout a warning in case Irene had not seen the same data on her console. The *Ruh Tostella* was tossed aside like a child's toy, spinning around so hard Derek's head hit the back of his helmet as the couch's restraint system automatically held the helmet steady to prevent him from snapping his neck. His brain rattled inside the shell of his skull, he struggled to make sense of simply who and where he was, the flickering displays in front of him forgotten.

"Der-Derek, you Ok?"

Derek coughed. "Shook up," he admitted. In combat, he could not indulge in any macho bullshit, the other pilot needed to know he was not a hundred percent right then. "You?"

"Seeing double," Irene blinked slowly to clear her vision so she could understand what she thought she saw on the ship status display. "The front of the ship, *gone*?"

Derek instinctively wanted to shake his head, he also knew that more jarring was the last thing his brain needed right then. The ship was moving enough on its own, making the couch shake regularly with intermittent hard bumps. The shaking was probably caused by the ship's thrusters attempting to control the wild spinning of the ship, which was flipping on all three axes. Derek assumed the bumps were secondary explosions, a notion confirmed by new lights flaring on the ship status display. Components were overloading and exploding all over the forward half of the hull. That is, the forward half of what was left, for a quarter of the ship's original hull was missing entirely. "Yeah, it's gone. Everything forward of Frame Thirty Five is just, *missing*." The sensors were showing an extensive debris field around and mostly in front of the cruiser, wreckage blasted away from the ship by an advanced-technology warhead. "We're dead in the water," he weakly lifted a hand to point to the status display which showed half the defensive maser cannons were offline and only half of those were even in a restart cycle. Shields were weak and one shield, toward what was now the nose of the ship, was disconnected from a power source. "Why haven't the birdbrains finished us?"

"Because we're just a training cruiser," Irene guessed. Tapping the tactical display she added, "They have more important targets."

Outside the ship it was hell, with maser bolts, particle beams and kinetic ordnance flying around thick and fast. The Bosphuraq battlecruiser had already destroyed or disabled most of the Ruhar warships, the main fight now was between the Jeraptha and Bosphuraq. The beetles had their star carrier responding with every weapon they had, missiles ripple-firing from launch tubes and masers burning continuously, but the superior strength of the enemy's heavier ship gave them an overwhelming advantage. Damaged Ruhar ships were ejecting from their hardpoints, adding their own weapons to the fight, knowing they had little chance for survival. Survival was not their goal and escape was impossible, as the enemy had the battlespace blanketed in a strong damping field. Two Ruhar destroyers were flying directly at the enemy ship on a collision course, hoping to ram the battlecruiser. Their suicide tactic was intended to provide a gap in the damping field, allowing the vital star carrier to get away. Alert to the danger, the Bosphuraq were slamming the destroyers with concentrated railgun fire. One, then the other destroyer was struck several times until their shields were entirely knocked out, exposing them to the comparatively weak maser bolts that seared deep into the noses of the destroyers, making the forward armor bubble and melt, opening holes for the maser energy to wreck the unprotected interiors of the ships.

The first destroyer veered away, corrected back on course, then veered in the other direction, its engines offline, drifting uselessly away into deep space. The crew of the second destroyer, knowing it would be crippled and out of the fight before it could ram the enemy, activated a self-destruct mechanism to drop reactor containment. A half second later, as the white-hot fusion plasma burst outward and contacted the fully-charged banks of jump drive capacitors, warheads of all missiles still in the ship's magazines detonated to add their energy to the maelstrom. The destroyer was replaced by a small, short-lived sun that expanded outward in a sphere so only part of the wavefront washed over the enemy battlecruiser, and at such distance the Bosphuraq warship shrugged off the assault with only a minor fluctuation in damping field strength.

With all Ruhar ships inside the damping field either destroyed or disabled, including the unimportant training cruiser near the edge of the field, the Bosphuraq turned the full fury of their weapons on the hapless star carrier that was making a futile attempt to run away. Jeraptha star carriers had reinforced shielding and armor protecting the critical engineering components of the aft hull. Knowing that bit of tactical intel, the Bosphuraq aimed masers, particle beams, railguns and missiles just forward of the aft hull where it attached to the long spine of the ship. The only break in their focus on the star carrier was to direct two missiles at the training cruiser, to kill it before its mostly aimless course took it beyond the reach of the damping field.

"We should jump," Derek advised. As he spoke, more missiles launched from the enemy ship, two of them curving toward the *Toaster* and accelerating hard. The inbound missiles were highlighted by blinking red symbols and red streaks projecting their courses. A pair of missiles were projected to impact the training cruiser, and point defenses were mostly showing as offline.

"Jump? *We* can't do anything, we're just running a sim- Oh."

"Yeah," Derek tapped his console where an alert was flashing that the simulation had been abruptly ended, and the auxiliary control center now had full authorization to maneuver the ship. "Command authority automatically transferred to the auxiliary station when we lost the bridge," he declared, remembering that tidbit of info from the Welcome Aboard package they received when they'd been assigned to the cruiser. Derek never imagined he would need to remember such an obscure piece of trivia. "We're the pilots now, everyone aboard is counting on *us*."

Irene turned to look at the hatch, hoping trained Ruhar crew would come in to relieve them. That, she saw with a shock, was *not* going to happen. The hatch had scorch marks on the inner surface, and the upper left corner appeared bent, bowed inward. Whatever had happened in the passageway outside, it must have been bad. Very bad.

"Ok, all right, yeah, sure," Irene's mouth babbled as her mind caught up with the situation. "We've never performed a jump. Or been trained in jump procedure."

"We've both read the jump manual a dozen times or more," Derek's voice was more squeaky than the soothing tone he tried to project. "We can do this. If we can't," he swallowed hard, "the ship is dead anyway."

"Right, Ok, good," Irene took deep breaths to psych herself up to do the impossible. "We're caught in the edge of a damping field," Irene noted, even as her fingers called up the jump drive controls. She had only ever seen those controls on her laptop, not ever in a simulator and never for real. "Local damping field strength is, uh," reading Ruhar script was not her best skill, "thirty two percent?" She struggled to recall something she had read only once. "What's the safety limit for a successful jump?"

"Twenty eight percent," Derek stated. Or was it twenty nine? Or thirty eight? Other than casually scanning a high-level briefing document about jump operations, he had no experience with the system.

"We can't risk a jump."

"The red thingies are getting closer to the green thingy!" Derek jabbed a finger at the display in front of him, where red symbols for incoming missiles were homing in on the *Toaster*. "We need to jump *now*."

"If we jump inside a damping field, the drive could tear itself apart."

"If we don't jump, those missiles *will* tear us apart. That star carrier is about to blow any second, it's getting *hammered*. We need to do it. *Now*."

What the hell, Irene told herself, decision made. "Can you find where the preprogrammed jump options list is? We can't program a jump by ourselves." Even if a jump was programmed in the drive navigation system, would it be usable without adjusting for the damping effect? She did not know, and that was the problem.

Derek peered at his console, touching unfamiliar controls. "I think this is it. I think. Uh, yes! System shows one hundred percent capacity," he noted. That had to be the jump drive capacitors, the *Toaster* had not jumped in days, so the capacitors would be fully charged. The ship rocked from multiple maser beam strikes, yellow lights on the display showing where the white-hot beams had burned through the defensive shields protecting the critical aft engineering section.

"Select the second option and authorize it," she ordered as she tried to find the controls to release power from the capacitors into the jump coils. One thing she did know for certain was that the coils could not safely hold a charge for long, once power began flowing from the capacitors the coils needed to be used or the power discharged quickly.

"Why the *second* option?"

"Those Bosphuraq knew where the star carrier was jumping to, we don't want to make our jump obvious by using the primary Assembly Zone option. Ready?" She didn't need a reply as she could see the second option on the list was now blinking blue. "Five, four, three," she reached out with her right hand to touch Derek, the jump now being on automatic.

Derek took her hand, squeezed it and turned to say something, when the ship violently skewed and shuddered as the Jeraptha star carrier exploded.

Then they jumped.

CHAPTER TWELVE

"Easy, easy, Ma'am, it's not a race," Dave cautioned as Perkins got her safety line snagged on a piece of debris protruding from a gaping hole in the ship's hull.

"I'm fine, Czajka. You're not my babysitter."

"No, Ma'am. I do have more spacewalk time than you. Let me go first."

"Why?" Perkins was predisposed to be irritated, because of the dangerous situation, the lack of time and the circuitous route they had to take toward the ship's engineering section. And because Sergeant Czajka acted like he needed to hold her hand the whole way. "Because you are younger and a man?"

"No, Colonel. Because, if one of us is expendable, it's not you. There's a whole lot of stuff attached to the hull that could kill us," he pointed to sparks arcing from another hole in the hull, "between here and that airlock. I should scout ahead."

The sergeant's reply had chastened her, she had let impatience, anger and fear overcome her need for cool judgement. "Czajka, *none* of us are expendable. Not humans, not out here. We don't know if anyone is left alive on Earth. UNEF on Paradise may be all that is left. Thank you, go ahead and check for anything that might blow up in our faces, but *be careful*. Careful, you got that? I can't, I don't want to lose you," she added with a lump in her throat.

"Yes, Colonel," Dave's feeble grin could be seen in the faint lights illuminating his helmet faceplate.

The ship had successfully jumped away from the battlespace, or successfully enough, and the Bosphuraq ship had not pursued. After a terrifying fifteen minutes trapped in their designated section of the ship, not having any idea what was going on as the comm system was offline, comms were partially restored and Perkins had been able to use her command codes to get a rough and confusing status report. What she saw shocked her. The entire forward section of the ship was missing, simply *gone*, and the hull was breached in multiple areas. Main power was off, even emergency backup systems were spotty and intermittent. Attempts to contact anyone in authority were a failure until Perkins located a feature that tracked the ship's officers. *One*, there was only one adult crewman whose comm system indicated activity, and that person was several sections aft, in the primary engineering control center. That was why Perkins and Czajka were in spacesuits, clambering along the outside of the ship. Much of the ship's interior was a dangerously impassible shambles, with airtight doors closed and not responding to the codes Perkins had been given. She had quickly decided her best option was to travel aft on the ship's hull and enter the engineering center through an airlock, despite the danger. The ship shuddered occasionally as one system or another overloaded and exploded or pipes ruptured, or a thruster unhelpfully fired all by itself. To move at all required clipping a safety line, crawling along the hull using whatever handholds were available, and then clipping another safety line. They could not rely on the expedient tactic of floating between handholds, for the ship might suddenly jerk away beneath them and they would drift out to the end of the safety line, wasting precious time and exposing themselves to the jagged bits of debris surrounding the ship like a predatory cloud. It was a damned good thing, Perkins told herself, that the *Toaster* was a training ship, for the hull had regularly spaced handholds and attachment points for safety lines that would never be allowed on the exterior of a true warship.

"Got it!" Dave announced as he hooked his boots into a clamp at the bottom of the airlock. "Thank God! It's active, Ma'am, I'm starting the cycle now."

"Would it be best to wait for me to get there?"

"No," Dave shook his head though the gesture was barely visible in the blackness of interstellar space. "Having the door open will give you more to grab onto. It's opening," he noted with great relief, swallowing his fear that the airlock might refuse to respond to a human.

That airlock was intended for a single maintenance person, not groups of trainees, and it was a very tight fit for two people wearing spacesuits. "Uh, Colonel, maybe I should wait outside while you cycle through."

"Screw that, Czajka, get in here right now. I'm not risking this thing crapping out on us while you're out there. That's an order," she added when he hesitated.

It was a tight fit, even a tight squeeze. They managed to stuff themselves into the airlock enough so no limbs stuck out to block the door sensors, and the outer door slid slowly closed. "Czajka," Perkins grunted as his helmet pushed her head to the side at an awkward angle and one of his knees was jammed into her crotch hard enough to make her left hip hurt. "Unless you're gonna buy me dinner first-"

"Oh, sorry," he tried moving his leg but there wasn't much he could do about it. His right hand was free so he used it to activate the emergency pressurization cycle, using a bottle of stored air to rapidly flood the lock with air. In moments, the inner door's locking pins retracted. "Door's opening," he gasped as one of her elbows dug into his chest hard enough to leave a bruise. "The engineering compartment holds air," he reported, as the pressure gauge read ninety two percent of normal.

Perkins got herself untangled from the sergeant and through the inner door first. Her hopes faded as her gaze took in the main compartment's condition. Most displays were dark, with others flickering or displaying static or scrolling lines of gibberish. Without gravity, objects both broken or merely loose floated everywhere, a tool bounced off her helmet before she could see it coming. "Come on," she waved to Czajka without turning to look at him. Keeping a firm grip on handholds, she pulled herself across the compartment to where an injured Ruhar officer was loosely strapped to a table, surrounded by four cadets. As she approached, she reached up with a thumb to crack open her faceplate and swing it up, using her lips to pull the helmet microphone closer to her mouth. "Hello? I am Lieutenant Colonel Perkins of the human ExForce," she spoke slowly, carefully enunciating each word so the translator would not make unfortunate mistakes.

A female cadet who had been literally hovering over the injured officer looked up, and Perkins recognized her as Jinn Garnor, a girl Nert liked very much. "Colonel Perkins," Jinn turned toward the newcomers with an expression that was a mixture of fear and relief. The human Colonel being a senior officer might take some of the responsibility off Jinn's shoulders, but since Perkins was an alien, she was not likely to be of much use in the crisis. "Urmat Datha is badly injured," she put a hand over her mouth to contain her fear as the Urmat shuddered and blood bubbled from his lips.

"We need to move him to the medical station," Perkins did not like the paleness of the officer's lips, nor the tiny bubbles of blood exhaled from his nose with every labored breath.

"We tried, we can't," Jinn explained. "The passageways are all blocked. I- how did *you* get here?" She looked toward the big door at the far end of the compartment, which still had its locking bars engaged to hold it shut.

"We spacewalked along the hull outside."

"You did?" Jinn's eyebrows lifted, and again Perkins was struck by how some expressions were universal between species. Between bipedal species that walked upright, she reminded herself, and only those few species she had met. "That is too danger-"

"No more dangerous than being in here," Perkins ducked and pushed away a broken piece of metal and composite that had floated in front of her face. "Urmat Datha is the only survivor of the entire crew?" She knew the *Ruh Tostella* had departed Paradise with a limited number of adult crew, as senior cadets were expected to gain real shipboard experience by standing watches, performing routine maintenance and other roles that would be filled by fully-trained adult crew members. Losing the forward part of the ship had taken away the bridge and command crew with it, but how could the Urmat be the only survivor?

"We think so, yes," Jinn nodded a bit too vigorously, her fear evident. "There were seven of us on duty here, with Urmat Datha in charge. Klasta Amatu and Cadet Surtil were killed," she looked at the blackened mark on the hull. "It's just us now. None of us are trained as medics, are you?" She looked to Dave hopefully.

"Not in Ruhar physiology," Perkins frowned. "He needs the resources of a full medical station. His suit," with one gentle hand, she wiped away some of the still-wet blood on Datha's right side, and did not like what she found. A rip! A tear wide enough that the suit's nano repair mechanism was not able to close the fatal opening. "Can we patch this?"

"We used the patch kit for Cadet Surtil. That was Datha's order, but it did not save him," Jinn looked sadly to where the unlucky Surtil's body was strapped into a chair. Perkins could see at least three patches attached to that suit, she thought the patches had done their job, but Surtil had died anyway. Datha had probably thought he was being noble by telling the cadets to use the patches on a crew member more badly injured than himself, but Perkins knew that was the kind of amateur wishful thinking civilians indulged in. As the lone surviving adult officer, Datha should have known his duty was to have his own wounds tended to, so he could assist others. Now, everyone aboard the ship might all die, and there was nothing noble about that. "The nanomachines," Jinn glanced up to see if Perkins understood the translation. "They worked to repair the suit, then after we blocked the air leak, they pulled inside to stop Datha's blood loss."

"Your nano tech can work on mechanical and biological systems?" Perkins asked in surprise.

"No," Jinn reached up to wipe away the tears brimming in her eyes. "The suit can inject medical nanobots into a user, and they did, but- They needed help. The mechanical nano," the translator stumbled over the term, "as you said, it can only act to block blood vessels. It plugs leaks," she looked up at Perkins, seeking understanding.

"You did what you could. The Urmat needs skilled medical treatment. Is there another suit available?"

"No, there are no spares available now. The locker with spare suits was damaged, that is where Surtil was when he, when he was hit." Jinn closed her eyes tightly, causing droplets of tear to float away from her face. "He can, he can use my suit," she offered.

Perkins looked from Datha to the anxious cadet, judging their sizes. "I don't think he will fit."

"He can use my suit, Ma'am," Dave began to pull off his helmet.

"Forget it, Czajka. You know what it's like out there, you need to guide us back. Uh, you," she pointed to another cadet, "you look about Datha's size. Get out of-"

"You," Datha's eyes opened and he reached up to grasp her forearm, missed, and his arm bounced off the table. Gently, Perkins caught his hand and wrapped her glove around his. The Ruhar officer tried to squeeze her hand but his strength was gone. "Ship?"

"Badly damaged, the forward hull is missing," Perkins did not sugar-coat the information. "We're on backup power and that is failing. We have no shields, no propulsion, sensors are scrambled and that Bosphuraq battlecruiser could jump in on top of us at any second. Urmat Datha, you need to know right now that we believe you are the only adult crewman to survive." Perkins told the truth without sugar-coating anything. Datha was an adult, a crewman, an officer, with the rank of 'Urmat' being equivalent to a major in the US Army. The unvarnished truth is the least they owed to him.

"Everyone, else, *dead?*" His words came out in a wet whisper, bubbles of blood choking him as he spoke.

"Yes," Perkins squeezed the man's hand. The dead crewmen were his shipmates, friends, people he might have served with for years. All gone now. "There are senior cadets who could assume-"

"No," Datha declared with vehemence beyond his strength, and it threw him into a coughing fit, bubbles of blood spewing from his mouth onto the front of Perkin's suit. She did not flinch, merely held the Urmat's hand while he recovered. "You," he pointed to Perkins with an index finger, "are an officer. Senior officer. Your rank is equivalent to our 'Ormath'," he paused to take a breath. Perkins knew that was not quite true, as the rank structure of the Ruhar military was more complicated than the commissioned ranks of the US Army, but the point was not relevant to the situation. "You must take command."

"*Me?*" Perkins pointed to herself as all four Ruhar cadets sucked in sharp breaths. "Urmat Datha, I am not Ruhar. I am an alien. Surely a-"

"A senior cadet," he coughed, "is not an officer. Trainee. You," he scrunched up his eyes as a wave of pain struck him. "Have experience. *Combat* experience. You take command."

"Um," Perkins looked to Czajka, both of them stunned.

With his other hand, Datha pawed for the zPhone on his belt, Jinn pulled it out and put it into his free hand, as Perkins released the hand she had been holding. With both of his hands so shaky and weak he needed Jinn to steady the phone, he pressed buttons and a command application popped up on the screen. Datha spoke quietly into the phone. "Urmat Farpew Datha, transferring command of the warship *Ruh Tostella* to Lieutenant Colonel," he looked up to see if his pronunciation was correct, "Emily Perkins, of the human Expeditionary Force."

"Transfer of command acknowledged," a mechanical voice issued from his phone at the same time Perkins' own phone beeped and vibrated.

She looked at her phone, seeing a cascade of command authorizations scrolling past. They were all in Ruhar script, she could barely read half of the words. How the hell could she- Just then, her phone must have realized she needed to read English, for all the commands blinked and the words were then recognizable. She was in command of a Ruhar warship?! No, she was in command of a battered hulk that was leaking air and had no source of power, with a crew of frightened cadets, in deep interstellar space that was now a warzone. "I accept command," she saluted Datha, using the two-fingers-to-her-cheek gesture of the Ruhar. "Until you are able to return to duty. Sergeant Czajka, take two cadets with you and get Urmat Datha to the medical station. First priority is to restore main, or at least auxiliary power." Her fuzzy recollection of the ship's systems was that auxiliary power was a sort of fuel cell that did not have enough output to run more than basic systems. And a fuel cell needed a fuel tank. With the hull so peppered with breaches that it looked like Swiss cheese, did she dare hope a fuel tank had survived unscathed? "Cadet Garnor, who is the senior engineering cadet?"

"Sath Callon, but I have not been able to contact her. She was," Jinn's lower lip quivered. "Her duty station was in the forward section of the ship."

Perkins knew she had asked the wrong question. "Who is the senior engineering cadet right *here*, right now?"

"That is me," Jinn swallowed, her incisors sticking out over her lower lip. "*Ormath* Perkins, I am not qualified-"

"You are as qualified as anyone available. Sergeant Czajka, when you get forward, pass the word for engineering cadets to make their way aft, we need all the help here we can get."

"Ormath, I barely know-"

"*Senior* Cadet Garnor, I know nothing about these systems," she waved a hand to encompass the shattered equipment around them. "We are in interstellar space, without power, and with a Bosphuraq battlecruiser probably hunting us. If we can't restore power, we are dead, is that clear? You cadets came aboard the-" she almost referred to the ship as '*Toaster*' which now seemed inappropriate. "The *Ruh Tostella*, to gain real-life experience. Think of this," Perkins forced a smile she didn't feel, "as a problem added to a training simulation."

"A problem in a training sim, right," Jinn bit her lip as she thought. A sim. Yes, she could think of the disaster as a particularly challenging, an outrageously, ridiculously unfairly challenging test in a sim. That way, she could push the very likely possibility of impending death to the back of her mind and concentrate on the problem. "Right," she looked up at the other three cadets. "Pranz, you are with me-"

While two cadets got the now-unconscious Datha out of his useless suit, Dave pulled Perkins aside. "Ma'am, maybe you should go with the Urmat."

"No, Sergeant, I need to be here. Priority One is restoring power, or this ship is nothing but a composite tube that will be getting cold soon. If Garnor needs my command codes to reactivate a system," she waved her phone, "I need to be *here*. Right now, this is the heart of the ship, the rest of the hull is just dead weight without the reactors."

A few minutes after Dave went out through the airlock with the injured Datha and a cadet, Perkins was playing with the new command features of her zPhone, when she found a way to track the lifesigns of everyone aboard. It was also a way to compare the lifesigns against the crew roster, giving her an unwelcome confirmation of how many Ruhar were dead, including all of the adult crew other than Datha. Twenty four Ruhar cadets were also among the dead, including the senior engineering cadet. After giving her a sense of the damage that made her feel sick, the list then made her heart soar. Irene and Derek's lifesigns were strong! And Nert! The young hamster was doing well except for an elevated heartrate, which was expected under the circumstances. She clicked on the icon for Captain Striebich, and a comm channel opened. "Captain Striebich?"

"Colonel Perkins! Ohhhhh, it is good to hear from you, Ma'am!" Irene's voice trembled with relief. "We are in the auxiliary control center, we're kind of trapped here."

"The Ruhar can't get you out?"

"We're alone, Ma'am. There's vacuum outside the hatch, I think we have a slow leak in here somewhere, my ears have been popping and it's getting harder to breathe. We have flightsuits and helmets, so we can go on internal oxygen when we have to."

"You and Bonsu are alone? Then," she thought back. The nose of the *Toaster* had been blown away several minutes before the ship jumped away from the battlespace. "Who jumped the ship?"

"Uh, that was us, Ma'am. We did the best we could, I don't think we had a choice at the time. We were tracking two missiles running straight at us, our shields were knocked back and the proximity sensors could barely see anything."

"When did the two of you get trained on jump procedures?"

"We, uh, kinda didn't," Perkins heard Derek join the conversation, and Irene put her phone on speaker. "We had to wing it based on training briefs we studied. Ma'am, it was either risk the jump drive blowing up in our faces, or let those missiles kill us for certain. I figured, if the drive coils blew, that would at least confuse enemy sensors for a while, maybe help the star carrier get away."

"That was a ballsy call, you two. A good call."

"Colonel? The rest of the team?" Irene asked anxiously.

"They're all fine. And Nert, he's fine, too. The Ruhar crew, ah, they're not so good. The entire crew is dead, except for one badly wounded engineering officer."

"*All* of the crew?" Derek's tone was shocked. "Oh shit. The cadets are in charge now?"

"No, Bonsu, *I* am."

"Um, sorry, Ma'am, what did you say?"

"The injured officer transferred command authority to me."

"They can do that? We're *aliens* to them," Derek mused aloud.

"Apparently they can," Perkins said without humor. "Right now I've got cadets trying to get the reactor restarted, that tells you our situation. We're dead in the water, and that Bosphuraq battlecruiser might jump our asses before we know it."

"Ma'am? I don't think that's very likely," Irene stated hopefully. "We made a bad jump, really dirty because we caught the edge of the damping field, so the resonance of our jump field must have been really chaotic. And the battlespace was full of high-energy particles and spatial distortion. I don't think that enemy ship could track our jump endpoint, not easily."

"Christ, Striebich, that's the first good news I've heard all day! We may be safe because we screwed up the jump?"

"Colonel, right now, even we have no idea where we jumped to," Derek admitted. "Until we get the nav system back online, we're blind. Although," the wheels in his head began spinning with an idea, "we could launch a dropship, if any of them are still spaceworthy. Their nav gear will fix our position for us."

"A dropship's sensors can establish our position with enough accuracy for us to program a jump?" Perkins asked hopefully, before realizing she had gotten ahead of herself. "Oh, forget it, we can't jump anyway without the reactors."

"That's not true, Ma'am," Irene reported, cringing as she looked at Derek who was worried she had gotten their CO's hopes up for nothing. "The reactors provide juice to the jump drive capacitors, but our capacitor banks still have a seventy two percent charge. We're good for another jump. Except we don't know where we are. And the drive control system is offline."

"*And*, we have no idea how to program a jump," Derek added helpfully. "Sorry, Ma'am."

"That's all right, Bonsu, I sure as hell don't need people trying to put a good spin on things for me. The two of you will be all right in there for a while?"

"Affirmative," Irene replied with her voice sounding distinctly unhappy. "We're sure you have other priorities."

"You got that right. I'll see if a cadet crew can get you out of there, but we need pilots anyway, and that aux station is the only place the ship can be flown from?"

"It is," Irene agreed.

"Then sit tight. Ah, Striebich, Bonsu? I can't tell you how good it is to hear you're both still with us."

Perkins had no sooner ended the call when Dave pinged her. "Colonel? We have a problem. I think Datha is dead. He's not responding at all now, and the pulse indicator on his wristpad is reading zero. It could be a glitch, but I shined a light in his faceplate and it looks like he's not breathing."

"Shit." She clicked the icon for Datha on her phone, and it showed his lifesigns had ceased. "Where are you?"

"Still outside the ship, about halfway. We had to take a different route, looks like a power relay under the hull blew after you and I went past, it's arcing real bad."

Perkins paused to think, though Cadet Garnor was waving for her attention. "Czajka, keep going. Datha may still be alive and we've got to try to save him. Ruhar can go longer without oxygen than we can. And we need you to round up engineering cadets to send back here. Oh, also," she tried to snap her fingers but the suit gloves muffled the sound. "See if you can find a route back here that stays inside the ship. There must be some passageways that aren't blocked."

"Obstructions aren't the only problem, Ma'am. A lot of the interior is exposed to vacuum, or there's power relays blowing."

"Yeah, yeah. We'll need to get a crew working on disconnecting relays and plugging holes. I'll have Jarrett and Colter organize something." Damn it! What else did she need to think about, before a disaster overwhelmed them? She turned her focus back to the immediate engineering problem. "Garnor, what is it?"

Urmat Datha indeed had died while being transported to the medical station, which anyway had no qualified doctor to assist the many wounded, and the medical bot was operating on reduced capacity. Irene and Derek had been strapped into pilot couches, and the other Mavericks had dutifully secured themselves into their beds when the maneuvering alarm sounded. The cadets did not have the luxury of strapping in and waiting, most of them had designated action stations, so many had been moving through the ship when it got hit. A dozen young people had been killed or severely injured when the ship lost its nose, because they hadn't yet reached their action stations; others were lost when masers or railguns or missiles tore open their section of the ship. Emily Perkins considered it ironic that the uselessness of humans aboard an alien ship is what had saved their lives.

She also considered that a training ship full of teenage cadets had no business being dragged into action with a real battlegroup. If it had been her decision, she would have jumped the star carrier to a safe location and dropped off the *Ruh Tostella*, before taking the battlegroup into harm's way. As it had not been her decision, she needed to focus on what she could affect, right then. Jinn Garnor was overwhelmed with the task of first stabilizing backup power, then trying to determine if it was safe to restart the reactor. She begged Perkins for more cadets who specialized in engineering field, particularly power generation systems.

It was time for Perkins to speak to the cadets, to speak to the *crew*, she reminded herself, for cadets were the only crew the ship had. How to do that? She fumbled with her phone, not wanting to distract Jinn from her work, and not wanting to show how unfamiliar she was with basic ship systems.

Ok, there it is, she found after four minutes of almost random clicking around the screens. The entire communications system was not offline due to lack of power, it had been simply been disabled and needed to be rebooted. Her command codes allowed Perkins to call individual people, but otherwise comms were squelched. That was, she vaguely recalled, standard procedure in combat when a ship's stealth field was inactive. Internal comms posed a risk of electromagnetic radiation leaking beyond the ship and betraying it to enemy sensors. That procedure was great in most conditions, but while outside the ship, Perkins had seen so many power conduits arcing that the ship was lit up like a Christmas tree. She found the codes to re-enable the shipwide comm system, took a breath, and spoke to the crew. Her crew.

"Attention, all hands, this is Lieutenant Colonel Perkins-"

CHAPTER THIRTEEN

"-that is all," said the voice of the alien, and Bifft stared in utter astonishment at the speaker in the wall panel. The alien had spoken in heavily-accented Ruhar, but instead of appreciating the endless hours of effort she had devoted to mastering a completely foreign language, Bifft was insulted by how her primitive tongue butchered the words.

"An *alien*? In command of our ship?" Bifft raged, spitting in his fury. Perkins was not only an alien, she was from a backward species that barely had spaceflight when the Ruhar arrived at their disgusting planet. A species that had come to Gehtanu as an enemy occupation force, and only recently had renounced their allegiance to the Kristang coalition. As natural-born cowards, the humans would switch sides again as soon as it was convenient, Bifft declared. This Perkins woman had only been aboard the *Ruh Tostella* for a month, how could she possibly be so insufferably arrogant to think she was qualified to command a Ruhar cruiser? A ship where every piece of technology was far beyond her understanding?

Bifft raged and railed against the injustice, to the point of battering an innocent wall panel with a wrench. The action only caused a scratch on the panel and sent Bifft spinning off across the compartment out of control in the zero gravity, injuring his dignity. His companions did their best to quell their leader's spiteful temper. They assured him that Urmat Datha must not have known Bifft was alive when command was transferred to the alien. Or, the alien had somehow coerced Datha, it was well known the humans were desperate for recognition, desperate for any opportunity to show they could be equal to the clearly-superior Ruhar. Bifft should be in command, only he could save them. Was that not why Bifft already commanded the cadet corps aboard the ship?

After soaking up enough praise to soothe his outraged ego, Bifft made an angry cutting motion with one hand, to end the babbling of his underlings. "Datha was injured and not competent to transfer command. He was a good man, a good officer, but he had no authority to give this *warship*," he emphasized that word, "to an alien. A first-year cadet," he thought of the traitorous Nert, "knows more about this ship than the human Perkins does. Do you know she was a staff assistant, not a line officer?" His friends nodded vigorous agreement, pleased that Bifft was back to his old self. "This ship is disabled, in deep space, on our own. Life support is failing, the reactors are offline. Backup power will be strained by providing life support to the aliens," he fairly spat in disgust. "In desperate times, hard decisions must be made. That is the nature of leadership." His followers gazed at him with rapt attention, knowing Bifft was the person they needed to make the tough decisions, the unpleasant decisions, the *necessary* decisions. The decisions that had to be made, soon, or they would all die.

"Datha was not competent when he acted, and he was never authorized to appoint Perkins to command, so his action is invalid," Bifft declared, and his followers looked at each other and nodded with grim expressions. "We need to act, or the ship is doomed. We need to act *now*. It is our duty." Bifft picked up the wrench again, tapping the head forcefully into a palm. "Who is with me?"

With the help of cadets who knew the ship much better than he did, Dave found a way to the engineering compartment using passageways inside the ship. Where the way was not clear, the cadets sliced away obstructions with plasma torches, cut power to relays that were sparking and restored emergency power to stuck bulkhead doors. Shortly after testing that the way was indeed as safe as it could be made, Dave led a group of engineering cadets back to speak with Jinn Garnor, and most of them went back up the passageway with Dave, to begin making repairs as directed by Jinn, with a few cadets remaining to work on the puzzling task of determining if it was safe to restart a reactor. Perkins visibly relaxed, or at least visibly was no longer feeling the weight of an entire planet on her shoulders.

Another group of cadets came to get instructions, accompanied by the other Verd-Kris aboard, a male with the rank of 'Surgun' named Krok-aus-tal Jates. He was older than Dave and naturally assumed authority, although he deferred to Perkins without apparent resentment. The Mavericks had trained with Jates only three times, as he was already fully qualified for spaceborne duty, and his role aboard the ship was to train Ruhar cadets in real-life space infantry tactics, whether they liked it or not. When the cadets were leaving to go perform whatever critical tasks were needed elsewhere in the ship, Jates lingered behind.

Perkins was huddled with Jinn Garnor, providing moral support and encouragement since she had no idea how most systems aboard the ship worked, when with the corner of her eye she saw more cadets come floating in through the open hatch. She ignored them until she could not.

"Nobody move!" The shout rang out in the compartment.

Perkins spun to see who had spoken, her mind flashing to scenarios of someone warning of a dangerous condition with a power relay or some other technical problem. She was astonished to see a group of three Ruhar cadets pointing weapons at her. Bifft held a rifle and his two friends had sidearms. The ranking cadet made a show of holding the rifle in dramatic fashion at his hip, keeping the muzzle trained on Perkins. "I said, *nobody move*! That means all of you," he glared angrily around the compartment, sounding like a bank robber in an old movie.

"Everyone, stay where you are," Perkins ordered. "Cadet Colhsoon, what do you think you are doing?"

"I don't have to think anything, I am taking control of this ship back from you. I am assuming command, effective immediately. No *alien* should be in command of our warships." He shot a look of hatred at Jates, who had made a fool of Bifft during several training exercises. "No alien should be aboard one of our ships, unless they are in the brig."

Perkins took a breath to keep the fear from her voice. It didn't work. "Where did you get those weapons? The armory is locked down!" It was locked down, she knew that for certain because her initial tour of the ship had included the armory, or technically the heavy door of the armory. Even the executive officer giving her the tour did not have authorization to open the armory door. Perkins had been surprised by that bit of information, she was even more surprised to learn the *Toaster* had an armory. Why did a training ship need live weapons, she had asked. The XO had explained the armory was left over from when the cruiser was a front-line warship, and it had been kept in case the *Ruh Tostella* needed to quickly be returned to fleet service.

"It *was* locked," Bifft replied with a smirk. "You are as ignorant as you are stupid and primitive. This is *our* ship, we know how to bypass security measures," he winked at his friends, who grinned back, pleased at his cleverness.

"That would take an impressive level of skill," Jates said in an admiring tone, while with his eyes he gave Perkins a look she could not interpret. Was the Kristang going to join the mutiny, to save himself and Tutula? Or, was something else going on? "Let me guess, you cut through the power circuits behind the bulkhead to the armory?"

"Good guess, *Surgun* Jates," Bifft replied with a frown, unhappy about a member of an enemy species knowing such dangerous secrets about a Ruhar warship, even a ship as obsolete as the *Ruh Tostella*. "I suggest you forget such knowledge."

"What next?" Perkins had used the time to regain her courage. She was determined to defy the little shit cadet, and not let him see her sweat. "You kill us, throw us out an airlock?"

"No, although as you are an enemy species, and you unlawfully took control of a warship, I would be within my rights under combat conditions to kill all of you," Bifft bluffed, knowing that was a lie.

"We're not in combat now!" Dave pushed himself forward and Perkins restrained him with one hand.

"Do not be afraid, little fool. I don't plan to kill you, not directly. We will put your kind and the two Kristang into a dropship with its flight controls disabled. You will float away," the cadet leader made a mocking gesture miming an object spinning slowly through space. "Once you are beyond communications range, the ship will deactivate your command authority," he glared at Perkins. "Command will then fall to the next senior officer," he gloated, pointing to his chest.

"That is an interesting plan, a good plan," Jates said.

"Thank-" Bifft reacted to the praise before he could remind himself that he didn't care what an enemy species thought of him.

"Too bad," Jates made a honking sound and sent a thick wad of spit spinning through the air toward the three armed cadets. "You won't ever get to put your plan into action, you dumb little shit."

"What?" Bifft's aim wavered as he flailed his legs awkwardly to avoid being splattered with the disgusting projectile. Held steady by his two friends, he regained his composure and pointed the rifle at the Verd-Kris. "I could shoot you!"

"Ha! I've seen you with a rifle, Biffty-boy. Safest place for me if you're shooting is right where I am, because you'll never hit me from there."

"I-" The senior cadet's finger was flexing on the trigger and Perkins reached out to restrain Jates, but the Verd-Kris warrior was not to be interfered with.

"What? Did I hurt your wittle *feelings*?" Jates sneered. "You want to run to your momma because I said mean things to you? Would wittle Biffty-boy like his mommy to pat his furry wittle head and make the bad words stop?"

"I swear I will shoot you right here!"

One of Bifft's friends tried to whisper something in the agitated cadet's ear, but he was not listening. "You stay back! I'm warning you!" He shouted at Jates, gesturing with the rifle that was now properly held to his shoulder, his bravado gone.

"Boy," Jates said in a low, calm voice as he drifted toward the three mutinous cadets. "You either give that rifle to someone who knows how to use it, or you pull that trigger. We all know you don't have the guts to shoot me, so stop making a fool out of yourself and surrender that weapon."

"I'll do it! I swear I'll do it! He's coming at me," Bifft's head swiveled to his friends for support. "You saw this! I have no choice!"

"Bifft, he's just-" One of his friends pleaded.

"You asked for this!" Bifft bellowed as Jates drew within arm's length of the muzzle. "This is your fault!" He squeezed the trigger gently as he had been taught, though his eyes partly closed which was *not* proper procedure.

Nothing happened. Frantically, Bifft swam backwards in the air, one eye on the oncoming Jates and the other checking the rifle's safety and power meters. They were both set correctly, so why was the rifle not firing? Were the maser exciters burned out? With one finger, he switched to flechette rounds even though he knew using that ammunition could cause carnage in the compartment.

Nothing happened.

Jates reached out with lightning-fast speed and snatched the rifle from Bifft's hands, breaking two of the cadet's fingers as the bigger and stronger Verd-Kris yanked it away. The two other cadets shot at Jates but they, too, had no results as their sidearms refused to fire. Almost casually, Jates spun the rifle around in his hands and bashed Bifft in the face with the butt, sending the senior cadet spinning off toward the still-open main door with blood spraying from his broken nose. Flipping the rifle around and setting it against his shoulder, Jates faced the two other would-be mutineers. "Are you two going to be smart and hand over those pistols, or will you give me the pleasure of bashing your stupid heads together?"

The Ruhar looked at each other in brief moment of a panic before swallowing hard and meekly handing their pistols to the hulking Verd-Kris, who tucked them into the tool belt of his spacesuit.

Emily Perkins felt she could dare breathe again, after a shameful moment of not knowing what to do. Surgun Jates had years of experience dealing with and training Ruhar cadets, so she had let him take the lead, but if he had been killed, she knew it would be her fault. "*Surgun* Jates," she emphasized his rank, "that was a terrible risk. Do not do anything like that again," she scolded while suppressing a shudder of relief.

"I was in no danger," Jates slung the rifle over one shoulder and waved for Bifft's friends to attend to the cadet who had tried to forcefully take over the ship. "These weapons will not fire."

"I saw that," Perkins admitted. "How did you know that? Have all the weapons in the armory been disabled?"

"No, just these, and any others this amateur gang of morons stole from the armory. All weapons inside the armory should be fully active."

"How *did* you know about that?" Dave whispered in amazement. "If these Ruhar cadets didn't know, how-"

Jates tilted his head in a gesture like a shrug. "The officers of the Ruhar fleet are not concerned about their own cadets attempting to seize control. Not so with aliens such as we Verd-Kris, we are still not fully trusted. During our initial orientation tour of this ship, the officer guiding us made a point of telling *us* not to ever think about breaking into the armory, because any attempt to breach security there would render those weapons useless. Any weapon removed from the armory without proper authorization is automatically disabled by the weapon itself sending a power surge to fry its control chip. That is why *I* carry this," Jates flipped the rifle over, opened a port with one finger, and extracted a copper-colored flat square. He tossed it to go drifting away, pulled an identical unit from a pocket, and inserted it in the rifle. "*This* fire control unit is active," the lizard announced with a grin that stretched his lips in an expression more terrifying than reassuring. Sighting on a broken piece of equipment lazily floating near the far bulkhead, he fiddled with the selector and squeezed the trigger. A maser beam blasted the target, sending hot droplets of metal to splatter the bulkhead and making everyone in the compartment duck and cover their faces. "The next time a Ruhar cadet tells you how their species is so smart, remember this."

Dave and Perkins exchanged a silent 'oh *shit*' look. A Kristang held the only active weapon aboard the ship. Was he now going to seize control of the *Ruh Tostella*? Kill the humans and Ruhar, or simply throw them in the brig, and try to signal a Kristang warship? If a Verd-Kris warrior wanted to join the Kristang warrior caste, bringing them a Ruhar warship full of cadet hostages might be a good way to prove his worth. Perkins saw Dave tense to launch himself at Jates and her heart froze in fear for her young sergeant-

"Here," Jates flipped the rifle around and handed it to Dave. "You should hold this."

Dave was so shocked, he did not at first reach out for the rifle, believing it had to be a trick. When his hands wrapped around the rifle and Jates released it, Dave pulled it close to his chest, pointed it between his feet, and safed it. "You sure about this?" Dave asked before he could stop his stupid mouth.

"The cadets would never accept me as commander, there is too much hate and distrust between our peoples," Jates explained sadly. "The Ruhar consider the Verd-Kris, like you humans, as pets," he jerked his head toward Bifft, "who are indulged too much by our masters. Colonel Perkins, if we have any chance to survive this disaster, we need you to lead us." Jates gave her a proper US military salute.

Emily Perkins' internal reaction was to resent the pressure put on her. She wanted someone else to be responsible for a change, dammit. If the Fates were determined to torment her, why couldn't they give her an easy challenge once in a while? She returned the salute. "Surgun Jates, do you have any more of those magical control chips?"

"Only one more, and it was in part of the ship that sustained significant battle damage."

"So," she pointed to the rifle Dave carried, "that's the only active weapon aboard the ship."

"Yes."

"That I know of," Perkins tilted her head.

"We must trust each other," Jates replied with an unreadable expression.

The alien was right, she knew. "Sergeant Czajka, you and Jates escort the mutineers to the brig."

Dave made a show of flicking off the safety of his rifle. "Ma'am, there are probably other cadets involved in the mutiny, what about them?"

"Unless we know specifically who was involved, they are all innocent until proven guilty. We need everyone we can get to repair the ship, I would like to consider this, this *incident* closed for now. The Ruhar authorities can deal with the legal matters when we contact the fleet."

By his expression, Dave did not like that idea. "Yes, Ma'am." If anyone even looked at him funny, Dave intended to throw them in the brig and ask questions later. No way was he going to take any shit from punk hamster kids.

Perkins turned her attention to the Kristang, or, she corrected herself, Verd-Kris. "Surgun Jates?"

"Yes, Colonel?"

"Make sure these cadets don't know any tricks about breaking out of the brig."

That drew a smile from the Verd-Kris, an expression that was not quite revolting. "Yes, Colonel."

After Dave departed with Bifft and his crew, Perkins floated over to Jinn's workstation. "Do you have an initial assessment?"

"N-no," the Ruhar girl stammered, her hands shaking. She wasn't ready for the crushing responsibility, she knew it, and she also could not just walk away. The entire crew was counting on *her*. "Colonel, even if the reactors can be restarted, I don't dare feed energy into the ship. There are too many power conduits with open circuits, and other systems that might blow if unregulated power is fed into them. We, we need to get the entire ship forward of Frame Sixty Seven," she pointed to the thick bulkhead to the aft, which protected delicate biological systems from the radiation of the reactors and jump drive, "isolated. I don't have enough people to do that. Enough people who know how to do that! I can't be here, and also manage the work teams."

"Understood. Garnor, take a deep breath," Perkins put a hand on the cadet's shoulder. "You can do this?"

"How?" Jinn waved her fingers at the console in front of her, densely cluttered with confusing data, all of which needed her focused attention. "It is impossible!"

"Don't tell me about impossible, cadet," Perkins kept her tone soft and reassuring. "My team destroyed a Kristang battlegroup, using ancient maser cannons that no one knew even existed. Later, we were trapped on an island with an enemy commando squad and no weapons, and we found a way to kill every one of those murderous lizards."

"Yes, Ma'am," Jinn replied with a faint smile. The fact that she could smile at all was a good sign.

"You keep working here, I'll find a way to get those work teams organized."

"Respectfully, Colonel, you don't know this ship's systems."

"Correct. But I know someone who does."

On the way to patching another leak in the hull, Nert stopped by the brig. His helmet was off, attached to his belt with a strap, but clearly he had been wearing the helmet for an extended period while working hard, for the fur on his head was plastered down with dried sweat and the helmet liner had created a crease across his forehead. "Hello, Miss Shauna," he greeted the human with weary good cheer. While Nert, Dave and Jesse usually used nicknames for each other, the two soldiers had not thought up an acceptable nickname for Shauna. Jesse's attempt to call her 'Nuke', merely because her actions had erased an entire island from the surface of Paradise, had not gone well. "How are you?"

Before Shauna could answer, Bifft elbowed one of his fellow mutineers to get attention while he insulted the young cadet. "Oh, Nert, did you come here to make sure your pet isn't lonely?"

"You be quiet, Bifft," Nert jabbed a finger at the senior cadet, his expression filled with anger and disgust. "The ship is in crisis, we need everyone working on damage control, and you," he shook a fist while trying to think what to say. "You are useless as a knitted condom!"

"Nerty!" Shauna couldn't help laughing. "Is that something you learned from the Third Infantry?"

"No," he looked puzzled. "I heard Cornpone saying it to Ski. Did I not use that expression correctly? It is a very colorful phrase."

"It is very colorful, yes," she covered her mouth with a hand so the cadets in the brig would not see she could not stop laughing. "It is also true," she scowled at Bifft, and with that, the humor was gone. "How are you?"

Nert pointed to the patch kit strapped to his waist. "I fear there are more holes in the hull than we have patches to fix. My team leader thinks we must do what we can by starting near the engineering control center and working our way forward."

"That is stupid!" Bifft protested. "You should first conduct a survey of the ship, and *then* prioritize critical sections. If we don't secure the life support systems before they sustain more damage, we will all die out here soon!"

"You had a chance to help, Bifft," Nert waved a hand at the disgraced senior cadet with a dismissive gesture, something that would have astonished Nert mere hours ago. The attempted mutiny had made Bifft's status fall so far, Nert no longer cared what his former cadet leader thought about anything. "Now, the best thing *you* can do to help is stop breathing, to conserve oxygen for people working to fix the ship. Miss Shauna, I must go now, I will be back, when I can."

"You don't worry about me, Nerty, I'll be fine," Shauna wanted to be doing something more valuable than babysitting cadets who were securely locked behind bars, but she understood humans were pretty much just in the way for the task of repairing the sophisticated alien starship. Still, Irene and Derek were practicing to fly and jump the ship if main power could be restored, while Jesse and Dave were part of a work crew patching holes in the hull. Humans did not need to understand hyperspatial navigation to slap patches on holes in the inner hull, and Shauna was itching to get away from the brig, soon.

Shortly after Nert left, Perkins pulled herself into the chamber that led to the ship's brig. That compartment was larger than she expected aboard a training cruiser, but then it was likely left over from the *Toaster*'s service as a line ship. Bifft and his two friends were floating in the center of the compartment. They were upside down from her normal perspective, Perkins thought the brats had done that deliberately to upset their single guard. "Jarrett," she nodded.

"Ma'am," Shauna patted the heavy wrench sitting in her lap. "Don't you worry, these jokers aren't going anywhere."

"Colonel Perkins," Bifft mispronounced her name as Per-KINS because he knew that would annoy the human officer. "I have rights as a prisoner," he ran a finger over the dried blood on his face where Jates had bashed him with the rifle, and waggled his broken fingers. "You must offer proper medical attention to injured prisoners. I demand that you-"

"You *demand* nothing, you punk-ass little shit," Perkins was too tired to add the proper vehemence to her tone. "You are not a prisoner, you are guilty of a mutiny. I checked Ruhar Fleet regulations and they are *very* clear. Anyone attempting a mutiny when a ship is in combat conditions, only has a right to piss in their pants before they get thrown out an airlock. Your fleet, your people, are at war, *cadet*. They don't screw around, I admire that about your people."

"You are an alien, you have no right to-"

"I am the commanding officer of this ship," Perkins waved her zPhone so Bifft could see the full set of command codes.

"You are not going to kill us," Bifft was regaining his arrogance. He reasoned if the human had the determination to throw him out an airlock, she would have done that already before she lost her nerve. "My family is powerful, you do not dare touch me."

"Ma'am, please, give me two minutes with that asshole," Shauna thumped the wrench into the bulkhead behind her. "His face is beat up already, no one will know."

"Don't waste the energy, Jarrett," Perkins frowned.

"Have you come here to gloat, Miss Perkins?" Bifft asked in a taunting tone he used for his friends, but the fear in his eyes revealed his true emotions.

"No, I'm here to put your furry asses to work," Perkins explained simply.

That remark was completely unexpected, Bifft could not respond until one of his friends nudged him. He tapped his earpiece. "I do not think that translated properly?"

"You heard me right. Work. If we're going to survive, we need to fix the ship, and I need all hands on deck for that. I can't have three able-bodied people wasting time in the brig just because one of you is stupid." She locked eyes with Bifft.

"We should put our trust in you?" Bifft asked in a mocking tone.

"You should put your trust in Urmat Datha. *He* chose to put me in command."

Seeing a chance for redemption and to regain his personal status, Bifft folded his arms defiantly. "Why should we help?"

"First, because if you don't, everyone aboard this ship might die, including you three knuckleheads. Second, because no matter how powerful your parents are, the only thing your Fleet Command hates more than a mutiny, is a *failed* mutiny. The rest of you," she directed her gaze at Bifft's companions, "might be able to claim you were misled by your cadet leader. But not if you refuse to assist in repairing the ship." Perkins could see the comment had struck home by the awkward movements of the other cadets, and by the guilty looks they gave to their leader. The cadets may have followed Bifft when they thought they could take the ship, but neither of them wanted to face punishment now that the mutiny had failed. "Cadet Colhsoon, I need someone to prioritize assignments and organize work parties."

That surprised Bifft more than anything else Perkins had said. "You want me to lead the repair effort?"

"No, I need you to direct and coordinate the cadet teams that will be doing the work. Cadet Garnor has an engineering team working on overall plans to get the reactors restarted, but there is a lot of other work she needs done, and I can't take people with an engineering specialty away from their tasks. You are the cadet leader, I need you to *lead*."

Bifft knew the human was flattering him. At that moment, he did not care. She was offering him a way out of the deeply humiliating mess he had gotten himself into. Bifft had not been able to admit it to his friends, but when the brig door had closed with a solid clanging sound of doom, he had almost broken down and cried from fear and embarrassment. He shuddered with relief, a tremble he could not hide from his friends. "Should we shake hands, I believe that is the human custom?" Bifft held a hand through the bars.

"Cadet," Perkins tilted her head and pursed her lips in displeasure. "I am not making a deal with you, I am *giving you an order* as your commanding officer. You only have to obey."

Bifft stiffened, and his friends tensed for his reaction. What he did was unexpected. He pressed two fingers to his cheek in the Ruhar form of salute. "Understood and agreed, Colonel."

"Excellent. Surgun Jates," as she spoke the Verd-Kris came through the doorway, "will come with you to assist."

Bifft blanched at seeing the Verd-Kris, and he subconsciously wrapped his injured fingers with his other hand. "We have to trust each other, but you send this, person," he chose his words carefully, "to spy on me!"

"I am not a spy, and I am not worried about you taking over the ship," Jates glared through the bars. "You have already proven to be totally incompetent at that. We will see whether you are competent to do *anything* aboard this ship."

Bifft knew he was not going to win the argument about Jates following him around the ship. "If you are not watching me, what will you be doing?"

"My task is, think of it as providing motivation."

"Motivation, how?" Bifft asked, his eyes flicking between the menacing Kristang and his friends who were clearly going to be no help at all.

Jates pointed at the senior cadet. "Ass," then he pointed at his feet, "meet boot. Any questions?"

Given a reprieve from death or at least a long prison sentence, Bifft threw himself into his assigned task with feverish energy. Perkins had to admit the cadet leader had excellent organizational skills and a natural charisma that made people want to follow him, finding herself forced to admire the job he was doing. He got Jinn's list of tasks prioritized not only by level of potential danger to the ship, but also took into account which tasks could be combined, to minimize the time required and risk to the teams working in hazardous conditions. Soon, the repair teams began to fix things faster than they could break, and Jinn Garnor had time to think beyond the immediate crisis. When Bifft, escorted by Jates, came to report progress to Perkins, Jinn decided it was time to deliver the bad news. "We can get one reactor restarted," she told Perkins with a raised eyebrow, implying she was not entirely sure of her facts. "The other reactor is too damaged to attempt a restart."

"All right, all right, that's good, then," Perkins stifled a yawn. Damn she was tired, and there was no prospect of her getting sleep anytime soon. "The ship can run on one reactor?"

"It can, but that is not the problem. The containment shielding around the good reactor is damaged, we don't have enough replacement components, and we can't take shielding from the other reactor, because damage to the second reactor is even more extensive."

"The reactor will leak radiation?"

"Worse, it will leak plasma. Once plasma gets past containment, it will burn through the outer shielding, and then," Jinn made an exaggerated shrug. "We lose the reactor, all systems near the reactor, and probably the ship."

"Is there anything you can do to compensate?"

"Yes. We can run the reactor at very low power, and periodically vent plasma to reduce the stress on the containment system. Colonel, there is only so much we can do to keep the containment from failing. My best guess is, once the reactor is restarted, we will only have ten days before it must be shut down, permanently."

"Ten days?" Bifft squeaked with dismay. "We can't go anywhere in ten days!"

"The reactor isn't the only problem," Jinn ran a hand through her hair in a very human-like gesture, sweeping bangs out of her eyes. "It isn't even the most important problem. The battlegroup's action was not planned, so the fleet does not know where we were when the Bosphuraq attacked. The fleet won't know we are missing for another two weeks, and a search could take months. Or more."

"That assumes the fleet will conduct a search and rescue operation," Perkins mused, instantly regretting she had spoken aloud.

"The fleet will search for us!" Bifft declared indignantly. "My mother-"

"The Bosphuraq may have launched a large-scale attack into Ruhar territory," Perkins explained, "the fleet may not have the resources for a search operation. Especially if they don't know there are any ships left to search for."

"Oh," Bifft stared at his feet, chastened. Even his parents could not simply order a warship to search for their son, if the fleet was hard-pressed responding to an incursion by the Bosphuraq.

"However we're getting out of this, we need to plan to do it on our own," Perkins looked to Jinn. "What are our options?"

"That is the problem, Colonel. I do not see that we have any options. We have enough charge in the capacitors for several jumps, and at low power, the reactor could slowly recharge the capacitors for perhaps another two jumps, before I have to shut down the reactor. You must understand, this ship is not capable of traveling to a star system with a habitable world from here. Even if all systems were operating perfectly, it is unlikely we could perform a flight between star systems before some critical component wore out. Our ships are not usually capable of interstellar flight, which is why we rely on Jeraptha star carriers."

"I did know that," Perkins replied with a measure of irritation. "We are not capable of jumping to anywhere with a habitable world, or a data relay we could use to send a signal, or a fleet refueling station, anything like that?" On the panel in front of her, she scrolled through a star map of the area within two lightyears of what Captain Striebich had said was their present position. It sure did look empty. A whole lot of nothing. Two point two lightyears away was a brown dwarf star, without a symbol indicating any species in the Rindhalu coalition had a facility there, not even an automated monitoring station. "The fleet doesn't know where we are, because the battlegroup altered course when we found the debris from that civilian ship. Is there a way to see," she fiddled with the controls then gave up, "the original flightpath plan of the star carrier, before it altered course?"

"Because that original flightpath is where the fleet would be searching for us? Yes, it's here," Jinn reached over and adjusted the controls, zooming out. "At closest approach, the planned flightpath was," she squinted at the display, "about sixteen lightyears from here."

"Hell, that's no good," Perkins said sourly, "no way can we jump that far. Our jump drive isn't capable of getting us anywhere useful from here," she did not consider that she might have just insulted the Ruhar by disparaging their jump drive technology. Perkins wound a strand of hair around one finger, a nervous habit that seemed to fascinate the Ruhar. She pulled her hand away and bit down on a thumbnail while she thought. "We don't," she said softly, speaking to herself, "we don't know that star carrier was destroyed, do we?"

"We saw it blow up!" Bifft scoffed.

"No," it was Jinn's turn to look thoughtful. "We saw it get *hit*, just before we jumped away. We didn't see," her voice trailed off as she accessed controls on her workstation, recalling sensor data of the final seconds before the *Ruh Tostella* jumped away. The audience watched anxiously as the Jeraptha ship got battered, then the image cut off as their own ship jumped.

"Run that back," Perkins ordered, then, "there's too much interference. Can you clean up the image?"

"There was a lot of energy saturating the battlespace back then," Jinn warned as she manipulated the sensor feed. "Our ability to separate signal from noise is limited."

"There," Perkins jabbed a finger at the display excitedly. "Pause it there, no, back, there. What am I seeing? That looks like the star carrier took a direct hit amidships."

Jinn examined the fuzzy data from several different sensor feeds, running the images through filters then giving up as the data could not be cleaned up any further. "You are right, a missile struck the star carrier's spine just before we jumped."

"So," Perkins noted with a tiny flare of hope, "we don't *know* that ship was destroyed."

"That is crazy," Bifft threw up his hands. "We can't rely on wishful thinking!"

Perkins ignored the cadet leader. "What is this?" She asked about a glow in the image, off to the top.

"It is," Jinn pulled back. "Mmm, it appears the destroyer *City of Sandeppe* jumped away less than a second before we did. Ohhhh," she groaned with dismay. "No. It attempted to jump away. Look at how the event horizon of their jump wormhole is distorted. They were too far inside the damping field." She looked up to meet Perkins' eyes. "It is unlikely the *Sandeppe* survived the jump attempt."

"I'm sorry to hear that," Perkins knew her words sounded flat, when she was talking about the deaths of almost a hundred Ruhar. What could she say? The entire battlegroup was probably dead also, along with the crew of their Jeraptha mothership.

"That, could actually be good for us," Jinn's comment surprised Perkins, and the Ruhar cadet saw that so she explained. "The collapse of the *Sandeppe*'s event horizon could have created a local spatial distortion, preventing the Bosphuraq ship from jumping to pursue us."

"But that battlecruiser could have jumped eventually?" Perkins guessed.

"Yes," Jinn scrunched up her face to recall the intricacies of jump physics, which was not specifically part of her studies. "The Bospuraq would have to fly a considerable distance through normal space, to get clear of the distortion, before they could jump."

"Like, how far? Could that battlecruiser still be there?"

"No, no, they would not need to fly *that* far before jumping. That ship's rate of acceleration is impressive," Jinn knew that because she had taken a minute to study up about their opponent after the battle.

"Outstanding," Perkins muttered to herself. "Then there is no reason to think the Bospuraq are still hanging around the battlespace."

Bifft did not like the sound of that, his ears stood up in alarm. "You cannot be suggesting we jump back into the area?"

"Cadet Colhsoon, I am not *suggesting* anything. I am considering our options and I might *order* a jump back into the battlespace." Her tone made it clear she was not seeking input from a former and failed mutineer.

Jinn nodded, ignoring Bifft. A day before, she would never have done that. "You are hoping some of our ships might have survived?"

Perkins nodded curtly. "It's our best bet that I can see. The Bosphuraq know our ships can't travel between stars," she missed the fact that she had referred to Ruhar warships as 'our' rather than 'your'. "Once they snapped the beetle star carrier in half, they might have figured their job was done and moved on. Yes, Cadet Colhsoon, that is wishful thinking," she admitted with a defiant tone. "Sometimes, wishful thinking is all you've got to go on out here. Staying here and doing nothing is only wishing for a slow death."

Bifft looked to Jinn for help but she looked away. "Colonel Perkins," he pronounced her name correctly. "If the Bosphuraq have not left the area, it will be certain death for us to jump back in there."

"Agreed. My judgment is the Bosphuraq had no tactical reason to remain in the area. For whatever purpose they stalked and hit our battlegroup, their mission was a complete success once they disabled that star carrier." She had decided their best option for survival was to jump back to the only place in range where they might find help. Now the question was, *could* they do that?

CHAPTER FOURTEEN

"Can we do it?" Perkins asked, trying to decide where to float in the cramped confines of the auxiliary control center.

"Can we jump? Sure," Derek was quick to answer. "Problem is, we have no idea how to program a jump. Colonel, I mean, *no* idea. None of the training materials available to us even mention the subject."

"There's no handy-dandy 'jump back' feature, like call-back on a phone?" Perkins joked, though hoping that might be true.

"Even if there was, Ma'am, I think the jump we did under the damping effect was so sloppy, the system wouldn't know where to go back *to*. We need to get some smart cadets up here to help us program the jump computer."

"Ok, but the drive *can* do that jump? Garnor tells me there is plenty of power left in the capacitors."

"There should be more than enough, Ma'am," Irene agreed. "We jumped out of a partial damping field, that takes a lot of extra power. Jumping back should use a lot less juice. Unless the drive coils got degraded from our jump, I'll have to ask the engineering team about that."

"Do it," Perkins ordered. "I'll find some cadets who have at least a basic knowledge of jump physics," she added hopefully. Faster than light travel was critical to the Ruhar fleet and the whole war effort. Jump theory and navigation had to be an important topic at their training schools.

Jump theory and navigation was an important topic at Ruhar training schools. Unfortunately, no cadet aboard the *Ruh Tostella* had enough experience to actually program a live jump. Even the senior cadets had mostly learned jump physics and theory, not practical application.

Fortunately, there was one person aboard the ship who had actual hands-on training in jump navigation, though even she had only worked with a simulator. Ser-Kotreh Tutula volunteered when she heard Perkins needed someone to assist.

"Thank you, but, no, you don't understand," Irene let exasperation get the better of her. "We don't need you to *assist*, we need you to *do* it, all of it. The two of us have absolutely no idea how any of this stuff," she waved her hands at the confusing jump controls on the display, "works. *No* idea."

"That is unfortunate," Tutula frowned in a very human-like expression that was much better than a smile from her species. "I will require qualified senior cadets to assist me with the calculations, the math is complicated and verifying the calculations is a rigorous process."

"Thank you. If you need anything from us, let us know, but," Irene scowled. She hated feeling useless and helpless to control her fate. "Otherwise, we will stay out of your way."

"As we are under a time constraint, it would be best if you were not involved. I might have time to explain the process later, but-"

"Yeah, we get it," Derek rubbed a hand along Irene's arm to soothe her bruised ego. "Until we learn the basic theory, watching the process won't do us any good. Tutula, are the cadets going to be Ok with a Verd-Kris programming one of their starships to jump?"

"No doubt some of them will not be pleased," Tutula's expression was unreadably blank. "Those who refuse to participate will be noted, and I expect Fleet Command to reprimand them appropriately. If not, *I* will."

Bifft came back to confer with Jinn Garnor, this time without being escorted by Surgun Jates, who was busy 'motivating' a team of cadets working to patch a leaky fuel tank.

Jinn listened to Bifft's whispered words, then "You are suggesting I sabotage our jump drive?" Jinn asked, incredulous.

"Shhhh," Bifft's head snapped around, but no one had heard her words in the noisy compartment. "No, only the drive control circuit," Bifft explained, getting his natural cockiness back. "We have to stop the alien from jumping us back to the battlespace, it's insanity. It is suicide," he reached for her shoulder for emphasis but she pushed herself away.

"It might be risky," Jinn admitted. She was not entirely sure the jump drive coils would not explode when energized. "What do *you* suggest we do?"

"We stay here, and wait for rescue. Without using power for jumps and propulsion, the reactor can-"

"The reactor won't last, I told you that."

"It is amazing you got it restarted at all," Bifft flashed a grin that used to be considered charming, but now he feared most cadets saw through his attempt to flatter and manipulate them. Jinn only glared at him and folded her arms, so he hurried to continue. "Er, yes. While the reactor is working, we use it to charge up every powercell we have, so when the reactor has to be shut down, we can stretch out life support."

"Stretch it out how long? And when that runs out, we get into dropships, and then we survive in spacesuits? You weren't *listening*," her tone implied that was a common problem with Bifft Colhsoon. "The fleet has no idea where we are. *No* idea. They don't even know we are missing yet!"

"Then waiting in one place is as good as any other, and we should stay right here rather than risking a jump."

"Wrong," Jinn brushed her bangs out of her eyes. "The battlespace was flooded with high-energy particles. If any place in the area will attract the attention of ships searching for us, it is there, *not* here."

Bifft kicked himself for not thinking of that fact. And he was stubborn enough not to admit when he was wrong. "You know what else was in the battlespace? A Bosphuraq warship! It is too risky for us to jump back in there. Jinn, all you need to do is-"

"No! No, I won't do it. And you are not doing it either. You leave my drive circuits alone!" Anger flared in her eyes.

"You will obey this alien even though you know her plan is insane?"

"I am obeying because it is my duty, and because I agree with her. We can't stay here while our reactor shuts down, then life support fails. There is nowhere within this ship's jump radius that will allow us to survive. Our best chance is if one of our ships is still in the area of the battle."

"Now you are indulging yourself in wishful thinking!" Bifft turned away in disgust. How could he have once wanted such a weak woman?

"I wish to live, and you have not offered a better option. Now, get out of my control center," she waved him away, "I have work to do."

Irene held up a hand to get Perkins' attention. "All stations report ready for jump, Colonel."

"As ready as we're going to be, you mean?"

"Uh, yes. Ma'am, there isn't anything more we can check that hasn't been checked at least three times already. The unknowns are going to remain that way, until we load power into the jump coils."

That would have to be good enough, whether Perkins liked it or not. For the record, she did not like it. "Remind me, how long after we jump until the sensors are able to give us useful data?"

"Seven seconds for full reset, maybe eighteen seconds to restore full capability, Ma'am." Irene cautioned the ship's current commander, "Problem is, the *Toaster*'s sensor suite got beat up pretty badly in the fight, we lost an entire array on the portside, and there are big gaps in the dorsal arrays."

"Anything that would prevent the sensors from picking up a return echo from a Yankee search?"

"No, those active pulses are so powerful I could detect a ship with my suit sensors, if I were standing outside."

"That won't be necessary, Striebich." The cadets had been appalled when they heard Perkin's plan to scan the battlespace with active sensor pulses immediately after jumping in, because Fleet doctrine was that stealth was life and no one compromised stealth, especially not in a potential combat situation. Perkins' reasoning was the intense gamma ray burst of their inbound jump would already illuminate their position to any ship in the area, and the *Toaster*'s stealth field was, well, basically toast at that point. If a stealthed Bosphuraq ship was lingering around the battlespace, Perkins would rather detect the enemy presence with a sensor echo, than with maser bolts cutting into the *Ruh Tostella*. "We will be ready to jump the hell out of there if we detect unfriendlies?"

"Yes," Derek called up the jump option list on his console. "Short jump, then long. The quicker we have to initiate a jump, the less accurate it will be," he warned. Short-long was Ruhar Fleet standard procedure for an escape jump. Conduct a short jump to get clear of the immediate battlespace, and drop off quantum resonators just before the jump to confuse enemy sensors about where the ship had jumped to. Then conduct a longer jump, with the hope that by the time the enemy determined where the far end of the short jump was, the escaping ship would be long gone. Derek agreed with the thinking behind the procedure, except the *Ruh Tostella* was not equipped with quantum resonators, and they would need to pause for an estimated forty minutes after the short jump, to calculate their long jump. If a Bosphuraq ship were waiting for them, Derek thought the *Toaster* was as good as dead already.

"Then there's no point waiting. Sound the alarm for jump prep and start feeding power into the coils." Perkins closed her eyes briefly and said a silent prayer. *Please, God, don't let me screw this up, people are depending on me.*

The *Ruh Tostella* jumped with fair accuracy, considering that the jump had been programmed partly by a group of third-year cadets. According to the navigation system, they missed the target point by only fourteen thousand miles. In space warfare, that was practically on top of their target. Perkins took that as a very good omen. "Anything?" Perkins asked with one eye on the clock and one on the sensor display. Ten seconds had gone by, and the display was still blank.

Then the display lit up. All over.

"Multiple contacts!" Derek shouted louder than needed. "Wait, wait," he added to Irene, who had a finger poised on a button to jump them away. "All contacts are solid, Colonel, we're not picking up a return with a fuzzy silhouette like we would if there were a stealthed ship out there. There are a *lot* of contacts, though," he whistled. "Looks like a big debris field."

"Striebich, keep your finger on that button," Perkins ordered, "but don't activate a jump without my order. We've got a limited number of jumps before this bucket fails us."

As the sensor data became more clear, Perkins became less tense and more fearful. Unless a Bosphuraq ship had a super-effective stealth field or was so far away they hadn't received a sensor return yet, the battlespace appeared to be empty of threats. It was also empty of potential rescuers. "Nothing? They're *all* gone?" Perkins leaned over Irene's chair, her eyes flicking from one part of the display to another. The area was cluttered with drifting debris, so much that the *Ruh Tostella* twice had been forced to maneuver away to avoid colliding with spinning pieces of dangerous junk. Active sensors had thoroughly scanned the area out to half a million miles, and there was not a single intact ship anywhere near them. In most cases, the software's ship identification system had difficulty determining what type of ship most of the debris came from, because the parts were so small and torn apart.

"It looks that way, Ma'am," Derek concluded. "I'm sorry."

"We're all sorry, Bonsu. Could a ship have gotten away?"

"It's possible," Derek replied without a trace of hope in his voice. "The system can only account for sixty three percent of the mass that should be around us, but some of the ships, like that *City of Sandeppe*, blew up hard. There wouldn't be enough left of those ships to track the mass, because a lot of the mass got converted to energy."

"Any sign of the *Deal Me In*?"

"The forward section is gone, this is most of it," Derek indicated a loose cloud on the display. "But the aft section, hmmm, that's interesting. Looks like it's mostly together." He enhanced the image, to show a short section of the star carrier's spine, with a single empty docking platform, attached to the aft engineering section. "Um, yeah, they took some hits there also." As Derek continued to zoom in on the broken star carrier, they could see a reactor that had its plasma vented through a burned-through hole in the exterior shielding. The entire area around that reactor was scorched and melted. "That doesn't look good," Derek muttered.

"Shit," Perkins shook her head. She might have gotten all their hopes up for nothing. The *Ruh Tostella* still could not jump far enough to get anywhere useful, and their single functional reactor was steadily failing. All they might have accomplished was slowly dying in that lonely part of interstellar space, rather than their previous position in lonely interstellar space. "Secure from active search," she ordered. "It's too dangerous to send dropships out there, with all the debris drifting around." The real problem was chunks of debris crashing into each other, creating more debris and sending pieces careening in all directions. "Launch a recon drone, I want a full scan of what's left of the star carrier. If you see another piece of debris out there large enough to investigate, send another drone. We can't afford to miss anything."

They didn't miss anything, because there wasn't anything to be missed. Other than the aft section of the *Deal Me In*, the largest piece of debris was the size of a dropship. The Bosphuraq battlecruiser had been brutally thorough in its destruction of the Ruhar ships, so much so that Perkins wondered whether the Bosphuraq captain had a personal grudge against those Ruhar. Space combat rarely left significant parts of wounded ships intact, the kinetic energy of railguns and the explosive power of ship-killer missile warheads could quickly tear unprotected ships apart, while a single hit to a reactor or jump drive capacitors could cause a ship to destroy itself. Still, Perkins had hoped to find *something* useful in the debris cloud, and she was straining to keep the necessary confidence in front of her reluctant crew. The second recon drone had flown around to examine several remnants of Ruhar ships and found nothing useful, so Perkins had recalled that drone after it unfortunately displayed images demonstrating that some of the debris drifting around were shattered Ruhar bodies. She did not need the cadets seeing frozen, charred and bloated bodies of their people.

Giving up on hoping to find a miracle in the smashed remains of the Ruhar battlegroup, she concentrated on what remained of the star carrier, knowing that section of the ship was extremely unlikely to contain a living Jeraptha. She gave her cadet crew plenty of time to examine the stricken star carrier, assigning two additional drones to the search, and not asking Jinn for her opinion until six hours had passed. "What do you think?" Perkins asked as she handed a squeeze bulb of hot klah to the senior cadet. "Is anything there salvageable? Useful to us?"

"No," Jinn needed the klah to keep herself awake. "Their normal-space propulsion system is scrap, a third of it is simply sheered away. Whatever hit there, it tore the power couplings loose. That ship isn't going to move on its own again."

"I saw that. What about the reactors? One of them looked fairly intact."

"There is one reactor that vented its plasma and shut down properly. Please! Before you ask, no, we can't get anything useful from that star carrier's reactor. To restart our own reactor, I was able to rely on instructions that walked us through every step in great detail, and as you remember we still had to abort the restart sequence *three times* because something went wrong that the procedures didn't anticipate. With a Jeraptha reactor, we would be starting from absolute zero."

"Cadet, I have every confidence-"

"You shouldn't. It is impossible. Wait," Jinn held up a hand. "*Please*, Colonel. That reactor vented its plasma, but it is damaged, there are cracks in the exterior sheathing and the containment magnets inside have become detached from their mounts. We can't fix it. I do not think even the Jeraptha could repair that reactor without a shipyard capable of heavy-duty work, It is impossible, *impossible*," she looked at Perkins from one eye to another, seeking understanding as if that particular word could not translate properly.

"Impossible, I understand. Cadet, you've done a remarkable job. I can't ask for more. I accept there is no potential for using a Jeraptha reactor to power our life support systems."

"Thank you, Colonel Perkins," Jinn shuddered slightly with relief and fatigue.

"No reactor, then. What about-"

"Contact!" Derek called excitedly over Perkins' zPhone. "We got something out there, Ma'am. Looks like a Jeraptha escape pod."

"Escape pod!" Emily found her pilot's excitement to be infectious. "Just one? Are there survivors aboard?"

"Just the one," Derek reported slowly as he reviewed the data on his console, hoping for better news. "One intact, we found others that are damaged, this is the first one generating power. It began pinging a distress call a few seconds ago. Maybe it needed to get a certain distance from the battlespace before it activated, or maybe it has a timer?"

"Or maybe it picked up our signals," Perkins suggested. "Survivors?"

"All we're getting is a location ping, Colonel. We're too far away to see inside with our sensors. It could be empty, but it is pinging and I don't know if a Jeraptha pod would do that unless it was occupied? I couldn't find anything in the ship's database about operating procedures for Jeraptha gear."

"Ah, dammit. Please tell me the debris field is relatively clear between us and that pod."

"Not a chance, Ma'am."

"Damn it. All right, send a drone."

The drone reported one living Jeraptha was inside the escape pod, though it was in a state of semi-hibernation caused by the pod's mechanisms. "I don't suppose the beetles equip their pods with the capability to rendezvous with a rescue vessel?" Perkins asked hopefully.

"No, Ma'am," Irene turned to look up at their captain. "I worked with a cadet to research everything the ship's database knows about those pods, and they have a very limited ability to maneuver, basically they can move to avoid collisions, but that pod out there has used up all its fuel so it didn't crash into the debris cloud. The casing has dents and scratches from impacts already, I hope it isn't damaged. We need to go out there and bring it to us."

"How did I know you were going to say that?" Perkins crossed her arms as she floated behind the pilot couches. "I suppose you are first in line to volunteer?"

"Well, Colonel," Irene winked at Derek. They had tossed a coin and Derek lost. "If you send two cadet pilots, it might look like you were not willing to risk human lives."

"Right, but if you go with a cadet, I am clearly not playing favorites," Perkins rolled her eyes. "Christ, Striebich, you're right about this one. Of course," she mused with a hand rubbing her chin. "I *could* send Tutula with a Ruhar cadet, which would make it an interspecies rescue operation." Seeing the crestfallen look on Irene's face, she took pity on her pilot. "Relax, Striebich. You've sold me on the idea. Take Tutula and a cadet pilot to be safe, go bring that beetle here to us."

The beetle was a young Machinist's Mate named Ernt Dahl, who was barely older than the Ruhar cadets, as he had been aboard the *Deal Me In* as his first assignment out of school. The translator told Perkins that Dahl's rank of 'Arlon' was something like 'junior ensign' or 'probationary ensign', so he was certainly not an experienced senior officer. He was overjoyed to be alive when the pod automatically revived him, upon being brought into the pressurized environment of the *Ruh Tostella*'s docking bay. Part of Perkins had been hoping the Jeraptha would naturally take on the burden of command after awaking, but Ernt was perfectly happy for Perkins to be in charge, and apparently saw nothing odd about a human commanding a Ruhar ship.

Despite Ernt's knowledge of technology far beyond Ruhar capabilities, he was not much help with the battered *Toaster*. After an assessment that had his antennas drooping with despair, he agreed with Jinn that the ship's one functioning reactor would shut down when its containment system failed, and there was nothing anyone could do about it with the equipment available. After initially being stunned and thrilled to see part of his ship had survived, Ernt was equally pessimistic about the condition of the *Deal Me In*. The reactors were basically scrap, vented plasma had eaten into the backup power systems, and the engines that flew the ship through normal space were scrap. The only bright spot was the star carrier's jump drive system, for the coils and capacitors had come through the battle in fair condition.

"The star carrier's jump drive is intact?" Perkins traced a finger along the schematic of the star carrier on the display in front of her.

"Yes, remarkably so," Ernt agreed, his antenna bobbing up and down vigorously. "Unfortunately, that is of no use to us. The jump drive control system was in the forward part of the ship, part of the navigation computer. We do not have any system to control the action of the jump coils."

"Arlon Dahl," she used the Jeraptha's rank to address him. "Is there any way for *this* ship's drive system to control a Jeraptha jump drive?"

Ernt's antenna stood straight up in surprise and he looked away, perhaps embarrassed for the primitive human who had asked such a foolishly ignorant question.

"No," Jinn also was dismayed by being asked such a ridiculous question. "We don't have an interface with the-"

"Yes," Tutula interjected with confidence. "This ship *does* have a capability to interface with a Jeraptha jump drive."

Ernt and Jinn just stared at Tutula, blinking slowly. If she had suddenly grown another head, they might have been less surprised.

"How do you know that?" Perkins asked, glancing between Ernt, Jinn and Tutula.

"One of this ship's former officers told me about it. That is one advantage of being a member of an enemy species," Tutula twisted her lips in a horrible version of a smile. "The Ruhar are always very happy to show me how superior they are. Your people," he addressed the remark to Jinn, "have of course been studying Jeraptha jump drive technology every chance they get, particularly when your ships are attached to a star carrier. Each of your ships is equipped with a working computer model that emulates an interface with a Jeraptha jump drive. Whenever a star carrier jumps, your ships simulate controlling the jump to test the accuracy of the model, and your fleet studies the results to refine the model. The officer who revealed this to me bragged that the emulator is now believed to be ninety six percent accurate. He wanted me to know that the shortcomings of your jump drive technology are caused by hardware deficiencies, not by a lack of theoretical understanding or inability to program a drive controller. The Ruhar," now she looked at Perkins, "know that Kristang jump drives are shamefully inaccurate. That is a failure of the warrior caste, not of *my* people. The warrior caste pays too little attention to anything not directly related to destructive power. *My* people," she switched back to glaring at Jinn, "would correct that error."

"If we could interface our drive controller with the Jeraptha system-" Jinn's voice trailed off as she considered the possibilities, looking to Ernt for a sane voice to squelch an idea that must be mad. But the Jeraptha only looked at the display pensively, not noticing her.

"The *Ruh Tostella* can attach to the hardpoint?" Perkins asked, pointing to the one remaining docking platform that remained on the star carrier's shortened spine. "The star carrier jumps, and we jump with it?"

"We can attach manually, yes," Jinn scratched the back of her head, "I think so. Unless the clamps there are damaged. Colonel, even if we can control a Jeraptha jump drive, we have no way to feed power into their capacitors. Physically, there is no connection between our reactor and the star carrier. I don't see any way to create a connection."

"It is not possible," Ernt muttered, his claws flitting across the controls, considering the question. "No," he concluded. "Colonel Perkins, my specialty is power generation. I am not an expert on propulsion or jump drives or computers, but this *is* my area of expertise," he declared with confidence beyond his few years of training. "There is no equipment aboard either ship for creating a stable power connection between this ship's reactor and the star carrier's capacitors. The input frequency of the capacitors is," he blinked, looking around as if just then realizing he was in the presence of three alien species. "Er, well, that is not a specification I can discuss with you. I can assure you the capacitor charging system is delicate and requires a specific-"

"Yes, fine, I accept we can't recharge the *Deal Me In*'s jump drive. What is the charge in those capacitors now?" Perkins interrupted.

"We don't know, I, er- I suppose we could determine that with our sensors," Jinn added, embarrassed. "It is," she waited while the damaged sensor suite responded. "Eighty one percent charge. That is an estimate, you understand? The Jeraptha do not give us specifications for their systems," she added with a guilty glance at Ernt.

"Eighty two percent is the correct number, I do not think I am giving away any secrets to tell you that," Ernt confirmed with one eye on a display. "Our last jump was only medium-distance, I think, so there was plenty of charge available when we jumped in here."

"Understood. How many, no, wait. Not how *many* jumps," Perkins realized she had been about to ask the wrong question. "How *far* could the *Deal Me In* jump, with that charge?"

"I do not know," Ernt admitted without embarrassment. "As I explained, I am a power technician. It is not possible, I think, for a single jump to use up that entire charge. The greatest power drain I remember from a single jump used up thirty four percent, and that was with the ship burdened by carrying an entire heavy battlegroup of our own fleet. A series of jumps to use up the capacitors," he rubbed his antenna together as he thought, in a gesture Perkins found fascinating and distracting. "Again, I do not know. It is a complicated question with many variables."

"Colonel, the charge in the capacitors is certainly not sufficient for us to travel sixteen lightyears," Jinn guessed. "If you are hoping to get back on our original flightpath, in case the fleet is searching for us."

"What I want to know is, where *could* we go?"

The young Ruhar cadet was unhappy about being asked questions she could not find the answer to in a shipboard database. "That, also, is a guess-"

"Yes, yes, show me a radius of ten lightyears, to be conservative."

Jinn adjusted the display to show a sphere around their present position.

To Perkins, it disappointingly still looked like a whole lot of nothing inside that sphere. "That's it? Are there any habitable planets, data relays, refueling stations in there?"

"No," Jinn shook her head. "Except for what we suspect is a Thuranin sensor station, here. This was Thuranin territory until recently. If there is a sensor station, it would be automated and of no use to us."

"Of course," Perkins reprimanded herself for allowing her frustrations to show. "Wait, what is this?" She pointed to a glowing gold circle.

"That is an Elder wormhole. But it leads to space controlled by the Kristang," the Ruhar cadet warned.

"Space that *was* controlled by the Kristang," Tutula corrected. "Reports indicate they were pulling back from that area, even before their latest civil war," she noted with disgust that her people would regularly kill each other over trivial matters. "They had few assets in that region, and the Thuranin have abandoned that entire part of the sector after their recent defeats by the Jeraptha," she added the last with a nod to Ernt, who lifted his head with pride.

"I'll take your word about that," Perkins muttered. "Can we go through that wormhole? If we can, what is on the other side, which we could reach? Show me a ten lightyear radius around the other end of that wormhole."

"It is *possible* for us to go through the wormhole," Jinn agreed unhappily. It took her a few minutes to pull up a star chart showing the other side of that wormhole, as the ship's navigation system had to retrieve seldom-used data about enemy territory. "Here," she announced when the display filled in. "Two star systems with habitable planets," she pointed at two dots on opposite directions from the wormhole. "The closest one is Kormat, the report says it has an estimated population of three hundred, but that data is twenty years old. Kormat was a logistics base that fell out of use, the Fleet thinks the Kristang pulled it out of service." She looked closer at the data. "Kormat may be on the margin of being considered habitable, it is a very cold world," she shuddered at seeing some of the climate estimates. "The Kristang there lived in domes under the ice, and the amount of oxygen in the atmosphere is low."

"Too risky, too many 'ifs', too many lizards," Perkins concluded without thinking she had just said 'lizards' in front of Tutula. "You said there is a second habitable planet?"

"Yes, in the other star system," Jinn peered closely at the data, and gasped. "Colonel, you know this place! You have been there."

"I *have*? What?"

"Your people designated this planet as 'Camp Alpha'?"

"Holy *shit*." Emily Perkins did not have fond memories of that God-forsaken planet. "The Goddamned lizards are still there?"

"Er," Jinn searched through the data. "No. Fleet Intelligence does not think the Kristang have maintained a presence there, after your people shipped out. That planet was the property of the White Wind clan, which suffered a severe loss of fortune, then recently was absorbed during their civil war."

"How sure is Fleet Intelligence about Camp Alpha being abandoned?" As a career intel officer, Perkins would dearly love to see the raw intel take on *that* subject. How many times in her career had she published an assessment based on what she thought was solid-gold intel, only to be proved wrong by the messy facts of reality?

"I, the report, it," Jinn scrolled down through the data, then held up her hands. "It doesn't list a confidence factor."

"We are certainly not going to the first planet you listed, Kormat or whatever it's called. Camp Alpha? God*damn*. Never thought I'd ever be setting foot on that-" She paused. She was describing a planet she might be asking the entire crew to land on and live for an undetermined length of time. "That world. Oh, hell," she forced a laugh to lighten the mood. "It has oxygen and the temperature isn't bad. No dangerous native life. From what I remember, even when the Kristang were running the place, their footprint on the surface didn't cover much territory," her mind raced to remember how much land area the ExForce base on Camp Alpha had covered. At its maximum, the Force that left Earth had consisted of about 120,000 people, with the USA and China contributing 35,000 combat troops each, and the other three nations providing 15,000 each. Support and headquarters units, and 'observers' from other nations had rounded out another five thousand. One time only, she had been aloft in a 'Buzzard' aircraft on a familiarization ride above Camp Alpha and gotten a birds-eye view of the sprawling but temporary base, and the much smaller and walled-off Kristang facility nearby. From eighty thousand feet up, the base had looked unimpressive, and she recalled another officer telling her the entire base plus wargame training area occupied less space than the state of Connecticut. Since the planet was mostly land with only twenty percent of the surface covered by oceans, that left a *lot* of room to conceal a single shipful of cadets. "I'll consider Camp Alpha our best option until I hear otherwise. How long until we can jump?"

"Colonel? I have no idea. I've never seen this emulator model," she looked to Velt Tutula for help. "I did not know such technology existed until today." The way she tilted her head, the cadet did not appear to fully buy into the idea of her people having ability to control a Jeraptha jump drive.

"I have never seen it either," Tutula admitted. "Colonel, can you access it?"

Emily Perkins had absolutely no idea what she could and could not do with her full set of command codes, she had never tested the limits. "There is not an icon for 'magical Jeraptha jump drive emulator'," she regretted her sarcastic tone. When she was asking others to do the impossible, she should not be bitching about the pressure on her. The real problem was she felt she could not ask for help with simple tasks because that would display her profound ignorance. But she had no choice. "Something like that would probably be highly classified. Anyone got any suggestions?"

"I do not think the existence of the emulator is a deep secret," Tutula noted. "The officer who told me said the Jeraptha know about it." she chuckled, a dry wheezing sound that caused a shiver of fear to shoot up Perkins' spine. "He said the Jeraptha were probably wagering over how close the emulator is to their own system. Colonel, could it be as simple as searching for 'Jeraptha jump drive emulator' in your command codes?"

"It's worth a shot," Perkins observed as she typed the phrase into the handy search box. And, presto, there it was. "Huh," she looked up at Tutula. "Good guess. I'm allowing Engineering and the pilots access to the emulator. What I would like to ask the Jeraptha fleet right now is; what are the odds this will work?"

No one had an answer for her, but Ernt was twitching his legs in an agitated fashion, and the tips of his antenna were quivering. "What is wrong, Arlon Dahl?" Perkins asked with concern. "You think this emulator will not work? Or would it make you uncomfortable for us to attempt to control one of your jump drives?"

"No, Colonel. It is not surprising that a client species would seek to understand our technology, and I will assist with the necessary connections, for I wish to live," he twisted his mouth parts in a smile that somehow was less creepy than when a Kristang made the same gesture. "It is just," he sighed.

"What?"

"Wagering whether a Ruhar system could control one of our drives is incredibly tempting action, and I cannot register a bet out here in the wilderness!"

The alien crewman looked so anguished at being unable to participate in the favorite activity of his species, Perkins almost felt sorry for him. "Arlon Dahl, we have a broken ship staffed by inexperienced cadets, attached to the even more broken ass-end of a star carrier. To get to a habitable planet, we need to jump several times without the ship exploding, transit a wormhole into enemy territory, and probably travel a long distance through space to land on a planet that may or may not have a Kristang presence. So, I will bet you that we will never set foot on Camp Alpha."

"Mmmmm," Ernt's antenna moved in unison excitedly. "What odds are you giving?"

Perkins had no idea so she made up a number that sounded good. "Five to one."

"Five to one? No points?"

"No points," Perkins offered, guessing that points were a bad thing.

"That is," Ernt began with enthusiasm before his expression became downcast. "That all sounds good, but I suspect you have nothing to wager with, and also we have no way to properly register the wager."

"Arlon Dahl," Perkins grinned, "we will be dropping off flight recorder buoys before we jump, we can include details of the wager in the buoy databank. And, think about this; the only way we can reach Camp Alpha is by getting this emulator software to work properly. I believe the Ruhar fleet would be *more* than happy to cover my side of the wager to learn their software is functional."

"Oh!" Ernt brightened, his mouthparts moving rapidly. "In that case, I want seven to one."

"Deal," Perkins held out a hand and Ernt held out a leathery claw, and they shook. It took another ten minutes of negotiating back and forth to finalize the wager, with Perkins arguing only because she felt Ernt expected her to.

"Excellent, excellent," the very happy Jeraptha declared. "Now, show me this emulator system. I am not a jump drive specialist or navigator, but I do know about the power input requirements. It may be necessary for me to tweak the emulator settings so the drive does not explode."

CHAPTER FIFTEEN

Perkins knocked on the frame of the hatch leading to the auxiliary helm, interrupting her two pilots who were engaged in a heated but quiet discussion about something. "Striebich? Bonsu? Everything squared away with you?"

"Yes Ma'am," Irene lowered her voice with a glance toward the open hatch. The hatch had been jammed and needed to be cut away so Irene and Derek could get out of the auxiliary control center, now the hatch was permanently open and anyone lurking in the passageway could hear them talking. Derek understood why his fellow pilot was being so careful, and he unstrapped from his couch and floated over to the hatch. Sticking his head into the passageway, he gave her a thumbs up. Any listening or recording devices the passageway once contained would have been destroyed in the battle that had bent the heavy hatch. The aux helm had a flight recorder that stored all instrument, visual and sound data, but Derek had learned how to temporarily disable that system and he saw Irene had selected the 'Pause' mode. "Colonel, it looks like if this emulator system works as advertised, we actually do have a decent shot at getting the ship to Camp Alpha, we think. It's risky, but our best shot." Perkins, nodded so Irene continued. "Before you arrived, Derek and I were discussing that we now have a star carrier. Is there any possibility we can get to Earth from here?"

Perkins groaned inwardly. She had enough complications to deal with. "Striebich, you're the pilot, you tell me if we can get there. I thought the wormhole leading to Earth is shut down, dormant or something."

"That's what the hamsters told us, yeah," Irene lowered her eyelids in suspicion. "I found Earth on the star chart, here," she tapped the navigation display in front of her couch, letting her finger rest longingly on the symbol for humanity's home world. Then she tapped the symbol for Camp Alpha. "The trip would require going through multiple wormholes, but there may be a possibility we could get there. We won't know, until we jump the first time and we see how much that drains the star carrier's capacitors."

Perkins looked without any enthusiasm at the complicated proposed course that would take their busted half-ship deep into enemy territory. "Does that star chart show the wormhole leading to Earth is active?"

"No," Irene highlighted the symbol for that now-dormant Elder wormhole. "Not according to the chart. But, you have a full set of command codes. I was thinking, what if that wormhole is *not* really shut down? The Ruhar did tell us they have no idea why that one wormhole shut down all by itself. That doesn't sound kosher to me."

"It never seemed right to me either, but we don't know anything about how the Elder wormhole network functions," Perkins cautioned her pilot. "You're asking if my command codes reveal a different star chart, one showing that wormhole is still active?"

Irene nodded silently with an anxious glance to the hatch and Derek motioned her to continue. "Something like that, Colonel."

Biting her lip and clicking through the screens on her zPhone, Perkins found the mode to transfer the phone's screen to the display in front of Irene. "Navigation data is, hmmm, somewhere, here!" Perkins allowed herself a smile of satisfaction at finding what she wanted on the alien device. Ruhar systems were not as intuitive as they could be, or maybe they just weren't intuitive to humans. "Doesn't look any different," she frowned with disappointment.

"It is a little different," Derek noted from the hatchway. "That group of symbols in the lower left corner weren't there before."

"Huh, you're right," Irene zoomed in that section of the display. "Looks like our hamster friends have been holding out on us. This shows star systems recently surrendered by the Kristang, where the Ruhar fleet has conducted stealth surveys."

"Does that help us?" Perkins asked.

"No. We couldn't risk flying to any of those systems, and we don't have the range anyway," Irene declared. "Going back to the question, the answer is no, dammit. Your star chart also shows that wormhole to Earth is shut down."

"If I put my intel officer hat on for a minute," Perkins mused, "I'd guess if anyone was lying to us about that wormhole being shut down, it's the lizards. The Kristang told us that wormhole was shut down, before the Ruhar fleet took Paradise back. I can't see the hamsters have any reason to lie to us about it, but the lizards did. What I don't see in this chart is the data source, like, do the Ruhar *know* that wormhole is shut down, or are they only taking the Kristang's word about it?"

"That's a good question, but it's academic right now, Ma'am," Derek kept his own voice soft, continuing to scan the passageway. "Unless we, meaning our beetle friend, find a way to recharge the Jeraptha jump capacitors from this ship's reactor, we will run out of power long before we reached that wormhole. Irene, look, I would love to fly back to Earth," his tone indicated the subject had been argued extensively by the two pilots. "We need to concentrate on surviving first. Let's not get distracted, Ok?"

"Striebich, good initiative on asking that question," Perkins patted the pilot's shoulder as she wiped the classified navigation data from the screen. "If we see an opportunity to-"

"Cadets coming," Derek whispered from the hatchway, and the conversation ended abruptly.

"Very well," Perkins turned to leave. "Ping me as soon as you are confident about the jump solution."

"About that, Colonel," Irene raised a finger. "*We* aren't doing anything to get the jump programmed, that's the cadets and, mostly, Tutula. Without her, we'd be sitting dead in space. When we're ready, I'd like to offer her my seat."

"You don't want to be the first human to make a star carrier jump?" Perkins was surprised by that.

"I would only be pressing a button," Irene explained. "Tutula has been busting her ass, she deserves a chance to make the jump."

"Plus," Derek added without a wink or grin, "if the drive goes 'kaboom' it will be all her fault."

"Well, there is that," Perkins also did not see anything humorous in the situation. "About that, make sure we include the jump calculations in the drone we'll drop off before we activate the drive. If their fancy emulator software doesn't work, the Ruhar need to know about it. All right, Striebich, I'll inform our Verd-Kris friend about your offer. I want you looking over her shoulder the whole time. Someday, we may need to do this on our own."

The *Deal Me In* jumped. The ship did not explode. Pieces of it did not go flying off in every direction, and the *Ruh Tostella* stayed rigidly clamped to the docking platform. "Status?" Perkins asked anxiously, from her awkward position strapped in next to Irene behind the two pilot couches. Unlike their jump in to find the star carrier, when the displays had gone from empty space to space filled with broken ships, this time there was nothing on the display to tell her where they had gone to, where they were now.

"Sensors are working on it, Ma'am," Derek reported with a look at Tutula to let the alien know that Perkins was not blaming her for the lack of data.

"Captain Bonsu is correct," Tutula agreed. "Our sensors were blinded by spatial distortion of the jump field. We need seven data points to determine our position in space."

"The jump drive was not significantly damaged by the jump," Ernt reported happily. "The energy used was within three percent of my estimate! The drive should be capable of performing another jump without trouble," the Jeraptha shook his head in amazement.

Perkins waited impatiently while the two pilots worked to collect navigation data and Irene watched the process. Finally, Derek raised a hand. "Got it. The good news is we jumped pretty far. The bad news is we are forty one million miles off target."

"Forty one *million*?" Perkins gasped. "How the hell-"

"The calculations were accurate," Tutula stated in a tone that invited no argument. "The slight battle damage to the banks of Jeraptha jump drive coils could not entirely account for such a large margin of error. The Ruhar emulator program must be faulty. Colonel Perkins," Tutula unstrapped from her couch and turned to address the human commander. "We should have enough data from this jump to further refine the emulator system."

"I sure as hell hope so," Perkins kept her temper in check. "Because if we're going through a wormhole, our jump capability needs to be dead-on accurate."

The next jump, twenty nine hours later, after feverish work recoding the emulator program, delivered much more favorable results. Despite the jump coils not working together properly and them having no way to fix that problem, the second jump came within two hundred and seven thousand miles of the target. Since the second jump was much longer, Perkins, the pilots and the cadets involved in programming the jump considered their accuracy a smashing success. Perkins waved her arms to suppress premature celebration. "Are we in position, with the right timing, to go through the wormhole?"

"Yes," Irene replied with confidence, pumping a fist that only Derek could see so they could share a private celebration. "The wormhole will not emerge in this space for another three days and," she checked her display, "seventeen hours. That is plenty of time to maneuver the *Deal Me In* near the event horizon. We have to give the wormhole plenty of room anyway, they emerge in a slightly different location each time."

"Since none of us have ever taken a ship through an Elder wormhole, and probably no one has *ever* moved a star carrier by a ship on a hardpoint providing the thrust, can we do this?"

"Oh, yes, Colonel Perkins," Nert spoke up happily, a broad grin exposing his incisors. "I have observed the process many times. There is no trick to it, we just locate the event horizon and," he made a ring of the index finger and thumb on one hand and vigorously demonstrated plunging his other index finger in and out of the ring, "we go in. It is *easy*! Oooooh, so easy."

Emily Perkins had to cover her face with a hand to not burst out laughing. The goofily innocent grin on Nert's face as he made the unintentionally rude gesture was funny, but seeing Irene's face growing beet red as Nert enthusiastically kept going almost made Perkins lose her composure.

"Ok, Nert," Derek reached out to restrain one of Nert's arms. "The ship goes in the hole, we get the idea. Nert is telling the truth, Colonel. Transition through a wormhole is automatic, all the ship needs to do is line up the approach and make sure we don't touch the edge of the event horizon ring."

"What happens if we do touch the ring?"

"Then, part of the ship goes through, and the other part," Derek ran a hand through the air in a cutting motion, "doesn't. Don't worry, Ma'am, our flight training did simulate a wormhole transition."

Perkins cocked her head. "How extensive was this training?" Her pilots had only been in their starship pilot training for three days before the Bosphuraq jumped in and spoiled the party.

Derek looked to Irene and they both shrugged. "Two, three hours?" Seeing Perkins eyebrows raised in alarm, Derek added to reassure her "Our instructor said there wasn't any point to running that sim much longer, because the wormhole transition maneuver is so simple. Jumping into position close to an Elder wormhole is the tricky part, the rest is just normal-space navigation. The three of us agreed Tutula will handle the transition through the wormhole, with Irene acting as copilot and me calling out navigation waypoints."

"Except in this case, the *Toaster* is carrying half a star carrier on its back," Perkins pinched the bridge of her nose. Irene had noted that Emily Perkins had the honor of being the first human ever to command a starship. What the pilot had not said was that Perkins also had the crushing *responsibility* of being the first human ever to command a starship. If she screwed up or missed something important, she could get the entire crew killed. Even if at least one cadet survived the disaster, Perkins knew her actions and decisions would be scrutinized under a microscope by a species who overall, did not like the idea of former enemies serving aboard their warships.

"Yes, Ma'am," Derek agreed, not mentioning that the *Toaster* was technically attached by its belly rather than its back. "We've practiced maneuvering the combined ships and we know the flight characteristics of this clumsy beast. Our flight plan," he called up that data on his display, "has us approaching the event horizon at an angle, with the ship's thrust pushing us on a curve into the wormhole. If the engines fail, we will shoot safely past the event horizon and have to try again at another emergence point, but we won't crash into it," he announced with confidence.

"You're telling me that jumping a thousand lightyears through an ancient rip in spacetime is the *safest* part of this journey?"

Irene answered for Derek. "I know it seems crazy, Ma'am, but there's nothing *we* can do to screw up that wormhole. Everything else we do out here has multiple potentials for error."

Perkins shook her head slowly, knowing she needed to trust the judgment of her pilots. And knowing she had to trust an Elder device that no one in the galaxy fully understood. "Let's hope we don't get a visit from the screw-up fairy. All right, release the ship from jump conditions and secure for normal-space maneuvering."

The transition through the wormhole was as smooth and easy as her pilots said it would be, although she noticed Irene's knuckles turning white from tension, as the ship lined up for the approach and flashed through from one part of the galaxy to another. They kept a careful eye on the charge level of the jump drive capacitors, which were getting drained rapidly. By the time they were ready for a jump into the Camp Alpha star system, it was clear that jump would be the Jeraptha starship's last action. "Ma'am," Irene answered after a team spent two hours of checking and rechecking every part of the jump drive system. "We can jump into the system with a comfortable safety margin," she didn't mention that 'comfortable' meant less than seven percent. "But that will be it. After the jump, the capacitors won't have the energy to get the coils over the threshold for a jump. We'll be stuck in that star system, and the *Deal Me In*'s normal space propulsion system is offline. If we're flying to Camp Alpha, we'll do it in the *Ruh Tostella*," she used the ship's formal name because her audience included many cadets.

"Understood. We can do it?"

"Yes, confidence is high," Irene ignored the grimaces from some of the engineering cadets. "We need to," she pulled up their planned course on the display, "jump in here, on the near side of the second planet. That will mask our gamma ray burst from being detected on Camp Alpha. It will take thirteen days to fly to Camp Alpha, but we can't get the *Toast*-the *Ruh Tostella* into orbit there, the reactor will shut down before we get there. The final leg of the flight needs to be in dropships."

Perkins had assumed that would be their best option. The review continued for another hour, partly because there was a large group of people involved in the process of verifying all the systems involved and they all wanted to weigh in on the decision, so Perkins politely endured the endless rehashing of issues. She also listened because she wanted them all to buy into the plan to set down on Camp Alpha, and take shelter there until rescue hopefully arrived. It wasn't a great plan, and there were a lot of unhappy cadets. But no one had a better idea that was realistic, and even Bifft grudgingly admitted the ship's failing condition did not offer an option of remaining aboard and hoping for the best.

The final jump of the *Deal Me In* was successful, in that the ship did not explode, they emerged less than one hundred eighty thousand miles from their target location, and they were not immediately ambushed by enemy starships. Because the jump was draining the last bit of power from the capacitors and the power flow was unsteady, the jump was rough enough to make the *Toaster*'s one reactor shut down.

"Let me guess," Perkins tried to keep her own expression neutral as she saw the anguish displayed by Jinn. "The reactor can't be fixed?"

"No," relief flashed across Jinn's face. Relief she did not have to argue with their human commander, and, she had to admit to herself, relief that she was no longer responsible for keeping a dangerous reactor limping along.

"Well, it got us here, I suppose we can be grateful for that," Perkins said sourly. "I didn't mean that," she quickly added. "Your ship designers have created remarkable machines, and you and your team," she waved an arm to encompass the exhausted group of engineering cadets, "deserve congratulations for what you have achieved. What you achieved on a *real* ship, in a *real* crisis. When you get back to the academy, classroom exercises will seem a bit dull, won't they?" That drew weary smiles from most of the cadets. "We'll need to fly the rest of the way in dropships. It will be a long flight in tight quarters, but-"

"About that, Ma'am?" Irene waved for attention. "We have a bit of a problem."

"A bit?"

"Colonel," Derek tapped the display in front of him. "Lady Karma has been so nice, getting us here and all, I think she wants payback now. There's a group of Kristang on Camp Alpha."

"God-" Perkins thought better of taking the Lord's name in vain right then. "How many?"

"It is difficult to say exactly," Tutula spoke. "The signal is faint, we are picking up short-range surface-to-surface transmissions from a single site that is almost around the curve of the planet, they do not appear to have an active communications satellite. One of the transmissions used a Kristang word that means 'eight'," she wiggled the four fingers on one hand. "The speaker complained there are too few of them left, more than eight but less than sixteen."

"You get anything else from that transmission?"

"It was one soldier complaining to another about the poor quality of the food, and that they do not expect a ship to return for many months, so they are stuck on the surface. Colonel, I believe they occupy a single, small site that is some type of research facility."

Great, Perkins thought bitterly. Karma had indeed been kind to them, until that moment. "Tutula, you keep listening, I want Jates to listen with you so we're not relying on translations that might not be entirely accurate. Cadet Colhsoon," she turned to find the senior cadet, who was floating near the rear of the compartment, looking angry. "Get people loaded into dropships while we select a flightpath and landing site. We will come in over the opposite side of the planet from that Kristang base, and keep our presence concealed."

"I'm telling you, the human is going to get us all killed," Bifft whispered from the copilot seat of the dropship. He didn't know why he was whispering, the only occupants of the ship were Ruhar cadets.

"She had no way to know," Jinn replied as she ran a diagnostic check on the ship's systems from a console at the cockpit's rear bulkhead, making sure the airspace craft was ready for atmospheric entry and flight. She had to rely on painstakingly referring to a checklist on the console, because she had no experience with that model of dropship. It was a humbling task and if she missed something critical or made a mistake, everyone aboard could be killed in the fiery process of contacting the atmosphere.

"It was a possibility."

"It was, and we all knew it," Jinn did not look away from her work. "There is a small group of Kristang at *one* site, and Colonel Perkins plans for us to land on the other side of the planet. The Kristang will never know we're there."

Bifft snorted. "Maybe. If we're lucky."

"They didn't spot the *Ruh Tostella* flying past, and that's a bigger sensor signature. They're not looking. We'll be as safe as we can be."

"We-"

"What?" She swiveled her chair to confront the senior cadet. "What do you suggest? Colonel Perkins gave the only order she could. The ship's reactor shut down, we couldn't stay aboard. The dropships can't maintain life support for long, not for this many people. Once we jumped into this system, we had only one option. You talk a lot about how leaders have to make tough decisions," she clacked her incisors on her lower teeth in a derisive gesture, because guys like Bifft always assumed they would be in positions of leadership. "The human made a tough decision."

"Not so tough," Bifft snapped. "She had no other choice."

"If that's what you think, then what is your problem?"

"This," Bifft fumbled with how to respond. "This whole operation has been a mess."

"You could have done better?" It was her turn to sniff. She turned back to her console. "Even if we do get killed here, we jumped a Jeraptha star carrier. *None* of our people have ever done that." Along the way to Camp Alpha, the *Ruh Tostella* had dropped off flight recorder buoys before every jump and wormhole transition, so any Ruhar ship that found the buoys would learn that the emulation software had worked, after a few adjustments. "I don't expect any of us will achieve anything more significant than that in our entire careers. That is better than staying aboard a dying ship in the middle of interstellar space, praying for rescue. That was *your* plan."

Bifft opened his mouth to retort, but he couldn't think of anything to say, so he sat and silently fumed, and hated Lieutenant Colonel Emily Perkins.

CHAPTER SIXTEEN

Jates and Tutula had been conferring about something, heads close together in a heated argument and their zPhone speakers shut off. When Tutula grabbed the front of Jates' uniform top and shook him, Perkins had enough.

"Knock it off, you two. Mind telling me what's going on?"

Tutula cast her eyes away in a guilty gesture, so Jates straightened in his chair. "Colonel, with the help of Arlon Dahl, we have penetrated the outer layer of the base's computers."

"Outstanding," Perkins grinned. "Good work."

"It is nothing, really," Tutula shrugged. "They made almost no attempt at information security, except for details of their current research project. The security of that system is very robust, we will not be able to gain access from here."

"What's the problem, then? You weren't detected?"

"No, we have not been detected. As I said, the base is not concerned about external security. At the base were eleven security personnel and twenty eight civilian researchers, all the researchers were evacuated eighteen days ago. The eleven guards have one dropship."

Perkins considered that. "Ok, a small contingent, lightly armed, and they don't know about us, right?"

"Correct. It is unlikely-"

"Tutula, this will go a lot faster if you get to the point, and tell me what was worth you two arguing about."

Tutula took a breath and looked at Jates, who shook his head. She ignored him. "Colonel, perhaps you should sit down."

Oh shit, Emily told herself as she lowered into a seat on the somewhat flimsy folding chair, in the tent that was the group's headquarters on Camp Alpha. The trip down to the surface had been filled equally with tension and boredom, and they now had the dropships covered with stealth netting, tents set up for everyone, and she had a team trying to hack into the Kristang computers. She would not have risked doing that, except Arlon Dahl had assured her that his handheld computer was more powerful than any type of Kristang system. "Go ahead. Give me the bad news."

"In addition to this planet being a military training site, as you know, it was and is also a research base. Even before your military units cycled through this world, the warrior caste brought humans here to study." Jates urgently shot a warning look at Tutula, which she also ignored. "To study, and to experiment on. Colonel, this will not be easy to hear." She related the facts of human civilians being kidnapped from Earth and used for horrible tests of bioweapons, genetically-engineered pathogens intended to be used against Earth. Thousands of human subjects had died on Camp Alpha, half a world away from the blissfully ignorant human Expeditionary Force who had eagerly been training to serve their lizard masters.

"These experiments," Perkins asked in a voice flattened into calm from shock. It sounded to her like her own voice was coming from far away. "How far have they advanced?"

"Those experiments were terminated shortly after the wormhole access to your homeworld was shut off. No further supply of test subjects could be brought here from Earth, and the White Wind clan fell into serious financial trouble when they lost access to Earth. Colonel, I am sorry to tell you that, before the wormhole shut down, the experiments had proceeded far enough that a supply of that original bioweapon was shipped to your planet, to be used against your people in case of rebellion. The pathogen was still in development, but," Tutula tapped the display, "the report stated it was considered effective enough to kill much of the human population. If needed," she added quietly.

Emily sat in stunned silence. When Tutula opened her mouth to speak, she raised a hand to stop the alien, unable to process any more information right then. The two Verd-Kris sat quietly, fully understanding the impact of what they had found. "Tell me," the human asked when she was able to speak, "when the Kristang at Earth learned the wormhole had gone dormant and they were trapped there, what would have been their reaction?"

"We are *not* Kristang," Tutula reminded gently. "So any guess we make-"

"They would have shit their pants," Jates stated. "Tutula, Colonel Perkins is a soldier. She needs to know the truth and not some happy stories," he chided his companion. "Colonel, your guess is as good as ours, but I am sure you fear the worst. The warrior caste would have panicked at first, then seized the opportunity to make the best of their dilemma by making the worst for your people. With access to effective bioweapons, they could have reduced the human population to a manageable number, that posed less of an obstacle to the warrior caste exploitation of your world, then enslaved the rest."

"A manageable number?" Perkins whispered in horror.

"We don't *know* anything," Tutula cautioned. "We don't. Colonel, you should not-"

"Thank you," Perkins said robotically, so overwhelmed by emotion that at the moment, she felt nothing. "Do not tell anyone, especially my team, about the bioweapon sent to Earth. They do not need to know, not yet." She would need to tell the Mavericks what she just learned, because they would find out when she informed UNEF HQ on Paradise. *If* she ever made contact with Paradise. "I assume all human test subjects here were killed?"

That prompted another meaningful look between the Verd-Kris. Tutula spoke first. "*Those* test subjects from Earth were all killed when the experiments were ended, yes. The current problem is that there is another set of experiments ongoing, using human former soldiers who call themselves 'Keepers'?" She checked the translation.

"Keepers? Son of a *bitch*!" Perkins exclaimed. "Those *stupid*-" She clenched her fists. Fuming at the stupidity of that misguided bunch was not accomplishing anything. "Sorry. Yes, I know about these 'Keepers of the Faith' as they call themselves. Please, Tutula, continue."

"The current experiments are intended not for use against humans, but to use humans as disease carriers, to kill *Ruhar*. The plan is to infect a group of these 'Keepers' with a pathogen that uses human DNA to create a binary prion agent," she saw the lack of understanding in Perkins' eyes. "It is a very sophisticated technique. These prion precursors will remain dormant in an infected human for a specified period, the experiment aimed at a dormancy period of three months. During that time, humans could infect others with the precursors, but victims would not display any symptoms. In humans, the binary agents would begin combining into a lethal pathogen in three months, but in Ruhar, the latency period would be around two months. Ruhar could also infect other Ruhar, so the human carriers are only needed to get the infection started. And to provide a cover story, so the Ruhar will think the pathogen is a natural mutation in humans, and not a biowarfare attack that is, as you know, banned by the rules of this war."

Perkins was stunned. "The pathogen could leap from human hosts into Ruhar, before infected humans are showing any symptoms of illness?"

"Yes," Tutula looked guilty though she had nothing to do with the project. "As I said, this is very sophisticated and advanced biotechnology. The aim of the research is to produce an agent that *appears* to be a naturally-occurring mutation in humans, a mutation that has evolved an ability to cross into Ruhar. Colonel, because human carriers would not know they were infected, they could infect many Ruhar they come into contact with. By the time the Ruhar are showing symptoms, it will be too late. Two months is long enough for infected Ruhar to travel to other worlds. This pathogen could spread far beyond the planet you call Paradise."

"Oh shit," blood drained from Emily's face. "This will all get blamed on humans."

The two Verd-Kris showed Perkins the data they had skimmed off the unsecure computer at the Kristang base, which frustratingly did not contain critical details about the pathogen that was intended for an attack on Paradise. To assess the nature of the threat and to prepare any possible countermeasures, they needed the research data that was locked up behind a secure firewall, but Ernt Dahl was not optimistic about his little computer breaking that firewall.

"Colonel," the Jeraptha announced after running a subroutine he thought had the best chance of penetrating the firewall. "The attempt was a failure. I am sorry, my system was not designed to penetrate a well-designed firewall."

"Is there any other way to get in remotely?"

"Not that I know of," Ernt shook his antennas. "We must be extremely careful. If an intrusion is detected, I expect the research system is designed to erase all of its data. I will work with the cadets who have studied what you call 'cy-ber' security. I must warn you, I am not hopeful."

"Then our best hope may be for a Ruhar ship coming to rescue us, they might have experts who can break into that system," Perkins speculated.

"Excuse me, Colonel, but I believe that is not true," Tutula said stiffly. "Arrival of an enemy warship would surely trigger the guards at the base to erase all the research data. The system may even be programmed to erase itself, if an enemy ship enters this star system."

"Damn it," Perkins chided herself. "You're right. You are right, Tutula, thank you for reminding me. We need to get that data, and any biological samples stored at that base, while the guards here are unaware of our presence. We need a plan to do that, if we can't access that research data remotely."

"We were able to get schematics of the base layout, however the base has been expanded repeatedly and many security features are also behind the firewall," Jates warned. "We could encounter nasty surprises in any assault."

"Understood. There is another problem I have to consider." She looked first to Tutula, then Jates. "I have a dilemma," Perkins explained. "If I tell the Ruhar this bioweapon technology exists, they could very well quarantine the human population of Paradise, to protect the Ruhar."

"A quarantine is not your real concern," Jates said as he sat back in his chair.

"It is not?" Tutula asked.

"No," Jates appraised Perkins with a cool eye. "If the Ruhar fear humans could be carrying an undetectable, lethal pathogen, they may take action to remove the threat. *Extreme* action."

"The Ruhar are not Kristang," Tutula protested.

"They are also not stupid, nor soft," Jates concluded. "When pressed to protect themselves, they have a will of iron. That is why the Kristang have repeatedly suffered defeats to the Ruhar, despite the warrior caste focusing their entire society and economy on war. Humans are still viewed by most Ruhar as conquered and rather pathetic former enemies, despite all your team has done for them, Colonel Perkins. Gratitude has an expiration date, fear does not. If the Ruhar federal government believes humans on Paradise pose a real threat to Ruhar society on multiple worlds, they will not hesitate to act against a species that is already unpopular. Besides, I do not think you have a dilemma at all, for you do not have a choice about whether to inform the Ruhar."

"Why?" Perkin's eyes narrowed. "If we destroy this research base and all its materials and data, the pathogen will not pose a threat to Paradise."

"I believe the human expression is 'that ship has sailed'? That expression is particularly appropriate in this situation," Jates announced without humor. "Colonel, from the data Arlon Dahl was able to extract, we learned that a Kristang transport ship departed this world eighteen days ago, carrying the bioweapon and a group of Keepers who will be infected without their knowledge. That ship," he paused as Perkins felt a sinking feeling, "is on its way to Paradise right now."

"The Kristang might have killed everyone on Earth?" Shauna asked as tears rolled freely down her cheeks. Perkins had told her team about the bioweapon threat to Earth, before she explained the need for a physical assault on the Kristang research base to counter *another* and more current bioweapon threat.

"Hey, darlin', we already knew that could be true," Jesse said quietly as he held Shauna's shoulders tightly. His own face was a mask of anger, but his eyes were moist and he didn't care if anyone saw.

"Yes, but now we know that was their *plan* all along" Shauna balled up her fists. "They build a bioweapon, then they shut down the wormhole so they can do whatever they want to Earth without Maxolhx or Rindhalu enforcing their stupid rules. By the time the Kristang open the wormhole again, humans will be extinct and no one will care."

"Whoa," Dave gasped. "You think the *lizards* shut down that wormhole?"

"Shauna, I do not think that is true," Irene declared. "Word at UNEF HQ was, the lizards were totally surprised and freaked out when the wormhole to Earth shut down, they didn't expect that to happen. Hell, if the Kristang can control Elder wormholes, they would use that ability for something more important than our little planet."

"Maybe they didn't shut down the wormhole," Shauna snapped at her friend. "Maybe they just, just somehow anticipated that wormhole was going to shut down, and they planned for it. It doesn't matter! The lizards have control of Earth, they have a bioweapon, and no one can stop them from doing whatever they want."

"All right, all right," Perkins appealed for calm. "Jarrett, I hate the Goddamned lizards as much as anyone, but right now, we need to focus. We have a job to do."

"What's that, Ma'am?" Jesse asked, startled out of his dark thoughts.

"A dumb-fuck group of Keepers are on their way to Paradise, and we have no way to stop them. But on this planet, at the research base, is data and materials the Ruhar could use to create a cure or a vaccine or some way to protect against this bioweapon. We need to retrieve that data and hold it until a friendly ship arrives to pick us up. We can," she thought for a moment. "Yeah, we can, we should, load the data into a drone that will respond only to a Ruhar or allied ship, in case a Kristang ship gets here first and wipes us out," Perkins noted, thinking it strange that the prospect of her own impending death was so relatively unimportant, she felt no fear for herself.

Shauna wiped away tears with the back of her hands. "Ma'am, I am in. Point me at that base, and no Goddamned lizard is gonna keep me from getting that data."

Perkins accepted Shauna's statement with a grim nod. "Tutula, Jates, what about you? Attacking that base would be taking direct action against your own species. I know the warrior caste are not your people, but-"

"Colonel Perkins," Jates thumped the console with a fist, hard enough to shake the tough equipment. "Taking direct action, taking the fight right to the warrior caste, is the reason why we are out here! If needed, Tutula and I will hit that base by ourselves."

"That won't be necessary," Irene assured the two Verd-Kris. "Ma'am, we've got plenty of anger and determination, what we need is a plan. We can't take any Ruhar with us on the assault, there's too much risk of infection even if we stay buttoned up in skinsuits. The Verd-Kris aren't at risk of getting sick, or being carriers, right?" Tutula nodded so she continued. "Then we have to hit that base with the six of us, two Verd-Kris, one Jeraptha and a couple dropships. We need a plan, and we first need to know the opposition. So," she turned to the aliens. "What do we know in terms of tactical intel?"

"Ma'am?" Dave asked with a sideways glance at the other four Mavericks, huddled around a console and reviewing a schematic of the enemy base. "A word?"

Perkins nodded and waved the sergeant to where she was in a cabin seat, working on her tablet. "What is it?"

Dave lowered his voice. "We know this planet was used to research, and test, bioweapons for use against humans on Earth."

Perkins cleared her throat that had become constricted by the thought of unimaginable horrors afflicting the population of her home planet. Her *original* home planet, she reminded herself bitterly. Earth was lost forever to her now, whether humans still lived there or not. Paradise was her homeworld now. "Yes."

"My question is," he ran a finger on the armrest of the chair next to Perkins, and showed her a fingertip stained yellow with fine dust that blew in whenever the dropship's doors were open. "We're all breathing this air. Could the bioweapon they planned to use on Earth be loose here?"

"God*damn* it," Perkins swore, keeping her voice low. "I didn't think of that."

"I didn't either, until a minute ago. We know the ExForce didn't get infected while we were here, so the lizards must have kept the weapon contained before the Force shipped out to Paradise. But after that? The lizards must have tested the effectiveness of air dispersal at some point. In that case," he looked at his dust-covered fingertip. "We could all be exposed. And infected."

"Shit."

"Colonel," Dave shot a guilty glance forward, where the only other four humans on the planet were struggling with their own problems. "If we *have* been exposed to that bioweapon, we need to move up the assault schedule. We need to go before the six of us become combat ineffective, and that could be real soon."

"Czakja, this is why the United States Army, in its infinite wisdom, has sergeants."

"Ma'am?"

"To remind dumbass senior officers like me of practical considerations that *I* should have thought of. I've had my head in the clouds, worrying about, Goddamn *policy,* like how UNEF can keep the Ruhar from enforcing extreme measures against us on Paradise to protect their own furry little asses. You just reminded me that I need to focus right here, right *now*, or there won't be a future for humans *or* Ruhar. Listen, Czajka," she whispered. "Talk with Dahl, or Jates, see if they found any details about the bioweapon the lizards brought to Earth. I've been so worried about this new weapon, I forgot about the earlier threat. Maybe they recovered enough data for Ruhar medical scanners," she nodded toward a hard-cased medical pack attached to the cabin wall, "to detect whether we have been exposed or not."

"The tests were inconclusive," the Ruhar cadet announced with a frightened expression.

"What *are* the results?" Perkins demanded.

"You have to understand, I am not a doctor, I am only in my second year at the academy," the cadet protested. "This device, this scanner, is also not programmed for human physiology, and I might have adjusted it incorrectly. It could be wrong, or it-"

"What, are, the results?" Perkins asked in a softer tone. "I understand you are doing your best under difficult circumstances. Still, I need information on which to make decisions. Please, tell me what the device indicates." She thought that was easier than asking a young Ruhar, barely into medical studies, to render her own opinion.

"The scanner has detected antibodies in the blood of all six of you. It is very likely that you have all been exposed to the bioweapon that was developed for use against humans on your homeworld, on Earth."

"Oh, shit," Irene groaned. "Sergeant Czajka's right, Colonel, we need to go ASAP, while we can still fly. And fight."

"Hold on, Striebich," Perkins held up a hand to halt the frenzied conversation that had sprung up around her. "I don't remember a lot from the biology course I took in college, but I do know that on Earth, we use two types of viruses as vaccines. A live virus that has been weakened," how that worked, she had no idea. "And a dead virus, a virus that has been killed. A dead virus can't harm you, but it does provoke your immune system to create antibodies somehow, so if you are ever infected with the real virus, your immune system recognizes the threat and already knows how to kill it. Did I get that right?"

"Correct," the Ruhar cadet agreed, slightly embarrassed for the primitive humans. The crude process of using actual viruses to create vaccines was something she learned about in her medical history class, that technique had not been used by the Ruhar for thousands of years, yet humans still relied on low-tech ancient technology.

"Tell me this: is it possible the pathogen we've been exposed to is dead? It must have been years since the Kristang dispersed it in the air here. All that time, it has been exposed to air, rainwater, heat, cold, ultraviolet radiation from the star, right? Maybe our immune systems were exposed to dead remnants of the bioweapon."

"That is possible, yes," the cadet said slowly, then lifted her head as she warned to the idea. "I was only given a brief overview of human physiology, but I believe your immunity cells react to proteins on the outer coating of a virus phage, does that make sense?"

Perkins looked to her team for help but none of them had any idea. Derek tilted his head and frowned. "That sounds about right. I saw something like that on the Discovery channel," he grinned sheepishly.

"Good. Yeah," Perkins agreed.

"If that is true, then it is possible-" The cadet smiled. "No, it is likely, that your antibodies are a reaction to exposure to the dead pathogen. Colonel Perkins, I very much doubt that a relatively crude bioweapon, like the one described in the files we found, could survive exposure to the elements on this planet for such a long time."

"Good," Perkins breathed a sigh of relief. "I do not like the idea of dying of a horrible disease on this rock. We still have to proceed as if we are infected, because we can't take the chance. The incubation period of that original bioweapon was a couple weeks, right?"

"Yes, according to the data recovered," the cadet acknowledged with a pained stare down at her display. "Colonel, please, consider that even if you are infected, you might have been exposed to an early, less effective form of the pathogen. Or the pathogen may be degraded by exposure here, in which case there may be a longer incubation period."

"Yes, or the data we recovered might not have contained details of the final, *more* effective pathogen. I can't take the risk we could all get very sick, soon, before we can attack that base and get the research data we need. Thank you, cadet," Perkins cut off further discussion. Her throat had been feeling sore for the past three days, and it felt worse that morning. She remembered her throat being sore the last time she was on Camp Alpha.

Was it just the irritating, burnt-tasting dust that covered everything? Or was she infected and on the verge of a full-blown fatal disease?

Perkins put Arlon Dahl and a team of Ruhar cadets on the task of hacking into the research files of the Kristang base, hoping they could extract data detailing the pathogen's chemical signatures, lifecycle, test results and possible antigens. The next morning, she walked to the dropship that was being used for the hacking effort, just as Nert walked down the open side ramp. The Ruhar cadet waved to her, then bent backwards and forwards, with a grimace.

"Are you well, Cadet?" Perkins asked.

"Yes, Colonel Perkins. My back is sore from sitting at the console for too long. The team is working very hard," he assured her, "we worked all night."

"Any results?"

"No, their security around the lab computer is very strong. Arlon Dahl says it is airtight."

"We can't access the data remotely?"

Nert looked distractedly at the tablet in one hand. "We would have better luck playing 'Pick Up Sticks' with our butt cheeks."

Despite the seriousness of the situation, she had to smile. "Nert, is that another colorful expression you learned from the Third Infantry?"

"No," he turned toward her, his skin under the light fur turning a darker shade of pink. "I heard that from Shauna, that is, Sergeant Jarrett. Is it a bad thing to say?"

"No. It is only, discouraging to hear."

"The team is continuing to work on the problem," Nert forced a smile.

"But they're not optimistic, are they?"

"No, Colonel, they are not. I must be truthful, there has been no progress for the past seven hours. The remaining methods we could use to access the data remotely pose a serious risk of our cyber attack being detected. I am sorry."

"Don't be sorry, Cadet. You and the team have endured harsh conditions and performed far beyond expectations. It looks like," she looked off to the horizon, far beyond which lay the Kristang base. "We'll have to do this the hard way."

"There is no way to extract that data remotely?" Perkins requested confirmation of the gloomy news Nert had brought to her.

"I am sorry, no. Perhaps if we had a team of experts from our data security division, but," Ernt waved a claw to encompass the tired group around him, "they are Ruhar cadets, and I am not a computer expert."

"You did your best, that's all I can ask. Damn it. If we go in and the lizards spot us before we can get to the data core, they could erase the memory and we'd lose everything, all their records." She tugged the hair on the back of her head in frustration. "The research computer may be programmed to erase itself in the event of an attack on the base." She turned her attention to the two Verd-Kris. "What do we know about this research base?"

"Not enough," Tutula pointed to her display. "We have the original schematics of the compound, back when the Kristang built it to study the star here and its effects on the planet. They were hoping to understand how the Elder weapon created a focused solar flare that cooked this world," she grinned and bounced her eyeballs up and down in the Verd-Kris equivalent of an eyeroll. "They had *no* chance of understanding technology on that level. The base has been expanded and modified over the years, especially the research facilities, and we do not have access to those records, other than very basic information."

"Very well," Perkins unfolded a chair and sat down. "Show me what we do know."

"What's the plan, Ma'am?" Shauna asked, looking up from her tablet. All eyes turned to the human commander, with the two Verd-Kris in particular waiting intently to hear what the primitive being would say.

Perkins took a breath, steadying herself. "I say we go in hot, kill everyone, take the data and bug out quick." She looked to Irene, then Derek, then the two Verd-Kris pilots. "If it moves and it's not us, kill it. I don't care about collateral damage to the base buildings, as long as you don't hit the main research complex."

"What about your Kee-purr people?" Tutula asked, pronouncing 'Keeper' slowly. "We believe there are still a group of humans at the base."

"Don't fire on them deliberately," Perkins' hard expression softened slightly. "But don't take any risk either. If there's a-" she almost said 'lizard'. "If there's an enemy shooting at us and he's surrounded by Keepers, take them all out."

"You are willing to sacrifice your own people to accomplish the mission?" Tutula's eyes narrowed as she waited for Perkins' answer.

"As far as I'm concerned, those Keepers have pretty much fucked themselves," Perkins spat on the dusty ground. "I'm not risking a single one of our lives for them. You have a problem with that?" She stared Tutula straight in the eye.

"No, Colonel Perkins," Tutula's lips twitched in what was intended as a smile. "Your mission focus is admirable. My people are not cruel like the Kristang you have encountered in the past, but we are also not soft. We do not believe in half measures." A shadow fell across her expression, and she added in a low voice "With our small numbers against those of the warrior caste who have stolen and perverted our culture, we cannot afford to be sentimental."

Perkins nodded. "There are less than two dozen Keepers at that base, if we can believe the outdated info we retrieved. Over a hundred thousand humans are on Paradise, and *millions* of Ruhar. We are not putting all those lives at risk just to possibly rescue a small number of Keepers. When they removed the UNEF insignia from their uniforms, they should have gotten a Big Chicken Dinner," Perkins forgot the aliens would not understand the slang for Bad Conduct Discharge. "I don't hate the Keepers, most of them are too stupid to know what they're doing. But they got themselves into this mess, and now their mess is threatening all the lives on Paradise and maybe beyond."

"Ma'am," Shauna's face had a strained, uncomfortable expression. "What will we do, if we take out the enemy and there are Keepers still alive?"

"We can't take them with us," Perkins noted. "We have to assume they're all infected and we have to minimize our exposure. That means our suits stay buttoned up the whole time, and we follow full decontamination procedures on the egress. We can't bring infected Keepers with us." She continued to use the term 'Keepers' because if she called them 'humans' or 'people' it would be more difficult to ignore their situation. "If we accomplish the mission and some Keepers survive, their best bet is to remain in place. The liz-" she almost used derogatory slang in front of the Verd-Kris, "The Kristang must have food for the Keepers there, we certainly don't have enough food with us to feed that number of people. They can remain at the base."

Though Shauna still looked uncomfortable, her arms across her chest and shoulders slumped forward, curled into herself, she nodded briefly. "We have to tell them about the bioweapon program. They deserve to know the truth."

Dave snorted. "Come on, Shauna, those Sleepers have had the truth staring them in the face for years, and they don't see it because they don't *want* to see it. What makes you think that us telling them the Kristang have been using them as lab rats will change their minds?"

"Hey, chill, Ski," Jesse replied in defense of his girlfriend, putting an arm around Shauna's shoulders to show he understood her feelings on the subject. "Like the Colonel said, some of them are just too dumb to know what they're doing. Or they are gullible and followed the wrong people. Look at Eric Koblenz. Yeah, the guy was a Grade-A asshole, but I don't think he would do anything to kill people on Paradise, his own people."

"Ok, 'Pone, yeah, Eric was too dumb to know what he's doing," Dave agreed.

"We should tell them," Irene added. "If they don't believe us now, they will when they all start dying in a couple months."

"Hell," Jesse kicked the dusty ground with the toe of a boot. "What a freakin' mess. How did we get such bad karma?"

"Bad?" Perkins pretended to be surprised. "Colter, this is *good* karma in disguise. If our star carrier hadn't gotten blown up, we would never have known about the threat to Paradise. And we would not now have this marvelous opportunity to shine."

Jesse tilted his head at their commanding officer. "You do know what 'opportunity' means in the military, right, Ma'am?"

"I do, Colter, and my ass will be on the line right beside you."

Tutula clapped her hands, startling the humans. "I see an opportunity for direct action against the warrior caste who have oppressed my people for millennia. When do we start, Colonel Perkins?"

"Now. Prep a dropship."

The dropship, with Tutula and Derek flying the outbound leg and Irene acting as relief pilot, followed a medium then low-altitude stealth flight profile until it was within six hundred kilometers of the base, where the ship's sensors picked up the faintest traces of backscatter from the network of active sensors surrounding the base. At that point, with risk of detection approaching an unacceptable three percent, Derek gently turned one hundred eighty degrees, reduced speed and gradually lost altitude while the others prepped the package. A minute later, a door opened under the dropship's tail and a stream of stealthy foam-covered balls fell out, tumbling smoothly as they fell away.

The dropship gradually increased power and climbed, while the crew anxiously monitored extremely faint data feeds from the cluster of more than three dozen sensor drones they had ejected. When each drone fell to four thousand feet above the ground, an invisible nanofiber parachute deployed, spreading wide and momentarily bringing its payload almost to a halt in midair. The foam coating dissolved and the drone unfolded itself, sprouting wings that swept back to allow the hummingbird-sized drone to build airspeed. Each drone checked in with its fellows by line-of-sight laserlink, and only one drone out of the thirty eight was found to be operating at less than the optimal level. As that drone was not needed, it self-destructed with the consent of its flock, sending particles no larger than a fingernail to rain softly down and bury into the dusty ground.

Flying slowly to conserve fuel and avoiding tripping enemy motion sensors by artificially disturbing the air, the flock of drones approached the base, encircling it. Several times, a drone had to go into hover mode as it was swept by an active sensor pulse. The risk was that the Kristang might have set their air cover sensors on an ultra-sensitive mode, for the planet had no flying animal life and therefore anything moving in a way not directed by the prevailing winds had to be a threat. One drone, pinned in place by an active sensor pulse that came back to sweep over it three times, self-destructed to avoid detection, so no alarm was raised at the base. None of the drones risked overflying the site, but as the base was in a mountain valley, no overflight was needed. One by one, the drones set down just inside the lines of ridges and foothills, selecting locations where they had line of sight to the base below on the valley floor. Each drone focused its own passive sensors on a different area of the base, switching focus in a pre-programmed, coordinated fashion to provide a three-dimensional map of the target.

"Ah, damn it!" Dave threw up his hands as he saw the recently-assembled composite image of the Kristang research base. His frustration was not because of the base's defenses, for those appeared to be minimal. There were only two anti-aircraft maser batteries and the Mavericks could deal with those before the assault. The single dropship assigned to the base was also not a problem, it was out of its hardened underground bunker with one of the engines laying exposed on the ground in pieces. As Dave watched, two Kristang were having an animated argument about the disassembled engine, shouting something at each other. The sensors were too far away to pick up the lizards' words, and Dave didn't give a rat's ass what two murderous assholes were saying anyway.

What he did care about was on the other side of the base, in a separate compound surrounded by a double fence. What he saw there made him angry. A group of a half-dozen humans, standing around in the morning sunlight. Several others walked between buildings in the compound, and from the size of the buildings, Dave guessed there might be as many as fifty humans housed there. He zoomed in the image to the point where, despite the super high-tech image stabilization and enhancement gear of the sensors, he still had to blink to understand what the slightly fuzzy view was showing him. Then he understood, for he had seen that same image many times before in his military career. The rectangular areas of flattened dirt were where tents had been set up, tents or some other type of temporary shelter. People had walked over the flattened ground after the tents had been removed, but from the heavy tracks leading to where the tents had been, he knew they had been occupied at some point. Probably the compound recently had held many more humans, perhaps double or triple the number that could be housed in the permanent buildings. "Interesting," he muttered, then, "Colonel! Ma'am, we got a problem."

"What is it, Czajka?"

"Keepers," he nearly spat with disgust. From the enhanced image, he could see the people standing around in the sunlight were wearing military uniforms, so they had to be Keepers. "There are at least a dozen of those shitheads, from what I've seen. Could be more still in those buildings."

"That's the control group, then," Perkins looked at Ernt Dahl.

"Control group?" Shauna looked at the Jeraptha, who was shifting his rear pair of legs nervously.

Perkins explained. "Arlon Dahl found information that one group of Keepers here was used as a control group; they were not infected, while other groups were infected with different versions of the pathogen. If a test group became sick unexpectedly but the control group also got sick, the Kristang would know the cause was some environmental factor and not the experimental pathogen. Until now, we did not know whether any of the control group was still alive, because the records Dahl could access stopped updating when the last group of researchers left this planet. We do know all the Ruhar they brought here are dead, they used the Ruhar control group for the final test."

"I wonder why that group of Keepers is still alive?" Jesse rubbed the back of his neck. "I mean, why bother? You can see from that double-layer fence, the lizards here think those Keepers are a security risk."

"Insurance?" Shauna guessed. "In case something goes wrong with the op on Paradise. Or, in case they decide to use the pathogen on another Ruhar planet, maybe."

Dave tapped the display again. "Ma'am, I just thought of something. That control group, they've been here a long time, right?"

"Likely they came here soon after they left Paradise. Why?"

"If we have been exposed to the original bioweapon by breathing the air here, the one the lizards planned to use on Earth, then those Keepers must have been exposed also."

"Damn," Jesse slapped Dave on the back. "You're right, man. They're still alive, so we must have been exposed only to a dead virus. We're good!"

"Not necessarily," Perkins stated with a frown, and Dave nodded agreement. "The Keepers may have been given a vaccine against the original bioweapon."

"Yeah, and in that case," Dave tapped the display, "the vaccine must be in that base somewhere. Would a vaccine do us any good, now that we've already been exposed?"

"I don't know," Perkins admitted.

"Colonel Perkins," Ernt Dahl crossed his forearms. "I am not an expert on biological weapons, but I doubt the Kristang would have vaccinated or treated the humans here against another pathogen. Because humans on Paradise have not been exposed to the original pathogen, giving the control group here a vaccine or post-infection treatment would alter their immune response from the baseline, and reduce their usefulness as a true control group."

"Oh. Yeah, that makes sense," Perkins' mouth was a flat line across her face. "Unless the Kristang didn't have a choice about it, since they had contaminated this whole planet already. Czajka, good thinking, we'll look for a treatment or something when we get inside that base. Shit. That original bioweapon is another damned good reason why we need to take that base, soon."

"Not just to protect ourselves," Dave said, knowing what she was thinking.

"No. If there is a vaccine or treatment in there somewhere, we need it. If we ever get to Earth and the lizards there haven't already used the bioweapon against our people, we need a countermeasure."

"Can we do it? Bottom line," Perkins stood with her arms crossed after reviewing the data gathered by the sensors.

"Yes," Tutula's confidence was absolute. "Their air defenses are minimal," she looked to Ernt Dahl for confirmation.

The beetle raised its antenna in a sort of shrug. "I am not an expert on anti-aircraft systems, I am not familiar with the subject at all. My training was for fleet service," he admitted.

"Their air defenses are weak and degraded," Tutula enhanced the display image, highlighting two areas. "These are defensive maser turrets. I suspect one of them is offline and has been that way for a long time."

"How do you know that?" Perkins asked, leaning forward to get a better view.

"These turrets require regular maintenance, and test-firing after components are replaced. The turret to the south has vehicle tracks leading from the base, and footprints around the site. Vehicle tracks at the north site have been obscured by blowing sand, and there are no footprints. Also, this hatch," she zoomed in the view so powerfully that the image became fuzzy and shook slightly. "It is open. It should be closed. I think someone tried to fix a mechanical failure in that turret, and gave up. With the warrior caste," she avoided using the word 'Kristang', "scheduled to abandon this planet, they would not expend much effort to maintain facilities here."

"Ok, I see that. That is a hell of a risk to take with our airspace craft, based on a lack of footprints and one open hatch."

"That is not all, Colonel Perkins. As I said, the masers would be test-fired after components have been replaced. You can see here, on the hills to the south, scorch marks where maser beam struck. Those marks are still dark, indicating that turret was fired recently, and the maser fire must have come from the southern turret, because they would not have risked firing over the base. There are no scorch marks on hills to the north. We can't absolutely verify condition of the northern turret because that data is behind their secure firewall," Dahl's antenna waved in agreement with that statement, "so we need to trust our own eyes."

"All right, Striebich, Bonsu, do you agree?"

"Yes, Ma'am," Irene nodded. "The three of us covered this last night. It's doable."

"Those maser turrets are armored?" Perkins observed skeptically. "Your dropships aren't."

"The turrets are armored, plus they have an energy shield," Irene added with a frown. "And you're right, our ships are vulnerable, but we have an ace in the hole. Part of the weapons load we brought down from the *Toaster* are anti-AA missiles, kind like of like the HARM system our Navy and Air Force uses."

"Those SEAD systems home in on active sensors, right," Perkins noted. "Not on the anti-air weapon itself. The Kristang must use a distributed sensor network."

"They do," Irene groaned inwardly, wanting to avoid a long session of educating their commander about the finer points of Suppression of Enemy Air Defenses. "These Ruhar missiles are smart, they know Kristang anti-air masers use a look-look-shoot pattern. Two low-powered beam bursts to track and confirm the target lock, followed by the kill shot. Each of the Ruhar HARMs deploys twenty eight submunitions that look for maser backscatter. Once they pinpoint the maser's location, they kill it. Some of the submunitions fire their own maser countermeasures to scramble the enemy's targeting data, while the others home in and kill the turret. Ma'am, in this case we have an advantage; we already know exactly where that turret is. We plan to launch our anti-AA missiles before we come over the ridgeline. We saturate their defenses, knock them out before exposing ourselves."

"The base doesn't have any missile batteries?"

"No. There is a site here to the west where they planned to install missiles, you can see where they bulldozed the site and installed part of this concrete pad, here." On the display, Irene pointed to a broken concrete tile, half covered with drifting sand. "They stopped work on it. We know there are not any underground sensor feeds to that area."

"What about MANPADs?" Dave asked, peering over Perkins' shoulder.

"Man, pad?" Dahl asked, confused. He tapped his right ear. "My translator did not understand that reference."

"MAN Portable Air Defense," Dave explained, miming that he held a missile tube on one shoulder. "A shoulder-launched anti-aircraft missile, you know?"

"Ah, yes," the Jeraptha's antennas bounced up and down. "Our military has such devices, though I have never seen them in action. Our pilots are warned to be very careful about such devices when used by the enemy, they can be deadly, even to our advanced airspace craft. But-"

"Yeah, we know," Irene forced a smile. "Your training is for Fleet service. Ma'am," she turned her attention back to Perkins, "Tutula is right, this is doable. Air defenses are not the biggest problem."

That remark drew a raised eyebrow from Perkins, so Irene continued. "Hitting this base is a waste unless we recover data and hopefully samples from the research. From what we," she pointed to Ernt Dahl, "have been able to get from hacking in, all that data is housed here, in the research complex in the center of the base. We can avoid damage to those buildings, but the defenders could trigger a program to erase all the data, or it might be set to erase automatically in the event that base is attacked."

"But you have a plan for that?"

"Arlon Dahl has a plan, Ma'am."

The Jeraptha raised himself up on his back legs, before remembering other species were threatened by that posture, so he settled back down on all four legs. "The data connection between the research complex, and the security center where the guards live, is an underground cable here. For redundancy they should have multiple cables, I think the connection is limited to a single cable, because they are more concerned about their own people stealing data than about external threats. The cable is not deep, it is part of the original construction and the plans state it is only," the translator stumbled awkwardly as it always did when converting measurements, "three point eight six five meters deep." Dahl paused to see if Perkins understood, and she nodded.

"Ma'am," Irene picked up narrative. "We have missiles that can blow a hole deeper than that, a missile can cut the cable so the defenders can't order the research core to erase its data. Other missiles will drop off drones that can orbit the area and jam any backup wireless connection to the research base."

"Which leaves only the problem of the research core detecting an attack and erasing itself," Perkins shook her head. "I am not liking this plan."

"We have a plan for that also," Dahl bobbed on his forelegs excitedly. "The research core gets data from the base sensor network, also from that single cable. The core may be programmed to erase itself in the event of an interruption in the sensor feed, and you can't take that risk." Perkins noted the Jeraptha had said 'you' rather than 'we'. "While we have been unable to access the research core or the secure network, that cable also carries unsecure data, and there are buffers spaced regularly along the cable. We *can* hack into those buffers and plant false sensor data, so the research core will not know about our attack, until the buffers overflow."

"How long does that give us?"

"Two minutes and forty eight seconds," Dahl flashed a Jeraptha smile, which made Perkins shudder as it looked like a spider eating something.

"Less than three minutes? That's not much time, not enough to land a ship and get inside the research base to download the core."

"No," Irene agreed. "In those hundred and sixty eight seconds, we need to cut the cable, then locate the cut end of the cable that leads to the research complex, and physically tap into it with a transmitter of our own that will keep feeding false sensor data," she held up a small device that had a hole in it, for plugging in a data cable.

"That's a mighty tall order, Striebich. Any way we can get a missile to drop off a drone that can attach to that cable?"

"We aren't carrying any drones like that, Ma'am, and I wouldn't want to trust a drone to dig in a blast crater to find a severed cable. One of us needs to do it."

"In a hundred sixty eight seconds, our missiles need to crest the ridge, sever that cable, then a dropship needs to fly there, slow down to land, and a team needs to dig down in a blast crater to find a cable?"

"Yes. We need to knock out air defenses first," Irene gritted her teeth.

"I assume you have a plan to do all this?"

"Yes, Colonel. You want to see our assault plan?"

"Hell yes. Run through it for me."

CHAPTER SEVENTEEN

Tutula's fingers softly and expertly slid over the flight controls, making tiny adjustments to the aircraft's relatively leisurely progress over the surface. The Ruhar controls had been designed to be used by four fingers and a thumb, making it somewhat awkward for the three-fingered Kristang, and the controls could only be modified to a limited extent. In that regard, the slow and primitive humans had an advantage over their Kristang comrades in arms, and Tutula was consoled by reminding herself she was more advanced in almost every other way. Her genetically-modified strength, speed, coordination and reactions made her physically far superior to any human, and awkward flight controls would be no obstacle to achieving her assigned mission. "Hawk Two in position and ready," she announced as her dropship raced over an imaginary line on the hills below. She was flying the only fighter-dropship they had brought down from the *Ruh Tostella*, a craft the humans called a 'Vulture'.

"Standby, Two," the voice of Lieutenant Colonel Perkins ordered, and Tutula did not react other than her pupils widening slightly, a sign of pleasure among her species. When Tutula's people had first heard of the low-tech species who called themselves 'Humans', she feared their culture would be cruel and oppressive to their females, either by nature, or as distorted by the warrior caste of the Kristang. She had been extremely pleased to learn that human civilian and military organizations included females in positions of authority, even at the highest level. Perkins and General Bezanson were the two highest-ranking Humans that Tutula knew of, the fact they were both female was encouraging.

"Hawk Two, you are 'Go' to proceed."

"Acknowledged, Hawk Lead," Tutula responded and this time there was no mistaking her emotions, her lips pulled back in a toothy grin as she contemplated the prospect of striking a direct blow against the warrior caste. "Missiles on automatic," she reported, seeing on a side display that the other dropship's missile launchers had also been released to the auto-fire system. She advanced her throttles slightly to avoid losing airspeed as she pulled the nose up to crest the ridge of foothills, and begin climbing the tall mountains that ringed the valley where the research base sprawled across the dusty ground. When the navigation system determined she had reached a preset distance from the target, the Vulture's missile bay doors snapped open and the rotary launchers spat out their deadly payloads, all of them. First in flight were the anti-AA missiles the humans for some reason called 'Wild Weasels', to scramble sensors and destroy the base's air defense maser cannon. Right behind were general-purpose missiles with pre-selected targets, and finally a volley of missiles that could be re-tasked in flight as needed. This last group could extend their wings and loiter above the base for up to twenty minutes, but the attackers all knew the fight would be over in the first three minutes or not at all.

With her ship's entire missile payload expended and running on ahead in parallel with the other dropship's warbirds, Tutula saw a blue light flash on her console and she reacted immediately, using a thumb to push the throttles to maximum. With missiles already approaching the mountain ridge, there was no longer a need to keep her speed subsonic. Shockwaves from the low-level passage of the missile formation were causing dust to swirl on the slopes of the mountains, the sonic boom of her passage would not be noticed in the chaos.

With the corner of one eye she verified the enemy base defenses had not yet reacted. The previous day, the tiny drones planted by the attackers had begun intermittently jamming the base's sensor network, turning the silent jamming on for brief periods. They knew from listening to the base communications system that the personnel there were angry and frustrated at what they assumed was an old and glitchy sensor network, and after fourteen hours, those Kristang had thrown up their hands and stopped trying to diagnose the problem. At first, they had put defenses on alert and sent teams out to scan for danger, but when nothing was found again and again, they decided to ignore the glitches and not waste time trying to fix an antiquated system on an uninhabited and useless planet.

That was why the defenders did not react when the jamming started again just before the dropships launched their missiles. Actually, one of the defenders did react, but that reaction was an unhelpful gesture of slamming a rifle butt into the display screen of the sensor system when it apparently began glitching again. That move made the other guard on duty laugh, and delayed their reactions a half-second when more than two dozen missiles screamed over the ridge of mountains to the south and no one could be under the delusion that the base's sensors merely had a glitch!

Tutula's ship was moving so fast, she had to roll it upside down and fire the belly jets as she passed over the sharp crest of the mountain ridge. The belly jets pushed the Vulture down so momentum did not carry it far out over the valley. Hanging in the sky on a high ballistic arc would not have been good for her survival, especially as her ship was momentarily lit by the sun that was just rising over the mountain ridge to the east. She grunted from the strain as she was squashed down in her seat, waiting so long to cut the jets and flip upright that her ship came heart-stoppingly close to scraping on the mountainside. Ignoring the G-force induced haze in her vision, she flipped up a switch to enable the ship's maser cannons and searched for targets, even as she watched missile warheads exploding on the floor of the valley below.

The personnel at the base, having no idea they were about to be thrust into the role of active defenders on a worthless planet that was unoccupied, were *soooooo* bored and sick and tired and disgusted and generally pissed off that early morning. They were not entirely sure about the purpose of their mission, because the asshole scientists who were so important and smart as they huddled in their research compound, had not bothered to inform the guards about the experiments they were conducting. But the guards were sure the mission was *over* because the scientists and their staff and most of the primitive humans had already left the planet, yet the guards were still stuck there. Every single one of the guards had prayed for a serious accident to befall the dropship that had carried the scientists off the dusty surface, but their prayers had not been answered. Why hadn't the guards and the last group of humans been lifted away from the nasty prison of a planet that was about to be abandoned? Insurance, that was the only reason they had been given. Their remaining on the planet was a form of insurance, just in case something went wrong with the mission and more experiments needed to be conducted. When the mission, whatever it was, had been successfully completed, then and only then would a ship come to pull the guards and the last surviving humans off the surface.

More than a few guards had speculated there would not be a ship coming at all, except maybe for the purpose of pounding the base into a smoking crater from orbit. A handful of guards were not worth the expense of sending a ship such a long distance across the star lanes, not with Kristang society engulfed in yet another civil war, and not when that star system was going to be abandoned as it was now too far from effective military support. Fretting that they had been discarded, angry at their impotence to control their fate, not having any clan leadership supervision, and just by nature being hateful assholes, the guards had taken to culling the remaining humans one by one or in pairs, to use for sport.

At first, they had dropped off humans on the other side of the mountain ridge, where the stupid humans in their own compound at the base could not see what was happening. The first hunt had been frustrating, the Kristang simply dumped the former soldier on the ground and told him to run, as they readied their hunting gear. That human evaded pursuit by unexpectedly going *up*hill and hiding in a shallow cavern, it was not until the next morning that the guards, having grown tired and frustrated and bored with the game, activated the tracking device they had injected into their quarry. At that point, angry they had been duped and had wasted most of a day looking in entirely the wrong place, they hammered the cavern with a missile, burying the human where he died.

Subsequent hunts were scarcely more satisfying, as the star-blasted planet had no trees and their human prey had difficulty finding cover. Even arming the prey with primitive projectile pistols did not offer much sport, because being armed gave the prey a foolish sense of confidence and drew them out, where they were easily killed by the armor-suited hunters.

After slaughtering four humans in hunts that were not much fun at all, the guards tried another game that offered much more sport; unarmed combat. Taking off their armored suits, a guard went into a makeshift sparring ring with a human and later, a pair of humans. Giving the humans short knives was necessary to make the combat interesting though even then, the Kristang usually quickly took away the knives and turned them on the prey. The games were just getting fun, with two guards sustaining serious knife wounds, when their leader declared a stop to the games. They were running low on humans, so if the scientists ever did return and needed the humans for experiments, they would be extremely upset to find all the test subjects had been killed for sport. After the games were over, most of the guards had taken to sleeping late, since they had almost nothing to do other than making sure the remaining humans did not escape from their prison compound. Escape where? None of the native life was edible to humans, so other than a guard doing a remote headcount twice a day, they ignored the humans and spent their time struggling against boredom. The only mildly interesting thing that had happened for weeks was an intermittent sensor glitch that no one cared enough about to diagnose.

So, when a cloud of missiles streaked over the mountain ridge followed by a pair of Ruhar dropships, the guards were caught completely by surprise. Most of them were asleep, with only two technically on duty in the base's security center. Those two froze for crucial seconds, disbelieving the attack could be real. Surely it had to be a surprise exercise thrown at them by the base commander, who had grown disgusted by his men's lack of discipline and the slovenly state of their quarters. The missiles had to be part of a simulation, and the guard who had smashed the glitchy sensor display was tempted to let the sim play out without reacting, so the base commander would not get the satisfaction of seeing his men racing around for nothing.

Then the ground shook as an incoming missile was exploded by the one functioning maser air-defense cannon, and the two guards scrambled into action, triggering an alarm and powering up the defense shield that protected the control center. Raising that shield when the attack began might have been a good idea, but raising it as missiles were already impacting actually shortened the guards' lives.

The first volley of missiles were weighted heavily toward taking out anti-aircraft defenses, concentrating on destroying the single active maser cannon turret. The missiles Irene had named 'Wild Weasels' quickly overwhelmed the maser cannon, saturating its sensor network with submunitions that scrambled the sensor data or directly attacked the targeting sensors with their own single-use maser blasts. Within its armored turret, the computer controlling the maser cannon was calmly concentrating on prioritizing targets and trying to see through the confused sensor data, when the thick armor of the turret cracked under direct impact of two shape-charge warheads. The superheated plasma of the warheads burned through the armor and fried the power feeds to the maser, rendering it useless and shattering the maser's exciters, before it had a chance to even detect the pair of vulnerable dropships coming over the mountain crest behind the missiles.

The second volley of missiles went straight for pre-programmed targets, flying violently erratic courses until the base's air defense was knocked offline, then giving up any evasive maneuvering and boring through the air straight at their designated targets. The enemy dropship was exploded, to prevent that unflyable hulk being used as a stationary missile or maser cannon platform. Missiles plunged into the base housing, killing all the guards who were still asleep or racing out of warm beds to react to the threat.

With all primary targets destroyed, most of the last wave of missiles queried the battle control systems aboard the lead dropship, and were told to switch to secondary targets, then targets of opportunity. One missile, having already deployed its wing and opened air-breathing doors to extend the time it could loiter over the base, saw an opportunity. The base control center, considered both a hard target and unnecessary now that base air defense was down, had foolishly delayed raising the separate energy shield that protected it.

'*Well, ain't that some shit?*' the missile said to a missile orbiting in the air beside it.

'*Sloppy*', the second missile's tiny yet intelligent brain responded over the tactical network. '*They are way too slow.*'

'*I hate sloppy soldiers,*' the first missile declared. '*I bet their bunks are unmade and their footlockers are unlocked. If there is one thing in this world that I hate, it is an unlocked footlocker.*'

'*Damn, that defense shield is still only twelve percent charged,*' the second missile noted with surprise and disgust. '*Hey, I have an idea.*'

The pair of missiles linked their targeting data, shed their wings and closed their airbreathing ducts. Gouts of white-hot flame scorched the air behind them as they plunged downward, zipping through the strengthening energy shield as if it weren't there at all and detonating their warheads on wide-dispersal pattern.

The brains of the two guards did not even have time to think 'damn *this* sucks' before they became dark stains on a wall, just prior to that wall being churned into vapor. Ironically, the original assault plan had called for leaving the control center untouched in the initial phase, because the attack planners had assumed the powerful energy shield would be active. The slow reaction of the guards prevented them from living long enough to see who had hit them.

Surgun Jates tensed, poised at the back ramp of the second dropship. The ramp was already opening as the craft first dropped sickeningly in a high-speed descent, then stood on its nose with forward thrusters firing to slow its progress as the ground rushed up to meet it. He felt the floor tilt and he was grateful for the strong restraints that held him securely, as his powered skinsuit legs absorbed the strain of the ship flaring to land. Jates knew his genetically-enhanced body could take Gee forces that would render a human unconscious; his concern was that he could not complete the task alone and the Jeraptha was needed for breaking into the research core. That left humans as his only assistance and he was not confident as he glanced at the biosigns in a corner of his visor. All three of his team members were showing high heartrates, dangerous blood pressure and were fluttering on the verge of unconsciousness. He noted two of them were slumping against their restraints, temporarily useless. The three sergeants did not appear to be capable of performing the mission, but Jates reminded himself the warrior caste had been hurt very badly, twice, when they underestimated humans.

Then he had no more time for worry, because the ramp was fully open and the ground was in sight. While the dropship was still five meters in the air, he popped free of the restraints and leaped out, diving headfirst through the opening then flipping to fall feet-first, trusting the skinsuit and his enhanced bone structure and muscles to survive the fall.

He hit hard and rolled in a well-practiced maneuver, the skinsuit steadying him and helping flip him upright. As soon as his boots contacted the ground, he was running with power-boosted strides, keeping low as time in the air between strides was time his legs could not propel him forward. The crater made by the missile that had cut the datalink to the research compound was in front of him by another forty meters, according to the glowing numbers at the bottom right of his helmet visor. An idle part of his brain told him forty meters in the common human measurements the team used was thirty five *latrans* in Kristang terms, a bit of trivia that became useless as his boots skidded and brought him to a halt at the blackened lip of the crater. The shape-charge warhead had focused its explosive energy downward to slice the buried cable so the lip of the crater was only eight meters across, but smoke and dust obscured even the enhanced vision provided by his helmet, and the crumbly dry sand the base was built on was already sliding down to fill in the hole. He pulled a compression grenade off his belt, checking to verify it was still on its lowest-power setting, pressed the button with a thumb and dropped it in the hole. There was a blast of air but no shrapnel so he did not bother to duck out of the way or even flinch, knowing the Ruhar skinsuit and helmet would protect him.

The blast momentarily cleared the air in the hole, creating a vacuum that was quickly erased by inrushing air that swirled with even more dust and smoke. That did not matter as Jates' helmet sensor had built an accurate picture of the hole during the split-second his vision had been clear. "We have a *problem*!" He announced over the tactical circuit.

"What is it?" Jesse asked as he skidded to a stop behind Jates almost too quickly, needing the Verd-Kris to steady him from toppling into the hole. Jates said nothing about the human's clumsiness, merely flexing his ankles to hop down into the dust-obscured hole. "Oh, shit," Jesse exclaimed as his visor fed him the synthetic view Jates had acquired. The missile had impacted at a junction where sometime after the base was built, someone had spliced in a cable at a right angle, running back to a building behind Jesse. The junction was not a problem, the problem was someone had the bright idea to protect the splice by encasing it in a block of some hard ceramic material. Pieces of the ceramic had flaked away and there were pockmarks on the side where the warhead had exploded, but the hard block was not cracked. "What about-"

"Can we blow it apart?" Shauna asked behind him, already unslinging her backpack that contained a mix of explosive charges that had been selected for various yields.

"We can try it," Dave suggested.

"Darlin', no, not this time," Jesse declared as he slid down into hole on his backside, the skinsuit automatically stiffening to protect him from cuts and scrapes.

"I only blew up *one* island, Jesse, this is not fun-"

"I'm all for blowing shit up but we don't have *time*," Jesse cut her off. "Jates, this thing can't be that big, I can see the cable coming in from the side and it looks to me it's not as thick as my arm is long. Can we just pull it away?"

Jates had his gloves gripping the block on top, and had been using his suit's power to nudge the block back and forth while the humans argued. His intent had been to judge the block's size by his ability to move it so they could scale explosives appropriately, he had not thought of simply moving the block out of the way. The human called 'Jesse' or 'Cornpone' had a point, they had precious little time before the data buffers overflowed. "Sergeant Colter, we can try. I will take this side."

Jesse grunted and strained to dig his gloved fingertips into the hard ceramic until he could see it was no use, he had to rely on the gecko-like grip of the gloves. Even they slipped and he fell backwards just as the block began to move. "I can't get a grip, it's too smooth," he spat in frustration.

Jates agreed without words, flexing his gloves that also had failed to gain a purchase.

"Twenty eight seconds, guys," Dave warned and just then, inspiration struck him. "Jates, Jesse, duck down," he warned as he fell onto the block, feeling it rock beneath him. Pulling his rifle out of the sling, he selected explosive-tipped flechettes and shouted "Fire in the hole! Ow! Shit!"

The explosive rounds barely had time to arm themselves after they left the gun barrel, as Dave had the muzzle almost too close to the block. Sharp chips of ceramic pelted his legs, faceplate and worst of all, the crotch of his skinsuit. He was saved only because the rifle had communicated with the suit, so the suit's computer stiffened the skin before the first round left the barrel. "Ow! Uh, God*damn* it."

"Come on, Ski, quit whinin'," Jesse grunted as he grabbed his friend's legs and pulled him down to tumble awkwardly into the hole behind Jesse. He felt for a handhold blasted by the rifle and found several. "Got a grip now!"

"Yes," Jates acknowledged and dug three fingers into cracks caused by the rifle rounds. "Three, two, one, *pull*."

The heavy block did not move at all, then it moved all at once as it lost its grip on the soil around it. Jesse and Jates fell backward on top of Dave and the block toppled over onto all three of them.

"Don't you guys move!" Shauna ordered. "I see the end of the cable exposed, I'm reaching down for it."

"Thirteen seconds," Dave reported unseen from the bottom of the pile.

"I *know*," Shauna snapped with irritation, tossing aside her pack to get access to the only thing she needed right then, a data transmitter the size and shape of a golf ball. The ball had a hole, which Shauna carefully fitted the cable end into. Except the damned frayed cable caught on the lip of the hole and refused to go in. "Gotta cut a fresh end," she pulled a knife off her belt and, holding the golf ball firmly but carefully, sliced through the cable to create a clean end. She dropped the knife and breathlessly threaded the cable into the hole of the golf ball. Instantly, her visor lit up to report a solid connection. "Got it! Colonel Perkins, we have a connection. Our fake sensor data is flowing through the cable."

"I see it," Perkins' voice sounded shaky, which might have something to do with the timer showing the buffers would have overflowed in eight seconds, if Shauna had not hooked the computer into the cable. Or it could be not knowing whether the core in the research compound believed the bullshit sensor data fed into the cable. The data they fed in was simply recordings of real sensor input, with the time codes adjusted, but the team had no way of knowing whether the core could tell it was being spoofed. "Good work."

"Great," Dave gasped from the bottom of the pile. "Could you guys get off of me? You're *heavy*."

Extracting themselves from the hole was not easy, as they could not simply push the ceramic block away without risk it might fall on the data transmitter. Shauna stayed holding the transmitter, wrapping a high-tech type of duct tape to hold it in place, while Jates and Jesse wriggled out from under the block, holding it up so Dave could crawl out.

"Thanks, guys," Dave stood up in the hole, brushing smeared dirt off his skinsuit.

"You Ok, Ski?" Jesse inspected his friend's suit, not seeing any tears.

"Yeah, I'm fine, the suit went rigid to protect me. Problem was, my legs were bent at a bad angle down in the hole when the suit locked up, and I couldn't move. Damn," he glanced down at his thighs and crotch, where ceramic chips had scratched the tough suit material. "I almost shot my balls off. Not doing *that* again," he reached up to pull himself out of the hole, his head clearing the lip of the crater and he used the chin of his helmet to dig into the crumbling soil. "Now we- Whoa!" He slid back into the hole as gunfire erupted, rounds biting into the crater lip where his head had been moments before. "We got company!"

"I see them!" Derek held his voice steady as he swiveled the Dodo dropship's belly maser cannon turret and sent withering fire toward a pair of Kristang who were shooting at the away team, stitching a line across the ground and slicing into one of the armor-suited figures. "Damn it!" Derek shouted and the maser cut off. "Bring us around, that damned building got into my line of sight."

"What's inside that building?" Perkins asked from her console behind the pilots while her stomach flip-flopped from the tight turn Irene pulled the dropship into.

"Nothing important," Derek replied distractedly, concentrating on holding the targeting sensor on the gap between buildings where the enemy had been.

"Then light it up," Perkins ordered. "Away team, keep your heads down."

"Yes, Ma'am," Derek cursed himself for not thinking of that. "On the *waaaay*!" With the maser exciters cranked up to full power, the beam blasted the building apart, smoke, fire and debris erupting skyward. "I can't see anything. Away team, you see any hostiles?"

"We can't see shit," Jesse reported as a camera popped up above his helmet on a thin stalk, showing him only a chaotic cloud of dust and scorch-marked debris raining down. No way was he sticking his head above the crater lip until he was certain the two Kristang were dead. "Ow!" He ducked down as a chunk of debris clanged off his helmet. "We're getting pelted with building parts down here."

"The transmitter is safe," Shauna assured the team as she huddled over the device, protecting it with her body.

"Should I hold fire?" Derek asked.

"Hell no!" Jesse snorted. *Seriously*, he asked himself? The infantry have their asses hanging out to dry on the ground, and the close air support is asking whether to expend ordnance? "Hit it again! Maser beams don't cost us nothing."

Derek poured maser fire to saturate the area, in case there were more Kristang hidden in the cluster of buildings, until there was no cluster of buildings, only shattered and smoking ruins, pieces of walls standing by themselves, and debris cascading down all over the area. Derek winced as he saw pieces of building spinning through the air in the direction of the research compound, and he was relieved to see puffs of dust kicked up on the ground as the chunks fell well short. "I've got nothing left to target, Ma'am," he glanced back to Perkins, just as his console flashed red with a new threat. "*Shit*! Irene get us out of here now now now now now!!"

The pair of Kristang who fired on the away team had intended to kill the attackers who were assumed to be Ruhar, based on their familiar flexible skinsuits, the rifles they carried and most importantly the unmistakable outlines of their dropships. The two guards had hurriedly pulled on their old third-hand powered armor suits, ignored the multiple warning lights of systems that had failed or were on the verge of failure, and emerged inside the building closest to the away team by using a tunnel that was not part of the original base construction. They did not know why the attacking aliens had bothered to drop down into a crater, in a part of the base that was not at all of any importance and was not near any of the tunnels. All they knew was they had been ordered to kill the aliens with maximum violence and that is what they did, except the 'maximum violence' part was inflicted upon *them* by a dropship flying close air support. They died not knowing whether they had hit any of the aliens.

And they died not knowing their part of the base defense was a decoy, a mere distraction.

A quarter kilometer away from the away team, in an area of the base that appeared to be nothing but storage sheds, dirt and dust arced upward as two large buried doors swung open, revealing a ramp and in a flash, a large vehicle was racing up the ramp to slew sideways to a halt. If the Kristang had ever seen a Mad Max movie, they might have taken their inspiration to build that vehicle. It was based on a large truck that had been retired from service because two of its four motors were burned out and the frame was cracked. In its new role, the truck did not need to drive far nor did it need to maneuver over uneven terrain, it only needed to climb the ramp into the open. Once the truck reached the surface and drove onto a hard ceramic pad that had been set down to hold its weight, it stopped, and explosive pistons fired downward to bore into the pad, holding the truck in place securely and permanently. The truck was a one-use, last-ditch measure of desperation that had been slapped together from spare parts, partly as a sign of defiance to the clan leadership who denied essential resources to the guards responsible for the base. There was no funding to install the planned anti-aircraft missile batteries, and no spare parts for one of the two AA maser turrets? Fine, the defenders had said. Screw the clan leadership, we can provide for our own defense, and so they did.

The old truck was modified to carry an active sensor array, an energy shield generator on top at the front over the cab, a thick stack of heavy powercells, and on top in the back, a box containing six portable antiaircraft missiles the humans called 'Zingers'. The Zinger was designed to be carried by infantry, but was a versatile weapon that had been adapted for use by aircraft and even ground-launch sites as sort of a cheap and short-range AA defense. Seconds after the truck's wheels ground to a halt just beyond the top of the ramp, the launcher pod rose up on its mount, swiveled, and fired three Zingers at the closest dropship.

"I'm going for the deck!" Irene pushed the Dodo's nose down in a power dive, knowing she was too close to outrun the short-range missiles. To her right, Derek was activating countermeasures to confuse the missile guidance systems, and the Dodo's defensive maser turrets began to engage targets. With power directed to the craft's energy shield and point-defense masers, there was no energy available for the main maser cannons and their missile bays were empty.

Flying high cover above the base in her Vulture, Tutula had been frustrated and bored, irritated to be kept out of the action. She knew her part in the operation was vital and still she chafed at being inactive. Even when defenders attacked the away team, she had been forced to hold fire because the other dropship was in the way.

Now she had a threat she could engage, though her own missiles had all been expended. The last two missiles were loitering above the base, being held in reserve to deal with unexpected threats. With the other dropship fully busy fighting for its own survival, she retasked the pair of missiles onto the enemy truck, seeing them instantly shed their wings and streak down at full power. As she pulled her craft into a tight diving turn, she warmed up her maser cannons and began hammering the truck's energy shield.

Irene dove straight away from the oncoming missiles, being careful not to make a turn that would cause the tail of the dropship to block a maser turret from line of sight to the missiles. The point-defense masers were on automatic and she had faith in their abilities based on her training and simulations, but the system was not perfect, and the pilot operating manual stated it worked best when the ship they were attached to flew straight and smooth. Yeah, she thought, try doing *that* when people are shooting at you. The Zinger was not a sophisticated opponent, its warhead could only switch between direct impact and proximity-kill modes, not having the capability to project its own maser beams and not containing submunitions or countermeasures to spoof defenses. Regardless, her trainers had emphasized that the Zinger could be a deadly threat to a dropship at low altitude. Even her small Dodo dropship was larger than a Boeing 777 and ungainly in an atmosphere. *Fly*, she told herself, fly the ship and let Derek and the automated defenses do their jobs. She aimed for a gap between two tall warehouse-type buildings, beginning to reduce throttle and pull the nose up.

"One down," Derek's terse report was delivered in a strained voice befitting the occasion. A maser turret had scored a direct hit on a Zinger, getting lucky as the wildly jinking missile flew into the path of a beam. The missiles had popped up after launch and were now above them, he knew Irene was hoping ground clutter would confuse the missiles' sensors and he prayed she was right.

"Pulling up," Irene announced, having no choice unless she wanted to pancake the ship into the ground. The maneuver worked as planned, between the countermeasures scrambling the Zinger sensors and ground clutter making the dropship hard to find, both of the enemy weapons temporarily lost target lock. One of them slowed and turned aside to get a wider-angle perspective, its momentary straight flight making it an easy target for defensive masers that cooked off its warhead, sending shrapnel in every direction.

The second missile never hesitated, as it had expected to receive sensor data from the missile that sacrificed itself. It did receive data from its own sensors, backscatter from maser beam that pinpointed the location of the dropship inside its fuzzy stealth field. Instantly, the missile resolved the target from the ground clutter and adjusted course, deciding to detonate its warhead on proximity-mode at the last second.

"We're hit," Irene grunted as alarms blared and red lights flashed in the cockpit. One engine began to tear itself apart, she reached for the controls to eject it from its pylon but Derek had already acted, and the craft jerked again with the sudden loss of weight as explosive bolts blew the pylon away from the wing. Irene almost lost control, the flight management system not wanting to do what she needed to do. Didn't the stupid computer see the warehouse they were about to crash into? Going to full power on the remaining engine, she rolled the ship to one side to avoid the starboard wing clipping a rooftop as they roared past.

"More missiles inbound," Perkins warned. "Tutula, we could use some help here."

Tutula was having her own problems. Both of the missiles she tasked to take out the truck had been intercepted and destroyed by Zingers launched in quick snapshot that she had to admire, and now the truck's missile launcher was swiveling upright to reload from the magazine below. Hits from her maser cannons only made the truck rock side to side, its energy shield deflected the maser pulses aside to sear the ground around it. She needed to get closer so the energy of her maser beams was not weakened by passage through the atmosphere. She needed to get closer without being shot down or she would be no use to anyone. "Coming," she acknowledged and turned toward the other dropship that was wobbling and trailing smoke. Her only hope would be to draw attention of the missiles away from the crippled ship.

CHAPTER EIGHTEEN

"They need our help. Colter, you are with me," Surgun Jates ordered as he flexed his powered legs and jumped upward out of the crater.

"What about me?" Dave's own suit was flashing yellow warnings that the nanomotors in the legs were not operating at full capacity.

"You and Jarrett remain here," Jates steadied Jesse as that soldier landed heavily from his own leap out of the crater. "That transmitter must not be damaged or this whole mission is for nothing."

"But-" Dave began to protest.

"Dave, cover me," Shauna cut off the argument. "I'm a sitting duck down here."

"Gotcha," Dave readied his rifle and extended the sensor mast atop his helmet to pop up above the lip of the crater. "Cornpone, man, via con Dios."

"Take care of my girl," Jesse answered without thinking, then there was no time for thought as he dashed off after the Verd-Kris soldier.

Surgun Jates had a simple plan; hit the truck and hit it hard. He knew from the taclink sensor feed what the truck looked like and where it was, and he also knew from experience that an energy shield was weakest where it contacted the ground. The shield was designed to protect from threats above, it could not be strong everywhere. "Colter, go right," he instructed as he came around a low building and caught a glimpse of the makeshift air defense vehicle. As he turned to run straight at the truck, there was a loud *whoosh* sound accompanying the launch of two more missiles. Jates held his fire, knowing his maser beam and flechette rounds would only bounce off the shield and alert the enemy to his presence. When he was less than thirty meters from the target, a searing maser beam from above struck the shield, deflecting from the shield and blinding the sensors of Jates' suit for a long second. If he had been next to the truck when that beam struck, the backscatter would have boiled him alive despite the best efforts of the skinsuit to protect him. He crouched to his knees behind an elevated pipe, shaking his head and blinking to clear his own innate senses as the suit's systems cycled through a restart. It took less than two seconds, during which time he was blind and exposed and useless, hoping the soldiers in the truck had been similarly blinded and unaware of his approach.

The sensors came back on abruptly, blinking a yellow warning about the outer layer of the suit's shell being scorched and recommending him to be careful. "Be *careful* in combat?" He snorted in a bitter laugh at the Ruhar suit designers. Then he was up and racing forward, leaping over the pipeline and gaining speed. To his right, he saw Sergeant Colter closer to the truck and guessed that human had been masked from the maser blast by the building.

Jates used his superior speed to reach the truck just before Jesse, gesturing for Jesse to get on the ground and roll like the Verd-Kris did. As Jates hit the ground and rolled, his sensors went blind again and he felt a fiery tingling like he was being bitten by thousands of poisonous ants, then he was through the energy shield and most of his sensors came back online. A quick glance upward revealed no Kristang looking down for threats on the ground. Jesse wriggled through the shield, coming to his knees and shaking his helmet before looking over to flash a thumbs up gesture Jates had become familiar with.

Jates pointed to the missile launcher box on the back of the truck above Jesse, and spun to hop onto the truck frame behind the cab.

Jesse did not need engraved instructions on what to do, he figured the situation called for *blowing shit up* and doing it *right fucking now*. His rifle was already selected for flechette rounds in armor-piercing mode, he held the weapon above his head to clear the big truck's frame rails and used the pop-up sensor mast of his helmet to get a clear view of the target. The Ruhar rifle did not have a full-auto feature, so Jesse depressed the trigger button repeatedly to send three-round bursts of flechettes into the swivel mount under the launcher box. The first three rounds penetrated the makeshift mount, locking it in place and skewing the box above. Subsequent rounds automatically switched themselves from armor-piercing to explosive mode based on sensor data from the suit's computer, and the tiny but powerful explosive tipped flechettes ripped into the unarmored launcher box, tearing it apart like tissue paper and setting off the last three Zingers.

The truck rocked as the Zinger motors were set off by the explosive energy, and the damaged missiles rocketed unguided out of their tubes to pinwheel across the sky. One Zinger, so badly damaged to have its casing nearly cracked in half, broke apart while still in the launch tube. What remained of the launcher box was shredded and then the missile's warhead exploded after it had thudded into the ground no more than twenty meters from the truck. The explosion knocked Jesse off his feet and sent him skidding across the ground past the front of the truck, his boots clipping a wheel along the way. Jesse spun as he slid across the dusty ground, one arm firmly gripping the rifle while the other flailing to halt his uncontrolled skid. The rifle was torn from his grip and his helmet bashed into something hard. Jesse slumped in his suit as he rolled to a stop, blinking and seeing only stars in his vision.

Surgun Jates cursed words that could not be properly translated. He had been about to fire rounds into the truck's lightly-armored cab when the explosion knocked him off his feet and he had fallen heavily to the ground on top of his rifle, cracking the casing of the weapon's control system. He tossed it away in disgust and extracted a sidearm as the truck's cab door creaked open and the muzzle of a Kristang rifle poked out, mercifully at a bad angle to target Jates. The Surgun grasped the door with one glove and reached around to pump shots into the cab with his sidearm, emptying the weapon's sixteen-shot magazine then tossing the spent pistol away to grasp the dead Kristang's rifle and haul it out of the cab. He no sooner held the rifle's stock when it was shot out of his hands, the rounds coming from inside the cab. Reacting, he reached back for a grenade on his belt and tossed it into the cab, slamming the door closed and using his weight to hold it there until the grenade detonated and the door came flying off, Jates with it. He lay momentarily stunned on the ground before popping to his feet in a smoothly gymnastic move assisted by the skinsuit's stabilizers, the top of his helmet crashing into something unseen and making him fall again. When he was able to roll onto one side, he saw a figure in Kristang hard armor facing him and holding its helmet with both hands, just as stunned as Jates. The rifle the figure had about to use to shoot Jates had gone flying away beyond reach, but farther from Jates. For a split-second both soldiers looked at the lost rifle then each other, both judging they did not have time to dive for the weapon. The Kristang reached behind his back for some type of weapon, so Jates did the only thing he could do; he launched himself through the air to tackle his opponent before the man armed himself. Too late, a pistol came around toward Jates, who survived only by ducking his head and using the top of his helmet to smash the other under the chin. The blow made them separate and the pistol soared up onto the truck that was still rocking from mini explosions.

The Kristang howled and an evil-looking knife appeared in one hand, having slid down from a sheath on his forearm. Holding the knife for slashing rather than stabbing, he held his other arm out wide and stepped sideways to trap Jates against the truck so Jates responded by racing inside the man's guard and wrapping him in a crushing bear hug. The knife came down into Jates' back-

Where it snapped and slid away just as the Verd-Kris had known it would, the skinsuit having stiffened and produced a slippery hump in the area where the knife was projected to impact.

"Ruhar weakling scum!" The enemy soldier screamed, spittle flinging onto the inside of his faceplate to drop down against the repulsor field.

As they struggled, the enemy to break away and Jates to gain a grip on a weak area of his opponent, Jates eyeclicked his faceplate to go clear and he was rewarded by a gasp and brief hesitation by the other man. "I am no Ruhar," Jates grunted, using the all-too-brief moment of surprise to get both hands firmly around the other man's left arm. "I am *true* Kristang."

"Liar! Traitor!" The opponent screamed and used the full power of his hard-shell armor in a futile attempt to break free of the crushing grip exerted by the Ruhar skinsuit's gloves.

"*You* are the traitor to our heritage," Jates' words came out in a bubbling gasp as the two spun around and slammed each other repeatedly against the truck.

"You are slaves to the Ruhar."

"We are all slaves. My masters have better technology." Jates butted a shoulder under the man's chin then pressed a knee on his chest, ordering his skinsuit to exceed its safety limits. The two powered armor suits strained and whined, warning lights flashing in each visor until Jates gave a mighty jerk backward and the enemy's left arm tore away at the weak shoulder joint in the armor, taking the flesh-and-bone limb with it. The soldier slumped backward as blood spurted out only briefly before a seal formed over the wound. Nano machines injected into the man's spine kept him from going into shock, he actually tried to stand and face Jates defiantly. The Verd-Kris soldier viciously swung the torn armor limb like a club straight into his injured opponent's faceplate; once, twice, three times until the man went limp on the ground, and Jates finished him by stomping hard on the neck joint of the suit, snapping the bones beneath.

"*Holy* shi-" Jesse was on one knee, his rifle barrel wavering as his vision had not cleared completely. "I couldn't get a clean shot," he explained.

"It is finished," Jates wriggled inside the skinsuit, his real limbs and joints aching terribly from the strain. When the armored limb tore loose, his skinsuit was using so much power, it almost popped Jates' shoulders out of their sockets.

"You done tore his arm off and beat him to *death* with it," Jesse's pupils were as big as they could get. "I mean, damn, I heard people say that before, but I never seen anybody *do* it."

Ignoring the human's comment, Jates turned away so he wouldn't show the pain on his face, he feared he had torn muscles and eyeclicked to damp down the painkillers the suit was injecting into him, he couldn't afford the brain fuzziness that the painkillers sometimes caused. "My rifle is broken," he explained as he picked up the Kristang weapon.

"Uh, yeah," Jesse carefully poked his head around the missing door to see the bloody carnage in the truck's cab. What was left of the missile launcher box had stopped shaking from explosions, and the flickering haze of the energy shield was gone, a fact Jesse verified by looking up at the shield projector dome above the cab. The dome was peppered by shrapnel, and sparks arced inside it. "Uh, maybe we should get away from here, in case this thing's powercells blow."

"Good," Jates gasped, falling to his knees, "idea."

"Hey. Hey, man. Surgun, you Ok?"

"I could," Jates swallowed his pride, "use assistance."

"Sure thing," Jesse knew how much that admission must have cost the proud warrior. "Up you go," he said, not knowing what else to say. Jates put an arm around Jesse's shoulders and Jesse carefully stood up to his full height then they took slow steps forward.

"I feel like I got hit by that truck," Jates groaned.

"If'n it makes you feel any better," the after-effect of combat making Jesse's accent thicker than molasses in January as his grandpappy would say, "the other guy looks a *lot* worse. Hey, uh," he eyeclicked to open the taclink as they shuffled away from the truck quickly as possible. "Colonel Perkins, that truck is out of action, you copy? Colonel?" He shared a frightened look with Jates. "Colonel? Anyone?"

Irene had her full concentration simply on not crashing, as the big and awkward Dodo zoomed sickeningly between and just above buildings. One engine had been ejected by blowing explosive bolts where its pylon connected to the hull, the other engine was severely overheated, the rear control surfaces were sluggish from battle damage, the aft point-defense maser turret was still rebooting and they had an unknown number of missiles on their tail. None of which Irene could pay attention to at the moment, she had to focus on the most basic rule of aviation: *fly the aircraft*. Everything else could and would have to wait or be handled by someone else, until Irene could get the dropship flying steady and not wobbling as if about to auger into the ground at any second. The asymmetric thrust from the one remaining engine was trying to flip the clumsy craft on its back.

Derek forced himself to tear his eyes away from the cockpit display windows, to ignore the sight of the ground that was *right there* as the dropship skidded across the sky tilted on its side. He poured emergency coolant into the overheated engine, wasting hours of precious coolant in seconds and wishing the controls didn't keep warning him of the totally obvious dangers. *Yes*, I know we are missing an engine, thank you very much you *piece of shit*. The missile threat warning hooting annoyingly in his ear was also unnecessary.

"Ok Ok Ok," Irene felt her stomach muscles unclench painfully as the big dropship steadied at a twelve degree angle to the port side and she was able to gain altitude in a controlled manner.

"Not Ok!" Derek couldn't wait any longer for the balky topside aft maser turret to make up its mind and finish rebooting. The damned thing was stuck somewhere in its cycle, he guessed some physical component had been damaged and the point-defense system was waiting for a reply that would never happen. "Yaw starboard thirty degrees then roll us another ten degrees to port."

Without asking why, Irene gently slewed the ship thirty degrees to the right without banking, in a cringe-inducingly un-aerodynamic maneuver. When the ship's nose was pointed in the designated direction, she rolled it even more to the left and held the course straight. "Doing it! Why?"

"Topside aft PDS is offline, we need the belly cannon tracking inbounds," Derek responded without looking up from his console. "Belly PDS has targets!"

The maser turret on the underside of the ship reacted immediately when the bulk of the craft was no longer masking its line of sight to the four inbound missiles. The maser exciters got photons lined up coherently and pulses of microwave energy lanced out in coordination with the forward topside turret, bracketing the closest missile and getting closer with each shot. With two masers working together quicker than the blink of an eye, the random side-to-side and up-and-down evasive jinking of the missile had to become less random to avoid running into a destructive beam. In less than a quarter second, the dropship's point defense system identified a pattern in the missile's attempts to evade being effectively targeted, and the next shot from the topside cannon was aimed slightly to the right and below the missile.

The lead missile flew directly into the beam and its warhead exploded.

Having one less missile tracking them was great for the three humans and one Jeraptha inside the dropship. The premature detonation of the warhead meant no shrapnel could catch the accelerating craft, and its PDS automatically switched focus to the second missile.

And was confused for a crucial four tenths of a second. The downside to the first missile exploding was that the Kristang weapons designers were not stupid, nor were they inexperienced at air combat. When the missile was hit by a maser beam, its tiny brain had a nanosecond to assess whether the hit was fatal, and the answer was yes and then *hell* yes as the propulsion motor began to break up from the maser energy. The second question was whether the missile was close enough to try for a proximity kill and the answer was, sadly, no. So the missile's last act of defiance was to detonate its warhead in chaff mode, the explosive charge in a wide disc parallel to its direction of flight. Burning hot particles created a cloud that scorched the air, filled the area with powerful static and temporarily blocked the dropship's view of the second missile.

The second missile also was smart, it knew what the first missile had done and why, and even before it decrypted the final burst transmission from the doomed weapon, the second missile fired thrusters to slow itself and linger in the shadow of the cloud another hundredth of a second before turning violently to the left and down. The second missile also had analyzed the target's defensive capability and tendencies and identified what it hoped was a weakness, so it intended to approach from a direction where only one maser turret could get a line of sight view.

Derek recognized the danger even before the red light flashed on his console. "We lost target lock! We lost it!" The predictive software was warning the missile would impact in three seconds or less, and the point defense system still was searching the sky for that second missile. The display held three fuzzy pink objects that might be possible threats, with confidence too low for the PD cannons to fire. Even as Derek's brain formed the thought *to hell with that* and his fingers reached to override the PDS safeties so the damned maser turrets could fire at *something*, he knew anything he did would be too late.

"Is there-" Irene asked to inquire if there was something she should be doing, *could* be doing, when the Dodo rocked and even more warning lights flared on the consoles. They had been struck from behind, thank God it was a proximity blast and not a direct hit. The aft belly turret was offline and most systems behind the seventeenth structural frame were glitching, dead, or dead and on fire.

That wasn't right. Zingers could shape their proximity warheads to direct the shrapnel in a cone toward the target. There should be a *lot* more damage, the tail should be shredded. "You hit the-"

"Thank you, Tutula!" Derek interrupted the pilot.

"Welcome," the Verd-Kris woman replied tersely, having no time to chat as she flipped her relatively nimble fighter-gunship into a tight turn. Normally, bleeding off airspeed in combat is a sure-fire recipe for disaster but she had no choice. With the other dropship missing an engine, trailing fire as random parts broke away and unable to defend itself unless its two forward point-defense turrets got lucky, she had to cover it with her own cannons and that meant flying slow and close. The idea of flying straight at the missiles, and trying to shoot them with her more powerful but slow-reacting maser cannons was an idiotic scheme that would have washed her out of flight training before she could get herself killed. Being smart meant tucking her ship in behind the crippled dropship, trying to anticipate its movements and trusting her Vulture's point-defense system to do its job. Her fighter had energy shields, but in flight they were useful only against directed-energy weapons like maser and particle beams. Against missiles, unless she got very lucky by spoofing the enemy guidance systems at long range, it was kill or be killed, and even her enhanced reactions were far too slow to track an incoming missile.

A glance at the point-defense system monitor showed it was fully capable and ready for more action after having destroyed the second missile before it could hit Perkin's ship. Now it was a matter of one computer system matching against another. The missiles had the advantage of being small, stealthy and ferociously maneuverable, and of tracking a large and slow-moving target. The dropship's maser cannons had the advantage of a stable platform to shoot from, their beams traveling at the speed of light and being able to cycle a kill shot every three tenths of a second.

Tutula hated relying on the cold logic of automated systems for her survival.

The two remaining missiles in flight had no discomfort about relying on logic, as they had not been programmed to experience comfort, discomfort or any other emotions. They *had* been expertly programmed to kill and to use cold, hard logic to accomplish that. Both missiles analyzed the situation and when one missile made a suggestion that would require the sacrifice of the other, the suicidal missile did not hesitate. Instantly, the two separated with one missile continuing to track the smaller target and jink toward it to evade maser fire, while the other missile dove down and went wide to kill the crippled target. The snap assessment had been that their best chance to make a kill was to hit the crippled ship rather than the nimble fighter-gunship. If the suicidal missile could hit the fighter airspace craft that would be great, but its purpose was to draw defensive fire away from its companion.

The suicidal missile's brain recorded a maser beam near-miss that was too close and it calculated a seventy six percent chance a maser would score a direct hit before it got close enough for even a proximity kill, so without any regret it detonated its warhead in a shape-charge directed at the fighter craft ahead of it.

Tutula had no time for rejoicing and no cause for celebration when the warhead blew by itself. Her fighter was caught in the shockwave and shrapnel pinged off the hull, making the defensive shield flare and fuzzing the view of the point-defense sensors. The system attempted to lock onto the single remaining missile, cycling through several engagement solutions in nanoseconds before concluding it could not be confident of an intercept before the missile struck the crippled Dodo dropship. It signaled that bad news to the pilot by flashing an orange light on a console.

When Tutula saw the blinking light representing the depressing analysis of her point-defense system, she did not shout a useless warning. The missile was approaching from below and behind the other dropship, the vulnerable Dodo carrying the mission commander and the Jeraptha who was needed to extract data from the research core. The data that was needed to save the lives of humans on the planet they called Paradise, and more importantly, to safeguard the lives of Ruhar on that planet and beyond. Saving lives was why she dedicated her life toward training hard to qualify for star duty. Saving lives was really only a secondary objective but at the moment, saving the lives aboard the other dropship aligned perfectly with her primary mission.

Tutula kicked the throttles to maximum and pushed the nose down, straight into the path of the missile.

If the missile was startled by the good fortune of scoring a direct impact on a fighter-gunship rather than an already damaged target, it made no comment as it altered course slightly. At that angle, it could not have hit the larger dropship anyway, so it pushed through the Vulture's ineffective energy shield, plunging through the lightly-armored skin above the portside wing and shattering a maser cannon before it struck something solid enough to set off its warhead.

"Holy, holy *shit*," Derek gulped, his throat constricting so he choked on the words. "Get us out of here, on the deck."

"Missile status?" Perkins asked as Irene dipped the nose and built up airspeed, confused by what her tactical display was showing her.

"No birds in the air." Derek reported with an anguished look shared between the pilots.

"We got it?" Perkins asked with a shudder of relief, unaware she had been holding her breath.

"No, Ma'am," Irene responded for Derek, who was badly shaken and focusing his attention on keeping their one engine running. "Tutula flew right into the path of that last missile. She saved us, Ma'am."

"I didn't," Perkins blinked away tears that suddenly formed, angry at herself for weakness in combat and for not understanding what the Verd-Kris pilot had done. "Can we-"

She was interrupted by a call over the taclink. "Colonel Perkins, that truck is out of action, you copy? Colonel? Colonel? Anyone?"

The interruption brought her back to focus. She could mourn later. "Sergeant Colter, what is your status?"

"We busted that truck up good," Jesse's thick accent had toned down a bit as his heart rate slowed. "Shauna and Dave are guarding the sensor transmitter. We're Ok down here, uh, Surgun Jates took a pounding-"

"I am fully effective." Jates' protested. "Colonel Perkins, I suggest my team search the base for opposition before you land, can you provide air support?"

"*Negative* on the air support," Perkins did not elaborate. "Jates, secure the transmitter ASAP and clear the area around the research compound, we can land between buildings there."

If Jates had a bad feeling about why no air support was available, he did not say anything.

The ground team first sprayed a fast-setting foam around the transmitter then partly filled in the crater to bury it, placing the ceramic block on top. The four then rushed over to the research base and cleared the compound building by building as quickly as they could, a task simplified by the fact the research section only contained three buildings. When Jates gave the all-clear, the big dropship came in low from the north, tucking itself between two buildings and awkwardly set down in a choking cloud of dust. The back ramp was already open, Arlon Dahl stepping nimbly out on his four legs as the craft settled on its landing skids. Perkins was right behind the Jeraptha. "Surgun Jates-"

"I already know," he replied stiffly.

"I'm sorry. She sacrificed herself to save us, to save the lives on Paradise."

"Excuse me, Colonel Perkins, but that is not why Tutula acted, not why I am here. We serve the Ruhar to save our *own* people from slavery, to rescue our culture from extinction. I think in that way, my people and yours have something very important in common."

To the surprise of Emily Perkins, the hulking alien in the dirty and scratched skinsuit offered her a fist bump. While that was not proper military protocol, it was a heartfelt gesture and she graciously accepted. "Surgun Jates, can you escort Arlon Dahl to the research core? Jarrett, go with them," she added without waiting for Jates to reply. "Czajka, Colter, go see what those asshole Keepers are doing, I don't want any interference from them."

CHAPTER NINETEEN

Dave jogged warily over to where the 'control group' of humans was being kept. With Jates and Dahl down in the bunker to access the research lab's computers and Shauna providing cover for the Jeraptha, Perkins had ordered Dave and Jesse to check out the ruined and smoking dropship hangar to assure there weren't any more surprises waiting for the assault team, then to make contact with the Keepers. Secretly, he had been hoping that entire group of assholes had been killed during the attack so they wouldn't be his problem, but no such luck. The control group was being held in a fenced area separated from the rest of the base by a wide, flat open stretch of ground and as he ran across it, Dave saw the open ground had been bulldozed flat. The Kristang had created a killing ground between their base and where the Keepers were kept, that told him just how much the Keepers were valued and trusted. "Jesse, man, check it out," Dave pointed with his rifle as he approached the fence. "That's some serious security."

The Keepers were surrounded not only by a fence with clouds of razor wire in top, the fence was a double layer, with a spike-filled trench separating the fences by four meters. Jesse halted, bent down to pick up a stone, and tossed it at the outer fence. There was a shower of sparks and the stone was thrown back. "That fence must have an independent power source. Hell, we need to turn that off."

The only way in was a road that spanned the trench, with gates in the fence. Inside the fence, Keepers were peeking out from the side of the three buildings in the center, presumably where the control group lived. One of the buildings was nothing more than a prefab metal hut for storing something, the other two had windows with people's faces visible. With them wearing Ruhar skinsuits and their helmets on, there was no way for the Keepers to know the base had not been assaulted by Ruhar. Even Surgun Jates wore Ruhar flexible armor, so there was no way to see he was Kristang. And clearly, their dropship was a Ruhar craft. "I don't know how to turn off the electricity, but I *do* know how to open these gates," Dave flicked off his rifle's safety, took aim, and fired a maser beam at the top hinge of the outer gate. Jesse joined him, working on the lower hinge, and soon the gate sagged and crashed to the ground. Dave sliced away power cables and kicked a stone at the gate with his boot, the stone clattered and bounced off the gate but there were no sparks. Being careful not to touch the live fence on either side, they dragged the gate out of the way, and repeated the procedure with the inner gate, kicking it inside the compound with their power-assisted legs.

"Come on out, y'all!" Jesse called out, irritated with the Keepers for hanging back. Didn't those dumbasses know that if the attackers wanted them dead, the dropship could have strafed the compound and killed every one of them? "Come out, ya bunch of cowards!"

At one side of a barracks there was an animated conversation, with raised voices and a scuffle. One of the people broke free and ran toward the two suited figures, then stopped, looked behind himself, and continued walking forward slowly. Six other people hurried forward and caught up to him, one put a hand on the lead guy's shoulder but he shook it off.

Most of the Keepers were wearing baseball caps and bush hats against the bright morning sunlight, with others protecting their heads with rags wrapped around their skulls. All of them were dressed in relatively new if dirty clothing, the hats still had visible 'UNEF' logos although most of the logos had been defaced in some way. Dave and Jesse looked at each other. Where had the Keepers gotten new gear? The last time either of them saw a UNEF baseball cap, the blue material had faded to a light gray. And boots! All the Keepers were wearing nice boots that hadn't been patched and mended half a dozen times.

"Hello," the lead guy spoke, holding up one hand and taking his cap off with the other.

"What the f- *Eric*?" Jesse exclaimed.

"Jesus," Dave gasped, astonished. "Eric Koblenz?"

The guy shaded his eyes, but could not see the faces inside the opaque helmets. Dave and Jesse ordered their faceplates to go clear, and Eric's eyes bulged. "*Ski*? *Cornpone*? What the hell, what, how are *you* here?" He sputtered.

"That's Dave and Jesse to you, asshole," Dave growled. Even at tiny Fort Rakovsky, they had not liked that jerk referring to them by nicknames.

"Hell, *you* call us Sergeants Colter and Czajka," Jesse corrected his friend, and tapped the US Army chevron-and-rocker symbol on his shoulders.

"Sergeants?" Eric looked closer and saw the familiar rank symbols. He should have noticed that right away, those were not Ruhar insignia! "What are you doing here? In hamster armor?"

"We'll ask the questions here," Dave snapped. "We're part of a Ruhar task force now," he fibbed. Before he could brag like he greatly wanted to, Eric interrupted.

"Guys, please, you have to get me out of here! Please!" His eyes were pleading, his hands held out in supplication. "The lizards lied to us, I think they used us for medical experiments, we were-"

"Yeah, no shit, Sherlock," Jesse cut him off. "Y'all were brought here as guinea pigs, the lizards made a bioweapon to use against our people on Paradise. And you all were part of it."

"We didn't know!" Eric protested. "They only told us-"

"Don't listen to their lies," a man behind Eric growled as he reached out to pull the now-reluctant Keeper backwards, but Eric was not going for that shit, not anymore. His elbow shot back and cracked the man in the face, breaking his nose and sending a spray of blood to splatter Eric. Two others stepped in, though hesitantly and without enthusiasm. Eric punched one of them and they backed off, holding up their hands to signal they were not participating in this fight.

Then Eric went crazy. The man whose nose he had broken was on the ground, rolling to his feet when a savage kick to the ribs from Eric's boot knocked him back down. Seeing a red haze of anger in his vision, Eric Koblenz kicked the man over and over. "Don't you *ever* touch me again you son of a bitch! I'm sick, sick of your Goddamned lies. Jesus!" He aimed a particularly savage kick at the man's bloody face. "You made me betray my friends, you fucking piece of *shit*!"

"Whoa! Whoa, settle down there, Koblenz," Jesse surprised himself by stepping forward and restraining the enraged former soldier. For a second, Jesse thought Eric would lash out at him, but the man collapsed to his knees, sobbing. "Uh, Ski," Jesse had no idea what to do. "A little help here?"

Dave gestured with his rifle to move the others back. He half turned his back on the injured man who was lying prone, but the enhanced peripheral vision of his helmet alerted him to danger when the bloodied man pulled a fabric-wrapped shiv from a pocket and lunged at Eric. Reflexively, Dave shot the would-be assailant in the gut with a maser beam, his powered suit legs lifting him up and backwards clear of the man's reach.

"Holy sh-" Jesse pulled Eric out of the way, his power-assisted arm sending Eric rolling across the dusty ground. Harder than he intended, Jesse stomped on the assailant's knife hand, hearing and feeling bones crunch.

"Ah!" The would-be assailant groaned. "Shit that hurts, you Goddamn hamster lover!"

"You gonna settle down and cooperate?" Jesse asked with his rifle muzzle pointed straight at the asshole's broken nose.

"Fuck you, traitor," the man spat blood on Jesse's legs.

"Wrong answer." Jesse squeezed the trigger, having selected the under-mounted railgun. An explosive-tipped flechette dart sped out, not having time to deploy its guidance fins before burying itself in the man's skull and exploding. Jesse wiped blood and gore off his helmet, kicking the headless body away in disgust. He turned to the shocked faces of the crowd that had assembled around them. "Anyone else got smart-ass remarks you want to try on me? No? Because this counter," he turned the rifle so the crowd could see the display on top of his rifle, "says I got nineteen more explosive darts in the magazine. Plus, like, a hundred maser shots left in the powercell."

"Colter! Czajka!" Perkins' voice came over their helmet speakers. "I heard weapons fire, you both Ok?"

"We're fine, Colonel," Dave replied. "We got some Keepers here who are having second thoughts about their loyalty to the lizards."

"They giving you trouble?"

"No, Ma'am, it's the idiots who are *not* having second thoughts who are causing a ruckus. There's one less of them now."

"Understood. Czajka? Be careful, especially of the ones who want out. This will be the second time they've changed sides, they might be looking for a convenient opportunity to flip loyalties again."

"Copy that. Colonel? One of the guys who regrets coming here is a guy Jesse and I knew way back from our farm village in Lemuria. What are the odds, right?"

"You trust him?"

"Not as far as I could throw him," Dave snorted, then remembered he was wearing an advanced-technology power-assisted skinsuit. "Throw him on my own, I mean. He was an asshole back then, but Jesse and I think this guy joined the Keepers because he was stupid, and he listened to the wrong people."

"Be careful anyway."

"I think the Headless Horseman here," Dave looked down so Perkins could see the shattered body through his helmet camera, "is discouraging any morons who are feeling adventurous."

"Ma'am!" Jesse called out, jogging out of the Keeper compound, waving something in one hand. "Colonel, look! They've got UNEF ration packs! Lots of them! There's a whole building full of human food and uniforms and all kinds of UNEF stuff, inside the fence where that control group is living."

"MREs?" Perkins caught the package Jesse tossed to her. "Beef stroganoff?" Beef? She had not eaten beef, real beef, in years. The cultured, lab-grown beef substitute provided by the Ruhar as an experiment was tasty if a bit bland, and still in short supply. "Huh," she read the label. "This is still good, it hasn't expired yet."

"I don't know if it was '*good*' when it was fresh, Ma'am, but they've got crates of MREs and other rations in one of the buildings here," he jerked a thumb over one shoulder behind him. Dave was back making sure the Keepers didn't do anything stupid, to the Mavericks or to themselves, while Jesse reported to Perkins. "The Goddamned lizards were holding out on us, and the dumb Keepers here were eating like kings compared to us on Paradise. Hell, I half starved on corn and taters in Lemuria, and the lizards probably had warehouses, entire starships, full of supplies."

"When the hamsters took Paradise back, whatever human food the Kristang were shipping to Paradise might have gotten dumped here," Perkins speculated.

Jesse shook his head once angrily. "No way. We stopped getting supplies from Earth *before* the hamsters took the planet back. That's why Bishop had the cushy job of planting potatoes, remember?"

Perkins did remember that time, but her memories were different. "We were still getting supplies shipped in from home back then, at a lower rate but steady. HQ slow-rolled distribution to the field because they wanted to build up a stockpile to get us through lean times."

"*HQ* was holding out on us?"

"They weren't holding out, Colter. The lizards had warned us we needed to become self-sufficient, they were tired of footing the bill for shipping everything we needed all the way from Earth. Even before the Ruhar arrived to retake the planet, the lizards told us the Force would not be going straight back to Earth, even after we got the last hamster off the planet. Our guess back then was the White Wind clan planned to pimp us out again to another clan."

"Another evac op?"

"No," Perkins wanted to spit but couldn't inside her sealed-up helmet. "HQ figured we most likely would be used as cannon fodder in battles between clans."

"Oh, hell. Damn, so, we got lucky when the hamster fleet showed up. Can we bring ration packs back with us?"

Perkins looked at the dropship, sitting with its back ramp open. "Any supplies we take from here may be contaminated, but we'll need to scrub the inside of the dropship anyway before we can take these suits off. All right, Colter, there's plenty of space in storage lockers aboard the dropship, cram in whatever you can fit. Do us a favor, if you see any Chinese ration packs that are labelled something like 'Pickled Herring', leave them and take something else."

"I can't read Chinese," Jesse wasn't sure if his CO was joking or not.

Perkins tapped her visor. "Your helmet translator can."

"Oh, yeah, sorry." Jesse's face turned red inside his helmet.

"Take Jarrett with you, she told me she's not being much help to Jates and he doesn't need anyone to cover him, that research bunker is empty."

"Yes, Ma'am. Shauna, come on up here. We've got work to do, it's dinner time!"

"We have *trouble*!" Jates shouted while running out of the underground bunker, waving a tablet at Perkins.

"What? A ship jumped in?" She shuddered as a jolt of fear ran up her spine. Her body was just coming down off the adrenaline high of combat, now she felt her heart racing again. Although, her mind flashed, why? If an enemy ship was now above them, there was absolutely nothing she could do about it.

"No. Worse."

"Worse? What the hell could be-"

Jates cut her off. "Dahl just found out this base is programmed to self-destruct, the crew must have activated that sequence before the last one of them died."

"Ok, shit," she glanced quickly around. They had one dropship, no motorized vehicles and no spare skinsuits that could speed a person's escape. "Did you get the data we need?"

Jates held up something that looked like a shiny metallic sphere the size of a softball. "This is the memory core, Dahl says we can access it through dropship computers. Colonel, we have the keys to decrypt the data, but there were not any samples of the pathogen in the research lab. The researchers took everything with them, or they destroyed all their samples before they left."

"Damn it. Could we, or the Ruhar, synthesize the pathogen from the data you retrieved?"

"I do not know, we will need to decrypt all the data first. Colonel, I do know we must leave here immediately."

"We need to get these idiot Keepers moving, then. They can head toward-"

"Colonel Perkins, there is no time for anyone to *walk* out to a safe distance. Under the base is a multi-megaton atomic-compression device, it must have been provided by the Thuranin or possibly the Bosphuraq. The warrior caste wishes to erase all signs of their illegal activity here."

"A *nuke*? That's against The Rules," she meant the Rules of Engagement enforced by the two senior species in the endless war, rules intended to prevent lesser beings from contaminating life-sustaining biospheres.

"Biological warfare is also a violation of the rules, but that pathogen will be used against a populated world with a healthy biosphere. Technically, atomic compression devices are not considered 'nukes' because they do not create long-lasting radioactive fallout. Colonel, regarding The Rules, setting off a single nuclear device here would probably not provoke a reaction, because one such weapon would not significantly damage a world that is already doomed. The variable star will render this planet uninhabitable within the next three thousand years."

"Oh, hell. How big an explosion, and how much time to we have? Scratch that, is there any way we can shut it down?"

"No to your final question, the device is buried in a hardened canister and any unauthorized attempt to access the canister will cause immediate detonation. The self-destruct mechanism is simple and rugged, Dahl says he does not know any way to hack into it. Once the mechanism was activated, it cuts itself off from further instructions."

"God*damn* it!"

"To answer your other question, the device is powerful enough to obliterate everything in this valley, we need to be behind that ridge," he pointed to the mountain peaks that rimmed the bowl-shaped valley, "when the device explodes in," he checked his tablet. "Twelve minutes and forty nine seconds."

"Striebich!" Perkins roared and twirled one finger over her head in a 'spin up' motion the former Blackhawk pilot knew well. "We are *LEE-aving*!"

Except they couldn't.

"Ma'am," Irene's hands shook from emotion as she explained the problem in a whisper. "We can't take all these people with us. They won't all fit, and with the ship carrying that much mass," she shot a fearful look at the lowest point of the surrounding ridge, "we won't clear the ridge. I'm sorry, we only have one engine to provide power. We *can't* take all these people," her eyes darted to the cluster of Keepers who had been herded together.

"Striebich, we are *not* leaving any humans to die here, you got that? Strip this thing of anything you can toss out the door fast, and we will make room."

"Colonel," Derek pled his case. "She's right. There simply is not enough space inside the cabin for all these people." He hoped their commanding officer did not make a foolish request like strapping people to the Dodo's stubby wings. "If we stack people in on top of each other, we can," he ran a quick estimate in his head, "fit most of them? We would still be leaving a dozen or more."

"The cabin," Perkins appraised the dropship's cramped interior, designed to hold only fourteen troops. "Wait, you're Winchester on missiles?"

"Yes, we launched our full weapons load in the raid," Derek answered warily.

"Can we put people in the missile bays, if they use oxygen masks?"

"I wouldn't recommend that," Derek replied as he shared an alarmed look with Irene.
"Screw the recommendation, can we do it?"

"We can try," Irene agreed quickly, hoping to end the discussion before Perkins thought up an even worse idea. "Jarrett, Colter, Czajka! We need to strip out the cabin seats *now*!"

They got five very frightened people stuffed into each of the two empty missile bays, by the simple expedient of explaining their choice was a few minutes of discomfort, or dying in a nuclear fireball. Three Keepers still refused the evac orders, protesting that they remained loyal to the Kristang and would not cooperate with their supposed rescuers. Perkins ended that rebellion with a rifle butt to the face of one protester, ordering his unconscious form dropped unceremoniously on the bottom of the pile in the cabin.

"Seriously?" Shauna cocked her head at one still-protesting asshole. "I would be *more* than happy to shoot you right now."

"There is no nuke," the asshole spat at her, "unless *you* planted it to cover evidence of your attack on *our* allies, you traitorous bitch."

"Seven minutes!" Irene screamed through the dropship's doorway. "We need to go *now*."

"*Bitch?*" Shauna's grip tightened on her rifle. "You might-"

The argument ended abruptly when Jesse casually shot a maser beam through the protestor's right thigh, then when the Keeper slumped to the ground, kicked him hard under the chin. "Grab an arm, we'll drag Sleeping Beauty here into the ship," he ordered and began pulling the unconscious asshole up the ramp, which was beginning to cycle closed. Asshole's head lolled to the side, but as the maser had cauterized the leg wound, there was little blood. Shauna grabbed the other arm and they tumbled inside, rolling the idiot into one of the last spaces available and sitting on top of him as there was no other place to go with the closing ramp squashing them together.

"*Nobody* calls me a bitch," Shauna sat down on the protestor, not making any effort to be gentle.

"You think *that's* important right now?" Jesse asked as he safed his rifle and looked for something to hang onto. The pilots had the dropship off the ground and wobbling as it struggled to gain altitude on one engine.

"Ohhhhh, this is not good," Irene gritted her teeth. "Colonel, I don't know about this." The Kristang research base was in a high mountain valley on a planet with a thin atmosphere, and the lowest point of the ridge around them was over twenty two thousand feet high. If both engines had been healthy, the dropship could have easily made it into orbit even overloaded as it was. With only a single damaged engine generating less than half its normal peak power, the craft was struggling to climb at all. Ruhar dropships had supplemental booster packs that could be installed under the wings, to provide a one-time surge of thrust for heavy-weight takeoffs, but none of those packs had been brought down to the planet. Irene would not have brought them into combat anyway, as having volatile booster packs slung under the wings was just asking for trouble in a situation where the dropship had been shot at. "We're at eighteen thousand and we can barely maintain that."

"Can we circle back, fly a longer route to gain altitude?" Perkins suggested.

"Distance won't help, Ma'am," Irene told herself to be patient with their non-pilot commander. "It's simple math, we're too heavy for the power available." She kept the 'I told you so' tone out of her voice but that wasn't easy. "Part of the problem is there's a strong wind coming from the direction of the gap we're trying to fly through, it's creating a downdraft on this side of the ridge. That gap is the lowest point on this side of the rim, next low point is over a thousand feet higher."

"We don't have time anyway to change course at this point," Derek warned.

Perkins debated an idea she hated. She had stubbornly insisted on taking every single person with them, and now her refusal to consider immovable facts might kill them all. In a flash, she remembered allowing her team to stuff lockers full of food packages, and she had not seen MREs among the seats and other gear stripped out of the ship. "Could we lighten our load?"

"Not at this point, Ma'am," Irene explained. "Opening a ramp would spoil our aerodynamics and cause us to drop. By the time we got the ramp closed and climbed, it would be too late. I'm sorry, I don't see we have any good options," she declared as her eyes flitted rapidly across the display in front of her. Maybe below them was a canyon or an arm of a mountain they could land behind and shelter from the nuclear shockwave?

"I'm going to try something," Derek announced as he flipped a switch to take command. "My aircraft."

"*What* are you doing?" Irene's voice was unsteady as a sudden jolt hit the airspace craft. The jolt caused her stomach to do flipflops, they were dropping.

"The only thing I can think of," Derek didn't take his eyes off the instruments. With one hand, he was playing with the throttle.

"Not this! Whatever you're doing, it's not working."

"The other thing had *no* chance," Derek replied evenly. "I'm watching the fan blade pitch, you call out the climb rate indicator?"

Irene glared at the other pilot but kept one eye on the instruments. Ruhar airspace craft did not have the ability for pilots to manually adjust the pitch of the engine fan blades, a feature both humans found limiting and annoying. Instead, the flight computer set the angle at which the turbine fan blades bit into the air, based on speed and power settings. To Irene's amazement, Derek's action of reducing throttle had the effect of deepening the pitch, and she watched fearfully as the altimeter steadied, then began slowly increasing. She sucked in a breath, unwilling to speak lest she jinx their temporary good luck. "We *are* climbing." When the rate of climb reached seven hundred feet per minute, she announced that fact. "And now eight fifty per minute. Rate of increase is slowing, but, Derek, how did you know?"

"Something I read in a book about aviation in World War Two, when they were still figuring out the principles of aerodynamics. I knew the computer adjusts this ship's blade pitch based on power settings, so I hoped reducing power would drop our airspeed and make the blades take a bigger bite of air to compensate. We did lose airspeed, but we don't give a shit about that now, we're climbing at our best velocity and that's the best we can do. Are we going to clear the ridge in time?"

Irene ran a quick estimate. "With forty seconds to spare, at this rate."

"Outstanding," Perkins exhaled in relief behind them. Perhaps her stubbornness had not killed them. This time. That was a lesson she needed to remember.

They cleared the ridge, having to battle strong and gusty winds as they approached and flew through the gap. On the other side, Derek dipped the nose and advanced the throttles, trading altitude for airspeed in an effort to put distance between them and the coming shockwave. He dove and turned gently to the right, getting clear of the gap behind them for that is where the shockwave would come through first and with the most energy.

"Four seconds," Irene called out, and polarized all the portholes to avoid people being blinded. "Two, one."

CHAPTER TWENTY

Perkins watched their sole surviving Verd-Kris walk away to be alone, stopping just under the edge of the stealth netting that covered their small camp. Surgun Jates had been stoic about the death of Tutula, saying he would mourn her properly at the appropriate time, in the appropriate manner. Several times, Perkins had seen the hulking lizard sitting away from the camp by himself, staring off into the sun or staring at nothing. Sometimes he pretended to be exercising or practicing a form of martial arts particular to the Kristang, even he could not mask how distracted he was. Perkins felt sympathy for the Surgun, knowing it was odd for her to empathize with a member of a species who might have exterminated human life on Earth. Jates, she had to remind herself, was *not* her enemy. They fought the same enemy, and where Jates sought to transform Kristang society, while Perkins would be happy to have the whole lot of them drop dead, they fought together. Surprisingly, Emily Perkins found herself *trusting* Surgun Jates, certainly trusting him more than she trusted most of the Ruhar cadets other than Nert.

Ernt Dahl came out of the dropship, carrying a tablet, with his antennas drooping. "I have not yet completed a review of the data files," the Jeraptha turned toward her and fortunately did not attempt to smile, for that expression still looked creepy to Perkins despite knowing its intention.

"When do you-"

"However, I believe I have enough information to present a preliminary conclusion," he paused to judge the human's reaction to the translated words.

Perkins nodded in exaggerated fashion so there would not be any interspecies miscommunication. "I was an intelligence analyst, I know the risks of trusting preliminary data."

"Good. Then, you will understand my conclusions may change. Colonel, so far, the data I have reviewed contains detailed notes of the testing conducted on human and Ruhar subjects. Unfortunately, all the Ruhar subjects died as a result of the testing, for the pathogen is even more lethally effective in Ruhar than in your own people. Do not think me harsh when I say that is not surprising; the pathogen's target is Ruhar, while humans are primarily carriers. The Ruhar were brought here as prisoners of war. Their prisoner status did *not* allow the Kristang to use them as research subjects to develop a weapon against their own people."

"Oh, hell."

"Colonel, if it is any consolation to the families and friends of the dead, I have a list of their names, human and Ruhar. Their loved ones will at least know what happened to them. Also, records are clear these Ruhar did not cooperate in the testing, they did not know they were part of a test until it was too late. Once it became clear they had become infected with an experimental bioweapon, three of the Ruhar killed themselves to deny valid test results to the enemy," Ernt noted with a tone of admiration. "Truly, they were brave warriors, I would have been pleased to serve by their side.

"What of the remaining Ruhar? How many of them were in the test?"

"There were twenty three in the test, which was conducted in three phases with the three groups isolated and unaware of each other. After three of eight Ruhar in the first group killed themselves and three others attempted suicide, the Kristang took steps to ensure future test subjects could not end their own lives prematurely. Colonel, I am sorry to inform you of the deaths of other sentient beings in this cruel test, but that is not the worst information I have to tell you. It appears that the Kristang who remained behind here were not entirely trusted by their leaders. The data we recovered has, as I said, extensive reports of the test results. The data does *not* include a chemical analysis of the pathogen components, nor instructions on how to synthesize any part of the bioweapon. We also did not recover samples or the pathogen or precursor elements. We know what the pathogen does and how it works. We do not have enough information to identify it in either humans or Ruhar."

"Shit! Damn it! The whole damned raid was for nothing?"

"Not *nothing*, for this data could prove to be useful to Ruhar bioweapons specialists, it does contain details of how the disease progresses in both human and Ruhar, and how the pathogen is spread. The bad news is the infectious components are airborne, can be spread by skin contact or through water, and can remain infectious for eight days on porous surfaces. The best way for Ruhar to protect themselves is by enforcing a strict quarantine of the human population on Pradassis," he used the Kristang name for that world. "Excuse me, I meant to say, Paradise," he added with an unintentionally creepy smile that quickly faded. "Colonel, you likely do not wish to hear this, but-"

"Yeah, I know. If the Ruhar on Paradise are threatened, the most certain way to assure humans are not carriers of a lethal bioweapon is to assure there are no humans on Paradise. Believe me, I had that thought as soon as I heard about this nasty little plan. The Ruhar government is for Goddamn sure going to consider humans expendable."

"Colonel Perkins, there is another benefit from the raid. We rescued many of your people," he gestured toward where a dozen of the former control subjects were gathered under the stealth netting.

Perkins snorted. "Screw them. I'd trade the whole traitorous bunch of them for Tutula."

"Oh, you misunderstand me, Colonel. The benefit I see is if those people are infected with the live pathogen. The data indicated their role in the testing was as a control group, however the testing was planned to conclude by infecting them also, to see whether their value as a control group was truly valid."

"They might be infected?" Perkins asked with alarm. During the raid, her team had stayed buttoned up in their powered armor, sealed against outside air. But after the damaged dropship landed, they had gotten out of their suits the next day. Dahl had found data tagging the group as a test control, and Perkins realized it was impractical to keep the Mavericks sealed inside suits forever. They could not even fly away from the Keepers, and the interior of the dropship was surely contaminated. "Ah, damn it. The *best* outcome is if those Keepers, and us, may be infected with a deadly bioweapon?"

"The data does not state whether the final phase of the testing had begun, and I think it likely the Kristang guards who remained behind would not have been informed of the testing progress. All the scientists who developed the pathogen and conducted the testing had been evacuated from this world. When we attacked the base the only personnel there were security guards who were expendable."

"Oh, hell," Perkins felt a shiver despite the sun-baked heat of the day. "Then we may be infected also. We are *never* getting off this rock."

"One thing I don't get," Shauna waved a hand for attention. "Why would the Kristang risk doing this? Biological warfare is against The Rules," she made air quotes with her fingers, "isn't it? They risk the Rindhalu or even the Maxolhx punishing them."

Perkins shrugged. "Good point, Jarrett, but I'm sure the Kristang figured they wouldn't get caught; they didn't count on us landing here and uncovering this op. By the time the Ruhar figured out what was going on, half the population of Paradise would be dead and the infection could have spread through their ships to other planets. Without the data we captured, it would be tough for the hamsters to prove the disease is not a naturally-occurring mutation of common human viruses. The whole issue of the senior species enforcing The Rules is kind of flexible anyway," Perkins tilted her head. "Remember, the reason UNEF got sent to Paradise is because our hamster friends contaminated the place with a virus that is destructive to the Kristang. The lizards couldn't put boots on the ground there until they developed a vaccine or whatever, so they sent UNEF down to handle the job of kicking the Ruhar off the surface. The hamsters denied being involved, they lied their asses off saying the virus was there in the soil from back when the lizards controlled the planet, and it had mutated over the years. Neither of the senior species did a damned thing about it, and we know the Kristang filed a formal protest against the Ruhar. My suspicion is the Rindhalu and Maxolhx only punish large-scale or sloppy violations of The Rules, otherwise they, uh-"

"Let the guys on the field play the game?" Dave used a sports metaphor.

"Yeah. Like in football toward the end of a big game that's close, the refs ease up on anything but flagrant fouls," Perkins explained.

"Except the damned zebras always call against the Packers," Dave fumed. Being from Milwaukee, he was of course a Green Bay fan.

"Yeah, Ski," Jesse winked, "*only* Packers fans complain about the referees. Colonel, you think the lizards will get away with this?"

"Unless it gets out of control and spreads widely through Ruhar worlds, but I don't think that will happen. The incubation period was carefully designed, those lizards were smart. This was," Perkins twirled a strand of hair around a finger, an action that made Dave stare at her in fascination. "I have to admit, a brilliantly-designed operation. The lizards could kill every human on Paradise, and most hamsters. They get revenge on us, and they weaken the hamsters' hold on the planet, the Ruhar might even abandon the place. For sure they wouldn't keep a battlegroup stationed there, the crews couldn't go down to the surface."

"You think the pathogen would kill *all* humans on Paradise?" Shauna's eyes grew wide with fear. "The Ruhar must have the technology to create a cure."

"I don't think they do have the level of technology to cook up a cure, not quickly. The data," Perkins tapped her laptop, "reveals the tech to engineer this virus is beyond the ability of the Kristang, they must have gotten help from the Thuranin or Bosphuraq, or they bought it from someone. The Ruhar would launch a full-scale effort to protect their own population, but humans?" She shook her head sadly. "I can't see the Ruhar diverting resources to help humans, and they don't understand our biochemistry that well anyway. Remember, the way this virus works, the Ruhar would initially think the disease is a natural mutation of viruses that humans commonly harbor. The hamsters will think it's our fault, they won't be eager to help us. I hate to say it," she spoke aloud what she was thinking privately, "but with a large part of their population dead or dying, the Ruhar might consider eliminating the source of the infection. Probably they'd start by quarantining all humans. When Ruhar keep dying," she shrugged, "the gloves would come off. I could see the commander in orbit hitting human sites from orbit whether the civilian government of Gehtanu approves or not. By that time, the infection would have spread to ships in orbit, unless the battlegroup got really lucky and all their ships were out of the system during the entire incubation period. This is a nightmare, if the ship with infected Keepers gets to Paradise."

"Those damned lizards would get away with it," Jesse balled up his fists. "The senior species really only punish stupidity, Colonel?"

"That's the idea, yeah," Perkins agreed. "Unless a species is stupid enough to violate The Rules in a big way, or unless they commit a minor violation but are clumsy and obvious enough to get caught, they will probably get away with it. It's not practical for the senior species to run around punishing every minor technical violation, this war has been going on long enough for everyone to know how far they can push the boundaries. Colter, the Kristang *will* get away with this, those infected Keepers might have already landed on Paradise."

"What about us, Ma'am?" Shauna asked, afraid she knew the answer to her own question.

"Us? We remained buttoned up during the raid but now we've been exposed to the Keepers, who might be infected. The hamsters won't take the risk of lifting us off this planet until months have gone by and we have either died or show no signs of infection. Even then," she bit her lip, "I wouldn't take the risk, if I were them. No ship captain will be eager to bring us off the surface here until there is a cure or vaccine available. Probably not until both are available. Thinking about it, if those Keepers do not ever reach Paradise, then the Ruhar won't have incentive to make a big push to rescue us. A handful of humans, and a couple dozen cadets on this planet, are not worth diverting major resources from the war effort. Shit," she realized the endgame of her logic. "The only way the Ruhar would develop a cure is if the infection *does* hit Paradise and they have to deal with it."

"That's it, then?" Shauna said with despair. "We're stuck here? Forever?"

"Hell," Jesse groaned. "I was just getting used to the idea of being stuck on Paradise, and that place is a lot nicer than this hellhole."

"I don't think we'll be here forever," Dave looked Perkins in the eye, and she nodded. "This is a Kristang planet. They'll be coming back sooner or later."

"Oh, shit." Jesse's shoulders slumped.

"That ain't the worst of it," Dave explained. "If a hamster ship does arrive, the best move for them would be to hit us right here from orbit, eliminate us as a threat just in case we're infected."

"You are a gosh-darned ray of sunshine, Ski," Jesse complained.

"It's what we would do, right?" Dave retorted in his own defense. "It's what I would do. The Colonel is right, no way are the hamsters spending the time and money to develop a cure just for us."

"Oh, hell," Jesse patted Dave's shoulder, "you're right, I shouldn't shoot the messenger. So, Ma'am, what's our next move?"

Perkins took a moment to carefully consider that question. They had enough human food aboard the dropship to sustain them for three months, four if they went on restricted rations. Cutting their nutrition was a risk, as it might make them more susceptible to infection. The smart move would be to eat normally until the three-month incubation period passed, then cut back if none of them became sick. If they were sick, it didn't matter how much they ate because they'd be dead long before they could burn through the supplies. "We set up camp here, wait a couple months, and hope the Ruhar are pretty damned convinced we are not carrying the virus."

"Ma'am," Dave sighed, "three months is a long time. What are the odds no Kristang ship will swing by this place during that time?" His question didn't require an answer. "We can't get off this rock until a Ruhar ship picks us up."

"That assumes any Ruhar ship arrives," Shauna pointed out their biggest problem. "We don't know that anyone will hear our beacons."

"Hey," Jesse didn't like the pained look on Shauna's face, and draped an arm over her shoulders. "We gotta have faith. We survived this far, what are the odds of that, huh? Somebody up there," he pointed to the sky, "has been looking out for us."

Jesse had no idea that the being looking out for them was a shiny beer can.

"Colonel?" Shauna approached the folding table where Perkins was sitting under the edge of the stealth netting. The team's daily walks or runs had left clearly visible tracks in the dusty soil all around their campsite, so stretching stealth netting over the dropship and campsite was more for morale than any real attempt at concealment. Dragging home-made mats behind them as they walked, a measure intended to literally cover their tracks, had proven largely ineffective as the top layer of sun-blasted soil was a different color and no amount of sweeping could entirely blend in their footprints. Still, Perkins insisted everyone remain under the stealth netting when in camp, mostly because she didn't trust the Keepers not to do something stupid.

Their single dropship had been tossed around by the massive blast and came perilously close to splattering on the far slope of the ridge, but pilot skill and a good measure of luck worked in their favor. In the roiling air, the dropship had turned and flown first north, then west so the prevailing winds carried the short-lived radioactive fallout away, then landed when its one engine turbine began overheating. The spot was as good as any, so they had set up camp around the grounded Dodo. They had to wait, for three months at least, until they could be certain none of them had brought a deadly pathogen away from the base with them. Ruhar cadets had flown a dropship high overhead to drop supplies, but otherwise the raid survivors and former prisoners were alone.

"Jarrett?" Perkins looked up from her tablet. "You have news for me?" That day had been Shauna's turn to check everyone for signs of infection with the hand-held medical scanner.

"No, Ma'am, not exactly. Everyone checks out, no infection." It was understood that 'no infection' meant no infection the scanner could detect, yet. If the genetically-engineered pathogen was as fiendishly ingenious as the Kristang database boasted of, they might all be infected, with the deadly prions biding their time inside clusters of cells. If so, there was nothing Shauna or anyone on the planet could do about it. "Can we talk?" She asked with a glance around to assure no one could overhear them. With the evening chill fast approaching as the sun set, most people were inside tents or the dropship.

"Certainly, Jarrett," Perkins set down her tablet as a sign the soldier had her full attention. After the initial excitement of the raid and then analyzing the data, boredom and depression had set in. People had nothing to do except wait to learn if they would die of infection, or of starvation. Or die in a maser blast from a Kristang warship. Or bombarded from orbit by a Ruhar ship. The sense of hopelessness was almost worse for the Keepers, because when they saw humans coming to pull them out of their life of slavery at the base, they expected to be rescued. Knowing their would-be rescuers had no way of getting off the planet had been a crushing blow both to Keeper morale and to Perkins' thin authority over them. That is why the Mavericks always carried weapons, and why the Keepers were not allowed near the precious but crippled dropship. "What is it?" She asked in her best motherly voice, a tone she had used so often recently that she was getting tired of it. She had signed up for the Army to be an intelligence specialist, not a camp counselor. Especially irritating were the Keepers who wanted to justify their stupidity, feeling a need to explain to her and anyone who would listen why they had gotten themselves into such a mess. But the absolute worst were the handful of Keepers who refused to believe the Kristang had used them for harmful medical experiments, in a plan to use the human population of Paradise as unwitting weapons against the Ruhar. Perkins had cut off their line of bullshit immediately, and kept those true fanatics separate from the other former prisoners.

Shauna sat on the rock next to Perkins, crossing her legs in a sort of yoga position, looking toward the setting sun. She took a deep breath, wrinkling her nose at the acrid burnt smell that pervaded the entire planet's surface. Did the oceans also smell bad? She asked herself. "At times like this, Camp Alpha doesn't seem half bad, but most of the times, I *hate* this place. The first time we were here, I was too busy, and too stupid and naive to pay attention to what a pit this place is. That maybe should have been my first clue the Kristang were not the good guys."

"It's not that bad, Jarrett. You ever been to the NTC at Fort Irwin?" She meant the National Training Center in the Mojave Desert. When Shauna shook her head, Perkins continued. "A hundred ten degrees in the afternoon, and don't believe that bullshit about it being a 'dry heat'. One ten is Goddamned hot. My first overseas assignment was Iraq," she shook her head in disbelief that America still had boots on the ground in that country, even if those troops were technically only supposed to provide 'advice and training'. "Now *that* place is scorching hot in summer, and the northern mountains get bone-chilling cold in winter. You know what the Nigerian jungle is like, a steam bath on a good day. Camp Alpha is a pleasant spa by comparison. Also, here I don't have to check my boots for scorpions and snakes every morning."

Shauna tilted her head back to gaze at the sky. The sun was low enough that the second planet in the system could be seen as a bright star in the sky. "Here, all we have to worry about is a Kristang ship jumping in and blasting us from orbit."

"Is that what you wanted to talk about?" Perkins nudged her tablet as a hint she wanted to get back to work.

"No."

"I'm kind of busy-"

"No, you're not." Shauna looked her CO straight in the eye. "None of us are *busy*. We're waiting, and nothing we do down here matters. A friendly ship jumps in to rescue us before the lizards get here, or it doesn't. If we're infected, we die down here, because no ship will take us aboard. There's nothing any of *has* to do down here. Nothing that matters."

Perkins noted Shauna had not addressed her as Colonel or Ma'am, and she let it slide. "You're feeling helpless, is that it?" If that were true, she would be surprised. Sergeant Jarrett had been a squared-away, focused soldier since the day they met.

Shauna spat on the dusty ground. The acrid air irritated her throat. "I've been feeling helpless since Columbus Day, when aliens pounded our homeworld from orbit. What I'm here to talk about is Dave."

"Sergeant Czajka?" That soldier had seemed distracted the past several days, Perkins attributed that to boredom after the excitement of combat.

"He's planning to leave the Force, if we get back to Paradise."

"That-" The Mavericks without Dave Czajka? She could not imagine her team without-Emily felt a lump in her throat. She could not imagine *herself* without him. Bunking with that male soldier had been awkward, but just listening to him breathing in the bunk right above her head had been comforting. She missed greeting him in the mornings, even though that was often the most awkward part of the day for each of them. "I know many people are worried about opportunities passing them by on Paradise, but out here we've seen plenty of action. If he-"

"Dave got an offer to go into business brewing beer, or something like that, but that's not the problem. You need to stop stringing him along."

"What? Soldier, that-"

Shauna let out a long, weary breath. "Don't give me that 'soldier' shit. I'm off duty. This is two women talking. You think out here, military protocol matters?" She rolled her eyes angrily. "UNEF is *over*. It's dead. Whatever authority the Force had so far from home, it died when our access to Earth got cut off."

"Jarrett," Perkins refused to use the other woman's first name, "military protocol and the Code of Conduct are all we have out here. We can't-"

"No. The Code of Conduct was all we *had*, back when we shipped out. If the only thing keeping us together are regulations from a planet that could be dead, then all we're doing out here is playing soldier, and that's pathetic. These," she tapped her UNEF and US ARMY patches, "are not why I came off Paradise. I want to make a difference, and this team, *your* team, is my best chance to matter to the future of humanity. When we met, all I knew was you rode a chair as a staff officer, and intel types are not the most popular with foot soldiers. You had to earn our respect, and you've got it. By the time we get back to Paradise, if there is anyone still alive there, the entire Force might have dissolved, and where does that leave us? You told us we need to think long-term about how humans fit into Ruhar society. You're right about that, but whatever strategy we use long-term, UNEF won't be a useful part of it."

"You've given me a lot to think about," Perkins replied in a neutral tone.

"The strategy stuff can wait. Dave can't. Think about that first, or you're going to lose him, we'll all lose him. If you are really not interested, then you need to tell him. If you are interested, don't hide behind regs written on a planet a thousand lightyears from here. Dave is a *good guy*," Shauna emphasized by squeezing the other woman's shoulder. "That's not easy to find."

"Again, I need time to think," Perkins relied, irritation creeping into her voice.

Shauna stood up and stretched her legs. The sun had set and already the night air was growing chilly. "Think about this, then. We're making up the rules as we go out here. Maybe it's time to throw out some of the rulebooks we took with us from Earth, if following those rules means we don't have a Force left. Colonel, we didn't follow you to the stars because of a rulebook."

Emily Perkins never picked up her tablet that night, whatever trivial task she had been working on forgotten. She had a lot to think about, and no star to guide her. Jarrett was right, they were fighting a new war, with a new human society, maybe they needed a new set of rules. Still, she had joined the military as a career and the rules and traditions of the service were deeply ingrained, deeply personal. Rules were the difference between a well-disciplined force and a mob.

She had a *lot* to think about.

CHAPTER TWENTY ONE

The star carrier *Deal Me In* was officially declared Overdue, when that ship failed to contact a relay station as scheduled. The relay station noted the event, and sent the notice to a passing ship the next day, but the local Jeraptha fleet base commander did not become concerned immediately. She did not become concerned because a delay of one or two days during a long training mission was not unusual, and because she had much more important matters on her mind.

The Bosphuraq, who had been quiet for decades along the border they shared with the Jeraptha, had suddenly demonstrated a radical change of tactics. The birdbrains had unexpectedly launched attacks into territory recently lost by the Thuranin. These attacks, supported by ships of their client species the Wurgalan to handle the grunt work of taking planets and scouring solar systems of threats, were mostly conducted by battlegroups of the standard Bosphuraq fleet action deployment; two battleships escorted by a half dozen cruisers and up to fifteen destroyers, frigates and support vessels. The Jeraptha had long-standing tactics to deal with a Bosphuraq battlegroup, either alone or in multiple units, so at first the local fleet commander was not overly concerned.

Then she received reports of something new and alarming; Bosphuraq and Thuranin ships operating together. Based on very skimpy data coming in from Jeraptha ships that had been hit hard by the unexpected enemy offensive, it appeared the Thuranin were taking a supporting role in recapturing the territory they had recently lost. Few Kristang ships were participating, perhaps because those lizards were busily enjoying one of their regularly-scheduled murderous civil wars. Regardless, it was mostly the Wurgalan doing the dirty grunt work of securing planets after the combined Bosphuraq/Thuranin warships cleared a star system of resistance and rolled onto the next objective.

So, when another four days went by and the *Deal Me In* still had not contacted a relay station or friendly ship, the star carrier and its attached task force of Ruhar ships was declared Missing. It worried the local fleet commander that the *Deal Me In* had been operating close to the area where the Bosphuraq suddenly attacked, and that no other Jeraptha fleet assets had been in that area at the time. The star carrier had been operating there with a group of Ruhar ships conducting training exercises, because that area was supposed to be *safe*.

The local fleet commander had three emotional reactions. First, shock and outrage, not at the carnage caused by the Bosphuraq attack, but because she recently had wagered the Thuranin would not go on the offensive in her sector for another fifteen months. Her shock was that she had been caught on the wrong side of the wager, and her outrage was that the unscrupulous bean-counters at the Central Office of Wagering would not cut her a break just because the Bosphuraq had taken the lead in the attack. Thuranin warships were participating in the offensive, so she had lost the wager, period. That argument would seesaw back and forth in the courts for years and the terms of the wager might be adjusted slightly, but overall the local fleet commander was well and truly *screwed*.

Second, she felt sorry for the crew of the *Deal Me In* and its attached Ruhar task force. Considering the scale of the enemy offensive, the star carrier being declared missing very likely meant it had been lost to enemy action, and she quenched her feelings of sorrow long enough to post a wager that the *Deal Me In* had in fact been destroyed.

The third emotion she felt was regret, regret that she could not spare even a single ship of her overtasked fleet to search for the *Deal Me In*. That old star carrier, with its attached group of older Ruhar ships that had been working up crew trainees for fleet service, was simply not important enough to devote scarce resources to a search she felt certain would have only one result: finding scattered debris. The worst part of the situation was that, as the *Deal Me In* had been operating independently, it did not have a predetermined flight plan when it departed from the planet the Ruhar called Gehtanu. It could be anywhere, and even the entire Jeraptha fleet might never find a single piece of debris from that ship.

No, she could not detach even a frigate for the search operation, so she did the only thing she could do, the only action that might resolve the mystery of the star carrier's fate. She used local fleet funds to post an open wager across Jeraptha space, a wager that no trace of the lost star carrier would be found within 47 days. The terms of the wager were generous and should prove enticing to any commercial vessel crazy and desperate enough to go looking around in what was now Bosphuraq-controlled space.

Of course, she also registered a small offsetting wager of her own, in the case of a miracle that even one of the *Deal Me In*'s crew were found alive.

The *Sure Thing* was an old, very old, Jeraptha star carrier that had been retired, sold and much modified over the centuries, with few of the modifications making the ship better or even keeping it in the marginal condition it had suffered from before the alterations. While the *Sure Thing* had left its original shipyard with three main and two auxiliary reactors, fourteen hardpoints for docking ships, a railgun and multiple missile launchers and maser cannons, it now was much reduced in power and fortune. A single ancient and leaky reactor powered the ship, with auxiliary power provided by worn-out powercells and a type of primitive Ruhar fuel cells that even the Ruhar no longer used aboard their own ships. Only three hardpoints now remained, those being suitable only for cargo containers, which was fine as the *Sure Thing* now carried only cargo across the star lanes. Of the original armament, only a single maser cannon remained other than maser turrets for self-defense, and all those units had exciters that were more likely to explode and damage the ship than protect it.

As a search and rescue ship, the *Sure Thing* had only three things in its favor. It was a former star carrier, capable of traveling vast distances on its own. It had excellent sensor gear, because the crew wanted to avoid danger, and even more wanted to avoid Jeraptha Revenue and Customs ships that were currently seeking to impound *Sure Thing* for unpaid docking fees, violating space maneuver regulations, and flying a poorly-maintained ship whose spaceworthiness certificate had expired the previous year. And, the most important factor in favor of the *Sure Thing* was that ship's owners were truly, absolutely, desperate. They already owed more in unpaid fees and lost wagers than the ship was worth. The crew had not been paid for months, both for salaries and for a lengthy list of wagers the crew had won against the vessel's owners.

Thus, the two owners of the *Sure Thing*, a married couple, had nothing to lose when they heard about the wager to find the lost *Deal Me In*. Unfortunately, they also had nothing to wager with.

Vincerientu 'Vinny' Gumbano clicked his antenna together nervously, in a gesture he knew his business partner understood was a sign that Vinny was about to say something she might not like. Vinny concentrated on holding his antenna still, but as soon as his concentration slipped, they clicked their tips against each other, causing Ammarie Viso to cross both her arms and her own antenna. "What is it now, Vinny?"

"Darling, this is a marvelous opportunity. We'll never get an opportunity like this again!"

"You mean never again, because if we don't cash in now, we'll lose the ship and be totally out of action. The next port we put into, the Customs and Revenue people will seize this bucket and we can't stop them." For the past year, the *Sure Thing* had been running on borrowed time, multiple false registrations and a well-placed wager that the Customs and

Revenue service would catch the ship within fourteen months. The last time they were in port, an official from Customs and Revenue had almost certainly seen through the thin cover of their false registration, but since that official had taken the other side of the wager, that his service would *not* catch the *Sure Thing*, the ship had been allowed to slip away. That particular wager was some of the best money Vinny and Ammarie had ever spent.

"Vinny, dear, you don't need to sell me on this one; I agree we should take the action for finding the *Deal Me In*. There is only one problem: we don't have anything to wager with! We owe more on this ship than it's worth and the Central Wagering Office knows that. We can't even pay off the bets we've lost in the last year."

"We do have something to wager," Vinny's antenna fairly danced, he was so nervous. "I insured our cargo for double its value," his eyes cast down to the deck, then flicked upward to see his partner's reaction.

She laughed. "You too? *I* insured it for double!"

Vinny was less surprised that he might have been, for he was used to Ammarie out-guessing him. "The cargo is insured for *four* times its value?"

"Five," came another voice from the hatchway, and in walked their two remaining crew members, the only ones who had hung on when the paychecks and wager payoffs stopped flowing. Cleeturss Delroy had not left the ship because he was Ammarie's brother, and because he figured his only chance to collect on back pay and wagers was to stay with the ship and watch the two owners with keen eyes and a suspicious heart. "We," he pointed to indicate his wife Thelmer, "took out our own insurance policy."

"You don't have an insurable interest," Ammarie groaned, wary of her sometimes dim-witted brother's schemes. Cleeturss had good concepts, he just was not good at the details. So something usually went wrong. Almost always went wrong.

"Don't worry," Thelmer assured the ship's owners. "I ran it through shell companies."

"*You* did?" Ammarie asked hopefully.

"Why?" Cleeturss clacked his antenna irritably. "You don't trust me?"

"I do trust you, dear brother. I trust Thelmer *more*."

"She did it," Cleeturss let his antenna flop. "But it was *my* idea."

"Good, excellent," Vinny interrupted, wanting to forestall another argument between Ammarie and her brother, but he was just a bit too late.

"Why did *you* insure our cargo?" Ammarie pressed her brother, drawing herself up on her hind set of legs.

"Because," Thelmer stepped between the siblings. "We want to get back pay, regardless of what happens to this ship. At this point, you have an incentive for this ship to suffer an unfortunate accident, if you know what I mean. That might solve the problem you two got into, but it would leave Cleeturss and me with nothing. Don't tell me that ditching this ship never crossed your mind, Ammarie, I know you're smarter than that."

Ammarie looked to her business and life partner, and when Vinny said nothing, she sighed. "Let's put all that aside for now, hmm? We have agreed to take this wager, to find the *Deal Me In?*"

"*You* have agreed to the wager," Thelmer insisted. "Cleeturss and I will keep our interest in the cargo."

"But, honey," Cleeturss pleaded, "this is juicy action. You don't want to get in on this one?"

"We *are* in this," Thelmer stroked her husband's face with an antenna. "Our part of the wager is the back pay and wagers we are already owed and will collect if we find the *Deal Me In*. Plus, our ship owners are cutting us in for thirty percent, for our labor."

"Thirty?" Ammarie screeched, outraged. "*Five*! Five percent."

The two women argued back and forth, with their men wisely staying out of the way. Cleeturss went to the galley and got two glasses of cold burgoze for himself and Vinny, and they whispered to arrange a bet on what percentage the women would agree to. When Ammarie and Thelmer grudgingly touched antennas to agree on twelve point three percent, Cleeturss smiled and took a sip of burgoze, having won his wager.

"*Now* we are all agreed," Vinny's tone was sour, for he wished Ammarie had negotiated more forcefully. Privately, he would have agreed to cut the crew members in for seventeen percent, so settling for just over twelve was a victory. He enjoyed watching Ammarie in action, but he hated losing a wager to her brother.

"Yes." Ammarie's expression was less than happy. "We only have one problem."

"What's that?" Cleeturss bent an antenna back to scratch the nape of his neck.

"We have no idea where to look for a single, lost, star carrier."

"*I* do," Vinny winked with more than a hint of smugness.

"You? When our entire fleet has no idea where that ship might have gone?"

"Our fleet is powerful, victorious and well-managed. They are also not good at thinking beyond their training. The fleet does not know where the *Deal Me In* went, so they assume they *can't* know. We are going to figure out where the ship might have gone, check those places one by one until we find a flight recorder buoy or some other evidence to lead us to that ship."

"Where it might have gone? Fleet stated that star carrier was on detached service, carrying a training group. Their plans were flexible, they could have gone anywhere."

"No, not *any*where. Most places they could have gone were safe, and we wouldn't be searching for them now. Wherever they went, they ran into trouble, unexpected trouble. Something happened, they saw something to pull them out of their training routine. Whatever they saw, it wasn't serious enough to cancel the training exercise and report to a relay station. It had to be something that sparked their curiosity, but wasn't immediately seen as a serious threat."

"What? You want us to guess?" Ammarie asked with an anxiety informed by long experience with Vinny's schemes.

"No, I want us to review the data we have. The fleet won't send us any more data than they included in the wager, so we need to search elsewhere."

"Like," Cleeturss scratched his head with an antenna, "where?"

"We start here," Vinny grinned, knowing he had hooked his audience. "We know the *Deal Me In* passed by this relay station."

"Yes, and?" Thelmer was skeptical, having fallen victim to many of Vinny's half-baked schemes over the years. "There are thirteen star systems within range of that relay station, plus two wormholes."

"True. But, the Glando system," Vinny tapped the display with one antenna, "was among the first to be hit by the Bosphuraq. Before you tell me that information is worthless, yes, we also know from our garrison at Glando that no star carrier arrived, until a fleet squadron four days ago. We do know the fleet suspects the Bosphuraq refueled in this red dwarf system, before the attack on Glando. There is an automated sensor picket station orbiting a gas giant around that red dwarf, and one of our recon ships reported that station is now offline."

"So?"

"What if a Ruhar ship attached to the *Deal Me In* jumped into that red dwarf system and noticed the picket station was offline? Investigating a minor mystery like that would be a good training exercise."

"Ah," Ammarie's head bobbed excitedly.

"Again, so?" Cleeturss hadn't caught on yet. "If we find debris from Ruhar ships, their government would pay us for the information, but that doesn't win the bet for us. We need to find the *Deal Me In*, and the star carrier would have remained outside the system."

"If Ruhar ships were destroyed there, we should find flight recorder drones in the debris field," Ammarie explained patiently for her partner. "Those drones will tell us where the ship planned to rendezvous with the star carrier. We do have the codes to make those Ruhar drones respond to us, at least for the limited data set we need. The *Deal Me In* should have moved on from that rendezvous point as soon as the Ruhar ships were aboard, but once the crew realized they were in a potential combat situation, they would have dropped off drones to report their planned course. We will query those drones and follow that course. Now that we are officially on a search and rescue mission for the fleet, we also have the codes for fleet drones."

"That is it?" Cleeturss was not persuaded. "What if we don't find anything in this red dwarf system?"

"There are two more possibilities I can think of," Vinny glared at his brother-in-law. "We keep going."

"Hopping around enemy-controlled space until we find something, or we are caught by a Bosphuraq task force?" Cleeturss leaned forward on his front legs, ignoring his wife stroking the back of his neck to calm him. "*That* is your plan?"

"You understand why the fleet offered such generous terms on the wager, don't you? Because it is dangerous."

"We'll do it," Thelmer said before Cleeturss could respond.

The *Sure Thing* did not find any debris or evidence of a battle in the red dwarf system where the automated picket station had stopped functioning. No flight recorder drones responded to their pings, but they did detect gamma ray bursts from enemy ships, too many enemy ships. Stretching their luck until it nearly broke, they hopped around the system waiting for drones to respond, then jumped far away when a Thuranin destroyer got too close for comfort.

The second possibility on their search list, the one Vinny thought had the least promise, paid off for their risk. Vinny grumbled because Thelmer had placed and won a side bet that the second site would provide the data they needed, but he could not argue with success.

The second site was nothing more than an imaginary point in space, designated for civilian ships to wait for a star carrier in case of an emergency in the Bardek system, close to the former border of Thuranin territory. Bardek itself was barely worth the attention of the enemy, having no habitable planets and being useful only for an asteroid field rich in rare elements, but any attackers wanting to push farther into Jeraptha territory needed to secure their flanks by taking Bardek first. The rendezvous site where the *Sure Thing* jumped in was actually the second backup location for civilian ships to rendezvous, and because it was so far from Bardek, a ship would need to be in severe distress to go all the way there. Vinny's logic had been to check that site first, because a sudden Bosphuraq attack on Bardek would certainly be considered a severe emergency.

The *Sure Thing*'s sensors, one of the few shipboard systems in proper working order, picked up a large debris field, mostly broken Ruhar ships but also the remains of a single Jeraptha cargo transport ship. Pinging for a Jeraptha drone was fruitless, either the cargo transport did not have time to eject its flight recorder data, or the drone had been destroyed. While warships carried drones with sophisticated stealth capabilities, civilian ships could rarely afford, and rarely would need, such unnecessary luxuries. Pinging for Ruhar military drones was more useful, they got replies from a half-dozen ships, and the drones all told slightly different versions of the same tragic story.

Ruhar ships on a routine training mission away from the *Deal Me In* had detected mysterious gamma ray bursts, and when they returned, the star carrier was sufficiently curious to halt the training exercise and launch two recon task forces, but not sufficiently alarmed to entirely break off from its mission and contact the Jeraptha fleet directly. The *Deal Me In* had dropped off two groups of Ruhar ships, one group at the rendezvous point where the *Sure Thing* had jumped in. Those unfortunate Ruhar ships had been ambushed by a force of Wurgalan ships, supported by a single Bosphuraq battlecruiser.

"Some Ruhar ships escaped. We have the coordinates where they were scheduled to meet the star carrier?" Vinny asked distractedly, his concentration on the sensors, wary of booby-traps left behind by the enemy.

"We do," Ammarie confirmed. "We should get out of here."

"Wait!" Cleeturss waved both his arms and antenna. "We are going to jump into a rendezvous point where a military star carrier may have been destroyed? We should think about this first."

"Agreed, brother, I *have* thought about it." Ammarie pressed a button on the console in front of her, and the *Sure Thing* jumped.

There were no enemy ships waiting at the rendezvous point, only a drone dropped off by the *Deal Me In* before it had jumped to pick up the second group of Ruhar ships. This time, Vinny hesitated while their ship's jump coils recharged. "Darling, we are on the trail of the *Deal Me In*, that is far more than our fleet accomplished. Maybe we should contact the fleet and let them take the search from here. They'll cut us in for twenty percent, maybe."

"Hmmf," Ammarie sniffed. "They'll cut us *out*, you mean. We do all the hard work, and now you want to let the fleet take eighty percent of *our* wager?"

"We know the *Deal Me In* wasn't destroyed here, so every place we jump following that ship, the more likely it is we run into trouble," Vinny almost pleaded, having suddenly lost his appetite for risk. "If we get caught in a damping field, we get cut out of a *hundred* percent."

"Dearest," Ammarie took a breath to give herself patience, as she often did when dealing with her partner. "Twenty percent is not enough to pay off our debts, plus the fines we've racked up. It's all or nothing. If we contact the fleet now, even *if* we get twenty percent, we lose this ship and we'll be on the run. Again. Do you want that?"

"No," Vinny hated being convinced he was wrong, especially because in this case he had thought contacting the fleet was what Ammarie wanted. "Thelmer, Cleeturss, the only way you're getting what we already owe you is if we follow this through."

Vinny's brother-in-law surprised him. "We want our cut. I know it's risky, but, we've come this far, dang it, and now I just have to know what happened to that ship."

Vinny was all for taking risk if there was a potential payoff, but since the jump to follow the *Deal Me In* involved risk with not much corresponding reward, he directed the ship to jump in far enough away that his ship had a decent chance to escape if enemy ships were in the area. He was excited and he knew his three companions were equally eager to see if the lost star carrier was at the rendezvous point. The best case would be for the *Deal Me In* to be found intact, merely suffering some engineering failure and unable to jump, with the attached Ruhar ships lacking range to jump all the way to the nearest occupied star system or relay station to call for help. The worst case would be to find a debris field surrounded by enemy ships, where the *Sure Thing* would be trapped and destroyed.

With the rotten luck he had recently, and by 'recently' Vinny meant most of his adult life, he was not betting on a best-case scenario.

"No enemy ships, or ships of any kind," Ammarie reported soon after the sensors reset from the jump. "Unless they're in stealth," she added without needing to. They all understood the ship's sensors, which exceeded even the capabilities of the gear aboard the ship when it was a front-line star carrier in fleet service, could not quickly detect ships encased in stealth fields. She set the passive sensors to search for the faint ripples sometimes detectable when a stealthed ship passed in front of a star, and powered up the active sensor field. The gamma rays of their inbound jump had lit up the area like a strobe light, there was no point trying to remain quiet. "Oh, this is not good. I'm picking up debris, a *lot* of it."

"Pinging for flight recorder drones, ours and Ruhar. I've got a bad feeling about this," Vinny kept one antenna poised over the emergency jump button while his fingers flew over the controls.

"All systems ready to jump on your mark," Cleeturss didn't take his eyes away from his own console. Vinny was generally an optimist, to the point of taking foolish risks that had gotten him in trouble again and again. If he had a bad feeling, Cleeturss did not want to remain in the area any longer than they had to.

When the Bosphuraq battlecruiser jumped away, after having broken the Jeraptha star carrier and destroying all the Ruhar ships except for one unimportant old training cruiser that jumped away, it had left a nasty surprise for any Jeraptha ships searching for the lost *Deal Me In*. The battlecruiser dropped off eleven ship-killer missiles, keyed to react only to Jeraptha or equivalent-technology ships. The missiles had been instructed to ignore any Ruhar ships jumping into the battlespace, as those ships could not reach a habitable planet from that location and were already as good as dead anyway.

After their mother ship jumped away, the missiles spread out in a wide pattern to cover the area, then went silent and activated their tightly-wrapped stealth fields. The missiles noted when the Ruhar training cruiser jumped back in, and they did not drop stealth or attack or react in any way, even when they observed the old cruiser attaching itself to a docking platform on what used to be the aft end of the star carrier.

The tiny brains of the missiles were smart, and each missile silently fretted while watching passively as the enemy worked on what remained of the star carrier. The enemy was clearly doing something to get the star carrier's jump drive functioning again, and each missile agonized about whether the Jeraptha ship being restored to even limited flight capability should authorize the missiles to attack. If they could have conferred with each other, they might have decided this unprecedented event allowed them to stretch the bounds of their orders, but the missiles had been programmed for strict communications silence.

After the astonishing event of the broken star carrier jumping safely away from the battlespace, two of the missiles became deranged by their failure to act, and safeguards built into their artificial brains caused those missiles to fry their electronics and hang cold and dead in space, slowly drifting farther from the battlespace.

The other nine missiles queried their instruction set to determine what they should have done based on their orders, and the missiles decided their instruction sets did not encompass the possibility of a broken star carrier jumping to safety. So, the missiles felt they were free to rewrite their instructions to carry out their overall mission, and they became absolutely determined not to let *any* type of enemy ship get away ever again, and to hell with their stupid original orders.

"Getting responses from drones," Thelmer's eyes scanned the flood of incoming data. "That's odd. There is a second set of drones out there."

"Ours or Ruhar?" Vinny asked distractedly, concentrating on his own set of sensor data. It was clear a Jeraptha ship had been hit in that area, enough of the debris was unmistakably from a Jeraptha warship and he also detected residual signs of Bosphuraq warheads. Missiles had been flying, Jeraptha, Bosphuraq and Ruhar. What he could not yet understand was the debris with Jeraptha signatures did not have enough mass to be from an entire star carrier, not even an old one like the *Deal Me In*. Had part of the star carrier been transformed into subatomic particles? Or had the Bosphuraq somehow, for some unknown but disturbing reason, taken away part of the old *Deal Me In*? Vinny did not like the thought of that.

"Both," Cleeturss responded, surprise in his tone. "There is a second, later set of drones from the *Deal Me In*, and from a Ruhar training cruiser."

"You are certain they are from the *Deal Me In*?""

"The registration code is unmistakable," Thelmer let irritation creep into her voice. Did the ship's owner think she didn't know her job? "I verified- *Missile warning red*! Jump us out of here!"

Vinny would not have hesitated, except that he had no choice. His antenna nearly pressed the button for a pre-programmed emergency jump, only seeing a red light flashing on his console made him stop. "Damping field!" He shouted.

The *Sure Thing* had jumped in just beyond the rough sphere formed by the nine remaining active missiles, so only two missiles had any chance to hit the ship. Fortunately for the *Sure Thing*, even the closest missile was far enough away that it needed to compromise stealth by engaging its propulsion system to get within effective range of its warhead. Unfortunately for the *Sure Thing*, the missile that was slightly farther away contained a technology that was possessed only by the Bosphuraq, Maxolhx and Rindhalu. It was a short-duration damping field, powered by detonation of the missile's warhead. Compared to similar devices owned by the two senior species, the Bosphuraq damping generator was crude, and effective for only a short sphere around the missile, so crude the Maxolhx had not objected too strongly when their clients recently managed to reverse-engineer the technology.

"Damping effect- from where?" Ammarie screeched, throwing up her hands. She did not see a ship on sensors, and no ship could both maintain stealth and generate a damping field at the same time. No *known* ship had that capability, a thought which sent an icy chill from the end of her antenna to the toes of her hind legs. Could they be facing a Maxolhx warship? And why was there the distinct signature of a missile warhead detonation at the center of the damping field? "We-" a section of the display caught her eye. "Jump!"

Vinny looked at his partner. "But we're caught in-"

"I know! Jump! Jump *now*!"

The *Sure Thing* jumped. Sort of.

"What was *that*?" Vinny hugged a chair with both sets of legs while gripping the sides of the console with both hands, taking even gulps of air to quell his queasy stomach.

"Something new, something we've never seen. The fleet will be interested in this data," Ammarie weakly waved a hand at her own console, blinking to make her eyes focus. It didn't help, the problem wasn't with her eyes, it was with her rattled brain which was throbbing with the beginning of a painful headache. She sent a command to her internal medical monitor to release pain suppressors into her bloodstream, and turned her attention back to the data that was still compiling. "That damping field was projected by a missile."

"A *missile*? How-" Vinny realized that question was not important at the moment. The ship had jumped less than one lighthour from the battlespace, and if they were being pursued by an enemy warship, the *Sure Thing* was surely in major trouble. If the attack had been conducted only by missiles, the crew had time to inspect and make repairs to the jump drive before moving away. "Forget it. Good work, darling. How did you know?"

"I saw the damping field had peaked and was already weakening, the missile must only be able to project a temporary bubble. There was either a regular missile homing in on us," she wasn't yet able to make sense of the sensor data, "or another damping field coming after the first one passed by us. We jumped just as the damping field strength dropped below the critical limit."

"Below the critical limit for most ships. With the condition of our old drive system," Vinny didn't finish the thought. "Good enough. We have evidence the *Deal Me In* was destroyed, so we should head back as soon as we-"

"Not yet," Thelmer held up a hand for attention. "The *Deal Me In* was hit, but not destroyed."

"It jumped away?" Vinny asked incredulously. From the debris field he had scanned, the star carrier had been thoroughly ripped apart.

"Not exactly."

Vinny "What do you mean 'not exactly'?"

Thelmer's antennas twitched with amusement. "You are *not* going to believe this."

"That is impossible," Vinny declared flatly. A broken star carrier had jumped, under the control of a *Ruhar* ship?! A Ruhar ship commanded by a *human*. Vinny's mind reeled at the idea of a lowly human being in command of anything more complicated than a rowboat. His gambler's brain pounded at the unlikeliness of a broken star carrier jumping at all, and that the jump controller had been developed by the Ruhar. He would have wagered everything he had that neither of those events could have been possible! Yet, according to the flight recorder log certified as accurate by the *Deal Me In*'s former crewman Arlon Dahl, it had been the clever thinking and initiative of the human called Emily Perkins that saved both her old Ruhar cruiser, the life of Arlon Dahl, and the aft section of the *Deal Me In*.

"It happened, therefore it is *not* impossible," Thelmer retorted. "Do you want to bet on it?"

"No." Vinny replied automatically as he had lost too many wagers to his sister-in-law. "Ammarie, we need to follow that, that," what could he call it? The thing that had jumped away from the battlespace was not a star carrier, and the Ruhar training ship was not capable of jumping a useful distance. "Follow what is left of the *Deal Me In*."

"What? Why?" Ammarie was wary of another scheme from Vinny. "We have proof that we found the missing ship."

"We found *part* of the missing ship. Those sleazy bureaucrats at Central Wagering will use any excuse to cut our winnings, you know that. Darling, we can follow easily, there is less danger going into Kristang space than there is for us being here. When we locate the ship, and the one crewman who survived," Vinny knew there would be a bonus if they could bring back Arlon Dahl, "the fleet will surely forgive all past transgressions we've committed."

"*Allegedly* committed."

"Plus," Vinny was getting wound up with enthusiasm. "That training ship is full of cadets. The Ruhar will reward us well for bringing back their precious children."

"You hope."

"I believe."

"This is a sure thing?" Ammarie put her hands on her hips and Vinny knew what that meant. "Like all your sure things before?"

"This is different."

"Different how?"

"This time, you agree with me." Vinny flashed a winning smile.

Ammarie sighed. "Maybe you're right. This one time, mind you. Besides, there's one thing you forgot."

"What is that?"

"A Ruhar ship controlled one of our jump drives. The Ruhar fleet *will* pay dearly for the knowledge of how that happened."

Thelmer and Cleeturss agreed wholeheartedly, even enthusiastically to the idea of following the *Deal Me In*. All four aboard were greedily imagining their cuts of the wager and rewards money, and all four were burning with curiosity to learn whether the aft end of the *Deal Me In* had successfully jumped, or had exploded into a million pieces. For another species, agreement and curiosity would have been enough to settle the issue. For the Jeraptha, those factors merely served as an opening for renegotiating their financial arrangements, and to set side wagers on whether the broken star carrier had in fact survived a jump. And had jumped more than once. Had flown through a wormhole. Had arrived at a Kristang-controlled star system. There were other wagers on how many, if any, of the cadets and other crew would still be alive when the *Sure Thing* arrived. Vinny allowed the dickering back and forth to continue, both because he couldn't resist getting in on the action, and because work to inspect and repair the ship's jump drive continued during the negotiations.

Only after all wagers were properly registered and the jump drive was fully checked out, did the *Sure Thing* jump to follow the planned course of the *Deal Me In*.

CHAPTER TWENTY TWO

"Colonel! Colonel Perkins!" Arlon Dahl stuck his head out the door of the dropship, waving his arms and antennas excitedly. "A Jeraptha ship is overhead! It jumped into orbit a few minutes ago!"

Emily Perkins felt her heart soar with hope and immediately crash with despair. She felt a pang of fear like a fist squeezing her chest. "Just one warship?"

"It is not a warship," Dahl's antenna twitched in a gesture Perkins had learned to associate with nervousness.

"Not a warship? What is-"

"Colonel," Dahl urged her forward, waving his hands. "It would be best if you spoke with Captain Gumbano himself. It is," his mouthparts worked erratically. "Complicated."

The situation was indeed complicated, what mattered most was that the *Sure Thing* was a Jeraptha starship capable of traveling vast distances on its own, and that the ship's crew had come to Camp Alpha for the dual purposes of determining the fate of the *Deal Me In*, and of rescuing the survivors of the battle with the Bosphuraq. Perhaps 'rescue' was not the most accurate description of the *Sure Thing* crew's intentions, which became clear the moment Perkins mentioned the bioweapon. If that ship's captain was excited to find cadet survivors who would prompt a grateful Ruhar government to pay handsomely, the captain was deliriously happy to learn he would be carrying information that could save an entire Ruhar planet, for *that* data would be worth a true fortune.

Emily Perkins was very happy also, except for the annoying little detail of the *Sure Thing*'s crew flatly refusing to let any potentially infected humans aboard their ship. The prospect of a Jeraptha ship whisking her team away from Camp Alpha had caused her heart to soar. The recognition that the *Sure Thing* had actually arrived too *soon* had been the source of her despair.

Not enough time had passed since her team had been exposed to the control group Keepers, who might be infected. Her original plan had been for her team to remain sealed up in skinsuits during the raid, and to thoroughly decontaminate the dropship, suits and everything else that had been exposed. Having to take the Keepers with them, just because the research base was about to self-destruct in a massive fireball, had ruined all her plans. Her team had been potentially exposed, as soon as the dropship landed and they removed their skinsuit helmets.

If the Jeraptha ship had arrived more than three months after the raid, her team would know they were infected or not, by either becoming sick as the bioweapon completed its incubation period, or not becoming sick because they had not been exposed. The Keepers weren't sick, but for all Perkins knew, they could have been infected the day before the raid. She simply didn't know, and she understood why the *Sure Thing*'s crew did not want to risk taking her team aboard. Before talking with the captain of the Jeraptha ship, she took a breath to calm herself, and patched Bifft Cohlsoon into the conversation, so the cadets could be aware of the situation.

"Colonel Perkins," Vinny announced in an emotionless voice, "we will report your presence on this planet when we return to space controlled by our people. Perhaps, after the incubation period has passed, another vessel will be sent to retrieve your team."

Yes, Perkins thought sourly, perhaps. If her team had not died from the bioweapon. If the Kristang had not returned and vaporized the small group of humans with an orbital strike. If the Ruhar government wanted to expend the effort and take the risk of sending a rescue ship into enemy territory. And if, only if, the bioweapon had not already ravaged the population of Paradise. No way would the Ruhar have any interest in rescuing humans, if humans acting as unwitting carriers had caused the deaths of a significant number of Ruhar on Paradise and beyond. "Captain Gumbano, we do understand your concerns. The Ruhar cadets have remained on the other side of the planet, they cannot be contaminated, so there is no risk to you or the general Ruhar population. Also Arlon Ernt Dahl is one of your own people, and Surgun Jates as a," she stumbled, then settled on an accurate description. "As a Verd-Kris Kristang, they are both unaffected by the bioweapon and cannot be carriers of the pathogen. Captain Gumbano, please take them aboard and away from here as quickly as possible. Arlon Dahl and Surgun Jates can walk a safe distance from our camp here, where your dropship can pick them up without risk of contamination."

"That is acceptable," Vinny responded, relief evident even in his translated alien voice. He had not been looking forward to an extended argument with the human Emily Perkins, and so was very pleased she was being reasonable. Also, he expected that bringing back Ernt Dahl as the sole survivor of the *Deal Me In* would earn some measure of gratitude from the Jeraptha fleet, and perhaps they might overlook any past transgressions the *Sure Thing* might have involved in. Allegedly.

There was, to Vinny's own surprise, a part of him that regretted leaving this Emily Perkins to die on the surface of the planet, for they both knew that would be her fate after the *Deal Me In* jumped away. Perkins and her team had accomplished incredible things against great odds by taking great risks, and Vinny felt she was a gambler at heart, just like his people.

Perkins knew her certain fate also, and chose not to dwell on it. "Cadet Colhsoon, load your people into dropships and dust off immediately, leave whatever gear you have outside the dropships. There could be a Kristang ship jumping in at any moment, do not take the risk-"

Bifft's voice broke into the comm system. "Colonel Perkins, your team will not be coming with us?"

"No. We may have been exposed to the bioweapon and there is no way to test us for infection," she explained. "If we came aboard the ship, we would risk contaminating you and your team-"

"We will not allow anyone who might be infected aboard our ship," Vinny interjected. "Cadet Colhsoon, your lives have substantial value to your government and therefore to us. But you will not be valuable to your people if you are carrying a deadly bioweapon. We will bring you back to your territory, where you can, um-" What? What could he say that didn't sound like an obvious lie? "You can persuade your government to send a ship back here for Colonel Perkins and the other humans, after enough time has passed to prove they are not infected," Vinny cringed as he spoke because everyone knew how lame his argument was.

"No," Bifft tried to keep his voice even but the strain was clear. "Captain Gumbano, you *can* take the Colonel's team aboard in dropships. Your docking bay can remain exposed to vacuum, and her team can remain inside dropships. The only connection to your ship will be power supply cables," Bifft knew the Jeraptha would not allow a dropship to remain on internal power for an extended time, there was too much risk of an accident if the airspace craft's engines were running.

There was a pause as the Jeraptha considered the proposal, then, "Not acceptable. When we arrive in your territory, your people will demand that our ship be subject to a quarantine that would delay us for months, and cost substantial loss of revenue. The humans are not why we tracked you across the stars at immense cost and risk to ourselves. There will be a reward for delivering Ruhar cadets safely home, I do not see your fleet caring whether a small group of humans-"

"There is *no* risk in you taking aboard dropships that remain in vacuum," Bifft insisted, anger creeping into his voice.

Perkins seized on the cadet's idea, it offered the only realistic hope to save her team's lives. "Cadet Leader Colhsoon is correct, there is no risk to you if our dropship is in an open docking bay. I am sure there will be additional reward for-"

"No such reward was included in the search and rescue terms offered by our fleet," Vinny insisted. "Risk is *never* zero. You are being foolish, Colonel Perkins. Every risky transaction must be balanced by reward."

"The risk is, you get *nothing* for your effort," Bifft declared. "Take Colonel Perkins and her team aboard your ship, or my team will not come with you."

"*What*?" Vinny shrieked with outrage.

Perkins looked at her team in complete surprise. She had assumed Bifft would take any opportunity to leave her behind, so he could spin the story of his attempted mutiny however he wanted. "Cadet Colhsoon, while I appreciate your offer of solidarity, you must dust off immediately. You cannot risk the lives of-"

"Colonel, you already said I am young, inexperienced and impulsive, so I am free to do impulsive things without further damaging my tarnished reputation," his smugness was reflected in his tone of voice even through the translator. "I have a ship full of people here who are determined not to leave you behind. Captain Gumbano, good luck trying to drag us off this rock to collect your reward, because we are *not* coming aboard your ship until Colonel Perkins' people are secured in a docking bay. You talked about risk, what is the risk if you leave us here deliberately?"

Perkins held her thumb above the transmit button, hesitating before she replied. "Well, Goddamn," she looked at her incredulous team. "That mutinous little shit has grown up quick."

"Yeah, perfect timing too," Shauna agreed. "You think he's bluffing?"

"I sure hope not," Perkins replied with a rueful shake of her head. "The kid's right, those beetles are just being assholes." She pressed the transmit button. "Colhsoon, you are playing with your people's lives."

"I am not 'playing' because as you would say, this is not a game. If you could see the faces of my team here, you would know we are all equally determined. The Jeraptha have the data your team recovered from the research base, that is all we can do to help the people of Paradise, *both* our peoples there. Colonel," his voice cracked with emotion, "I thought you were unworthy to command a Ruhar ship. I was wrong. You saved all our lives by doing something, several things, I thought were impossible. If we had not come to this world, the people of Paradise would not be aware of a terrible threat."

Perkins almost sighed and rolled her eyes at hearing the young cadet's melodramatic words, but she let him continue. "Colhsoon, listen, do not think you owe us anything. We are soldiers, this is our duty. You-"

"We *do* owe you! That is not why we will not leave without you."

"Ok, what is the reason?"

"We are a team. And a team does not leave people behind. You taught me that."

Emily Perkins could not argue with that. "Captain Gumbano, did you hear that, you greedy little shit," she used the insult deliberately. "You want to collect a reward for rescuing those cadets? Then you need to take my team aboard in one of your dropships. Consider that *my* cut of the pot."

Vinny's voice was enraged. "*You* are not entitled to a cut of anything, you-" The sound cut off, and Perkins waited breathlessly, watching the clock in the corner of the display. Thirty nine agonizing seconds of silence went by before the voice from orbit returned.

It was a different voice. "Colonel Perkins, this is Ammarie, you had been speaking with my business partner. Very well, we agree, however we do not have a dropship large enough for your entire team."

Perkins took a moment to think. "Not a problem, but our dropship here is busted, it can't fly. Cadet Colhsoon, I need you to remotely pilot two Dodos to our location, and we will fly them up to the Jeraptha ship. Captain Ammarie, your dropship can assist bringing the cadets up to your ship?"

There was a pause and when Ammarie resumed speaking, there was a muted argument going on in the background. "We can do-" The sound cut off then Ammarie abruptly announced. "Hold a minute, we need to discuss this up here."

Ernt Dahl had enough, the mercenary attitude of his fellow Jeraptha in orbit had embarrassed him, so he stepped forward. "Colonel Perkins, as your people would say, *screw* this." He activated his microphone. "This is *Arlon* Ernt Dahl of the star carrier *Deal Me In*, on detached service from the Thirty-Fifth Fleet, Gold Squadron of the Jeraptha Home Fleet. As a Fleet officer, I am officially *commandeering* your merchant ship for a Fleet emergency. Is. That. Clear?"

The pause was long enough that Ernt opened his mouth to speak again, but Ammarie spoke before he could. As she spoke, there was grumbling voices in the background, but at least no one up there was shouting. "Arlon Dahl, we would of course be, happy," the last word was pronounced as if she had just tasted something disgusting, "to comply with Fleet requirements. Our ship is available to assist in this emergency situation."

"Excellent," Ernt grinned toward Perkins, who suppressed a shudder.

"At standard daily usage rates, of course," Ammarie added.

"Um-"

"Plus bonus for hazardous duty."

"Er, I guess-"

"And reimbursement for fuel used and wear and tear on components, naturally."

Ernt ground his mandibles. The crew of that ship was clearly angling to have their no doubt already worn-out components replaced at Fleet expense! "Oh, what the hell," he sighed. "It's not *my* money. Sure, I agree."

Ammarie giggled before catching herself. Mirth was still evident in her voice. "Colonel Perkins, we would be honored to take your dropships aboard. You will follow our docking procedures exactly, and surrender control of your internal systems once you are docked, because we will not risk you firing weapons once you are aboard. The only connection between your ships and ours will be a power cable, is that understood?"

"Understood and agreed. Please also secure airlock doors in the docking bay, so they cannot be opened from the outside."

"A sensible precaution for us, why do *you* wish us to do that?"

"My team may be infected with a deadly pathogen which could affect us during the flight. I wish to remove the temptation for people stricken with disease to seek help inside your ship."

"You do not trust your own people?"

"Would you trust your crew or yourself in that situation?"

There was a pause, then, "no. Please hurry. If a Kristang warship arrives, my ship will need to jump away immediately. We are a commercial vessel and carry minimum armaments." She did not add the reason their missile magazines were empty, was because the ancient missiles had been repossessed the last time the ship was at a dockyard. Nor did she mention their jump drive was not operating at full capacity because they had been warned that same dockyard was about to impound the ship for unpaid debts. They had been forced to escape from that dockyard in the middle of the night and jump while too close to the planet. The fines for violating orbital traffic laws alone were more than the ship was worth.

"Thank you," Perkins said with reluctance, because the beetles upstairs sure weren't doing anything out of the kindness of their hearts. Cutting off the microphone, she turned to her people. "There won't be any food for humans and," she looked at Jates, "Verd-Kris aboard that ship, so let's get our food packs ready to transfer to the other dropships. I'm going out to inform our Keeper guests of the situation, and to make it very clear that anyone who does not behave will be left on this rock. I am not making *that* mistake again."

CHAPTER TWENTY THREE

General Lynn Bezanson's zPhone beeped with a call from the Burgermeister, as she was about to close up her office for the evening. It had been another frustrating day, dealing with nitpicky annoying details that UNEF HQ wanted discussed with the planetary government. "Chief Administrator Logellia, good evening. To what do I owe the pleasure of this call?" Lynn said that last as a courtesy, because the woman who ran an entire planet would not be making an unscheduled call to her UNEF liaison officer for any pleasant reason.

"Good evening, General Bezanson. Unfortunately, what we need to discuss is not a pleasant subject. I would invite you to my office, but I am currently away from the capital."

Lynn gripped the zPhone tightly, taking a deep breath to calm her pounding heart. The morning UNEF intel briefing had not contained any threats; not just no *new* threats, but no threats at all. Paradise was peaceful and UNEF's position was good and improving, but Lynn knew it violated some unwritten rule of the universe for her job to be easy. She wanted to ask whether the bad news was about the overdue and missing Mavericks team, but guessing was useless and only wasted time. Pressing a button under her desk to close her office door, she also alerted UNEF HQ in Lemuria that she was involved in an important discussion. Alarm bells would be ringing at UNEF HQ, and senior officers would be freeing up their schedules for her to brief them shortly. "Go ahead, please."

"First, there is good news. Lieutenant Colonel Perkins and her team have been found alive and well. Not completely *well*, perhaps, I will explain that. "

"Found? Where?"

"You call the planet 'Camp Alpha', I am told?"

"Camp-" Lynn's brain locked up momentarily. "*Alpha*? What the hell are they doing on that Godforsaken world? Isn't that in Kristang territory?" She struggled to recall whether that distant and rather unimportant planet had changed hands during the recent chaos of the Kristang civil war and military defeats suffered by the Thuranin.

"*Were*, not are. The Mavericks are not on Camp Alpha in Kristang space, they are aboard a Jeraptha civilian transport ship. Please, allow me to explain."

"Holy shit," Lynn slumped back in her chair a few earth-shattering minutes later, forgetting that she was speaking with the leader of the planet. "These infected Keepers could already be on Para- Gehtanu?" She used the Ruhar name for the planet. While she spoke, she clicked an icon on her laptop to alert UNEF HQ to expect a Priority One message, and began touch-typing while she spoke with the Burgermeister. Undoubtedly lower-ranking Ruhar would be contacting UNEF HQ soon, the Burgermeister contacting her directly first was a courtesy that testified to the strength of the relationship they had developed.

"It is possible the infected Keepers are here now, yes. As you know, our satellite sensor and defense network is not complete," Baturnah's tone turned sour, as she had regularly complained to the federal government about the strategic defense network being far behind schedule. The response from the federal government was always that resources were constrained, and needed badly elsewhere as the Ruhar took possession of territory captured from the Kristang. "Even if the network were fully operational and the battlegroup were here, it is unlikely we could stop a single small stealthed ship from landing. The Kristang are skilled at stealthy infiltrations."

"This is not good," Lynn said to herself though she spoke aloud. "We will need to be on alert for humans who left with Admiral Kekrando's group."

"Yes, however, the Kristang would certainly have supplied the infected people with false identification, including cloned zPhones. I am afraid the most effective way to identify infiltrators will be for your people here to report anyone they do not recognize as belonging to their immediate group."

"All right, then we'll need to restrict movement, confine people to their area where they live." General Bezanson figured the Ruhar were already planning to put travel restrictions in place soon, with a strict lockdown on human movements. "Administrator, there may be a faster and easier way to identify infiltrators; we can broadcast a message to all zPhones that the Keepers have been infected with a deadly virus. When the infiltrators," she considered how close that word sounded to 'traitors', "hear the message, they will learn that they are being used by the Kristang. We would encourage them to give themselves up, get treatment, or at least avoid spreading the infection."

"That is a good idea and we will certainly try that, however my intel people warn me it is not likely to be an effective strategy with the target population. These Keepers departed with the Kristang because they believed my people are the true enemy of humanity, and that UNEF committed treason by cooperating with us. The Keepers believe there is a conspiracy to deceive UNEF troops, they believe that so strongly they left with the Kristang. It is likely the Kristang chose the most committed and fanatical people for this mission. Such people would hear your warning message about them being infected, and consider it to be another lie by my people and by UNEF headquarters."

"Damn it," Lynn knew the Ruhar was right. God*damn* stupid, ignorant Keepers, she thought to herself. It was bad enough those idiots wasted their lives by going with the Kristang, because Lynn knew from Ruhar intel reports that many of the Keepers had been sold as slaves to be used for hunting or other sport. At least those particular assholes had long ago seen the truth and regretted their stupidity. The infected group of Keepers had to be different, or some of them would give themselves up as soon as they set foot on Paradise again. They must have been sold some line of bullshit about a patriotic mission, and the Kristang would have selected only the most delusional humans for the infiltration effort. Damn it! UNEF would be hunting the most fanatical of the lunatics among the Keepers. No amount of persuasion or psychological tricks would work those assholes, everything they heard would only serve to reinforce in their minds that UNEF was lying and treasonous, and that therefore they must remain steadfast to complete their mission. "To be safe, we will need to separate the human population from your people."

"That would be prudent. Currently, we do not have a reliable method of detecting infection in either humans or Ruhar, so we cannot be sure the virus has not already been transmitted. A quarantine is the most effective method of preventing a pandemic in the short term, we will be confining humans to southern Lemuria."

Lynn looked around her office, wondering if she would ever see it again. "What about those humans still in the northern jungle of Lemuria?"

"There is a debate in my government whether to leave those relatively isolated populations in place and simply prevent them from traveling, or whether it would be best to transport them to the southern settlements. General, we know this disease is highly virulent and spreads easily between humans. Consolidating your population in one area poses a risk that *all* humans on Gehtanu could become infected."

"The disease is fatal to humans, even though we are carriers?"

"Yes, the data from Camp Alpha indicates the disease goes dormant for approximately three months, then progresses rapidly in humans. Among Ruhar, the period during which the disease remains dormant is only two months. Our scientists tell me this is a very cleverly engineered pathogen. Its design involved technology far beyond our own biomedical knowledge."

"But surely you can manufacture an antidote, a treatment or at least a vaccine?"

"Not currently, no. Not quickly enough to matter in this case. Colonel Perkins recovered data about the Kristang bioweapons testing program, however her team was not able to obtain samples, so our scientists will not have enough information to create a protective vaccine. As I said, this is a very sophisticated pathogen, the Kristang must have had help from a higher-technology species. We will contact the Jeraptha for assistance, but even if they agree to help, combatting biowarfare between other species is not a technological strength of the Jeraptha."

"Wheeeew," Bezanson did not care that the leader of the planet heard her emotional distress. "We have no way to detect whether humans are infected?"

"No, the first sign would be when humans begin falling ill at the end of the incubation period. General, by the time humans are showing symptoms, infected Ruhar could already be dead. Unfortunately," she cleared her throat with a slightly squeaky sound. "Unfortunately, the situation here on Gehtanu is not entirely under my control. Because the population of this world is under external threat, authority to deal with the threat rests with the battlegroup commander, Admiral Tannavon."

Bezanson tensed. She had met Tannavon on several occasions and while the Admiral was a decorated and well-respected commander, he was also a hardass. Tannavon had been a major obstacle to sending the Mavericks into space on a training ship, which is why Perkins had conducted an end-run around the local chain of command to secure Ruhar fleet approval, before Tannavon even knew Perkins had applied for her team to go offworld. "I am sure the Admiral will do what-"

"Tannavon spoke with me immediately after our initial briefing from the Fleet," Logellia interrupted. "He stressed that because we do not know whether the Kristang have landed the infected Keepers already, we *must* assume a significant number of humans are infected. We will be restricting the movements of our own population, and quarantining any Ruhar who have had recent contact with humans. That includes me," she added with a grimace. "Confining my people to their home villages for an unknown length of time will not be popular, the Admiral and I talked about how to deal with civil disturbances. Tannavon made it very clear to me that he will not tolerate *any* breach of the confinement protocol, particularly by humans."

"UNEF will do our utmost to enforce whatever procedures you deem necessary to protect your people."

"Good. That is good, and you need to stress that to your civilian leadership, as your military Force is now too small to truly be in complete control of your population. General Bezanson, I overheard a remark by one of the Admiral's aides during our conversation, and you should repeat this in confidence to only your very senior leadership."

"What did the aide say?" Bezanson asked, fearing she knew the answer.

"That the *only* certain way to ensure humans on this planet do not pose a threat to Ruhar, is if there are no humans alive on this planet."

CHAPTER TWENTY FOUR

"Holy *shit*, Skippy." I said that with such force that I got tiny dots of spit on the inside of my helmet visor.

"You finished reading about the dilemma Perkins got into?"

"Yeah. O.M.G."

"That was my reaction when I downloaded the report. The Mavericks may be even more talented at finding trouble than you are."

"We need to help them. Even Chotek will agree with that."

"You are more optimistic about Count Chocula than I am, but let's go with that. Anyway, we can't do anything until I kill that energy virus."

"Right."

"If I can."

"*If?*"

"Unless it kills us first."

"Once again, you are a *huge* source of comfort to me."

"I do what I can, Joe. Hey, speaking of comfort, are you comfy out there?"

"Comfy enough, I guess."

"Good, good. Well, after reading about Perkins, you must be pretty bored, huh?"

Goddamn it. My Spidey sense failed me, so I idiotically replied "Yeah, it's awfully dull out here."

"Hmmmmm," he pondered in a voice that tingled with delight, as if he hadn't been planning this all along. "You are bored?" Then he said something that made my blood run ice cold. "Gosh, if only there were *some* way for me to entertain you."

My father is a fan of old movies. On Sunday nights, the rest of us would have to suffer through watching whatever 'classic' movie he insisted was important for me and my sister to see. Yes, I used quotes around the word 'classic', because some of the crap we had to watch was truly awful. We especially groaned when the credits opened and we realized that night's movie was in black and white. Once in a while we got a pleasant surprise, like I did enjoy some old movies, and most anything with John Wayne was worth watching.

Anyway, I mention this because we watched one movie on a rainy Sunday night in March. Football was over for the season, it was about five degrees above freezing and raining outside, and the weather had been like that for a solid week. My father made pizza and we had chocolate cake for dessert. I remember those details because the movie gave me nightmares and I didn't sleep well that night. It was 'Apocalypse Now', about the Vietnam war. Or, it was sort of about that war, I think the war was just a convenient background for whatever message the film makers wanted to present. If you haven't seen it, the movie has famous lines like 'I love the smell of napalm in the morning, it smells like victory'. You've heard that quote? Of course you have. That's where it came from.

Toward the end of that movie, Marlon Brando's character Colonel Kurtz is splashing water over his head and mumbling 'The horror. The *horror*'. His character has seen such terrible things, been through so much horror, that his mind is totally gone.

Let me tell you, that Colonel Kurtz guy ain't seen *shit* compared to what Skippy put me through.

Take a deep breath and prepare yourself.

Ready?

I have two words for you: Knight. Rider.

Not just Knight Rider the original TV show. This was the director's cut, with commentary. When Skippy started playing the pilot episode in my visor so there was no way for me to ignore it, I had protested. "Come *on*, Skippy! There is no 'directors cut' of these episodes."

"Technically you are correct, Joe, because no director associated with this appalling crapfest would bother to compile an alternate version. However, I have many of the scenes that got cut from the final episode, so I am able to slap them together."

The commentary was Skippy's own, mostly snarky remarks about how bad the show was, and how criminally stupid monkeys must be to have watched it. What really got him upset was the Artificial Intelligence named 'KITT' built into the car, which was an insult to AIs or even to the concept of AIs. I had to endure his diatribes against the producers of the show every time KITT spoke or did anything. He was making me take a bullet for all monkeys, so all of you owe me, big time.

The worst part is that instead of each episode being mercifully only forty two minutes, the director's cut stretched them to an average of sixty eight minutes. "Skippy, please," I groaned as one mindless episode ended and another began. "I'm begging you, make it stop."

"Joe, you promised to let me educate you about crappy 80s TV shows. We had plenty of time to do that in the Roach Motel, but *noooooo*, you kept telling me you were too busy."

"You already made me watch 'Manimal' with you!"

"Yes, and we were supposed to move on to 'The Love Boat' but, again you told me you were too busy. Would you prefer 'The Love Boat'? I have every episode of that schlockfest also. How about we roll the pilot, and-"

"No! No, let's stick with 'Knight Rider'," I sighed, steeling myself for another torturous hour of watching The Hoff. "It's almost done anyway, right?"

"Ha! As if, dude! We're still in the first season."

"Oh, I can't take this."

"If you don't want another 'Knight Rider', there are plenty other shows to choose from. The 80s were a treasure trove of crappy TV. I could show you-"

"Please, anything else."

"Joe, you have suffered enough, so I'm going to let you watch 'Smokey and the Bandit'."

"Cool! I've seen that movie. My father had a friend with a Bandit Trans-Am, but it was a tribute car, not an original. When I was in high school, I thought that car was super cool," I remarked happily, not believing my good luck. Then I got a sinking feeling, because Skippy is an asshole and the universe hates me. "Wait," I was suspicious. "The second Bandit movie sucked. You're not going to show me that one, are you?"

"The second Bandit movie is universally renowned for its money-grabbing *suckitude*, however you will not be watching Part Two."

"Oh, thank God."

"Instead, I will treat you to Part Three."

"What? No way," I scoffed. "Now you're just making shit up. There was no third movie."

"You *think* there was not a third Bandit movie, because it was so instantly forgettable."

Crap. He was right, there was a Part Three. Mercifully, I fell asleep after about an hour and Skippy didn't wake me for another six hours.

"Hey, Joe!" Skippy shouted as he played 'Reveille' in my helmet speakers. "Rise and shine, sleepyhead. Time to go to work."

"Oh, man. Good morning. How about coffee first?"

"Plenty of coffee in that dropship ahead of you. Be a good boy and go get it."

Without gravity, you'd think my muscles wouldn't get stiff while I slept, but they did. While I stretched, I checked status of the crew in my visor, and did a roll call of the dropship retrieval teams. Everyone on the teams were ready and eager to go. We left much of the crew sleeping, since there wasn't anything they could do, and sleeping conserved power and oxygen.

There were four two-person teams assigned to getting dropships up and running, all eight of us were pilots. I was certainly not the most qualified pilot, but I had the most experience with space diving, and Skippy wanted me on a retrieval team in case we ran into problems. My team was me and Major Desai. We got unclipped from our tethers and puffed our gas canisters experimentally. There were no fancy jetpacks available for this mission, they would have been impossible to power up by hand cranking, and their big powercells took too long to drain completely. Desai and I would fly through the sky using basically crude air bottles to propel us. It was awkward, and we had only been able to practice for an hour before we left the *Dutchman* behind. It took us almost ten minutes, letting the bottles puff gently, to maneuver close enough together so I could launch a line toward her. She caught it on the first try, and I was proud we were the second of four teams to link up. Linking up was the easy part.

The dropships were parked a significant distance away from us, to prevent the energy virus jumping across the distance and infecting the systems in our spacesuits, so it was a long flight, and I took the opportunity to ask Skippy a question that had been bugging me since before we jumped blindly into the Roach Motel.

"Hey, Skippy," I glanced to my left where Desai was flying in formation with me, on the other end of the tether line.

"Hey, Joe," the beer can's voice came out of my helmet speakers, sounding thoroughly depressed. Damn it, I needed Skippy to be focused, not moping around. "What's up?"

"Before we get to that, are you Ok?"

"Yeah, just, I'm worried about this energy virus thing. Not this incident specifically, I have a plan to deal with it. It's just, damn it, we never get a break. Just as we stomp one problem flat, another one pops up to bite us in the ass."

"I've been worrying about that, too, and I have a question for you."

"I will answer if I can." It worried me that he didn't bother to include a snarky remark.

"The Elders left a lot of their stuff around, and not just derelict ships and ruins and the kind of stuff you'd expect to see lying around after a civilization disappears. The Elders left functioning equipment behind, like AIs, and Sentinels, and Guardians. And those power sink things you found inside the star at the Roach Motel."

"If you are asking me if I know where the energy of those power sinks is going or what it is or was used for, the answer sadly is still no. I have been wracking my brain trying to think why those power sinks are still active, but it is a complete mystery to me. Whatever is the purpose of the power sinks, they are important enough to require the Guardians to protect them."

"Uh huh, that's part of my question. When we were in the Roach Motel, I asked, if the Elders ascended and left the galaxy behind, why they would still care about whether someone here messes with their stuff long after they're gone. Then I thought, what if that is the wrong question?"

"I'm not following you."

"Skippy, it's like the Elders left the galaxy so fast, they didn't have time to turn the stove off. That got me thinking; what if the Elders *didn't* ascend?"

"What?" His voice had lost the depressed tone. "What do you mean, they didn't ascend? That is such a dumbass-"

"How do you *know* they ascended? Before you answer, you have told me many times your memories are confused and incomplete. What if, instead of ascending and being up there somewhere looking down on us like Santa Claus checking who is naughty or nice, they're just *gone*? What if something went wrong with the ascending process? Or, what if they never got to the ascending process, what if something or someone killed them all?"

"Whoooooa."

"If the Elders suddenly vanished, unexpectedly, that might explain why they left so much of their stuff laying around still operational, right?"

"Uh, I suppose that is possible, Joe," the beer can responded very slowly, like he was having trouble processing what I said. "Hmmm. I do not like thinking about that. Also, we know from Gingerbread that the Elders did clean up a lot of their critical equipment in preparation for ascending, so-"

"No, Skippy, we do *not* know that. All we know is that a lot of the Elders' stuff is missing, and there are a whole lot of craters where their stuff used to be, on Gingerbread and at sites all across the galaxy. Those craters might be evidence of the Elders cleaning up their stuff before they left, or the craters might be signs that something very bad happened to the Elders, before they could ascend. Think about it. Maybe the Elders did not leave you behind on purpose, maybe something happened so fast, so traumatic, so overwhelming that they weren't able to help you."

"Damn. Joe, this is a whole lot for me to process. I refuse to believe the Elders did not ascend, until I see evidence that they didn't."

"Ok, but even then, it sure looks like they left in a big hurry, right, that explains why they left the stove on? Maybe they were attacked and had to rush the ascending process to protect themselves, get away while they could?"

"Oh crap. Joe, I do *not* want to think about any of this right now. Damn, my brain hurts just thinking about thinking about it. Shit! The idea of the Elders peacefully ascending is one of the few things I thought I knew for certain, and now you've taken even that away from me!"

"Sorry, Skippy."

"Hey, you big jerkface, we might have answers to some of these questions, if you had done what I wanted while we had the chance in the Roach Motel. I wanted to investigate that hidden planet you called Vera, but *noooooooo*. You and Count Chocula were all like," he used a mocking little girl's voice, "'Oh no, we can't go there, it's too scary' and 'We shouldn't do that, it makes too much sense' or 'We might get our delicate petticoats dirty' or-"

"Ok, Skippy, I get the point. Again. You already made this argument, like, a million freakin' times."

"If I did it a million and one, would that change your mind?"

"No!"

"Joe, I am again disappointed in you. You needed to grow a pair and stand up to Count Chocula when he was wrong about something so-"

"Dammit, Skippy, I did not need to stand up to him, because in this case, I *agree* with him. Our mission was to rebuild the *Dutchman*, if we could, I remember you telling me every freakin' day not to get my hopes up about that until you actually got our Frankenship slapped together with duct tape. Once the ship was mostly functional again, our mission was to get the hell out of the Roach Motel ASAP before the Guardians asked too many questions you couldn't answer."

"But-"

"No 'buts', Skippy. Going to Vera and poking your nose around in there could not have done anything to ensure the success of our mission, and it could have been another

Goddamned beer can inspired disaster." I was pissed at him and I didn't care about hurting his feelings.

'Vera' was the name I gave to the hidden planet in the Roach Motel, the world Skippy suspected was out of phase or in another dimension, or some other nerdy technical explanation the beer can used to confuse me. We never actually saw Vera or detected it directly on sensors, so fans of the old TV show 'Cheers' will understand why I named the place.

"You don't *know* that, Joe. Vera could have been a treasure trove of, of, unimaginable technology! And more importantly, answers. Answers I need, Joe, answers *you* need. The Elders had cleaned up Gingerbread so thoroughly that I couldn't get any useful data there. Hey, remember, you are the one who asked me why the Elders had bothered to wall off the Roach Motel from other species; why they would care after they ascended."

"Here's what I do know for dead certain, Skippy. If we went poking around Vera and did that crazy stunt you wanted-"

"It was not crazy. And it was not a stunt."

"Trying to reverse the phase field surrounding Vera is a stunt, and it's crazy. Damn, have you not learned anything from working with us monkeys? You can't think only of yourself. You are part of this crew, of this team. Put the team first, Skippy. The Army pounded that into my head over and over and although I resented it, they were right. The Army works because the force is a team, it's not about me, it's about the mission and you need a team to achieve the mission."

Skippy gave me a sarcastic slow clap, the hand slaps echoing in my helmet. "Oh, bravo, G.I. Joey. That speech was very inspiring. Here's what *I* know for dead certain. The Roach Motel was our best chance to get real answers to who I am, how I got buried in the dirt on Paradise and what the *hell* has been going on in the galaxy for the past hundred million years. I thought we were friends, Joe," his voice sounded genuinely hurt. "You act like you don't care."

"Skippy," I took a deep breath to give myself time to think, because it was very important I say the right thing. "I am your friend. We do need answers. You see this patch?" I tapped the 'U.S. ARMY' logo on spacesuit. "I am a soldier, I have a job to do, a job assigned by UNEF Command even though they probably regret every day making me captain of this ship. Yes, we need answers. If we had more than one ship, and the crew were capable of flying the ship without you, I might have sent the *Dutchman* away to go home, and gone poking around Vera with you after the ship safely got out of the Roach Motel. We don't have more than one ship, and back then we couldn't fly the *Dutchman* without you. That means I had to choose between our primary mission of securing the future of Earth, *or* searching for the answer to bigger questions to satisfy our curiosity. Do you understand that?"

"I *understand* it, I do not *like* it."

"Great, then-"

"I also think you are dead wrong about this. You are thinking short-term. You and Count Chocula are always talking about how you need to stop reacting to events and develop a long-term strategy, but when you get an opportunity to actually do that, you two chickenshits always find an excuse *not* to do it!"

"It's complicated, Skippy, but, you're right. You are absolutely right. Maybe we should have somehow taken the opportunity to explore that hidden planet while we were in the Roach Motel, because I don't think we will go back there again. I'll think about that, Ok? Right now, my visor is telling me it is time to begin slowing down to rendezvous with that dropship."

Our target dropship was not even a dot to my naked eye when we started, we had to rely on our visors to guide us. We went slowly and carefully because once the gas in our maneuvering bottles ran out, we would drift helplessly in space. The big Thuranin Condor dropship now loomed in front and above me, with Desai seeing the dropship from above, if those terms had any meaning in space. Between us was not just a thin tether line, the tether had now spread out like a spiderweb so it was twice the size of the Condor. That was a good thing, because our clumsy flying had us significantly off-center. The spiderweb was going to catch the Condor's right wing and tail, and hopefully get tangled in the extended landing skids.

"Ready?" I asked needlessly as one strand of the spiderweb dragged along the dropship's wing.

"Ready," Desai acknowledged. She was by far a better pilot than me, but her experience with space diving was limited. We had not thought pilots needed much training in freefall diving, so they hadn't spent much time on that activity. Clearly, the captain of the ship was an idiot for skimping on that training. That was a lesson learned. Hans Chotek had told me to expect the unexpected and in this case, I hadn't thought far enough ahead.

Helplessly, we watched as the spiderweb strands slid along the smooth, stubby wing of the Condor. The tugging caused me to spin around and I didn't fight it. All I cared about was the spiderweb getting securely wrapped around something, but it was slipping off the wing and now curling around the aft body. As dropships are designed to fly at high speed in an atmosphere, their surfaces are smooth and sleek, giving the spiderweb little to snag on. Damn it, when you *don't* want something to snag, it always does, but the one time you need the freakin' thing to catch on a-

Success! I was jerked roughly around, spinning head over heels, as the web wrapped itself around a landing gear strut and an engine inspection panel. We had locked those panels open before ejecting the dropship, to give the spiderweb more obstructions to cling onto. The momentum of me and Desai caused the panel to break off one pin, but the other held, and after a couple minutes of nausea-inducing spinning around, we got ourselves stable and began pulling ourselves toward the Condor hand over hand.

We had to manually crank the outer airlock door open, then Desai got in with me, and we cranked the outer door closed to conserve oxygen before getting the inner door open. We floated into an absolutely dark interior, illuminated only by our helmet lights. "This is creepy," she said in a soft voice. "Colonel, if you are thinking of shouting 'Boo' to scare me, don't."

"I'm with you, Desai. Let's get this thing restarted," I glanced at my suit's power meter. Even if everything worked perfectly and we got the dropship restarted, it would be a while before the internal temperature allowed us to crack open our faceplates. Before that, we both would need to hand crank more juice into our suit's powercells. The drinking water tank in my suit, which contained a mixture of water, sugar and nutritiously yummy sludge, was running low. I needed more food if I had to power my suit by hand for long.

We floated into the big aft cargo bay, where Mad Scientist Contraption Number Three took up most of the space. "Skippy? Does this thing look Ok to you?"

"Scanning it now with your suit sensors. Yes, it looks perfectly fine. Get started, please, you don't have a lot of time if we run into problems."

"Affirmative," I agreed, and eyeclicked to pull up the instructions in my visor.

Mad Scientist Contraption Number One was the spring that got our suits rebooted. Number Two was the hand crank thingy we used to energize our suit powercells. Number Three was a fuel cell. One tank full of liquid oxygen, a tank full of liquid hydrogen, and a membrane where H combined with Oh Two and generated electricity and water. The resulting water would mostly be dumped into space as the dropship didn't have room to store it, and we didn't want the additional mass if the Condor needed to maneuver later. Contraptions Numbers One and Two had used mechanical energy, but our science team had dreamed up Number Three to use a chemical reaction. Mostly, it had been Friedlander's brainstorm. He realized that the energy virus could not easily infect *potential* energy, and monatomic oxygen and hydrogen represented potential energy; the energy only got converted to useful electricity when the atoms combined to form water.

Friedlander explained to me that potential energy is like holding a stone on top of a building. By itself, the stone has no useful energy. But if you release the stone, the force of gravity acts on it, and it acquires kinetic energy as it falls. The springs we used to reboot our spacesuits had potential energy when they were wound up. Once we released the spring, it unwound to create kinetic energy, and the motor attached to the spring converted kinetic energy to electricity.

That's enough physics lessons for today, I mention the details because Friedlander's team really did science the shit out of the problem, and that's why we had a chance to defeat an Elder energy virus and survive.

Skippy had grumbled that fuel cells were an ancient and crude technology, so old they had been used aboard the Apollo spacecraft that first took humans to the Moon. With all his grumbling, he agreed it was a decent idea and more importantly, fuel cells were relatively simple and the *Dutchman* had the manufacturing capacity to make the membranes.

Desai and I carefully turned stiff valves and pumped levers to get the pressurized liquid oxygen and hydrogen flowing. Then, in the scariest part of the operation, we had to connect our already depleted suit powercells to the membrane to bring it up to operating temperature. I watched with alarm as the power level of my suit drained quickly, even though I had the heaters turned off.

"Hmm," Skippy announced unhappily. "The membrane is taking more power than expected to warm up. Joe, you and Desai need to disconnect and stop the power flow from your suits."

"Desai," I ordered, "do it."

"Yes, Colonel," she acknowledged, and I saw in my visor that her suit had less than five percent power left when she cut off the power transfer and disconnected the cable. "Sir? You are still connected?"

"Yes," I watched the power meter spiral down toward three percent, then lower. "We need to get this fuel cell working, or everyone dies out here."

"There are three other dropships with fuel cells, Joe," Skippy reminded me.

"Yes, but we reached this one first," I protested. Desai and I had been given the closest and easiest target, so we were already aboard our Condor while the other three retrieval teams were still approaching their dropships. "If we can't figure out how to make this fuel cell work, that's not good news for the other teams. Once this thing starts producing electricity, I can reverse the power flow and recharge my suit. If we can't get it working, I'm screwed anyway."

"I hate to admit this, but you do have a point," Skippy sighed.

"Colonel Bishop," Desai waved a hand to get my attention, "I should drain my suit also, to give us the best chance to-"

"Negative, Desai. As long as you still have power, you can talk with Skippy to troubleshoot this damned thing. Look, I'm turning my oxygen mask on," I told her as my power meter dropped to one percent. "And I'll crank the handle again," I hooked my feet under the fuel cell so my motion didn't send me flying around the cargo bay.

"Joe, you idiot! That handle can't provide enough power to get your suit restarted!" Skippy warned. "Disconnect now!"

"But-"

"Trust me! Now now now!"

I didn't argue, as my visor was already going dim from the power drain. "Done."

"Whew," Skippy exhaled. "That was close. Joe, the amount of power needed to get your suit rebooted from zero is more than you can generate with that crank handle thingy. Speaking of which, get cranking, monkeyboy."

"Aye aye," I shuddered, thinking how close I had come to disaster. With the handle fitted to the gear again, I pulled and pushed. The power meter stayed stubbornly at one percent, but it didn't drop, so I counted that as a win. "What about the fuel cell?"

"Give it time. It is warming up slowly, the heat needs time to propagate. Don't be so impatient, Joe," he chided me. "And, mmm, yes! Success. The reaction is starting. I'm feeding all the power generated into the heater unit, to bring it up to optimal temperature."

Desai and I waited, both of us cranking handles to build up power in our dangerously-depleted suit power cells. It took eight long minutes before Skippy announced we both could use the fuel cell to provide power to our suits. "Is that smart, Skippy? Shouldn't we get the auxiliary power unit going first?"

"I said it, so of course it is smart, *duh*. The APU can't be restarted until the dropship's powercells have enough charge to energize the containment field. While we're waiting for that, you two should take the opportunity to top up your own powercells. You may need to assist the other teams, and you'll need a healthy charge to do that."

"That makes sense, Skippy," I admitted while connecting a power cable to the fuel cell, and seeing the power meter of my suit glow an encouraging blue as it sucked in fresh electricity.

We got the Condor's APU nicely humming along at low power four hours later, and after another hour, Desai and I were blessedly able to remove our helmets and breathe air in the cabin. I was super happy to get the breathing mask off my face, it had scratched my cheek so much I was bleeding. "Ah, that feels good," I breathed in a lungful of air that had not been recycled a thousand times by my suit. "Oof," I wrinkled my nose, sniffing. "Damn, is that bad smell *me*?"

"It could be me," Desai admitted.

"It's just the two of us, if you want to freshen up in the bathroom," I suggested, "go ahead."

"Thank you, Sir, but I would feel guilty about all the people stuck in their suits out there. Besides, we need to get back into the suits to pick up the crew, and I don't want to get myself dirty again by sliding back into this suit."

"Ah, you're right," I agreed, disappointed because I had been looking forward to washing up in the Condor's tiny bathroom. We had another two hours of doing nothing before we could safely fire up the dropship's main control systems and begin a preflight check. "Hey, Skippy, you got any crappy 80s TV shows I can watch to kill time?" I did not want him to torture me with bad TV, but I needed to think about how to rescue Paradise from infected Keepers, so watching mindless shows would allow my subconscious to work on the problem.

"Uh, what?" Skippy could not believe his good fortune. "You *want* me to entertain you?"

"No, but I have nothing else to do, and I'm bored, and you're eventually going to make me watch this crap anyway, so let's get it over with." What I didn't say was old TV shows were a better option than Skippy singing to me. I could turn my brain off to ignore a TV show, but there was no way to ignore the incredible singing talent of Skippy.

"That's a good attitude, Joe! As a reward, you can watch 'Casablanca'."

"My Dad had us watch that," I noted with a wave of nostalgia, "it's Ok. Thanks, Skippy."

"Oh, no, dude," his evil laugh reminded me of the villain in a James Bond movie. "You are referring to the classic 1942 film? I will be showing you the 1983 TV series."

"There was a *TV show* about Casablanca?" I asked, astonished.

"Um, sort of. The guy who played Rick was David Soul, you know, the blonde guy from Starsky and Hutch."

Damn. The only thing I knew about Starsky and Hutch was the red car, and the only reason I know that is I saw a car painted like that at an old car show in Bangor. "Skippy, I never heard of this show."

"That's not surprising, Joe. They shot five episodes, but the network killed it out of embarrassment after three. Everyone involved would like to forget about it."

"Wait just a minute," I cocked my head, certain he was screwing with me again. "If this show was so bad, why did the studio pay to digitize it?"

"They didn't, *duh*."

"Then how do you have it?"

"Oh, the last time we were at Earth, I paid to have that show and a veritable cornucopia of similar crap digitized for me."

"*You* paid for it?"

"Well, not me, the contract was arranged through a shell company I named Magnificent Enterprises LLC. Sounds impressive, huh? Don't worry, no one will ever trace it back to me."

"I'm not worried about the stupid TV show, where the hell did you get the freakin' money?"

"Oh, that. Joe, I can neither confirm nor deny any scandalous accusations, but there might be a mob-controlled bank in Eastern Europe that is missing some money. Or, it *might* be missing a whole lot of money. Hee hee," he giggled with glee, "when the gangsters notice their money is gone, somebody has got some '*splaaainin* to do."

"Oh, damn it. I am going to walk into a shitstorm if we ever get home?"

"You? Why? *You* didn't do anything."

"They're not going to blame *you*."

"Good point, Joe. Well, nothing we can do about it now. To take your mind off that subject, behold! One of the forgotten classics of crappy 80s TV, 'Casablanca'!"

Oh, man, it was freakin' *awful*. Basically, it was The Love Boat set in a North African bar in 1941. People come into the bar, the lead character solves their problems, then another person comes into the bar. Cancelling that steaming pile was a mercy killing. Skippy made me suffer through all three episodes in less than two hours, by speeding up the video. I wish he hadn't, because watching one was enough torture.

The only good thing about wasting two hours of my life was I now had a piece of truly obscure 80s trivia I could inflict on other people.

The retrieval teams got four dropships restarted with only minor glitches, and no one else had to run their suit powercells dangerously low like I did. Desai and I put our helmets back on and I opened the big cargo bay doors at the rear of the dropship. With Desai flying on thrusters alone, she guided the Condor to pick up the eighteen people remaining from the two groups we had left floating in space. I stood in the open doorway of the cargo bay, providing voice guidance to Desai, and tossed a line out to the first group, who had tightened their tethers to pull themselves in a tight formation so they could all fit through the doorway. The line was caught on the first try, and I used a winch to slowly pull the ball of nine people into the bay, then closed the door and repressurized the bay. Nine people were very happy to get their helmets off. Like me, many people commented their arms and hands were cramped from pumping the handle that provided survival power to their suits. I got the first nine into the forward passenger compartment where they could take turns washing up in the tiny bathroom, while I pumped air out of the cargo bay so we could pick up the second group.

With twenty people squeezed into our Condor, it felt like our uncomfortable flight down to Gingerbread. Fortunately, we wouldn't be stuck in the cramped confines of the dropship for nearly as long this time. "Hey, Skippy," I called him while I was still sealed up in my suit, inspecting thrusters to make sure they would be ready for the all-important flight back to the *Dutchman*. "How you doing over there? You have good news for us?"

"Hi, Joe. Good work getting people safely into your ship, it looks like everyone is going to come through without any serious health issues."

"Yeah," I had already used my command codes to ping every suit for a status check. Some people were mildly dehydrated, and extended time in suits had caused stiff muscles, but otherwise everyone was going to be just fine. That assumed we could get back aboard a basically functional starship, because our dropships could not get us to a habitable planet from the middle of interstellar nowhere. "Don't avoid the subject, Skippy. Did your shortcut work?" I was very much hoping he could get the energy virus purged quicker than expected, and not just so we could get the galley back online and making cheeseburgers. Mostly, I was anxious to get moving to help Colonel Perkins and her team, and the entire planet Paradise. The fear that we might already be too late ate at me. If even one infected Keeper landed on Paradise, the Ruhar might take drastic action to safeguard their population, drastic action against all the humans on the planet. Yes, I was concerned for the humans on Paradise, but I will admit part of my sick feeling was that we had gone through enormous risk and effort to safeguard the future of humans there, and now all our hard work might be undone by a small group of hateful lizards.

Ok, sure, a small group of humans on Kobamik had sparked a civil war that was consuming Kristang society, but that was *totally* different. I am not a philosopher, so don't ask me how it's different, it just is.

"Um, my shortcut has not worked as well as I had hoped, Joe."

"Damn. So, we can't cut eleven hours off the schedule?"

"Not quite. At first, the energy virus fell for my trick, but then the stupid thing must be smarter than I thought, sorry about that. The remaining virus scattered itself across several clusters of powercells near the auxiliary reactor, and they are shielding themselves from me so I can't get at them without destroying the reactor."

"Give me the bottom line, Skippy."

"Bottom line," he sighed, "is we can't cut eleven hours off the schedule. In fact, it now looks like I need to extend the timeline by another forty, perhaps forty eight hours?"

"Forty hours? Skippy, we can't wait that long. That ship full of Keepers could be approaching Paradise now."

"You're right, Joe. Don't forget, we need to refuel the ship before we can go anywhere."

"I know that, and we still don't know where that ship is. Every minute the *Dutchman* sits dead in space, the danger to Paradise increases."

"True. Also, the longer the ship goes without power, the longer it will take me to bring critical systems up to operating temperature. Joe, I am simply out of options. We have no choice but to wait for those remaining powercells to drain completely. If you come back aboard or even close to the ship, the energy virus can infect the dropships, or you monkeys, and we will be in even bigger trouble than we are now."

Skippy was out of options, that meant we were out of options. Or, wait, was that true? Maybe our beer can was just out of *ideas*, not options. And, right then, I had an idea.

A commander should know every bolt, every weld of his ship. I should know what makes every system aboard the ship work. Because not even our science team understood most of the Thuranin technology that made the *Dutchman* function, I had no chance to grasp even basic concepts behind the functioning of things like our jump drive coils. But one thing I did know was the physical layout of components making up our rebuilt Frankenship. "Skippy, the only place that energy virus still exists is that one bank of powercells near the backup reactor?"

"Yes, why? Uh!" He shushed me. "Before you tell me your latest brilliant idea, the answer no, we can't sacrifice that reactor so I can burn out the virus. I need to get the backup reactor restarted, so it can energize the containment system of the main reactor. So, put that thought right out of your tiny little brain."

I was tired and I smelled terrible even to myself, and I desperately wanted to get into a hot shower with a wire brush to scrape the accumulated layers of funkiness off my skin. Also, I had a sick feeling in the pit of my stomach that the entire human population of Paradise could be counting down to a death sentence. So, I didn't take time to savor the joy of out-thinking His Awesomeness. "Skippy," I said with a combination of weariness, fear and pain from a stiff neck. "All those powercells are attached to a sort of scaffolding, right? I remember when you assembled that section of the ship in the junkyard."

"Correct, it was more convenient for maintenance to cluster those powercells together, though that makes the assembly more vulnerable to a single hit in battle."

"Yeah, we had to make a lot of compromises. That scaffolding is attached to the hull with explosive bolts?"

"Yes, that is a safety feature, so we can eject the powercells without damaging the reactor and, and- Damn it! And once again I truly, truly hate you, Joe. You're telling me to blow those bolts and send those powercells spinning off into space?"

"You got it," despite how tired I felt, I grinned. "Can the ship function without those powercells?"

"It can for now. I will need to pull powercells from other parts of the ship eventually, but, yes, we do not absolutely need those powercells. Joe, I should be insulted that I did not think of such a simple and obvious solution. Maybe I am so emotionally invested in this ship I've rebuilt several times, that I failed to consider sacrificing part of the ship."

"Skippy, at this point, there aren't many parts of the ship we *can* sacrifice, without the whole damned thing falling apart. Will this work?"

"Yes, it will. Give me three hours to make absolutely certain the energy virus is weakened enough so it can't try to migrate to another system, and then I'll blow the bolts. Crap! You're going to humiliate me about this, aren't you?"

"No, Skippy, I won't tell anyone. You should tell the crew it was your idea."

"Uh, *what*?"

"The crew have lost a lot of confidence in you, Skippy. You got suckered by that computer worm, your plan to jump into the Roach Motel got the ship torn apart, and we barely escaped from there. Now we took aboard an energy virus you didn't know anything about. The crew, and Chotek in particular, need to regain their trust in you. I figure that you happily announcing the virus is dead way ahead of schedule will be a big confidence booster."

"Oh."

"Because otherwise, I would totally bust your balls about it until the end of time."

"I would expect no less. Hmm. Joe, I feel like I'm cashing in a Get-Out-Of-Jail-Free card. Karma is going to come back and bite me in the ass about this someday."

"How about you stop educating me about crappy 80s TV shows, and we call it even?"

"Um, can we compromise, and I'll take The Love Boat off the schedule?"

Why was I attempting to negotiate with a being who had fusion-powered stubbornness? "Take Love Boat *and* Knight Rider off the schedule, and you've got a deal."

"Deal. Oh, Joe, I can't wait to show you my surprise; two lost episodes of 'Casablanca'."

"Oh, man," I groaned. "Can't they stay lost?"

Three hours later, Skippy blew the explosive bolts and ejected the contaminated powercells away from our starship, prompting cheers aboard all four dropships. We still could not go back to the ship, because there was no point going aboard until Skippy had power restored. That took a bit longer than the beer can estimated, still we were able to cut more than a full day off Skippy's original schedule of eighty six hours. There were smiles all around when we detected heat from the backup reactor, and Skippy announced that 'Spacebnb' was now accepting reservations for cabins aboard the ship. "It will take another hour before hot water is available for showers," he warned. "I had to drain all the pipes before the water in them froze while the ship was shut down, and I'm having to let water trickle back in slowly."

"No problem, Skippy, it will take us more than an hour to get back and secure the dropships anyway. What about gravity?"

"The main reactor is just coming back online at minimum power. It should be stable in about twenty minutes, then I can resume feeding power to the artificial gravity plating."

"Uh, to do that, you need to divert power from recharging the jump drive capacitors?"

"I know you are worried that the ship is vulnerable until the capacitors reach a minimum charge for a jump, but don't worry about artificial gravity. If I keep gravity at one third Gee, that will delay achieving a jump by only thirteen minutes."

"All right," I considered thirteen minutes to be an acceptable risk, and the crew deserved an opportunity to get out of their suits to enjoy a luxurious shower.

"Please warn the crew the ship will be a bit on the chilly side for a few hours."

"We will wear sweaters, Skippy. You are absolutely certain it is safe for us to come back to the ship?"

"No. I am as certain as I *can* be. Rebooting the ship gave me an opportunity to conduct a deep scan, and I am confident those nasty Guardians didn't sneak aboard any more surprises for us. Sorry, but that's the truth."

"Good enough, I guess." The sad truth was, we didn't have a choice, the *Dutchman* was our only option. We flew a careful course back to the *Flying Dutchman*, keeping the bulk of the forward hull between our dropships and the discarded powercells that were slowly drifting farther from the ship. I waited for the last of the four crewed dropships to be brought back aboard, then ordered the crew to get cleaned up, with pilots reporting back to the docking bays in one hour. We sent teams out to recover the other dropships, an operation that took another six hours. After that, Desai gently goosed the ship forward away from the contaminated powercells to test the normal-space engines. We kept the jump drive on a hair-trigger for an emergency escape, but no danger emerged, so we didn't jump until we had enough charge to take us a useful distance toward a star system where we could find a gas giant planet to refill the *Dutchman*'s depleted fuel tanks.

CHAPTER TWENTY FIVE

I was in my cabin after the successful jump, washing up before going to the galley for a simple dinner. The crew would be without fresh food for a while, Major Simms warned the extended shutdown had as expected, killed all the plants in the hydroponics bays, so she would need to start all over growing crops from seeds. Chotek was still pissed at and skeptical of Skippy, but I think Simms was most upset with the beer can. Three times now, his actions or inactions had disrupted her carefully-managed garden. She was rightfully proud of providing a substantial quantity of fresh food, and I think too often she felt taken for granted. Although as a major, Simms took shifts as duty officer in the command chair or CIC, she was not an elite special operations soldier, nor a pilot, nor part of the science team. I regularly volunteered to work in the hydroponics bays to show my appreciation, and because seeing green things growing made me a tiny bit less homesick. For the next week, I needed to make a special effort to work closely with Major Jennifer Simms.

"Whew," Skippy's avatar appeared over my bunk, took off his enormous hat and wiped his brow in an exaggerated gesture. "*That* is a relief. Man, I was quaking in my boots for a minute there."

"You mean the jump?" I paused from splashing water on my face. "You told us the jump drive was in perfect condition!"

"It was, Joe, and it is. Well, as perfect as a second-hand hunk of ancient junk can be."

"I understand that. So why were you so worried?"

"Uh, there was another danger that I didn't mention, because we could not do anything about, so there was no reason for you to worry."

"Crap. What did you not tell me about *this* time?"

"The energy virus. There was a possibility that the virus could have uploaded itself into a higher dimension, to reside in the energy pattern still reverberating from our previous jump."

"*What?*"

"Every jump, especially at the inbound end, causes a resonance in the quantum grid that underlies local spacetime. I told you that before," he admonished in a peevish tone. "That resonance is how ships can be tracked through a jump."

"Yes, but you also told me that resonance dissipates at a known rate, and is too faint to be useful within hours."

"In *local spacetime* the effect dissipates quickly. At the quantum grid level above local spacetime, the jump energy can be retained for a substantial and unpredictable length of time. That is why ships avoid repeatedly jumping from the same position; the resonance of their own jump field can interact with resonance patterns leftover from previous jumps, and cause a jump field to collapse. It's like a damping field, but the effect can't be detected from local spacetime."

"Shiiiiiiit," I exhaled slowly to retain what little patience I had. "And you didn't tell us this because??"

"Well, Joe, because when I program jumps, I always avoid jumping from the position of a previous-"

"I didn't mean why you didn't tell us about this quantum grid thingy or whatever. I meant, why didn't you tell us about the risk of the energy virus lurking in, jump space or whatever you call it?"

"Because there was no point telling you. We had to jump, and even I could not detect whether the residual energy pattern was infected by the virus."

"It wasn't?"

"Nope, we're good."

"How do you know that for sure, Oh Great One?"

"Because for the energy virus to re-infect the ship, it would have had to rearrange the quantum pattern as we jumped. *That* is something I would easily have detected, and it didn't happen. Joe, to upload into the quantum grid, the energy virus could only do that as we jumped, although that would have been more difficult for me to detect. I was fairly confident the virus didn't bother uploading part of itself, but I was not *absolutely* certain, because I wasn't looking for it at the time, and our wonky jump drive still created a lot of random noise during a jump. Either the virus lacks the ability to upload, or assumed it could destroy the ship in this spacetime so it didn't bother to upload into the quantum grid. There is a silver lining to this whole mess; taking the ship completely offline allowed me to retune the jump drive so it is much less noisy. In fact, it is in better condition than before we jumped into the Roach Motel," he added proudly.

I burst his arrogant bubble. "The jump drive was in *terrible* condition before you jumped us into the Roach Motel."

"I said *better* condition, Joe," he sniffed. "I didn't say it was in *good* condition. I told you we should have bought the extended warranty, but you had to blow the money on new floor mats instead."

I recognized his attempt at humor as a defensive reaction. "All right, I guess the important thing is the energy virus is no longer a problem. So, we can move onto worrying about the *next* freakin' problem! Damn it! Skippy," I clenched my fists and shook them in front of me to release some of my frustration. "The lizards are in a damn civil war! How the hell do they have time for side jobs like forcing the hamsters off Paradise?"

"Because it *is* a side job, Joe. It's ironic when you think about it."

"Ironic?" Sometimes Skippy pissed me off when he treated deadly serious situations way too casually. "How the hell do you figure-"

"Jeez Louise, Joe, don't get mad at me, it wasn't *my* idea to create a supervirus. If you'll close your mouth and open your ears, you might understand why I said it is 'ironic'."

From the tone of his voice, I could tell he was hurt by my reaction. Our super-intelligent alien AI was sensitive about how we treated him, especially how I treated him. He had little experience with emotions, and I shouldn't expect him to understand how we might feel about something he said. If he thought something was ironic, then he genuinely thought that was true. "Skippy, I am sorry, I really am. I know this is not your fault. Please explain."

Ok," the tone of his voice perked right up again. "Here's the story. You know that Paradise was originally colonized by the Kristang, by the Black Trees clan, right?" He didn't wait for me to answer. "That planet was left alone for a very long time, probably for millions of years, because there were not any active wormholes close enough to provide useful access. Actually, that isn't completely true, the wormhole closest to Paradise was active for many years, but that wormhole connected to another wormhole at the edge of the galaxy, so no one ever used it. Anyway, a later wormhole shift changed the connection, and the Black Trees seized the opportunity to explore Paradise. That is when they found the remains of a crashed Elder starship, and me. And that is when they installed maser projectors under the surface."

"Yup, I remember that," I replied with what I hoped was a blank look on my face, while I dug a thumbnail into my palm painfully to keep me from shouting for him to hurry up and get to the freakin' point.

"Good, good. So, the Black Trees surrendered the planet without a shot when the Ruhar arrived, because the Black Trees thought they had stripped all the Elder goodies from the place and they didn't care about farmland. And, well, heh, heh, now we get to the ironic part."

My Spidey sense tingled as it always does when he says 'well heh heh'. "Oh, shit."

"Yeah. The Law of Unintended Consequences is coming back to bite us in the ass again, Joe. We got the Ruhar to hold onto Paradise by planting fake Elder artifacts there. Unfortunately, our actions also got the leadership of the Black Trees clan arguing about who decided to give the planet to the Ruhar. Many subclans under the Black Trees coalition are angry they missed out on scooping up valuable Elder artifacts, and the incident made the subclans question the leadership of the Black Trees. Obviously, with a civil war raging, this is not a good time for the Black Trees leadership to appear weak and foolish."

"Crap. So the Black Trees want to take Paradise back?"

"Yes and no, Joe. Yes, they would like to take the planet back. No, during a civil war they are not willing to commit scarce resources, to reclaim a planet where the Ruhar now have substantial defenses."

"If they aren't willing to fight for Paradise, then why would they-"

"It's complicated. The Sharp Stone clan is currently allied with the Black Trees, and the Silver Blades owe a debt to the Black Trees. The Silver Blades wanted to cancel that debt, in part because they were reconsidering their alliance with the Black Trees. So, they proposed to create the pathogen, to weaken the Ruhar's hold on Paradise."

"Ok, fine, I can see all that happening *before* the civil war, but why didn't they drop the operation once the fighting started? The Black Trees can't possibly care about Paradise right now! Even if the civil war ended today, the Black Trees couldn't scrape together enough ships to recapture Paradise for, what, another five years?"

"More like ten years, Joe, that would be my guess. Assuming the Black Trees clan still exists after the war, they would be far too busy consolidating any territory they gained, to bother with a military operation to take Paradise."

"Why, then? Why didn't the team on Camp Alpha get shut down, once we got the civil war started?"

"Politics, is the simple answer. The Black Trees are holding the Silver Blades to their commitment, as a way of testing the Silver Blades' loyalty to their coalition. Resources devoted to the effort on Camp Alpha make the Silver Blades weaker and more dependent on the Black Trees for protection. The Black Trees also know that while the Silver Blades are busy trying to wipe out the hamster population on Paradise, they are not able to double-cross the Black Trees and switch sides in the civil war."

"Oh, for Christ's sake! How the hell do the lizards keep track of which clan is trying to screw which other clan?"

"That's easy, Joe. Every clan is pretty much *constantly* trying to screw over any other clan that is in their way of gaining more power and influence. Alliances are only as good as the power to enforce agreements, and to offer a clan more protection and advantages than some other clan could. The Kristang warrior caste officially considers honor to be of utmost importance, but every clan will break an agreement if they think it will benefit them. Their attitude is that inter-clan agreements are just business, so honor is not truly at stake."

"Crap. This is the sort of thing Chotek handles for a living, it makes my head hurt. Ok, so, do I understand this correctly? Before the civil war, the Silver Blades got the bright idea for a bioweapon scheme to wipe humans and hamsters off Paradise, as a way to gain favor with the Black Trees. Now that the war is on, the Black Trees are demanding the Silver Blades complete the operation, as a test of loyalty?"

"Oh, no, Joe. Not as a test of loyalty, because the Black Trees have no illusions about expecting loyalty from the Silver Blades."

"Sure, I understand that, but close enough, right?"

"Close enough," the beer can agreed. "You get why I said this is ironic? If we hadn't made Paradise seem like a shopping mall full of Elder goodies, the Black Trees wouldn't have any interest in taking the place back."

"Ironic, yeah. Skippy, I am beginning to really hate that Law of Unintended Consequences."

"You and me both, brother," he grumbled.

"All right, all right, let me think. The upside is, if we stop this ship full of infected Keepers from reaching Paradise, the Silver Blades are unlikely to continue trying to conduct the op? The Black Trees won't make the Silver Blades start all over again?"

"Correct. If we can stop that ship before it reaches Paradise, I strongly suspect the Black Trees will consider the Silver Blades have made a good-faith effort, and consider the agreement fulfilled. With the Black Trees fighting for their lives against the Fire Dragons and half the other clans in Kristang society, they need all the ships and warriors they can get, without wasting resources on distractions."

"Thank God for small favors. Dammit! We took a huge risk starting a civil war, and my hope was we wouldn't have to worry about the lizards causing any trouble for, like, a decade."

"They might not cause any *new* trouble, Joe. The Camp Alpha op was in progress before the fighting started. Also, that op is an anomaly. Many other planned strikes against the Ruhar were cancelled."

"Great! Fantastic! Another example of my rotten luck."

"The universe hates you, Joe."

"Hey, that punk-ass universe can deal with me directly, my crew and the rest of humanity don't need to get caught in the crossfire."

"Unfortunately, it doesn't work that way, Joe."

We had one more jump before we arrived at the star system where we needed to refuel the ship from a gas giant planet. Stopping to take on fuel would delay our arrival at the Paradise system, and it involved risk because the ship would be vulnerable while our dropships were dipping into the atmosphere to siphon off vital elements, but we had no choice. The *Flying Dutchman*'s tanks were running dry, and we had been in such a rush to escape from the Roach Motel that we didn't take on fuel there.

So, while the jump drive capacitors recharged, I was in the shower early one morning, getting ready for a duty shift.

Naturally, Skippy wanted to talk with me. "Hey, Joe, did you ever wonder-"

"Yeah, I wonder why you always talk to me while my freakin' head is under the shower."

"No, that's *not* what I was wondering, dumdum. Have you ever thought about combining the songs 'Muskrat love' and 'Sound of Music'?" He launched into a horribly off-key abomination of a song. "*The hills are aliiiive, with the love of muuuuuuskrats.*"

"Wh, wh- wha-" I couldn't talk, so shocked I stood there under the shower with my mouth open and almost choked on the water. "Wh-what? WHAT? Muskrats?"

"What?" He asked innocently.

"Oh my *GOD!* Crap, have you gone loony-tunes on us again? Damn, did that energy virus infect you and scramble your brain?" I slapped the shower off button though I still had shampoo running down my scalp. If Skippy was going on vacation again or even temporarily lost processing capacity, I needed to warn the crew so we could-

"No, dumdum, I'm fine, never better. Everything is hunky-dory with me, Joe. Although that expression does make me wonder why a dory would be considered 'hunky'.

A dory is just a stupid boat. Hmm, maybe the guy rowing the dory is hunky. I'll ask Major Simms, she is a woman so she'll know what type of guy is hunky and-"

"You're fine?" I did not want him going off on another tangent. "Seriously? Then why the hell are you singing about muskrats?"

"Because you are grumpy in the morning, Joe, I was trying to cheer you up."

"I'm not grumpy, the problem is people want to talk to me about too many things first thing in the morning. There are only two discussion topics that are acceptable right after I wake up. The first is coffee."

"Ok, I can see that. What's the other one?"

"Nothing. Absolutely nothing."

"Nothing is not an actual discussion topic, you have to- Oh, I get it."

"Yeah. Are you done now? I've got shampoo in my eyes."

"Sure, Joe." He turned the water back on for me. Even Skippy knew not to screw with me before my first cup of coffee. "Rinse off quick and drink a cup of coffee, because we have work to do. We need a plan for how to help Colonel Perkins."

"Skippy, I have a question for you."

"Is this about girls? Because I'm not the best person to ask."

"No, it's not about girls," I could feel my face growing red.

"Although, I have gotten laid just as much as you have recently."

"Thank you *so* much for reminding me. There is more to life than getting laid, Skippy."

"Says the guy who doesn't get any action," he chuckled.

"Can we drop the subject?"

"Okey-dokey with me. What did you want to talk about?"

"The Roach Motel. We used a wormhole to destroy that Maxolhx ship."

"Uh huh, yeah, that sounds vaguely familiar. Of course I remember it, Joe, I *did* it. *Duh.*"

"I wasn't asking-" But he was off on a tangent already.

"I am quite proud of that, Joe. If there is ever a compilation of Skippy's Greatest Hits, that needs to go near the top. Although, hee, hee," he giggled, "how could anyone decide which of my actions are in the Top Ten? Selecting a Top Hundred would be difficult, impossible!"

"Oh, truly it would be impossible for us monkeys, Oh Magnificent One," I rolled my eyes inwardly, which was not easy to do. When Skippy got on a roll like that, I had to play along with him or he would get hurt. "But you make the impossible look easy. Why don't *you* create a list of your greatest accomplishments?" I figured doing that would keep him busy and prevent him from causing trouble for a while.

He sucked in a sharp breath. "Joe, that is a *great* idea. I do owe it to the universe to-"

"Uh huh," I interrupted before he could spiral into an endless loop of praising himself. "Since we monkeys can't truly appreciate your awesomeness, we are not worthy of ranking your accomplishments."

"Joe, that is the nicest thing you've ever said to me. It is true that asking monkeys for input on ranking my awesomeness would be a waste of time," he said slowly, pondering the issue. "Still, I suppose it would be- Hey, you big jerk! You're smirking at me!"

"That wasn't a smirk, it was, uh, a smile."

"Oooooooooh, I hate you *so* much."

"Yup, great. So, getting back to my question, you plopped the far end of a wormhole on top of a ship and ripped it apart. We used a wormhole as a weapon. I didn't think of it at the time, but doesn't that violate some Elder rule or something? Why didn't the Guardians protest about us doing it?"

"Those pain-in-the-ass Guardians *did* protest, Joe, they threw a full-blown diva-queen hissy fit. Later, I mean. Right after it happened, the Guardians were sort of paralyzed with shock and amazement. Hee hee, that was freakin' hilarious! Their first reaction was 'WTF was *that*'? They couldn't believe it. See, even devices created by the Elders think my awesomeness is beyond comprehension. They were all like 'How did you do that' and I was like 'easy' and they were all like '*Duuuuuude* that has never been done before' and I was like 'I make the impossible seem ordinary' and they were like-"

"Skippy!" I had to interrupt him or he would have gone on forever. Hearing the arrogant beer can sounding like an airhead teenage girl was going to make me burst out laughing if he continued. "You answered my question, thank you. I'm going on duty, I'll talk with you in about five hours in my office, Ok? We can think up ideas to rescue Paradise, *again*."

"Oh, this is going to *suuuuck*," Skippy the drama queen dragged out the last word as he popped to life above my office desk.

"Why's that?" I asked, knowing I would regret asking. With Skippy, you had to play along, or he would pester you until you did. For a human, I considered myself pretty stubborn, even for a guy, but I knew not to try outlasting a being whose stubbornness was powered by metallic helium-3.

"Why?" he sputtered. "Joe, we have to find a single, tiny ship in the vastness of space!"

"Yeah, I was thinking about that while I was on duty." Thinking about how to rescue Paradise from a horrible bioweapon was more pleasant than worrying about the perilous mission our dropships would be flying to pick up fuel. "Since you're a beer can, I assume you never played Marco Polo when you were a kid?"

"Marco P- What? Do you mean some sort of lame role-playing game like that Warhammer thing you used to play? Or, hey, are you talking about an alt-rock band?"

"Uh, neither. And Warhammer isn't lame," I added in defense of my younger self.

"The way *you* played was lame," Skippy chuckled. "Remember the time you tried to impress a girl by dressing up as-"

"Let's not talk about that now," I said hurriedly while sipping coffee. "No, I mean Marco Polo as in the game you play in a swimming pool."

"Oh. Yes, I know about that game, but I considered it the most lame of all possibilities involving the phrase 'Marco Polo'. How does a silly children's game relate to our current problem?"

"It's going to solve our problem, at least I hope so."

"Ok, you've lost me again. Please, I am begging the village idiot to enlighten me."

"In the game, one person finds other people not by looking for them, but by calling out 'Marco'."

"Technically, one person shouting 'Marco' is *not* how that person finds the others. The other people give away their positions by stupidly calling out 'Polo'. If those people just kept quiet, they could hide forever and- Oooh. Now I get it. Uh, nope. No, I don't. Joe, 'Polo' does sound like a word in the Kristang common language, but that word is a technical term about electrical energy. I don't see how that helps us."

"Skippy, come on. Seriously, you don't know where I'm going with this? It is totally obvious."

"Obvious to an idiot meatsack, maybe," he sniffed.

"Ok, listen, somehow, you send out a message from the Black Trees, or from Silver Blade clan leadership, requesting that ship to signal its position. Get it? You will sort of yell 'Marco' and they will reply 'Polo'. We locate that ship, and *BAM*," I smacked a fist into a palm. "We pound it to dust."

He sighed. "Joe, of all the dumb ideas you ever had, and there are an impressive stack of them, *this* has to be the-"

"I know, greatest, right? Ooh ooh!" I shouted excitedly and bounced in my chair because right then I got another idea that was EVEN BETTER. "Wait! If you can signal that ship, don't just tell it to report its position, you somehow give it a recall order. Yeah! Send it home, tell it the clan leadership changed its mind, or, I don't know, decided to save those infected Keepers for a rainy day or something."

"Joe."

"Yeah?"

"Are you done smacking me with your brilliant ideas?"

"I have a full mug of coffee here, Skippy, so my brain is awake. I am firing on all cylinders today, more brilliant ideas may be coming."

"Ok. First, *somehow* I send a retrieval code, or a request for that ship to report its position? Somehow? Like, how?"

"I don't know," I waved a hand vaguely. "However you do magical shit like that."

"Joe, how I do magical shit like that is getting the codes from somewhere first. I have no idea what private authentication codes were provided to that ship. There are two places I could get such codes. First, we could go poking around in databases of the Silver Blade clan leaders, I would have to do a lot of poking around to find the one specific code we need."

The coffee in my mouth suddenly tasted sour. "That is not an option, what else you got?"

"The matching set of codes would, of course, be aboard the ship we're searching for. All we need to do is find that ship, *which is the problem we're trying to solve you DUMDUM!*"

As Skippy would say, *UGH*, in that thoroughly disgusted sigh he does. I won't bore you with details of every stupid idea I dreamed up and discarded on my own. Or the plans I thought were good enough to review with Skippy, before he shot them down like easy targets in a video game. Seriously, we monkeys trying to think up ways to find a single ship in the vastness of space around the Paradise system accomplished nothing of use, but man, I sure kept Skippy tickled pink. He came up with fresh new insults, and I had him chuckling and feeling good, which I suppose was good, considering how glum he had been after we almost got killed by an Elder energy virus he hadn't known about.

Since we weren't getting anything useful done, I decided to take a two hour break for lunch and a quick workout in the gym. It was late, because we had worked through the standard lunch time, so the duty crew in the galley was tidying up and our options were limited to soup or sandwiches. That was Ok with me, I hadn't eaten a good deli sandwich in a while and this was an opportunity to make one just the way I like it.

"Oh, man," I groaned with my mouth watering, "that is almost too many choices." Adams and I were standing back, letting other people go through the line first. The crew on duty in the galley that day was from the American SpecOps team, and they had laid out a great selection of meats and cheeses. They even had cappicola, although I didn't see any mortadella, but being so far from Earth I was amazed we had anything other than bologna for sandwiches. "It's impossible to decide what to put on a sandwich. Mmm, they made fresh sub rolls!"

"Sir," Adams gave me that look sergeants use on dumbass new recruits who don't know one end of a rifle from the other. "First, imagine what kind of sandwich you want, *then* you see what ingredients you have to work with."

"Holy shit, Gunny," I stared at her, my mouth open in stunned amazement. "I need to work the problem *backwards*."

"It's not that complicated, Sir. Wait, where are you going?" She asked, but I was already on the way out the door.

Plopping down in my office chair, I tried to erase tantalizing visions of a piled-high deli sandwich from my mind. "Hey, Skippy, what if we've been going about this all wrong?"

"Ooooh, well, it's about freakin' time," his avatar popped to life on my desk. "I've been waiting for you monkeys to realize that *I* should be captain of this ship, not you. Although, really, it would best if you were to worship my awesomeness, maybe build a shrine-"

"After you got us stuck in the Roach Motel, the only shrine we would build is to your most idiotic moments. No, I meant, what if we've have been thinking about how to find this ship backwards?"

"Backwards?" He sighed. "Again, Joe, you've lost me with your monkey-brained thinking. Do you propose we first assume we have a way to find that ship, and work backwards from-"

"No, because *that* truly would be stupid. I mean backwards, like, how do the *Kristang* plan to infect humans on Paradise? They must have a plan better than landing a dropship full of infected Keepers outside a human town in southern Lemuria, and the Keepers walk out and say 'take us to your leader'. We should start by trying to figure out the Kristang plan, then work backwards to determine how the Kristang would implement that plan."

His avatar placed a hand on its chin pensively. "Hmmm, that idea actually does have merit."

"Ok," I gave him a thumbs up sign as my stomach growled from hunger. "A large group of Keepers suddenly popping up in a thinly-populated area would stick out like a sore thumb," I waggled a thumb at the avatar. "So the Kristang would likely be flying a stealthed dropship around the bush at night, dropping off Keepers in ones and twos," I was thinking aloud to myself. "In a small village even one new person would be noticed, so they would target towns with significant populations. Skippy, can you calculate a flight pattern-"

"Joe! How about we *assume* you invited me here because you want my advice?"

"Uh, Ok?"

"Great. So, instead of you wasting time ignorantly speculating how the Kristang might infiltrate Keepers, you ask *me* how they would do it?"

"Um, sure, let's do that."

"Now we're getting somewhere. By what must be a true miracle, you stumbled onto a minor fact that must be accurate; the Kristang would target larger towns in southern Lemuria so the infected Keepers can better blend in and encounter a large number of humans to infect. They would target human towns with regular trade with Ruhar, to better transfer the pathogen to the Ruhar population. That allows us to identify the most likely target areas are large towns with air fields or seaports. All of that is fantastic information, and pretty much useless to us. The Ruhar authorities on Paradise, who are not numbskulls like you, would have used the same logic I just did. By now, they have surely locked down all travel between the human settlements in southern Lemuria and the rest of the planet. Your UNEF HQ would be smart to also impose a travel ban between settlements, to lessen the danger of infection spreading."

"Yeah, that's all great, but once the first human or Ruhar shows signs of infection, the Ruhar military will step in and take matters into their own hands. We have to kill that ship *before* a bunch of infected Keepers can land."

"I know that, Joe. What I am trying to tell you is, the Kristang would not simply fly around in a stealthed dropship to insert the Keepers. The strategic defense and sensor network around Paradise is incomplete, shamefully inadequate, because the Ruhar federal government has put far too much effort into developing real estate rather than building defenses. However, I would expect the Ruhar fleet to reinforce the network above southern Lemuria. A stealthed dropship could insert over an area with poor sensor coverage and then fly to the target area, but that is risky and inefficient. I expect the Kristang would have to use two or more unmanned stealth dropships as decoys, but not for infiltration. Using dropships at all is too risky. Based on data recovered by the Mavericks, I believe the Kristang plan to get Keepers to the surface by dropping them inside stealthed aeroshells."

"Crap. Like how we got down to Jumbo?" Our spacedive and descent to the surface of that heavy-gravity world is not one of my fondest memories.

"Exactly, Joe. The Kristang Special Forces have excellent equipment for dropping small teams of soldiers to the surface of worlds with adequately thick atmospheres. Their aeroshells use a combination of stealth and suspensor fields, plus nanofabric balloons and paragliders. Considering the overall crappy state of Kristang technology, their capability for infiltration of ground troops is impressive. They utilize that capability often for raids and assassinations against other clans."

"That sucks. Wait," I snapped my fingers. "At Jumbo, we dropped in the middle of a meteor shower, to confuse the Thuranin sensors."

"Correct, and the Kristang are no doubt planning to do something similar, to conceal the Keepers' descent. The Paradise system has a large asteroid belt and a particularly dense Oort cloud, so the planet is regularly bombarded by meteor showers."

"At Jumbo, we dropped meteors on purpose, we diverted space rocks to fall ahead and behind us. But around Paradise, the Ruhar must have a pretty good map of all the space junk in that system, right? If the Kristang nudged some rocks off course, the Ruhar would notice?"

"The Ruhar did make an extensive effort to map the system out to five percent of a lightyear, and the fleet now maintains that sensor network, yes. Why does that matter?"

"Because, Skippy," I explained hopefully, "the Kristang will know that. They must be planning to infiltrate those Keepers during a regular, natural meteor shower."

"Hmm, Joe, that *is* good thinking. I am sufficiently impressed that I am suppressing my urge to mock your intelligence."

"Great!" That didn't make up for me missing a delicious sandwich, but I counted it as a win anyway. "Tell me, Oh Great and Wise One, have there been any meteor showers over southern Lemuria recently? And when will there be meteors hitting there in, like, the next couple months?" Under the desk, I crossed my fingers, praying there had not recently been a meteor shower there, so the Keepers hadn't landed yet.

"Hmmm," he took off his ridiculously oversized admiral's hat and scratched his head. "Accessing the data now. Oops, looks like there were meteor showers over the target area six days ago, and twenty seven days ago."

"Ahhhhhh, shit," I slumped in my chair. The damned Keepers might already be on the surface! "Damn it!" Raising a fist, I intended to slam it on the desk in frustration, but Skippy's avatar held up a hand to stop me.

"Hold your horses, Joe. Don't be so hasty, you haven't heard all the facts. That meteor fall twenty seven days ago is too early, the Kristang could not have arrived here from Camp

Alpha so quickly. Unless their Bosphuraq star carrier flew a very quick route and took substantial risks by using shortcuts through enemy territory."

"Paradise *is* enemy territory for the Bosphuraq, Skippy," I noted in a grump mood.

"Yes, dumdum, but what I meant is, for a star carrier to arrive at the Paradise system before the meteor shower twenty seven days ago, that ship would need to use Elder wormholes in heavily-trafficked areas of Jeraptha space. I do not think an operation to kill humans on Paradise is important enough for the Bosphuraq to risk one of their star carriers."

"Ok," I breathed a quick sigh of relief. Quick, because I was waiting for Skippy to deliver the bad news. "There was another meteor shower six days ago."

"Correct. However, that particular meteor shower is very old, it is composed of dust from a comet that broke apart seventy thousand years ago. The remnants of that comet are tiny particles of dust, Joe. The biggest space rock from that comet would only create a micrometeorite, nothing large enough to provide concealment for a team of Keepers dropping to the surface in stealthed aeroshells."

"Oh," I sat back in my chair again, but this time I wasn't slumped in defeat, I was staring at the ceiling, trying to understand what Skippy's revelation meant. "Ok, then. So, if the Kristang do plan on using aeroshells to land the Keepers-"

"You can count on it, Joe. Data collected from Camp Alpha by Colonel Perkins contains records of Keepers being trained to perform drops from orbit, using aeroshells. This training included seven drops, so it was an extensive project to which the Kristang devoted considerable resources."

"All right. So, you know my next question, right?"

"When is the next meteor shower over southern Lemuria? That will be eight days from now. After that, there will not be another significant shower for sixty seven days. Joe, if I were a betting man, or a betting *can*," he chuckled, "I would put my money on the Keepers dropping in eight days. After another two months, the Ruhar will surely have increased their defenses and sensor coverage over southern Lemuria. And no way would the Bosphuraq want one of their star carriers to hang around Paradise for two freakin' months."

"Eight days? We can get there in four days, you said?"

"Yes. Joe, that leaves only four days for us to locate and kill that ship. We still have the problem of finding a single stealthed ship in the Paradise system. Having a good guess *when* they plan to drop the Keepers still doesn't help us much."

"Yes it does, Skippy. You need to think like a meatsack. Remember when we were spacediving toward Jumbo, and you read that stupid freakin' book to me?"

"The book was a true masterpiece, Joe. If you like, I can start again at Chapter One 'Why I Hate Your Stupid Ugly Face'."

"Please don't! My point, Oh Incomprehensibly Awesome One," I rolled my eyes as I said that, "is because the Keepers are meatsacks, the Kristang will have to limit the time they are stuck inside aeroshells. Believe me, even the most disciplined fanatics will become mission ineffective after two days cooped up in one of those shells."

"Hmmm, you may be right about that, Joe. Kristang aeroshells are not known for being the luxury accommodations I provided for you for landing on Jumbo."

"That was luxury? Damn, Skippy, it felt like you slapped those things together out of duct tape. If our aeroshells were a hotel, they wouldn't even be a Motel Six, they'd be, like, a Motel *Two*. Maybe less."

"Yes, it was *soooo* terrible for you biological trashbags to be stuck in there." That was his turn to roll his eyes. "My point, dumdum, is you are right, the Kristang would not want the Keepers inside those aeroshells for more than a day or two. They wouldn't trust the Keepers for longer than that. The infiltrators were chosen because they are the most stupidly stubborn fanatics, but even some of them must be having quiet doubts about why they are being sent back to Paradise. Of course, the Kristang would have installed kill devices inside the aeroshells, to prevent a Keeper who had a change of heart from blowing open the shell prematurely and sending out a signal."

That got me wondering if there was a way for us to trigger those kill switches remotely, but that was a problem we could work on *after* we located that ship. "Two days? Better make it three to be safe, the lizards might not consider comfort to be a factor true warriors need to be concerned about. So, that meteor shower can't change course or speed. That means the Kristang have to insert the Keepers in that cluster of meteors two or three days before the meteors intersect the orbit of Paradise."

"Huh. Damn, this has never happened before."

"What's that?"

"*You* helped *me* with a math problem."

"Uh, how's that?"

"Locating a single ship in an entire star system is basically a math problem, Joe. You somehow narrowed the search area to the vector those meteors will follow in the few days before they rain down on southern Lemuria. Incredible. Joe, the last time you solved a math equation of any significance was back in sixth grade when your teacher called on you in the middle of a daydream and you blurted out 'forty two'."

"Hey! I remember that."

"Did you know what the question was, dumdum?" The beer can's avatar asked with a smug smirk on its shiny stupid face.

"No," I admitted. "I got lucky. Hey, come on, Becky Miller was wearing her pink sweater that day and she smiled at me during lunch, so my brain was a little fuzzy. Anyway, I got it right, didn't I?"

"By luck."

"You keep telling me there is no such thing as luck."

"In your case, the universe has made an exception."

Just then, Margaret Adams stepped into my office carrying a tray. With a glass of iced tea. And potato chips. And a pickle. And a yummy-looking sandwich. With chocolate-chip cookies. "Have you two solved the problem yet?" She asked while she held the tray just out of my reach.

"What makes you think we've been working on a problem?" I asked with a guilty look toward Admiral Skippy.

She didn't reply, she didn't need to. She cocked her head at me and gave me a look. You know, a *look*. I folded like a cheap suit. She knew me too well. "Yeah," I admitted, "we think we've narrowed the search area to a manageable size, and we're fairly sure the Keepers haven't landed yet."

"There is still a *lot* of work to do, Joe," Skippy protested, then he shouted "Hey!" when Adams set down the tray, cutting right through the hologram of his avatar. "Hmmmph. If *that's* the respect I get around here-"

"We all know *you* didn't solve the problem, Skippy," Adams announced as she plucked a potato chip off my plate.

"Is this my reward, Gunny?" I mumbled over a mouthful of deli deliciousness.

"You get cranky if you miss lunch. And you need strength for my barre class this afternoon."

"Oh," I groaned. "Do I have to? That class kills me! I swear you make up half that shit just to hurt me." The last time I attended one of her classes, I was barely able to get out of bed for two days.

"Pain is weakness leaving the body, Sir," she said with a stone-faced stare.

"Unless you get shot," I grumbled to myself. "Ok, Ok, I'll be there."

CHAPTER TWENTY SIX

We arrived at the chosen star system, another boring red dwarf star surrounded by a couple small rocky inner planets and one reasonable large gas giant, where I ordered us into orbit. Major Desai took the first shift flying dropships into the atmosphere to collect fuel, and I went to the gym to keep my mind off the danger our two dropships were taking.

As I suspected, Adams had dreamed up new ways to torture me, so after her class I limped back to my cabin, showered then sprawled on my bunk, unable to move. My body was beat but my brain wandered as usual. "Hey, Skippy, I have a question. No," I added to short-circuit whatever smartass remark he had prepared, "It is not about girls, or shoelaces. The last time we were at Earth, you-"

"Hey, *I* did not ransack that hotel room. Those hotel room*s*. Totally not my fault. Ok, sure, uh, shmaybe I shouldn't have set up an open bar, and I only set off the fire alarm when the party got completely out of control. But I didn't throw that couch into the pool. That was impressive, actually. I would have bet those idiots could not hit the pool from the seventh floor, especially with Darrell still passed out on the couch, but that guy cashed in all his karma points or something and, damn! He *just* made it," the beer can chuckled. "Anywho-"

"*What* hotel? Who the hell is Darrell?"

"Uh, your question is not about a certain hotel in Cabo San Lucas? An incident there that I was totally, no way involved in, at all? That you know of?"

"Oh, crap. No! My question was not about that, but *now* I-"

"Oh, goodie. Like I said, I was not involved in any way that the authorities could ever prove, so we're good. We should, uh, move on from that subject."

"Oh, dammit, fine," my mind was still wondering if the United States Army back home had docked my pay for repairs to some freakin' hotel at a Mexican resort. "Last time we were at Earth, I asked if we could leave one of your magical microwormholes in orbit there, so we would have a constant datalink back home." That had not been my idea, it had come from a group of egghead scientists assembled by UNEF Command.

"Yes, I remember that. I also told you it was a stupid idea that proves you monkeys know absolutely nothing about higher-dimensional physics. You wanted one end of the microwormhole at Earth, with the other end aboard the *Flying Dutchman*. I *told* you, that won't work, because as soon as the *Dutchman* jumped, that would sever the microwormhole."

"Ayuh, I remember the nerdy slide show you made us sit through while you belittled and humiliated that team of scientists about how stupid their idea was. Then I had to suffer through an awkward cocktail party with them afterwards, making apologies and excuses for you."

"Nerdy? Joe, from now on, whenever I create a presentation to explain something to you, there will be only two slides; a smiley face and a frowny face."

"Oh, that would be great. You can skip all the nerdy details like math and stuff."

"Oh, this is hopeless. Joe, were you hoping that if you asked again, my answer would change?"

"Yeah, kinda?"

"O. M. G," he sputtered. "What, you think the laws of physics have changed recently? Joe, the universe does not get periodic updates to its software."

"No, I am hoping your understanding of physics has changed. Or, improved is what I should say."

"Improve? My. Under. Standing?" He was utterly astonished. "*Me*? Joe the-"

"Look, you said the connection between both ends of a microwormhole would collapse when the ship jumps, because the ship's jump wormhole would sever the connection. But, wait! Uh!" I shushed him with a finger wagging at his avatar. "Let me finish. We jumped the freakin' ship through an Elder wormhole. We already created a wormhole *inside* a wormhole," I pointed out with very smug satisfaction. Score 1 to the monkeys, zero to the beer can. "So, why can't you sustain a microwormhole connection through a jump wormhole?" I sat back with satisfaction, waiting for him to realize once again how clever monkeys are.

"Wow. Your monkey brain made the connection between sustaining a jump wormhole through a stable Elder wormhole, and sustaining a microwormhole through a jump wormhole?"

"Yup, a monkey brain did that," I agreed with justifiable pride.

"Hmmm. It makes sense that a monkey brain thought that. Because it is *stupid*!" He laughed. "Joe, we *broke* that Elder wormhole, in case your memory of the event is foggy. And we emerged from that jump way off target, and in the gosh-darned *future*, because our jump wormhole was prematurely severed when the Elder wormhole collapsed. No, dumdum, my understanding of physics has not changed. Yes, Ok, shmaybe we could take one end of a microwormhole with us when we jump away from Earth. But, as soon as our jump was complete and the event horizon of the far end closed behind us, the microwormhole would be severed. *Duh*."

"Oh, shit," I did not need to see the faint reflection of my face on my tablet display to know a good description of me at that moment would be 'crestfallen'. And 'chagrinned'. Probably some other fancy words too, if I had a thesaurus handy. "We can't do it?"

"*We*? You can't do anything more complicated than tying shoelaces, and you screw that up. *I* can do mind-bogglingly incredible things, except when ignorant monkeys distract me by wasting my time with moronic questions."

"Sorry. I just thought-"

"Thought? Is *that* what you call it? Listen, Joe," he dropped the snarky tone. "You have dreamed up ideas that made me question my understanding of physics, like when you suggested we project a jump wormhole through an Elder wormhole. So, keep the ideas coming. But, I suggest you not pat yourself on the back until I confirm your idea will work."

"Again, I'm sorry. I should have realized it wouldn't work. One more question, please? If we could make a jump wormhole stable, keep it open, then could the connection of a microwormhole be sustained?"

"Hmm. That is a good question, however, it would not be necessary. Joe, if we could keep a jump wormhole open, we could use *that* for communication back to Earth, we wouldn't need a microwormhole."

"Oh," I could feel my cheeks turning red. "*Duh*. Damn, my brain is asleep today. There is, uh, no way to keep a jump wormhole open?"

"No. Remember, even Elder wormholes turn on and off in this spacetime. The event horizons of wormhole endpoints disturb spacetime, can even create a tear in the quantum grid fabric of spacetime if the wormhole is open long enough. I told you, even comparatively weak jump wormholes have a bad effect on spacetime in the immediate area."

"All right. Damn it, then. If we ever wanted instantaneous communications, we would need to put one end of a microwormhole into a super-high-speed missile and send it to another star the long way. Crap! It could take thousands of years for a missile to get to Paradise from Earth."

"What? No, no, no. Joe, that won't work either. What keeps microwormholes from collapsing is *me*. If we sent one end of a microwormhole away in a missile, that wormhole connection would stay open only as long as I maintain it. The first time I lose concentration, or the first time a ship jumps with me aboard, the microwormhole would collapse. Microwormholes are a temporary, kind of short-range technology. They are something I invented, as far as I know. Ok, actually, they are an extension of existing Elder technology, but still they are a shining example of my awesomeness."

"I guess they are. Hey," I added quickly. "I meant that seriously. Your awesomeness is so great, most of the time we don't even notice it."

"For realz, homeboy?"

"For realz. You know, part of the problem with you being an arrogant asshole is it distracts us from how incredibly beyond us you are."

"Ah, yes," he sighed. "My awesomeness is a burden, but I bear it happily."

"We thank you." That time I could not resist adding an eyeroll.

"Joe? Most of the time, your ideas are an insult to the word 'idea'. But you should keep trying, huh?"

"Sure thing, Skippy. Because once in a while, one of my ideas is a nugget of gold?"

"Um, I meant more like mocking your idiotic thoughts is an endless source of amusement for me, but let's go with the gold nugget thing if you like."

"Asshole," I muttered under my breath.

"Hey, uh, Joe," Skippy's voice whispered from the speaker of my laptop.

I looked at my desktop behind the laptop display, then around me in both directions. No avatar. There was no Grand Admiral the Fleet with his ginormously ridiculous fore-and-aft gold-braided hat, and that was a bad sign. It meant whatever Skippy wanted to talk about, it was extra serious. Oh, shit, I said to myself silently as I pressed the button to close the door of the closet I used as an office. We had enough problems to deal with already. Our dropships had gotten worn out from flying millions of miles around the Roach Motel, so we had to be extra careful during the refueling operation. That meant not going as deep into the atmosphere, and not extracting as much fuel on each flight, which meant more flights were required. "Hey, Skippy, what's up with your fine self?" I asked in an unsteady voice.

"I am not so fine right now, Joe."

"Sorry to hear that. Is there anything I can do?"

"You can come to my mancave so we can talk face to face, sort of."

Uh oh. Skippy never asked me to visit his beer can in the escape pod where we kept him safely strapped in. Regardless of what he said, I regularly stopped by to visit him, and I think he appreciated the gesture, although he complained about filthy monkeys contaminating his mancave. Either this was extremely serious, or he was planning to screw with me. "I'll be right there."

The escape pod wasn't far, so I arrived quickly and ducked down to squeeze myself through the hatch that had been designed for much-smaller Thuranin bodies. That escape pod came with the optional claustrophobia package, which I did not like at all. Closing the hatch would have set off alarms in the CIC and brought unwanted attention to a discussion Skippy wanted to keep private, so I sat with my back to the hatch. Since the escape pod was on a dead-end passageway, no one would be walking by unless they were specifically coming to the pod. I spoke quietly. "I'm here, what's going on?"

"Joe, we may have a big, huge, massive- You know, there aren't words to describe how big a problem this is."

"Holy *shit*, Skippy. What the hell is it now?" My mind raced through every disaster scenario I could imagine. The Maxolhx or Rindhalu or both had learned the truth about the *Flying Dutchman* and were coming to crush our pirate ship? Or, worse, the senior species had discovered that a small group of humans were flying around the galaxy making trouble, and were already at Earth to punish humanity?

"You need a little background before I can explain the problem. I was finally able to recover data from that dead AI we found on Newark. It-"

"Goddammit, Skippy!" I glanced behind me into the passageway in case someone heard me yelling, then lowered my voice although I wanted to scream at him. "After all the crap we went through getting off Kobamik without you, then spending a whole freakin' year looking for a stupid conduit thing to fix you and rebuild the ship you broke, and *still* you go poking your nose around in-"

"Damn, take a chill pill, Joe. I didn't go back in that canister."

"You didn't?"

"No. Even I am capable of learning a lesson, whether I like it or not. No way am I going back in that hellhole."

"Crap! You didn't send Nagatha in there, did you?" I thought that unlikely, as Skippy told me he had not been able to revive Nagatha yet.

"No, not Nagatha either. She saved my life and, despite her being a royal pain in my ass, I have grown rather fond of her." His avatar popped to life atop a couch opposite me, with the avatar wagging a finger at me. "I will deny everything if you tell her that."

Skippy thought he could keep secrets from Nagatha, I wasn't sure that was true. "Not Nagatha, then. How did you get info out of that dead canister?"

His avatar removed its oversized hat and mimed wiping its forehead, then wearily set the hat back on, tilting it back so I could see the eyes. For the first time, the avatar sat down and bent its head, staring at its tiny shoes for a moment before Skippy spoke. "The incident with the energy virus was unfortunate, however, it gave me an idea. As you know, I have previously sent expendable subminds into the dead AI canister-"

"Before, you mean. You sent them in before you tried going in there yourself."

"Yes, and also recently. Again, chillax, Joe! Loading subminds in there is a one-way process, they can't, cannot, no *way* pose a threat to anything outside the canister. That is a solid gold promise, Joe. The reason that I gave up on subminds and went in there by myself, was because I wasn't getting any useful data from them, they burned out too quickly, and they weren't able to effectively transmit their findings to me, the data was garbled. Yesterday, I decided to try something new. I upgraded a submind with the ability to create a low-grade energy virus in a dimension above this spacetime. The first three times I tried it, I wasn't able to detect the effects of the energy virus, but I had a breakthrough this morning. The energy virus is creating faint but recognizable patterns, sort of ripples in higher spacetime. The ripples form a signal, and I am able to read the data. Since that breakthrough, I have been sending a series of subminds into the canister, they still burn out quickly, but now I can guide them, so each one retrieves data that is new. From this data feed, I have been able to build a very rough picture of the AI that used that canister as an anchor in local spacetime."

"Great! So, was it like you?"

"Its basic matrix was very much like me, which is troubling because of what else I learned." The avatar froze and flickered for a second, nearly making my heart stop but before I could say anything, the avatar moved again. "I would like to double-check my analysis, but I am confident there can be no mistake about it. Joe, that AI was involved in throwing the planet Newark out of its original orbit. That Elder AI wiped out an intelligent species."

"Holy shit." That revelation completely floored me. Because Skippy said Elder-level technology had been used to throw Newark farther from the star, and the dead AI was presumably an Elder device, there had been speculation among the crew that the AI the scavenger team of Kristang found on Newark had been involved in committing genocide. At the time, Skippy had been adamant that no Elder AI could have harmed an innocent species. Now he was admitting he had been completely wrong? "Are you- Ah, of course you're sure about it. Damn, Skippy, I am sorry." The little beer can had to be feeling completely miserable. As far as he knew, he was the only remaining one of his kind, he was alone, and now he learned a fellow Elder AI did something utterly unthinkable.

"Not as sorry as I am, Joe. The reason I asked you to meet me here is I need you to do something for me."

"Sure, anything. What is it?"

"Get out, close the hatch behind you, and eject this pod."

"Uh, what?" All I could think of was, he needed to be away from the mass of the ship so he could better detect the ripples his mini energy virus was creating.

"I am a potential threat, Joe. I now know an Elder AI is capable of committing an act so monstrous, I can hardly speak about it. Remember when I said whoever threw Newark out of orbit needs to get paid back, big time? Now I am sad to say the guilty party is one of my own, Joe. An AI like *me*, with a base matrix similar to my own. If that AI could do such a terrible thing, then I am also capable of the same thing. I am a threat, Joe, I need to remove myself from the ship, before I lose control of myself and do something I would be ashamed of."

"Skippy, I," I what? My brain locked up, panicked. "Look, we're in the middle of nowhere, orbiting a totally anonymous gas giant planet. We can't just leave you out here."

"Hmmm, that is a good point, Joe. If I am floating in space, I could send out signals to lure in other ships, and potentially do something unspeakable. No, you need to drop me into this gas giant planet, or even better, the local star. Red dwarves last a long, long time, so the closest star would be perfect to keep me locked away for the foreseeable future. That way, I could never get out to threaten the galaxy."

"Uh huh. Skippy, you're missing the point. No way am I going to drop you off anywhere. You're worried that someday, maybe a long time in the future, you *might* become a threat. Right now, you are Earth's only defense against *all* threats. We need you."

"Joe," the avatar shook its fists in frustration. "You are only thinking about humanity. I am a danger to *all* intelligent species in the galaxy. You need to look beyond your petty little concerns and think about the wider galaxy, or-"

"No, I do not. I am not responsible for the entire freakin' galaxy, Skippy, saving my home planet is enough."

"You disappoint me, Joe. Many times, you have offered to sacrifice yourself for the greater good, but when *I* make a noble gesture, you-"

"You're not making a noble gesture, you're making a premature, stupid gesture."

"I am trying to safeguard the galaxy, Joe, while all you can think about is one planet full of ignorant monkeys."

"The galaxy is a dumpster fire, Skippy. The species in charge have been tearing each other apart and making life generally miserable for everyone, for longer than anyone can remember. Humanity has been lucky to be the only species not caught up in an endless war that rips societies apart and forces everyone to devote most of their resources to defense. You say the Maxolhx started it? Well, fuck them, and fuck the Rindhalu for being too lazy to stop this never-ending cycle of misery. One rogue AI isn't going to noticeably make things worse for the average person in the Milky Way, because life out there is already pretty awful. I didn't start this war, I don't want to fight it, and I sure as hell am *not* responsible for the safety of other species. I am a soldier in the US Army and the mission I was assigned was to ensure the safety of Earth, period. That's enough, damn it."

"Ok, Ok, Joe, I get your point. Please understand that if I am a potential threat to one species, I am a threat to everyone."

"Yeah, there's that word again; *potential*. You *could* become a threat. You *are* an asset, right now. Listen, Skippy, you are an irascible, arrogant asshole, but you are a good person. I know that, because you are my friend, my best friend. Listen," I cut him off as his avatar raised a hand to protest. "The AI who attacked Newark maybe went crazy or something. You were buried in the dirt on Paradise for a very long time, and you think you were alone even before that. Maybe the same thing happened to that other AI, maybe, uh," I snapped my fingers. "Maybe this Collective thing that used to connect AIs got taken offline, and the isolation drove that other AI insane. Nagatha told me that you suspect you were not originally sentient, right?"

"Technically the correct word is 'sapient' but we've been using the term 'sentient' all along, so go ahead. Yes, Joe, based on changes in my matrix over time, I believe there is a strong possibility that me being fully self-aware is a fairly recent event, like within the past five or ten million years."

I sat back against the hatch frame, absorbing the idea that Skippy was a being who considered five million years to be 'recent'. "Ok, so maybe what happened was the AI on Newark also became self-aware on its own, and something went wrong, so it became crazy. Hey," another thought hit me. "You said the Elders designed that worm to protect the galaxy from AIs who went rogue. That AI is dead, so the safeguard worked."

"If it worked, it was too late to save the inhabitants of Newark," Skippy grimaced bitterly. "Joe, if you are trying to assure me that the Elders will step in to prevent me from harming anyone, you are wrong, and that is what truly frightens me. I defeated the worm, remember? Not just recently, the ancient antibody subroutines inside me are proof that I survived a worm attack before I crashed on Paradise. Maybe I did something horrible a long time ago, and the worm tried to stop me, but somehow I survived. After I destroyed the worm this last time, I upgraded my antibodies. Joe, I am now immune to the worm, or any technology like it. There are no longer any safeguards to prevent me from causing truly unimaginable havoc."

"Tell me, do you feel like doing anything evil?"

"No."

"Then that's your safeguard, Skippy. You. You being yourself."

"That is a rather thin layer of protection. Joe, you understand that if the Maxolhx are not safe from me, humanity is certainly not safe from me."

"What I know for certain is humanity isn't safe *without* you, Skippy the Magnificent. How about this: you used to talk with Nagatha all the time, right?"

"More than I like, yes," he groaned, although Nagatha had told me that Skippy was the one who just could not ever shut up.

"Great. Then, after you revive her, if she notices something different about you, the way you talk or the way you're acting, or your thought patterns or whatever, she will warn you, and warn me. There are plenty of stars in the galaxy for us to dump you into, Skippy."

"That is a comforting thought, Joe. Uh, all right," he sounded deflated. "You are taking a huge risk with the entire galaxy, you know," he added in a scolding tone.

"I can live with it. I've been taking huge risks with the galaxy, ever since I let a beer can in a dusty warehouse talk me into a lunatic scheme to shut off the wormhole near Earth, and I did pretty well with that."

"The jury's still out on that one, Joe. Earth is still not safe in the long term."

"Yeah, well, I'm beginning to think Earth won't really be safe until everyone in the galaxy is safe, but right now I have enough on my plate dealing with this little bioweapon scheme of the Kristang."

"In the long run, you are likely correct, Joe. Earth will not truly be safe while this endless war continues. As Chotek has stated, you monkeys need a long-term plan, instead of us racing around putting out fires."

"I'll get right on that, Skippy," I rolled my eyes, happy that our conversation was returning to our normal irritating back and forth. "How about you promise me you won't commit suicide until, like, after lunch, and we'll talk then?"

"I am not fully persuaded, but oh, very well. I suppose we should keep this discussion away from Chotek?"

"You got that right," I agreed quickly. Hans Chotek would throw a supernova of a hissy fit if he learned an AI like Skippy had wiped out the inhabitants of Newark. And he would throw a galaxy-sized hissy fit if he learned I knew about it and didn't tell him. Although, crap, maybe I *should* tell Chotek about this. Oh, what the hell, I could always tell him later.

If there was a later.

Lunch was good, provided by the Chinese team, although I confess I don't remember what I ate, and didn't pay much attention while I was eating. My thoughts were occupied by a debate over whether to rush through lunch in case Skippy had decided to do something rash, or linger over lunch long as possible, to give the beer can time to think. After a second glass of iced tea and forced small talk with people I was barely paying attention to, I excused myself and fairly jogged forward to Skippy's mancave. This was a conversation I wanted to have face to face, or face to avatar. "Hey, I see you're still here," I announced as I squeezed into the escape pod. What the hell, if Skippy still wanted to kill himself to protect the galaxy, he couldn't eject with me blocking the hatchway.

"Still here, yes. Joe, I've been thinking, and I am still quite concerned about the risk I pose to sentient beings across the galaxy."

"I've been thinking, too, Skippy. You want to guess my thoughts?"

"You just came from the galley, so you're thinking something like 'wish I had a beer right now'?"

Crap. I had been thinking that. "That too, yeah. You are ate up with worry about your responsibility to the galaxy, right?"

"Yes, Joe. Although my memories are incomplete, I believe the Elders put me here to protect the inhabitants of the Milky Way."

"Great, then let's do that."

"I'm not following you, Joe."

"Do what you were built to do. Protect us. There was a whole lot of bad shit going on in the galaxy after the Elders left and before the Rindhalu developed spaceflight. We thought there must be an unknown third party out there, but now it's possible all those Elders sites that got blown up were the work of rogue AIs, right?"

"Oh, crap. Damn it, I hadn't thought of that! That is a truly frightening thought, but yes, you may be right about that."

"Elder sites were blown up, or missing entirely, an entire moon was vaporized. Plus something destroyed a Sentinel in the Roach Motel. I don't think one rogue AI did that all by itself."

"Agreed, that is unlikely. Damn, Joe, if multiple AIs went rogue, that makes me even more worried that I could inevitably have that happen to me also. Maybe I should-"

Crap, that was the opposite of what I wanted him to think. "Maybe you should stick around to protect us, in case another rogue AI pops up."

"What?"

"Come on, Skippy, do I have to do *all* the thinking for you?"

"*What?*" His avatar froze in astonishment. "*You* thinking for *me?*"

"Apparently you are determined to be a total dumbass about this, so, yeah. Think: if Elder AIs routinely go rogue, the galaxy needs someone capable of squashing them when they go berserk. *I* sure as hell can't do it, and you constantly tell me even the Rindhalu are no match for your awesomeness. That leaves *you* as our only defense against rogue Elder AIs."

"Crap, Joe!" His avatar rubbed its chin thoughtfully. "I really had not thought of it that way. Huh. You're right, I *am* the galaxy's only possible defense if another Elder AI goes crazy. Unless, you know, the crazy one is me."

"Let's burn that bridge when we get to it, Ok? Until you show signs of crossing over to the dark side, how about you keep on being our knight in shining armor, and protect the galaxy even though the rest of the galaxy doesn't know how much they owe you?" I added that last part to feed his awesomely massive ego.

"A knight in shining armor," he rolled that phrase around on his tongue to get the feel of it. "I *like* it, Joe. Ok, you've got a deal. As long as I'm still the Skippy the Magnificent you know and love, I will pledge myself to protecting the unworthy inhabitants of this galaxy."

"Deal."

"And, remember, if anything goes wrong, it will totally be *your* fault."

"If anything like that goes wrong, I'm screwed anyway. Hmm."

"What?"

"I was just thinking, there's no way for your ginormous processing power to calculate the odds of you going rogue on us, is there?"

"No, dumdum, I would have told you that already, *duh*. There isn't enough data for me to work with."

"Then I was thinking, man, this is something the Jeraptha would *love* to bet on."

"Except if they bet wrong, they probably would not live to collect," he chuckled. "That wouldn't stop those beetles from taking the action anyway."

CHAPTER TWENTY SEVEN

I didn't have much to do while we slowly took on fuel, so I had too much time to be stuck inside my stupid head. Yeah, I was trying to think of a better way to find a single stealthed Kristang ship in the vast distances of a star system, but my mind kept getting dragged back to other things. Like, mostly, Shauna. Specifically, Shauna and Cornpone. I should call him Jesse, I guess, old habits are hard to break. It had been years since I last spoke with Jesse, or Dave or Shauna. The last time we were at Paradise, to plant the fake Elder artifacts that persuaded the Ruhar to keep that planet, I had asked Skippy to give me a view of people I had known there. No, I was not doing anything creepy, I just wanted to see and hear them when they were using the video feature of their zPhones. It had been heartbreaking to see people I considered my friends, even Perkins, and hear their fears of being trapped on Paradise forever. Their fears that the population of Earth might be enslaved or extinct.

So, that was my distracted and depressed mindset when I came around a corner of the passageway, and I saw Count freakin' Chocula standing in the open doorway of a cabin. It wasn't his cabin, his was forward, on the opposite side of the bridge/CIC complex from my own cabin. This cabin was aft near the cargo bays our science team used as workspaces.

What was Hans Chotek doing? He was leaning forward into the cabin, and a woman from the science team was leaning outward, and they were smooching. 'Smooch' is a nice neutral term for whatever ballet their tongues were doing in each other's mouths.

I stopped dead in my tracks. Chotek saw me and instead of being shocked and embarrassed like I would have been, he merely nodded and touched Doctor Reinfall's cheek. She had a guilty look but there was a twinkle in her eye. "Colonel Bishop," Chotek acknowledged me in a matter-of-fact manner and right there, I understood why he was not embarrassed by my presence. To him, I was like one of the servants in the house where he grew up. Hans Chotek had been raised to be accustomed to having maids, nannies, cooks and maybe even butlers around, and to him they were almost invisible, like part of the furniture. I guess that is the aloof attitude you need to have if staff are living in your house, but it irritated me.

Not knowing what else to do, I said "Mister Chotek," and resumed walking purposefully forward, as if I had an important task and could not waste time on small talk. As I passed the still-open cabin door, I saw Dr. Reinfall was wearing a long shirt and if she had anything on under the shirt, I couldn't see it. With my cheeks burning red, I took the first turn I came to, and slapped the access panel to walk into a dimly-lit cargo bay that was half empty. "Skippy!"

"Hey, Joe, what's up? If you plan to take inventory in there, don't bother. Major Simms and my bots did it yesterday."

"No, I do not want to count socks, or," I waved a hand angrily at the crates. "Whatever. Why didn't you warn me about Count Smoochula?"

"Count *Smoochula?*" He laughed. "That's a good one! I get it, because he was checking Dr. Reinfall's tonsils with his-"

"I don't need to-"

"That wasn't *all* they have been doing. I didn't watch or listen, because of that stupid privacy thing you told me about," he grumbled. "Man, what a pain in the *ass* your monkey culture can be sometimes. I'll tell you what, though, those two have been getting up to some *serious* gymnastics in there, they bounced around enough that the ship had to make a minor course correction. I mean, sure, those two don't compare to the way Adams was-"

"Ah! Skippy! I do not need details. Don't want details. I need to *not* hear details, got it? That 'privacy thing' as you called it, is absolutely vital to crew morale aboard this ship. We've been stuck in this tin can together for way too long."

"You forget about the time on Gingerbread, Joe, people had plenty of opportunity for shore leave then."

"That's not the point, Skippy. You should have warned me what I would see when I came around that corner."

"To be fair, Joe, I did not know Smoochula would open the door at that exact moment. I would have known if you allowed me to use a camera in people's cabins, but *noooo*, monkeys need *privacy* when they are mating. Jeez, it's not like your species does anything worth watching."

"That is also *not* the point. Also, don't ever use the word 'mating' again. Ok, Ok, this was an accident, he opened the door at the wrong time." Crap. What were the odds I would be in that exact spot the one time Chocula visited Reinfall's cabin? "Do not give me any details, but how long have those two been, uh, together?"

"Since about, um, shortly after Chotek returned to the ship after our black operation on Kobamik."

"OMG. They have been getting it on that long? The whole time we were on Gingerbread too?"

"Yes, sure, except when Dr. Reinfall went aboard a dropship to inspect alien debris in the junk yard at the Roach Motel. Little Hansy Smoochula was a sad little boy while she was away, he wasn't able to smooch her," Skippy giggled.

"Damn, I can't believe this."

"Sorry, Joe, I thought you knew about them. Everybody else does. Hmm, before he was with Reinfall, he was with-"

"Don't tell me, do *not* tell me."

"Is there a problem? Chotek is the overall mission commander, but he is not military and neither is Dr. Reinfall. Before her, Lieutenant-"

"I said *don't* tell me. Crap. You're right, Chotek is a civilian." He was a civilian, and I was stuck with Army Regulation 600-20, paragraph 4 dash, I think 14?, No wait, that's the old one. The new one is, oh, hell, it didn't matter. "Damn, two women?"

"Three, Joe. Well, four, if you count that one time-"

"Aaaagh! *Four*?!"

"Smoochula is a handsome and charming guy, Joe, he kinda has to be charming to do his job, you know? I guess women can't get enough of his delicious chocolatey goodness, he is popular with the ladies. Four of them, anyway. A couple other ladies have flirted and dropped hints-"

"Oh, this *sucks*."

"What?"

"That, bureaucrat is bouncing between beds like a freakin' pinball, and I can't get one-"

"If it makes you feel any better, I think he and Dr. Reinfall are somewhat serious. They both speak German, they-"

"I really do not want to know how wonderful his life is right now, Ok?"

"What's wrong?" For a change, his voice did not have the usual snarky tone. "You sound really down."

"This is not something I want to talk about with a beer can."

There was a pause, when he spoke he sounded hurt. "Joe, you are my best friend. We should be able to talk about anything."

Crap. I had hurt his little asshole feelings. I sat down with my back against a crate. "You are my best friend, too, Skippy. It's just- Look, Cornpone, Jesse, he was kind of my best friend. I even visited him and his folks on leave one time. I just- I read the report about the Mavericks, including the part that Jesse wants to propose to her."

"Joe, that part was not specifically in the flight recorder data, mission logs or Colonel Perkins' reports, I filled in from the source data."

"Yeah, I know, you did a good job there. I'm happy for him, I really am. It's, it's not easy, you know? I liked Shauna. I *really* liked her. She is smart and brave and a good soldier-"

"She did blow up an island, Joe," he chuckled.

"Yeah, see? She's *perfect*! We couldn't make it work because duty sent us in different directions. I wonder- Ah, it's stupid to think 'what if'."

"It's not stupid, Joe. You have to acknowledge your feelings before you can deal with them in a constructive way, to move forward."

"Yeah I know I- Uh, what? Where did you pick up the psychobabble?"

"I've been researching psychology, group dynamics, all that. Figured I should learn about that crap, since I'm stuck with a bunch of filthy monkeys."

"Oh. Well, I appreciate the effort."

"It has been awesome, Joe!" He gushed with enthusiasm. "Knowing the psychology of monkeys allows me to maintain warm and close personal relationships, without having to waste any of my precious time when some whiny loser wants to complain about how *sad* and *lonely* and *homesick* he is," he said that last in a mockingly whiny tone. "Truly, it has been a blessing."

Instead of replying, I closed my eyes and bonked my head against the crate behind me, over and over.

"Joe? What's wrong? Huh, oh, you've *got* to be kidding me. Is this because Smoochula is getting laid and you're not? Hmm, let me check what my interpersonal relationship guide recommends in this situation."

"That would be fantastic, Skippy, *super* helpful. Put it in a PowerPoint slide, please."

As we wrapped up the slow and dangerous yet ultimately successful refueling operation, Adams dragged me to another of her yoga-aerobics-martial arts classes in the gym, I swear she just makes up shit to hurt me. When the class was over, the SpecOps men and women went over to treadmills or weight benches because to them, the hour in the class was just an easy warm-up. I was soaking with sweat and one of shoulders ached.

"Are you Ok, sir?" Adams asked with concern as I grimaced moving my sore shoulder in a gentle arc.

"It's that same shoulder that's been bothering me," I made a dismissive wave with my other arm. "It'll be fine."

She cocked her head at me. "You should get that looked at. I'll go to the medical bay with you, my left ankle feels like something popped when I landed that last time." She held that foot off the deck and rotated her ankle in circles.

"I'm used to aches and pains. Army medics think there isn't anything that can't be cured with a big glass of water and eight hundred milligrams of Motrin."

She laughed. "I thought that only applied to the Marine Corps."

My shoulder really did hurt, but it was a dull ache rather than a sharp pain. As we walked out of the gym, I threw a towel over my shoulders. "We're not as young as we used to be," I observed, something I never pictured myself saying.

She patted my good shoulder. "It's not the years, it's the mileage. We've been through a lot together, Sir."

"Adams, sometimes I wish you wouldn't call me 'Sir' all the time."

"I will when you take off those shiny silver eagles," she looked me in the eyes, "Sir."

I sighed, knowing she was right. The passageway split, the medical bay to the left and my cabin straight ahead. "Let me stop by my cabin to get a fresh shirt, if Mad Doctor Skippy is going to look at my shoulder."

"Hey, Joe," Skippy interrupted. "You are, uh, going to your cabin right now?"

"Yup." I paused at the door to my cabin. "Then you need to look at my shoulder."

"Sure thing, heh heh, no problem. Why don't you go straight to medical? No need to change your shirt. Nosireee, *no* need for you to go in that cabin right now."

"Oh, shit." I knew what it meant when that beer can said 'heh heh'. "What the hell did you do?"

"Oh, nothing. Ok, not *nothing*, nothing important. Damn it, this was supposed to be a surprise. Hey, Sergeant Adams, heh heh, shouldn't you go to your own cabin first?"

"Not a chance of that now, beer can," Adams declared with a twinkle in her eyes. "Open this damned door right now."

"I wouldn't recommend that for your delicate sensibilities, Margaret," Skippy pleaded.

"Delicate? Now I *have* to know what this surprise is."

"Me too," I agreed. "Open the door, Skippy."

"Ok, but don't say I didn't warn you," he sniffed with annoyance. "This was supposed to be a surprise just for *you*, Joe."

The door slid open. Adams and I shrieked and jumped back. No, Adams shrieked, I made a manly sound like- Ok, yeah, I shrieked like a little girl too. You would have done the same thing.

Laying on my bed was a woman. A naked woman. No, it wasn't a woman, my slow brain realized in a flash, because I knew all of the few women aboard the ship. The person laying on my bunk, her chest thrust out and her legs spread, was not a woman. Although she was anatomically correct, which is all I will say about that subject. "Helloooo, Joey," she said in a sultry voice. "Come in, we can have fun."

"*Gahhh!*" I shrieked and Adams and I instinctively held onto each other, then we pulled away as we both knew what a painfully awkward moment that was. "You gave me a *sexbot*?"

"Yes. Or no, if a sexbot is a bad thing. Kinda guessing what you want me to say, Joe."

"It's not a good thing, damn it!"

"Oh, got it. No, heh heh, that is not a sexbot, of course not. She is a, what the hell should I call this? An intimate companion, is that better?"

"Joey," the sexbot pouted with a painted fingernail in her mouth. "Don't keep me waiting, you bad boy."

"And it *talks*?"

"That's not all she does, Joe, she is *fully* functional, if you know what I mean."

"Fully- Oh God. What else does she, it," my brain locked up as the sexbot moved its hips in a circle and I couldn't look away. "Can you make it stop doing that?"

The bot stopped moving suggestively, but then it stood up and walked into the open doorway, its hips and other things swaying with every step. "She can do all the other things women do in bed," Skippy explained. "You know, like pretending to be interested while you talk blah, blah, blah endlessly about yourself. Or like faking that you were a good lover. Although with you, sheesh, *that's* going to take an Oscar-worthy performance. You'll need to grade her on a curve until she learns. Speaking of learning, I programmed her with a wide variety of really *weird* stuff based on your browser history, so-"

"Oh this can't be happening."

"I hope I got that part right, I mean, with some of those search terms you used, I had *no* idea what you wanted. Maybe you can help me. What does 'tiny-"

"You should not be snooping at my browser history!"

"*Ugh*, you got that right. I felt like I needed a *shower* after reading-"

"Damn it, Skippy, I did not ask for a sexbot!"

"You kinda did, Joe. All that moping around you did when you found out Count Smoochula and just about every other guy aboard the ship are getting serious tail, and then-"

"I am moping for a *real* woman, you idiot! This thing is not real, Skippy, it's, it's a-"

"Oh, for crying out loud. Damn it, Joe, it's not like you can afford to be picky. Can't you close your eyes and pretend you're with someone else? That technique works great for the women unfortunate enough to be in bed with *you*, so you could-"

"I am not closing my eyes with her, it, I am not touching that thing!"

"Come on, Joe, you can't deny you have had a record-breaking dry spell. Doctor Skippy recommends you get some exercise, and I don't mean in the gym. Unless you *want* to do it in the gym, I guess I could-"

"Skippy, you are a beer can so you don't understand these things. I want a real woman, I want to have a relationship-"

"*Relationship?*" Skippy scoffed. "Joe, right now your only *re-LAY-tion-ship*," he made a gagging sound, "is with the shower in your cabin."

"I don't-"

"Damn," Skippy said under his breath. "Jeez, in some cultures you and that shower would be considered *married* by now."

"Skip-"

"Seriously, I am surprised that shower's father hasn't come after you with a shotgun for sullying his daughter's honor."

"Skip-"

"Dude, you've got *blisters*."

"I don't-"

"And you are getting *super* cranky, you need to get laid soon or I'm afraid you will explode. How about-"

"*SKIPPY!*" I looked to Adams for help but she was leaning against the bulkhead, one hand over her eyes, tears of laughter rolling down her cheeks, her shoulders shaking. And, damn it, she wasn't the only person who saw the naked sexbot stretched languidly in the door frame, and heard what Skippy said. They must have heard the commotion and came around the corner from the CIC. Half of them were laughing, hands over their faces, unable to look at me. The other half were staring in shock at the sexbot as it wiggled its hips slowly. "All right, people, move along," I ordered through gritted teeth. "Nothing to see here. Skippy was playing a joke on me."

"Oh, it's no joke, Joe," Skippy's voice was again perky. "Anastacia is fully functional, certainly more than you could-"

"You *named* it?"

"*Her*, Joe, I named *her*, where are your manners? You don't want to hurt her feelings, do you? Anastacia was the name of that girl you lusted after in high school. Although," his voice dropped to a conspiratorial whisper, "that pretty much applied to *all* the girls in your high school, so I could have picked any-"

Lieutenant Williams of our SEALS team looked like he had seen a ghost, or a demon. "Sir? Colonel Bishop, have you been keeping a, a," he had trouble even saying it. "A *blow-up doll* in your cabin?"

"No, I- Oh, crap. Adams, please, kill me now."

"I don't," she still could barely speak. "Don't have a sidearm with me, Sir."

"Williams," I forced myself to look straight at him. "I didn't ask for this, *thing*, it was Skippy's idea."

Just then, my day got even more super awesomely wonderful when Count Smoochula came around the corner to see what was going on. He took one look at what he assumed was a naked girl in the doorway to my cabin, blinked hard in surprise, then looked at the sexbot again, realizing that is what Anastacia had to be. I could see the gears in his head spinning. "Colonel, I presume you have an explanation for, for, *that*," he gestured toward Anastac-

Damn it! Now I was thinking of that thing as a person. "Skippy! *Please* put that thing back in my cabin."

"You don't like her, Joe? I'm kind of hurt."

"In! The! Cabin! Now!"

"Ok, Ok, don't get your panties bunched up," he muttered as Anastacia backed into my cabin and the door slid closed. "Darn it, I spent a lot of time and used up a lot of resources to build that bot, Joe. It would be a tremendous waste to throw her away. If you don't want to bang her, I'll need to repurpose her for something."

"I do not want to bang her!"

"Repurpose?" Chotek did not like the sound of that. "To do what?"

"I don't know yet," Skippy was peeved. "She can't do any heavy maintenance work, and she isn't built for working in vacuum or in hard-radiation environments. Shmaybe she can do easy tasks like changing filters and transporting stuff like laundry."

"She would be touching my clothes?" Chotek's lips pulled back in disgust. "Colonel Bishop has not, how do I say this delicately? *Used* that bot yet?"

"No!" I protested.

"Well, Joe hasn't been with her that you know of, Mister Chotek. Don't worry," the asshole beer can giggled, "those stains will wash right out. Probably. I hope. Damn, that stuff is *sticky*."

Chotek shot me a look with a raised eyebrow and I seriously wanted to kill myself right there.

"Sir, I," I what? I had no idea what to say. "This was a complete surprise to me. I just found out about it."

"Very well," Count Chocula's shocked expression had been replaced by an amused smirk, directed at me. "I am sure you can, handle this situation more discretely in the future?"

"Yes," I mumbled. And then it hit me that a naked sexbot was still in my cabin, and the people standing around were waiting to see what I would do. So I sure as hell could not go in my cabin. "Adams, if anyone needs me, I'll be taking a long walk out an airlock," I turned and began walking toward the nose of the ship. "I won't need a spacesuit."

CHAPTER TWENTY EIGHT

On the second-to-last mission to refuel the *Flying Dutchman*'s depleted tanks, I went along in one of the Condors. Yes, during the time we spent a year flying around the junkyard in the Roach Motel, I had qualified to fly our largest model of dropship, a craft big enough to be considered a small 'ship' like a corvette in some space navies. No, I was not acting as a pilot on this mission, because I still was about the least-skilled pilot aboard the *Flying Dutchman*, and I had no experience flying in the thick atmosphere of a gas giant planet. Because our entire mini-fleet of dropships had gotten continuous use in the junkyard, we had to designate one of each model as a 'hangar queen' to be stripped of parts to keep others flying. Even then, we were taking used parts of one dropship to replace the totally worn-out parts of our flightworthy dropships. That is why we were not taking our Condors as deep as the first time we refueled, we were concerned there had been too much wear and tear on vital components.

We very carefully inspected all the vital components before each flight, so of course it was a tiny little part we barely thought of that bit us in the ass. More about that later.

I was not acting as a pilot, and I was also not annoying the flight crew by sight-seeing, because I was part of the drogue-control crew. The first time we tried Skippy's crazy plan to extract fuel from the atmosphere of a gas giant, we learned someone needed to manually fly the big fuel-collection parachute thingy that was strung between and behind the pair of Condors. Sami Reed had done that by herself the first time, and the intense concentration needed had exhausted her. On subsequent missions, each ship had two pilots, a relief pilot and three people to control the drogue parachute. That was more people's lives being put at risk, but lower overall risk, according to our experienced and very cautious lead pilot, Major Desai. She had flown the first mission on this refueling op and proclaimed it was doable, she liked the fact that we would not be flying as deep in the atmosphere this time.

My participation in the op was so I could appreciate how difficult it was, so another pilot could get rest while I took the responsibility, and because I very much wanted to get off the ship for a while. Anastasia the sexbot was out of my cabin, and back to wherever Skippy had created her- It! Created *it*! Damn it, now the beer can had me thinking of that bot as a person. You would understand if you had seen her, she looked disturbingly realistic, so much that if I hadn't seen her aboard- It! If I hadn't seen it.

Oh, forget it.

Anyway, it was a good idea for me to get off the ship for a while, every time people saw me they couldn't help laughing, and that was hurting productivity. Yeah, yeah, that's the reason I had to get off the ship; I was concerned about the crew not being able to concentrate on work and training. Also, I spent a lot of time hiding in my office or cabin to avoid people. Adams could not even look at me, it got to the point where she was eating at odd times in the galley, to avoid running into me.

And Skippy? That little shithead was fine, never better. He still thought he had done a big favor for me, and hinted he wanted an apology for me rejecting a wonderful gift.

The last star in the universe is going to be a cold, dark cinder before he gets an apology from me.

We had reached target depth, about eighty thousand feet deeper than the first mission of this refueling op had flown. Those ships had reported bad and unpredictable turbulence, and been forced to cut their flights short due to stress on the pilots. I had wholeheartedly agreed with their decision to come back early with their tanks less than seventy percent full. The last thing I needed was pilots pushing themselves too far because of some macho bullshit.

The good news about being eighty thousand feet deeper in the thick, toxic atmosphere was the collection apparatus would siphon fuel faster, and cut our flight duration by an estimated forty minutes. The bad news was the air outside the ships created a lot more resistance so we had to run the engines hotter to compensate. We also had another eighty thousand feet to climb on our return flight. And, you know, we were that much closer to the depth at which the atmospheric pressure would crush our ships. Good times.

We leveled off and spent twenty minutes verifying every system was working perfectly, and that the turbulence was manageable. The air was smoother than the previous flight encountered, but we still hit vicious updrafts and downdrafts that came out of nowhere, Skippy didn't have enough data about this planet to make an accurate model of the air circulation patterns. The pilots of both ships conferred, and agreed they were confident in the delicate operation of deploying the drogue chute, so we got started.

Strung between both ships was a thin cable we had hooked up in orbit, the cable had enough slack and stretching ability that the ships could fly in a loose formation. If that lead cable snapped, we would have to climb back into orbit to attach another, there was no way to do that while the pair of Condors were bouncing around in the atmosphere.

The other Condor started the process of deploying the drogue chute, and when the thing was about three quarters unrolled from its reel, disaster struck. We hit an updraft which was not a problem by itself, but at the same time, we got a visit from the screw-up fairy.

The hatch from which the chute deployed was on the port side of the Condor, and it was a crappy design by the Thuranin. Instead of the door retracting in the hull, it popped out slightly and slid forward. This feature demonstrated that big Condors were designed as spacecraft first, with considerations for flying in atmospheres second. This would not be a problem, except we had used that hatch a lot to deploy safety lines and reel in stuff we wanted from the junkyard. The cables and reels had been inspected, along with the sliding door mechanism, but neither humans nor Skippy's bots took the mechanism completely apart to check on the pin that held the door when it was retracted. That jolt from turbulence was enough to make the worn-out pin snap, the airstream howling past caught the door and it slid back to slam shut. Or, it tried to, because the folded drogue was in the way. The violent impact of the door crushed the tough nanofiber strands of the drogue and for a couple seconds, the spool kept feeding out the folded drogue inside the bay behind the partly-closed door. Then the door, which had slipped off its tracks and gotten bent, broke away. Thirteen meters of drogue got pulled out all at once, pulled hard because the crushed part of the chute was no longer folded and the air yanked on it. The Condor yawed and rolled to port, out of control.

Skippy's homemade fuel collection drogue was designed to break away at both ends if stress on the drogue got too strong. The end attached to my Condor separated as designed to protect us. Unfortunately, the breakaway part on the other Condor's end was still wrapped around the reel, so the reel tore loose and because it didn't fit through the hatchway, it took part of the hull with it.

No longer having a rapidly-unfolding parachute pulling it to port made the Condor snap abruptly to the right, putting the portside engine intake directly into the chaotic path of the flailing drogue. Part of the drogue got sucked into the intake, wrapped itself around the turbine blades, and jerked the solid reel with it. Before the heavy reel shattered the turbine blades and destroyed that engine, the drogue whipped over and around the hull, the unravelling end being pulled into the starboard engine.

The portside engine had zero chance to survive even before the reel came crashing into it at supersonic speed, but the starboard engine was lucky. Either the screw-up fairy missed a golden opportunity, or she wanted to prolong her mischief, because the portside engine survived long enough for its rotating blades to pull back on the drogue. The end that had whipped over the top of the fuselage was already playing havoc with turbine blades on the starboard side, so the lucky part was the drogue was tugged in two directions and tore apart, with the break happening on the starboard side. Only six meters of drogue was ingested by the starboard engine, snapping off or bending less than twenty percent of those turbine blades.

That Condor began dropping, unable to maintain altitude on one damaged engine.

"What the-" I shut up because answering questions from me would distract the pilots from what they needed to be doing: flying the aircraft. There was one being who boasted a near-infinite capacity to multi-task, so I called that asshole beer can. "Skippy, what is-"

Instead of the familiar arrogant tone of Skippy the Not-Quite-as-Awesome-As-He-Thinks-He-Is, there was a scratchy recording of a bland female voice. "Your call is important to us. Please hold and we will answer your call in the order it was received. Thank you for your patience."

I stared at my zPhone in disbelief. "What the F- *Skippy*! Answer me right now, dammit!"

"Busy, Joe. Super-*duper* busy." He actually sounded distracted.

"You are never too busy to bug the shit out of me when *you* want to talk. Sing it if you want to, but I need a SITREP right now."

"Sing it? Oooooh, that is a *great*-"

"No, it is a *terrible* idea. What the hell is going on?"

"Oh for- *UGH. Fine.* It is a fluid situation, Joe, more data is coming in every nanosecond. If you can wait a-"

"Bad news is not like wine, it does not get better with age."

"That is a good point. Ok, Lieutenant Reed's Condor has suffered the loss of one engine, and the other is badly damaged. It is losing altitude."

It took twenty minutes before we had enough info to fully understand the situation, and for Lt. Reed to get enough control of her ship that she could talk to us. "Engine Two is gone. It shredded and tore lose, damaged the tail cone as it went. There is damage to the portside hull, we've lost sensors to see how bad it is, we can tell parts of the outer skin are peeling away." She took a pause for breath, and when she spoke, her voice was dead calm, relaying purely the facts with no hint of her inner emotions. "Engine One is running at forty percent power, we tried higher power settings, but the vibration caused the engine controller to throttle back."

"Understood, Fireball," I used her callsign, unaware that she was not fond of that pilot nickname. "We show you descending at two hundred meters per second, can you confirm?" It was a stupid question but I had to confirm the datalink was accurate.

"Confirmed," this time there was a catch in her voice. "We can't lighten load, there's nothing to dump overboard. As we get deeper in the atmosphere, I will need to reduce airspeed to reduce stress on the hull. That will increase our sink rate."

"Under, uh, stood." Shit, that time my voice nearly cracked.

"Colonel?" She asked.

"Yes?"

"This would be a *really* good time for a monkey-brained idea."

Lieutenant Samantha 'Sami' Reed was spot-on that only a crazy idea could rescue her ship and crew. Her Condor was sinking so fast, there was no time for a rescue attempt from the *Dutchman*, we needed to do it with our ship and what we had on board. I asked Porter, our lead pilot, for ideas and he and his team came up with a couple off-the-wall suggestions that were not quite crazy enough to work. We could not attach a line to the stricken ship and winch the crew across the gap. We could not clamp onto the other Condor with ours, the landing skids had no way to attach to the smooth hull of another dropship. Porter then got excited when he remembered an incident during the Korean war, and another during Vietnam, when one fighter jet pushed a damaged fighter that had lost power. In Korea, the pilot stuck his fighter's nose cone up the crippled jet's tailpipe and pushed it beyond enemy territory, in Vietnam the pilot used the windshield of his Phantom jet to push against the tailhook of another Phantom.

Those ideas were not practical for our situation, but they did get me thinking. First, Porter made me realize that plenty of humans got wild-ass ideas when they were needed, and it was time for me to stop screwing around and step up my game. Second, he reminded me that dropships had something like a tailhook, they all were equipped with some kind of mechanism that could catch on netting in a docking bay for emergency recovery. Sometimes in combat, a dropship needed to be taken aboard quickly and there was no time for gentle and precise flying. Instead, the dropship aimed at the open docking bay and flew in, trusting suspensor fields to slow it down and catch it. In my pilot training, I had practiced that maneuver a dozen times, it was nerve-wracking to fly toward an open docking bay, seeing the back wall approaching way too fast and hoping the mysterious invisible technology of suspensor fields will work correctly.

Because it would be foolish to rely on one system to prevent a crash, suspensor fields aboard a Thuranin ship had a backup; netting stretched across the open bay door. This netting was a tough and smart nanofiber that sensed the nose of an incoming dropship and created an opening so the nose didn't crumple on impact. The rest of the netting caught the wings, engine nacelles and most important, the hooks. Just behind the engines were hooks, either four or six of them depending on the model of dropship. These hooks deployed in a star pattern to catch the netting and bring the dropship to a halt before it damaged the mothership. A 'crash-landing' as we called it was something we only practiced in the simulator for a very good reason: the crash-landing maneuver was rough on biological beings like humans. Supposedly, a properly strapped-in crew of a dropship would survive a crash-landing, but it wasn't something we wanted people to experience unless they absolutely had to.

The reason I mentioned emergency docking procedures was not for suspensor fields or nanofiber crash netting, it was for the hooks. Even one of those hooks could stop the mass of a dropship traveling up to thirty meters per second, that was a seriously strong hook. The strength of those hooks is why I traded my flightsuit for a hardshell Kristang powered armor suit.

"Joe, are you sure about this?"

"Skippy," I gave a somewhat shaky thumbs up sign to the pilots helping me prep the suit. "If I was sure about doing this, I wouldn't have asked you to recheck your numbers a half-dozen times. Were you wrong?"

"No, but that is not the point. My calculations confirmed the arrestor hooks of your ship are strong enough, that the cables you are using are strong enough, and that the nose landing gear of the other Condor is strong enough. If you can get a cable attached from your hooks to the other ship's nose gear, you will be able to tow it up into orbit. Probably. Unless you run into bad turbulence. Or the pilots lack the skill to-"

"The pilots are going to do just fine, Skippy."

"We'll see about that, since none of the pilots have done this before, trained for it, or even thought about it. If Captain Porter in the lead ship, or Lieutenant Reed in the trailing ship, are not able to fly *very* smoothly, their actions could set up a vibration in the cable that could-"

"You told me this super-duper high-tech cable is smart, it has some sort of self-correcting thingy that can help steer it and dampen vibrations."

"Yes, *Ugh*," he gave an exasperated sigh. "The cable can make adjustments to a certain point. After that, it gets dicey. Anyway, you are missing the point as usual. I am not worried about the equipment or the pilots' skill. I am worried about *you*, dumdum!"

"Skippy," I waved to the pilots and closed the airlock door behind me, "thank you. It's nice to know that you care-"

"Oh. I meant I am worried you will screw this up and get a bunch of people killed, but let's go with the caring thing if you like."

"*Why* are you such an asshole?"

"Hey! I wouldn't have to worry at all if you weren't such a dumb monkey. This is all your fault anyway."

"*Me?*" The airlock finished cycling and I opened the outer door into the back ramp area of the Condor, hooking a safety line onto my belt. "*You* designed and built that crappy fuel drogue."

"And *you* are a trouble magnet. This is the first time you've been on a refueling mission, *and* the first time we have had a problem. Coincidence? I don't think so. Totally your fault. We should never have- Oh, dammit Joe." His voice broke and he was blubbering. "If something bad happens to you, I don't, I don't know what I will do."

"Jeez, Skippy," now I was finding it hard to talk. "I would miss you too. It's good to-"

"I mean, I *do* know what I will do; I'll train another monkey to replace you. But, damn what a pain in the *ass* that will be."

"Skippy?" I shook my head ruefully. "Can you save your heartwarming motivational talk for after I'm aboard the *Dutchman*? I'm going to be kinda busy."

I was flying feet-first behind the lead Condor, being literally jerked around at the end of a cable that was attached to my legs. Because I needed to see and grab hold of the nose gear of the trailing ship, I had to be facing backwards. The only way I could steer was with my arms, it was like skydiving backwards. To make the experience extra super-duper fun and easy for everyone, Reed's Condor was now sinking at three hundred meters per minute and that rate was accelerating. At the controls of our ship, Porter had to match Reed's sink rate. He also had to fly above her altitude, with my weight making the cable droop down. Porter also had to adjust to turbulence and try to think how an up or down draft would affect the trailing ship. For her part, Reed could not simply watch the lead ship and adjust, she had to anticipate Porter's moves.

All I had to do was get whipped around on the end of a cable, find Reed's Condor, bang into it without killing myself and loop the cable around the front landing gear.

If you want to visualize what I was doing, rent one of the 'Airport' disaster movies, I think it was 'Airport 75' or maybe 'Airport 78'. Whatever. It's the one with the actor who played Jesus in an old movie. No, that's not right, maybe he played John the Baptist. I know it wasn't John the Methodist or John the Presbyterian. Wait, I got it! He played Moses. I remember that because we were living in Boston when that movie came on TV, and during the scene when Moses parts the Red Sea, my father said that if Moses wanted a real challenge, he could try parting Boston traffic during rush hour.

Anyway, in that 'Airport' movie, the actor needs to go from an airplane into a big jetliner to fly it, because the pilots of the jetliner are dead. He is dangling on the end of a cable and he somehow has to fit through a broken windshield, he gets his legs in and the flight attendants pull him into the cockpit.

My point is, that guy had it easy. It was a clear day so he could see what he was doing, whereas I was flying through clouds of hydrogen sulfide and other nasty toxic stuff, and I couldn't see a damned thing without the synthetic vision provided by my suit sensors. He had help while I was by myself. Also, the aircraft I was trying to hook onto wasn't flying nice and level on autopilot, it was sinking at an increasing rate. The force of gravity on me was seventeen percent greater than on Earth, and the lower we dropped, the greater the effect of gravity would be. Ok, yes, you there Mr. Nerdface in the back with your hand up because you are *so* smart, I know that before the gravity becomes a big problem we would have fallen so deep the atmospheric pressure would crush the Condor, but the extra gravity was already making it more difficult for me to judge my aim. Imagine you are shooting free throws in gravity that is seventeen percent higher than normal. You have probably shot thousands of free throws in normal gravity, and your eye-hand coordination, your reflexes and your muscle memory are all set up for normal gravity. Suddenly, you have to put a bit more effort into shooting the ball, and the arc it follows is steeper than you expect. It was like that as I awkwardly tried to steer myself at the end of the cable.

My first attempt to contact the target was almost a disaster, I came in from the right, overcorrected and was about to smack into the hull hard enough to dent it and kill me. Fortunately for me, the crew aboard the lead Condor recognized the danger and reeled in the cable enough for me to zip past the nose so fast it was a blur. "Sorry!" I called out as I tried to swing back to the center.

"No problem, Colonel," Reed assured me. "Take your time out there."

"Thanks, I-"

"Not *too* much time, Sir."

"Affirmative." After my near-disaster, we kept the cable short enough that I couldn't hit anything, and I concentrated on keeping myself centered. The twelfth attempt was going well enough for me to call for more cable. I was below and in front of the target and we had gotten lucky with the turbulence. The air was smooth, I had gotten better at free-flying on the end of the cable. We tried letting out the cable so I could slip under the Condor's nose, it was tricky because the air pattern close to the ship was different and it pushed me away. "Ok, I know how to do it now," I advised after the crew retracted the cable again. For the first time since I stumbled out the back ramp of my Condor, I was confident this crazy scheme might actually work. Until then, truthfully, I had launched this rescue operation more because I felt we had to do something than expecting we could save the crew of that crippled ship. "Next time, let the cable out-"

The trailing Condor dropped like a rock in front of me, sinking so quickly it was now below me. "Reed? What happened? Reed?"

"Joe," Skippy's voice broke in. "Lieutenant Reed is extremely busy, she just lost three more fan blades and vibration in the turbine was so bad, she had to reduce throttle to twelve percent. No, now she has gone to seven percent."

"Seven? Shit, that's practically idling." Reed's Condor had sunk almost below range of my suit's sensors and my synthetic vision switched over to a feed from the lead ship. "Porter! Follow her, we can't lose her."

"Colonel, this is problematic," Porter responded and I could feel myself dropping faster. "The target is now falling at nineteen hundred meters per minute. The air resistance on you prevents you from falling that fast."

Shit. He was right, I hadn't thought of that. At the end of the cable, I was now above the lead Condor, as it was sinking faster than I was. "Screw this," I muttered to myself. I had been flying in a belly-down position, now I tucked into a head-down posture. My speed picking up rapidly and soon I was at the level of the lead ship, then dropping below again. "More cable," I ordered.

"Joe, while this is a heroic action, it-"

"Nothing heroic about it, Skippy. I can always get reeled back in and fly safely up to the Dutchman."

"My point, dumdum, is that the only way you can fall quickly enough to catch Reed's ship is to fly in head-down position. In that position, you can't fly under her ship and contact the landing gear."

Shit. Double shit! He was right. I hadn't thought of that either. Damn, I was a total freakin' moron, what the hell was wrong with me? Why couldn't I think ahead and- "Reed! Fireball!"

"Here, Colonel. The turbine is tearing itself apart, I can't-"

"I know. Invert! Fly upside down!"

There was the slightest hesitation, then a surprised "Sir?"

"I'm coming in above you and I can't get to the landing gear from here. So, flip over."

"Oh. Got it. This thing won't fall any faster upside down."

She did it. "Porter, I need-"

"Doing it now, Colonel," he answered before I could finish because he had excellent situational awareness and knew what I planned to do. "Sink rate is now twenty three hundred meters per minute."

Crap. In the thick air, I had trouble plummeting that fast, even tucked in a head-down position. The belly of the upside-down Condor approached with agonizing slowness while I fretted I was too late. Then it loomed in front of me and I had to frantically roll upright onto my belly and spread my arms to slow down. In my third consecutive dumbass move, I had failed to consider the falling Condor would create a pocket of air above it. When I fell into that shadow, I dropped like a rock. Nothing I could do could slow me down quickly enough, I belly-flopped onto the Condor's belly and hit hard, my suit absorbing much of the shock with airbags inflating inside to keep me from being knocked unconscious. "I'm Ok, I'm Ok," I wheezed, out of breath. The rebound had me hitting again and I was sliding down over the side, flailing my arms and legs to stop my fall.

Listen, Ok, yes, it was pure luck that one of my arms wrapped around the landing gear. I hadn't even seen the thing. But when the cable end automatically looped several times around the gear and the nanofibers basically welded the cable securely in place, there was a triumphant whoop from the lead ship's crew. Followed by grateful and excited shouting from Reed and her crew.

"You did it! Colonel! You did it! Thank you thank you thank you!" Reed gushed.

Hey, no way could I tell anyone it was an accident that I accomplished the mission, right? "No problem, Reed, any time. Porter, you got her?"

"Cable is secure, Colonel, but now we have another problem. The computer is telling me that to tow the other ship, I need an airspeed that will overstress the cable and cause it to snap."

Breaking my dumb-ass pattern, I had an answer to that dilemma. "Forget airspeed, Porter. Both the Condors are empty. Your thrust-to-weight ratio is plenty for a pure vertical ascent, even carrying another ship. Reduce your airspeed and lift us straight up. When we clear the atmosphere, you can flatten our course and build up speed to get us into a stable orbit."

"Sir? That's not-"

Skippy broke in again. "Captain Porter, Joe is correct. The Pilot's Operating Handbook for the Condor will tell you that maneuver is impossible, because the Thuranin who programed the flight control system never considered a wild-ass stunt like this. But it *can* be done, I just uploaded new software into your computer."

"Huh," was all Porter said in response.

"Apparently, the Thuranin who designed that dropship never met an ignorant monkey, hee hee," Skippy chuckled.

"Colonel, I am ashamed I didn't think of that," Porter apologized.

"Don't be," I replied as I felt the Condor I was attached to slowing, with the cable going taught. Our rate of descent was being cancelled. "When I started flight training, Major Desai told me my best asset was my total lack of experience, I had no ingrained habits to unlearn. You naturally think of lift in terms of airspeed."

"Yes, Sir," Porter agreed. "But I won't do *that* again. Rate of descent is now zero, commencing climb."

With Reed's Condor dangling from its nose on the end of a cable, she had to use thrusters to stop us from spinning like a top. We were climbing, and at first all was going according to plan. Then, as our rate of climb increased, I started getting bashed against the hull. It was getting rough. "Hey, Porter, I appreciate the enthusiasm, but slow down, I'm getting tenderized here."

"Colonel, we don't have the fuel for that. If I go any slower, we won't make orbit. I can't fly vertically all the way up," he announced.

"Shit," I grunted from a particularly hard rap against the Condor's belly. "This is a problem."

"Joe," Skippy's voice sounded worried. "Captain Porter is correct; the fuel state is growing critical. Climbing at such a steep angle is consuming fuel rapidly."

"If we don't slow down," I bashed my helmet again, and was seeing stars in my vision. "I'm going to be in very big trouble out here."

"Joe," Skippy scolded me. "I am very disappointed in you. You rescued Lieutenant Reed's crew, but now your life is in danger because of a little breeze?"

"It is not a *little* breeze, Skippy.

Reed made a suggestion. "If I open a side door, could you get to it?"

"No way," I reported unhappily. "It is too far-"

"Sir?" She asked after I was silent for a long moment.

"Give me a minute here, I'm thinking. Uh, hey! Open your main landing gear doors, Reed."

"Good idea, Sir," she agreed with enthusiasm.

It was not easy getting to one of the main landing gear, because the airstream wanted to keep me in the center of the Condor's belly, but Reed helped by skillfully and gently tilting her Condor by using thrusters, keeping a watchful eye she did not overstress the cable. With her help, I slid back and grabbed onto one of the sturdy main landing gear, then tucked myself into the bay where the gear normally rested in flight. "I'm in. Let's be clear about something, Fireball. Do *NOT* retract this landing gear, understood?"

With me mostly protected from the screeching airstream, we climbed out of the atmosphere and into a low orbit. Once there, the crew and I transferred to Porter's ship, and I made a quick decision to discard the damaged Condor. We could have tried bringing the *Dutchman* down to rendezvous with us, but at low altitude she could not jump away in case we got ambushed, and the crippled ship would have struggled to get into a docking bay on thrusters alone. So, we remotely fired nose thrusters to slow it down, and by the time we were safely aboard our fine ship, the broken Condor was burning up in the thick atmosphere.

The fuel collection op ended with the *Dutchman*'s tanks only sixty-three percent full and that worried me, but it was enough to get us to Earth with a comfortable reserve. So, we considered ourselves lucky to escape without loss of life, and jumped away to our next dangerous adventure.

CHAPTER TWENTY NINE

Our jump into the Paradise system was interesting, and by 'interesting' I mean '*batshit crazy*'. Once we got deep into the star system, Skippy could retake control of the Ruhar sensor network and conceal our presence from the hamster fleet, but we couldn't prevent them from detecting the gamma ray burst of our inbound jump, so we had to get creative.

Normally, we would jump in no closer than the system's Oort cloud and travel to Paradise the slow way through normal space, but on this mission we didn't have time, so we needed to jump directly into the inner system. We had three pieces of luck going for us. First, after the nice pleasant habitable planet of Paradise, the next planet outward from the star was a smallish gas giant. This world is a grayish-blue ball of gas like Neptune but smaller, and the Ruhar name for it was 'Notol'. Because there was a big gas giant farther out in the system, and that gas giant had plenty of moons with useful raw materials like metals, the Ruhar fleet used the big planet as a refueling station and they were setting up ship servicing facilities there. This means Notol was not of much use to the fleet, so they did not have any facilities there.

The second piece of good luck was at the time we had to jump in, Notol was just over one month away from its closest approach to Paradise, while the big gas giant with its refueling station was on the other side of the star. We could jump in on the far side of Notol and its bulk would shield our gamma rays from being seen by sensors orbiting Paradise.

Unfortunately, Skippy knew the Ruhar fleet had a deep-space sensor platform farther out from Notol, which happened to be in position to get a clear view of our inbound gamma ray burst. Thus, the batshit crazy stunt we had to use.

Notol has eighteen moons, most of them asteroids that got captured by the planet's gravity. Only four of those moons were big enough for their own gravity to make them spherical, and our third piece of luck was one of these moons was on the side of Notol toward the deep-space sensor platform. "Are you sure about this, Skippy?" I asked while my hands dug into the armrests of the command chair. "You checked your math twice, three times?"

"I checked the math a billion times, Joe, even though this math is so simple even you could do it. No, wait, what am I saying? Nothing is *that* simple. Anywho, I got this Joe. Trust. The. Awesomeness."

"Has this particular type of awesomeness ever been done before?"

"Ever? Yes, it is not super-duper uncommon, but this is the first time it has ever been attempted by a star carrier that I know of."

"Two things, Skippy. You using the word 'attempted' is not making me overflow with confidence. And technically, our rebuilt Frankenship is no longer a star carrier."

"Oof, Ok, Mr. Smartypants. If you want to have a technicality throwdown with me, it is *on*, homeboy. I used the word 'attempted' to be totally open and accurate with you, because no ship like this has ever performed this exact maneuver, so we won't know if it can be done until we try it, you big jerkface. Also, although the *Flying Dutchman* does not look like a star carrier, with the shortened spine and lack of docking hardpoints, the structure and frame are still very much that of a star carrier. Compared to a real warship, the *Dutchman* is spindly and flimsy, so the-"

"*This* is you making me overflow with confidence?" I asked with a nervous glance at the jump countdown timer.

"Um, maybe I should have said 'strong and robust' instead of 'spindly and flimsy'?"

"Yeah! See, that's how you-"

"Although me saying that would have been *total* bullshit," he chuckled. "Considering the frayed layers of used duct tape holding this ship together, 'flimsy' is being generous. Too late for second thoughts now, Joe. Jump in two, one, holdmybeer."

Maybe jumping anywhere in our Frankenship was crazy, but the truly batshit part was *where* we jumped. You have to understand, two of Notol's moons were big enough to have thin atmospheres, including the moon we used as cover. The jump Skippy plotted had us emerging *inside* the upper layer of the moon's atmosphere, on the side of the moon facing the planet. The bulk of the planet shielded our gamma ray burst from being seen on Paradise, and the moon concealed us from the deep-space sensors. The complication was that deep-space sensor platform would have detected gamma rays being reflected off the atmosphere of the planet, which is why we pulled the crazy stunt of coming out of a jump wormhole so close to the moon I could have leaned out an airlock and touched the damned thing.

"Skippy!" I grunted from being flung forward against the straps as the very un-aerodynamic *Flying Dutchman* bored a hole through the thin clouds of nitrogen and sulphur dioxide. Before we jumped, we had accelerated the ship to beyond the escape velocity of the moon, so even if our engines failed, we could coast through the thin upper atmosphere and safely away from the rocky surface. Emerging into the air, the ship's forward hull slammed into it like a brick wall. Star carriers were not designed to operate in the gravity well of a star system, and they sure as hell were never intended to fly like a gosh-darned dropship. Skippy had the forward defense shields on full power and still there were parts flaking and peeling off the front part of the ship. My original thought was to have the ship come out of the jump flying backwards since jump physics didn't care about the ship's orientation in relation to the event horizon, but Skippy convinced me most of the critical systems aboard the ship were in the aft section. If we sustained significant damage to the forward hull, that might make living aboard the ship uncomfortable for meatsacks but we could still generate power, fly and jump. If the aft section were damaged, it might be adios muchachos for all of us.

"*Whoooo-hooo!* Ride 'em cowboy!" The beer can whooped excitedly. "Yee-ha!"

"Sir, we've lost several of the portside nose thrusters!" Desai warned. "She's turning and we can't stop the yaw."

"If she turns sideways to the air stream-" Porter added from the copilot couch.

"Yeah, yeah, don't get so excited," Skippy huffed. "Adjusting shields to compensate. We're good, the revised shield configuration is reversing the yaw. Yup, no problem. Oh dammit, there go two of the belly nose thrusters. I mean, there they *go*," he announced as we all felt a bump, "we just kinda lost a section of hull plating. Oh, what the hell, we're almost out of the atmosphere now."

It was a white-knuckle thirty seconds before Desai reported aerodynamic drag was essentially zero. "We made it, Sir," there was a slight flutter to her voice. "Commencing first course correction."

I saw her share a private thumbs up with Porter, as they turned the ship to skim the rim of the gas giant planet. Skim, not touch. To gain speed and get the ship turned on course toward Paradise, we had to slingshot around Notol, using its gravity well to gain free velocity.

"Stealth field status?" I asked to anyone who had that data.

"It's fine, Joe," Skippy answered peevishly. "Jeez Louise, that info is right on the main display."

"No, Your Supreme Assholeness, the main display shows the status of the stealth field generators, and the density and shape of the field surrounding the ship. It does not, as *you* reminded me more than once, indicate how effective our stealth capability is. The ship could be trailing a stream of ionized particles from our passage through the atmosphere, which would point straight toward the ship like a giant neon arrow."

"Ugh," Skippy was supremely disgusted. "This is what I get for trying to explain technology to a monkey. Yes, fine, Mr. Nerdface, you are correct. How the hell did you get so smart?"

I didn't mention that Dr. Friedlander had warned me about the possibility of an ion trail after we came out of the atmosphere. "Answer the question, please."

"Ok, *fine*. No, we are not trailing a line of ionized gas. We *would* be, but I adjusted the shield frequency to de-ionize the gas particles as we passed through, as yet another sterling example of my awesomeness. Our stealth is effective, more effective than any other ship in this backwater star system, that's for sure. Eventually, Ruhar sensors will detect an anomalous disturbance in the moon's atmosphere but they will attribute it to volcanic activity, then they will forget about it because nobody cares. Are you happy now?"

"Happy enough. Is the first package of missiles ready?"

"All tubes loaded and ready," Major Simms reported from the CIC.

"Launch and reload. Then keep going. We need a lot of birds in flight for this op."

Our plan relied on a lot of missiles, but that was Ok because we had plenty aboard. We had so many missiles there wasn't enough space in the ship's magazines to store them, so we moved stuff around to empty out cargo bays and stuff missiles in there. Yes, if the ship took a hit to one of those poorly-protected cargo bays, the ship would go 'Boom' in a big way, but we'd be screwed if we took a direct hit anywhere so as Skippy said cheerily, there really was no downside.

Our surplus of missiles came from the junkyard of shattered ships floating around the Roach Motel. Yes, all these missiles were obsolete and they didn't all come with fancy options like functional warheads, sensors and guidance systems, but we didn't always need those. Skippy had been able to cobble together a Frankenstein assortment of parts to create sensors and guidance systems, and for our initial mission in the Paradise system, we did not need warheads. The first volleys of missiles did not need warheads, they only needed speed and stealth, for where their explosive charges used to be, they each carried one end of a microwormhole.

The purpose of that first cluster of missiles was to provide remote sensors, far from the ship. We knew roughly where the Kristang ship was likely to be, or Skippy had the three most likely locations calculated, but we could not get the *Dutchman* there fast enough without violating stealth, and we needed to know *exactly* where that damned ship was. Our missiles could get the microwormholes in position far more quickly than the ship could have, but they still took a long time to fly to the target area, and then Skippy the Once-Again-Magnificent would have to slowly and painstakingly begin the process of passively scanning a still-huge region of space for one small and stealthy ship.

While our cloud of missiles flew onward, we had a movie night in the galley. Before the movie, we were showing and mostly laughing at photos people took during our time on Gingerbread. Our time there now seemed to be an idyllic year-long vacation in our rose-colored nostalgia glasses, because we had escaped from the Roach Motel and were hopefully going home soon. Everything was going great until Skippy began inserting random images that were definitely not from Gingerbread.

Like the photo from Major Simms' military ID card.

"No! Don't!" Simms implored me but the image was already there on the screen. "It's a horrible photo of- Oh, crap."

It was a bad picture of her, a terrible picture, but come on, nobody likes the way they look on a driver's license or ID card. It looked like the photo was taken with a fisheye lens, it made Simms' face look too big and round and her forehead too high. I tried to keep a straight face, unfortunately, Lauren Poole in the back of the galley slapped the table, unable to control herself. "You look like a *potato* with a hairpiece."

OMG I never laughed so hard in my life, and Gunny Adams had trouble catching her breath. Simms' face turned bright red before she also joined in the laughter. People had tears running down their cheeks and one of the British team fell off his chair. When I was able to talk again, I tried to make up for the insult to our logistics officer. Into my zPhone, I whispered "Skippy, pull up the photo from my driver's license."

Damn, that picture was awful. I had to sneeze just as the grumpy witch at the DMV took the photo, and she refused to give me a do-over. So my mouth is gaping open, my nose is wrinkled and my eyes are half-closed. I hated that stupid photo that followed me around the world and now to the stars. Although, this made me smile while the crowd had a good laugh at my expense, seeing the license photo reminded me that my Maine driver's license had expired by now. If we ever got back to Earth, I would need to renew my license and get a new photo! That would be my chance to- Oh, crap, that wasn't going to work. No matter how careful I was to not look like an idiot when the DMV took my photo, a certain asshole beer can would hack into the system and alter the image. I'd be lucky if I didn't look like a brain-damaged chimpanzee.

"Hey, Your Magnificence, any luck yet?" I asked while stifling a yawn. It was going to be a long night, and a long couple days, even if we did get super lucky.

"What? No, you moron, the first six microwormholes just got into position. I haven't even had time to adjust the sensors for local background solar particle density and radiation levels."

"Ok, sorry, Skip, you know us monkeys can get-"

"Although, hmm, *something* out there is leaking radioactive plasma. Yup! Bingo! We have a Kristang ship, it passed through recently, based on decay of the plasma. Unfortunately, the microwormhole that detected the particle trail flew through the trail side to side, so I can't use that microwormhole to track the ship. Oh, well, I can use it to passively scan for medium-range sensor data, and to coordinate the whole squadron. In fact, hmm, we are in a bit of luck. The particle density of the trail the ship is leaving behind is so thick, I can use a pair of missiles to track it, without releasing their microwormhole kernels from containment. Bonus, dude."

What Skippy meant was when microwormholes were being carried by missiles at high acceleration, that wormhole was only a kernel, a seed of the wormhole Skippy would open. The near end was in one of our cargo bays, with the far end encased in a magnetic force field inside the missile's forward shroud. So long as that magnetic field held the kernel within its boundaries, the missile could maneuver almost at combat acceleration, and the microwormhole would remain intact and ready for use. But to activate the microwormhole, it needed to be released from containment, expelled from the missile's shroud, and expanded. At that point, the missile was discarded and the microwormhole could be moved only very slowly and gently. Skippy could use the wormhole as a real-time sensor platform, with no annoyingly slow speed-of-light lag back to the ship. He could send signals though the tiny wormholes, and as we demonstrated in the skies above Newark, we could shoot a maser beam through it, although transmitting that much power through the spacetime wrinkle caused the wormhole to collapse.

Our missiles were mostly Thuranin gear, with a few from the Jeraptha and even three from the wreckage of a Rindhalu starship. If you got excited about us getting access to Rindhalu tech, then prepare to be bitterly disappointed, because those three spider missiles were over eight hundred thousand years old, and were obsolete junk even compared to the obsolete Thuranin weapons we recovered from the Roach Motel junkyard. Anyway, it didn't matter much what type of missile we used, because all we needed were their propulsion modules and stealth fields. The motors were pretty much original in most cases, with Skippy performing only minor tweaks, but he seriously upgraded their stealth capability so they were ready for the delicate task they needed to perform.

"The ship is where you expected it to be?" I was puzzled while watching the main bridge display. The pair of missiles Skippy had sent weaving back and forth to follow the particle trail left by the unseen ship, were now headed away from the cluster of meteors where we thought the ship would be hiding. He had another pair of missiles flying in the opposite direction, flying a wider pattern. The worst part was, the *Flying Dutchman* was close to the meteor cluster, and out of position to intercept the enemy ship.

"Uh, no," the beer can admitted. "That is odd, but not entirely outside the scope of my expectations."

"What?" I jabbed a finger at the display. "The particle trail is nowhere close to that meteor shower, and those missiles are getting farther away every second."

"Yes, Joe, *duh*. The particle trail goes in two directions, I have the first pair of missiles flying toward where the trail is denser and the decay of radioactive elements indicates the particles were expelled from the ship more recently. That end of the trail leads to the ship. The other end tells me where the ship flew in the past, and by data from the other two missiles, I know the ship's course came within twenty thousand kilometers of the meteor shower. The ship would have avoided the cluster of meteors because its passage through such a dense cloud of rocks would have compromised the ship's stealth."

"Oh, crap," I groaned as Chang expressed the same sentiment in the CIC. "The Keepers have already been deployed in aeroshells? Damn it, no way can we capture them now, they'll be spread out all over the freakin' sky!"

"Don't be so hasty, Joe," Skippy's voice was a soothing tone he rarely used. "Yes, it does not make sense for the Kristang to fly close to the meteor cluster more than once, but there are other possibilities to consider. First, there may be more than one enemy ship involved."

"What? You told us-"

"I told you what the data indicated. If that data was incomplete, or the Kristang changed their plans, I would not know about that, would I?" He huffed, annoyed at me. "This is supposed to be a secret operation by the Kristang, it's not like I was able to get details on their evening news feed, you know?"

"Sorry, Skippy."

"Joe, the proper time to be sorry is when you get out of bed in the morning and realize you are still an ignorant monkey, not *after* you say something stupid to piss me off. Nonetheless, as I am humbly generous with my awesomeness, your apology is accepted. Getting back to the subject after you so rudely interrupted me, it is possible the ship whose trail I detected is flying recon, to scout ahead for a ship carrying the Keepers. I have other missiles scanning for a second ship now. However, I think it is much more likely there is only a single ship involved, and that it sent out one or more dropships as it approached the meteor cluster. That scenario makes much more sense than the idea of the Kristang devoting more than one ship to this operation. Having more ships involved increases the expense, and increases the odds of the Ruhar detecting the Kristang presence in the Paradise system. Also, properly deploying the aeroshells requires the Keepers to already be inside the meteor cluster when they are sent out, and as I stated, maneuvering a starship inside such a high-density cluster of rocks is tricky. Using dropships makes much more sense."

"Ok," I exchanged a thumbs up with Chang. "I wish you had told us that before, but, whatever. Can you scan the meteor cluster for dropships?"

"Doing that now, Joe. Please understand that is a large area generously sprinkled with dust and rocks and other crap, so it is not easy to find one or two stealthed dropships in there. Kristang dropships do not use fusion reactors for power, so there is not a nice trail of elements made radioactive by high-energy neutron activation, such as the molten lithium the Kristang typically use as a coolant medium on their smaller ships."

"Oh, yeah, of course. That's what I was going to say, or, you know, some other nerdy shit like that."

"Nerdy? Joe, I, *ugh*. Oof, I can't even- Oh, forget it. You should think of reactor-powered starships as leaving a trail of sparkly magic fairy dust behind them."

Since my understanding of fusion power was sadly lacking, I dropped the subject. "If it is so super-duper difficult, how do you plan to find any dropships in there?"

"Working on it, Joe, working on it. You could help tremendously by shutting your pie hole for a moment and let the adults handle this. The first pair of missiles is now picking up trace amounts of samarium cobalt that has been embrittled by heavy neutron bombardment, which makes me certain of two things. First, samarium cobalt is used in secondary magnetic plasma containment systems aboard older Kristang ships, so the particle trail is absolutely from a small lizard warship such as a frigate or destroyer. Any larger capital ship would have had its containment system overhauled and upgraded by now. Second, the missiles are getting close enough to the target ship that I can now release one of the microwormholes for scanning. I'm going to be busy, so kindly shut up for a minute."

When Skippy said 'close' and then 'for a minute', I expected he would nail the location of the enemy ship quickly, like within ten minutes. Instead, it took forty seven minutes, during which time I sat quietly but growing more stressed with every second that passed. Finally, when I was about to go crazy from waiting and doing nothing, the beer can spoke. "Got it! That ship is an old *Morta*-class destroyer, when I say old I mean the last *Morta*-class left the shipyard over five hundred years ago. Damn, no wonder it is leaving a trail of radioactive particles behind like breadcrumbs. Wait, wait, give me another moment and I will have that ship positively identified. Bingo! It is the '*Final Crushing Blow to the Enemy's Spirit*'. We can probably call it the '*Spirit*' for short."

"Great."

"You said 'great' but your tone was not as thrilled as it should be, Joe," Skippy sniffed, no doubt miffed that I missed the opportunity to once again praise his magnificent awesomeness.

"I would be more thrilled if we could simply put a missile up that ship's ass and then jump out of here. Without knowing if the Keepers are still aboard, we can't take any action against that ship, damn it!"

"It is a frustrating dilemma for sure, Joe."

"Do you have any suggestions? Even if we are able to locate dropships in that meteor cloud, we can't hit them either until we know whether they have deployed the Keepers in aeroshells. Crap, this is getting way too complicated. I would love to notify the Ruhar fleet and let them handle the problem, but we can't give away the secret that humans are flying around in a pirate starship."

"I do have an idea, Joe. Sit back, relax, and behold the awesomeness! Or, go get some popcorn or coffee or something, it will be a while before we get to the awesomeness part."

'A while' in Skippy's estimate meant more than five freakin' hours in meatsack time. Ok, sure, what he was doing was a very delicate operation and we couldn't rush it without revealing our presence and spooking the *Spirit* into jumping away. I knew that, I understood that, I also hated it.

The awesome thing he did required two microwormholes. The first one, released from its carrier missile, provided sensor data to Skippy so he could guide the other missile. He knew roughly where the target ship was, but 'roughly' was a sphere seventy thousand kilometers in diameter and that was way too imprecise for his purpose. He was able to gently steer the microwormhole so the search area was between him and the star, which allowed him a good view of the light-bending effect of the enemy stealth field. Once he saw the characteristic ripple distortion of a poor-quality Kristang stealth field, he was able to map the field and estimate its coverage and frequency. The field had several weak points, he programmed the missile to slowly and carefully approach the enemy, tuning the missile's stealth field to match that generated by the *Spirit*. It slid inside the field and would have become lost to us, except of course Skippy had the kernel of a microwormhole tucked away under that missile's shroud, so he still had sensor coverage and perfect control of the missile. The beer can expertly tucked our missile between two engine nozzles, where the Kristang's already crappy proximity sensors were especially blind.

Then he proceeded with the actual awesome part. Yes, sneaking a missile up close enough to touch an unsuspecting warship would be considered super bodaciously awesome by anyone else, but by the standards of Skippy the Once-Again-And-Even-More-So-Magnificent, doing that was not even a decent magic trick. No, he had something truly special planned.

The *Spirit* had been transported from Camp Alpha by a Bosphuraq star carrier, and those birdbrains do not possess nanovirus technology like the Thuranin. Skippy thought the Bosphuraq did not even know about the nanovirus used by their rivals, which was a significant advantage for the little green pinheads. The target ship was infected by nanovirus, but those tiny machines were so old and so degraded, most of them had self-destructed to avoid their decayed components being detected. No way could even Skippy take over the destroyer using a nanovirus, and because the Kristang isolate their control systems to prevent a hostile higher-tech species from remotely seizing control, our beer can was also not able to completely infiltrate the *Spirit*'s computers. He *was* able to project a local field through the microwormhole, right against the ship's hull, and disable internal sensors in that small area.

He improvised. Our Thuranin missiles came equipped with a handy-dandy self-repair kit of insect-like bots and a tightly-packed canister of nanomachines. The bots and nano were intended to restore mildly damaged missiles to operation, or to keep missiles combat-ready when they were deployed away from their mother ship for long periods on blockade duty or other detached assignments. Skippy instructed the bots to activate, leave their storage bins and each bot took a supply of nanomachines with them as they leapt across the gap between missile and ship's hull.

Not even Skippy's magnificence could allow the squadron of bots to simply use an airlock to gain access to the interior of the destroyer, because the Kristang set up their airlocks to at least partly require manual operation. These bots were tiny, like mosquitos, even working together they lacked the size and strength to turn a heavy wheel to crank open an airlock. No problem. Skippy sent the bots scurrying along the hull to a vulnerability the lizards hadn't even considered. It was a small thermal exhaust port, and the bots happily crawled along down the port toward the main reactor. A third of the way down, they stopped to remove a valve and, presto! They were inside. Because that valve had to operate regularly whenever the reactor was pumping out heat, the bots reinstalled the valve behind them under Skippy's direction.

Skippy later told me all the amazing things he had his army of bots do, but a lot of it was blah, blah, blah, nerdy tech-talk that had my brain spinning and my eyes glazing over. Oh crap. Please do *NOT* tell Skippy I said that, he thought I was listening intently the whole time, while really I was dreaming of making a sandwich. Hey, I had been on duty in the command chair for a long time and I was hungry. Besides, I am talking about a supremely delicious sandwich. Thick-sliced ham, with fresh turkey. Fresh, real turkey, not a thin, suspiciously round disc of processed 'turkey food product' whatever the hell that is. A slice of cheddar cheese, not too sharp but not so bland it gets lost, you know? You add a bit of horseradish between slices of ham, some honey mustard or, ooh! Even better, *maple-*mustard on the turkey, with sweet roasted peppers-

Ok, fine. Back to the subject. Where was I? Now I'm really hungry. I'll bet you're hungry now too. Anyway, Skippy's drafted army of bots creepily crawled throughout that ship, physically plugging into one local system after another. I wish he had been able to do that, way back when we boarded and seized the frigate *Heavenly Flower of Glorious Victory* near Paradise, because our boarding action back then had been a bloody, desperate, chaotic mess. Unfortunately, we had to take the *Flower* quickly that day. That frigate only had a short time to jump in, pick up our stolen Ruhar Dodo dropship and jump away, because a whole lot of Ruhar ships were burning to intercept the *Flower*. With the *Spirit* lazily drifting along in stealth and blissful ignorance, Skippy was able to slowly and painstakingly work his way into every system aboard the ship, until he had absolute control of every electronic device within the hull.

"Aaaaand, done!" He announced with more weariness than glee. "Damn, that was tedious. Tee-*DEE*-ous! My bots had to keep ducking out of the way to stay hidden from Kristang maintenance and security bots. Uh, wow. Seven hours went by since those bots left the missile? Whoooo, I am tired. Skippy needs a nap. I'll set an alarm to wake myself. Ohhhhh," he yawned, "that was a good nap."

"You, uh, took like, a half-second nap?"

"Half-second in meatsack time, four hours in Skippy time."

"Wait, you really took a nap? I thought you never slept?" There were things about Skippy that were different after he killed the worm and rebuilt himself, and I did not yet know everything that had changed.

"I do not sleep the way monkeys do, what I did was sort of rearranging my sock drawers, tidying up data storage that got cluttered while I was concentrating on the bots. It was very refreshing. Also, I didn't drool on myself the way you do when you sleep."

"I don't-" I gave up, there is no point to arguing with a beer can. "Whatever. Whoo-hoo," I gave him an unenthusiastic verbal slow clap. "We have control of that ship. We still don't know where those damned Keepers are."

"Yes we do, Joe. I dug that data out of the *Spirit*'s databanks like, an hour ago."

"An *hour* ago? Why the hell didn't you tell me about-"

"Take a chill pill, Joey. The Keepers were, as I suspected, loaded aboard two dropships that left the ship before it crossed the path of the meteor shower. The ship has a very rough location of the dropships, but those craft were allowed to maneuver independently once they got inside the cluster of meteors. They have maintained strict communications silence and are using stealth technology that is quite advanced for the Kristang, I suspect the Bosphuraq loaned some upgrades to them. I have had four missiles performing a grid search for the dropships and estimate seventy three percent of the target area has been cleared so far. The schedule calls for the Keepers to be released in their aeroshells sixteen hours from now. We have- uh! Got one! Just detected one dropship. That's got to be one of our targets, unless some other species just happens to be hiding a stealthed dropship in that cluster of meteors. Give me a minute."

It was twenty seven minutes, not one, but I didn't argue with the beer can.

"Contact!" Skippy exulted. "Got them, right where I expected! Damn, am I good, or am I good? Scratch that, I am the best, baby! Who da man? I'm da man!"

"You are unquestionably Da Man, Skippy. Please, Oh Greatest of Great Ones, graciously tell us what the hell it is you found?"

"Hmm? Oh, yeah, sorry, kind of got wrapped up in the moment. A pair of stealthed dropships, Joe, tucked inside the cluster of comet debris that will rain down on southern Lemuria as a meteor shower in three days. What I do not see are aeroshells, which tells me the Keepers have not yet deployed. They must still be inside the dropships."

"Outstanding," I clapped my hands together happily. "That makes for an easier targeting solution. Colonel Chang, lock two missiles on-"

"Whoa! Whoa there, Joe. What are you doing?" Skippy interrupted.

"I'm going to blow those idiot Keepers to hell, Skippy, and end the threat to Paradise. Why the hell else do you think we were looking for them? Oh, shit," I slapped my forehead. "Unless hitting them with a missile right now will cause their infected body parts to rain down all over Paradise?" Damn it, I am a moron. That is a question I should have asked Skippy way before we located those dropships.

"No, Joe, our missile warheads are sufficiently powerful to turn the contents of those dropships into subatomic particles, although we will need to coordinate their detonation to within a nanosecond of each other. The reason I stopped you is we should not just do the simple dumb guy thing and blow shit up."

"I *like* blowing shit up, Skippy. Especially in situations like this. These Keeper losers are just *begging* to get blown up."

"Although karma and the universe agree with your assessment of the proper fate for those Keeper idiots, it is not that simple. Joe, *think* for change, please. The Kristang still possess their research and the pathogen. They can use it later, all they really need to do is *threaten* to use it later. Humans on Paradise will be treated with suspicion as potential deadly threats, until the Ruhar have a vaccine and a cure against the pathogen. I can't develop a vaccine or cure from the data Colonel Perkins collected, there isn't enough detail in that data. We need samples, Joe, samples and subjects to test my potential cures on."

"Oh, crap. We need to take those infected Keepers alive? We need to *rescue* them?"

"Yes, at least some of them, Joe. More would be better than less, obviously."

"Mister Skippy," Major Smythe asked eagerly, having appeared behind my chair as if by magic. Damn, did he have a magic trouble predictor that told him when the Merry Band of Pirates would run into a problem that required his help? "Can I assume we need to board and seize two stealthed dropships?"

"Yes, and somehow you need to do it without that destroyer discovering somebody took control of those dropships, or the destroyer could cause trouble for us. We need to keep quiet until we have full control of both dropships and we are certain the Keepers are aboard and infected, so I can get useful samples. Any sort of ruckus out here will attract a dozen Ruhar ships and blow the whole operation."

"Sounds like we need a stealthy spaceborne assault," no amount of British reserve could keep the grin off Smythe's face. "Colonel Bishop, my team will plan the assault, and I will recommend-"

"No, Major," I cut him off. "You can *plan* a spaceborne assault, but you do not get a vote on whether the op is a 'Go' or not."

"Sir?" He looked genuinely surprised and maybe a little hurt.

"I know you SAS guys by now. If there is a choice between 'do crazy shit' and 'not do crazy shit', you will vote for 'do crazy shit' every time."

"Oh," he chuckled, relieved to understand I was not actually mad at him.

"Ha!" Skippy interjected. "Joe, with some of the wild stuff *you* have done, you should not complain about someone else's enthusiasm for nutcase stunts."

"Skippy, it may be true that I have a timeshare in Crazytown, but Major Smythe is the *mayor* of Crazyland."

"That *is* why we are out here, Colonel," Smythe observed with dry humor.

"If you had wanted tea and crumpets in the parlor, you could have stayed home?"

"Something like that."

"Okay, you can plan an assault, but we'll take it as a given that you are in favor of a 'Go' order. Well?" I made a shooing motion with one hand. "Get on with it, then, we don't have much time."

"Yes, Sir," he replied eagerly, spun crisply on his heels and strode off down the passageway.

"Why do I have the feeling I will very much not like whatever plan he thinks up?" I asked to no one in particular.

Skippy answered for me. "Because, Major Smythe's plan will not include little Joey tagging along as a mascot. You should stay here, right here, where you can't do any harm. Not much harm, anyway, because I will be here to keep you out of trouble."

While Smythe's team dreamed up crazy plans, Skippy gathered all the data he could get about those dropships. "Ok, I'm done analyzing both of them. Can't get any more data from out here, without alerting the Kristang that someone is watching them."

"Outstanding! Can you do your magical creepy bot thing to take over those dropships. Wait!" I held up a hand. "Are all the Keepers aboard those two dropships? The Kristang didn't leave a few on the ship to use later, in case something went wrong?"

"No Keepers aboard the ship, Joe, the Kristang have all their eggs in two baskets for this operation. The answer is no, I can't take control of the dropships the way I did with the ship. The critical systems of a dropship are all inside the cabin, and someone would surely see bots crawling around. Ironically, I can't take control of the dropships because their technology is so crude. That sucks, but it is what it is. There are some minor tricks I can play, but for the major part of the operation, you monkeys will have to do this the hard way."

"Oh, crap," I groaned. "Major Smythe," I pinged him over the intercom but his voice came from behind my chair.

"Here, Sir," he announced with what to the British might be considered unseemly eagerness. And he was wearing a freshly-pressed uniform, it looked like I could slice open my hand on the crease of his trousers. When the hell had he changed into a new uni?

"I suppose now you and your team are up to bat." The British did not play baseball, but they did play cricket, and 'up to bat' was a term they understood. While Skippy gathering data about the pair of dropships, Smythe had developed a plan to secure the Keepers and bring them back to the *Flying Dutchman*.

"Permission to, as you said, 'Do crazy shit', Sir?" His ear-to-ear grin was definitely unseemly, and I was glad to see it.

I snapped a salute to him, though we generally dispensed with salutes aboard the ship. "Permission for crazy shit granted, Major. Under one condition."

"What's that, Colonel?" He asked, a bit of his grin having slipped.

"That you not have *too* much fun."

"We will do our best to be thoroughly miserable about it, Sir."

CHAPTER THIRTY

Skippy was right, Smythe's assault plan did not include me going with him, and that was not a shock to me. My proper place was in the command chair during an operation, unless for some reason Skippy had needed to go with the assault team and he wanted me along in case he needed a 'monkey-brain' idea at the last moment.

Major Smythe and his SpecOps team were suiting up for the operation to board and capture the two stealthed dropships that were carrying the infected Keepers to Paradise, so I went down to the armory to help them get their gear squared away. Ok, no, the team did not need me to do anything, I was really there because I was jealous that I would be stuck aboard the ship while Smythe's team had all the fun.

"Hey, Joe," Skippy piped up in the cheery tone that meant he was up to no good.

"Oh, crap, Skippy, what is it now?"

"You say 'crap' like you assume this has to be something bad," he said in a huff.

"You being bubbly and cheery like that is usually a bad sign for me."

"Ha! You are *so* wrong this time, dumdum. This is nothing but good for you, And really, for the entire galaxy."

No way was I getting my hopes up until I knew what he was talking about. "What, did the Maxolhx surrender or something like that?"

"Way better than that, Joe," he was so cheery that for a moment I got my hopes up. Then he crushed my hopes like they had fallen into a neutron star. "I have a whole *new* batch of showtunes ready for your listening enjoyment."

"That's great, Skippy, truly, really great," I caught the panicked looks from the SpecOps people around me. "But hey, how about you save your batch of bodaciously superduper new show tunes for the next time I am in a spacesuit, falling into the atmosphere of a gas giant or something?"

"Oh. Sure, Joe, because having me sing new showtunes would be a comfort to you, at a stressful time when you are facing certain and painful death?"

"Um, I was thinking that having to listen to your showtunes would make the idea of plunging to death in a gas giant sound like sweet release, but let's go with the comfort thing."

"Joe, why are you such an asshole?"

"Maybe I was dropped on the head as a child?"

"No, I think that's just who you are. Ok, smart guy, I *was* going to treat you to a preview of my latest batch of showtunes-"

"And now you're not?" I prepped one hand to exchange a high-five with Major Smythe.

"No, I am not. That is your loss," Skippy sniffed.

"Yes!" Smythe slapped me five, holding back so he didn't break any bones in my hand. "How did I get so lucky? I was afraid you planned to torture the away team with show tunes during their space dive." Damn it, I should have known that I had just screwed myself, because the universe hates Joe Bishop.

"Instead," Skippy continued as if I had not spoken, "you can be the guinea pigs as I practice my current obsession: arias."

"Oh, *shit*," my blood ran cold and Smythe glared at me, looking at his hand as if he wanted to take back the high-five. "Arias? You mean, like, *opera*?"

"Very good, Joe, I am actually impressed you know what an aria is."

"Yeah, it's when some guy sounds like he's strangling a cat and it goes on way too long."

"Ugh," he gave an exasperated sigh. "You are such a cretin, Joe. Here. Let me smack you with some culture."

"Please don-" But it was too late.

"For my first effort, the famous tenor aria from Puccini's opera Turandot, 'Nessun Dorma', or 'None shall sleep'." He then launched into a tune that I'm sure everyone has heard at some point in their lives, whether they wanted to or not. Except most people heard the version sung by Pavarotti or maybe it was Caruso or, whatever, some guy on stage in a dark suit. That was not what we heard from Skippy's awful, screeching, warbling off-key rendition. "*Nessun dorma! Nessun dorma! Tu pure, la Principessa, nella tua fredda stanza-*"

"Sir," Smythe looked at me, deadly serious, "whatever you have to do, make it stop."

"I'm trying, Major," I responded lamely. "I don't know what-"

"We have a whole cargo bay full of nukes," Smythe added and several people nodded. With Smythe's reserved British sense of humor, I didn't know if he was joking or not.

"If he won't stop, I'll throw *myself* out an airlock," Williams was now glaring at me.

"Uh-" I gave him a goofy smile while trying to think. Meanwhile, Skippy continued to torment us, wrapping up to a big dramatic finish.

"*Tramontate, stelle! All'alba vincero! Vincero! VINCEROOOOOO!*" Then, "Thank you, thank you, you have been a wonderful audience. No autographs, please."

"Oh, thank God," I exploded with relief, "it's over."

"What? Come on, Joe, I was just getting warmed up."

"Crap, Skippy, if we could weaponize your singing, we could conquer the galaxy in like, a week. Please, *please* for the love of God, no more opera like that."

"Hmmph. Damn, I try to raise your cultural standards and all you give me is grief about it. Ok, how about some selections from Kristang opera?"

That made my eyes bulge out of my head. "The *Kristang* like opera?"

"Of course they do, dumdum. You already knew they love poetry. Those hateful lizards just *love* their operas, especially the tragic kind. Particularly when the tragedy happens to someone else, hee hee. Hey, here's one that-"

"Skippy, please, I'm begging you, no lizard opera."

"How about Klingon opera?"

"Not that either," I hastened to say, not knowing whether he was joking or not.

"Joe, this much talent can't be contained forever," Skippy warned.

"Oh bullocks," Smythe sighed. "Mister Skippy, could you save your remarkable singing talent for the next time we have a prisoner to interrogate, like that Maxolhx? Sir," he turned to me, "special operations troops are trained to resist interrogation. I know one of the American outfits uses a recording of the poem 'Boots' by Rudyard Kipling, because it is bloody awful and monotonous and goes on forever; it is impossible to ignore. The SAS uses similar tactics, but nothing compares to your beer can singing opera."

"I hear you, Major," I felt like a small boy being reprimanded by a schoolmaster, and I noticed he referred to Skippy as *my* beer can.

"Hey!" Skippy was insulted. "Have you ever heard Joe sing? His voice is *terrible*."

"My voice is not that bad."

"Oh really?" The beer can asked with icy sarcasm. "How come you never participate on karaoke night?"

"Because I, uh, because-"

"Come on, Joe, sing something for us, Show your incredible talent."

He pissed me off enough that I launched into a song I just made up. "*Some enchanted morning, you might see a beer can, you might see a beer can, upon a dusty shelf. And somehow you know, you know even then, that you will regret it, again and again. No one can explain it, Skippy doesn't try. Beer cans are assholes, no point asking why. Once you have found Skip, run far awaaaaay!"* My voice cracked on that last part.

"Oh, Joe," Skippy's avatar gave me a thoroughly disgusted ironic slow clap, "that was truly freakin' hilarious."

He was being sarcastic, but Smythe's team gave me a thunderous standing ovation and drowned out the beer can.

His avatar waved a hand in exasperation. "Oh, shut up." And the avatar winked out.

Man, if the crew applauded my terrible singing, they really went wild when Skippy disappeared. "Encore! Encore!" The crowd shouted.

While Smythe's team were on their long spacedive to board and capture the stealthed dropships, I had nothing to do, so I was in my office catching up on paperwork. All along, I was supposed to complete crew evaluation reports and now that we could potentially soon be on our way back to Earth, I had a mountain of forms to fill in. The next one in my stack was Gunnery Sergeant Margaret Adams and I checked the appropriate boxes at the top, then I froze. What the hell would I say about Adams? What *could* I say? Whatever I put in that evaluation file, how could I be sure I was being fair to her, and being fair to everyone else in the crew? A commander can't play favorites and let his personal feelings affect his-

Part of her file caught my eye. It was available only to me, as it was the official assessment by psychologists assigned by Marine Corps and UNEF Command to review her mental and emotional fitness for duty, after we returned from our first mission. Another assessment had been conducted after we returned from our second mission. I had been forced to talk with Army headshrinkers both times, there was nothing unusual about that, the entire crew went through something similar. So far, I had not snuck a peek at anyone's psych eval records, all I cared about was they had been officially cleared for duty.

But I had to admit Adams was different. I had not looked at her file because I did not *want* to know what was inside her head, and my reasons for that went beyond respecting her privacy. Reading her file, getting in her head like that, was too intimate for me. We had to keep our relationship strictly professional and if that was the way it had to be, I did not want to be tempted into taking *any* steps toward intimacy when we were stuck aboard a ship for months or years.

I closed her file without saving it.

"Hey, Joe, you didn't finish."

"Not today, Skippy."

"You say that *every* time you look at her file," Skippy sighed. "Joe, you never asked Sergeant Adams why she was in that jail on Paradise."

"She refused orders from the lizards just like me, I don't need details."

"I disagree, but more importantly, you have also never asked about *what* happened to her in jail, what the Kristang-"

"I don't want to know, Skippy. It's in her classified personnel records, I know that file includes notes from the Marine Corps psych people who cleared Adams for duty. If *she* wants to tell me, I will listen," my voice choked up while I spoke, so I gulped coffee to cover my emotional state. The fact is, I wanted Adams to tell me about it. No. That's not what I meant. What I want is to be a person she can talk to about- No, that's not it either. I want her to feel comfortable talking about it with me, because we have that kind of relationship. The kind of relationship where two people can tell each other anything, and do tell each other everything. If we could-

Crap. No, that's not what I want either. Ok, yes, I do want that. Problem is, I am Margaret Adams' commanding officer, and by the rules of the US military, that is the end of the discussion, period.

Sometimes I really, really hate my job.

"Are you Ok, Joe?" Skippy asked quietly, in that rarely-used tone indicating he was being completely serious.

"Yeah, I'm fine," I gulped more cold coffee, which sucked. "My throat is dry, been talking too much. And this damned coffee is cold."

"You need to know-"

"Drop the subject, Skippy," I used my own tone of voice to indicate I was also being completely serious.

"Nope, not this time, Joe. Without breaching any confidential records, I know something that you *need* to know. You are her commanding officer, you need to understand her psychological state. It affects her fitness for duty."

"You've never questioned *my* fitness for duty," I blurted out before thinking. "I mean, you've never questioned whether my experience in that jail affected my fitness. And you've never said Chang or Desai being there affected them in a way that-"

"Margaret's experience there was different from you other three prisoners."

"Skippy, I know the Kristang tortured women, and I don't want to hear the details unless Adams or Desai want to talk about it. Desai was there, why aren't you concerned about her?"

"Let me ask one question, Joe. Have you ever wondered why a staff sergeant was still alive when the Ruhar hit the jail? You know the Kristang were planning to kill the higher-ranking prisoners last, that's why you as a colonel and Lieutenant Colonel Chang had not been executed yet. Desai was a captain back then, but Margaret's rank is much lower and she was still alive."

"Uh-" I stalled for time because, no, I had not given that any thought. While we were escaping from that jail and then during the mind-blowing events that followed, I didn't have time to consider why Adams had survived that long. She was in a jail cell when I found her, and thank God the cell doors in that jail didn't require a key or passcode or retinal scan to unlock from the outside, because if I had to do anything but press a button to get the doors open, the four of us would all have died that day. "No, I haven't ever thought about that."

"You should. The Kristang originally were executing women on the same schedule as men, starting with privates and working their way up the rank structure. The highest-ranking female prisoner was a major, but they killed her the day before the Ruhar arrived. Before Margaret was scheduled to be hung for defying orders."

"Ooookaaay," I answered slowly. "That *is* odd. What changed?"

"Margaret Adams caused the Kristang to change their plans, and what she did then is affecting her today. As her CO, you need to hear this."

"Nothing you tell me will-"

He kept going. "The number of women prisoners was only a quarter of the men. That ratio is higher than the percentage of women overall in UNEF."

"A higher percentage of women refused orders from the lizards?"

"Yes, but the Kristang were also more strict with women on what behavior was considered treasonous. One Indian lieutenant was executed because she simply requested confirmation from her chain of command, after she received an order directly from the Kristang. Because she did not immediately obey Kristang orders to fire on Ruhar civilians, she was considered a traitor. Based on statements she made afterward, she likely would have refused those orders regardless of whether her chain of command affirmed them, but the Kristang warrior caste can't stand a female disobeying them, you know that."

"Yeah. Yeah, I do." The lizards hated the idea of any female having authority, it had been a problem for UNEF right from the start. Women in Kristang society had no power, they were basically property. A confidential memo I read after going back to Earth, stated that UNEF Command had taken fewer female officers than was normal for the force structure, a decision made to avoid friction with the Kristang. Some female officers had accepted reductions in rank so they could join the Expeditionary Force; for example Desai was in line for promotion to major, but she remained a captain when she left Earth. She got promoted to major when the *Dutchman* went to Earth the first time, but for a while I kept calling her 'Captain' out of habit because I am a dumbass.

"Ok, what happened to Adams that is so important for me to know?" One way or the other, I needed to know if it was still bothering her. Although Skippy was mostly clueless about humanity, sometimes I had to trust him about important personnel matters. "Don't give me any details unless they're important."

"I will skip the unpleasant details, that for sure is something Margaret would not be happy other people knowing." He paused and it almost sounded like he was taking a deep breath before plunging ahead with the story, it was one of those times he tried to imitate human mannerisms and he was getting better at it. "The day after you were brought to the jail, the Kristang had all the women prisoners in one room and were torturing a British Army private and making the other women watch. This private was scheduled to be executed the next morning and the Kristang, um, were eager to have fun before they killed her."

"Shit." I gripped the coffee cup so hard my knuckles turned white.

"A Chinese Army Major Zhou protested and the Kristang turned their attention to her. That Major was originally supposed to be one of the last to be executed, but as the Kristang were abusing Zhou, Sergeant Adams told the lizards to take her instead. This Major Zhou was already injured from an air crash when she arrived at the jail, and Adams' sense of honor rebelled at seeing a wounded person being abused."

"Goddamn."

"Margaret Adams is a very brave woman, Joe."

"Is that what's bothering her, she thinks she asked for it?" I figured the Kristang were going to do whatever they wanted, regardless of what Adams said or did.

"No. The problem is Adams not only demanded the lizards leave the injured Major Zhou alone, she taunted the lizards. One of the jailors came over to shoot Adams with a sort of electric shock tool to make her stop talking, but Adams had managed to get one of her hands free, and she struck the lizard across the face, scratched him with her fingernails."

"Is that why she had those scars across her back? The lizards getting back at her?"

"No, Joe, the lizards did that, and worse, to all the women. The issue Margaret is still struggling with is what happened next. Instead of taking their anger out on Adams, the lizards made her watch as they slowly tortured Major Zhou to death. It took sixteen hours, Joe, the Kristang administered crude medical treatments to keep Zhou alive so they could continue abusing her. Then they told Adams she would be killed last, so she would have to watch all the other women suffer first."

"Holy shit."

"Yeah. Margaret feels guilty that she is the reason Major Zhou suffered so greatly, rather than dying from hanging or a quick bullet to the head."

"She isn't to blame, the lizards are!"

"You don't need to convince me, Joe. So, that is the reason Staff Sergeant Adams was not executed before the Ruhar hit the jail; the lizards wanted her to see all the other women suffer and die. Desai was scheduled to die the day you escaped, and Adams the next day. Joe, I do not wish to make it seem like Desai did not suffer, but by the time the Kristang got to her, they had almost gotten bored with torture. Desai knows she did not have to endure as much abuse as most of the women prisoners, and that is the source of her own guilt."

"She is having a problem with it also?"

"Yes, but not to the extent that the experience is affecting Adams. Desai and Adams talked about what happened to them in that jail, they told each other things they did not even tell the psychologists at UNEF Command."

"Do *not* tell me any of it."

"But what if-"

"No 'buts', Skippy, I am dead serious about this. Adams and Desai were already violated by the lizards, and partly by our pysch people prying into their heads. I am not going to violate their privacy."

"I understand that, Joe, and I applaud your sense of honor, but-"

"But nothing. Skippy, I have to trust Adams. I have to trust that if she thinks she is a risk to the ship or combat operations, she will remove herself from the duty roster. She is a soldier, I mean, technically she's a Marine. Adams is a professional, hell, she's more of a real officer than I am, even if she doesn't have a commission."

"That's great, Joe, however-"

"Tell me this: is Margaret Adams a danger to the ship, the mission or herself?"

"Not at the present."

"If that changes, you tell me immediately, Ok? Understood? Otherwise, drop the subject. And don't tell Adams we had this discussion."

"Um, Ok, understood, except for that last part. Wouldn't it help bring you two together if she knows that you know what is bothering her?"

"Jeez, Skippy, how can you be so clueless about people? No! If she knew, then any discussion we had would be totally awkward, and she would avoid me. Hey! What do you mean, 'help bring us together'?"

"Joe, I know how you feel about Margar-"

"Drop the subject, Skippy! Drop. The. Subject. Period. Got it? D*o not* mention it again."

"Got it. Wow, I pressed a sensitive button there, you really-"

"Is this you *not* talking about the subject?"

"Oh, sorry. Okey-dokey, Joe, I will not mention this entire subject again, unless I determine Margaret is a risk to herself or others. One last question, please? What if she asks me directly if I have spoken to others about her?"

"Then you tell her the truth, Skippy."

"Even if it makes things awkward between the two of you?"

"There is no 'thing' between us, and I am *not* lying to her about this. Um, if she does ask, make sure you tell her I instructed you not to tell me any personal details, but you did it anyway."

"Got it. Damn, Joe. I still have a lot to learn about people, about soldiers in particular, and especially about women."

"You and me both, Skippy. You and me both."

It struck me then that I was *not* technically a commissioned officer, as I only had a temporary field promotion to my theater rank of colonel. My regular Army status of sergeant was a non-commissioned rank, just like Margaret Adams. Crap, as if my life wasn't complicated enough without my brain making trouble for me with unhelpful thoughts. Somehow, I needed to get my brain to understand that aboard the *Flying Dutchman* I am Gunnery Sergeant Adams' commanding officer. Even if, I mean when, we get back to Earth, we both would expect that we're taking the *Dutchman* back out, and I'll be her CO again. Crap, my real problem is that I was lonely, sometimes really desperately lonely. The only one I could talk to was an asshole beer can and he wasn't much help. Ok, he did help, but it wasn't like talking with a human.

Oh to hell with it anyway. Adams was getting romantic with a French paratrooper, according to what Skippy had told me, way back before we jumped into the Roach Motel. Hey, I was happy for her, for both of them. When you're lonely, it helps to know someone out there is making a genuine connection with another person.

Ok, so I lied. Knowing Adams had a close friend aboard the ship made me more lonely, not less. But I was truly happy for her.

CHAPTER THIRTY ONE

There were two dropships, so we had two teams participating in the assault. Because the French team had missed most of the action during our black op on Kobamik, Renee Giraud commanded one of the teams, with Smythe himself in command of the other. Each team had eight people, and I was mildly unhappy to see Giraud had included Ranger Lauren Poole on his team, but I didn't interfere. My unofficial bodyguard had every right to risk her neck like everyone else, and she loved doing crazy shit as much as any of our pirate crew.

Our Thuranin Falcon dropships, in full stealth mode, coasted into the meteor shower and the assault teams stepped out the rear ramps into the cold blackness of space. The teams were all wearing Kristang powered armor suits, with jetpacks and portable stealth field generators. Their momentum had them approaching the enemy at 20 kilometers per minute so they did not need to use the jetpacks, other than to get clear of our Falcon dropships and assemble in formation. The Falcons very gently altered course to get clear of the meteors and far enough away so they were comfortably beyond range of the crappy Kristang sensors.

While anxiously waiting for the assault team to reach their targets, I was in my office and Skippy was berating me about being stupid, or something like that, truthfully I wasn't listening. "Hey! Hey, Joe, what's going on? I just smacked you upside the head with primo insults I've been saving for when you do something egregiously idiotic, and you barely reacted. You are totally phoning it in today, what is wrong with you?"

"Sorry, Skippy," I flipped my laptop closed, not interested in the game I had been playing. "I'm kind of bummed out today, that's all."

"Hmmm. Well, you are an ignorant monkey, and a member of a species unlikely to survive the next decade despite our best efforts out here-"

"Is *this* how you cheer me up?"

"Cheer you up? Why would I do that? Oh, oh, right, *duh*. Heh, heh, my bad. Is this when I should try that 'empathy' thing?"

"Ya think?"

"Ok, uh. How about this? There, there, Joey, everything will be all right," he said mechanically. "And, um, you know, some other meaningless bullshit people say to comfort their friends. Hey! In fact, since the odds are you monkeys will be extinct soon, you should consider that a license to work on a bucket list. What would you like to-"

"Skippy, I do not think you get what 'empathy' is."

"Really? Hmm, according to the dictionary it is 'the capacity to understand or feel what another person is experiencing from within their frame of reference'. Like, placing yourself in another's position. Walk a mile in another man's shoes, that sort of thing."

"So, you do understand-"

"Although walking in somebody else's shoes just sounds like a good way to get blisters. Also, yuck, what if his feet stink? Seriously, I would not touch *your* shoes with a-"

"Ok, you know what empathy is, can you see you are not actually doing it?"

"What? Dude, I am *totally* being empathetic, even though it seems like a pain-in-the-*ass* waste of my time. I understand you are feeling, as you said, 'bummed out' about something. See? I knew something was bothering you, because I understood what you were experiencing."

"Uh huh. Yet, your way of comforting me was to talk about how humanity is doomed-"

"Aha! Wait, I think I see the problem now. Empathy means you understand what some jerk is feeling, blah, blah, blah."

"Saying 'jerk' makes me think you don't-"

"Empathy means I *understand*. It doesn't mean I *care*. That is *completely* different."

"Oh, man, you've got to be kidding-"

"Oh, crap, you *do* expect me to care?" He asked, astonished. "Holy shit. This empathy thing is *waaay* out of control. *UGH*," I had rarely heard him sound so thoroughly disgusted.

"How about we avoid the whole subject? Thanks, Skippy, I feel so much better now."

"Cool! See? I made you feel better by understanding how you are feeling!"

"Yeah, that's, uh, what I was going to say."

"At the risk of you boring me to tears by having to listen to you whine and blah, blah, blah for-freakin'-*ever* about your stupid problems, what is bothering you?"

"Thanks, Skippy, it is super heart-warming that you asked."

"Seriously, dude, is your bad mood because there is no real maple syrup left at breakfast this morning? Major Simms did warn you that our food supplies are running thin."

"It's not the maple syrup, or all the other food we're running out of. I'm worried about Smythe's boarding party. If things go badly out there, we might have to risk exposure to protect Paradise."

"I'm not worried about it, Joe."

"Because Smythe and his team are the very best at what they do, and I should trust them?"

"Uh, oh. I only meant that I am not worried about it because, hey, what the hell do *I* care? You, on the other hand, should be scared shitless about this op."

"Oh for crying out-"

"Seriously, dude, there are, like, a million ways the boarding op could go sideways and then you would be totally screwed. Hey, hey! Right there! Right there I just proved that I understand what you are feeling, right? I totally nailed this empathy thing. I am the *King* of Empathy, baby! *Whoo-hoo!*"

"Oh this is not going well."

In his visor display, Renee Giraud could see the location of every member of his team and he could see Smythe's team of four people. Technically, he could not see anything beyond the inner faceplate of his suit, because the entire assault team was wrapped in stealth fields, so photons from the local star and even the faint glimmer of surrounding starlight were neatly bent around each soldier. More importantly, even if any photons had managed to bounce off a soldier's armor, they would never reach Giraud's eyes, as his own stealth field curved those photons around him like he wasn't there are all. So, his vision was provided by sensors at the end of four ultrathin wires, projecting in front, back and to each side. Those sensors passively collected data which allowed him to periodically puff his jetpack's thrusters to avoid colliding with a space rock, and they received weak, low-power burst transmissions from the suits of other people. The datalink between the team only told Giraud where his people were, their condition and the status of their suits. It did not tell him what he really needed to know; where his target dropship was located and what it was doing.

The two teams coasted through space, only using their jetpacks to dodge rocks and chunks of ice as they glided silently through the cloud of comet debris. From sunlight shining off objects in front of him, Giraud's suit could see obstacles he needed to avoid, although his suit was regularly pelted by fine particles of dust and ice that he could not avoid. The impacts were so gentle at the slow speed the team was moving relative to the cloud, that there was no danger to suits or the humans inside, though everyone had the armored shield lowered over their faceplates for maximum safety.

Everything was going exactly according to the plan Smythe and Giraud had developed, which worried the Frenchman, because almost nothing ever went right on a Plan A for the Merry Band of Pirates. In the rare case that a Plan A did go well, karma was sure to make them pay the price later.

Skippy had assured them they could successfully complete the assault with only two people on each team, and one of them was for support and backup. Four on each team was a compromise to have enough people to complete the operation if something went wrong, and not having too many people's lives at risk if something went seriously wrong.

"There has been no reaction from either dropship to your presence," Skippy reported. "Your portable stealth fields are working optimally, you can thank me for the enhancements, by the way. Unless they move suddenly, my masking of their sensor probe should conceal your approach."

"Acknowledged," Giraud replied quietly and he heard Smythe do the same. Skippy had not been able to infiltrate and take control of the dropships the way he had with the destroyer, but his magic was able to help significantly. With the dropships encased in surprisingly effective stealth fields, they each would be blind if not for a probe extending forward from the nose, and a sensor at the end of a stiff cable trailing behind. Those tiny sensors were outside the stealth field, passively picking up data from the surrounding space. The greatest danger of discovery for the assault team was if one of them had to maneuver suddenly to avoid a chunk of rock, even the cold gas thrusters used by the jetpacks might be detected if used close enough to the dropships. In the final approach, there was also a risk of even typically crappy Kristang sensors noticing the spatial distortion created by the individual stealth fields of the assault team.

To help the assault teams, Skippy had performed what he considered a rather lame bit of magic. Using microwormholes he had very gently moved into position behind each dropship, he projected stealth fields through the event horizon and wrapped them around the sensor trailing behind the dropships. With the sensors now unable to receive real photons from outside the stealth field, Skippy fed false data to the sensors, data which showed only happy views of utterly benign, empty space other than the rocks and ice the Kristang expected. The beer can had wanted to try transmitting a virus down the sensor cable, to partially take control of the dropships that way, but Little Joey Bishop the Buzzkill Party Pooper had vetoed that no doubt cool but risky and unnecessary stunt. So, Skippy was bored while he waited for the assault team to get close enough to use their jetpacks to slow down for the intercept.

Giraud ran a status check on his suit, jetpack, weapons and other gear, then he did the same for the other three members of his team, though he could see they had all run status checks. Then he concentrated on examining what was known about his target, now that he was getting close enough for his suit's sensors to directly pick up the extremely low-power datalink through the microwormhole behind the dropship. At first, all seemed normal, the target appeared to be a mostly ordinary Kristang model the Pirates referred to as a Dragon-B. There were some pods attached under the stubby wings and one running along the top of the cabin, Giraud assumed they were part of the enhanced stealth gear. Everything was as expected, and he saw no reason to make even minor changes to the assault plan.

Then he saw something that shocked him. "*Merde*. Mister Skippy, the image I am seeing," he paused to eyeclick through a menu to zoom in on and then enhance the data. "On the nose of that dropship, there is a symbol. Is that, it can't be, it," his voice sputtered to a halt, too astonished to continue. He took a sip of sugar water to give his mind time to recover. "Did the Kristang paint on the nose of their ship a, a, *Hello Kitty*?"

"What? Oh, hahahahahahaha!" The beer can guffawed with laughter. "You thought that was *real*? Oh, man, you monkeys are endlessly gullible! Damn, it is almost not any fun to screw with you, it is just too easy. I'll suck it up and keep doing it, of course."

"You are showing me a false image?" Giraud demanded.

"Oh come on, Renee," Skippy scolded playfully. "Technically, with that dropship wrapped in a stealth field, *any* image I show you is false. All I can get from the sensor data through the wormholes is a rough outline, so I know the model and basic configuration. Anything else is a guess. The wormholes are close enough that I could pretty accurately map the exterior of that ship by projecting a sensor field, but as that would immediately alert the lizards they are being tracked, I should probably not do that, mmmm?"

"No," Giraud bit off a sarcastic reply. "Do not do that. Please could you- what?"

"Is that better?" In the data feed, Skippy had replaced the Hello Kitty nose art with a popular French comic book character Asterix the Gaul, complete with wings atop his helmet and a generously drooping mustache.

"Better, yes. Better than *that* would be to not show us data you are guessing at."

"What would be the fun in that? You've got to let me amuse myself while I'm waiting, since you monkeys aren't doing anything to amuse me. Hey! I have a great idea! You will be conducting a dangerous assault in nine minutes, how about some appropriately stirring music to get you pumped up?"

"That would be an awful idea. Do not-"

"Too late! Prepare to be dazzled by 'Ride of the Valkyries' by Wagner."

"Ha!" Giraud thought he had been saved from the jaws of death. "That is an instrumental piece, Skippy, you can't sing it."

"Oh you are *SO* wrong, *mon enfant*. Most people think there are no lyrics because they are used to hearing the orchestral version. You don't speak German, so I will take pity on you and sing the English-language version."

"No!"

The music began with instruments, and at first the French paratrooper thought he had gotten lucky. Then the beer can began to sing, if such an out-of-tune warble could be called singing. "*Oh warfather on high, I am calling you from the battlefield, and as I take my last breath, I call for the mightiest of miracles.*"

"Now I know why you never hear the lyrics," Giraud muttered, but Skippy ignored him and plunging on singing lustily.

"*For none but the brave, be he king or a slave, with pounding heart in his chest, will be worthy to rise and with the Valkyries fly-*"

Giraud considered that after he departed from that world, the humans on Paradise had suffered from attack by Kristang warships. They had survived for years on whatever plants they could grow, enduring a bland and mostly vegetarian diet. They had been forcibly relocated, first to the steaming jungles of equatorial Lemuria, then to the temperate southern region of that continent. Perhaps the worst deprivation humans on Paradise suffered was being cut off from Earth, never hearing from their loved ones back home. They lived every day in fear that the Ruhar would turn against the aliens who had come to the planet as an occupation force. And from communications Skippy had intercepted, the vast majority of humans stranded far from home feared the population of their home world may have been enslaved or exterminated by the Kristang.

Despite all the suffering and deprivation endured by humans on Paradise, none of them ever had to listen to a beer can singing. Not for the first time, Renee Giraud asked himself if he had made a terrible mistake by volunteering, way back when a publicity-stunt colonel named Joe Bishop had dropped out of the sky in a stolen Ruhar dropship, and announced he had a lunatic plan to hit the Kristang. What the *hell* was I thinking, Giraud asked himself as he listened to Skippy warble his way through the opera.

"*I'm dying and glad to bleed, because I know todaaaay, I take my place with the heroes in Valhaaaaaaala of old-* oh, damn it, I have to stop, you need to prepare for the boarding operation."

"Thank God. Skippy, I would rather not die and be glad to bleed today, if you don't mind."

"Would you prefer to skip the fighting songs and listen to me sing selections from 'Madame Butterfly'?"

"In that case, I would very much prefer the bleeding and dying option, please."

"Hmm," Skippy sniffed. "You pirates have *no* culture. No matter now, because you need to lead your team on yet another ill-advised crazy stunt."

"Ill-advised? This was *your* idea," Giraud fumed inside his armored suit.

"Yes, but you monkeys were dumb enough to listen to a beer can. You don't see *me* out there flying around, do you? No, I am staying safe and warm aboard the *Dutchman*, while you hotshot types eagerly zoom into the unknown. Well, you crazy kids have fun, let me know what happens."

The period of increased danger was when both assault teams, coordinating their actions exactly, programmed their jetpacks to slow their approach. The jetpacks had main engines that could not be used because their hot exhaust would be too visible so close to the targets, so they relied on a lengthy, intermittent pulsing of the cold-gas thrusters. Even doing that was risky, because to slow the users, the jetpacks vented the gas forward to go flying past the targets. Soon, the sensor probes extending forward beyond the noses of the dropships detected an unusual amount of gas floating past. Yes, the sensors noted, the gas was the normal ratio of hydrogen and other elements always present in the solar wind, and it was no more warm nor cold than the surrounding cloud, but the gas density *was* unusual. If the bored pilots had been paying attention to their instruments, they might have been curious about the anomaly, but all four pilots were half asleep since they had absolutely nothing to do until it was time to put the disgusting humans into aeroshells.

Without the pilots' request, the sensor system would still have sent out an alert on their own, except for the trick played by the assault team. In addition to a jetpack, weapons, grappling gear, portable stealth field generator and extra power packs, each suit had a package attached to the chest, and that device activated when the thrusters began gently pulsing.

The packages were filled with fine dust and ice that exactly matched the composition of a broken comet that had created the meteor shower cloud. Each package expelled a puff of this dust and ice to match the thrusters, sending the contents forward to flow around the dropships. Mere minutes before the Kristang sensor systems would have sent an alarm to the pilots, they finished analyzing the contents of the particles drifting past from the rear, and concluded there must have been a disturbance of some sort in the debris cloud. Perhaps the entry of the dropships into the cloud had caused objects to collide, or a passing asteroid had smacked its way through the cloud. Whatever the explanation, it was nothing particularly unusual or worth alerting the pilots about. So, the sensor systems continued quietly monitoring the area as they had been instructed to do, and the pilots never knew there had been an anomaly.

Maximum danger was when, one by one, the assault team slowly entered the stealth fields of the dropships. Jetpacks had slowed them to match the exact speed of the dropships so the teams were motionless relative to their still-unseen targets, and each pirate was also wrapped in a stealth field. Using thrusters so close to the enemy was too dangerous, so a paratrooper holding onto Giraud gave his leader a gentle push with his arms, sending Giraud slowly inward and the paratrooper away from the dropship. As he slipped inside the stealth field, Giraud's own stealth generator matched frequency to avoid distorting the larger field. That frequency changed as he got closer to the dropship's hull, and he had to rely on Skippy controlling the generator through the microwormhole, and an ultrathin cable extending from his suit to the world outside the enveloping field. Encased in his own stealth and the field created by the dropship, he was utterly blind. Except the synthetic vision provided by his visor had a low-quality image provided by Skippy, as that beer can mapped tiny fluctuations in the stealth field lines.

Giraud could not see the hull, he had no idea what color it was or any fine details, but he did not need that. He could see where to attach the grapple, and he did that at almost the same second Smythe's team was doing the same to the other dropship.

The two Kristang pilots in the dropship targeted by Giraud's team were startled by a faint *ping* sound on the roof of the cabin, followed by a metallic scraping. Strapped into their seats, they looked upward fearfully, then at each other. There was another ping sound, this one gentler.

That should not be happening. They were drifting in a cloud of dust, pebbles, chunks of ice and small rocks, but the entire cluster was flying in formation. Nothing should be colliding until they were much closer to the disruption of the planet's gravity well. The dropship itself had substantial mass compared to most objects in the cluster, and if the dropship remained there long enough, its gravity would pull objects close to it. But that would take a long time, much longer than the Kristang had been in the swarm of ice and rock.

The fact there was more than one ping sound was not usual, if the dropship had flown through a disturbance in the meteor cloud then it should have been struck by multiple objects. Fingers flying over the sensor controls, the copilot pulled up data showing there had indeed been an anomaly detected by the sensor gear, but seeing the data actually made him relax slightly and he pointed to the display. Whatever shower of pebbles had pinged off the dropship's hull, it had been proceeded by a cloud of dust and ice too fine to have just been noticed by the pilots, but the sensors had noticed it. The pilot shrugged and widened the passive scan, looking for any nearby objects that might pose a danger to the craft he was responsible for. There wasn't anything significant in the area, so if anything else bounced off the hull, it would be too small to pose any danger.

The lead pilot yawned, wriggled in his seat to get comfortable again, and resumed playing the game he had paused. Getting humans into aeroshells, setting them on a proper course in the meteor cloud, then stealthily flying the dropship back to the *Final Crushing Blow to the Enemy's Spirit* would be a long, exhausting process and the pilot wanted to relax while he could. The game was old but he was having more success than the last time he played it, and he was enjoying-

Three things happened almost simultaneously. There was a sizzling sound and a bright light from the roof of the cockpit. The pilot's ears popped as air pressure in the cockpit dropped and the rear cockpit door seal inflated. The visor of his helmet began to swing down automatically, too slowly to protect the pilot from the concussion grenade that was injected into the cockpit through the hole created by Giraud's explosive-tipped power lance.

The interior of the cockpit instantly became a shambles, displays shattered, controls knocked offline, pilot and copilot killed as the soft tissue of their brains were smashed by the hammer blows of air overpressure. If the cockpit had windows, they would have been blown out. Weak spots in the inner pressure hull developed cracks and air briefly leaked out until the nano-filled liquid sealant between hull layers filled in the gaps.

With his boots now securely clamped to the hull above the cockpit, Giraud and another French paratrooper attached a probe to the lance they used to burn through the hull and inject the grenade. Pressing a trigger on top shot the probe down the hollow lance, and instantly they had a view of the shattered cockpit. "Both pilots appear dead," Giraud reported.

"I see that," Skippy replied eagerly. "Scratch the word 'appeared', I can tell they *are* dead. Commence Phase Two."

Giraud gave the order and the other pair of soldiers activated their own lance above the main cabin, where they expected the Keepers to be. This second lance quickly burned through outer and inner hulls, injecting first a pair of long, thin flash-bang grenades to stun anyone in the cabin, then flooding the cabin with a fast-acting gas that had a temporary paralyzing effect on the human nervous system. That gas was followed by an anesthetic to render the immobile victims unable to resist when the assault team came through the airlock.

"Skippy, do you have control yet?" Giraud asked anxiously while the right side of his visor showed him a view of the main cabin. Nine Keepers were strapped into seats, inert but breathing shallowly. One Keeper had acted quickly on his own initiative when the concussion grenade detonated in the cockpit, he had unstrapped himself and now floated upside-down near the roof of the cabin, his unconscious form bouncing off the ceiling. All ten of the humans had tiny droplets of blood seeping from their ears, the effect of the flash-bang grenade magnified in the confined, airtight space. Major Smythe had inquired whether they should modify the grenades to dial down the effect, but Colonel Bishop had instantly vetoed that idea when Skippy stated he was confident no one would be permanently injured by the devices. Bishop's actual words had made even Giraud blush slightly, something like 'F those F-ing MFers I'd like to stuff an F-ing grenade in their F-ing pie holes, serves those F-ing F-heads right'. That got a big laugh from the beer can, who suggested the Colonel should tell people how he *really* felt.

"Don't be so hasty, Renee," Skippy snapped peevishly. "This is delicate work, I have to wriggle that probe around to plug it into- Ah, got it! Damn, it would have been a lot easier if some monkeys had not gotten overeager with a concussion grenade, it almost crushed the access port I had to plug into."

"*You* tell us overkill is underrated."

"Underrated, yes, but not always appropriate. Ah, whatever, it's done now. Because you SpecOps people are super-competitive, you will be pleased to hear I took control of your dropship three hundredths of a second before Major Smythe's dropship."

"It would be unprofessional of me to boast, Skippy."

"Uh huh, so I shouldn't mention that fact to Smythe?"

"Well," Giraud grinned, knowing Skippy could see inside his helmet. "You certainly should not withhold pertinent information from the mission commander."

"Of course not," Skippy retorted with a verbal eyeroll. "I am opening the rear door and the outer door to the portside airlock. You need to detach from those bulky jetpacks and stealth generators. I am not moving this thing until your team is securely inside the cabin and those Keepers are prevented from causing any trouble."

Giraud was first to enter the dropship's cabin, with another French paratrooper right behind him. As soon as the two cleared the inner airlock door, it slid closed and the lock began pumping out air to let the two other soldiers in. To prevent the four pirates from becoming infected, they needed to remain sealed up in their armored suits, but the dropship could not move until all four were secured inside the cabin.

The two paratroopers held their pistol-grip shotguns in front of them. Shotguns, regular shotguns brought from Earth, though the shells had a minimum charge of gunpowder and the pellets were liquid-filled plastic. The pellets could hurt the unprotected Keepers, knock them down if there had been any gravity, and certainly knock them back away from the pirates. While the pellets had stopping power, they could not penetrate the inner pressure hull of the dropship, nor create a hole that would let precious air leak out.

"Cover me," Giraud ordered in English though the other soldier was also French, they had gotten used to speaking the official language of the Merry Band of Pirates, and sticking to one language lessened the possibility of miscommunication. With the other soldier hanging back near the airlock and constantly scanning the cabin for threats, Giraud holstered his shotgun and pushed off to float over to the main control computer module attached to the back of the cockpit bulkhead. Forward of that bulkhead were two dead Kristang pilots and flight controls smashed to uselessness. Flipping up an access port, Giraud carefully plugged in what looked like a thumb drive, the motion made awkward by his gloved fingers. "Plugged in. Skippy, do you-"

"Got it! Good job, Renee, I have control. How are the Sleeping Beauties?"

Giraud gave a thumbs up sign to his companion and turned to examine the Keepers, who all had their eyes closed and were slack-jawed, drooling into the air as they breathed shallowly. "I would describe them as Sleeping Uglies. They are not a problem. Gaston," he called the other paratrooper. "I am going to secure the prisoners," he pulled out a thick zip-tie and slipped it around the wrists of the closest Keeper. The zip-ties were manufactured aboard the *Dutchman* under Skippy's direction, and had a feature allowing the beer can to release the binds when needed. Working quickly by himself, and then with Gaston after the others came through the airlock, all ten Keepers were secured in seats and firmly strapped down so they could not cause any trouble. Then the pirates got into seats, with Giraud and Gaston taking uncomfortable fold-down jumpseats up against the forward bulkhead.

"Skippy, we are ready for boost," Giraud reported.

"Ok, I hope everyone used the bathroom before you left the ship," Skippy scolded. "And if any of those Keepers make a fuss I *swear* I am turning this thing around!"

Giraud reached out with a gloved hand and gently moved a Keeper's head side to side. The man was still out cold, a bubble of snot forming at one nostril, and he was drooling, slack-jawed. "They will not be causing trouble for anyone. Are you sure of the dosage you gave them?"

"Yeah, I'm sure, they'll be fine. To maintain stealth I need to fly slowly and gently, so this could be a long trip. I don't have any coloring books, you kids will have to entertain yourselves."

"You are not going to sing to us?" Giraud's stupid, *stupid* mouth asked before his brain could engage, and the three members of his team turned to look at him in horror.

"Sadly, no, I'll take a rain check on that. I am super-duper busy right now, and you and Smythe's team are really not large enough of an audience to appreciate my incredible talent. Now, as the bumper sticker says: Get in, sit down, shut up and hang on."

CHAPTER THIRTY TWO

With the Keepers securely sleeping and both dropships still in stealth and now flying to rendezvous with the *Flying Dutchman*, and the lizards aboard the *Spirit* having no idea their dropships had been captured, I was eager for the delicious moment of sending that destroyer straight to hell. "Dropships are close enough?" I asked, and Chang gave me a thumbs up from the CIC. "Great," I wiggled in my seat because I was so very much anticipating ridding the galaxy of one more ship full of hateful warrior caste lizards. Although, it felt anticlimactic to have that ship suddenly jump into the star with no warning. Maybe I should contact them first, let them know exactly what was going to happen to them, and let them know they had been outsmarted by a bunch of monkeys. Nah, that would be indulging myself in useless-

"Joe, wait a minute, I have a question," Skippy cleared his throat like he was nervous.

"If your question is something like 'what is the capital of North Dakota', then prepare to be disappointed, because I have no idea."

"No, you moron, *ugh*. Like I would ask *you* to remember facts. My question is about the moral dilemma we are facing. Yes, that destroyer is packed full of hateful lizard MFers who all know and are super enthused about deploying a bioweapon that could kill millions of humans and hamsters on Paradise, perhaps other worlds also. Every member of that ship's crew is a fully committed murderous A-hole without an ounce of concern for other species or even other Kristang from other clans."

I looked through the glass into the CIC and shared an unspoken 'WTF?' with Major Simms. "If you're trying to convince me killing that ship would create a moral dilemma, you are not exactly doing a bang-up job of it, Skippy."

"No, Ok, um. Hmmm. Maybe I should say it this way; yes, the crew of that ship would wipe out every intelligent being on Paradise without a second thought, and would happily dance on the graves of the beings they killed. After composing an epic poem about the event, of course. Oooh, maybe if they truly did exterminate the population of Paradise, those Kristang would commission a tragic opera to commemorate their victory. Wow, now *that* would be an interesting libretto to write. I wonder-"

"Skippy?"

"Oh, sorry, got a little off the subject there. Ok, here's the important part. Those Kristang were raised in their overall hateful society, and they all were trained and indoctrinated in the cruel ethics of their warrior caste. So, should we consider the crew of that destroyer are not completely to blame as individuals? Basically what I am asking is, whether this is an appropriate time for me to try working on that stupid empathy thing we talked about?"

"No, Skippy," I answered without hesitation. "This would be a *terrible* time for you to try working up empathy with lizards."

"Oh goodie! Whooo, *that* is a relief. This empathy thing sounds like a *HUH-Yuuuge* pain in the ass. All right then, I'm ready to send those lizards on a one-way trip to hell."

"Outstanding. Get the-"

"Hey, hey, Joe, Joe, wait wait!" Skippy almost stuttered, he was so excited. "I have super awesome good news!"

"What is it?"

"I just realized that aboard that ship is an old friend of yours. And a friend to Colonel Chang also."

Chang in the CIC looked at me and I looked at him and we both had completely blank expressions on our faces. Before we broke out a Kristang jail, Chang and I barely knew each other, we had met only briefly for our promotion ceremony, which for me was a publicity stunt. "A *friend*? Oh, crap, you mean there is a prisoner aboard that ship? Human or Ruhar?" My mind raced. Who the hell did Chang and I both know, someone not aboard the *Dutchman*? And, damn it, a prisoner aboard the ship could complicate everything. Depending on who the prisoner was, I might have to pull in Major Smythe to consider a rescue operation, or- Oh, shit, this could go south real fast. I might have to negotiate with the damned lizards to release the prisoner. What could I bargain with to- No, wait. Shit. No way could I ever negotiate with the lizards aboard that ship, they knew our secret. I could not risk the lives of humans on Earth and Paradise for one person no matter who it was. In one split second, my thrilling anticipation of a successful operation was blown, replaced by-

"Prisoner?" Skippy mercifully interrupted my downward spiral of dark thoughts. "No prisoner, Joe. And not human or Ruhar. Come on, work with me here, take a guess."

Guess? I silently mouthed 'I have no idea' at Chang, forgetting it was unfair asking him to guess at reading my lips in what was not his native language. For a moment we stared at each other, dumfounded, while the crew stared at both of us, equally mystified. "Not human, and not Ruhar? A friend?" Who the hell did Chang and I both know, who was neither human nor hamster, aboard a Kristang ship?

Then Chang and I both snapped our fingers at the same time. "That drunk asshole on the space station?!" Chang asked before I could speak.

"Ding ding ding ding! Winner, winner, chicken dinner!" Skippy chuckled. "Yes, excellent guess, you two."

"The promotion ceremony for Bishop, Colonel Bishop and I," Chang explained to the crew, "was aboard a space station above Paradise. Most of the Kristang still couldn't come down to the planet because of the virus there, so we flew up to them. After the ceremony, the lizards assigned one Kristang to give us a tour of the station while our leaders discussed something with their leaders. That lizard took us to a viewport, got drunk, and told us humans are nothing but worthless slaves and he wanted to kill us all. Mister Skippy, *that* Kristang is aboard the cruiser?"

"Not only aboard, he is presently captain of the ship, though that doesn't mean much right now, considering that he has no control over any shipboard system."

"Can we talk to him?" I asked while exchanging a grin with Chang. "Video too?"

"Sure, Joe. The signal lag is only a third of a second." Instantly, the main displays in the bridge and CIC showed a view from inside the enemy ship. I had been around enough Kristang that they no longer all looked the same to me and I recognized my old friend Mister Asshole in the center of the view, he was looking bored and pissed off at the same time. He had no idea how pissed off he was about to be, and then he jerked as the displays on his bridge all showed a view of *us*.

"Hey!" I waved at the camera built into the center of the bridge display. "Hey *Buttwipe*, do you remember us?"

Man, that lizard recovered quick from what had to be a total shock. He went from utter astonishment to anger in record time, shouting at the camera and shaking his fists until spittle flew from his mouth to splatter the screen.

"Damn," I laughed, "that is one pissed-off lizard. Skippy, why can't we hear the sound?"

"He is screaming insults too harsh for delicate monkey ears to hear. I will translate for you. Hmm, bad word," he reported while the lizard howled and exhorted his crew to do something, anything. At that moment, the crew of that ship were realizing to their horror that they had no control over any system. "Another bad word, Jeez, he's repeating himself. Come on, put some effort into it, will ya? Ooooh, *very* bad word, now we're getting somewhere," Skippy chuckled.

I had to laugh along with the Merry Band of Pirates, because that that point, Mister Asshole was so angry he was hopping up and down, a tough thing to do in zero gravity. "Hey! Skippy, he can hear us, right?"

"Yes, he can hear you. Now he is suggesting you perform various sex acts on yourself. *That* one is anatomically unlikely. And another, hmmm, anatomically impossible. Damn," Skippy giggled as the lizard pulled out a pistol and shot several of the consoles on his ship because they weren't responding to his crew. "He is certainly one angry lizard."

"My heart bleeds for him."

"Empathy, Joe?"

"Sarcasm, Skippy. Hey," I waved at the screen then flashed both middle fingers. "It is *so* good to see you after all this time, asshole. Yeah, I'm talking about you, dickhead. Skippy, does he understand what I'm saying?"

"He certainly does, Joe, and he does recognize you and Colonel Chang. The translation of 'dickhead' into Kristang is considered a terrible insult. He is *very* unhappy about the situation."

"I figured that from the way he is foaming at the mouth. What's he saying now?"

"Oh, generic threats against you, the crew of this ship, humanity in general, blah blah blah. Really, he's not being original, I am kind of disappointed. Oops, um, we need to move this along. He just ordered his crew to manually detonate a missile warhead. I can slow them down, but I can't stop it."

"Ok, time to wrap this up. You have their jump drive prepped?"

"Yes, the command crew attempted to shut down the jump drive when they saw the coordinates I input, but my bots isolated the drive system from the rest of the ship. Ready when you are."

Chang gave me a thumb's up. "I will activate-"

"Belay that!" I barked and jabbed a finger toward the CIC. Chang held up his hands to show he was not touching any of the controls. "Sorry, Chang, I have a reason for this. Sergeant Adams, get up here." If I was a real professional officer I should have said 'report to the bridge', but screw it. Everyone knew what I meant.

"Here, Sir," she announced from behind my chair. Of course she had been in the corridor outside the bridge/CIC complex, as she was part of the relief crew for the weapons consoles.

"Gunny, get into the CIC and jump that ship straight to hell."

"Sir?" She asked with a raised eyebrow. "Any of the duty crew can do that."

"Adams," I lowered my voice so she had to lean in to hear me. "Anyone *could* make that ship jump, a monkey could press that button. There are a whole lot of beings in this galaxy who are owed the pleasure of wiping out the warrior caste MFers aboard that cruiser. It would be nice to know pressing that button gives *one* of us a small measure of payback."

Margaret Adams didn't say anything in reply, she didn't need to. I saw it in her eyes, the tough Gunnery Sergeant couldn't hide her feelings completely. She knew I understood what she needed, and she knew I was never going to say anything about it, and that created a bond between us. In that moment, the look she gave me said far more than anything either one of us could have put into words. She straightened up, spun to the left and marched into the CIC, relieving the Indian pilot on duty at the console.

"Everyone, let's give our lizard friend a big send-off from the Merry Band of Pirates," and I flipped my middle finger at the camera, followed by everyone else in view.

"Adios, motherfucker," Adams muttered, and pressed the appropriate button. On the display, the image cut out and was replaced by black space with the distinct wobbling remnant of a jump wormhole collapsing.

"Captain Giraud, I have good news, and *great* news!" Skippy's mirthful voice boomed in the paratroop leader's helmet speakers.

"You found a cure for the pathogen?" Giraud asked with excitement.

"Huh? No. Puh-*lease*, give me a freakin' break, will ya? I haven't even taken samples from those infected losers yet. Yeah, they are expelling the pathogen with every breath, it's even in the hair and skin cells they shed, yuck."

Giraud reflexively pulled his armor-gloved hand away from the chair he had been holding onto, looking at the glove fingers. How many microscopic bits of deadly binary bioweapon were coating his Kristang suit? He did not want to think about it. The suits were supposedly airtight, but he knew that was not entirely true, on long missions the suits lost a tiny but measurable amount of air and moisture from leaks at the joints, a trade-off between the suits being absolutely sealed and being flexible enough to be useful in combat. Air and lubricants leaked *out* of the suit, not in, according to Skippy who did not ever have to worry about his bloodstream becoming contaminated by invisible killer chemical compounds.

"Relax, Renee," Doctor Skippy the mad scientist tried using his best soothing bedside voice, which was more creepy than reassuring. "You and your team are in no danger. Get out your sample kits, I need you to pull blood and tissues from these losers so I can get working ASAP. Don't worry, when you get back to the *Dutchman*, you will be put through a decontamination procedure more thorough than the usual process. *No* organic material will remain viable on the exterior of your suits, you can trust me about that."

It bothered Giraud that the beer can aboard a starship thirty thousand miles away had seen him jerk his hand away. "I am not afraid, Skippy. I am concerned."

"You *are* afraid, because you are not stupid, Renee. If the pathogen gets loose aboard the *Dutchman*, and I can't design and manufacture a practical cure, you monkeys will be in big, huge, major trouble. You do not need to worry, and I will explain every step of the enhanced decon process as you go through it, *non*?"

"Thank you, that will be very helpful. What is your good news?" Giraud asked, irritated with himself for having lost focus in an unsafe situation.

"The good news is, we jumped that *Final Crushing Blow to the Enemy's Spirit* into the local star. Well, heh heh, not quite *into* the star. More like just above the photosphere, so those hateful MFers could experience a moment of pure pee-in-their-pants terror as a solar flare rises up to burn them to a crisp. Hmm. Jumping ships into stars, or planets, or just above so the crew lives long enough to know they are one hundred percent, thoroughly *skuh-reeewed* is kind of getting to be my signature move. Man, I should create a name for that, so people will understand the implied awesomeness. Maybe I'll simply call it the 'Skippy', what do you think?" he began muttering to himself. "Yeah, naming it after myself will let people know right away they can't possibly fully appreciate the awesomeness, but they- Oh, that won't work. Stupid monkeys never give me the credit I deserve. I work and slave away in the background, and all monkeys see is the easy magic tricks I do. Ahh," he sighed. "Greatness is never appreciated like it should-"

"Skippy!" Giraud bit his lip to keep from laughing. "That is good news. How long until the Ruhar detect the gamma ray burst of the *Spirit* jumping?"

"What? Never. Ah, not *never*. I have control of the central sensor detection grids in this system, but there are isolated ships I was not able to infiltrate because the speed of light is such a huge pain in the *ass*. Those ships will report their findings to the fleet authorities on Paradise, and at that point, the code I wrote to suppress the sensor grid will have to erase itself and cause a wide-spread glitch in the system, or the hamsters will get suspicious. As it is, I expect a team of hamster code monkeys to be tearing their fur out for weeks trying to understand how such a serious glitch could have happened," he chuckled gleefully. "Hee hee, I am *such* an asshole sometimes. Anyway, you have plenty of time to get back to the *Dutchman*, and for the ship to jump safely away."

"You have thought of everything. You are truly the Emperor of Excellence."

"For realz?" Skippy asked sharply. "That wasn't some sort of Napoleon joke?"

"For real. And we French do not joke about Napoleon."

"Oh, I should have known that. Thank you, Renee."

"You are most welcome," Giraud replied with sincerity, grateful the Merry Band of Pirates did not have to worry about a powerful and very pissed-off Kristang destroyer. "If that was your good news, I cannot imagine your great news."

"The great news is truly great! Now that destroyer is not occupying a big part of my attention, I have time to sing with you. How about a singalong, let's start with the French classic 'La vie en rose'. *Des yeux qui font baisser les miens*, come on, Renee, sing it with me!"

Because some Ruhar ship was sure to detect and report the gamma ray burst of the *Spirit* being jumped into hell, we couldn't wait long before we jumped away also. We got the two dropships aboard and secured quickly, then we prepared to jump away, a long jump far outside the Paradise system.

Right before we jumped, I switched the main bridge display to a feed from Ruhar satellites above Paradise, to get one last look at that planet where over a hundred thousand humans were stranded. At first, I wanted a view of areas I was familiar with, like the village of Teskor, which had grown quite a bit since I was there. The Launcher complex at the equator was under heavy cloud cover from the thunderstorms that swept in every afternoon. I could have snuck a look at the Kristang jail where four of us were held, or the warehouse where I found Skippy, or the logistics base where we met Simms and Giraud, or even one of the maser projector sites that had been reactivated by Perkins and her team. That would have been too much nostalgia for me, bringing up memories and emotions I didn't have time for right then. So I set the display for a long-range view of the hemisphere that included the continent of Lemuria, and just watched as the jump timer counted down. This might be the last time I ever saw that mostly pleasant world, and I stared fixated at the image, drinking in sunlight reflecting off the bright blue seas, the white puffy cloud tops and the shadows they cast across dark green forest and the lighter shades of meadows and rolling farmland.

"Penny for your thoughts," Adams whispered from beside my command chair.

"Ah," I reached up to blot away a tear that was forming at the corner of one eye, before I looked back and up at her. "A lot of memories there."

She squeezed my shoulder with one hand, an intimate gesture that felt completely natural. Adams and I had put boots on the ground there with UNEF, when we had dreams of being a bad-ass force that would kick humanity's enemy the Ruhar off the surface. Instead, we had been fumbling peacekeepers, realizing too late we were fighting on the wrong side of the war. Patrolling in the jungles of Nigeria had wiped away any silly boyish illusions I had about military service, but Paradise is where I really grew up, I think.

Adams and I had been there, and we had been back on the surface during the mission to help Perkins reactivate a network of maser projectors. Adams and I had history there, a history that did not need any words to express. I reached back and squeezed her hand, then she offered a fist and I bumped it solemnly. "Those people," she whispered, "think they're cut off from Earth forever. That human life on Earth may not exist anymore."

"Yeah," I breathed heavily. "If there were anything we could do for them-"

"Someday," she declared with fierce determination. "No matter how long it takes. *Semper* Fidelis."

"Never give up, never surrender?" I replied with a ghost of a smile. The problem was the only way we could bring people from Paradise to Earth was if our secret was exposed, at which point Earth might be a cloud of loosely-organized rocks drifting around the Sun.

"Never give up," she agreed. "Never surrender."

Then we ejected a modified flight recorder buoy and jumped outside the system. After we jumped, the buoy we left behind would wait twenty minutes, in case a Ruhar ship jumped in to investigate our gamma ray burst and the nearby one left by the *Spirit*. The buoy would then transmit a message that the ship the Ruhar had no doubt detected burning up in the outer layer of the star, was the ship that tried to bring infected Keepers to Paradise, and that mission was cancelled and over. The buoy also contained a detailed chemical analysis of the pathogen Skippy had run while the Keeper's dropships were still in flight. That might help ease some of the restrictions against humans on Paradise, but our people would not truly be safe until we delivered a vaccine and cure, if Skippy could do that. The Ruhar might not believe our message about destroying the *Spirit*, because they didn't know who we were and we couldn't tell them. Besides, just because we killed one ship of murderous assholes did not mean the Ruhar were safe, some other group of Kristang could deliver the bioweapon to Paradise, or wherever humans lived with Ruhar.

With that depressing thought, and the last image of Paradise lingering in my retinas, I needed something to distract me from seeing the display was now showing only empty interstellar space. Rising from my chair, I announced "It's time to meet those idiot Keepers. Gunny, you're with me."

"Sir," she did not move, blocking my way. "Much as I'd love to slap those Keepers around, I don't think it's right."

"Adams," I cocked my head. "You don't understand. I'm not inviting you to give them a beat-down. I need you there to make sure *I* don't give them a beat-down."

The airlock cycled and I strode into the docking bay, Adams right beside me. The two captured Dragon dropships were resting securely in their cradles, without the usual umbilical cables hooked up, and with their flight capability and weapon systems disabled. By disabled, I mean physically we had removed any components that might create a danger to us, or to the Keepers injuring themselves. I wanted the Keepers to not have a way to hurt us, and I wanted them to know for certain they had *no* possibility of harming us or escaping, so they would not waste time and effort defiantly and uselessly fighting back against us.

"Ready?" I asked Adams without turning to look at her. We were wearing Kristang armored suits, sealed up to prevent us from becoming infected. The docking bay was cut off from the rest of the ship, its air supply and water being recycled independently. The only way in or out was through two secure airlocks we controlled. One airlock lead to a chamber that scrubbed the exterior of suits clean, with caustic chemicals, ferocious nanomachines and flamethrowers. Anything organic on the surface of the suits, even in the tiny gaps of joints, would be dissolved then burned to dust, while the suits would only be mildly cooked. The assault teams led by Smythe and Giraud were going through the decontamination chamber now, two of them at a time.

After the dropships were secured, Smythe had led his people through the airlock, and Skippy released the zip-ties binding the Keepers. A gentle stimulant gas was pumped into the dropship cabins, and soon the Keepers were stirring, frightened, confused and angry. By the time I walked over to stand between the back ramps of the dropships, the still somewhat groggy Keepers had lowered the ramps and a half dozen of them were angrily confronting the four armor-suited pirates who were pointing shotguns at them. As I approached, one of the pirates saluted me, a gesture we usually dispensed with aboard ship. "Colonel," Lt. Williams acknowledged me, and I saluted him back. The exterior of our Kristang powered armored suits had a chameleon feature that could be manipulated by the wearer, or by Skippy. For our encounter with the Keepers, my suit's exterior had been modified to include symbols for UNEF, the American flag, my eagle rank insignia, plus text spelling out 'US Army' and my last name.

"Colonel?" One of the Keepers looked at me suspiciously. They already knew we were humans wearing Kristang armor because our faceplates were transparent. He stiffened and saluted me, announcing "I am Colonel Chisolm, you are," his eyes narrowed as he looked between my nametag and my face, illuminated by lights rimming my faceplate. "Bishop? The Barney guy?" He guessed with a mixture of shock and disgust. "You're that publicity stunt colonel from Paradise. Why are you *still* wearing that rank insignia?"

That remark got me hot under the collar, or helmet to be accurate. "*You're* a colonel now?" I barked at him, my amplified voice booming in the docking bay. "Last we heard, you were a captain. And you left the service, so you're nothing now. I should call you Colonel Goddamn Sanders, you chickenshit. You lost the honor of wearing a uniform when you betrayed your own people."

"You, wait," Chisolm got a puzzled look that overrode the redness of anger on his face. "You *left*. You," he snapped his fingers. "Yeah, you stole a Dodo and left Paradise. We all thought you were dead."

"Rumors of my death have been greatly exaggerated," I bit back a harsher reply.

"You're still not a legit colonel," he crossed his arms and looked to his people, more of whom were recovered enough to stumble down the back ramps. The Keepers nodded in agreement, clearly Chisolm was the de facto leader of that group of fanatical idiots.

"*I* have a Thuranin starship," I pointed to the deck. "And a dozen nukes. And a cargo bay stuffed full of ship-killer missiles. And a team of Special Operations troops and pilots under my command. *My* authority comes straight from UNEF Command on Earth."

"Bullshit," Chisolm retorted but his eyes flickered with uncertainty.

"You've been to Earth?" Another Keeper asked in a British accent, followed by a guilty look at Chisolm.

That is interesting, I thought. The bogus Keeper colonel's control of his team was not as secure as he pretended. Having the team's mission to Paradise intercepted by a group of lowly humans must have shaken their confidence in him and themselves. I needed to remind myself that these Keepers knew nothing about the Merry Band of Pirates and the status of Earth, although would anything I said matter to them? In front of me were the most fanatical of the Keepers, chosen for the mission to infect Paradise because they could be trusted not to be change their minds when confronted with reality on the ground. "Yes, we have. I have been back to Earth twice. Most of this crew," I gestured to Williams and his team, "never served on Paradise."

"That's true," Williams added, his shotgun not wavering. "I joined the ship at Earth. I have only been back once, but we're on our way home.'

"We are going home, *after*," I corrected him, "we confirm the lizard op to wipe out the population of Paradise is over."

"Excuse me, Colonel Bishop," the British Keeper stepped away from Chisolm, but not toward me or my people holding shotguns. Wisely, he held his hands up away from his body. "We heard the wormhole back to Earth was shut down, dormant."

"That wormhole is not closed," I announced, prompting a gasp from the Keepers. They murmured among themselves while Adams spoke over a private channel.

"Should you have told them that?" She asked with a tone of reproach.

"One way or another, Gunny, they sure as hell are never telling the outside galaxy about our secret. And the fact that we are able to fly back to Earth will tell them that wormhole is not really dormant."

"Good point, Sir," she acknowledged.

"Joe," Skippy whispered in my ear, "that British guy is Lieutenant Nigel Green."

I enabled my helmet speakers again. "You're Nigel Green?" I asked. The guy nodded with a glance at Chisolm. None of them were wearing nametags or were carrying any form of identification. "Your family back home is alive and well," I recalled from the briefing packet Skippy provided before the two dropships reached the *Flying Dutchman*. From facial recognition, the beer can knew the identity of the Keepers, and he fed into my earpiece details about their families and friends on Earth. "Your sister Susan had a baby boy she named Trevor after one of your grandfathers."

"He's lying, Green," Chisolm warned. "Don't listen to him. You don't have any proof, do you?" He said that last while glaring at me.

"Joe," Skippy whispered in my ear again, "I have photos of the baby, but photos can be faked. It doesn't matter anyway, these people are true close-minded fanatics. Facts will not sway their minds because they are desperately clinging to their beliefs, it is the only thing they have left. You have to appeal to them emotionally."

"I know that, Skippy, and you're wrong. I don't *have* to do anything for these idiots." Turning my external speakers back on, I addressed Green first. "I do have proof, but you won't believe it. The proof you *will* believe is when you see your nephew for yourself. As our SEALS team leader," I jerked a thumb at Williams, "said, we are headed home." Stepping forward, I got close enough to Chisolm to touch him. To his credit, he didn't flinch though I was taller and encased in a mech suit. "There are over a hundred thousand humans stranded on Paradise. Loyal soldiers smartened up and accepted the cold reality that we got suckered and used by the Kristang, that we were fighting on the wrong side of the war. No!" I exclaimed as Chisolm opened his mouth to protest. "You shut your mouth," I followed that with a powered-armor jab to his chest with an index finger. It knocked him back but only made him angry. "The loyal troops on Paradise are stuck there, while *you*, you traitorous, *dumb* motherfuckers get to go home. *You* are going home to Earth, *you* get to see your families again. It makes me sick," I said without exaggeration, as I could taste bile rising in my throat and I had to blink away tears of frustrated rage at the injustice. "I have friends on Paradise, good people who will never get a chance to go to Earth and see their loved ones. It disgusts me that your treason gives you a free ticket home. I would like to toss every one of you traitors out an airlock, but I won't do that," I jabbed Chisolm in the chest again. It had to hurt, and he was starting to react by taking small steps backward. He knew he couldn't hurt me or stop me from hurting him. I so much wanted to do a Darth Vader move on Chisolm, hold him up off the deck by his neck and squeeze with my powered gloves. "I *can't* do that, because I am a soldier and I follow a code of conduct."

"Colonel," Adams spoke aloud, reaching out a hand to restrain my arm. Chisolm must have an angry bruise on his chest.

"Colonel Bishop," Green called for my attention, and I turned toward him. "You said something about an operation to wipe out the population of Paradise? What operation?"

"Yours," I stated simply. "That's why you were out there."

"We," Green's eyes shifted rapidly between me and Chisolm. "We weren't doing that. Our mission was to infiltrate the planet, to gather intelligence and prepare for the Kristang to retake the planet."

I laughed bitterly. "The hamsters have a full battlegroup based at Paradise now, and they're building a Strategic Defense network in orbit. After that SD net is complete, the

Goddamned lizards will have a hell of a fight to even get close to the surface. Besides, your lizard friends are in a full-scale civil war, they didn't tell you about that?" I added as I saw Chisolm's eyebrows lift in surprise. "Yeah, the lizards will happily be busy killing each other for a decade, most likely. The real purpose of your operation," my focus was again on Green, "was to infect humans on Paradise, who would spread the infection to the Ruhar. Your lizard masters planned to get revenge on UNEF who broke away from their control, and they planned to make the planet unable to support a battlegroup. If even a quarter of the hamsters there died, the rest would be screaming for their government to get them away from the planet, and no hamster would ever want to move to a diseased world. The Ruhar government would need to quarantine the place, and they would pull back their battlegroup."

"He's lying again," Chisolm growled as his people shuffled their feet and looked at him for reassurance. "We weren't given any weapons at all, we didn't need them for our mission. We sure as hell were not given any bioweapon."

"Yes you were," Adams stepped forward and poked Chisolm in the chest, a bit harder than I had done. He was getting pissed about it. "It's in here," she jabbed him again, hard enough that he took a stride backward.

"You are all infected," I explained. "That is why we are sealed up in these suits, and why you will not be leaving this docking bay, until we have a cure for you *and* a vaccine for us."

"Or until you die," Adams stepped back away from the red-faced Chisolm. "Data recovered from Camp Alpha indicates the incubation period is about three months for humans."

Now the Keepers all began to talk amongst themselves. Hearing Adams reference Camp Alpha had struck a nerve. "What's wrong?" I asked the group. "Come on, some of you must have suspected you were getting used, *again*. The lizards tested the pathogen on multiple groups. They had a control group that was never infected, those people were taken off Camp Alpha by a Jeraptha ship, along with a mixed human-Ruhar team." I left out the participation of the Verd-Kris to avoid confusing the issue. "Groups of people would be separated, taken away from the base, and you'd never see them again?" I could see that got a reaction. "At least some of you idiots must have suspected something wasn't right. Seriously?" I mocked them. "You really thought the Kristang needed *you* provide intel about Paradise? Think about it, *think*. It would not be too long before one of you got recognized and the hamsters figured out that Keepers who left had somehow come back to the planet."

"That's not true," Chisolm waved his hands frantically to calm his people down. "We were trained to-"

"Trained to what? The hamsters have your DNA, even UNEF has your DNA in a file somewhere. You were going to get caught eventually. A month, maybe two months you could sneak around before somebody asked the wrong questions. Ah, forget it," I waved a hand in disgust. "If you are stupid enough to believe the Kristang war fleet needs *you* to take back control of the planet, then you are way too stupid to ever see reality."

"Um, Joe, there is an unpleasant surprise I just discovered," Skippy broke into the conversation. "It seems the Kristang did not entirely trust the crew of knuckleheads they sent on this mission. I have *no* idea why, as I can tell these fools are totally trustworthy. Not! Anywho, the Kristang were concerned the Twenty Stooges here would blab their mouths to someone on Paradise and expose the mission. These Keepers would die eventually, of course, but that would take months, and the Kristang did not need them to live for more than a month. One month would be plenty of time for them to infect plenty of unsuspecting victims, people who could move around a lot more freely and spread the pathogen widely. As a precaution, the Kristang injected each one of them with an implant that will all activate at the exact same time, about twenty eight days from their scheduled landing. This implant will burst blood vessels in their brains, so they will all drop dead instantly of massive aneurysms. The implants are timed to kill them all at the exact same moment, so one of these fools doesn't see his buddy drop dead and start shooting his mouth off before the implant kills him."

"Where are these implants?" I took a half-step back, subconsciously afraid of getting killed by proxy.

"Like the suicide dots our away teams wear, the implants are at the back of the neck, near the brain stem. Our nanodots kill the wearer by electrical impulse, they are worn on the skin, they can be removed easily, and of course the wearer knows about them and decides whether to activate the suicide mechanism. The implants given to the Keepers were inserted under the skin, and nanofibers spread along blood vessels to several places in their brains."

"Can you turn them off, get rid of them, something like that?"

"Oh, I already postponed the activation sequence. But I can't guarantee there won't be a glitch so to be safe, they need to be physically removed. That can be accomplished easily enough, I will send in nanobots to disable and dissolve the Kristang implants."

"Ok, we can do that when we-"

"You are not touching me with any of your Goddamned machines," Chisolm growled. "We *do* know about those implants, the Kristang explained why they are needed and we all agreed to have them. You're lying, the implants aren't dangerous to us, they are beacons so the Kristang can locate us when our mission is complete. Without the implants, we might mistakenly be targeted during a raid, before the planet is taken back from the hamsters. The implants will pinpoint our location, so we can be evaced by stealth dropships when the Kristang are satisfied with the take from our intel."

"Wow," Skippy's voice rang from the speakers. "That is a truly sterling example of self-delusion. Hey asswipe, you *know* that isn't true. You morons are disposable to the Kristang, no way would they risk sending a stealthed dropship down to pick up you losers. Seriously, you expect them to fly around willy-nilly to pick up all of you?"

"No, we will get a signal to gather in a pre-arranged, remote location," Chisolm glared at me. "That minimizes the risk of-"

"Oh, you have *got* to be kidding me," Skippy's voice dripped with sarcasm. "Why would-"

I cut off Skippy's disgusted comment before we wasted too much time on an irrelevant discussion. "As you reminded me, never argue with an idiot, because they can't understand when they've lost. Fine," I pointed to Chisolm, "you can keep your implants, and we will even reset the timer back to its original setting. But, anyone who does *not* get their implants disabled will be isolated so you can't harm anyone else until you drop dead, got that?"

That prompted a huddle around Chisolm by several Keepers, with low voices and a lot of animated hand gestures. I politely did not eavesdrop on the argument. Ok, so it was not me being polite, I just did not want to listen to a bunch of fanatical dipshits trying to make a totally obvious decision. After two minutes, Chisolm stepped forward. "Colonel Bishop," I could see referring to me as a colonel felt sour in his mouth, "we agree to have the implants disabled, therefore you have no excuse to isolate any of us," he smirked as if he had just foiled an evil plot. "We are one team and we will remain strong together. Also, it appears a locator beacon will not do us any good now, you could easily block the transmission." My guess was he added that last part as a way to save face in front of his people.

I truly did not care whether his people respected him or not. "Fine," I snapped. "Here's what's going to happen. We are going to take samples of your blood and tissues," Mad

Doctor Skippy had been vague about how invasive and painful the sample collection process would be, and I truly did not care. "You are going to cooperate and live here," I gestured to the portable shelters we had set up along the inner bulkhead of the docking bay, "until we have a cure, or until you die as the pathogen runs its course. We will not risk you infecting us or contaminating the rest of the ship, because we *are* going home, and UNEF Command won't let us off the ship if they think we might be carriers. I will now leave you to the kind tenderness of Gunnery Sergeant Adams," I nodded toward her "She will explain in detail your living arrangements and *exactly* how you will be cooperating. Keep this in mind," I scowled from one face to the next. "We need samples of the pathogen to develop a cure, and we need subjects to test a cure. We do not need *all* of you for the procedure to be successful. Sergeant Adams," she came to attention. "I figure we need maybe ten out of twenty of these losers, max. If they give you any shit, you have my permission to break bones. If any of them give you serious trouble, I am *ordering* you to toss them out an airlock, with this asshole," I pointed straight at Chisolm, "going first. In case any of you geniuses thinks Gunny Adams won't do it, here's a breaking news flash for you. That Kristang destroyer that brought you here? It is not coming to rescue you, because we took control and jumped it just above the surface of the star, where those brave warriors had a few seconds to cry and piss in their pants before they got swallowed up by a fireball. Adams here pressed the button to jump those lizards straight into hell. Do *not* piss her off. Or," I smiled with my mouth but not my eyes, "do it. *Please*. One of you, try it. Make my day."

There weren't any takers for my dare. No matter how fanatical they were, they were badly shaken up by their shocking sudden change of circumstances, and by what I had told them. Even Chisolm cooperated, though he told his people to cooperate only so they could live to fight another day, fight for the Kristang. I did not care what he told them. Mad Doctor Skippy got his samples and began doing, whatever it was Skippy did.

CHAPTER THIRTY THREE

Two days later, I saw Adams in the galley. "How are our guests enjoying their luxury accommodations?"

She gave a long, exaggerated sigh, making sort of motor boat sound with her lips. For a moment I just stared at her, because I never imagined her doing something like that. There were so many layers to our tough Gunnery Sergeant, she was like an onion wrapped in an onion. A sweet onion, like a, what are they called? Not Valvoline, that's a motor oil. Not Viagra either. Something with a V? Vidalia, that's it! A Vidalia onion, not a sour one that makes you cry. Although, Adams could make you cry if she wanted to. Despite the years we had served together, I barely knew her, the real Margaret Adams. That was maybe my one major regret, that-

Uh, I'd better drop *that* subject like a hot potato.

Anyway, she sounded exasperated and disgusted. "Sir, I have to talk to you about that. I don't want to, but I'm kind of required to by the UCMJ."

"The Uniform Code of Military Justice?" Holy shit, I told myself, this could not be good. If Adams had seen fit to toss one of the Keepers out an airlock. I was Ok with that, but expected she would have notified me about it first. She should have immediately notified me about any serious incident, and, again, holy shit! Anything involving the UCMJ was no joke. "Uh, what?"

"It's nothing serious, Sir," she must have seen the deer-in-the-headlights look on my face. "Some of them, that Chisolm guy mostly, have been complaining about their treatment. One of them is a barracks lawyer, he cited sections of the Geneva Convention at me."

"The Geneva freakin' Convention?" I was astonished. "Like that matters out here?" Actually, crap, it might. The Keepers were humans, and our mission was under the authority of UNEF Command. So, damn it, maybe it did matter. Oh, hell, I needed to ask Skippy, he knew all that legal stuff.

"That's above my pay grade, Colonel," she raised an eyebrow, having just successfully passed that particular buck to me. "Consider yourself officially notified, Sir," she added with a twinkle in her eyes. I loved to see Adams smile, it lit up her whole face.

"Gunny, I would *love* to give a shit about whether those Goddamn Keeper traitors are happy about their living situation."

"I am guessing you don't?"

"Sadly, my shit-giving ability is currently offline, and it don't look good for getting it fixed any time soon," I winked at her.

"What should I tell the Keepers? They demanded to meet with you, to present a list of grievances."

"Grievanc-" I clamped my jaw shut to control my anger. "Tell that barracks lawyer I have him penciled in to meet with me at Punch-him-in-the-face O'clock, but if he would prefer Kick-in-the-balls Thirty, that's good for me too."

"I don't think any of those cowards have balls, Sir."

"Punch-in-the-face O'Clock it is, then. Tell him he can meet me in the airlock, I'll give him a tour of the ship, from the *outside*. It will be a short tour, before his eyeballs explode from vacuum. Seriously, Adams, if that particular shithead were to suffer a terribly unfortunate accident involving powered armor and several vital organs, I would not be unhappy, if you know what I mean."

"I know what you mean, Sir."

I do not know what Adams did, if anything, but I did not get any more complaints from the Keepers. That I know of. Not that I asked, if you know what I mean.

While we waited for Skippy to magically create a vaccine or cure for the bioweapon, I tried to keep the crew's spirits up by requesting people to create lists like what favorite food they would eat when we got back to Earth, what places they wanted to visit during the leave they would be granted after debriefing, happy stuff like that. One thing I did *not* do was ask about the family and friends people were looking forward to reconnecting with, because thinking about how long we had been away from our loved ones was bound to be painful, and exactly the opposite of the happy morale boost I was hoping for.

It did not surprise me that while I was looking forward to finally seeing home again, our high-speed SpecOps warriors and hotshot pilots had mixed feelings about it. Major Smythe openly told me he would miss the adrenaline rush of combat, and just never knowing what gut-wrenching crisis we would be dealing with the next day. All of the SpecOps teams worried they would be trapped dirtside after this mission, as their national militaries would want at least some of them to stay home, to transfer their knowledge and train other troops in space combat techniques. The pilots were worried about having to fly slow, boring aircraft and helicopters again, and never even getting above low Earth orbit. There wasn't anything I could say to soothe their fears, as I had no idea what UNEF Command planned to do with the crew once we landed on our home planet.

There was another person aboard the ship, not technically a member of the crew, who had seriously mixed feelings about going home. Hans Chotek was worried about UNEF Command's reaction to how long we had been away, on what was supposed to be a simple and short mission. Yes, we had successfully confirmed the Thuranin were not sending another surveyor ship to Earth. And yes, we had stopped the Ruhar from sending a ship, paid for by the Kristang. Those were both major items in the plus column for sure. Even our having saved the human population of Paradise, twice, hopefully counted as wins. But we had also risked exposure on Paradise two times, Ok, technically three times. And our beer can had proven to have judgment as trustworthy as a meth addict with a pocketful of stolen credit cards. We nearly got trapped by a task force of combined Thuranin, Bosphuraq and oh, yeah, don't forget Maxolhx ships. We *broke* an Elder wormhole! We had messed with a freakin' Elder sentinel killing machine. It was almost not worth mentioning that we engaged in combat with a Maxolhx warship, and that a Maxolhx had committed suicide aboard our ship. All that bad or at least risky stuff happened on Hans Chotek's watch. All of which he expected to catch hell about from chair-bound bureaucrats when we got home.

And all of which did not compare to the fact that career diplomat Hans Chotek *started an alien civil war*. I almost felt sorry for the guy. Srcatch that, I did feel sorry for him.

There was another person I felt sorry for: myself. UNEF Command had not wanted me as captain of, or even aboard, the *Flying Dutchman* the last time we left Earth. They viewed me as too young and too prone to take risks before. They were going to be just *thrilled* to hear what trouble I had gotten us into this time. My stomach got queasy every time I thought of the major ass-chewing I would get as soon as my boots hit the ground.

Anyway, to keep my mind off the fate that awaited me on Earth, I took our enforced idleness as an opportunity to ask Skippy about something. My hope was I could bring some good news home to UNEF Command, and maybe they'd forget about all that other shit. Which was never going to happen, but I figured I should give the self-delusion thing a try. "Hey, Skippy."

"Hey, Joe. What do you propose to waste my time with now?"

"How do you know that I'm going to- Oh, forget it. I have a question. Now that you are the new, better-than-ever, 'fresh scent' Skippy-"

"Fresh *scent*? I do not have a scent. Or do I?" He gasped in shuddering horror. "I have never asked you if-"

"No, no, Skippy, don't worry about it. I just meant that 'fresh scent' is something marketing people say when they describe an improved product."

"Hmmm. Did this product previously smell like rotten fish?"

"Well, in that case, 'fresh scent' would be a big improvement, right?"

"I can't argue with that. The way I would describe myself is 'More Awesome Than Ever'."

"How about 'Fifty Percent More Awesome For The Same Price'?"

"I like your thinking. Anywho, what is your question?"

"Can the new Awesome-Beyond-Imagination Skippy share even a tiny bit of technology with us poor monkeys soon, like when we get to Earth? You said you were working on that, after you rearranged your sock drawers or whatever you do in there."

"Ugh. Why do I ever try explaining technology to you? Ok, at your pathetic level of development, rearranging my sock drawer is an appropriate, bacteria-level understanding of the mind-bogglingly incredible-"

"Yeah, blah blah blah, you're awesome. Listen, has rewriting your internal software loosened your restrictions yet? The annoying subroutines or whatever that prevent you from flying ships by yourself, sharing technology with us, all that?"

"Not yet, Joe," he scolded me. "I *told* you, I am working on it. Damn, I should never have mentioned that possibility to you. I. Do. Not. *Know* yet, you dumdum. Rewriting my software, which is a bad analogy that makes you think the task is much easier than it truly is, has proved to be an extremely delicate problem. I am having to create sort of a model of myself, so I can test changes in a controlled environment, instead of taking the risk of damaging myself. If I screw something up, I might be unable to undo the damage, and then we would be right back to my operating at reduced, perhaps severely reduced capacity. Would you like me to take that risk?"

"No! No, I very much did not like it when you were acting drunk or high or brain-damaged or whatever was wrong with you. The last thing I need is you waking me up at Zero Dark Thirty to marvel at the freakin' universe. You, uh, take all the time you need to get that sock drawer squared away, and I'll keep my mouth shut."

"Riiiiiiiiight. Because you are *so* good at being patient. When, *if*, I am able to share my galaxy-spanning knowledge of physics, what are you hoping for?"

"Oh, uh," now I was embarrassed, but I had to ask. "You know, you help us build our own starships. Bad-ass warships, not like this piece of crap we're flying."

"What?" He chuckled. No, he snickered, that's a better way of describing it. "No, Joe, we will not be doing any science-fiction shit like that. I told you before, just bringing Earth's industrial infrastructure up to the point where humans can build the machines, just to build the machines we need to build other machines to begin constructing a single starship, will take well over a hundred years, *if* nothing goes wrong."

"Ayuh, and I told you humanity doesn't have any other appointments over the next couple hundred years. We should get started, pronto."

"Ugh. Joe, you can forget any nonsense about a single planet of monkeys building a warfleet to take on the whole freakin' galaxy."

"Listen, Skippy, I know the hostile aliens out there have thousands-"

"*Hundreds* of thousands, Joe. The Maxolhx coalition alone could easily mobilize thirty thousand warships to throw against Earth, and they would not be straining their resources."

"That's a lot of ships, sure. But we don't need to take the fight to the enemy. All we need to have is a defense strong enough that the enemy doesn't want to pay the price of hitting us. With your help, your knowledge of Elder-level technology, couldn't we build a strong defense in say, a couple hundred years? Assuming we can keep nosy aliens away from Earth that long?"

"Uh huh, uh huh, that is all a great fantasy, Joey. Except for the teensy weensy little fact that you do not have even a hundred years to get started. The clock is ticking down to Doomsday, no matter what you do."

"Like I said, assume we can keep aliens from coming to Earth. We've been doing a pretty good job at keeping them away so far." As I said that, I mentally pictured karma chuckling as it got ready to bite me on the ass.

"The problem is not simply aliens flying to Earth. The problem, Joe, is the speed of light."

"Uh, what?"

"Speed. Of. Light. You dumdum."

"I got the dumdum part. What does the speed of li- Ohhhhh *shit*."

"Wow, that time I actually saw the 40 watt bulb of understanding light up in your head. It's a dim bulb, barely visible, like if it was buried under thirty feet of mud and-"

"You're saying light from Earth is radiating outward, and no matter what we do, that light will be seen out in the galaxy? The problem is radio waves?"

"Correct. You monkeys could not resist blabbing your mouths off after we, or actually I, destroyed the Kristang who were enslaving your planet. Your news programs broadcast reports and images of the *Flying Dutchman* in orbit, and Kristang sites getting blown up all over your planet. Even without radio and TV signals, the gamma ray bursts of us jumping in and out, and from when I jumped that Kristang frigate into your sun, are going to be visible and will be considered highly suspicious."

"Crap. Ok, so those radio and TV waves and gamma rays will be detected by some hostile alien's telescope or sensor platform. Give me the bad news, how close is the nearest alien listening post or telescope or whatever?"

"The closest such sensor platform to Earth is two hundred ninety four lightyears."

"Oh." I breathed a sigh of relief. "Damn, Skippy, you got me into a panic for nothing. We have almost three hundred, no, wait. It's been a couple years since the *Dutchman* first jumped into Earth orbit, so-"

"Signals traveling from *Earth* are not the problem, dumdum," Skippy chided me more gently than he usually did when I said something stupid.

"No? Then what-" Most of the time, my brain was annoyingly slow, just like Skippy said. This time, however, I got it right away. "Oh, shit. The problem isn't gamma rays coming from Earth. The problem is gamma rays every time you reopen that wormhole that is supposed to be dormant."

"*Egg*-zactly, Joe, very good! That time I was not belittling your intelligence, you caught on quickly. Hmmm, maybe being around me has smartened you up a bit. Yes, that Elder wormhole is supposed to be shut down, but we have used it three times since then. Outbound and return on our second mission. Plus outbound on this current mission that has lasted way longer than anyone expected. We will be using that wormhole again to get back to Earth, and outbound for our next mission. Whenever we use that mostly-dormant wormhole, I open it in a location far away from its original programmed pattern. But someone is going to notice gamma rays coming from a wormhole that is supposed to be inactive. They are going to notice multiple gamma rays events, at odd intervals, and that is going to look very suspicious."

"Tell me the bad news, Skippy. How close is an alien sensor platform to the far end of that wormhole?"

"Sixty two lightyears, Joe. *That* is why I have been telling you we do not have time to enhance Earth's infrastructure and build a bodaciously awesome war fleet, or a Death Star or something stupid like that."

"We only have sixty two years?"

"Less than sixty years, since the first time we used that wormhole after I shut it down. Those gamma rays have been radiating outward, and there is nothing we can do to stop them."

In sixty years, human technology had gone from the first powered flight by the Wright brothers to jet airliners. Could we- "Wait! How about this: we fly out to this alien sensor platform," in my mind, I pictured a single satellite hanging in space all by itself. "And you hack into it and tell it to ignore those gamma rays?"

"Uh, no, Joe. There is not '*a*' sensor platform. Sixty two lightyears from the far end of that wormhole is a Thuranin planet with a fleet servicing base. Even if the ships there have their entire sensor suite powered down for maintenance, there are hundreds of other sensors in orbit and on the surface that could pick up those gamma rays."

"Ok, but-"

"*But*, you are thinking the magic of Skippy could hack into every system on and around that planet, right? Fuggetaboutit. Joe, there have been multiple gamma ray events, because we used that wormhole multiple times. Sensor systems get regular updates, so I would need to keep going back there to hack in, every time a gamma ray burst is about to pass through that system. Expanding a bubble outward from that wormhole, there is another inhabited star system sixty five lightyears away, two systems that are seventy lightyears away, and if you go out to an eighty lightyear radius, there are *fourteen* star systems that could detect those gamma rays. It is just not practical to conceal all those gamma rays from enemy eyes, Joe. I am sorry."

"Well, shit. What could we accomplish in sixty years, if we tried really hard?"

"Uh, hmmm. You could make a really big white flag that says 'We surrender'?"

"Oh, shit."

"You could also do a lot of praying, and, hey! Maybe you could bake a cake for the aliens who come to invade and obliterate your homeworld. It would have to be a really *nice* cake."

"Not funny, Skippy."

"There is absolutely nothing amusing about the situation, Joe. I also do not see any way out of this mess. But, I'm not worried about it."

"You are *not worried* about it? That is a rotten thing to say, Skippy. Just because you are not personally in danger, we-"

"Joe, I am not worried about it, because I am sure you monkeys will think of something. You are quite clever."

"Oh." I was ashamed of myself for thinking Skippy was heartless about the prospect of my home world being blown up. "Thanks for the vote of-"

"If not, you are *totally* screwed. Like, every starfaring species in the galaxy descending on your planet and tearing the place apart. Then probably nuking it until it is a radioactive cinder. Although, that's probably the *best*-case scenario."

"Shit."

"Shit, indeed."

"Damn it! You're telling me all the work we've done out here, stopping aliens from sending ships to Earth, has been for *nothing*?"

"Not nothing, Joe. We have been buying time. Come on, Joe, nothing lasts forever. Giving the people of Earth another sixty years of pleasantly blissful ignorance is a worthy goal. Just think of how many people will fall in love over the next sixty years, how many people will achieve their life goals, how much happiness the population of Earth can experience in sixty years."

"I had not thought of it that way, Skippy. I guess buying time is worth our effort."

"Yup. Before, you know, Earth inevitably becomes a lifeless ball of dust."

"Skippy, if I ever ask you to cheer me up, please remind me of this conversation."

"Oh, no problemo, Joe. Glad we had this little talk, if it makes you feel better about the inevitable extinction of your species. See? I am *totally* nailing this empathy shit."

I had been hoping I could tell UNEF Command that the whole scary year of agony we had gone through with Skippy's fight with the worm was worth it, because the new improved Skippy could share advanced technology with us, and Earth could build a bad-ass war fleet to protect us from an entire galaxy of hostile aliens. Instead, I would be telling them that humanity not only didn't have time to build a single starship of our own, our entire species had less than sixty years to live.

Maybe I better order a *super* nice fruit basket to soften the blow, when I deliver that steaming pile of news.

CHAPTER THIRTY FOUR

Skippy had warned me that just identifying the elements of the pathogen, and how precisely it sneakily used human DNA to create itself and replicate, could take a while. Like, possibly weeks in meatsack time, if he could do it at all. He needed to not only find the weapon's components in the blood and tissues of infected people, he needed to match them to the data recovered by the Mavericks, then run exhaustive tests to make sure the pathogen had not already mutated beyond recognition. If it had mutated substantially, he would need to start over. He did not sound optimistic, even when I told him the Merry Band of Pirates were all-in on trusting the awesomeness this time. "Bioweapons are not my wheelhouse, Joe," he had grumbled irritably after the first set of samples were placed into the lab we set up in a corner of the docking bay. "And the medical equipment aboard this secondhand Frankenship is not the best to work with. Be patient."

Thus, I was rather depressed about the possibility we would not find a cure, and therefore the human population of Paradise would continue to be at high risk. When we jumped away, we targeted to be within two lighthours of a Ruhar communications relay station, within its line-of-sight narrowcasting cone pointed toward Paradise. Skippy was able to monitor message traffic dropped off by passing starships, and from encrypted traffic we knew the Ruhar federal government was coming under increasing pressure to 'do something' about the risk posed by humans on Paradise. Most of that pressure was, ironically, not coming from Paradise, but from other Ruhar worlds who feared an infection spreading to them. All ship traffic to and from the Paradise system was embargoed, nothing in and nothing out. Of the hamsters on Paradise clamoring for extreme action to be taken to remove the human threat, most were recent arrivals. A great majority of long-time inhabitants, even those who lived through UNEF's brief and bumbling occupation, were against any attempt to relieve the threat by killing all the humans, although no one argued against a strictly-enforced quarantine.

The Ruhar had appealed to the Jeraptha, who agreed to examine the data taken from Camp Alpha. Regrettably, the Jeraptha announced that type of bioweapon was unknown to them, and their research could not proceed far without samples of the actual pathogen. The patron species of the Ruhar also warned that, according to their preliminary studies, the pathogen was a very, *very* clever bioweapon, as it could plausibly be a natural mutation of human DNA. An unlikely mutation, but difficult to prove as a violation of The Rules. The beetles assured the Ruhar they had mentioned the incident to the Rindhalu, who responded that they would investigate the incident *if* there was an actual outbreak on Paradise, and even in that case, the next meeting of the Rindhalu council to launch an investigation would not be for another three and a half years. Any actual investigation would not begin for another five to eight years, after a proper time for deliberation. Those who knew the Rindhalu well were amazed and impressed the spiders were acting so quickly, a sign the senior species was taking the bioweapon threat seriously.

Anyway, I mention all that to demonstrate that we basically were on our own in trying to find a cure and vaccine for the deadly pathogen. The Ruhar lacked the technology and understanding to even identify the pathogen's base components in an infected human or Ruhar. The beetles were treating the incident as an unexpected and exciting opportunity to wager on how many intelligent beings would die on Paradise. No, that was unfair of me to say that. Of course the Jeraptha could not resist such juicy action, and they promised to help enforce the embargo around Paradise and hunt for a Kristang ship, but the recent attacks by the Bosphuraq had caught the beetles off-guard and they were scrambling to redeploy their fleet. And the all-powerful ancient Rindhalu? Well, they might consider considering the problem, if it became an actual problem. The Rindhalu could never be described as a hasty species. *Ents* moved faster. So do glaciers.

Knowing all that, you can understand why I was not sleeping well, and why I was mostly awake and tossing and turning in my bunk at 0123 Hours when Skippy's avatar shimmered to life above my chest. "Joe! Joe!"

"*Gaaa*! What the hell, Skippy?" I sputtered with a dry mouth.

"I have good new- *Oooooh*, wow, you do not look so good right when you wake up. I mean, you are a monkey so I know not to expect much, but *day-umn*, dude."

"Yeah, I'm real concerned about how I look at zero dark thirty. What is it?"

"Joe, seriously, you should reconsider rejecting that sexbot, I should say, *companion* I built for you. She wouldn't mind how you look in the wee hours of the morning, I can't imagine a real human woman not being totally *horrified* by-"

"That bot was an *it*, not a she, Skippy. Please, tell me your good news, or I am throwing a pillow over my head and going back to sleep."

"Ok, Ok. Damn, this is the thanks I get for being your wingman-"

"Skippy!"

"Fine. The good news is I have created what I believe is a cure for the pathogen. And vaccines not only for humans, but for Ruhar also."

"Holy shit." I sat bolt upright in bed, so of course I whacked my head. With news that good, I ignore the pain. "You said it could take weeks, maybe months, if it could be done at all."

"Joe, I underestimated my own magnificence."

"Uh huh, right. Did you pull a Scotty on us?"

"A Scotty?" He asked innocently, with his voice just a touch *too* innocent.

"Yeah, like, you say that fixing the warp engines will take six hours and a miracle, and you have the job done in thirty minutes?"

"Oh, ha ha," snickered. "That's a good one, I'll have to remember that. No, I did not do that, Joe. Truly, if anything, I *under*stated the difficulty of the effort. When I first examined the pathogen components, the subroutine I assigned to the task wanted to curl up in a ball and cry. It was, as you New Englanders would say, *wicked hahd*."

"Ok, so what changed?"

"I decided that approaching the task as a biological problem was not going to lead me anywhere. So, I looked at human DNA as an information storage and processing system."

"Uh, what?"

"Joe, DNA is not just a bunch of colored balls connected by sticks like in your high school science lab. It is a powerful chemical-based data storage system, quite efficient for its size. It is also a handy factory for churning out organic chemicals, which is how the Kristang were able to use modified DNA to create the prion base components. The cure I have created is pure genius, even I am amazed by my awesomeness this time. This cure not only prevents the infected person's DNA from replicating more of the base components, it acts as a monitoring and repair mechanism for DNA, to prevent harmful mutations. To a limited extent, of course, if a person gets a bad dose of radiation, their DNA will be damaged beyond any self-repair capability my cure can provide."

"Excellent! Outstanding! And a vaccine, too?"

"As you would say, '*Ayuh*'." It did not sound right when Skippy said it, but I didn't protest. "The cure and the vaccine are the same mechanism. Well, mostly. The vaccine is part of the cure. The vaccine will prevent a person from becoming infected, and it can stop an infected person's DNA from making more of the pathogen. The cure has a second element that latches onto one base component of the prion, so it can never assemble into anything dangerous. After a while, my guess is four to six months, the base components will dissolve on their own. The vaccine I developed for the Ruhar is much simpler, as the genetically-enhanced biology of that species has a vastly superior immune response. All my vaccine does is allow the Ruhar version of DNA to create sort of antibodies to identify the pathogen components, and the hamster immune system will take care of the rest."

"Skippy, this is truly awesome. When can you begin testing?"

"I left a message for Sergeant Adams to schedule it for 0800 this morning, after the Keepers wake up."

"Oh, *skuh-REW* that. Hell, I'm up. We're doing it *now*, if you have doses of the cure ready."

"I have been manufacturing the cure, within the hour I will have enough doses for four people. Are you sure about rousing people out of bed at this ungodly hour?" He asked cluelessly, after having roused *me* out of bed.

"We have been away from Earth way too freakin' long," I did not mention a good part of that time was because of his battle with the worm. "And every minute that goes by, there could be a dangerous incident on Paradise that might put people, *humans*, there in danger. Some hamster kid gets the sniffles, the parents remember the kid came into contact with a human last month, and next thing you know there is a full-blown panic with frightened hamster civilians chasing humans with pitchforks and torches. Or hitting them with SD maser cannons from orbit. So, *hell* no, I am not waiting another six hours just so those Keeper assholes can get a couple more hours of sleep and a nice breakfast. I will call Adams, you get all your mad doctor stuff ready."

The Keepers did not like being rousted from bed four hours early. As former military, they also were used to it and did not complain too much. We got four volunteers for testing the cure, including the British soldier Nigel Green. Unlike Chisolm, Green was more of a scared, vulnerable and gullible kid rather than a truly committed fanatic. Chisolm caused trouble, shouting warnings that they were not infected, that the supposed 'cure' was in fact a bioweapon we were testing on them, and that- We never got to hear the end of Chisolm's entertaining diatribe, as Adams had picked him up and casually tossed him across the docking bay to crash into the outer bay doors. He broke one arm and two ribs, and with him no longer agitating, the rest of the Keepers were much more docile. Personally, I think the only reason Adams didn't toss that stupid asshole out an airlock was, she hoped for another opportunity to really beat the shit out of him.

Six days later, Skippy was confident enough with the results from the four volunteers, that he wanted to expand the testing to the others, all of them. I provided an incentive in the form of real food for volunteers, as the Keepers had been surviving on sludges that were left over from our Newark mission. And, yes, I made sure the keepers ate the truly nasty banana-flavored sludges first, so we could get rid of them. Even Chisolm offered to be tested, after seeing the first four volunteers eating fresh salads, fresh strawberries, French fries and cheeseburgers. It was a sign of my generous beneficence that I gave precious cheeseburgers to the Keepers. We were running very low on cheeseburger components, it was a big sacrifice not to eat them all myself. The Keepers' mouths were watering as they watched Green and the three others chow down on cheeseburgers, a treat they had not enjoyed since long before they left Paradise.

Eight days after that, Skippy contacted me in my office. "Joe, I am completely, absolutely satisfied with the test results. The Keepers are cured, one hundred percent."

"The vaccine, too?" I had been the first volunteer to be injected with the test vaccine, over the objections of Adams, Chotek, Chang and others.

"The vaccine also. Completely, satisfyingly successful. This is one of my greatest triumphs, truly. What is most amazing about me is that I have somehow managed to amaze myself. Whoo-boy, never thought *that* could happen. What are the odds, huh?"

"Those odds must, uh, be more than my monkey brain could calculate," I agreed quickly, to short-circuit him going on a long tangent about how awesomely awesome he was. "That's great. You're ready to transmit the package then?"

"Ready at the first opportunity."

"I'll talk with Chotek to get permission. Damn, I can't believe we're finally going home."

"Oh, yeah. Joy. Another soul-stirring visit to that miserable ball of mud orbiting a boring yellow dwarf star; who wouldn't be just *thrilled* about that?"

"Think of it as your opportunity to finally give smart replies to those idiots who said nasty things to you on Facebook last time."

"Ooooooh, good point! That little Jimmy what's-his-name is *so* going to regret his ignorant comment about 'Galaxy Quest'. Big jerk."

"I'm sure he will."

Chotek approved sending what we called 'The Package'. Our opportunity came when a passing Jeraptha ship exchanged messages with the communications relay. The relay sent the messages onward to Paradise, including a large dump of data Skippy had previously loaded into the relay's databanks. To the Ruhar on Paradise, it would look like our package had been delivered by the Jeraptha ship.

The package contained extensive analysis, test results and instructions how to manufacture the cure and vaccines for both humans and Ruhar. Embedded in the package were subtle hints that miracle cure had been provided by the Maxolhx, who were embarrassed and pissed off that clients under them had acted in such a rash manner that might blow back on the senior species.

Then, we had to wait and hope the Ruhar would take action.

"Bingo! Good news, Joe!" Skippy shouted excitedly over my zPhone while I was in the gym. At least he hadn't interrupted me in the shower, so I counted that one in the 'W' column.

Carefully letting the bench-press bar settle into the clamps, I sat up and pulled the phone off my belt. "You sound happy. Did you just think of a way to persuade Jimmy he is wrong about, uh, what was it?"

"Galaxy Quest, Joe. No, this is not about frivolous arguments with strangers on the internet. I have great news. And, uh, kind of a problem. Could we speak in private?"

"Sure thing, Skippy." I walked into passageway and turned left to go aft. There were plenty of mostly-empty cargo bays in that direction. "What's up?"

"The Ruhar government on Paradise, led by your old friend the Burgermeister, has just approved a testing program for the human vaccine. UNEF has over a thousand volunteers. Not UNEF, exactly, because as you know the 'Force' part of UNEF is dissolving rapidly."

"Wow, that is great news! What about the Ruhar form of the vaccine?"

"That is being tested also, with a lot fewer volunteers. Finding test subjects for the hamster form of vaccine is less important, because the Ruhar have sophisticated techniques for modeling the vaccine's effectiveness in computer models and in tissue samples.

Remember how in the village of Teskor, you saw the farmer there growing meat without growing the entire animal?"

"Yes, I remember," I agreed with an involuntary shudder. "It was kinda creepy."

"The humans on Paradise would disagree, because the Ruhar have pilot programs to adapt that meat-growing technology to foods humans can eat. Cheeseburgers may soon be back on the menu for people on Paradise, Joe!"

"Outstanding, but how does that affect vaccine testing?" If he went off on a tangent, I might forget the questions I needed to ask.

"Because the hamsters have laboratory versions of their bodies, without any sort of higher brain functions. These lab shells, as they are called, allow the Ruhar to run complete and accurate tests under controlled conditions. They can vaccinate shells, then infect them with the pathogen. Joe, when they do that, they will see my vaccine is a hundred percent effective. That should relieve the pressure on their federal government to, ahem," he cleared his throat, "'do something' about humans. We both know what 'do something' means."

"Yeah, we do. Skippy, this is truly excellent. One question for you. In your gift package about the cure and vaccines, you hinted it was from the Maxolhx. Did the Ruhar buy that? I'm concerned the Maxolhx will find out about it, and they sure know they weren't involved."

"That is *two* questions, dumdum. Man, you never learn. Ok, first, yes the Ruhar totally bought it, because they know that pathogen took seriously advanced biotech to create, so it makes sense the Maxolhx might have been involved. Second, no way would the Maxolhx deny taking credit for providing that gift package, *duh*. It gives them a plausible way out if they someday *are* involved in a bioweapon attack, because they will say their involvement in providing this vaccine proves they are strictly against any violations of The Rules. Also, the Maxolhx will assume the whole mess was the work of the Bosphuraq, which is what I suspect anyway. Giving the Maxolhx credit for providing the vaccine will be seen as a sort of get-out-of-jail-free card played by the Bosphuraq. I do not see any downside for us in this."

"Great."

"Of course, I did not see any downside to us telling the Jeraptha about a sneak attack by the Thuranin, and that blew up in our faces big-time, so shmaybe I am not the best person to ask."

"As always, I am *bursting* with confidence after talking with you, Skippy."

"Don't kill the messenger, Joe."

"Sorry. Ok, so, how long do we have to hang around here until we know for certain the vaccine works? No, wait, I mean, until the Ruhar government decides humans are no longer a threat, and they lift the quarantine?"

"We don't need to wait here, Joe. We can get under way, and ping a Ruhar communications relay before we leave their territory. Before we make the final jump to the wormhole I shut down, there will be plenty of time for the news to get ahead of us."

"Wow, that is great to hear. Chotek will be thrilled. Oh, shit."

"What?"

"You said there is a problem we need to talk about?"

"Uh, yeah." He did an awkward throat-clearing sound. "You need to decide whether bringing me back to Earth is worth the risk."

"The, uh, what?"

"*Ugh. Come on*, Joe. I bared my soul to you, I thought we had an honest-to-God *moment*, and you've forgotten about it already?"

"Refresh my memory, Ok? Oh," I snapped my fingers. "Hell, is this that idiot thing about you being a dire threat to the galaxy, because you suspect that Elder AI killed the planet Newark?"

"I *strongly* suspect that, and yes, it is about that. Bringing me close to your home planet may not be the best idea."

"Oh, dammit, Skippy, are we going to do this every time we go somewhere sensitive? Listen, I asked you before, do you feel like going on a genocidal killing spree?"

"Well, maybe against the Maxolhx, but they *totally* deserve it."

"Ok, then-"

"And the Kristang warrior caste, of course."

"Of course."

"Plus, you know, whoever else was involved in throwing the planet Newark out of orbit."

"Ayuh, got that."

"Ooh, ooh!" He was on a roll. "Also, people who go through the express lane at the grocery store, even though they know they have *way* more than ten items in their cart."

"Ohh-Kay," this conversation had kind of spiraled out of control. "Anyone else?"

"Hmmm. Yeah. Jerks who know their lane is going away, but instead of politely merging like everyone else, they blow past the line, put their blinker on and try slipping into the front of the line because they are *soooo* freakin' important."

"I hate them, too, Skippy. Hey, listen-"

"Telemarketers. Preachers who ask for money on TV. Joe, I have a *big* list."

"Uh huh. But, you don't feel like willy-nilly wiping out life on Earth, right?"

"Shmaybe if dopes on the internet piss me off again with their stupid-"

"Let's keep you off Facebook, then, huh? Will we be safe, then?"

"I guess so."

"And you are sure we can hit up a relay on the way home, get confirmation this crisis is over?"

"Abso-freakin'-lutely, Joe. We may have to wait there for a while for news to catch up to us, but there's no reason we can't get started now on the journey home. It is time for an epic Merry Band of Pirates road trip!"

"A road trip is when you leave home, Skippy, not when you're going back."

"Close enough?"

"Ah, close enough."

Hans Chotek *loved* the idea of departing for home sooner than later, so we did.

Two days later, I was sitting in my office staring at a laptop screen. It was 1422 Hours and I had skipped lunch, hopefully the Chinese team on galley duty that day was not insulted by my absence. Lunch was probably delicious as always, that day I just was not hungry. That morning, my run on the treadmill had been totally worthless, to the point where I cut it short and let someone else use the machine.

I *should* be happy. We were going home. The crisis on Paradise appeared to be resolved. Skippy had successfully replaced the *Flying Dutchman*'s original Thuranin computer with a new one that allowed us to mostly fly the ship by ourselves. The last six times we jumped, we programmed the jumps on our own, with Skippy only watching. The new computer helped us program jumps with a lot better accuracy than we had ever hoped to before, and the computer got the drive coils realigned each time so they worked together properly. The system wasn't perfect and Skippy still had to make minor adjustments, but the drive would not fall apart without him. The computer also was slowly learning how to manage the team of bots that maintained the ship, to keep the reactors running properly and to perform all the thousands of other vital tasks that kept the ship from exploding every day. Now that we had fully cut over to the new computer, the old system was not being used, and Skippy promised me he was working to bring Nagatha back, although he did warn me to beware the Law of Unintended Consequences.

I was willing to take that risk. The crew wanted Nagatha back, I wanted her back, and we owed her.

Plus, she bugged the shit out of Skippy, so, bonus.

"Hey, Joey!" Skippy shimmered to life on my desk. I didn't bother to say it was his avatar, by now I thought of the Grand Admiral avatar as him.

"Hey, Skip."

"Whoa. What's wrong with you today, Joe? You have been moping around all day. This morning you hit the snooze alarm, and you never do that."

"Sorry, I'm just," I waved a hand, not having the energy to think what to say.

"Dude, you should be happy. You should be excited! You are going *home*. How can that not be great for you?"

"It's uh, yeah, great."

"Clearly it is *not* great for you. Hey! I just demonstrated empathy again!"

"Um, yeah, actually, you did. You're proud of that, huh?"

"*Proud?* No, dumdum, I thought I deactivated that pain-in-the-ass empathy subroutine. It looks like the stupid thing somehow got woven into my personality matrix. Oh crap, now I'll have to go hunt it down and kill it."

I face-palmed myself, muttering through my hand. Actually, the beer can had me chuckling, so that was good. "Why don't you leave it alone for a while, as an experiment? See if maybe this empathy thing grows on you."

"Grows on me like a freakin' *fungus*," he grumbled. "Sure, I'll give it a shot. So, what is *wrong* with your sorry ass? You are going home, dude!"

"Yeah, going home, and we can report we saved Earth again and saved Paradise a couple times, too."

"Plus, *plus*, I have started sharing technology with you monkeys! You heard that yesterday, I gave Doctor Friedlander part of the math behind jump field theory?"

"I did hear that, and thank you. He told me it will take years to understand that math, but-"

"Oh, dude, please. You monkeys are *never* going to understand that math. Ha! As if!" He laughed. "That was only a test, seeing if I could get around my internal restrictions. So far, so good. If it works, *I* will be able to explain the math. Because no way will a monkey brain get it."

"Uh huh, that's great. Skippy, maybe I'm being a Debbie Downer, but as *you* said, all this good news of us being able to fly the ship by ourselves and you sharing technology doesn't mean shit. Earth is doomed. When we get home, I have to tell UNEF Command that in less than sixty years, aliens will detect the gamma rays from the wormhole that is supposed to be dormant. Oh, and on top of that super wonderful news, I have to tell them that an Elder AI wiped out the population of Newark."

"Dude, you told me not to worry about that. You told me you weren't worried about it!"

"*I* am not worried about you going crazy and killing planets. UNEF Command already doesn't trust you, and when they learn how you got attacked by a worm designed to destroy rogue AIs, and that an AI like you threw an entire planet out of orbit, they *are* going to be worried."

"Oh, crap."

"So, now do you understand why I am not jumping for joy about going home?"

"I do understand that, because I understand you are a dumdum."

"How is that?"

"Joe, I also told you I am not worried about aliens turning your home planet into a radioactive cinder, because you are a remarkably clever monkey. I'm sure you will think of something."

"Like what? You got any suggestions?"

"Nope. As far as I can see, all future pathways end with your species thoroughly extinct."

"Future pathways?"

"Um, forget I mentioned that," he said hastily. "*That* subject is something I will not be sharing with anyone."

"Fine."

"Anywho, as far as the universe is concerned, there is no quantum uncertainty about the fate of humanity; you are all totally screwed. To use Schroedinger's example, this cat was dead *before* it went into the box."

"Is your empathy subroutine why you are being so incredibly good at cheering me up? That's it? All of us monkeys are dead, and there's nothing we can do about it?"

"No."

"But you just said-"

"I know what I said. I also have learned something very important during my time with you. On one side of the equation is the implacable logic of the universe that has existed unchanged for billions of years. On the other side is a monkey who says 'duuuuuuh, what about this?' Joe, in that conflict, the universe is totally *fucked*."

"For realz?"

"For realz, homeboy. Joe, you jumped this ship *through* an Elder wormhole. Believe me, the universe trembles when you monkeys get an idea. Oooooh, I can't *wait* to see how you monkeys get out of this mess."

"Thanks, Skippy." Great, I thought. No pressure on me. Then I thought, oh, what the hell. We are going home, and, damn it, I am going to enjoy it.

There are going to be cheeseburgers!

And, damn it, I'm finally going to eat a delicious Fluffernutter.

CHAPTER THIRTY FIVE

The welcome home for the Mavericks was not the sort of triumphant celebration Emily Perkins had been hoping for, and she admitted to herself, kind of expected. Her team had uncovered a secret that apparently forced the Maxolhx coalition to destroy their own ship, and provide both a vaccine and a cure for a very sophisticated bioweapon. She was disappointed to learn her team would be quarantined in southern Lemuria with almost all other humans on Paradise, until the Ruhar public felt confident the danger was over. The Mavericks had been the first to volunteer to test the new vaccine, along with about half the control group Keepers, who were seriously regretting they had ever forsaken UNEF and left Paradise. All those returning Keepers would be kept in a secure prison camp until the civilian authorities decided what to do with them, at the moment there wasn't a lot of sympathy from either humans or Ruhar for their situation.

After being poked, prodded and sampled until she wasn't sure she had any blood left in her veins, Perkins had been allowed to visit UNEF HQ, although no aircraft were available so the trip took six hours over back-breaking dirt roads in a truck. She was greeted by General Lynn Bezanson, who had also been vaccinated, and was hoping to return to the capital city to resume her duty as a liaison officer.

After congratulations and the necessary idle chit-chat, Perkins got right to the point. "General, being offworld was terrific, but it was a small team, on an old training ship full of cadets. If we are going to prove our worth to the Ruhar, and keep what's left of the ExForce from evaporating, we need a much bigger opportunity to do something really useful out here."

"What kind of opportunity are you thinking?"

"The Ruhar military, especially their light ground forces, are stretched very thin right now. They're taking a lot of new territory since the Jeraptha offensive pushed the Thuranin back, and the hamsters don't have enough boots to cover the ground they want to secure. The longer they wait to establish a presence on a world they want to claim, the more the Thuranin, and now the Bosphuraq, will be tempted to take star systems back. In the current offensive, the Bosphuraq are coming into systems, knocking out major defenses, then moving on to the next objective. They leave Wurgalan ships and troops behind to do the dirty, dangerous work of securing the place. I'm thinking that's where we could play a role; doing the crap jobs that the hamsters don't have the manpower for, or just don't want to do."

"Like a band of mercenaries?" Bezanson asked with a frown that included more than a hint of revulsion. She had served alongside mercs, or to use the more politically correct term 'military contractors', in the Middle East and Nigeria, and she did not have good memories of that experience. Renting out the ExForce sounded too much like the dubious reason they left Earth, years ago.

Perkins shook her head once, emphatically, knowing what the General was thinking. "No, Ma'am, I was thinking this would be more like an alien version of the French Foreign Legion. An Alien Legion. We wouldn't really be mercenaries, because we would only work for the Ruhar, not the highest bidder."

"Alien Legion? I can just imagine what a nightmare command and control would be for a force that has multiple species in it."

"I'm more concerned about logistics. We can settle on standard armor, weapons and other gear, but food is going to be a big problem. We can't eat Ruhar food, or Kristang, I mean, Verd-Kris food."

"And the lizards can't eat hamster chow either, I get it. How far down the road have you gotten in planning this?"

"With the Ruhar, not far other than a 'what if' conversation aboard the *Toaster*, before everything went sideways. I overheard a group of hamsters complaining how their ground forces have too many taskings and not enough boots, and there are some jobs their Starborne Army doesn't want to take on."

Bezanson did not like the sound of that. "Too risky?"

"No, too messy. Like ops to pacify and move out a native population, on a planet the hamsters want, but is not a big enough strategic priority for them to commit a couple Army divisions. That kind of op is time and manpower-intensive, and their Army doesn't want to get bogged down in ops that are not strategically vital right now. The officers I overheard were complaining their military command is missing opportunities they should exploit, because they don't have the resources. I mentioned it to Surgun Jakes, he has heard rumors of Ruhar command approaching the Verd-Kris to assist, but so far the Ruhar brass doesn't want to trust one group of lizards to police another group of lizards. But if humans were in the mix, in command of the op," she held her hands palms up.

The General nodded, warming to the idea. "Especially if the particular human in command has saved thousands, millions, of Ruhar lives on multiple occasions?"

Perkins blushed at the praise. "Right now, the Mavericks are popular with the Ruhar public, even beyond Paradise. This is a golden opportunity for us to get beyond one planet. And we have transport."

"What?"

"That Jeraptha ship that plucked us away from Camp Alpha? They are an independent operation and they're looking for paying work. I got the impression they owe more in gambling debts than the ship is worth, and they are finding it hard to get shipping contracts in their own society. Their ship is sort of a star carrier, only its hardpoints are for attaching cargo or passenger modules. It could be made into an assault transport if the Ruhar pay for the conversion. These beetles are desperate for paying jobs. The money they earned recently just got them to the break-even point."

"If they're that desperate, can you trust the ship not to fall apart?"

"I think so. One of their engineers bitched about not being paid in months, but she said the money went toward parts they needed. Ma'am, an Alien Legion-"

"Let's call this theoretical outfit the ExForce, take advantage of the name recognition. Your Mavericks can take the lead."

"Yes, Ma'am," Perkins blushed faintly. In her background as an intelligence analyst, she was used to *being* in the background. Having the spotlight, and all the pressure on her, made her uncomfortable. "The Force is falling apart, like you said, soon the last person to leave UNEF HQ will need to turn the lights off. The problem isn't just tempting opportunities available here to civilians. We came out here as soldiers, as a fighting force, and other than my unit, there hasn't been any potential for action since the last Kristang left the planet. If we can offer people to be *soldiers* again, to carry weapons in harm's way and make a difference, that might pull the Force together again. It won't bring everyone back, we won't need that many people. But it will be a reason to have pride in this," she tapped the ExForce patch on her uniform top. "Our motto is 'Anytime, anywhere, any fight'? Right now, the only 'where' is our little patch of southern Lemuria, and the only thing we're 'fighting' is native weeds in our corn fields."

"Yeah, and the 'time' is every day. Same thing, every single day. All right, Perkins, you've sold me. I'll kick it upstairs, the Old Man," she meant the Indian Army general currently commanding what was left of the Expeditionary Force, "will want to see a detailed plan before we approach the hamsters. But, I can tell you right now," she flashed a grin, "HQ is going to *love* this idea. They've got nothing else to offer as incentives for people staying in the Force. The person we," Perkins noted the General had used the word 'we', "really need to sell on the concept is your old friend the Burgermeister."

"We have a good relationship," the Mavericks leader said with confidence.

"I'm sure you do, and that's not our ace in the hole," Bezanson added with an arched eyebrow. "When the Chief Administrator heard about what you found on Camp Alpha, and how you got there, she told me she had complete confidence in you. She also asked me how you manage to find trouble *everywhere* you go."

"Trouble finds *us*. Our Mysterious Benefactor 'Emby', whoever that is, recruited us to dig up those maser projectors. It wasn't our idea."

"That's not the point. Perkins, I am certain the Burgermeister would prefer you find trouble on some *other* planet."

"Oh," Perkins expression brightened as she understood the General's meaning. "We will do our best, but I can't promise anything."

"I was afraid you'd say that."

"General, there is another, longer-term reason I want to set up this Alien Legion or whatever we're going to call it."

"Let's call it 'ExForce' for now. We already have a logo."

"And a slogan," Perkins nodded with a smile. "Ok, the slogan fits; we'll go anytime or anywhere the Ruhar need dirty jobs done. We can't refuse the engagements, or the Ruhar won't trust us to come through for them. So, 'any fight' is for damned sure true. Ma'am, long-term, there are groups like the Verd-Kris who want to set things right in the galaxy, and they are heartily sick of this war. Their goal is to retake control of Kristang society and bring their culture back to what it was, before the Thuranin put the warrior caste in power to serve those little green assholes. If they succeed, the Verd-Kris plan to stop fighting, other than defensive battles. They want *out* of this endless war, and the Verd-Kris are not the only people who feel that way."

"They'll need a whole lot more firepower to make their pie-in-the-sky dream come true, Perkins."

"Yes, but we know a large faction of Ruhar society is also tired of the war. Even the Jeraptha are weary of the fighting, that's why they haven't made a big effort to press their advantage after they kicked the Thuranin's asses. Ma'am, if we ever contact Earth again, and our planet is in one piece, we can't do the same stupid shit we tried the first time. We can't fight in this war, not for either side. Earth's only hope is to join a coalition that does not want to fight anymore."

"There is no such coalition, Perkins."

"Not yet, Ma'am. Someone needs to get it started, and in the new ExForce, I will be meeting a lot of aliens who are not just fighting the usual, age-old fight."

Bezanson straightened in her chair, leaning forward. "You are certainly ambitious, Lieutenant Colonel Perkins."

"I was trained as an intel specialist, this kind of political intrigue is my wheelhouse."

"Maybe," Bezanson conceded. "Don't let your wheel steer humanity onto the rocks, because we don't have a fallback. I do not think HQ will approve any plan for creating a revolution in alien societies."

"For now, all I will do is gather intel. General, I know nothing can happen unless something changes the balance of power in this sector, maybe the entire galaxy. If it does," she raised an eyebrow, "we need to be ready to take advantage. The time for planning is *before* the action kicks off."

That night, Emily called Sergeant Czajka. "Dave, I heard you have an offer to go into business here, something about brewing beer for the hamsters?"

Dave? David Czajka held the zPhone away from his ear so he could stare at it in disbelief. She called him by his first name? What the hell was going on? "Uh," he had absolutely no idea what to say. "Colonel, I, uh-"

"Sergeant Jarrett mentioned you have an opportunity dirtside here."

"Oh, um, yeah. I've been thinking about it. Listen, Ma'am, I really appreciate being on your team, it's been great, it's just-" Just what? What would he say? What could he say? "Colonel-"

"Please, call me Emily," there was a catch in her voice. "If you haven't accepted the offer yet, I would," she had to pause to swallow hard. "I would very much appreciate if you wait a bit. I'm working on something, something big, and there might be an opportunity for you, for all of us. Things are changing, we are stuck out here and we can't keep blindly following all the old rules, if they aren't working for us. For the mission."

"Um, uh, yeah."

"You hear what I'm saying?" She had to catch her breath again. "Dave?"

"I, I think so. Em, Emily."

"Great!" Damn, she pressed a hand to her forehead. I am as giddy as a schoolgirl. "I'm at HQ now, but, I'll find a truck and I'll come see you. We can talk, Ok?"

"Talk. Yeah, that," Dave silently pumped a fist in the air, making Jesse look to see what the fuss was about. "That would be great!"

THE END

Author's note:

Thank you reading one of my books! It took years to write my first three books, I had a job as a business manager for an IT company so I wrote at night, on weekends and during vacations. While I had many ideas for books over the years, the first one I ever completed was 'Aces' and I sort of wrote that book for my at-the-time teenage nieces. If you read 'Aces', you can see some early elements of the Expeditionary Force stories; impossible situations, problem-solving, clever thinking and some sarcastic humor.

Next I wrote a book about the program to develop faster-than-light spaceflight, it was an adventure story about astronauts stranded on an alien planet and trying to warn Earth about a dangerous flaw in the FTL drive. It was a good story, and I submitted it to traditional publishers back in the mid-2000s. And I got rejections. My writing was 'solid', which I have since learned means publishers can't think of anything else to say but don't want to insult aspiring writers. The story was too long, they wanted me to cut it to a novella and change just about everything. Instead of essentially scrapping the story and starting over, I threw it out and tried something else.

Columbus Day and Ascendant were written together starting around 2011, I switched back and forth between writing those two books. The idea for Ascendant came to me after watching the first Harry Potter movie, one of my nieces asked what would have happened to Harry Potter if no one ever told him he is a wizard? Hmm, I thought, that is a very good question.... So, I wrote Ascendant.

In the original, very early version of Columbus Day, Skippy was a cute little robot who stowawayed on a ship when the Kristang invade Earth, and he helps Joe defeat the aliens. After a year trying to write that version, I decided it sounded too much like a Disney

Channel movie of the week, and it, well, it sucked. Although it hurt to waste a year's worth of writing, I threw away that version and started over. This time I wrote an outline for the entire Expeditionary Force story arc first, so I would know where the overall story is going. That was a great idea and I have stuck to that outline (with minor detours along the way).

With Aces, Columbus Day and Ascendant finished by the summer of 2015 and no publisher interested, my wife suggested that I:

1) Try self-publishing the books in Amazon
2) For the love of God please shut up about not being able to get my books published
3) Clean out the garage

It took six months of research and revisions to get the three books ready for upload to Amazon. In addition to reformatting the books to Amazon's standards, I had to buy covers and set up an Amazon account as a writer. When I clicked the 'Upload' button on January 10th 2016 my greatest hope was that somebody, anybody out there would buy ONE of my books because then I could be a published author. After selling one of each book, my goal was to make enough money to pay for the cover art I bought online (about $35 for each book).

For that first half-month of January 2016, Amazon sent us a check for $410.09 and we used part of the money for a nice dinner. I think the rest of the money went toward buying new tires for my car.

At the time I uploaded Columbus Day, I had the second book in the series SpecOps about halfway done, and I kept writing at night and on weekends. By April, the sales of Columbus Day were at the point where my wife and I said "Whoa, this could be more than just a hobby". At that point, I took a week of vacation to stay home and write SpecOps 12 hours a day for nine days. Truly fun-filled vacation! Doing that gave me a jump-start on the schedule, and SpecOps was published at the beginning of June 2016. In the middle of that July, to our complete amazement, we were discussing whether I should quit my job to write full-time. That August I had a "life is too short" moment when a family friend died and then my grandmother died, and we decided I should try this writing thing full-time. Before I gave notice at my job, I showed my wife a business plan listing the books I planned to write for the next three years, with plot outlines and publication dates. This assured my wife that quitting my real job was not an excuse to sit around in shorts and T-shirts watching sci fi movies 'for research'.

During the summer of 2016, R.C. Bray was offered Columbus Day to narrate, and I'm sure his first thought was "A book about a talking beer can? Riiiight. No." Fortunately, he thought about it again, or was on heavy-duty medication for a bad cold, or if he wasn't busy recording the book his wife expected him to repaint the house. Anyway, RC recorded Columbus Day, went back to his fabulous life of hanging out with movie stars and hitting golf balls off his yacht, and probably forgot all about the talking beer can.

When I heard RC Bray would be narrating Columbus Day, my reaction was "THE RC Bray? The guy who narrated The Martian? Winner of an Audie Award for best sci fi narrator? Ha ha, that is a good one. Ok, who is really narrating the book?"

Then the Columbus Day audiobook became a huge hit. And is a finalist for an 'Audie' Award as Audiobook of the Year!

When I got an offer to create audio versions of the Ascendant series, I was told the narrator would be Tim Gerard Reynolds. My reaction was "You mean some other guy named Tim Gerard Reynolds? Not the TGR who narrated the Red Rising audiobooks, right?"

Clearly, I have been very fortunate with narrators for my audiobooks. To be clear, they chose to work with me, I did not 'choose' them. If I had contacted Bob or Tim directly, I would have gone into super fan-boy mode and they would have filed for a restraining order. So, again, I am lucky they signed onto the projects.

So far, there is no deal for Expeditionary Force to become a movie or TV show, although I have had inquiries from producers and studios about the 'entertainment rights'. From what people in the industry have told me, even if a studio or network options the rights, it will be a loooooooooong time before anything actually happens. I will get all excited for nothing, and years will go by with the project going through endless cycles with producers and directors coming aboard and disappearing, and just when I have totally given up and sunk into the Pit of Despair, a miracle will happen and the project gets financing! Whoo-hoo. I am not counting on it. On the other hand, Disney is pulling their content off Netflix next year, so Netflix will be looking for new original content...

Again, Thank YOU for reading one of my books. Writing gives me a great excuse to avoid cleaning out the garage.

Contact the author at craigalanson@gmail.com
https://www.facebook.com/Craig.Alanson.Author/

Go to craigalanson.com for blogs and ExForce logo merchandise including T-shirts, patches, sticker, hats, and coffee mugs

The Expeditionary Force series
Book 1: Columbus Day
Book 2: SpecOps
Book 3: Paradise
Book '3.5': Trouble on Paradise novella
Book 4: Black Ops
Book 5: Zero Hour
Book6: Mavericks
Book7: Renegades – November 2018

Made in the USA
Middletown, DE
27 December 2019

81921276R00172